Alison Scott Skelton is the widow of C. L. Skelton, who was the author of *Hardacre*. After Clem Skelton's death, Alison Skelton completed *Hardacre's Luck* and *Beloved Soldiers*, which her husband had left in draft. Both books were bestsellers.

Alison Skelton lives in Drumnadrochit, Inverness-shire, with her two sons.

ALISON SCOTT SKELTON

A Murderous Innocence

'Imagining in excited reverie
That the future years had come,
Dancing to a frenzied drum,
Out of the murderous innocence of the sea.'
– W. B. Yeats

This edition published 1994 by
Diamond Books
77–85 Fulham Palace Road
Hammersmith, London W6 8JB

Published by Grafton Books 1988

First published in Great Britain by
Grafton Books 1987

The four lines from Yeats's 'A Prayer for my Daughter' are reprinted from *THE COLLECTED POEMS OF W. B. YEATS* by kind permission of A. P. Watt Ltd. on behalf of Michael B. Yeats and Macmillan, London Ltd.

Printed and bound in Great Britain

Set in Times

For Juliet
and all the 'dear shadows'

Part One

1

I am standing at an arched doorway in a stone wall. There is a plank door, green-painted, and locked, and I am peering through a slit between the planks. Beyond I see, in a tear-drop frame, sea, sky and a headland. It is Loch Ewe, but I think it to be Ireland. Behind me, Clare, in a childish form of her strong, demanding voice is saying, 'You have left the age of innocence. You must pay for your own sins now.'

I am seven. It is my birthday. Therefore it is also Christmas Day 1900, and I know Clare is driving me to recant, but I will not, because I know I am innocent.

This is my earliest cogent memory.

I continue to peer one-eyed out of the tear-shaped split in the door and I say again, 'Persephone's coming,' in the pouting voice of the falsely accused. Already opposition makes me stubborn. Already contradiction drives Clare to rage. Long before the age of innocence departs, we set out on our paths of apostasy.

'Persephone comes in the spring,' Clare counters with mythic rectitude lost on my unschooled mind. But Clare is not thinking mythically, and understands no better than I why Mary Monogue is Persephone. And Persephone does always come in the spring, and is gone before winter begins.

'Persephone's coming,' I say once again and Clare explodes in her rage, as patterned and predictable as the seasons. She punches my back and shoves me down and I cower in a heap of now-muddy blue serge, my petticoats in the peaty earth below the garden wall. Her punches hurt. She is fourteen, and not gentle. The boys, who coddle me, tease her incessantly and have made her tough and vengeful, and I am their unintended victim.

'Nanny Hopkins,' I shriek, and Clare leaps on me. Her face is pink-cheeked with moist West Highland winter, and her yellow hair hazed with damp droplets of sea air, the maroon ungainly bonnet clamped down hard upon her head. Her pretty mouth is screwed up with raging. Then I bury my head in my sleeves, so my bonnet takes the battering, and ride it out. After a while, she subsides.

'Nanny will be *furious*,' she whispers coldly.'Your coat is a sight.'

'It's your fault,' I moan.

'It's *your* fault,' she says grandly. I feel the hollow weight of departed innocence once more. 'You're seven,' says Clare.

'I hate growing up,' I mourn, which is a lie, but the lie is an easy temptation, and I think it will please Clare. It does. She sits down beside me in the peaty earth, and leans against the wall. We can hear the sea breaking beyond on the weedy strand, behind our heads. Suddenly she is my compatriot. She holds my hand with her small cold fingers and says in an even voice, 'Why did you draw it, Justina?'

I shrink, miserable, under my blue hat. 'I dreamt it,' I say at last.

I know she will hit me again and she does, and I cringe because now my defences are weaker. Now I am lying. I did not dream anything. I stood at the sea gate and peered through my tear-drop of wood and I saw Persephone walking across the sea. She was there, and not there, at once. She was not there as the sea-gull flying by her left hand was there. But she was there in her own way all the same. It never struck me as odd to see her there.

Clare gave up hitting. Suddenly she looked very grown-up and sad, as if hitting her sister was a thing of her remote past. I almost wished she'd hit me again rather than sit with that look of adult sorrow that she increasingly wore.

'Did you dream about William?' I began to cry. Clare grew tender, 'Please, I won't strike you again. Promise I won't,' she paused, 'but please don't lie.' I looked up under the ribboned brim of my bonnet.

'I dreamt.' It was a lie, like the first lie, but I had no other words.

'What did you dream? Tell me all of it,' she whispered. 'Don't leave anything out.' I think she hoped some salvation lay unmentioned.

I shook my head. 'What I drew,' I sobbed. 'What I drew.' Clare's hand tightened around mine with controlled disgust. She said nothing. So there we were, back again where we started.

'Why did you give it to *Mother*?' she demanded at last in her cold and now adult voice. 'Even Father would have been all right, perhaps. But *Mother*.'

Oh, Father would have been all right. Father would have given it his accustomed glance, raised his theatrical eyebrows in astonishment at my brilliance and put it aside without having looked close enough to see what it possibly portrayed. He would have lifted me in his strong and embarrassing arms and made much of my prettiness in a manner that would, as always, leave me dissatisfied. My prettiness was less my doing than his. Everyone said I was his image. My drawings were *my* image, and it was them I wanted praised. So I gave my drawing of Persephone and William to Mother, as we sat down to a strange, tense Christmas dinner, and she raised her spectacles to her spectacularly beautiful eyes, looked carefully, and ran screaming from the room.

Whatever I lacked as an artist, it clearly wasn't impact.

I can remember at least something of almost all my paintings. Not everything, naturally, but the majority become engraved somewhere in the brain as the hand adorns the canvas. I can recall this one vividly, though naturally the circumstances aid my memory. It had already my usual flaws, my inability with hands and feet that Mr Yeats would later criticize; Persephone's thumbs were back to front. And it had a seven-year-old's logistic difficulties. My visual understanding of the effects of gravity were yet limited, and apart from the fact that Persephone was standing on the sea, her hair, although she was bending to look down on William, still paralleled her face and hence stood more or less straight up. I had drawn her with her hair loose, the way she looked when she stole into the nursery late at night to tell forbidden stories.

William was quite good actually, lying flat in his little tight-fitting boat like the Lady of the Lake. I dare say there were story-book influences on this disastrous work of my art, but the main of it came clearly from my wide-open dream receptacle of a mind, for thus it was in those days of rapidly departing innocence. I drew what I saw, like any good naturalist. What I *saw* in those days was another matter.

'But why draw William in a *coffin*,' Clare groaned. 'You little beast. You *vicious* little beast.' She meant that and I whimpered, 'It was a boat,' knowing now that no one was going to believe me, ever. I had never seen a coffin. Children did not attend funerals in those days in the Highlands of Scotland, not even imported children of the aristocracy such as ourselves. I drew what I saw through the tear-drop in the sea gate, and interpreted by my own limited lights, and I still thought I'd drawn a boat, albeit a remarkably small, odd-shaped and tight-fitting boat in which a five-year-old might just lie flat and encased, like a solitary sardine.

But coffins, not boats, were on everyone's mind that Christmas, unfortunately, and unbeknownst to me. While we gathered in that odd silence for dinner, my little brother William, the only member of our family actually younger than me, was lying in the third-floor nursery in his blue-painted little bed, red-faced and coughing. I thought he had a cold and I think Clare thought the same. What the boys, our three brothers yet at home, thought, I do not know. Something similar I imagine, because when the catastrophe precipitated by my drawing brought Christmas dinner to an untimely end, they got up in their noisy simultaneous way and bolted for the out of doors like the wild animals they were. They hardly seemed concerned either, though Mother was closeted wailing in her room and the doctor was arriving for the second time that day at the door. Father went out riding, as if nursery dilemmas, even of this magnitude, were not his concern.

'What about Christmas?' I cried as Nanny Hopkins dressed me in my outdoor coat with sharp rude jerks of sleeves and collar.

'Little brute,' she said and shoved me into Clare's presence and out of her own. 'Go out to the garden until you are called.'

And so we went, Clare coldly holding my hand, and myself whimpering sadly past the closed expectant door of the drawing room where we knew the tree was surely being erected, and the presents awaited us. But no one mentioned the tree, or presents, or Christmas, or indeed my birthday again. William died of diphtheria at three o'clock in the afternoon, and the age of my innocence was ended.

Clare and I, unaware of our loss and no doubt forgotten by the family, shivered in the walled garden until the light faded at four. Then, strictly against the rules, we made our way to the greenhouse where we knew there would be a fire in the stone cellar beneath the floor, generating heat for unseasonable flowers. Chrysanthemums glowed smugly through the glass. We descended the stone steps into the ground and knocked on the wooden door in the darkness. Donald Paul, the gardener, often sheltered in the cellar. He was the reason we were forbidden to go there. He drank and the little room smelled perpetually of his whisky and his urine. There was no answer, though, and when we pushed open the door the room was empty and glowing from the peat-fire on the hearth. We sat forlorn beside it in our Christmas dresses and Sunday coats and bonnets until we heard Nanny Hopkins's thin strained voice shouting in the garden above. And so we climbed up out of the ground and into the December night. A gale was blowing off Loch Ewe with snow in it that would not lie. We met Nanny beneath the cordoned apple trees on the inner garden wall. Wordlessly she took each of us by the hand and walked us to the house. Her silence, and the lack of chastisement for our forbidden sojourn in the greenhouse cellar, frightened us. Even Clare did not attempt to pull her hand free. We returned to a house in mourning: the holly was down from the mirrors and picture frames and a maid was draping them with crêpe. My father stood at the foot of the oak staircase, looking at the floor, his moustache drooping with frost and his riding crop yet in his hand. On the stairway, seeming quite unaware of his presence, my beautiful mother, dressed from head to foot in black, stood in silence. I never saw her in colours again.

She turned her face from us as we climbed the stairs. 'Take them,' she said to Nanny who seemed to know exactly where. We were led on up to the third floor where the nursery was. We passed our three middle brothers on the stairs, dressed in stiff collars and walking in line and in order of age: Douglas, who was almost as old as Clare, and Geoffrey, and then Alexander, called Sandy, who was just a year older than me. They were very quiet and ignored us, neither teasing Clare nor responding to my urgent little tugs at their sleeves. Sandy was crying.

Nanny stopped outside the nursery door and said suddenly with no explanation, 'You must bid your brother goodbye.' Then she opened the door, shoved us through in haste, and drew it shut behind us.

Clare and I were alone, it seemed, in the dark. But then I saw that there was light in the far end of the room, which had been changed around so William's bed no longer stood where it had, and in its place was a table, with two candles in tall silver candlesticks at either end. In the centre was William, white-faced in a white lacy dress, and, in the candlelight, so far removed from the William I knew as to pose no threat to my calm. He lay in his coffin already. Perhaps the doctor had brought it that morning. Diphtheria in a five-year-old, once diagnosed, was generally a foregone conclusion. Regardless, I knew now what a coffin was. Clare commenced shrieking behind me, but I did not really hear. Visual images overwhelmed all others. Before me was William in his boat, and standing gently smiling behind him, her black hair loose as I had drawn it, and falling in soft waves, her Irish pink cheeks glowing in the flare of candles, was Persephone. Never was death's harbinger more lovely.

'My darlings,' she said in her soft Sligo brogue, and stretched her arms wide, over our dead brother, to us. And I of course, brushing the coffin in my haste, ran at once into her embrace.

'Oh hush yourself, Clare Melrose,' she said with sweet

impatience, over the top of my head, cuddling me even as she chastised my sister. 'Keening like a washerwoman, and all for an innocent in the purest state of grace.' The words meant nothing to me. I was burying my nose up against her lace collar, seeking the smell of her like a nuzzling animal. 'Your brother's in heaven, bless his soul.'

'Persephone, when did you come?' I said. I think I had forgotten William. I was too young, and I doubt I realized death's permanence. I still expected William to emerge from the nursery next morning, padding in his nightgown down the corridor as he always did. The repeated reality of the customary I trusted to overwhelm this oddity of lying in lace in a boat. Clare was hiding in a corner of the room, her hands in fists before her mouth, sobbing with gasps like retches.

'Oh, such a carry on,' said Persephone, but sweetly still, and she crossed the room and gathered Clare in under her voluminous sleeve. 'Come, see the blessed little angel,' she said, guiding Clare to the coffin, and holding me over it. 'Come now, you must kiss your brother as he's leaving us,' she murmured. Clare wriggled and moaned, but I was unconcerned, only turning my face sideways as when I was asked to kiss anyone. 'Not his face, you'll find it cold. Just on his hair,' she instructed Clare. I kissed him, my hasty dry mumble of lips. He was not cold, and I remember no shock. I didn't see what Clare did, but it seemed to satisfy Persephone. Clare was calm now, quite white and silent.

'There now,' Persephone said. She set me down, and brushed her loose hair over her shoulder. 'The blessed little angel. And is it not yourselves the blessed ones as well, with a real little saint of your own in heaven to make your prayers to?'

There was a silence, while I considered this annoyingly awesome concept. William, my only lesser, now to be prayed to like Jesus? Never, I decided instantly. Just being dead was no reason to usurp my position as superior in the family. I stuck out my tongue at the coffin, but Persephone missed this charming gesture because Clare said suddenly, in her adult voice, 'We don't pray to saints.'

'Nonsense, of course you do,' said Persephone at her sweetest.

Clare's tone suddenly changed and became a mistress-to-servant voice, and she said again, 'We don't pray to saints, Persephone.'

'My name is Mary,' Persephone said, her sweetness unaltered, but the words in response to Clare's were a warning. Two can play that game, they said. Clare backed down.

'Don't be angry, Persephone,' she whispered, and was at once forgiven and allowed back into the secret fold.

Her name *was* Mary, of course. Which fact no doubt added to my early confusion of her with the Virgin Mary, whose picture travelled with her always from Sligo to Arradale Castle on Loch Ewe and back again. The picture resembled her; not surprising, it was of the cheap Irish art so popular among Mary Monogue's people and whoever the unknown artist was, he'd likely used an Irish peasant for a model. No doubt she'd been called Mary too; they almost all were. The Virgin Mary did not play so large a role in our lives; we were Church of England, virtually Protestant, a fact Persephone chose to ignore. Any reference, like Clare's, to a different style of faith was tossed aside like the stuff of fairy-tales. There was One True Church, and nothing more remained to be said.

Persephone was a lady's maid. To her singular personality may it be credited that my very first ambition in life was not art at all, but to be, like her, a domestic. She was the most glamorous person in my life, glamorous in the older sense of witchery, imbued with a natural drama, a truly haunting beauty, and a grand Irish flair for disaster. Persephone wore the black and white of service like the mantle of a queen, and she did not play strictly by the rules.

I was a considerably more experienced woman than my seven-year self before I realized that it was not customary for a lady's maid to fling herself giggling into her mistress's arms and tumble with her on the master's bed, whispering secrets. But she and my mother did, whenever alone. Like sisters they would lie together and whisper for hours, gossip and commiserations; husbands' failings and women's reprisals, all the undercurrent of treachery of two great houses, our own, and that other in County Sligo where Persephone belonged. Sometimes I was allowed to attend these grand seminars; I had early developed a style of play with small objects and an expression of remote absorption on my face that served as fine cover for my eager listening ears. I was wise enough never to answer my name on first call, or even to give that involuntary twitch of self-conscious awareness revealing I had heard. Adults often forgot I was even present, or at the least assumed me unconscious of their activities. One visiting lady was so impressed by my performance as to commiserate with a neighbour about my dimwittedness. On the next visit I was called forth to recite Shakespeare as antidote (I was five), lest Melrose honour be sullied.

To be fair to Persephone it must be said that she did not take liberties that were not offered. And to be fair to my mother, who offered them, there were circumstances of mitigation. My mother was a very lonely woman.

'But how are you *here*, Persephone,' I demanded again, my attention now turned utterly from William who wasn't doing much to hold it. 'It's *winter*,' I concluded almost tartly in my puzzlement.

'Hush, now,' she said. She was moving her lips, her eyes closed, looking *very* like the picture. Then she crossed herself, opened her eyes, still looking at William in his lacy dress and said, 'Now surely your good mother will be needing me here.'

I nodded, uncertain, though Clare said in distraction, 'How did you know *then*?' Clare, unlike myself, had a sense of time. One must recall that in the days of which I am telling the journey from the West of Ireland to the West Highlands of Scotland was neither easy nor swift, involving a complexity of steamers and railways and lesser vehicles, longcars and landaus and automobiles. There was no such thing as ready communication; telephone links were minimal, and between those two locales unimaginable. Persephone left Sligo a week ago, when William was happily splashing stones in Loch Ewe laying the foundations of his demise.

'Your mother will be needing me,' said Persephone stubbornly. Clare gave up. One did not push a stubborn Persephone.

She led us to the door where, to my surprise, my mother was waiting. Again she avoided our eyes, as if William's death had been something of unmentionable guilt, like wetting a bed. I was confused, not knowing who was guilty, she or I, and then remembering my drawing realized it must be me.

'I didn't mean it,' I said, tugging at her stiff alien black skirt.

Her hands lifted up and floated away from me. She did not want to touch me. I began to cry. 'Go with Persephone,' she said, her voice all on one level.

Clare suddenly rushed forward and flung herself at Mother. She too was turned gently away by the same floating arms, and I was relieved for myself, and sorry for her. '*We're* still here, Mother,' Clare burst out, 'and you can always have another William.' It was one of her rare moments of blurting outspokenness, like bright flashes in the gloom of her reserve. I was amazed to hear Mother laughing very softly and tiredly.

'I don't believe I will survive this,' she said suddenly, not to us but to Persephone.

Persephone turned abruptly, dropped our hands and took Mother by the shoulders and gave her two sharp shakes. 'Survive? Of course you'll survive. What choice have you?'

They stared at each other in silence and then Mother slipped into the nursery. Behind the shut door I heard her sobbing and wanted to comfort her, but Persephone was already hurrying us with whispered jokes and soft laughter to the kitchen for tea. Cook was shocked to see us stuff ourselves with bread and jam and cocoa, but Persephone silenced her with a look.

'William liked this jam,' I said with rather calculated sorrow.

'Then he shall have it in heaven,' said Persephone, unperturbed.

'That's impossible,' said Clare. 'The jam's here. It can't be in heaven too.'

'All things are possible for God,' said Persephone.

'Then why couldn't he make William better?' said Clare.

'William is better,' said Persephone, cuddling me.

'William,' said Clare, 'is dead.'

I gobbled bread and jam happily, and when Father with his lost look came creeping into the kitchen unnoticed by all but me, I brought everyone's eyes to him at once by shrieking gleefully, 'William's eating jam in heaven and we're eating it here.'

Father crossed the kitchen slates with clicks of his riding boots. Persephone never looked up. He cuddled me with his shaking cold hands and said in a mumbly voice, 'Oh my pet. My poor little pet.' Clare stiffened, watching us, and laid down her cocoa cup, ready to elude Father's embrace if he should attempt one. He was wiser. He turned to Persephone and, as cook had left the room, laid his bearded cheek against her black hair and whispered, 'Oh, Mary, how He punishes us.'

And there my memory ends of that day. Undoubtedly more happened; undoubtedly Clare and I spent the evening with Persephone telling stories around the fire in Clare's bedroom, or mine. Again the following days must have held events. William's funeral was logically one of them, though I have no memory of that, and I assume I did not attend. Others of my father's family must have gathered. And surely some effort was made to contact my eldest brother Jeremy, with his regiment in South Africa, to relay the tragic news. The house must have been in great uproar, but I cannot recall. All that is gone, anyhow; what remains is the last day of 1900 which, depending how one chooses to count could also be regarded as the last day of the nineteenth century. Regardless, on that day an era ended for us, and another began.

It was the New Year holiday, of course, a holiday of some note in that part of the world. This year there were no celebrations above or below stairs. My mother had retired to her bed some time in the week and remained there. Persephone waited upon her by day and came, in the evenings, to us. My father shuffled forlornly through the upstairs corridors outside my mother's door, and when no call to enter came, went out once more to his mare.

At bedtime, Persephone told stories. Nanny Hopkins was short with her that night; I suspect she was jealous; but anyhow Persephone always got her way.

'You're not to be frightening them.'

'Would I frighten you, my darlings?' Persephone's black brows arced wide over her wide blue eyes. The lashes swept down and up in innocence.

'We're not frightened,' Clare and I chorused.

'All very well, but who'll be up to you in the night if you wake with bad dreams?'

'I shall, shan't I?' Persephone said.

'Persephone shall,' we said together. Nanny put her lips together in a line.

'Fine words finely spoken,' she said. It was one of her standard replies, and like most of her conversation didn't really seem to mean anything. Nanny spoke in such phrases. All nannies did. I knew, because she was our third. We'd got rid of the first two, ourselves. Jemmy, my eldest brother Jeremy, had frightened away the first when he was twelve by letting a byre rat loose in her room, and then letting the cat in after by way of apology. (Jemmy was quick in remorse.) He was no concern of the second nanny, Nanny Fairweather, because by then he was at school in England, and now he was fighting the Boers so Nanny Hopkins was safe from him too. Nanny Fairweather was Clare's trophy. Clare sewed all the legs of all Nanny's drawers together, one night. Nanny Fairweather left in the morning, drawerless we always assumed. Now we had Nanny Hopkins and I felt her to be my responsibility since only William and I were truly in her care. The three middle boys simply ignored her, in spite of Mother's admonishments, and Clare was too old for a Nanny and only saw her for lessons and tea. Now that William was gone, I would have to undo this Nanny alone. I pondered how, as Persephone settled by the fire and prepared to speak, little aware that opportunity was falling into my hands.

'Tell about the swans,' I said, as repetitious as Nanny.

'No,' Clare argued. 'You always have the swans.'

'I want the swans,' I cried, and began to make an abominable fuss.

'Baby,' Clare said in disgust. 'Tell us Cuchulain fighting the sea.' Clare liked stories with fighting in them, stories in which the hero lost in the end.

I curled against Persephone's wide skirt, billowing on the hearthrug, and whimpered, 'Swans,' and began already to suck my thumb in anticipation. Persephone was still, allowing a theatrical silence to fall in the gaslit room.

'I will tell you,' she began then, 'of the fate of the Children of Lir.' I sighed with pleasure, having won. Her cadences were perfect, filled with drama and portent, as if the story she told had never been told before. Even Clare settled, lulled by the soft Irish voice and trusting Cuchulain to follow when I was asleep.

It was a simple story of an enchantment, four brothers turned to swans by an evil stepmother, and awaiting release. In Persephone's story their saviour was St Patrick, but sometimes she mixed it with another version that appeared in our story-books in which the brothers were seven and their magic release from swanhood was in the hands of their loyal little sister who must clothe them in garments of nettle leaves. Naturally, this was the version I loved.

The loss of William in no way lessened the charm of this story for me, for although I had five of the seven requisite brothers, I had never counted the fifth. He was my lesser, and it was my superiors, Douglas, Geoffrey, Alexander and glorious manly Jeremy, whose approval I sought. And how better to win it than to be thus the instrument of their salvation?

Sometimes, after the telling of this tale, I would go to the walled garden, to the corner where Donald Paul heaped garden cuttings for compost and allowed the wild nettle to grow. There, in secret even from Clare, I reached out determined hands until my fingers closed on the feathery grey stinging leaves. Fighting pain, I would stroke them, pluck them, even gather them in bunches, and imagine myself the sister of the story spinning them into yarn and the yarn into cloth and the cloth into coats, for only by such fiery garments might my brothers be freed from their swan feathers and returned to the world of men. I paid dearly for those fancies; my hands stung and swelled and caused great consternation from Nanny and Mother and my silence caused more. But I would return again and again to prove myself the equal of the swan-sister, and equal thus to a task of salvation that lay in wait in my future. Indeed it did, too, though in Victoria's last year, who would have imagined it? Nor, when it came, would coats of nettle-yarn, no matter how dearly bought, prove anodyne. Far better had I been Clare running at the heels of Cuchulain to do battle with the sea.

I must have fallen asleep on Persephone's knee because when I awoke I was in my bed and the sky beyond my window, over the back of the ben, was white with stars. Someone had called my name, so I sat up and said, 'Clare?' There was no answer, and with less confidence I now said, 'Nanny Hopkins?' You may notice I did not, as the modern child would, call for my mother. This was not because I did not love her, nor she me. Of course we did. It was merely a matter of proprieties. My night-time distresses were not her concern. We met each day at breakfast, when I was dressed and clean, and parted at tea time, when I again was clean, but now dressed for bed. Her night-time duties were to my father (whether or not she maintained them), and such duties were paramount, and not to be interfered with. Besides, her bedroom was not even on the same floor. Persephone's was, and I called the last time, 'Persephone?'

'It's me, Justina.' I peered into the darkness. 'It's just me.' The voice was low and sad and very masculine. My oldest, most adored brother stood there.

'Jemmy,' I whispered in puzzled delight. He was standing in the starlight, in his uniform. It looked tattered and old and even in that light I could see how tired he was. 'You're home,' I said. I floundered quickly in the bed, under the vast eiderdown and hampered by my yards of flannel nightgown.

'Don't get up, dear,' he said. 'I can't wait.' He hesitated by the window and said at last with great wisdom, 'I don't suppose I can kiss you, can I?'

'*You* can kiss me, Jemmy,' I whispered, but he shook his head and seemed to turn it as if someone spoke at his shoulder.

Then it began to happen. His uniform, which had seemed tattered and old, grew brighter, or paler, and began to change until it glistened and was almost white. I saw his moustache, that would tickle had he kissed me and whose tickle I yearned for now, grow white too, and then his face, and as he reached his arms up towards me, whiteness grew from them in long, sweeping tails, and then he began to turn and the wind came up through the closed window as if the starlight was blowing and Jemmy's shape blurred and whirled and lifted and launched itself with a great surge and, with infinite grace, spread wings and took to the sky. I cried, 'The window!' but no window could hold him now.

I was rather a sanguine child, as my reactions to William might have indicated, but this was strong stuff, even for me. I leapt up, shedding eiderdown like waves of the sea and stampeded out of the door and down the corridor. I passed

Nanny's door without pause and passed Clare's as well. Already I knew there was only one soul in the house fit to deal with this. 'Persephone!' I shrieked, 'Persephone!'

I could shriek well too. I had, have, one of those voices that 'carry'. I suppose I should have had a fling at the theatre along with everything else. In those days my ringing voice was cause for simple dismay. Time and again I was punished when all around me were equally sinning, because though all were shouting, 'It was you I heard,' Nanny would declare. Well, she heard me now.

Up and down in the house, all three turreted storeys, I was heard. Servants heard below stairs. Mother in her mournful bed heard. And Father heard. And yes, Persephone heard too, though it was not from her room, at whose door I had slumped howling, that she emerged, but from some other place, and Father was right on her heels.

'My darling,' she enveloped me in her arms.

'Justina, Justina, what is this?' my father demanded, pushing Nanny, who was scolding loudly, aside. I curled, in terror now of the fuss, against Persephone's sweet warmth.

'Jemmy's a swan,' I said.

I must have been a very trying child. Obviously, as an explanation for waking the entire household, that was not going to do. So the whole of it was dragged from me, in muffled wet sobs directed to Persephone's soft bosom. When I had finished and there was silence, I looked up. The entire household surrounded me. There is nothing more disconcerting for a child than to see elders unnerved. But how, in response, they all fell to type.

'You *would* have that swan story, wouldn't you,' Clare accused.

'She's lying, she's making it up,' Douglas and Geoffrey

said, neutralizing fear with scorn. And Alexander was thrilled and wanted it told again.

Father blustered lamely, 'Nightmares. Too much excitement at bedtime. Your fault, Nanny.' (Nannies were such easy targets.)

But Nanny rallied, retaliating primly, 'The child's demented. I always thought so.'

And Mother? Mother looked away from me, tilting her white neck back, distraught eyes wandering the corridor, across cornices and ceilings and draperies high above everyone's heads, as if sanity might reside in those airy regions.

'Such a fanciful child,' she said with a sad, perplexed smile. 'Such a fanciful child.' And then she turned and drifted away, leaving me in Persephone's arms.

Life is rarely just. I was the cause, Persephone was the catalyst, but the immediate casualty was Nanny Hopkins. Perhaps Father sensed the wings of ill-fortune over our heads, and like a vole on the ground, he jinked left and right to escape. As if to drive ill-luck from his door and disprove bad omens that he professed not to believe, Father turned on the one person least at fault. Nanny, who had told me no stories, nor awakened any dreams in all her tenure with us, was dismissed.

Three mornings later, her luggage was on the dogcart, and out she went, a scapegoat in black felt bonnet, into the wilderness at our door. But if Father truly intended by such a sacrifice to outwit fate, he surely failed. Barely had the dogcart vanished down the drive than the postman's son came up it, cantering on his pony, telegram in hand.

Clare and I, fresh from the triumph of watching Nanny's retreat, followed the small brown envelope on its journey through the house, from the kitchens to the butler's pantry and then on a silver tray through the corridors of the house to my father's study, and saw it vanish behind his closed door.

He emerged in what seemed only seconds without it. He was strange and changed, stumbling and holding the corridor wall with fumbly fingers. He did not see us, but rushed away, whispering my mother's name. Clare and I stared after him, and then stared at each other. I wanted to run after him, but Clare entered my father's study, walked straight to his desk and lifted the yellow paper in her hand. I saw her upper teeth move over her lip as she read, and slowly tighten until two drops of blood suddenly appeared.

'You're biting yourself, Clare,' I cried, alarmed. But she was more alarmed, looking from the paper to me with misery and awe.

And so the swans came home to roost. Captain Jeremy Melrose died of wounds sustained at Magersfontein while serving with the Highland Brigade, 31 December 1900, at the hour wings soared over my head. The War Office sent their regrets, and my reputation as Cassandra was assured.

2

Oh, my dears, what a grim beginning. I wonder that you have read on. But, since you have, let me hasten to reward your loyalty with reassurance. These things are at an end, for the meanwhile. This is not a Victorian melodrama, despite my Victorian childhood. Trilby exit stage left, Chatterton, stage right. My apologies to those I've upset, but it did need to be told, not for what it was (though it *was* true and that is precisely the way it happened) but for what it led to. Nor, I promise, will you be further inundated with eerie tales of the occult. That, too, more or less ended with the century of my birth. Dark wings may occasionally sweep my story, but they sweep everybody's from time to time. That personal touch they gave me in my age of innocence was soon gone. I regard it now a congenital gift, something from the waters of the womb. If, as the Darwinians say, we all grew as fish and had gills to swim those waters, perhaps those of us with this odd trait merely carry another kind of vestigial gill. Anyway, I lost mine. The future now is as blank a page to me as it is to any. That talent, whatever it was, I trust to have some explanation that will one day be found to be rational. So much in this awesome century has.

But what it led to, for that is my story: it led, actually, to Ireland. That was the short term. In the long term it led Clare and me out further and further in widening rings of apostasy. It led *me*, eighty-three years later, here. Poor Mother, she would have been devastated.

Devastated, naturally, was what she was, that first day of the year 1901. But let us hold perspective; she was no more ill-treated than many others, and better treated than some. Jeremy Melrose was not the only casualty of Magersfontein. Or the Modder River, or Colenso, or any of the battlefields of that or any of the wars of that lady Persephone called the Famine Queen. We lived at peace in those years but our Army was usually at war. Jeremy Melrose was a soldier and other soldiers' mothers also mourned.

And William? William fell on the battlefield of a far more universal war. No, Mother was not unfortunate. She bore seven and raised six to adult years. Few of her contemporaries were so successful. I must here ask you to cast your mind back to an era that is, in this way at least, incomprehensible. They were, my parents' generation, hostages to a terrorism of microbes. They lived in a world where a sniffle could escalate in startling leaps to bronchitis and pneumonia, and these things killed. Where a headache presaged scarlet fever, a cough diphtheria, and tuberculosis – not just the dramatic pulmonary form beloved of writers (there was a *reason* for all that melodrama), but the pervasive variants that ravaged all the body with heady virulence – could attack anyone's child. Imagine, if you can, that cancer were catching, a common complication of measles, or getting one's feet wet in the rain. Then perhaps you have it: the fear ever present, the anxious soundings of chests, the isolation wards, the hysteria over wet heads, or feet, the layers of foolish garments in which, summer and winter, we were wrapped, and the layers of superstition, the same. No, my mother was not unfortunate. Check any churchyard, and see beside each married pair the little posy of infants clustered there. Clare was quite right; Mother could always have another William. She was only forty-two, and that indeed was the response expected. That she chose not to was her own affair.

Still, let me not sound hard. I do acknowledge that Eleanor Melrose suffered perhaps unfairly, not in losing two children, but in losing two in one week, and not in the logical companionship of epidemic, but in two such divergent ways. And she lost two special children; her eldest and her youngest, her heir and her baby; it was a stunning blow. In days the whole shape of our lives changed completely, our family topped and tailed like a gooseberry. And whereas a week before we had comfortably spanned almost two decades, from Jemmy's twenty-one to William's scant five years, suddenly we were condensed, diminished, and crammed within barely seven. Suddenly Clare was the oldest (though *not* the heir) and I was the youngest. We looked at each other across the heads of the three brothers we now encompassed, and saw the family shifted into feminine hands. And a tight little army we now became, with Clare our wilful head.

So there we were, my mother and the five of us remaining, all in deep Victorian mourning, a veritable draper's stock of black crêpe; black arm-bands on the boys' sleeves, Clare, Mother and even I swathed in black veils, and behind us, Persephone, our black shepherd. And oh yes, my father, in deep mourning and deeper bewilderment. And so we migrated from Arradale on Loch Ewe, floating through railway stations and hotels, filling three railway compartments with our entourage of accompanying maids, the luggage cars groaning with our six months' further supply of black. From Achnasheen to Glasgow, from Glasgow to Liverpool, and at last aboard the vessel of the Sligo Steam Navigation Company that would bear us away, we moved in stately procession, Mother like some dark swan herself, with her veils and trains, and we paddling behind, excitement overriding the solemnity of our official mourning, bursting forth in illicit shouts and giggles, soon suppressed. Everywhere we went, all others stood solemnly aside to let us pass. Until, at last, we were lined up thus at the rail of the steamer, pulling out into the Mersey and waving small white handkerchiefs (small wonder they weren't black as well) at my forlorn and bewildered father, left behind.

So thus we left, for the first time, our native land. All except my mother and Persephone of course, whose native lands were both elsewhere, anyhow. Which, then, makes this as good a time as any to explain why that was, in Mother's case, and where in Ireland we were going now, and why. Of the latter, I can be brief: we were going to Temple House on the sea coast by Ballysodare, near the fine port of Sligo in the county of that name. It was the home of Sir James Howie, my father's cousin, and of his wife, Lady Eugenia Howie, the exquisite Lady Howie of Dublin society, and my mother's twin.

None of that of course meant much to us children. We had met none of these people (nor met their three children, our twice-over cousins so soon to be our dearest allies) nor seen any of these places. What we cared for was what we knew: we were going to Persephone's home. Sligo was her birthplace, and Temple House her abode since her twelfth year when first she went into service there to my mother's beloved sister. Around it stretched the landscape of all her stories, the land of my dreams.

But you will know already that this was not my mother's home; that she and Lady Howie were of course Americans. Nor was it likely to have been the landscape of her dreams. Wherever *that* place was, I doubt anyone other than Eugenia or Persephone knew, and perhaps not even they. Surely not Father; without a doubt it was a land in which he would never set foot.

Sligo itself he did know, though he did not accompany us on this journey, for it was in Sligo that he met and courted my mother in the spring of 1878, when she was just twenty years old and already a famous beauty. The Sargent portrait of her and Eugenia, painted but five years later on one of their rare reunions, in London, shows much of what Father fell for. Of course, there is a little uncertainty because, as Mother confessed years later, she and Eugenia, quite identical to all eyes but family, eased the tedium of sitting by switching positions whenever the poor young man was out of the room. So aside from being an interesting example of early Sargent, the portrait is of doubtful historical value, recording as it does two Eleanor-Eugenia composites, in sisterly embrace. In later years I found this story, which initially amused me greatly, less amusing, as my sympathies shifted solidly to the painter's side.

Still, I can tell you from memory that in feature at least it is amazingly accurate, and though time wrought varying changes on those faces, in those blossoming years the sisters' features were virtually the same. That was the woman I knew as a child, with her smooth oval face, the wide sweet mouth, faintly troubled at the corners, and the long, straight, perfect nose. And oh yes, the mountains, true mountains of that glorious deep brown hair that I, to my childhood dismay, did not inherit. Nor did I inherit those deep brown, gazelle eyes, that seemed as if they should stare out at one from a *chador*. But then they often appeared to, because even before the days of her mourning my mother, like all women of her age, went delicately veiled in the street. Eleanor Quigley Melrose, known to those close as Nell, a name I always hear as suppliance on my father's pleading tongue.

And yet, his pleas had won her once, if not to love, then to acquiescence to plans neither of his making, nor hers. They were the plans of Master Mariner Justin Quigley, whaler and seaman, shipowner, fortune builder, widower-father: my grandfather, for whom of course I was named. But not before every worthy Melrose ancestor was first commemorated, you may be sure. Nor did any Melrose son carry the Yankee seaman's name, though all grew, quite literally, in the shelter of his fortune.

Justin Quigley was born in 1828. The date was recorded in a family Bible, but not the place. He sprang to us placeless, a true American. He next appears, like the child Jesus, at the age of thirteen, though not in the Temple, but aboard a whaler sailing from New Bedford. It was the same year, and from the same port, that Herman Melville sailed on the whaling voyages that birthed Ahab. It would be nice to say it was on the same ship, but it was not. The ship was the *Pathfinder*, and of her history we know no more than the words Justin

Quigley scrawled in his Bible below the notice of his birth:

To sea on whale-ship *Pathfinder*, November, 1841.

He said nothing else, and the next event he considered worthy of mention was his marriage to Elizabeth Dunn in 1857. He was twenty-nine. A year later he was a father and a widower, both events recorded on the same day, and then he vanishes from history until the year 1878 when we find him, a man of wealth, power and substance, parading Sligo quay with a beautiful twin daughter on each arm.

Though Justin Quigley eludes history with all Yankee reserve, it is evident at once that his daughters were not to do the same. New York, America, knew them well already. Their charming double-act graced the cover of an early *Harper's Bazar*. Gossip columns recorded their comings and goings. Justin himself remained elusive; the 'shipowner father' of Eleanor and Eugenia Quigley. His fortunes were built on a small, swift fleet of middle-sized clippers, and his own acumen that kept them darting like hawks about the world's ports with the right cargoes at the right times. By that year in Sligo, he was shipping beef, both live cattle and carcasses, in refrigerated holds, from the eastern ports of America to Liverpool, Glasgow and Belfast. He loaded grain in Liverpool and delivered it, by the lengthy route we ourselves would travel, around the northern tip of Ireland to Sligo on the western coast aboard the flag-ship of his fleet, the one he captained himself, named, touchingly, *My Elizabeth*.

And it was aboard *My Elizabeth* that Eleanor and Eugenia travelled to Ireland when Justin Quigley determined it was time they were wed.

I have wondered why he chose Ireland, and not Dublin

either, but Sligo; in those days a very remote place. In the end I concluded that this, too, was a question of markets and ports, issues on which he was wise. I will not lean heavily on the too ready imagery of cattle-boats, and cattle-markets. If Justin Quigley was selling his daughters, he was doing no more than all men since Laban and before. Nor was it money that he wanted (money went with them), but a worthy place in the world, not for himself, clearly, but for them.

I do not doubt his intentions were high; even my mother acknowledged that. What else was there for them? New York knew them, but New York must have known him as well. He was a provincial, a self-created man, and the thirteen-year-old whaler-hunter could by no means have become a gentleman. Pretty faces might be courted in frivolity, but marriages among the four hundred were not made in frivolity. And London, too, and even Dublin would turn up noses at the tang of salt water and tar. But Sligo was provincial, as provincial as he. So there he brought his daughters, twenty years old, blushing and blooming, a perfect matched pair, and set upon them as high a price in title and land as the market would bear.

That Justin Quigley had social entrée in the district was evident. Scarcely had the Quigley sisters set dainty foot on Sligo quay, than they were whisked off to house parties and dances, luncheons and teas. My mother's diary for this brief period (the only period in which she consistently kept a diary, even then erratic and written in a yet girlish hand) records a score of place names – country houses and merchants' town dwellings – where some moment of gaiety or flirtation occurred. It was at one such townhouse the girls resided for months in the summer of that year when Justin Quigley sailed away again aboard *My Elizabeth*, back to his trade. And at another such house, a country house near Ballysodare, they met the young

James Howie and his handsome cousin Hugo Melrose, a meeting so impressive upon my mother that it filled two pages of that diary. By the time *My Elizabeth* again made Sligo harbour, both sisters were lost to romance. To read that diary, one would readily suppose that the meeting was chance and that indeed romance was the moving force. But something tells me otherwise. Mrs Moore, the lady of the townhouse entrusted with Justin Quigley's daughters, appears through my mother's witness as a woman of determination, chosen for a purpose. Her ready approval of each new meeting with the Howie-Melrose pair contrasts sharply with earlier moans and complaints on the part of Eleanor. Suddenly a strict termagant becomes a fairy godmother. I sense a set-up, and suspect that in later years Nell Melrose did, too.

And so, in July, *My Elizabeth* makes her way up the channel, past the Metal Man's pointing finger to Rosses Point, collecting her boatmen for the tow into Sligo harbour, and finally sets ashore there one Justin Quigley, master mariner. His plans, those of Mrs Moore, and those of his daughters seem to have reached a point of perfect agreement and fruition. Hugo Melrose has declared his devotion to Eleanor, and James Howie to the charming Eugenia. (Devilishness makes me wonder if any of that switch-about act practised on J. S. Sargent was indulged here as well.) Regardless, the two cousins somehow made their choices, and seemed able to tell their choices apart. The Howie family, possibly to Justin Quigley's surprise, were in happy accordance. Quite probably their ready acquiescence was due to a certain misunderstanding on both sides of the status of the other. My grandfather clearly possessed a talent for impressing people. We own no portrait or daguerreotype even, though a description circulates within the family of a tall, strong, heavily-bearded grey-headed man with a look of physical strength and mental power about him; a man to be noticed. That appearance, plus the grandeur of his fleet, may have given rise to a certain conviction among the Howies that their son was marrying into a Yankee family of renown. And on the other side, Temple House and its environs, the title borne by James Howie's father, Sir Michael, and perhaps most realistically of all, their close relationship with the Melroses, all must have combined to make Justin Quigley quite certain his daughter was marrying true gentry. And so, to some extent she was, though James Howie himself and his three brothers were rough and ragged shoots off the family tree; Irish squireens with a tough flavour about them that more suited the American West, they were at heart a brawling, hard-riding, hard-drinking crew.

Hugo Melrose, however, sprang from different sources. Though they were cousins (their mothers, the Guthrie sisters, May and Bride, for whom also I was named, bringing the one line of true nobility to both families, that of the Guthries of Argyll), they had roots in different countries, with different traditions. James Howie grew free and untrammelled by either much discipline or much education, in the Sligo countryside. As long as he rode well, and his aim was true, he satisfied family expectations. As he was among the finest horsemen in the country, and a legendary shot, everyone was happy. But my father was raised in Scottish tradition, Anglo-Scottish, I hasten to add, and educated ruthlessly, disciplined rigorously, and only allowed any element of freedom on his summer visits to Sligo and the Howies. No wonder he loved it there, no wonder he chose to marry there, as if in so doing he would marry that freedom to himself. But in the end, he must always return home, back to Arradale and the heavy awareness of the importance of his position. His parents joined two ancient lines, the Argyll Guthries whose land, a forfeit won from Jacobites the century before, he would inherit, and the border Melroses whose military tradition he must fulfil.

These were the Melroses to whom Justin Quigley hoped to join his daughter Nell. A fine hope indeed, for though they lacked the Howie title, they more than made up for it with Melrose pride. They were a lineage so old and self-confident as to seem to scorn such adornments anyhow. In like manner they had scorned the making of money, until midway through the nineteenth century when, much to their surprise, they ran out of the stuff. Desperate measures were needed. And desperate measures were taken. I've often in later years pictured the groanings and gnashings of teeth in old Arradale house, as the need to come to terms with Justin Quigley and all he stood for became apparent. But they came to terms. And what terms they must have been.

Suffice to say that when at the end of that year Hugo Melrose did wed Eleanor Quigley, and when, after a year's honeymoon wandering over most of the European continent, they returned at last home to Arradale, it was to Arradale changed indeed. The old house, a fine, dignified, unpretentious dwelling that a bit of modern attention and plumbing might have made pleasantly habitable, was gone. In its place stood Arradale Castle, a great red sandstone edifice soaring up to turrets and spires on the shores of Loch Ewe like a Bavarian folly. Folly it was too, a huge ungainly and unattractive pile, but follies were in vogue in those days, and tastes were different. Most of the younger generation have chosen to pretend that it was Justin who built Arradale, not, I suppose, wishing to admit that a Melrose could have had such appalling taste. But they had, and they built it. But every stone, every roof slate, every window, every chimney pot was paid for by my grandfather, and his fleet of clipper ships.

So there we were, a fairy-tale; seaman's daughter marries nobleman and lives in a castle, happily ever . . . ? But where's Eugenia, anyhow? And what of James Howie and Ballysodare?

Well, there's the rub. As I said, I do think Justin Quigley loved his daughters and intended them well. It was no accident that he chose cousins for them to wed, close cousins who spent their youth wandering the world together. They had ridden, hunted and played from Ireland to Persia. They were, one must remember, the jet-set of their day. London, Dublin, Paris, Vienna, Istanbul.

What a world of freedom they lived in, a world I can just recall, before one half of Europe and then another was closed to us all. And what a close youth they had; surely they were as close as brothers, and surely Justin Quigley had done as well for his inseparable daughters as if he had married them into one family, to blood brothers indeed. Though their homes would be some distance apart, they would all be under one flag, and they would travel as those of that class always travelled, at home in all the capitals of Europe. It was surely a happy picture, as happy a picture as he could have hoped to see.

Painters have an expression for certain unreliable pigments, those that deteriorate, that crack, pale, darken or fade. We call them fugitives. Sometimes we are tempted to use them, even though we know they are treacherous. Sometimes ignorance leads us astray. Many fine painters have been deceived and thus leave us with pictures that distort and crumble before our eyes. There were fugitives in Justin Quigley's picture too.

The first was, oddly, Eugenia herself. For though she too acquiesced, indeed as willingly as Eleanor, to the romance of the moment, her acquiescence was short-lived or, at least unsteady. Scarcely was her sister wed than she grew difficult. Mrs Moore, still in charge of Justin's remaining beauty, found her recalcitrant. An engagement was resisted, other suitors were encouraged, scenes developed, there was anger and shouting and tears. This we have on the evidence of letters, letters that followed the newly-wed Melroses about Europe. One in particular I find most significant:

Dear Nellie,

I cannot tell you how much I miss you. I am bored to the point of death. Mrs Moore is *worse* than you can imagine.

Yesterday James called again, but I was indisposed. I suppose he will call again today.

Oh do write and tell me you are so happy, my dearest sister and love,

Genie

There were three others, similar, dated the same week. There was no reply among Eugenia's papers. Eugenia's dearest sister and love was either too 'so happy' to find the time to answer, or her answer was not of a kind that a loyal sister felt wise to preserve. In either case, one hardly sees an eager bride-to-be in the lines above.

Wedding nerves? Perhaps, for after all that they were quite soon engaged, though it was to be a long engagement that gives the appearance in retrospect of being a long chase on the part of James Howie, and a wild flight on that of Eugenia. A year later it was still going on, the hounds in full voice and the hare jinking between her stern housemother, Mrs Moore, her powerfully persuasive father, returning with the tides to Sligo, and the ever-pursuant James. By then, of course, Hugo and Eleancr Melrose were home from Europe, via Persia and the Levant and temporarily resident at Ballysodare, while

Arradale Castle was building, Nell Melrose was pregnant with my dear brother Jemmy, and the two fond gentleman cousins were together once more, riding and hunting, fishing and drinking, as happily as ever before.

And here then came the second fugitive.

James Howie had a horse of which he was most proud, a four-year-old dun stallion he planned to run at Sligo races that year. It was a big, strong, mean animal and James prided himself most of all on the belief that no one but himself could ride it. Frankly, no one chose to try. It was a vicious brute and he'd encouraged its viciousness to flatter himself. Still, as you may have gathered earlier in my story, my father too was fond of horseflesh and proud of his abilities. To ride in those days was what it is today to drive: a thing a man had to do to carry on his daily affairs but also a thing a man chose to do with as much style and nerve as he could muster. A man who did not ride was hardly a man. A man who did not ride *well* was no gentleman. But Hugo Melrose was both.

One autumn day Hugo and James rode to the meet together, with Eugenia Quigley following a pace behind on a fidgeting, high-stepping chestnut mare. She told this story so many times since that I can even tell you the markings of that mare: it had three white feet, one more than acceptable, and a white blaze half-askew down its face, giving it a more wild-eyed look than anyone would like. Eugenia adored it because it terrified her and she liked life like that. At the front was James on the dun stallion, and Hugo on a big heavy reliable grey gelding. Eleanor, my mother, was at home at Temple House, 'confined' in every sense of the word.

It was a damp, misty day, the Ox mountains enveloped in grey as they rode out from Ballysodare into the wet green countryside. Far off the hare-hounds' yelping carried sharply through the still air. Every sound was magnified; the nervous feet of Eugenia's chestnut mare ringing on every stone of the unpaved roadway. Halfway to the house where the meet commenced, James Howie was caught by the call of nature, excused himself from his lady's presence and, leaving his stallion in Hugo's charge, made his way behind a fuchsia hedge. Hugo dismounted too, to tighten his girth but Eugenia, perched slightly precariously on her side-saddle, stayed where she was. I must add that neither of the sisters was an expert horsewoman; there was too much salt sea in their blood and their past. Eugenia could ride and she liked to ride, always a little beyond her abilities because she was quite fearless. But she was a learner and made a learner's mistakes. The mistake she made this time was to drop the reins of her mount over the upper pommel, and busy her hands adjusting the veil of her hat.

At that moment, around the bend of the roadway came a pedlar and a donkey cart. It was laden to twice its height with pots and pans and all manner of metal goods and the donkey, seeing the road blocked, came to a sudden jerking halt. One large tin chamberpot, pristine and gleaming, unloosed itself from the uppermost peak of the load and tumbled and rolled, ringing and clattering over its fellows, to the road, with a clang like three church bells. The donkey brayed, the pedlar shouted, and Eugenia's chestnut mare leapt two feet straight up and took off over the fuchsia hedge. Eugenia had just time to glimpse there what holy matrimony promised before the mare was over the neighbouring gate.

My father, seeing it all and knowing James was *hors de combat*, leapt to the rescue. But he had in his hands two sets of reins; one pair holding the reliable gelding with an undone girth, and the other holding the stallion that no one could ride. Of course he dropped the gelding's bridle and flung himself up on the dun. It shimmied with fury and he laid his crop across its pampered rump, and after a moment's surprised indignation it galloped obediently off after the mare. James Howie stared, unbelieving, and the reliable gelding reliably shed its saddle and went home, leaving him to re-do his fly-buttons at his leisure.

And so my father rescued Eugenia Quigley and saved her from breaking her lovely neck. (And what a difference *that* would have made to us all.) I think she ever after held a soft spot for him; but then, so many ladies did. When, fifteen minutes later after a long and hearty chase and a true rodeo style recovery, they returned to James, Eugenia, flushed and dusty, was riding tamely before my father on the back of the tamed stallion with the chestnut mare trotting behind. And there was James, unhorsed in the roadway, awaiting them, having endured fifteen minutes of country wisdom on the management of animals and women from the pedlar on the donkey cart.

'She's quite safe,' my father, breathing hard yet, shouted as they approached. 'Only frightened, that's all.' Eugenia nestled against him, did not look frightened. James Howie was silent, just the tip of his riding crop tapping against his boot, like the twitch of an angry cat's tail.

'James darling, I jumped three hedges and a ditch and then Hugo caught me,' Eugenia exulted, seeming as proud of the one thing as the other. 'Isn't he wonderful?'

'Was I not tellin' ye?' the pedlar said.

'Wonderful,' Eugenia breathed, turning under her tipsy hat and veil to look at my father.

'It was nothing,' said Hugo Melrose, looking modestly aside.

'Spoken like a true gentleman,' said the pedlar, beaming toothlessly at James Howie. James finally found his tongue.

'Are you quite done with my horse?' he said. Father, I

daresay, was taken aback, but only paused, and nodded, no doubt in his innocent puzzled way, and carefully eased Eugenia down from the saddle and got down as well. Eugenia was hovering awaiting James Howie's concerned attentions, which she would make light of, naturally, but to which she still felt an entitlement. But James Howie was only walking in a careful circle about the dun stallion, studying its legs. He lifted each hoof in turn and set each down. The stallion meanwhile was standing like a cart-horse nuzzling my father's neck.

James Howie rubbed his hands down its big blocky legs, finally straightened up, looked Hugo coolly in the eye and said, 'You were lucky. If you'd lamed him for Sligo races, I'd have thrashed you.'

'What?' Hugo whispered.

'You heard me.'

'You cad!'

'Why, Hugo!' said Eugenia, delighted.

'Rotter!' said James.

'Why, James!' said Eugenia.

'You *bastard*!' said Hugo and hit James in the jaw. James sat down hard on the dusty road, but was up and swinging in a moment.

'Ah, why not?' said the pedlar, settling on his cart to light his pipe and watch.

'James!' Eugenia squealed, and then 'Hugo!' but they were too busy to listen to her and remained so for so long, scuffling and punching and tumbling about on the country roadway, that Eugenia, briefly flattered, became thoroughly bored.

'Oh, *do* stop,' she cried petulantly, but both cousins were too absorbed to notice, and had quite forgotten that she, or the horse, was the grounds for the conflict. Pride had been hurt and pride must be assuaged. Eugenia's pride was hurt too, now. In pique she stamped away, suddenly grabbed the reins of the unridable dun stallion and leapt aboard astride, skirts hiked up and stockings and garters in full view of the now inspired pedlar. And away she galloped. The chestnut mare, unfettered, galloped after in the way of all horses, and Hugo and James were left forlorn, dusty, and unhorsed.

'Ye've a fine runner there,' said the pedlar, nodding down the road through a cloud of pipe smoke, though whether he meant the dun stallion or Eugenia was unclear. James Howie and Hugo Melrose looked once down the road, once at each other, then turned in opposite directions and stalked, booted and spurred, away.

They did not speak again for fifteen years.

And thus the fugitive colours fled from Justin Quigley's perfect picture for his daughters. Despite Eugenia's rather innocent flirtatious role in it, it was a definitively male folly. A point of honour, they maintained, and regardless how trivial, it could not be buried. A nonsense, a comedy, but it led to a tragedy: it separated my mother from the person dearest to her for most of twenty years. It took the double tragedy of my two brothers' deaths to throw even a partial bridge over the family chasm caused by the dun-coloured stallion and the chestnut mare.

My father returned to Temple House only long enough to collect his pregnant wife and move her into an inn for the night, taking her the next day back to Sligo and the ever-accommodating Mrs Moore. From thence they departed a month later, neither cousin having even seen the other, and the sisters still, at the final moment, striving ever more desperately for a reconciliation. By then they saw, already, what this trivial rift would mean. Of course, it nearly ended Eugenia and James' engagement. But, significantly, it didn't. Indeed, in a perverse way, it strengthened and cemented their union. Eugenia really did like life dangerous and flavourful. It was no wonder she found and adopted Persephone, and revelled with her in shared glorious miseries: the stage would have welcomed them both. Suddenly James Howie had arisen out of common country squiredom to something more; something dramatic, and doom-laden, glowering like Heathcliff one moment, flaring to passionate temper the next. He became, by his illogical pursuance of his ridiculous feud, a romantic hero; even about the countryside he had achieved a certain stature that he had lacked before. It was a very Irish victory.

For all that, Eugenia resisted, torn between devotion to her sister, and her growing real passion for James, and it was four whole years before she finally capitulated. By then she herself had become an institution, and her residence with Mrs Moore, who had grown from housemother to something like true mother, had become almost permanent. She could have stayed there. She could also have married some other of her many suitors. But in the end she did her father's will, wed James Howie in St John's church in Sligo, and stepped with reluctance to his side in the feud. From thence forward she and Eleanor would, she knew, in all probability never meet.

As for Justin Quigley, the work of his fatherhood was finally done. What had been embarked upon with confidence seven years before was finished at last in weariness and certainly pain. But it was over now, and one day he boarded *My Elizabeth* at Sligo quay and sailed away, past Rosses Point and Coney Island and out to the Western Sea. He went on about his seaman's life, for another seven years. He amassed more money, banked it, kept his affairs in order, and his fortune in trust for his married daughters and their progeny. He was a careful Yankee businessman all his days. We know all this because in the January of 1892, a year before I was born, that fortune was duly delivered, in equal shares, to the Melrose and Howie families (to the *men* of those families I hasten to add) by the hand of a San Francisco lawyer who held my grandfather's will. Inclusive in that inheritance were half shares in his yet thriving shipping company, which certainly hadn't died with him.

He chose a good moment to withdraw: my father had only just retired from his military career, a career which naturally enough did nothing to add to the family finances, and for that matter nothing else had added much to them since my parents' marriage a decade and a half before. The Melroses may have acknowledged the need to compromise with New Money. That did not mean any of them were about to actually *work* yet. Of course my father kept busy; he mismanaged the estate, he fished, and stalked and shot. Life was full. And we hardly went hungry. But that latest contribution from the clipper ships was certainly welcome. It set Arradale up for another generation, by which time, had things gone according to plan, I suppose Clare and I would have been married off somehow, and the boys would have brought home wealthy wives of their own. However, all that was soon to change, for us, and for everybody. Arradale was not fated to shine as a sort of Melrose stud farm after all. Nor was Temple House, which was as well, since the Howies had, at the time of my grandfather's exit, not yet produced a son.

A glance at our joint family tree shows something interesting: both Eugenia and Eleanor produced a child within two years of their wedding days. My mother conceived Jeremy at sea, during her long honeymoon, apparently somewhere between Istanbul and Athens. And Eugenia, with more restraint, still produced her eldest, Catherine, by 1886. That was also the year Clare was born, and the sisters bonded their daughters by names, and appointed each other as godparents, so that Clare was called Clare Eugenia, and Catherine, Catherine Eleanor. But both godmothers attended those christenings only in spirit. Spirits were not subject to the feud. But that was not what was interesting. That was only natural. Weddings in those days were always followed almost immediately by christenings. But afterwards something odd happened. For both Eugenia and Eleanor seven years would elapse before another child was born, after their first. That was not natural at all. Something happened in those twin marriage beds, or in those twin hearts that brought conjugal bliss to a sudden severe end. Whatever it was, it held out for most of seven years before each wife capitulated and granted her husband another child.

Hugo Melrose had at least the comfort that the inheritance was secure. His first, and for seven years, only child was a son, and Magersfontein far away. But Sir James spent seven restless years watching Catherine Eleanor grow to wilful girlhood, his only heir. But then came 1893, and while at Arradale I arrived, Michael James Howie made his entrance at Ballysodare. Parnell was dead, and Irish nationalism in disarray; the Howie succession, too, seemed assured.

Thus Clare and I each had a shadow in Sligo. For my mother, of course, the floodgates had opened after Clare. The reconciliation, or capitulation, was complete. In rapid succession had come Douglas, Geoffrey and Alexander. And after me, of course, came William. Eugenia, however, having provided the requisite son contented herself with one more daughter, Amelia May, born in 1894, slotting in between myself and William, and her broodmare duties were done. What arrangements she made with James Howie are her secret. Life held other interests for Eugenia now.

Throughout all this time, Eleanor and Eugenia could count the occasions of their own meetings on the fingers of a hand. The last had been, ironically enough, the short period in London just before Eugenia's marriage when the Sargent portrait was executed. For although James and Hugo would neither speak, nor countenance their ladies communicating except by letter, they had no wish of the harsh judgement of history. Tradition demanded a portrait; people marked major events in their lives with portraits in those days, thank God, or all portrait artists would have starved. And so, in a series of comically stilted letters, these two gentlemen arranged for the sitting with the young artist, arranged for the meeting of the two sisters on the neutral ground of London, and arranged to jointly pay the costs. And all this without a civil word passing between them. Had I been the artist, I would have been wary of this commission indeed. But the portrait was duly executed; the artist paid and, the sittings over, Eugenia and Eleanor made a farewell that would last until the century turned.

How dreadful for them to pose so sweetly, arms about each other's waist, smiling, young yet and flirtatious, as the artist recorded a family harmony that was, but for on his canvas, a total lie. I don't know who I pity most, Eugenia, torn as always by conflicting passions, or my mother, as always by conflicting duties. I doubt she, anyhow, would have survived those years were it not for Persephone.

For as they descended into the winters of their husbands' discontent Eugenia, quite by chance, discovered a secret spring. The details I do not have, only that Mary Monogue was taken into service at Temple House sometime in the first year of Eugenia and James Howie's marriage. She was twelve then, fourteen when Catherine Eleanor was born, and utterly devoted to her, as utterly devoted as she was to her mother. By then, she and Eugenia were already something closer than mistress and servant. Perhaps Mary Monogue was a replacement Eleanor already, a substitute sister. Perhaps she was a second daughter. Whatever she was, she became quite soon a confidante and thus she remained, Eugenia's secret resource, until the year of my birth.

It had been a cold, bitter, early winter, and my mother, heavily confined with my burdening weight within, cold winter without, and her own burden of loneliness, was very low. She was, in fact, quite ill and the subject of much concern. A few days before Christmas she had drifted off to her bed and lay there awaiting either my arrival or that of death. I suspect she did not much care which. Clare, who was old enough to remember all this, has told me of sitting sobbing outside Mother's door for hours. My advent was not Clare's happiest time; no wonder she pummelled me occasionally. She was sitting there, thus, one winter afternoon when a small light appeared at the end of the corridor, a candle flame held by a maid and, behind, a girl dressed in black, with shining black hair piled beneath her small hat and a bowl of white snowdrops in her hand. Clare insisted upon the snowdrops; I do know it was too early for them, but Clare had a vivid and good memory. I must include them.

Clare stood up and faced this stranger and said, with her customary tact, 'Go away.'

'But I've flowers for your mother,' said the girl.

'They're snowdrops. They're death flowers,' said Clare, recalling the superstition learnt from the servants who would not bring them in the house.

'They're spring flowers,' said the girl. She bent down over Clare and said, 'Perhaps I've brought the baby as well.' She was holding a velvet valise and she offered it to Clare. Clare pushed it away.

'Babies don't come that way,' she said. Clare was *born* knowing where babies came from, unlike myself, who did not believe the truth when told to me at a far greater age than seven.

'Sure and they don't. Such a wise little girl.' She smiled her beautiful smile and sailed by Clare with a cool light ruffling of her hair. The door stayed open for just a moment and swung closed, but Clare distinctly heard Mother cry out, 'Oh Genie, dear Genie. Genie's sent me spring.'

Snowdrops from Ireland in December; Persephone had entered our lives. And there, more or less, she stayed. At intervals she would appear throughout my childhood, though except for that first winter advent at my birth, and again, the last at William's death, her arrival coincided with that of the spring for which Mother and Eugenia named her. And like the legendary Persephone she brought light and happiness to our northern world, and in leaving each autumn for her six months' sojourn in unseen Ireland she took those qualities away. For Mother she was an extension, an astral projection, of Eugenia. She came as messenger, a living letter, a speaking diary, holding within her pretty head all Eugenia's dearest secrets, all the private thoughts saved for her sister. For six months, those private thoughts and dreams poured out in secret sessions with Eleanor and when, after summer's end, she returned to Sligo, she took with her a store of Eleanor's intimacies for Eugenia to savour through the winter. For seven years she bound their lives together, a living thread weaving back and forth across the Irish Sea.

And then in the spring of 1901 the delicate little thread wrapped right around us all, and for all Father's amazement and all his power, there was nothing he could do to keep her from drawing us away. Clothed in black, and sanctified by grief, Mother followed Persephone home.

3

We came to Sligo at dusk. All afternoon we had steamed southwards with the Donegal mountains off our port rail. The sea was calming, but Mother, who had been ill all the day and a half since Liverpool, still lay in her cabin. Encouraged by her example I had threatened seasickness too, until Persephone said, 'And you the granddaughter of a ship's master! Of course you're not ill!' Then I became too proud to be ill and joined the boys racing about the decks, to the crew's distraction. Clare was too old for such hypnosis. 'But I *am* ill,' she had insisted petulantly, and became so, all over our cabin floor, to prove her point. Now she languished with Mother and I felt very superior.

Just as the light began to fail we rounded a sand-scimitared headland and saw the pale shadow of a long, flat-topped mountain jutting its cliff face to the sea against the pearly sky. It was Ben Bulben, although Persephone did not name it then, but drew my attention to another low mountain across the water, that was rounder and had a knob on its top. 'The Queen is buried there,' she said. I thought she meant Victoria who had but recently died, and was quite mystified, wondering why she should be buried there, and not in London where I believed her to have lived. But Persephone explained she meant an Irish Queen, Queen Maeve.

'Wasn't Queen Victoria Ireland's Queen too?' I asked.

'No,' said Persephone. 'She was not.' We were alone at the ship's rail, and I wonder even now if she would have said that if we had not been. Then, I took her at her word.

The journey up to Sligo was tedious. The channel was long and slow and we were obliged to put in at the village at Rosses Point while some of the ship's cargo of grain was off-loaded from her holds into tenders at her side. Only then, suitably lightened, and with the tide favouring her, could she safely proceed up the Garavogue into shallower waters. It was nearly dark when we tied up at last at the quays within the town. Clare and Mother came shakily forth and we were loaded with our luggage on to a series of hired cars and transported through a steep confusion of cobbled streets to the Clarence Hotel on Wine Street, where we were to spend our first night.

Persephone, Clare, Douglas and I shared the first of the sidecars, sitting back to back with a stack of luggage between our seats. As we rode, the jarvey turned round on his seat, away from the horses, and spoke to Persephone in a foreign language. To my amazement, she answered in the same.

'What are you saying?' I cried, tugging at her skirt.

'That it is raining,' she replied, smiling at the driver who I am quite certain winked at her.

'Then why don't you say it?' I asked.

'But I *am* saying it. I'm saying it in Irish,' she said. 'The language of Queen Maeve.' An Irish Queen and an Irish tongue. I was impressed.

'Servants speak it,' Clare said suddenly. 'Just like at home. It's a servants' language.' I realized then she was right. It sounded very like the kitchen tongue of Arradale, the Scots Gaelic the maids spoke among themselves.

'Yes,' said Persephone. 'Servants speak it. Servants and Queens.'

In the morning it was raining still. It was a beautiful rain, a soft, warm gentle rain that would be nice to walk in. But because of it, closed carriages were sent to collect us, and the journey to Ballysodare was a misery.

I suspect James and Eugenia Howie had forgotten quite how many of us were arriving, and with quite how much luggage, for the number of carriages and sidecars that arrived in convoy from Temple House was barely sufficient. At first I was delighted with all the fuss of loading and squeezing and Irish cursing among the drivers, because I was certain that we children would be obliged to ride atop the luggage out in the lovely rain. But in the end it was the boys who were relegated to perches by the jarvey on the accompanying sidecars while Clare and I, accounted frail by virtue of our femininity, were forced into the stuffy confines of a brougham. This despite the obvious evidence in our family that boys, not girls, were the vulnerable ones. They'd been dropping like flies, after all, and Clare and I flourished. I tried to point this out but Persephone put her lavender-scented hand over my mouth lest poor Mother hear. Thus, in train, we moved out from Sligo and into the countryside.

But, of course, I saw none of it. Rain had fogged the windows, which were quite useless anyway, and sitting where I was, crammed between Mother and Persephone, all I could see was voluminous ruffled sleeves and bobbing hat feathers. There was a dusty leather smell that closed carriages always had, overlaid by a sickly mix of saddle soap and old tobacco smoke, that to this day I recall with queasiness. Carriages were not pleasant to ride in, particularly over rutted country roads. The brougham rocked and swayed like the ship we'd only just left, and creaked mustily on its unseen springs. I stretched my neck out like a tortoise for air and began to feel sick.

Outside, the boys' shouts of delight at the invisible was my frustrating introduction to Ireland. 'A donkey, a donkey,' cried Alexander, and my fury that he should see such a wonder while I saw but wet green blurs (through Mother's black veil but darkly) almost overcame the sickness in my stomach. We had ponies in Scotland, but not donkeys.

'Let me see, Persephone,' I begged, but she and Mother were rapt in conversation, and soon the donkey was gone. Other shouts greeted other Irish glories, but I had now sunk into a queasy self-involvement that no interest could penetrate. In desperation I hummed to the rhythm of the squeaking springs, hoping to befriend the sagging motion that sought to undo me. All failed. Just as I raised my dizzy head and blurted, 'Let me out, oh please,' the carriage came to a sudden halt. My stomach swirled, trying to reconcile itself, and Persephone, leaning to the window, cried delightedly, ''Tis the little ones, come to greet us.'

Doors were flung open and in the commotion I stumbled on to the road and staggered to its verge, hand over mouth. I barely saw the three children on ponies watching wide-eyed until I had finished being ill and Persephone, alerted now, was patting my damp forehead with her handkerchief. 'The poor lamb. The poor lambkins.'

'Which one is *she*,' said a cool young voice that reminded me of Clare. I looked up, awed, and saw a beautiful pale-skinned face beneath a riding hat, wearing a look of great scorn. 'Is *she* Clare?'

'Of *course* she's not.' Clare was standing aside with a matching look of scorn adorning her own face. 'She's just the baby, Justina. *I'm* Clare, naturally,' she added calmly. She reached up her hand to the girl on the pony with amazingly adult aplomb. Their two hands met and touched with the grace of two grand ladies meeting at the hunt.

'I'm Kate,' said the girl with the beautiful face. She looked again at me and shrugged, then said consolingly to

Clare, 'Never mind. We've a baby too.' She indicated with a slight further twitch of her riding-habited shoulder the fat child on the fat pony well below her. 'That's her, May. She doesn't get *sick*, though,' she added with another shrug. May was pink and white and blonde on a dappled grey pony with red leather tack. She giggled and beamed a gap-toothed smile at me, as if we were to be allies. She was a whole year younger than me, I knew. I gave her a suitable glare to remind her of her place and then raised my eyes to meet Kate's, ready to vent my outraged fury upon that beautiful pale face. But Kate and Clare were already walking down the road towards Temple House, arm in arm, with Kate's fine Connemara mare trailing behind. The adults were climbing back into the brougham. Persephone said to May, 'Go along now, Justina's unwell.' I think she felt my humiliation and sought to remedy it by giving my childish malady adult dignity. May giggled again and turned her sleepy fat pony, drumming its rump with a leafy switch.

Persephone reached for my hand. I turned in misery back to the horrible brougham but the softest of voices said suddenly, 'I shall look after Justina, Mary. She can walk with me.' I looked up. He had emerged from behind the sidecar where he had sheltered throughout Kate's speech. He held the reins of his own pony behind his back and was reaching his other hand gently to me. 'Please, you'll be coming with me?'

'This is Michael James Howie,' said Persephone. His hair was black like the hair of princes in stories, an animal black, like the wing of a bird, and his eyes were deep brown and dark with thought. At seven years old he had already the face of a saintly priest. I gave him my hand and we walked together behind the carriages and sidecars through the soft rain to Temple House. At seven years old, I was fatally, fatefully in love.

* * *

And so began our Sligo summers. They would continue, with some intermittence, for thirteen more years, until I was a woman and Michael James Howie was a man, and all of us about to step forth to the violent inheritance of our coming of age. The house to which I walked, my shy hand clasped in his, would be my second home. So well would I know it, so thoroughly would it work into my memories, that it and its environs would become as seminal as the cold hills of Scotland to all my future life. Until this moment I had thought, in the manner of most children, that the universe centred upon my own homely circle, that all beyond Arradale was periphery. Now I had two homes, and in years to come I would have others, so many, in so many lands, that any loyalties I once held to Queens, or tongues, or nations, would dissolve in the confusion until I had learned at last that the universe circles not upon any man, woman, land or people, but upon a great emptiness in which only God abides.

'It's little,' I said to Michael James Howie, as we stood at the gate of Temple House.

'No it's not,' he said, but happily, without argument. He tied his pony to the gate post.

'I like it little,' I said. We climbed up on the flat top of the low circling wall. The house lay beyond through a grove of trees. It was a square, dusty coloured Georgian structure of stuccoed stone, two storeys high with the typical mansard roof. Behind its architectured frontage additions rambled like afterthoughts. Country houses, like country matrons, never know when an issue is settled. There were stables, outbuildings, a further grove of trees and then another low wall, beyond which, over quite ordinary fields, was the sea. The sea light lay over all, giving a misty whiteness quite unlike the brilliant sharp light of Arradale. Over the doorway was a graceful Georgian fanlight, but it was the solitary decorative moment of all the house. The windows were tall, narrow and functional and somehow friendly, so that I knew even far away that they would be nice to lean against inside, and that cats would perch on their ledges without.

'Oh, I like it,' I breathed again and Michael said cautiously, lest I be disappointed, 'It's rather big around the back, you know.' But I did not mind.

Of course, it was not little at all. You must remember that I had always lived in a castle, and a child who lives in a castle takes castles for the norm. I was hardly a democrat in those days, after all. Highland black houses, and Irish peasant cabins, inspired in me only curiosity; my major concern being where they might keep their servants. And so I approached the family seat of Sir James Howie with gently patronizing affection.

It lacked grandeur. Arradale had grandeur, and I was too young to define yet the artificiality of Arradale. Temple House was like the Arradale House that had stood before my parents' betrothal and the advent of Justin Quigley's fortune. It was old, dignified, well worn and well used, and if there was a certain unpretentious shabbiness about it, that had less to do with Irish poverty (the Howies were not poor) than with Irish other-worldliness.

The Howies *themselves* were not other-worldly either, actually. That dreamy lack of serious concern for what Protestant man regards as the duties of life – work, production, creation, conservation – was not their inheritance. They were as Protestant as we were; which in their case meant Church of Ireland, in our case the English Church, and in both cases definitely not Catholic. That link with the next world that forever lets the works of this crumble away half finished was Persephone's blessing, not ours. But still it washed and pervaded all the land on which the Howies grew; like the underlying lime of the soil it dominated what sprang there, investing all with its own unique green. After six generations the Howies, once of Northumbria, were Northumbrian no more.

The walls about Temple House, on which Michael and I stood, crumbled gently in a dozen places into grassy green mounds.

'Shall I show you my room?' asked Michael.

'Please,' I said, shyer and nicer than I'd ever been in my life. He had a wonderful effect on me, at least at the start. We had crossed the stretch of field grass that served as a lawn and he led me around the corner of the house, towards the back. It was bigger there, but I was in love with it and it could do no wrong.

'It's up there,' said Michael. He was pointing to a first-floor window, a dozen feet over our heads.

'It's nice,' I said, trustingly.

'But I'll show you,' Michael insisted, and then, throwing his arms about a wide smooth tree trunk that leaned near the house he shimmied up it as easy as a cat, and turned and looked expectantly at me. So naturally I followed, not as easily as either a cat or Michael, but I made it to the wide branch on which he sat. The branch swept close to the western wall of the house, with only a small gap to the window sill. Michael stood on the branch without holding on and walked utterly calmly along its thinning length until he could step with one little hop on to the high window sill. The window was open, and holding the bottom of the raised sash with both hands, he swung neatly within. He looked out at me from the dark interior of the room.

'Come, Justina,' he said and held out his hand. There are men in this world that a woman would step across the Styx for, and Michael James Howie was one of them. I stood on the branch, and do remember my calf-length skirt, of black worsted, over white heavy cotton petticoats, and stockings and little leather buttoned boots on my feet with miniature Queen Anne heels. But it was none of those that undid me, but that little black hat with its mourning veil.

'Take my hand, Justina.'

'I can't see you,' I said, for the hat had slipped and I needed both arms to balance.

'Take your hat off.'

'I mustn't,' I said dutifully to Mother wherever she was, but I still reached both hands up prettily, to remove it. Shades of Eugenia and the chestnut mare. And so my tree bolted and threw me and Hugo Melrose was nowhere in sight.

I woke up a day and a half later in a strange bedroom with a very young Catholic priest sitting by the foot of the bed in which I was lying. That was Persephone's doing. She thought I was going to die and was determined I be baptized and anointed in the rites of the One True Church, before I did. This was very considerate but would have raised literal hell had my mother or the Howies learned about it, so in another moment the young priest, looking rather nervous, whispered, 'She's awakin' now, Mary, and none the worse for it, I'm certain. Will ye be showin' me the way out again.'

And Persephone, beaming with smiles, kissed me and said, 'Ah, the little lamb.'

She and the priest vanished from sight, to be replaced, in what seemed like moments, by a procession of Howies and Melroses, as if to the bedside of a queen. I had begun to look about myself and discovered that I was in a four-poster, which was rather a thrill, and that the room was large, prettily furnished with light chintzes, and lit by oil lamps. To my surprise I realized it was night.

'Why is everyone out of bed?' I asked, but then Mother

arrived, tear-stained and swollen-eyed, and in duplicate, since Eugenia was standing by her side. First one and then the other embraced me and kissed me and made me generally damp with tears and I said sharply, 'Stop it. It hurts.' They withdrew at once, favouring my bandaged head, which didn't hurt so much as feel slightly fizzy. Actually, I felt quite fine, but having lost a day and a half out of my life, I was still quite certain that I was in the room to which Michael had been trying to lead me, and hence Michael was right there somewhere. And I couldn't abide to have him see me kissed.

A big fair handsome man with mutton-chop whiskers was leaning over me and stroking my hair while another man, old, dressed in black and very professional was gripping my wrist. He was a doctor, naturally, and I detested him already because he smelled funny. I peered around him and refused to answer when he asked me how many of his fingers I was seeing. I wasn't seeing any of them. I was looking for someone else.

'Where's Michael?' I asked. And then suddenly I remembered everything and was filled with quite womanly concern. 'Oh, where's Michael?' I demanded. 'Did Michael fall, too?'

There was a long, pained silence, and finally the man with the mutton-chop whiskers grimaced and said wearily, 'Michael *never* falls.' He looked pained again and added suddenly to himself, 'More's the pity.'

No. Michael never fell. Not in those years, anyhow. Michael walked the high dangerous edges of life with the sure feet of a cat. And wherever he went, I followed. He was more careful of me in the future, having found to his intense chagrin that I *did* fall and was, although reasonably robust, still breakable. Michael would never willingly have let anything bad befall me. Michael cherished me.

But life with Michael, by what Persephone called in exasperation, 'the very nature of the creature', was dangerous. And filled with delight.

All that, of course, was in abeyance. My mother's understandable panic, neatly doubled by Eugenia's, and coupled with the medical tradition of the day (see above) ensured a lengthy and totally unnecessary convalescence. My first month at Ballysodare was spent in house arrest; confined first to the vast four-poster bed, later to the room, and just before my release, allowed the run of the upper corridor, I endured an unimaginable burden of frustration. Within two days I was as fit as I'd ever been, an energetic seven-year-old imbued with the excitement of that adventuresome place I'd only just glimpsed, and in which my sister and brothers now revelled. Paradise lay beyond the tall window but I, like Eve, had fallen and was barred. Unlike Eve, however, I had return visits from the snake.

Michael was banned from my company; Nurse Reilly, May's keeper and in theory his own, guarded my room door like the angel guarding Eden. She sat outside on a straight-backed chair whenever I was meant to be sleeping, which for some secret adult reason was a great deal of the time, her knitting-needles serving for the flaming sword. May was my only child visitor anyway. The adults, my mother, Eugenia, Persephone, and most of all, perhaps, poor dear James Howie, whose remorse for his son's behaviour far outstripped any he ever had for sins of his own, all spent long hours with me. The children, my siblings and cousins, as instinctively aware as I was myself, that I was a sham, abandoned me almost at once. Little May, as determined to win my affections as I was to lose hers, came whenever Nurse allowed, to read me babyish stories and enhance my boredom with her worshipfully boring presence. Under this regime I grew piggishly obnoxious, and even cruel. May usually left my sickroom in tears, and I soon realized that my condition was allowing me unusual graces, upon which I played ruthlessly. I stormed, cried, sulked and moaned, and rapidly convinced everybody except the children that I was in desperate straits. The family conviction that I was, if not demented, at least a little odd, born in Nanny Hopkins' accusations, burgeoned happily in this climate. People began to make exceptions for me, and 'Justina's accident' was dredged up as explanation as late as a dozen years later when I began my career in art. 'Tis an ill wind.

But all was not gloom. The angel in a nanny's cap might guard the way, but if anyone could find the back door to paradise it was Michael James Howie, who did not fall. There was, alas, no equivalent tree beside my bedroom window to the one that provided his private stairway to Temple House, but Michael, my beloved tempter, was a serpent of great invention. On the fourth excruciatingly dreary day on which I had lain counting every twist of the rose-trellis wallpaper, attempting to achieve a sleep my body did not need, I was stirred by a sudden tapping at the window and looked up to see a dark head swing gaily by, followed by an arm, and then in an interesting somersault entrance, Michael was standing on the window sill.

Somehow he had achieved the roof of Temple House and then progressed, serpentine and stealthily along the guttering until, with a rope tied around a chimney pot, he descended, more or less head-first, to his present perch. I leapt up at once, raised the ominously creaking sash with Michael balancing precariously outside, and let him in.

Thus forward, every afternoon was charmed by his secret presence. He brought me treasures from the world outside, rubbed sticks, favourite pebbles, a living snail, and a fossil clam from the limestone shore turned by time into a little stone. We sat together on the floor arranging them until four when we knew Mother and his mother would arrive in a stately procession for a formal nursery tea, held in my honour at my bedside. Then we would struggle with the heavy window once more, and Michael would flee up his rope to the roof and away. So confident was I in his father's assurance that it never occurred to me to worry over his safety; and indeed, Michael never fell.

Thus fortified, I was able to face my captors, and in a short while, with Michael's giggling encouragement, I began to play upon everyone's concerns and sympathies with dramatic relapses, occasional irrational ravings and periodic collapses. I knew I wasn't getting out of there for a month; they'd told me; so I had nothing to lose. Everyone else, however, lost a lot of sleep. I cringe with guilt recalling the nights Eugenia and my mother sat by me sleepless until dawn because I had put on a spectacular performance of fainting fits at tea. I didn't sleep much either, but lay in rigid silence, terrified that some bit of blatant normality would reveal me for the fraud I was. And my guilt is twofold; for lying there, eyes tightly shut, and ears open wide, I learnt things I was never meant to know, and some of which I'm not going to tell you. Suffice to say the years had diminished neither Eugenia Howie's beauty nor her passion. Poor James Howie was yet in pursuit of his wayward chestnut mare.

He won my sympathy, actually, partly because most men did; unlike Clare I was persuaded of their essential innocence; and partly because he was intensely kind to me. So kind that I wavered in my play-acting and almost confessed the truth when I saw in his eyes his utter genuine concern. But embarrassment, and loyalty to Michael, over-ruled. Still, I spared him my most dramatic efforts and I thanked him sincerely for all his many gifts, one of which was a greater gift than he could possibly imagine.

It was during my second week, when I was allowed occasionally to sit up and read. (Propped on pillows and smothered in comforters, I, who every afternoon romped barefooted on the floor with Michael in just my night-dress!) James Howie came in late in the evening, having been to the town of Sligo all day. He had a wrapped box in his arms; he always had, his generosity knew no bounds. Gleefully I unwrapped it, quite forgetting to make my practised little dizzy shake of the head that sent them all into panics, in my hurry. Fortunately, we were alone. I had expected chocolates, but found instead a wooden box, too heavy for chocolates and too permanent. Surprised, I lifted the lid and found awaiting me the companions of all my life. It was a set of oil paints; two rows of coloured tubes, a bottle each of linseed oil and turpentine, and three hog-bristle brushes, one round, one flat, and one filbert; the perfect gift for an invalid, everyone agreed. Or a demented seven-year-old going rollickingly out of her head.

Here was a delight of which I had never thought to dream. I scarcely even knew such things existed. Of course I always drew, and pencils and chalks were at my disposal. But there were no artists in my family, no artists among my list of nannies. Mother was gracefully musical, a decorative pianist. Father could sing, even well, but never thought of it. Persephone could, should, have gone on the stage. But nobody painted. I often wonder if that were James Howie's secret talent, hidden under his bushel of manly skills. If not, how ever did he think of such a gift? Or was it chance, a glance in a shop window, an impulsive fancy? Of such casual random moments lives are shaped, it is said. Though I, recalling distant swan wings, prefer to believe those many small moments join, if viewed from far enough back, to form a picture in the manner of the pointillists.

At once I set to their use, sitting there in the mountainous surrounds of the huge feather bed, with a bemused and delighted James Howie mixing the colours on the palette before me and then allowing me to dabble on the unprepared Academy board, as he ran back and forth to the door playing lookout just as Michael did in the afternoons. I cannot describe to you the excitement I felt at the expanding dimension of colour before me. It took all James Howie's sweetness and concern to persuade me, even after a full hour, to lay them aside. In the morning I was up and painting before anyone rose.

All morning I painted. My subjects were all around me, wherever my eye fell, bedstead and windowframe, china ewer and basin, Eugenia's vase of daffodils placed by my bedside. I'd barely taken one up when another demanded my attention, and I whirled from one board to another, and beyond to plain sheets of paper when the three boards provided by James Howie were all filled. Paint was spilled, and paper curled and the old table on which I worked was thoroughly ruined, but I hadn't time to worry, even to take breath. I had born in me instantly, full blown like arising Venus, the artist's delight and the artist's dilemma, the need to re-create and return the world to the Creator. My life's purpose was learned in a morning: I would be 'a master workman at His side'. I gulped my lunch with frantic haste that I might return to my paints, and even Nurse Reilly seemed aware of strange happenings in the room that morning and let me be.

Michael tapped at the window glass for a full half minute that afternoon, before I heard.

'I can't stop. I can't stop,' I gasped, letting him in. And I didn't stop. Michael folded his dirty bare legs and settled elfin on the floor, watching me. He sat utterly silent, joyful with my joy and made no single attempt, all afternoon, to lure me from my new companions. Many a man will tolerate competition for a woman's favours from another man; few will bear it from art. There was no jealousy in Michael at all. Late in the afternoon, with teatime approaching, and but one sheet of paper remaining to me, I suddenly saw Michael as I had seen the vase of daffodils, and at once I began to paint. His was the first human face I would attempt to capture in oils.

Of course these paintings were terrible. I was seven years old; I had no instruction, the medium was difficult and totally new. Again and again I sought a line so clear in my vision and found on the paper but a soggy blur. But I was undeterred. I knew I must learn. I never doubted I would learn. Impatience to learn drove me onward, and only exhaustion at the day's end made me stop. Michael started as from a trance when I laid my brush down, and we both remembered Nurse and tea. He was barely out of the window, and yet scrambling up the rope when the door swung open on the stately daily parade. I flopped suddenly into the chair by my table and my wilting this time was utterly real. I strove to hide my tiredness, and gathered my paintings before me in neat order, afraid that my benefactors would have second thoughts and take my gift away.

Unwittingly they had given themselves a great new power over me. Now I did have something to lose if I offended them and, aware of it, set about with determination to be pleasing to all. The improvement in my behaviour was at once remarkable to everyone. I would do anything as long as they would allow me to paint. I ate my meals without question, and as neatly as I could. I was polite to Nurse. I was kind to May. I even let her sit and watch me paint, and she was the subject of my second portrait. (The first I had carefully hidden away lest its presence betray Michael's.) I no longer whined to join Kate and Clare, and I waved cheerfully to my three brothers from my high window as they went their oblivious separate ways. I was a reformed character. Only the matter of Michael's secret visits remained, but since no one knew of them anyway, this one vice was allowed to continue, and the need to choose between him and my painting fortunately never arose.

Everyone was delighted, naturally, at the small ogre in the tower having metamorphosed into a princess. James Howie of the clever gift was everyone's hero. And he, unaccustomed to so much good favour from his female household, played shamelessly to the gallery. I was showered with further gifts, and by the time of my release from bondage two weeks later, he had added to my collection a proper and expensive beechwood easel, a whole stack of Academy board and a little blue cotton artist's smock.

Thus transformed, I set out to capture Ireland. Each day I went forth from Temple House, my wooden paintbox under my arm, my blue smock tied behind me in a big bow by Persephone, and a huge sunhat of Eugenia Howie's on my head. I had become 'the little artist' in Persephone's words, echoed now by all the staff of Temple House. Beside me was Michael, my most faithful companion, my beechwood easel under his arm. A beguiling twosome I imagine we must have made, because everywhere we went, either walking or riding in the donkey cart, we were greeted with laughter and cheers. Down on the shore, where grey limestone curved coldly into the Atlantic, the country girls paused in their gathering of seaweed to come and gather round wherever Michael set up my easel. They watched with child-like patience as my paints came out and the board was clipped in place, as if I would undoubtedly produce something quite wondrous. All the while I painted they ran back and forth from their work to see my progress, and exclaimed over it in Irish words I could not of course understand. Never again would I have so innocent an audience.

But innocence was everywhere that summer. The land itself lay fresh and virgin, green with soft rains, and brightened with soft sunshine. The West of Scotland, my home, is temperate, but the West of Ireland is balmy. Never had I known such lushness of growth, leafy hedges, lanes of thick trees, bounteous pastures. The air lay like velvet, sweet with the scent of peatsmoke, misty in morning and evening, sunsplashed in the day. From every hill the far sea sparkled, rimmed in a lace of white surf. Even the rocks of the heights were softened and blanketed with heather, and fields and hedgerows were tucked up like quilts beneath their limestone chins.

Men rode shining horses down the lanes and boys walked behind milk cows morning and evening, their bare feet silent on soft earth. No place could have been more gentle, more conducive to love, and no companion could have been finer than Michael. In the years that followed we climbed every hill, followed every peaty stream, explored every deep woodland that landscape had to offer. Never in all that time did he spare in his duty to show me the treasures I was, for both of us, to record. If we took risks, as assuredly we did, it was only to better grasp some elusive angle of sun or distant sea, and always Michael took them first and led the way. Neither Mother nor James Howie ever knew of the day we clung to the crumbling edges of the cliff-face of Ben Bulben in search of an elusive cave, or the night we ran lost in the mist along the dangerous causeway from Coney Island with the tide lapping our heels. I cannot even recall which year those adventures occurred, for the years of our companionship, repeating a pattern summer after summer, have now, with time, blended into a confusion of events impossible to date.

Of course, we were not always together, and when together, not always alone. He had two sisters, and I a sister and three brothers, and there were certainly occasions when the more normal divisions of boys and girls ensued. And many more occasions when we travelled the countryside in a great, loud, laughing and quarrelsome pack.

We would set out from Temple House in vast expeditions, with ponies and donkeys, carts and dogs and baskets of food, like a great emigration. And how pampered we were by the poor people of the district, who with that glorious tolerance of the oppressed could so happily indulge the oppressor's children. Jugs of fresh milk, great warm chunks of soda bread and fresh raspberries and plums were laden upon us, as if we, not they, had once suffered the famine.

Of course I must not give the wrong impression. James Howie was no famine landlord. He was a good man and there was never an eviction on his estate. But he was also a man of his class, and in the days of the Land Leaguers his family had been victims of sporadic violence, too. And too, the years of which I write were an odd time of innocence in that country. Behind lay the years of the Great Hunger, and the bitter years of evictions and land agitation, but a new era had been proclaimed. A policy of Kindness was in force, and between the two island nations that made the United Kingdom something called the Union of Hearts was aired about. Queen Victoria had but recently set her seal upon these national affections by a regal visit to Dublin. It was without doubt a time of peace, in the eyes of all but a few.

Persephone, however, was one of those few. It took me

some time to realize this, because she was subtle, if not discreet.

If the subject of Home Rule arose, as indeed it sometimes did, even in the household of the unpolitical James Howie, she would hold her tongue as he aired his conventional views, admitting past wrongs, proclaiming noble efforts to right them, and concluding eventually with the bright future of the Union. He would usually end with a little magnanimous eulogy to misguided Parnell and rule the issue closed. Eugenia would nod, uninterested, and Persephone would smile and go out whistling a Fenian tune.

We, not knowing one tune from another, would never understand quite why James Howie fumed. But fume was all he did, Eugenia had spread her protective wings about Persephone and James knew better than to offend, lest she raise those wings and take flight. I truly think that there was never a night of his marriage that James Howie went to his bridal bed quite certain that he'd find Eugenia there. And so, to keep his elusive wife, James tolerated revolution below his stairs.

I wonder would he have tolerated as much had he realized the rebellion she was firing above.

Young minds are all dry tinder, awaiting a match. I myself was alighted that summer with art, and love, closely mingled. But Clare and Kate Howie were bound for a different fire. Those two, both eldest daughters of passionate mothers and blundering fathers, had much in common. Already they detested men. Brothers were a bore and fathers were fools. Too young to seek beaux and too Victorian to even imagine sex, they sought comfort upon the backs of ponies which already they rode better, and harder, than the boys. And they sought release in opinions, making of personal dissatisfaction, political purpose. They were not unique; they were the last twisted flowers of the Victorian summer, nipped by the first frost of realism. There was a whole generation of them, and in one way or another, they set much of their world afire.

Whether that was Persephone's intention, I do not know. She was not, I think, strictly political, in the sense of our beautiful Sligo neighbour, the Countess Markievicz, who drilled boy scouts for war. She was, rather, an accidental firebrand, a sort of Midas of Fenianism; whatever she touched with her flamboyant imagination she set loose on the paths of insurrection. I have told you already of her stories, the mystical stories of Irish heroes by which she bewitched me at Arradale. They were only part of her fund. She had stories of Fenians, stories of the rising of 1798, and the landing at Killala, stories of Confederate Americans shipping arms to Sligo Bay. She wove them skilfully and with only the mildest regard for historical truth, in the manner of all true seannachies. What did it matter how the tale really ended, if a new end made it better?

And yet Persephone was never all she seemed. She may not have been a political schemer, but neither was she the innocent voice of the people that I may have inferred, and indeed originally thought. When I asked her who told her a tale, she would invariably say, 'Oh 'twas my grandmother, God rest her soul,' or 'I had it from the good Father O'Malley, who's dead now, may he rest in peace, but stopped once down by Glencar.' I accepted that all at face value but those references, I came to learn, were like the stories themselves, an artifice in the style of the folk idiom. Some indeed of Persephone's stories sprang from the Sligo earth. Not from her grandmother because her grandmother died in the Great Hunger, before she was born, but from someone's grandmother. But most of them, like the Irish language she spoke so lovingly and practised assiduously, were almost as new to her as they were to us. Persephone studied the Irish language with a group of earnest young women in Sligo, under the banner of the Daughters of Erin. They read books, performed plays, danced and sang and with innocent lack of self-consciousness, steadfastly learned to be Irish. Behind all this was nobody's Irish grandmother, but the beautiful revolutionary Maud Gonne.

Whatever their political pedigree, the tales Persephone told set a flame alight in Kate Howie and my sister Clare, who yearned to follow Cuchulain into battle with the sea. They began to borrow books from the Daughters of Erin, and read them in secret, and Clare taxed our innocent uncle James Howie with his part in the oppression of Ireland, while Kate took to using the Irish form of her name, and called herself Caitlin Howie ever after. James called her 'the pathriot' and was clearly not pleased.

None of this much affected Michael and me, that first year. I was merely confused and he had too much humour for the solemnities of political rhetoric. It became but one more thing we might tease them about. My brothers, however, were less amused. Geoffrey and Alexander, not so much older, were frankly bored, but Douglas was only a year younger than Clare. He remembered Jemmy in his British uniform, and he was surprisingly politically aware. He challenged Clare bitterly over the Irish Brigade who had fought with the Boers who'd killed our brother. It was a savage fight and brought the first adult shadow of dissent down over our previously united childish front, and a gap opened between them that would never fully close.

We were staying at the time in a beautiful house near the shore at Rosses Point, that belonged to James Howie's family, and where each summer we spent a fortnight for a 'change of air', something much believed in in those days when a twenty mile journey was a full day's event. It was a charming fishing community then, perched out on the northern arm of Sligo bay, and I sat each morning in the dazzling sea light, with Eugenia's sunhat pulled over my eyes, painting the small boats and the fishermen in their wide black hats. Michael had suddenly joined me from the house, which was only a few yards back from the sea. He crouched down beside me in his long, loose shorts, his legs skinny and scratched from climbing in the heather. 'Clare and Douglas are fighting *badly*,' he said. He looked in pain.

I followed him back to the house. All the windows were open and even outside the house I heard them shouting. There was a large bow-fronted room filled with faded chintz-covered furniture and sunlight filtering through climbing roses by the windows. When we entered, they were standing at opposite ends of it, glaring at each other with hatred.

'You're one of them, or you're one of us,' Douglas said.

'Then I'm one of them,' said Clare, shaking her blond hair back in defiant rage. And then he flew at her, punching and kicking, forgetting entirely she was a girl.

James Howie had to separate them. Clare was bleeding from the nose and bruised about the eyes and spitting her defiance yet at Douglas. James took Douglas behind the house while Mother and Eugenia tended Clare. Michael and I, unnoticed, followed, drawn irresistibly to what we feared to see. In the pretty courtyard by the stables James beat Douglas's bare back with his riding crop. I cried aloud with each stroke but Douglas took his punishment without a word.

From then onward, when Clare joined our company, Douglas left it for the day, and when he was with us, she and Kate went away, and the days of our great companionship were done.

Rosses Point was not our only other residence. The

Howies, like all of their class in those days, were great travellers. They had friends all over the county and in neighbouring counties, and in Dublin too. Throughout that first summer, and every summer there were periodic day-long journeys by sidecar with our nightcases behind our backs, or even longer journeys by railway to the houses of distant friends. These were mostly adult occasions, in which we were afterthoughts. Persephone travelled with us and we were either left in her care to see the local sights, or were thrust into strange gardens and commanded to play with strange children who we, out of prideful contempt, would instantly detest. There followed fights and alliances, and general hair-pulling sessions, in which our brothers chased their sisters and their brothers chased Kate and Clare and May. Michael and I usually took no part. We had our own alliance. We would hide somewhere, in a barn or up a tree or, with a vagrant curiosity we both shared, creep into the forbidden house itself and lurk behind doors, listening to the conversations within.

Some of those conversations must have been quite wonderful, because Eugenia Howie had an exalted circle of friends. James Howie's friends were exalted in their own way, gentlemen landowners like himself, clergymen, and the occasional Sligo merchant whose financial influence was significant enough to overcome any shortcomings in his bloodlines. They were as a rule Anglo-Irish of the Protestant Ascendency, though there were notable Catholic exceptions. It was not by any means a religious segregation being observed, but one of class, and as such could be counted on to produce a company at once gracious and rather boring. But Eugenia's circle was her own. I suspect that a good majority were simply former admirers; there were enough of those about to fill several drawing rooms. But without exception they were people of style. Eugenia was no intellectual, but she had a natural instinct for art and for artists. Just as she chose always to ride a saddle horse just slightly too strong and too spirited for her management, so she chose a company just slightly beyond her reach for friends. Her beauty gave her entrée, and once within the door her sheer charm overcame any difficulties. There is nothing, after all, that a brilliant man more enjoys than the chance to converse with a lovely woman not quite as brilliant as he. Those wide dark eyes were the pools into which gems of wisdom were cast again and again.

My great good fortune was to be trailed like a small lap-dog through the circles of the great, at Eugenia's pretty heels. My great misfortune was to rarely realize it at the time. A small child is quite conventional, usually, and thus has little tolerance for genius, with all its eccentricities. And also, genius often lacks an easy touch with children. Geniuses are all so often over-grown children themselves, and resent the competition. They lean down and say, 'Ah, Justina,' and make weighty pauses, as if great truth were being born, when in reality, like most adults, they can't think of anything to say, yet are restrained by their originality from saying the usual foolish things.

There were one or two notable exceptions. Three in fact, and all of them were painters, which may say something about painters, as opposed to poets and playwrights, or may have been simply chance. The first I met in that first year, during a visit to Dublin, where we stayed at the Gresham in much style, and Mother and the Howies were received at Dublin Castle by the Viceroy and Vicereine.

The first was Sarah Purser, the Dublin portrait artist whose painting of Eugenia hung in Temple House until it was sadly destroyed by fire during the civil war. I think we called upon her at her studio which I believe was in Fitzwilliam Square, though I may well have the place quite wrong. I think this was not a social call, indeed I am not sure Eugenia had a true social relationship with the formidable Miss Purser. Arrangements were being made for a portrait of Michael, a portrait which, in the end, was done by someone else.

I recall being dressed terribly carefully and neatly in a sort of sailor dress that matched Michael's sailor suit. We both hated these outfits, except for the fact that they made us alike, which of course enchanted us. I was doubly enchanted when Miss Purser, who seemed to have something else on her mind anyway, took us for brother and sister, obviously forgetting what children Eugenia possessed. Eugenia explained, rather hesitantly. She was just possibly afraid of this woman, or at least in awe. But I liked Sarah Purser. She was dressed handsomely and looked handsome with an intelligent, keen face. Her hair was severely pulled up and back, and I believe it was grey, and she wore spectacles, but there was an essential kindness that I as a child felt at once, and besides, she said none of the inane boring things, or the dramatic genius things, to either Michael or me. She said nothing to us at all beyond 'Hello' which was quite honestly all we warranted.

Michael was told to sit on a chair and she walked around him and studied him as if she were a dentist about to remove a tooth. He sat very solemn and looked stunning. After a while, Miss Purser said quite suddenly, 'I would wait a year. The face is forming yet. Next year we will see the essential lines that will not change, and you will have something permanent.' It seemed a very practical thing to say, as if she knew she was to give value for money.

Eugenia nodded, a little breathless and then suddenly

she did something terribly daring, and I realized why I had been brought along. Eugenia suddenly opened a large valise she had carried all the way from the hotel and laid on a small table two paintings. They were mine, and they were probably my best. She said, all in a hurry, 'I do know of course she is terribly young, and she's not even my child. But do you think she should train?'

Poor Eugenia. She turned quite red, quite beautifully blushing and very unlike herself. What a brave and foolish act to commit for me; it was the worst of classic provincial bad taste, the offensive child pianist thrust before the visiting master, the little scholar made to recite before the University don. Had Miss Purser swept them from the table and us from her studio she would have been fully justified, and Eugenia knew it. But she loved me, and more than me she loved art. Sarah Purser looked down, moved one painting one way, and one another. She never looked at me. Eventually she lifted them and replaced them in the valise.

'There's a modicum of talent there,' she said. 'I won't mention the technique.' She glanced across at me and almost smiled. 'Surprising,' she said. And that was all. It was enough. On such crumbs, however ill-deserved, sparrows feed, and on them, indeed, I fed, through all that cold Scottish winter ahead, and the following summer and winter too, until in the spring of 1903, I met Miss Purser's friend, that other wise genius, my mentor.

4

Recollections of my childhood history invariably evoke one particular question. So I shall settle this now. The answer is no, I never met William Butler Yeats. Though we shared a common landscape and our circles of acquaintance intersected, Sligo's chief genius eluded me. For one brief moment we more or less brushed shoulders, but it hardly counts. He didn't see me, and I didn't know who he was.

The occasion was a country house party and I cannot honestly recall which house, nor the name of our host. It was somewhere on the outskirts of Dublin, actually, perhaps no more countrified than Howth. If there was a garden, I always felt I was in the country, and anyhow would rarely know what lay beyond the encircling garden walls, unless there was a tree to scale and look over. We would arrive in a closed carriage from which I could rarely see out, and leave, often in darkness, in the same way. But this house, wherever, was the home of someone of note in the arts, because the gathering there was eminent.

It was late March in 1902. I can date it accurately from events that followed and also from the joyous surprise of finding myself so soon back in Michael's company, it being not even summer yet, but early spring. This happy early reunion was the fruit of another more belated reunion; after fifteen years my father and James Howie had settled their feud. They had met for ten minutes in a London hotel, shaken hands, and departed; James to return with us to Dublin and my father to take the boat-train to Dover and thence to the continent. They were hardly Jonathan and David yet, but a beginning had been made. Between Arradale and Temple House our own Union of Hearts was declared.

This reconciliation, like that other, had somewhat the forced ring of political expediency. Hugo Melrose knew he must make peace, for during the winter that lay between our first and second Sligo summers he had come to realize that the price of continued war would be too high. The price was Nellie Melrose; her health, her sanity, perhaps her life.

My mother had blossomed in Sligo, to the degree that a woman in mourning can be said to blossom. She recovered physical strength, animation, emotional resilience. She laughed again, enjoyed company again, rose above her losses at least enough to interest herself in the family that remained to her. She did not forsake her mourning dress and never would, but she took care now over its arrangement, chose fittings that flattered, jet jewellery that enhanced. If she bloomed but a black orchid, at least she bloomed. Once or twice I saw her virtually flirtatious, though not, I add hastily, with any of her conscious will. It was merely an old habit, or a natural instinct, biology reminding her of her fleeing fertile years. She brought no flirtation home to Arradale.

Winter came, we returned home. Douglas went off to school in England, Geoffrey and Alexander to their prep school in Perth. Clare and I resumed our lessons under yet another governess, Frau Leuchner, an iron-clad German fit for the Kaiser's navy. She took no nonsense from us and for once I achieved a small measure of education, and not before time. But into this orderly winter pattern Nellie Melrose descended like the original Persephone of legend. Her laughter silenced, her colour faded, her strength and her interest visibly declined. It was no act. I saw again and again her sad efforts to overcome that lethargy, to respond with motherly fervour to my conversations, my lessons, my paintings all proffered for approval. She simply could not. Arradale bereft of William and haunted by Jemmy's ghost imprisoned her soul. Father saw, watched sadly and hopelessly, and one particularly dark day in February wrote in desperation to James and Eugenia Howie. Thus our temporary refuge became our yearly retreat and over such a permanent arrangement the feud could not blithely continue. For Nellie Melrose my father laid down his pride, and for Eugenia, James Howie did the same. Justin Quigley's ghost had triumphed. Arrangements were made for our return to Ballysodare, almost as soon as the weather made journeying feasible. But with the boys yet in their schools, this time Mother and Clare and I would go alone. Father accompanied us to London, for his reconciliatory whisky and soda with his cousin, and then set out to tour Persia on his own. His interest in the East, a boyish fancy in the days of the James-Hugo alliance, began to take a solid form that year. Scholarship as a substitute for marital bliss was hardly what one would have expected of him, and in those early years I imagine there were other comforters on his journeys, and other adventures, unrecorded in his journal. But he was getting older too, and in the end his Persian fancy became the obsessive centre of his life.

Our first month that spring in Ireland was spent pleasurably enough in Dublin. We stayed once more at the Gresham and while Eugenia and Mother happily toured the shops of Grafton Street and the galleries and theatres, we were left in the rivalrous care of Persephone and the German governess. Each day a battle commenced shortly after breakfast akin to the primal conflict of the forces of darkness and light. They were evenly matched and one as likely as the other to triumph, so roughly half our days were spent over books in the sitting room of our suite, cheered only by the regular and sumptuous arrival of meals, and the other half in glorious abandon roaming the streets of Dublin with Persephone. Michael and Kate shared this uneven bounty, but May had returned with her father to Temple House, protesting sadly. Her lot could not have been happy, separated by merely a year from Michael and me and left so irrevocably behind. But in all those years her only response was respectful longing; I never knew a sweeter-natured child.

The last week of our stay, James Howie returned from the West and it was during that week that we attended the house party at which I did not meet Yeats. I almost did not even attend it, either, because I was quite thoroughly in disgrace. As in the now distant episode of William's boat, my art was again the source of my disfavour. Throughout my life it seems to have conveyed me as readily into disaster as into salvation, and I swung always between the two as between Persephone and the German governess.

As before, Persephone herself was my chief accomplice. On each of the days on which she had wrested us from the grasp of Frau Leuchner, our peregrinations assumed a distinctive and familiar character. Without exception we would turn left as we came out of the hotel door, and regardless of weather commence a long leisurely stroll down Sackville Street until we reached the Liffey. At that point there were two options; one to cross the street and make our way along Bachelor's Walk and Ormond Quay until crossing the river by the Metal Bridge and climbing up a narrow close to Dame St, College Green and eventually Grafton Street which, with our pace slowed to that of a snail as Persephone perused all the shop windows with country-girl's fervour, we would follow until our destination was achieved. That was Stephen's Green where trees, lawns, flower beds and a little boating pond combined to provide the miniature countryside that she, again as a country-girl, felt our health required. And indeed it was a great pleasure to stretch our hotel corridor and city street restricted legs and run, Michael and I rolling a hoop between us prettily, while Persephone walked as proper as an English Nanny behind. I think she liked this pose, because she would occasionally supplement it with admonitions that, with the prim voice in which she spoke them, were totally out of character. We ignored them, knowing it was but scene-setting, and Clare and Kate walked as far away from all of us as possible. They had their own acts. Sometimes they carried parasols à la Dublin Castle. At others they wore Aesthetic smocks and pretended great intellectual conversation, as if they were students of art.

From the Green we would return then directly by Grafton Street, back to College Green and across O'Connell Bridge to proceed back up Sackville Street to the hotel. The second option was, obviously, to do the whole circuit in reverse, and return back along the Quays beside the Liffey. Michael preferred that course, since his favourite part was then last. His favourite part was climbing up on any parapet beside the river that he could reach in the time it took Persephone to glance the other way. Her progress along the Quays was made in a series of panicky rescues. Once, when she had been distracted long enough to enter a small bookshop and study a volume, Michael managed to fall right into the Liffey, and had to be dragged out, half-drowned and totally cheerful, by passing tinkers. After that Persephone walked up Bachelor's Walk with her hand on his sailor collar.

The streets fascinated us, far more than the Green which was only a tame zoo-cage version of the wild country of Scotland and Sligo that we knew so well. But the streets had their own wildlife, beggars, street musicians, wandering dirty barefoot children, tatty tinker-women each with the ever-present baby, shawl wrapped on a bony hip. Barrow women sang the prices of fruit with melodies older than time. And on the wide pavement facing the noble exterior of Trinity College, street artists chalked masterpieces for pennies, to be washed away by rain.

Some, I suppose, were students, though hardly students of that august institution. Still, as near any University, the atmosphere was Bohemian, and Bohemians would gather. Others were simply beggars with a particular talent, like those who played penny-whistles or fiddles in the street. I, of course, was utterly intrigued. I begged Persephone passionately that we might stay and watch, and she generally allowed at least the partial completion of some one chalking, before we were made to move on. It was to me what the banks of the Liffey were to Michael.

Michael usually waited patiently, because this was my pleasure, though Kate and Clare would make loud comments and moan until out of sheer embarrassment I agreed to move on. But one day Michael, who was usually quite silent in his patience, suddenly spoke out. At his feet was appearing a solemn, bearded St Patrick with his crosier, a favourite theme. The artist, an older man in worn, dirty ragged coat, his face grimy beneath a stubble of beard, smelled of whiskey and worked with feverish intent. Pennies thrown into his cap on the pavement were pocketed by the artist at once, and the cap appeared to each newcomer sadly empty. Persephone always placed our penny in the cap at the beginning, almost as if she were buying entry to a play.

'Why give *him* the money?' Michael asked, as the artist scooped it up. 'Justina draws better than that, and you never give money to her.' The artist paused. He looked up at Michael. His hair fell over his eyes and he looked threatening, but his eyes then fell on Persephone and he seemed to regain humour for her sake.

'Will that be so, then?' he asked Michael. 'And who is your Justina, lad? Is it now this vision before me?' He was smiling slyly and looking yet at Persephone. He did not realize it was her penny in his pocket that Michael had begrudged. He had not seen the charity; only heard the familiar metallic sound.

'Get away with you, the tinker,' Persephone said, flirting, but Michael interrupted.

'No. That's *Persephone*. This is Justina, and she paints *much* better than you.' My eight-year-old and unimpressive self was thrust forward by Michael's proud hands. The artist rocked back on his heels. Persephone's charm yet surrounded him, keeping him civil.

'And does she?' He said wearily. 'And will she be choosing now to show us all?' He glared at Michael and then rather angrily at me, his humiliation before such a goddess as Persephone making him harsh.

'All right,' I said boldly. There was nothing else to say, after all. He nodded, assessing me, then stood and elaborately bowed, sweeping his arm in a circle to the watching crowd and back to me, announcing loudly, 'Ladies and gentlemen, *Madam* will proceed.' He stepped back from his unfinished St Patrick and suddenly, and quite savagely, sent his box of chalks skidding across the ground to me with the edge of his boot.

I caught them, nervously settling the few shaken loose from their places by his kick. Then I moved away from St Patrick and found an empty square of pavement. I looked around a little wildly and saw Michael.

'What shall I draw?' I whispered.

'Donkeys?' Michael suggested, a little uncertain. He was very fond of donkeys. I was doubtful. Dublin didn't seem the right place for donkeys. There was a silence. The artist tapped his foot.

'Draw *something*,' Clare hissed. She was torn between pride in me, and fear that I might disgrace us.

'Draw the Blessed Holy Mother,' cried Persephone with sudden fervour. It was quite the right choice. There was a cheer from the crowd and Kate, who had of late adopted a taste for Catholicism to match her nationalist aspirations, applauded. I got down on my stockinged knees and began to draw.

The pavement chalks were velvety soft and wonderful to work with. In moments I was lost in delight and would have worked all day. I worked actually for at least half an hour, and although my portrait was quite small, its colours were rich, and the face was quite beautiful, being of course Persephone's. Who else could I use for a model?

I sat back, at last, finished and happy. There was a silence and then much soft whispering, and suddenly the scraggy dirty drunken artist put his huge rough hand on my shoulder, gently, fumbly, like one long unused to tenderness and said clearly and aloud, 'Glory be to God, the child's blessed.' The crowd began to cheer, and pennies poured down on the pavement like bright and coppery rain. Michael began cheerfully to gather them even as they fell.

Then there were cries for more, and in keeping with the religious theme, favourite saints were requested on all sides. Happily, I began again. Saints were easy actually, because they all had their symbols; as long as I got the symbols right nobody cared that the faces were all alike. I did a chalking of St Anthony with his lily, and began St Catherine and her wheel and was possibly in danger of being canonized myself by the crowd which included now a brace of young priests and several nuns. My youth and the general air of holiness on the pavement was creating the atmosphere of a religious event. The displaced artist had become a votary, declaring me blessed with each chalk stroke.

But then quite suddenly the entire mood changed. A man had been watching at the edge of the gathering, quietly and steadily. He strode forward and crouched down beside me. He was a youngish man, dressed neatly and a little shabbily, and with his flat tweed cap and metal-framed spectacles gave the appearance of an impoverished scholar. He leaned close, so his clean-shaven cheek was by my own and whispered, 'Now, Colleen, give us Parnell.' He had spoken so quietly and yet everyone seemed to hear. There was whispering, and as he withdrew from his pocket a book and from the pages of the book a small printed portrait, one of the two priests in the crowd spoke clearly.

'You'll not be asking that of an innocent child.'

There was a murmur, and then some dissension, soft-voiced because of the priests and nuns. But one of the nuns said boldly and amazingly, in a country accent, 'And why not? Was there ever a finer man served his country?'

Shock gasped across the crowd. Persephone stared wide-eyed from nun to priest. The priest was reddening and the nun, her moment's rebellion over, scurried away. But the man with the spectacles laid his little portrait of a balding long-bearded man on the ground and I obediently began to draw. My new patron watched almost greedily as my reproduction emerged, in colour and filling a quarter square of pavement. He grinned with delight, enjoying the crowd's confusion and when my drawing was nearly complete bade me decorate the corners with green shamrocks. I complied, accepting them as necessary, like the symbols of the saints. At last it was done and the student stood, still grinning and, taking something from his pocket with care, took a last look at the portrait, lifted his small print, and turned away. As he did, he flung the something at Michael's cap and it landed with a healthy clunk. Michael scurried forward and shouted with glee.

'A whole half-crown,' he raised it for all to see. 'He's given a whole half-crown.'

There was a scuffle and the crowd faded back, I thought in reverence to our sudden fortune. But it was not that that parted them, but the advent of two elegant ladies returning from Grafton Street, trailed by servants and parcels. They looked down and then up with two pairs of identical liquid brown eyes and, as one, gasped, 'Justina!' Eugenia and Mother swept me up, one by each arm, scattering chalks and chalk box about me and hauled me away to a waiting closed cab. Michael, Kate, Clare and Persephone were left standing open-mouthed in the street as we clattered away.

I sat between my two beautiful executioners, trembling with terror. Once within the staid walls of the Gresham I was marched up flights of stairs to the door of our suite and thrust within. There, the German governess awaited to add to my misery, and I was in turn berated by Mother, Eugenia, and her awesome self, all of whom declared loudly and hotly about loss of dignity, lowering of standards, mingling with the masses and appealing to the hordes. With each new onslaught they grew more excited and I grew more confused. But the worst of all was clearly the taking of money.

'Like a beggar!' cried Mother.

'A tinker,' cried Eugenia.

'A woman of the streets,' declared the German gaoler. Eugenia and Mother turned as one, and two pairs of arched black brows rose higher 'Hardly,' they said coolly and the governess retreated to her room. There was the briefest pause. Eugenia and Mother marshalled their forces and I held my breath, but then the door swung open and in strode James Howie, pink-cheeked and happy, home from a day at the races, and at once and in unison they turned upon him with a recitation of my sins. At the end he turned to me and I hid my face in my hands before him. Very gently he leaned over and lifted me in his arms.

'And how was she to know?' he said very quietly. At once I began to sob, my arms wrapped about his neck and my face buried in his tweedy, tobacco and outdoors smelling collar. I heard through my sobbing his puzzled voice say to himself, 'Parnell?'

And so I was forgiven. There were no more street artist episodes; which we children all later concluded a terrible pity because we'd made a small fortune out of that one. And thanks to Persephone, we retained it, since she shamelessly preserved our hoard, and that night when I was in bed Michael crept into my room and laid a little purse full of coins before me, and on top of them placed the student's half-crown. With Persephone's willing compliance we treated her and ourselves to a fugitive and sumptuous tea at the Shelbourne the next afternoon and felt at once wicked, and redeemed.

It was on the following day that we were taken to that famous house party and all the way there I was reminded first by Mother, and then by Eugenia that I was *very* lucky to be included and by all justice should have been left at home for my sins. Repentance being at best a temporary emotion, I was already feeling ill-disposed to the whole event, and thoroughly sour by the time the carriage rolled through the stone pillars of our host's unfamiliar gates.

Persephone was not with us. Either she was banned as they had threatened to do with me, or Mother simply wanted me closely under her eye. Clare and Kate, now fifteen, were dressed like young ladies and were guests in their own right. Michael and I were suddenly the only children left. It was a lonesome feeling and we huddled together for comfort in the entrance hallway of the house.

The usual course was followed; the adults, which included now Kate and Clare, were welcomed into the mysterious confines of the house, while Michael and I were patted on the head by distracted hands and cast into the care of a servant girl who snatched a hand each and led us perfunctorily into the garden. It was a large and pretty garden full of box hedges and ornamented by a fish pond, and there were already several other children playing as best they could in the restriction of their party clothes. Michael and I felt less at ease than in the old days when we'd made such entrances amid our great family mob. We went to a corner beneath a yew tree and stood talking, while I rolled my dress ribbons up into snail shapes and we pretended we weren't interested in anyone.

After a while curiosity overcame us, as it usually did, and we decided to raid the house. Michael, of course, was most useful at such times, with his inclination to enter buildings from above. In no time we had found a tree and a drainpipe and, round a corner from the garden full of children, were making our way along the roof of a low portion of the house.

We were soon inside, scuttling through a spare bedroom and down the servants' stairs into a dark hallway. We followed the sound of voices to the inner sanctum, a pleasant sun-filled drawing room with numerous chairs and sofas covered in faded chintz, and a scattering of small tables, making islands of darkness in the pale brightness of the room. A dozen ladies in peach, and mint green, and pale blue, and ivory tea gowns clustered at the near end of the room, surrounding a tall man dressed in black. He stood with his back to us speaking in a voice in which I heard the dreamy cadences of the sea. I was fascinated by the voice, and so were the ladies, with the exception of Mother who, distinct in her mourning, as black as the gentleman's long coat, was seated alone at the far end of the room talking in her gentle way to a bearded man in a brown tweed suit. He sat on the arm of her chair leaning forward and nodding at each thing she said. Beyond her all the other gentlemen were standing in a dark cluster, like horses under a shade tree.

Michael and I crouched behind a sofa and settled down to listen. The tall man in black was talking about a play called *Deirdre* which excited me because Deirdre was one of the heroines of Persephone's stories, and it seemed quite odd to hear a stranger speak of her whom I thought to be Persephone's invention. I chanced a peek over the back of the sofa just as the man turned to answer a question. He had a long, intense dark face and very dark eyes, and his hair was as black as Michael's and fell in disarray over his ribboned pince-nez. He wore a white collar, a long loose cravat, and was startlingly handsome. He did not see me and I ducked my head down, but just as I did I suddenly glimpsed Clare at the elbow of the man in black, and indeed it was her question he had turned to answer. And Clare, unlike the man, did see me. Her eyes opened wide in amazement and her mouth opened as if she would speak. She was furious. I flattened myself on the floor by Michael and whispered, 'Clare's seen us.' So we jumped up to run, and just as we made the dark corridor collided with the bony tall figure of a man coming in. I yelped in alarm and Michael shouted, 'Who's that?' But the man just swept us up, one under each arm, and carried us off.

'Put us down,' Michael cried, squirming fiercely. I just hung there like a limp fish in my frilly party dress, quite amazed, and the tall bony man laughed under his breath.

'A proper little pirate,' he said at last of Michael, who he set down finally at the kitchen door of the garden.

'Let go of Justina,' Michael demanded, raising his fists.

'In time, my good man, in time. You'd not want me to drop her like a coal sack.' And with that he carefully lowered me feet first to the ground. I smiled up at him quite happily. He had a nice face, a nice voice, and I was inclined to trust men contentedly, anyhow. Michael glowered, but the man said quite cheerfully, 'Have you seen my ship?' Michael and I blinked and looked round the garden as if a yacht might be misplaced there.

'No, sir,' we both said politely, shaking our heads, and I added, 'Have you lost it?'

He looked grave. 'She has foundered,' he said solemnly. 'On a dangerous lee shore.'

'Oh dear,' I whispered. He took my hand and, with Michael following warily behind, led me across the garden to the fish pond upon which, her paper sails dipping into the placid water, was a tiny model boat, fashioned ingeniously from bits of wood, a tobacco tin and pieces of card. Perched in her bows was a tiny figure of a pirate, cut from card and beautifully painted, and from her mast flew a miniature Jolly Roger.

'Push her out again,' one of the other children shouted. 'Push her away from the shore.' The tall man got down on his knees and lifted his tiny vessel, set her down in deep water, and called us to blow into her sails. At once she soared prettily across the pond, and from all the children came a cheer.

And so we spent the afternoon, drawn in among the crowd of children, who were not so bad, we found, after all, constructing little boats with the guidance of our captor. When one was finished he would take out pen and ink that he had brought with him, and decorate it with ports and cleats and figureheads so that even the most mundane of our efforts emerged as a thing of beauty. At the end of the day when a great regatta was sailing on the little pond, the lady of the house came out, and a little fussily shouted, 'Jack? Are you there Jack? There is someone who *most* wants to meet you . . .'

'But do I most want to meet them?' said our shipbuilder to us, with a funny little smile.

'No,' said Michael bluntly.

'Wise pirate,' said Jack and he left us and our fleet.

Thus I was kept from meeting Ireland's premier poet by Ireland's premier painter, and all without my having the rarest idea who either of them was. And in the end it was neither of the Yeats brothers but yet another of that illustrious family who would make his indelible mark upon me.

Eugenia blushed and chatted gaily on the way back to the hotel. She had been more than a little enchanted by the party's famous guest and was now trying to convince James Howie of his true worth. She had an ulterior motive; Yeats was presenting a new play in Dublin and she wanted to attend. James Howie hated plays, hated the Irish Literary Theatre set that Yeats dominated, and hated Yeats' politics.

'But he's an *artist*!' Eugenia proclaimed. 'What has an artist to do with politics?'

'Ask him,' said James.

'All I want is to simply see the play. We don't have to applaud or anything *favourable*.'

'No.'

'James, you are too, too harsh.'

'Mr Yeats seemed such a nice man,' Mother put in suddenly in her dreamy, always-only-half-in-attendance, way. 'I'm sure his play couldn't possibly offend . . .' James Howie muttered something under his breath. As was so usual he was being out-flanked, and ever since Mother's devastation she could do no wrong at all in his eyes. James relented. Kate and Clare cheered so loudly that he didn't even have a chance to forbid their attending too, and of course all I had to do was cuddle a little closer on his knee, where I was riding, and my entrée and Michael's was also assured.

And so, on 2 April, at St Theresa's Temperance Hall in Clarendon Street, I had the rare good fortune to attend, at just eight years old, a moment of literary history. And leaving aside all rhetoric, had James and Eugenia Howie really wanted to know what art and politics had to do with each other, they were given the perfect opportunity to find out. On that night in Dublin art and politics made a rare marriage.

Of course for Michael Howie and me, the undercurrents of the event were all lost. We were thrilled only to be released from the German governess and handed into Persephone's care, and allowed to attend an evening adult occasion from which we would be ordinarily banned. We travelled in three closed cabs to this event, an expedition into the uncharted regions of the arts. James Howie trod as warily into the Hall as no doubt my father trod even at that moment through mapless Persia.

This was alien ground, and there was an air of the revolutionary all around. The hall was packed, rather to James Howie's surprise and, again to his surprise, we were thrown in amongst an immensely varied crowd. There were other of the city's established classes in attendance, dressed appropriately for a night at the theatre. But there were students, working people and tweedy Bohemians as well. James rebelled in sudden nervousness.

'We are not staying. This is hardly the atmosphere for children, Eugenia. Come. I'll summon cabs.'

'Oh James,' Eugenia sighed sadly, and we all chorused, 'We love it. We're most terribly happy.' And before

James could rouse us from our seats and begin shepherding us out, the door swung open on the darkening hall and a tall, cloaked and costumed figure strode into the main body of the audience, and walked right up through the waiting crowds like a ghost, her hair hooded and her eyes alight. The audience gasped and whispered until she slipped from sight behind the make-shift scenery, then settled with a rapturous sigh. What an entrance!

'She was *beautiful*,' Kate cried and, indeed, even costumed as a crone, she was.

'That Gonne woman,' James Howie fumed. 'What did I say?'

But the first performance began, and Eugenia in her unruffled way whispered, 'Hush, you'll spoil Mr Russell's play.'

So James was hushed and George Russell's *Deirdre* was not spoiled, indeed was a great success, though our small contingent, at least, was still rattled by the superb bit of upstaging committed by Maud Gonne. It was hard to concentrate while awaiting her reappearance and since it was only in the second play that she was to reappear, the first lost some of its glamour. But it was very charming for all that, and very romantic, which suited me very well. I liked sad romantic tales, like the swan story, and was contentedly curled against James Howie's sleeve, dreamily enraptured, when the curtain fell.

'See, dear,' Eugenia whispered in the darkness of the interval, 'that wasn't bad, was it?' She patted his opposite sleeve and was using her child-comforting voice.

'I'll answer that when I've seen this thing of Yeats',' James growled. But of course he never did; in the pandemonium that followed *Cathleen ni Houlihan* James Howie's theatrical criticism was forever lost.

It is hard, after all these years and all the history that followed, to convey to anyone not there what that evening was like. I have, in much, much later times, heard other young people describe some pivotal theatrical event, one of these popular music festivals perhaps, in such terms, as an event that changed their lives. It always seems false-messianic and silly, to outsiders, but is hardly so to them. It is, after all, in our inner selves that we are changed or not changed; the rest of history is only the outward visible sign. As I have said earlier, young minds are dry tinder, and in Dublin that year there was a kind of political heat about that dried the kindling further. Yeats possibly realized it, possibly did not. Surely he later expressed regrets. Miss Gonne certainly realized it, and expressed no regrets at all. She was to many young people, even to such as Kate Howie, a symbol of Ireland renascent, and on that stage she took just that role, so that her living presence and her mythic stance merged perfectly to the poet's beautiful words.

And yet, even so, it is such a little, simple play, a cottage scene, a visitant, a wedding doomed, father, mother and sweetheart forsaken for a nation's cause. Today, I cannot imagine myself how it did what I saw it do. I am left with the conviction that history just occasionally sets the stage on to which, foolish and innocent, we stumble, quite oblivious, and play our required role. Of our incongruous circle assembled that night in St Theresa's Temperance Hall, there would not be a one who would not feel in years to come the fiery hand of Cathleen ni Houlihan.

Maud Gonne finished her last lines off-stage, so that her exit, like her entrance, imposed a feeling that that drama was outreaching and unlimited to any proscenium. The curtain fell and the audience was on its feet. Michael and I were wildly excited, not so much by the play, or even the eerie Miss Gonne, but by the excitement around us. We jumped up on our seats and shouted like everyone else and cheered wildly, while James Howie, in a positive fury, was muttering, 'Treasonable, the whole thing's treasonable,' and Eugenia and Mother were laughing at him and cheering at once.

But Kate and Clare were also standing and they had linked arms with a young student and were singing with the crowd, 'A Nation Once Again', as the curtain dipped finally, triumphantly down. And that was too much for James, who pounced on them, physically separating them from their student and gathered them up, almost as Jack Yeats had hauled Michael and me from that drawing room, and hustled them out to the street. Eugenia and Mother began to follow with us but had to go back to fetch Persephone who was singing with a group of young men and had quite failed to see us leave.

That night in the Gresham Hotel there was a family conference of high order. James Howie was not at all amused. He had seen anarchy, in the hall, in the nation, and in his family, and he was about to set his house in order. Eugenia and Mother at first attempted to tease and cajole and remind him that he had seen nothing more serious than a play. But James was in a new mood of determination, and regarding the play, James was wiser than we.

'That is how one stirs the masses,' he said. 'It is very easily done. What is not so easy is the settling of them once stirred. And that, Catherine,' he addressed Kate, 'is a lesson you needs must learn, and soon.'

'My name is Caitlin,' she said and James Howie struck her across the mouth.

There followed a lot of crying and shouting on everyone's part but that of Kate, who spat blood out on to her glove and turned her back on her father. He blustered and then cooled and touched her shoulder. She shrugged off his hand in a gesture that was so cold that I leapt from the chair I had been told to sit silent in and threw my arms about his waist. Poor James. He stroked my hair absently, his imploring eyes yet on Kate's turned back. 'This damnable country,' he said.

Five weeks later Catherine Howie was enrolled in a girls' boarding school in Essex to which in the autumn she duly went for the edification of her mind and the taming of her spirit. She went willingly, not to please James but because Clare was to be sent there as well. They were overjoyed, free of the family for good, and together in happy rebellion. I was devastated. That winter when we returned to Arradale I was utterly alone, at the mercy of the German governess, her sole and recalcitrant charge.

5

It may occur to you to wonder if I ever had any formal education at all. The answer, I am quite ashamed to say, is essentially, no. This was not of my choosing although, in fairness, nothing in my academic performances under that variety of nanny-cum-governesses would have inspired anyone to consider me a likely candidate for schooling. And my parents, true to their own upbringing and times, and busy with other concerns, scarcely gave the subject a thought.

I suffered thus a fate common to many girls, and especially to girls of low standing in the family pecking order. May Howie was in like situation. For while Clare and Catherine, both at this time the eldest children of their families, openly rebelled against subordinating themselves to younger male siblings, May and I hadn't a hope. We were bottom of the heap in every sense and both learned shamelessly that easy, successful female tactic of employing pretty charm to oppose strength.

May, I must add, employed it better by far than I. She had far more of both charm and prettiness to begin with, and she was placid, gentle and loving by nature. I was less pretty than unusual in appearance, less gentle than sporadically remorseful of others' feelings, and less loving than prodigally passionate.

I loved with powerful intensity when I loved, but only those objects of my own choosing, such as Michael. I could be, and was, quite hatefully cruel to innocent bystanders like May, or my mother. And though James Howie, for instance, always aroused in me an almost motherly warmth, my own father, ever more lonely in Scotland and far Persia, slipped out of my heart quite early and became for a time only an occasional impediment.

On the question of my schooling, he was much in that latter role. It was not that I yearned for education, although in certain subjects I did. Literature, art of course, and history all intrigued me and the largely unused libraries of Arradale and Temple House were my frequent haunt. But the rest, mathematics, science, I felt quite happy at the time to do without. It was not learning that I wanted, but company. Douglas and Alexander and Geoffrey were all away so much of the year, and returned at holidays large, loud, and ever more remote. Clare now too was gone. And worst of all was the haunting knowledge that only a year or two remained before Michael also was snatched away into some school dormitory and, I feared, into that solely masculine world my brothers occupied and which I might not enter.

We made a pact (we made many) of course, that we would never be separated, never grow apart, never be prised apart by others. We wrote huge elaborate letters throughout our winter exiles. But that was not enough, I knew well, if ever that distorting mirror of the adult world cast its icy splinters into Michael's eyes, and sent him out on some Snow Queen's enchanted quest.

I determined to forestall such an event, and began to campaign that if Michael went away to school, then surely I must, at identical age, do the same. This suggestion was treated by my parents with the sort of distant amused compliance reserved for impossible Christmas requests that will be forgotten long before Christmas. For a while I believed they were really going to send me somewhere, but that was never a plan of theirs. There was still a lingering family conviction that I was faintly dim-witted, due to my still persistent dreaminess and, besides, they had other priorities. The boys' educations were an essential. And Clare, like many young ladies, was in school merely as a disciplinary act. They cared not at all whether she emerged knowledgeable in any field from St Margaret's as long as she emerged compliant. (Oh, blissful ignorance!)

As for me, beyond a faint unrealized inclination to 'do something about Justina,' nothing ever came to force. The German governess, for all I detested her, is solely responsible for what knowledge I have of the rather primitive science of my youth. She liked physics and mechanical things and made a wonderful imitation of a steam engine, kerr-thumping happily like a German band. As for languages, she knew no French, and I seemed utterly incapable of mastering German. Father himself taught me a fair smattering of Persian, a language in which he was both self-educated and quite knowledgeable and that surprising anomaly in my education proved far and away the most useful of all of it in later years.

I am still excruciatingly embarrassed at my inability to grasp elementary points of mathematics and my inherent weakness in those fields, coupled with virtually no training, made my eventual entrance exams to then unthought of art schools a nightmare. But it is amazing what one can learn, or at least parrot, when the need is pressing.

My parents were not without sympathy for my loneliness, however, and aside from importing other isolated girl children to cheer me on necessarily rare occasions, they did make one great concession. And that was that Michael, when he did indeed start his schooling in England, might spend some of his holiday breaks not at home, but with us. On this promise, I lived in hope throughout the next winter, until once more with the spring we journeyed to Sligo.

This was to be the last of our summers of true freedom. Michael was nearly ten, and at that painfully young age he, as many of his contemporaries, would be sent off to preparatory school. An English school, near in location to Clare's, had already been chosen. (James Howie was coming down heavily on the Anglo side of his Anglo-Irish inheritance, in response no doubt to the Irish side surging upwards around him.) In the future our visits would be shorter, and the great question mark of change hung over them, though for this spring and summer of 1903, we wandered freely in a last innocence.

But all around there were signs of danger; already our freedom was subtly curtailed. No longer could we expect lenience when we were found cuddled together illicitly in one bed, telling stories. Our bedrooms had become the separate citadels of adulthood. The dragon of sexuality, yet invisible to us, had risen up to frighten our keepers. Persephone scolded us for swimming naked together in the sea. We had shocked the good kelp-gatherers who had once loved my paintings. And my paintings too were censored, for I had painted Michael unclothed on his favourite sunny rock, and Mother had taken the painting away.

Those were not surprising strictures. They occur in time to all children whose baby friendships cross the sexual divide. But others, less common, arose. I was an underling child; not just a girl, but a second girl, the baby of the family, a scarcely essential afterthought. But Michael was James Howie's heir. He had a role to play, and needed a dignity to play it well. All his future life, or so it seemed, would be carefully calculated on its terms. His schooling, his friendships, even his marriage were not matters of merely personal concern. Importance began to hover about Michael, like a persistent summer fly, and though he swatted petulantly at it, it would not go away.

Now, when we attended adult parties, before our dismissal from the exalted company, Michael would be brought forth and introduced, and made to formally shake hands with all the company, while I hovered uneasily at the doorway, uncalled for. That Michael hated these episodes and mocked them was a comfort but not a cure. Forces were conspiring beyond our control.

And yet out of them came, quite by chance, my liberation.

Establishment families then, and perhaps now, shared an endearing and annoying trait. They had a sense of history. It endears because thus is the past, through diaries, letters, journals and portraits, preserved. It annoys because the record created is so irritatingly narrow and self-important. Who, after all, were the Howies of Ballysodare and the Melroses of Arradale that future generations should recall them? The answer is simple: they were those with finance, shrewdness and sufficient pomposity to record themselves for future eyes. Far more interesting lives were led perchance even in the poor cabins and black houses around them; but they are gone, and in written word, and painted canvas, their betters live on.

Eugenia Howie had been painted by Sarah Purser, William Orpen later immortalized Sir James. There were portraits done from time to time of Kate and May, at significant anniversary occasions, rather as royalty are even now recorded. But now it was Michael's turn, and the portrait sought from Sarah Purser a year and a half earlier, was now to be commenced. Much care was taken in this effort, the formal visual record of the Howie heir. Letters between Miss Purser and Eugenia sought an ideal location, timing, costuming. Arrangements were made and almost completed when something quite odd occurred.

About this time we, the Howies, Michael and I, and all attendants were invited to attend a country weekend at the home of a French count in Galway, a friend of the Howie family. It was a pleasant small house set in marshland by the sea, and Michael and I had a lovely morning there searching the waters for crabs and fish. In the afternoon we were summoned for the elaborate bathing and dressing ceremonies that always presaged an outing and shortly after, restricted once more in petticoats and elaborate skirt, coat, stockings and shoes and the inevitable useless hat, I was riding back to back with Michael on a longcar through the countryside. It was a long journey during which I amused myself by getting my white gloves as dirty as possible on the battered wooden structure of the car. Mother never understood how I managed to make myself so readily filthy with so little opportunity, but I had long perfected this rebellious art.

My clearest memory of illustrious Coole Park, our destination, was the wondrous dark archway of ilex trees at its entrance, beneath which we rode that late spring day. Michael and I leaned back against each other gasping with delight at the natural cathedral over our heads, as we rode up to the old Georgian house. It was a plain structure, of three storeys, with a square porch and flowering windowboxes before the many-paned windows. Thick vines grew up its front; the whole was rich with shadow. Within, it was shadowy as well, with fine furniture and art treasures and an air of genteel must.

There was, of course, a particularly nice garden and it being a splendid day, we were free to roam about it more or less untrammelled. There were endless woods and the lake that Yeats would make so famous. On that day it was more prosaic, decorated not with swans but with boating parties of household guests, larking about rather ridiculously. If the votary of the wild swans was in residence, as I imagine he quite likely was, I did not see him. His brother Jack was there, though, and that was the second, and last, time I met him. He remembered us, surprisingly, or at least he remembered Michael who most people did remember, and he took us out as his crew for a boat race against Robert Gregory, our hostess's son.

I suppose I was meant to be introduced to Lady Gregory, but Michael and I were up a tree at the time she was conversing with the Howies. (Not, I add, the famous autograph tree upon which the illustrious carved their names, but a quite ordinary apple tree.)

'It's Queen Victoria,' Michael whispered, staring through the branches.

'It can't be,' I said, 'Queen Victoria is *dead*.' I peered down. A tiny lady in black with a long veil was talking to James Howie, looking way up with her head bent back to see him, because he was so tall. 'I *think* Queen Victoria is dead,' I said, uncertain. There was a definite resemblance. But later I saw her eating a rock bun with her tea, and I knew Queen Victoria would eat nothing so ordinary.

We had our own tea in another corner of the garden.

There were other children, and tables of wonderful food. Just afterwards, Eugenia came and called Michael away. I watched them go, in a mix of annoyance at the curtailment of our playing, and slightly awed jealousy over the additional attentions so often showered upon him. They crossed to a table set beneath a huge beech tree and sat down with the lady and gentleman who were sitting there. I skulked around corners of the garden until I found a place beneath a box hedge where I could see them and listen. I saw, much to my surprise, that the lady was the painter Sarah Purser. With her was a tall lean old gentleman with grey hair and an untrimmed white beard and the most amazingly noticeable eyes, large and bright and vividly intent on first one of his companions, then another.

'My colleague and friend, John Butler Yeats,' I heard Sarah Purser say to Eugenia and James.

He stood quickly and easily for an elderly man and shook hands with the Howies and Michael, and then quite suddenly looked up, pointed right at me and said in a loud cheerful voice, 'What splendid big rabbits they have at Coole!' I leapt up, horrified, and trailing hat ribbons and petticoats, I fled like a rabbit through the hedges and away.

And that hardly promising occasion was my first meeting with the artist father of W. B. Yeats, the only one of the Yeatses with whom I had any real acquaintance, and the man who would be my mentor and inspiration. Many, many years later, in another far place, I reminded Mr Yeats of this, our initial contact. He denied all memory of it, possibly because he had forgotten it, but more I suspect because he was a little ashamed of the panic he had caused me. He had, most probably, expected me to simply come and join the party. Like many men of his era his natural liking of children was always confounded by a certain distancing that made understanding of their motives and reactions difficult. There were many other times when he managed to terrify me, in later years, though I am sure it was never his intention, any more than it was that day at Coole.

I never returned to Coole Park; none of us did, to my knowledge. Our invitation there was one of Eugenia's high leaps, upon which she perhaps came slightly unseated. Lady Gregory, a strong, intelligent woman, loved the company of intelligent men, and was not famous for her interest in women. Eugenia's charms were little help here; and the Dame of Coole liked her men friends more brilliant than James Howie of Ballysodare. The Howies were not asked back. But it was still a most significant afternoon of my childhood. From that scant and unpropitious meeting an avenue opened up, as straight and true as that beneath the arched trees of Coole, into the world of art.

A fortnight after that day, the Howie brougham returned from Sligo railway station, and drew up at the door of Temple House, and from it alighted John Butler Yeats. He had been commissioned to portray Michael James Howie in oils, on the urging of Sarah Purser. I know now that Miss Purser, his good friend and genuine admirer, had been actively encouraging his career for some time. The Howie portrait deflected in his direction was a deliberate act. Mr Yeats needed the work and Miss Purser did not. These were not terms the Howies, well-meaning philistines that they were, could be expected to understand, so the substitution of one artist for another was cloaked in various invented justifications. The portrait that emerged in time (in a great deal of time) was ample justification in itself. Mr Yeats was a master, and the portrait a little gem, lost, with so much else, in the fire that destroyed Temple House.

Mr Yeats began work almost at once. A north-facing

bedroom was chosen as a studio, furniture was cleared, except for a chair on which, before a backdrop of an old velvet drapery, Michael was enthroned. Mr Yeats set up his easel, and spread out the tools of his trade while Eugenia fussed about rearranging the drapery and discussing at length the costume her son should wear. Mr Yeats, however, had launched on a commentary about cats, inspired by a ginger tom he had met in Sligo Railway Station, and the further into details of the portrait Eugenia timidly ventured, the further into the philosophies of the feline world soared the painter. Eventually Eugenia quite gave up. Michael was presented in a prim costume of bright blue, with a frilly white collar which he of course hated, and tugged at constantly in annoyance, and which Eugenia as constantly rushed in to readjust. She might as well not have bothered because the whole emerged only as a faint white blur. Mr Yeats was not interested in collars.

The first sitting lasted half an hour, and from it I was excluded, though I sat outside the closed door listening. Mr Yeats was now talking about lions, as a progression from cats, and then London's Zoo as a progression from lions. Eugenia was still telling Michael not to tug at his collar. After half an hour Michael came fleeing out like a released lion himself, furious and fractious. I heard Eugenia apologizing, and Mr Yeats now talking about stone lions in Trafalgar Square. Eventually they both emerged and descended to the drawing room for tea.

There were to be several sessions, even by the original plan, and as it turned out there were several more beyond. Mr Yeats was naturally a guest in the house during this time and was a subject of much awed curiosity both above and below stairs as he wandered about house and grounds in his casual, comfortable and somehow flamboyant way. He was always talking, and always about the most interesting things, or so I felt. I followed him around just to listen.

For all my interest, none of this would have resulted in anything but entertaining amusement had not Michael, as the time for his second sitting approached, utterly rebelled. He was bored, the room was stuffy, the collar itched, he wasn't allowed to talk, he got hungry, thirsty, a stomach-ache, and the paints smelled funny and made his head hurt. Eugenia listened in desperate embarrassment before the waiting artist while this performance went on, and clearly knew not what to do.

But Mr Yeats was canny enough. He only said, 'Ah, shall we ask Justina to join us and play "I spy"?' And so I did. It was one-sided 'I spy', with me spying and Michael doing all the guessing, because he wasn't supposed to turn his head or look around. But even so we managed a fair enough game until I myself lost interest and began to stand at Mr Yeats' elbow and watch with widening eyes the magic on the canvas before me. By then Michael was mollified; my presence was all he wanted. Then, too, I could give him progress reports on his image emerging, which amused him endlessly.

'You've almost got an ear now. Now he's put a big dab on your nose. Your eyes are *splendid*.' He'd wiggled with anticipation for the end of the sitting when he would, himself, see, and forgot about complaining entirely. I think Mr Yeats' gratitude to me for that relief was a foundation stone of our rapport.

But his was not the only gratitude. I was enraptured. For the first time since James Howie had laid his wonderful gift on the foot of my bed two years before, I was receiving 'instruction'. Watching Mr Yeats was the first occasion on which I might even glimpse the true mechanics of my art. I was overwhelmed with waves of new knowledge because I had experimented enough to know how little I knew. Now effects emerged before me in an instant that days of experiment might not achieve. Fascination overwhelmed even my awed shyness, and as for Eugenia's admonishments, she might as well have begged silence of the sea.

'Why are you doing that?' I would demand, unable to suppress my hunger for knowledge. 'Why *that* colour on his nose? But what's that for now?' I would burst out in a torrent of words and then physically silence myself by covering my mouth with my hand. But Mr Yeats didn't seem to mind. Nothing in the way of noise or conversation upset him, he painted on complacently through all. Sometimes he made no answer for several minutes, until some detail successfully executed, he would quite suddenly explain his use of colour, his use of light, his concentration on the eyes; 'the soul is in the eyes, Justina. Painters paint souls. Photographs are quite sufficient for the mere corpse.' (Oh, that was a line I would remember one grim day.)

Were these great secrets? Was I shown mystic depths of the painter's art? Probably not. Whether Mr Yeats would have talked so freely to another adult as he did to me, a child, I do not know, but I suspect he would. He was voluble in the extreme, but more than that, he was electrically charged with ideas, and ideas were far more important in his conversation than any personal pride. It was the idea of painting he shared with me, and as he shared it he played with it, expanded it, teased it out like a fistful of new wool . . . and he might well have talked as happily to the blank unanswering wall. But I, unlike the wall, was listening to every word.

He never asked why I was so curious; he never asked if I painted. To him the subject was fascinating, so it was natural, I imagine, for him to find others fascinated. And I had no desire to speak now of my own dabblings in his art. Even before, I was not terribly prideful; my creative dreams always so outstripped my ability that I suffered enough constant and healthy humiliation to curb any pride. And now, watching the work of his masterly hand, my own childish efforts seemed too insignificant to mention. I would have died rather than have shown him my work.

After the fourth sitting the portrait was magnificent. Eugenia thought it was finished, as indeed it appeared, and went to send for James to see, but Mr Yeats forbade it. He looked depressed and I, in an instant, understood. He was experiencing that same humiliation, the gap between the vision and the reality. Or turned on its head, the reality and the vision. Before him sat Michael, exquisite as a medieval angel. On his easel was a splendid likeness, and everyone around was lauding it mightily, but he knew and I knew that something had fled between the two on silent wings.

'It was better at the beginning,' he said sadly, looking right at me, and I solemnly nodded my head.

Then began the second week of Mr Yeats' stay. He worked on, less happily, less boisterously. He still chatted, and still explained things to me, but the high, cheery certainty was gone. He repainted and repainted. Michael, like any child, grew restless. Eugenia grew uncertain. James Howie, art being a passing acquaintance at best, grew frankly impatient. The servants began to complain. Mr Yeats was a servants' nightmare. He dropped clothing in heaps about his room, got oil paint on towels, and was forever late for meals. The atmosphere at Temple House became confused and sullen.

On Monday of the third week James Howie said, 'He's going.'

'He's not finished,' Eugenia whispered, lest the painter overhear.

'He'll never be finished.'

'Of course he will. It's quite perfect really.'

'It was perfect ten days ago,' James said shrewdly. 'He's to finish by Friday. That's my last word.' It was, too, and James' last word being dutifully conveyed to the painter, Mr Yeats did, at last, complete the portrait. And it was indeed quite wonderful, though I, and perhaps everyone else, secretly felt it had been marginally more wonderful before.

But although the portrait was finished, the painter did not immediately depart. At the pace of an Irish country house that would have been unthinkable. He stayed on until early Tuesday, and now, with the pressure of work lifted, he rose again to his remarkably ebullient and entertaining heights. Dinners became major events, much looked forward to by the Howies and whatever fortunate friends made up each night's party. Mr Yeats presided over James Howie's table with more wit and grace than any Howie had ever mustered. Even the sea-mildewed walls seemed to brighten before his presence. Michael was allowed to attend these dinners, out of a concession of his central role in the whole occasion, and I attended too, specifically on Mr Yeats' invitation. Bursting with pride, I worked hard at disciplining my tongue so as to present a figure of silent listening perfection. I sensed already that the painter liked his youthful companions largely mute, when in adult company.

The adults too would have been wise to maintain silence, while such enchanting conversation poured forth about them. But adults, lacking any authority to bid them so, can rarely hold their own tongues. So each of Mr Yeats' delightful anecdotes was surmounted by one of infinite dullness of James Howie's, as he, playing the host, seemed to feel his duty. The conversation thus waxed and waned like the moon, or the waves on the shore of

Strandhill. But for all that, each evening was a major event, and only the servants, picking up socks and scrubbing out paint stains, could have wished Mr Yeats away.

Still all was not pure delight that weekend; it had its darker, more pathetic side. Mr Yeats was a gentleman. He came from very fine stock, finer than that of James Howie, though James was assuredly a gentleman as well. But a gentleman like James Howie was reared in a tradition of lordly disregard for matters financial and mundane. He followed the accepted vogue of paying one's tailor for last year's suit when this year's was completed. And to James Howie a portrait and a worsted suit were financially one and the same. It never occurred to him to even mention a fee.

As for Mr Yeats, I know now it must have occurred to him. Then as always, he floundered in a river of debts, grasping at financial straws. And although he did so quite cheerfully, the situation was often desperate. He had only recently returned to Dublin from years of struggle in London, and even now, widowed, and with his children more or less independent, he needed whatever recompense came his way. Sarah Purser had been well aware; that was why he was here. But being a gentleman, Mr Yeats would not bring himself to mention his commission either. And thus a sad stalemate occurred, throughout the long weekend. While we all bathed in the pleasure of his company, he kept his silence. And on Tuesday morning, his case on the sidecar and the family lined up to bid farewell, he kept his silence still.

He made only one protest, and that, quite oblique and inspired by myself, one word of irony. Somehow an underlying sadness infected me, seeing him about to leave. Perhaps I had picked up his muffled lonely sorrow about his yet unmentioned fee. Perhaps the sorrow was my own, because I saw going out of my life, presumably forever, the only person who understood the dearest subject of that life. I felt welling up within me a million questions, as if I could wrest from him in an instant on the steps of Temple House all the great knowledge of my art. And quite suddenly all that sorrow and longing, and communicated misery spilled up into real, wet and vigorous tears.

'Justina,' everyone gasped, but I ran to the painter and threw my arms around his long angular body and cried out, 'I want to be an artist, Mr Yeats. I want to be an artist too.'

He stepped back, detaching himself, not angry or precisely embarrassed but a little overwhelmed by my inappropriate display, and then laughing very softly he said, with wonder in his voice, 'Oh, child of Innocence!'

And then the moment was over, and he was riding away, his soft hat pulled down over his fine dark eyes, and his white beard blowing in the gentle wind. And that was the last I ever expected to see of him. But precisely a week later a small blue envelope arrived from Dublin, addressed amazingly enough to me, care of the Howies of Temple House. Within was a single sheet of paper:

7 Stephen's Green
3 May 1903

My dear Miss Melrose,

Would you be so kind as to call upon me at my studio (address above) at your pleasure, for further discussion of an issue raised?

Yrs affectly,
John Butler Yeats

6

It was a day in late August 1907, warm, with the gentle hazy sunshine of a Dublin summer. Outside, the faint shouts of children playing among the flowers and lawns of Stephen's Green could just be heard, mingling with the occasional muffled clatter of passing hooves, and the rumble of carriage wheels. The building itself, austerely graceful in the manner of that Georgian square, provided a refined mask for the clutter and confusion within.

An artist's studio, in the eyes of the world, is a cloister, a place of silence, solitude, and peace. But the world is much in ignorance of the ways of artists. It readily forgets how much they, and writers too, depend upon it; it is their wine and their meat. Nor is the artist an anchorite. He may be a solitary, indeed must be, according to my mentor, but that solitude is an inner monasticism, invisible to the observer. What the observer is likely to see, in observing the artist at work, is a man in the midst of the world. In observing the studio of John Butler Yeats, he would likely see as well a man in the midst of chaos.

It was a happy, friendly clutter, books, easels, paintings finished and unfinished, a few chairs, some bits of drapery to furnish backgrounds, a table piled with letters; all the pleasant accompaniment of the painter's work, which like the tools of any trade give a feeling of well-being and comfort. In the centre of the room stood an easel upon which the artist's current work awaited like a bride awaiting adornment. The room seemed to focus upon it, and its several occupants fell into the roles of bridal attendants. The painter himself stood several feet back from the easel, his long lean body tilted slightly backward as his eyes, quick and dark, darted from the work to the subject even as he talked. The brush remained steadily poised in mid-air and from time to time it darted forward as he strode to the canvas, worked steadily in momentary silence, and then retreated and launched into words once more.

Mr Yeats was carrying on four separate conversations that morning, balancing them with great deftness so that no one for a moment felt a lack of his attention. From time to time he would blend one with the other so that at one side of the room or another a new happy alliance was struck. He did this sort of thing all the time, without effort.

Each of the occupants of the room was there for a different purpose, had arrived at a different time, and had radically different views on life in general, but none of that seemed to matter. Central to the situation, I suppose, was the sitter whose portrait was emerging upon the easel and she, though perhaps the least at ease, had the most pressing need to be there, and thus she endured, rather than enjoyed. She was a lady of Dublin society, an acquaintance actually of Eugenia although that was incidental. She was a great beauty of about thirty years, tall and willowy with a mass of blond hair piled high on her head and the face, at once holy and sensuous, of a Renaissance saint. The face was an accident; she was a stupid woman of little charm and her efforts to genteelly evade Mr Yeats' conversation were comic moments of middle-class refinement. He had launched on the topic of agnosticism, in both its Protestant and Catholic variants, and worried it happily like a terrier.

In a corner of the room, gently puffing at a pipe and smiling through the haze of smoke, sat the poet and painter George Russell. He and Mr Yeats were discussing the work of the playwright Synge, a conversation that had continued at intervals all morning. In an opposite corner, sniffing occasionally into a decorative silk handkerchief, resided a beautiful young actress of the Abbey Theatre Company. She had arrived shortly after Mr Russell and was unburdening upon Mr Yeats her miseries regarding her treatment in the Company by his son. And then there were my sister Clare and cousin Kate Howie, in their Oxford Mackintoshes and felt hats, brims turned down over serious eyes. They had come half an hour earlier to collect me on their way to luncheon and remained yet, engaged in a debate about Christabel Pankhurst and the suffragettes.

Through it all, I worked on, silent out of the healthy realization that I had very little to contribute. Five summers of attendance at the studio of Mr Yeats had taught me the wisdom of silence in such exalted company, not an easy lesson for a young person whose tongue had always run far in advance of her thoughts. Sometimes, when vibrant opposition to some point made welled up in me I had need to clap both my paint-spattered hands over my mouth to imprison my words, but imprison them I did. And the rewards, in the end, had been plentiful.

Beside me, propped against a window-sill, sat a pencil sketch, recently executed by the artist. It showed a young girl's oval face, wide and large eyes full of uncertainty, a rounded rather pudgy nose, and mouth both full and wide. There was something faintly oriental in the stubby features of this face, a hint of other-race or other world that vanished before any attempt at speculation. The hair, marvellously executed in the artist's soft pencil, was mid-toned and wildly curling, drawn back from the face and already making good its escape from its ribbon bond. This was me, aged not quite fourteen, drawn by the hand of John Butler Yeats.

'Well, for instance, take Justina,' I heard Clare say sharply.

'Take her where?' said Mr Yeats, studying the tip of his long brush.

'You *do* understand,' Clare said petulantly. Two years at Oxford had given her enough self confidence to speak out to Mr Yeats, but she was still, underneath, rather terrified of him. 'Here she is, fourteen years old, with absolutely no education, no plans for her future, no attempt at any improvement . . . and where is her father?'

'Where *is* her father?' said Mr Yeats, anointing his canvas.

'I am being rhetorical,' said Clare. We all knew where my father was, roughly speaking, anyhow. He was in Persia, somewhere near the Caspian, and had been so for seven months. 'Where is her father in this matter of education? Totally uninterested. Do you imagine this would occur if Justina was male?'

'But you are not male, my dear, and you are at Oxford,' Mr Yeats returned amiably.

'Clare and I are at Oxford,' said Kate Howie, 'because our fathers thought education would cure us of our misguided ways. They were mistaken,' she added with a cool smile. She had grown into a breathtaking beauty, delicately white-skinned, with a long graceful throat, ascetic thin features, and pale blue eyes set under thin arching black brows. Her black hair was drawn up and back with a severity that only enhanced her grace.

'Then perhaps they wish not to repeat the mistake,' he replied, and added, 'Besides, will Miss Pankhurst's winning you the vote guarantee Justina an education?'

'The vote is the beginning,' said Clare. The sitter before Mr Yeats suddenly stirred into response.

'I've been a married woman and a mother for years, my dear, and I can tell you there is no way my situation would have benefited from having the vote. Far from it. I have enough to cope with without need or meddling in politics.' She sniffed and said, 'I do hope this costume will suit. Does it suit, Mr Yeats?' She batted her eyes, awaiting a compliment.

'Eminently,' said Mr Russell from his corner, puffing at his pipe and saving Mr Yeats the need of providing one. 'In a few years, Dublin will judge him fairly. 'Tis a thing of genius, his *Playboy*.'

'A pity then,' said Mr Yeats. 'Dublin may have her judgement. I doubt Synge has the years.'

'That dreadful play?' said the sitter.

'The trouble with Miss Pankhurst,' said the artist to Clare, 'is hatred. She is bringing hatred into the movement, and it will cause it to founder. It is a prison that entraps all who enter it. Hatred in politics leads always to an unfortunate end.'

'That dreadful female,' said the sitter, 'spitting upon an officer of the law. A shame on all decent women.'

'When the officer of the law has your arms pinned behind your back and another is kicking your shins, there is little else to do,' retorted Clare.

Mr Yeats left his central stance, circled the room once, glanced at my easel and said very softly, 'Justina, you are not looking at your subject. You are looking at your painting and putting there what you expect to see. Look now, your rose is not that colour now.'

'I'm sorry, Mr Yeats, but it's so hot that they've all blown.' I wiped sweat from my nose, and rubbed the palms of my hands down my smock. In this sticky heat I was still wearing the usual swathes of fabric that Edwardian morality decreed: high-buttoned, full-sleeved blouse, and woollen skirt over flannel petticoats and liberty bodice and black stockinette knickers. Over it all I wore the cotton painter's smock that would have in itself been garment enough for this day.

'Paint what you see, Justina,' he said, and turned away.

'I will be most interested in his *Deirdre*,' said George Russell.

'Ah, indeed. But then yours was a delight.'

Mr Russell shook his head, his shaggy beard brushing his tweed waistcoat, but said, 'Still, it was a fine theme.'

'I do hope this colour does me justice,' said the sitter, indicating her costume once more.

'Justice,' said Mr Yeats mischievously, 'is blind.' The sitter blinked her large vacant blue eyes and looked around once for support, found none, and lapsed into silence.

'Agnosticism,' said Mr Yeats, returning to his theme and looking down his long nose at the painting, 'is questioning. The Catholic agnostic questions within, into the depths of his soul, and grows humble. The Protestant agnostic questions without, into society, and grows judgemental. Do you not agree?'

'It would not do to be talking of politics and religion, Mr Yeats,' said the beautiful sitter with a prim set of her mouth. I looked across and hoped he would capture that tight little mouth in the portrait because it showed all her meanness that I detested. A muffled sob from the corner of the room suddenly interrupted the debate as the beautiful Abbey actress made her presence known, again.

'He is a brute,' she announced with another loud sniff.

'There, there,' said Mr Russell, not for the first time that morning.

'He *threatened* me.'

'Threatened?' said Mr Yeats, raising his black eyebrows.

'He sits there in the back of the theatre, in the *dark*, in all his black clothing, like a magician, and he looks at one with those eyes, and it's *threatening*.'

‘There, there,’ said Mr Russell.

‘Willie is rather a perfectionist,’ soothed Mr Yeats, dabbing at his canvas. The lady sitter was watching rather breathlessly at the entry into the conversation of the name of the younger Yeats.

‘He’s a brute,’ repeated the actress.

‘Oh no. He is really very, very human, when you get to know him,’ said George Russell.

‘He said he’d simply give the part to someone else. To think! I will not be threatened,’ said the beautiful actress and she began to sob.

Mr Yeats looked a little distracted and said softly, stepping back from his easel, ‘Willie is merely determined to *lose* his humanity for a while. He has become infected with Nietzsche. Pay it no mind; it will pass.’

‘A brute!’ cried the actress again and she got up and ran out of the studio, slamming the door.

‘There, there,’ said George Russell.

‘Women always take things so *seriously*,’ said Mr Yeats. Moments later, when the doorbell chimed and we all assumed she had returned for an encore, he said, ‘Justina, go and answer the door, please.’

I jumped up and went out, but found at the front door another Dublin lady, as elegantly dressed, if not as beautiful as the one whose portrait was in progress. She was looking worriedly down the street and said, ‘A woman just ran out weeping.’ I nodded.

‘She’s an actress,’ I said.

‘Oh, I see,’ said the lady, nodding wisely. She came in and greeted the sitter and fluttered about, a little awe-struck until her eyes spied the easel and the painting. Then her less than beautiful face set into mean little lines of suspicious envy and she sidled towards the easel like a farm dog approaching a post on which it will lift its leg.

‘Oh, Mattie,’ she whispered mournfully.

‘What’s wrong?’ cried the beautiful sitter, in alarm.

‘Oh Mattie, the colour! It’s all wrong, Mattie, it does you no justice.’

A silence fell on the room, and into it crept a vulnerability. Suddenly we, who were artists, were confronted with the awesome power of they who paid the piper, and all our cleverness, our intellect, our bright humour were as nothing. She, that stupid and beautiful arrogance in the subject’s chair, was now our master, and we waited in silence for her judgement. George Russell shifted his feet, and coughed behind a balled up hand. Clare and Kate looked young and uneasy, even in their Intellectual Woman’s garb. And I sat with my feet apart, my hands in my lap, awkward and schoolgirlish, my head bowed in misery.

The Dublin lady rose from her seat and crossed to the portrait in which Mr Yeats had, in three scant sittings, captured all her undeserved beauty forever. She looked down upon it, and upon her elaborate foolish dress and she looked at her friend. She fingered the edge of the stretched canvas, as if fingering the work of a seamstress, and said, wistfully, ‘Does it not? Such a pity,’ and then with strengthening resolve, ‘No, of course it doesn’t. You’re quite right, Nora, it won’t do.’ She straightened her back and turned to Mr Yeats. ‘It will have to be done again,’ she said. She lifted her cloak from the chair and turned to the door, ‘If you’ll excuse me now, I’ve an appointment for luncheon.’ And without a glance back, they both went out.

The room filled up with silence in their absence. Finally Mr Yeats turned from where he had stood in gentlemanly reserve and, looking about the room, let his eyes come to rest on me. He said patiently, ‘The woman has the face of an angel. I have done it full justice. What more can she possibly want?’ He was still looking right at me, and he wanted an answer, not from the others, but from me.

I took a deep breath, and said what I had seen: 'It's not to do with the painting. It's between the two ladies. One is beautiful and the other plain, and the beautiful one wants the plain one to say the painting is beautiful *because* the painting is so like her, and she knows it. And that was why the plain one must say something mean.' I closed my mouth and instinctively put my hands over it.

But Mr Yeats nodded slowly, looked away for a moment, and then his eyes shot back to mine. 'Would *you* behave like that?' he said, marvelling at the wiles of womanhood.

'I'm not pretty enough even to be jealous,' I said. George Russell laughed gently, but Mr Yeats said, 'Oh wise young Justina. Stay wise, though you cannot stay young.' He put away his paints, and cleaned his brushes carefully and sadly, and I did the same. Then I hung my smock on its peg in the cupboard and we all went out together, but he and George Russell walked off one way, into the trees and flowers of the Green, and I went with Clare and Kate down Grafton Street to the Liffey and Ormond Quay.

There was a café there, run by friends of Kate Howie, a young husband and wife, and the wife's sister. They were Theosophists, devotees of the renowned spiritualist Mme Blavatsky, and it was a vegetarian café, something for which there was a vogue in those days, and many of the patrons were students and artists and foreigners. We went there frequently, Kate and Clare and I, and Michael, May, my brothers Alexander and Geoffrey and of course Persephone. We travelled about the city in a great crowd, just as our younger selves had once roamed Sligo. Now, as then, Mother and Eugenia trusted in that unlikely adage of safety in numbers.

We knew Dublin well; the Howies had taken a town-house in Merrion Square in 1904, and spent much of their time there, or at least Eugenia did. The express purpose was provision for the need of the children to mix in Society, but since May was a year younger than me, Michael only a schoolboy, and Kate finding a very different society in London and Oxford in which to mix, the real benefits fell naturally upon Eugenia. Theatres, shops, and the Vice-Regal Court all beckoned and those were no doubt among her happiest years.

For my own family, the Dublin summers were surprisingly our time of greatest unity. For the rest of the year we were so fragmented and scattered as to hardly be a family at all. Mother and I grew close in those years. We were the only Melroses always together. Clare had gone on from her English school to Somerville College at Oxford, distinguishing herself academically, and raising eyebrows and tempers wherever she turned. The suffragette movement held her devotion now, as Irish Home Rule held Kate's and between the two cousins lay the same uneasy alliance that bound their two causes in Parliament. In neither case was there much time left over for family, and Clare rarely returned to Arradale. The boys too, were infrequent visitors. Douglas had dutifully followed his dead brother Jeremy into the family Regiment, taking on military duty with the same solemnity he took on everything else. Had he ever hopes and plans of his own, they were submerged forever upon his eldest brother's death. Inheritance and responsibility became his standards, and at twenty he had behind his new officer's moustache the serious face and humourless eyes of a weary middle-aged man. He was at Sandhurst and communicated with us all by stiff formal letters reeking with duty. Clare called him 'the Chocolate Soldier' but I felt sorry for him and thinking of him always made me sad.

Thinking of Geoffrey, on the other hand, made me laugh. I couldn't help it, try as I might. Geoffrey had adopted that familiar lesser son's ploy and gone into the Church. He was in his first year at the Episcopal Theological College in Edinburgh, and went about with a long clerical face and a stack of ecclesiastical texts under his arm, trying and failing to create an air of reverence. The failure was no doubt inherent in the lack of any real spiritual calling, at least at that early stage. Persephone had been quite awestruck at this turn of events, and although she did not equate our church's priesthood with that of her own, enough coincidental holiness rubbed off on to Geoffrey to thoroughly impress her.

'Will I have to be callin' him Father, now?' she asked me seriously every time Geoffrey was about to join our company.

'Not yet,' I would answer, smothering giggles. Poor Geoffrey, he was that sort of young man whose cheerful face, and precise neat dress always delighted adults and sent companions of his own age into hysteria. His collar was always too starched, his trousers somehow always too short, his braces too tight, so that his waistline rode up under his arms and he looked like Charlie Chaplin. His bright face, born for a freckly grin, was forever in his student years frozen in a rigid mask of respectability lest it break up into worldly mirth. Poor silly Geoffrey.

Still, scholarly pursuits kept Geoffrey also far from Arradale. Alexander was now at Eton with Michael Howie. Only a year apart in age, they had become good companions during term, and often returned together to Arradale for their holidays. For a while, we were a threesome, but the tightening strictures of femininity soon banned me from their company when they went off, with packs on their backs, to the hills. Michael had lost none of his desire to get on top of things, and had found a wonderful new outlet in the mountains of Scotland and Wales. For a while his schooling seemed threatened by an irrepressible urge to wander, often as far as the Grampians, even during term-time. But he was a serious student at heart, with a passion for science.

I, of course, went to no school at all. Frau Leuchner still instructed me and a French tutor was briefly imported one year, but essentially my education was in my own hands. I made good use of the Arradale library, and I painted and I was, actually, totally content. My loneliness was lessened by Michael's visits, and by his long wonderful letters. Nor was he my only correspondent. I wrote to everybody; Clare, Kate, May Howie who shared a similar homebound girlhood, to my brothers, to my often absent father, and of course I wrote to Mr Yeats, who answered with wonderful philosophical tracts miles above my eager head. We were a generation of letter writers, which was as well because we were also a generation doomed to separation.

Clare did often express concern about my educationless state, just as she had to Mr Yeats in his studio, but essentially her concern was political, as were so many of her emotions. I was a good example of neglected womanhood, and as such a weapon in her long-running battle with our father. I do not think she really cared much what happened to me; that sounds very harsh, but it is probably accurate. As for our father himself, he was the most elusive member of our elusive family, the Great Wanderer in a tribe of wanderers, our mysterious and amiable ghost.

What had begun undoubtedly as an escape, a fleeing from an unhappy marriage and a grief-stricken, unapproachable wife, had become now the centre of his life. It is difficult to imagine, looking over his journals of those years, and his huge and scholarly dissertation on the Babi Movement, unpublished until after his death, that those early journeys began as a dilettantish fancy. But if they did, it soon gave way to deeper things. My father, I suppose, was a man not unlike his eldest surviving son; like Douglas he felt obligated to take upon him duty and service. He had gone into the military because it was a tradition, and had never allowed himself to consider anything else. It was only by accident he discovered his true calling was scholarship.

Within two years he had mastered Persian and was at work on translations. He plunged into a study of the Islamic faith and in later years knew much of the Koran by heart. I can recall him in his study at Arradale chanting out whole suras in Arabic, and saying afterwards sadly, to me, 'It does not translate. It does not translate.' And assuredly the wonderful music of the original never did. Soon he was bringing home artefacts to the British Museum, and writing tracts about them for scholarly publications. Naturally his stays in the East grew longer and the gaps between them shorter, and his relations with much of the family grew thin to the point of breaking. And yet, it was in these years that I grew to appreciate my father for the wise, and foolish man that he was. And it was at his knee, quite literally, that I first learned of the lands and ways and mysterious faiths of Persia, that would haunt me the rest of my life.

Still, with Father so much away, and with her own health entering an ominous decline, Mother had become more a widow than a wife, a gentle, wanly beautiful defeated soul whom I yearned to protect. For her sake alone I made no strong plea to be sent away to school; I was her last companion. And so I remained there, studying my father's books, and wandering with my paints around the wild, West Highland countryside whose greater expanses became more attainable as my legs grew longer and my nature bolder. Michael had infected me with the excitement of the high country and I spent long days alone on the winter hills seeking to capture those lights and skies that elude me even today. It was, in spite of Clare's protests, an idyllic, if lonely, youth.

And then, of course, there were always the summers, in Sligo and more and more in Dublin, where my study of art progressed in its unique way under the casual and yet intense tutelage of Mr Yeats, an arrangement struck almost by accident out of a chance meeting, and for which he neither received, nor indeed expected, a farthing of pay. What had begun in my tenth year as an occasional visit, had become by my fourteenth a summer long routine, and what little chores I did about the studio, cleaning brushes and palettes, and seeing to the needs of visitors, could hardly have amounted to recompense. It was simply a gift, of immeasurable worth, and if my mother and the Howies regarded it with only a kind of tacit bemused approval, I myself was filled with such gratitude that I glowed with it, and Mr Yeats must surely have been aware. While Mother idled, and Clare fussed, and Father sporadically tossed scholarship my way, Mr Yeats in five summers laid my career at my feet.

Dublin meant more though, than this, although this was surely the centre. Dublin meant theatres, and cafés and conversation and a great, loud, chaotic gathering of Melrose and Howie young people, full of argument and dispute and conflict and delight. And most of all, Dublin meant Michael. Home from school, he had months of freedom and every hour possible was spent with me. Of course we were not alone in any sense. Clare, Kate, Persephone, May, Geoffrey, Sandy; always there was someone, and often everyone, as chaperone, if a chaperone was needed. But it did not matter; Michael and I had that rare ability of being alone together in the largest crowd, and over the table of the vegetarian café we communicated in whispers and giggles and grins.

There were eight around the table that day, squabbling

joyfully over our luncheon of nuts and goat's milk cheese. The table was a long, bare scrubbed deal affair and the furnishings of the café were equally bare, its walls dramatically adorned with life-size renditions of ancient Irish heroes and heroines, executed in bright clear colours and romantic simplistic style replete with symbolic flowers and flowing draperies.

The host and two hostesses drifted about in garments of exotic cut, fashioned in home-weave and unadorned by the conventional strictures of stiff collars and corsetry. I watched them in envy. I had only recently been encased in stays by Mother's directive and under their guardianship I itched and prickled in the sticky heat. To thus corset my skinny young body was as ridiculous as bolstering a birch tree with flying buttresses. But I was not a rebel, and never thought to even question my imprisonment. Nor, surprisingly, did Clare. For all her shortened straight skirts, flat heeled laced shoes and sober coat and hat she was, underneath, as wrapped up in Edwardian frippery as I. But then, we all were, and had few other examples. Mother yet went about the world black as a lady in purdah, heavy with veils, and Eugenia, in her frivolity, was laden with linen and lawn, and cascaded with lace, topped always with a hat of immense proportions and profusion of plumes and blooms. She did look amazingly wonderful in one way, and in another, like a square-rigged ship in full sail. Even Persephone, sitting at the head of our long table, was corseted up in a large-bosomed, top-heavy shape quite unlike her own natural form. She was dressed in a mauve linen suit, with the inevitable draped and drooping lace blouse and a collar four buttons high under her chin. Her hat swooped over one eye and was so feathered and flounced as to appear like the back of a living purple bird. She looked quite marvellous actually, with her pink cheeks and her black hair set against all that lavender splendour, and the young man at her side seemed unable to take his eyes from her for a moment.

Two things had happened to Persephone in the intervening years. The first was the culmination of a long, gradual pattern; she had slipped at last quite completely out of the role of servant, inasmuch as she ever had held such a role, and existed in Eugenia's household as a sort of hired companion, adopted sister, glorified and mysterious elder aunt to us all. She was hardly indeed so much our elder; there were only a few years between herself and Clare and Kate, and as they achieved adulthood, those years melted away. She was now more a contemporary and, as a companion, an odd sort of equal.

The second change was that Persephone was in love. This was of far more note to me, and far harder for me to accept. Persephone had never appeared to me as a servant; she did not behave like any of the others. But it had never occurred to me once that she might have a life beyond us, apart from us, private and her own. It was not unlike the chance discovery that one's own mother had a lover and was quite as disturbing. I did not want to think of her with a man, courting her and perhaps kissing her, and worst of all taking her away to live in a house and even have children, children other than us, whom she might love more than she loved me. From the start I disliked Padraic O'Mordha with a dislike both perceptive and unfair.

Padraic, or Patrick as he was before reverting to a more Irish style, was an actor. He had been with the Abbey Theatre Company of Lady Gregory, and George Russell and the younger Mr Yeats, until the previous year, when a tempest not unlike the one enacted that morning in the studio had flared up into open warfare and the eventual secession of a whole group of the actors and actresses.

The issues were a complex mix of politics, artistic standards and plain old theatrical bitchery, but at the centre was a deep and real schism: was art to be served first, or was Ireland? Padraic's first mistress was nationalism and he willingly followed the poet Colum and the schoolmaster Pearse into the new and radical Theatre of Ireland. I had been much aware of the conflict at the time because old Mr Yeats was, as often, in the eye of the storm, and letters and protests, and wailing actresses passed regularly through his domain. Mixed loyalties might have proved a problem for the child in the middle of it, but for Mr Yeats' perennial unrufflable tolerance, and for Persephone's own blithe cheerful calm. She had nothing against revolution, but saw it as no reason for people getting angry with each other. She painted backdrops and sewed costumes as she had for the Daughters of Erin and managed to stay on good terms with us all. James Howie was the exception: he forbade Padraic O'Mordha entrance to the house in Merrion Square. But Eugenia retaliated by providing Persephone transport to and from her assignations, thereby undoing his paternal decree.

Padraic himself was a tall, fierce red-headed young man, a little younger than Persephone. He wore his hair long and flowing in Shakespearean manner, and his red moustache bristled with general indignation. He was a man who could not get out of bed in the morning without having an argument with the bed-clothes and spent much of his time in furious debate. But in the manner of firebrands, he loved children, was fond of dogs and cats, and could be moved to tears by a peasant song. He was not a bad creature really, and was often amusing, but I never afforded him a moment of trust. Sensing this, no doubt, he did much to win me over, and met stubborn resistance all the way.

'Ah Justina, ye'll be sittin' beside me.' I scurried

instantly to the far side of the table. ''Tis fine she looks in that blouse, is it not?' I ducked my head and prodded Michael's foot under the table and we giggled behind our hands. Michael was fond of imitating Padraic's accent and declamatory style behind his back.

Padraic fell at once to arguing with Clare, as always. There was an uneasy tension between them. She found him handsome, but regarded him below herself, since he courted Persephone, and deflected his compliments with political dogma. She grew red and flushed, her sharp intelligent features trembling with a mix of anger and girlish desire. He was old enough to play her like a fish. Persephone watched, undisturbed. Class was a sure chaperone.

Clare smoothed back stray strands of her yellow hair beneath her brown hat and said coolly, 'What use to Ireland is a Home Rule Bill with no provision for Women's Suffrage?'

'First one thing and then the other,' Kate put in, but Padraic smiled his slow needling smile.

'Ireland's women know better than to be askin' nonsense,' he said, 'when there's serious issues at stake.'

'Now Padraic,' said Persephone, patting his arm as she would one of ours once, in the nursery, 'you're not to be gettin' excited.' But of course Clare exploded at once.

'What beastly arrogance!'

'Come now, Clare,' Geoffrey put in. He was eating a mouthful of nutroll, and crumbs sputtered out on to his waistcoat as he attempted the clerical role of reconciliation, as no doubt he thought his duty. 'Padraic may hold his opinion.' He nodded sagely, his curly hair bouncing up and down, 'And you, yours.'

'Oh stuff your Christianity,' said Clare.

'Clare Melrose!' Persephone whispered, shocked.

'Aye, listen to his Holiness,' said Padraic, gesturing one

big thumb towards Geoffrey, 'an' hold your tongue like a good Christian woman.' His mouth was scornful but his eyes full of a childish mischief. May Howie, who was sitting next to Geoffrey tugged his sleeve.

'Never mind,' she said. She was another peacemaker, though she had left Christianity behind some time ago, much to Geoffrey's dismay. May had become intrigued by our Theosophists and borrowed books by Mme Blavatsky from the café. To this day I find them undecipherable, but at thirteen May Howie read them all. She collected religions like other children collected agate marbles. With her long golden ringlets, she looked ten, not thirteen, and strangers in the café, hearing her happily debate the relative merits of Karma and Free Will reacted rather like the sages of the temple to the young Christ. Clare ignored both May and Geoffrey and commenced a diatribe against the Home Rule MP, John Redmond.

'Now don't you be gettin' excited,' Persephone said absently, as she buttered May's roll, forgetting for a moment that anyone old enough to read Mme Blavatsky was old enough to butter her own roll. May took no offence.

Padraic, however, grew suddenly gloomy and sour, which was a common occurrence, and he glowered into his herb tea and muttered dourly, 'Ah, Redmond's an ass. 'Tis not in your Parliament we'll win Home Rule, but in the streets.' He got up suddenly, bowed theatrically to Persephone and stamped out. Persephone watched him go and went back to buttering the roll.

'He shouldn't always be gettin' himself excited,' she said.

And so our luncheon broke up, gradually and piecemeal, and we all went our ways, sure that we would meet again tomorrow and the battle would again commence. It seemed that time stretched endlessly from Dublin summer to Dublin summer and we could laze happily onward, stretching our intellects and our artistry like so many awakening cats. Persephone walked home to Merrion Square, with her arms linked through Michael's and mine. She no longer needed to hold him firm lest he climb upon the parapets of the quayside, though now the bright glances of passing shopgirls offered another danger. Michael stood five feet, ten inches, slender and graceful, and with his black hair, dark eyes and skin looked, for all his stiff collar and tailored suit, more gypsy than gentleman. But although they looked, none approached, and it was not his youth that held them distant, for his youth was not at all apparent. He had a serenity that was virtually religious, and women stood back from him as good women stand back from a priest. And yet Michael was not religious, any more than I was. We both went to church as we did so many things, by parental dictate, and the strictures of Christianity were to me but another kind of unquestioned corsetry. Nor had Michael deeper respect. He had only his unmovable inner peace as if he possessed a secret about life's course.

We were laughing amongst ourselves as we climbed the short flight of steps to the brick-fronted house in Merrion Square, and Michael reached for the brass bell pull at the side of the polished, fanlight-surmounted door. But the door swung open before us as if someone had been awaiting anxiously our arrival. Mother stood there, thin and white faced, her cheekbones lit with a rare colour of nervous excitement. She was breathing heavily as if she had been running, and when she spoke her voice was filled with a puzzled child's amazement. Her words were for all of us, but it was really to Persephone she spoke.

'My darlings, we must return. We must return at once. Papa, Papa is *ill*.' Her eyes widened as she spoke and she shook her head again in bewilderment and collapsed weeping into Persephone's arms.

One final memory closes my childhood in Ireland. We had little more than twenty-four hours from that revelation on the doorstep until boarding the ferry at Kingstown, and in that time all our packing, our farewells, our scenes of worry, consolation and confusion over the scant words of the cable that summoned us home, must be enacted. Yet I was determined I would not leave Dublin without making my farewell to Mr Yeats. It seemed so churlish to do so, and even though I imagined I would return as always the following spring, the months between seemed intolerably long. But no one in our frantic family had time for my concern, and it was only by trickery the next morning that I escaped the house to set out, alone, the short distance to Stephen's Green. At once I was assailed by delicious fear and excitement: for the first time in my sheltered and typical life I was actually out in the streets of the city without accompaniment. I ran all the way, terrified that I would lose my direction and fail to return in time for the ferry sailing. I half believed they would go without me, so great was the haste being displayed at home. I suppose I should logically have been in more open fear for my father's condition, as was the remainder of the family, but it all seemed so unreal, distant, and unexplained, and I think even Mother still found it inconceivable that the big powerful body of Hugo Melrose could ever suffer any physical disability at all. To me it was all, as yet, mere inconvenience.

When I reached the address of Mr Yeats' studio, there was no one there. I stood confounded on the doorstep, pulling the bell-pull again and again. But there was no answer. It was not surprising, and yet I was shattered. It had never occurred to me in my determination to escape

Merrion Square that he might not be there when I arrived. I turned around forlornly on the step, and then glancing up the street, far away through clumps of hats and frock coats and ladies' bonnets, I glimpsed, or thought I glimpsed, his familiar soft hat, and a wisp of his white beard. 'Mr Yeats,' I cried, foolishly, and I started off after him, running, my skirts and petticoats flapping, my hat slipping over my eyes, holding up my hem with one hand and waving with the other. People in the street stopped and laughed, but I had no thought but closing the distance between me and my vanishing artist. I followed him, or what I took to be him, all the way down into Grafton Street, past Trinity College, and into Dane Street before I admitted to myself that I had lost him, if it were indeed him at all I had seen. Dejected and suddenly frightened I turned round amidst the busy, alien crowds and began, trotting and sobbing, to retrace my steps home. Dublin seemed cold and aloof, and I, very foolish and small. When I arrived home our luggage was on the car at the door and the family, frantic and furious, awaited in wrath.

After the inevitable chastisement, shortened by lack of time, I was left for a moment to wash and tidy myself for the journey. Michael, having learned of my fruitless mission, consoled me.

'Never mind. I'll go to the studio tomorrow and tell him for you. And you'll soon be back.'

'I won't,' I sobbed, deep in the visionary misery of adolescence. 'I know I won't. I'll never go there again.'

Michael, of course, kept his word, and not long after our return to Arradale a small parcel arrived for me, from Mr Yeats in Dublin. Inside was a letter in which he expressed his surprising intention to accompany his daughter Lily on a trip to New York. I thought this very brave, for New York seemed further away to me than

Persia, and quite as wild. He concluded, '. . . No doubt we will both have great adventures to share when next we meet.' Enclosed with the letter were his beautiful pencil sketch of me and, folded very neatly, my blue painter's smock.

7

Merrion Square
23 February 1912

Dearest Justina,

I am sending this on to Strathpeffer, hoping it will find you there. Thank you so much for the pencil sketch of Michael – *such* a true likeness. Mr Yeats would be very proud, I am sure. At Cuala they all say he is making a splendid triumph in New York, but he still *refuses to return home*! No one knows what to do, and it is four years now, and he is much missed. Just think, it is four years too since we've met! You must have changed so. Please *do* send a self-sketch. I should prefer that to a photograph. Your sketches are so much *realer*. As for me, I suspect I'm much the same. Yesterday a lady in Capel St insisted on taking my hand to 'cross me over' the road. Imagine, and I am almost eighteen! I shall have to do something terribly severe with my hair, but it will only all fall down again, I know!

Kate says I am to send love to you, but I fear *not* to Clare. K. is in High Dudgeon over Christabel Pankhurst opposing the Home Rule Party. She *must* understand that the Irish Party daren't weaken Asquith by supporting V. for W., with everything so delicate just now. Things are very tense, here, anyway, with Carson making threats in the North.

K. keeps very busy with the soup kitchens in the day, and warding off suitors by night! Everyone, it seems, wishes to marry her, but she is Devoted to Ireland. There was trouble in Sackville St over some soldiers and young women taunting them. K. was involved but denies it of course to Mother and Father. I am pledged to secrecy so tell *no one*!

I obtained a translation of the Upanishads from Q. of the

Order of the G.D. Please don't tell Geoffrey – it is only a curiosity with me, but he reads apostasy into the smallest act and he does worry so! Imagine carrying the whole weight of the Revelation on one's solitary shoulders! (Oh forgive me, I *am* naughty.)

Mother and Persephone are in Austria again. Persephone's cough is better, but Mother is cautious. Padraic misses her terribly, but why doesn't he *do* something when she is home?? She is hardly young, nor he, and if either are *ever* to marry . . . But here I go gossiping again. Do forgive.

I am enjoying my work at Cuala Industries. Lily Yeats is a *lovely* person. I am working with several other girls on an embroidered hanging for a church in Galway . . . St Bride! For you of course! Still I am more interested in the printing presses and would like to learn . . .

Please as always give my love to your dear Mama and kindest regards to your Father. I do hope there is some improvement.

As ever,
your loving cousin
May Howie

PS. Please, if in London, attempt to find translations of Egyptian Book of the Dead at Foyles. Have searched Dublin without success.

I put the letter away as soon as I heard Clare's step in the hallway outside the door. I knew it would only cause trouble. The wound of her argument with Kate was quite raw, and any reference to the Howies inflamed her. She had the same feuding nature as her father. She came in quickly, as she did everything, with tense, nervous haste. Without looking at me, or the letter I was concealing beneath a pile of sketch-paper, she crossed to the big cheval-glass by the window and peered at her thin cheeks. The winter light was harsh and clear. She pinched them abruptly between her bony finger and thumb.

'Have you some rouge?' she demanded.

I blinked stupidly. 'Of course not, silly. Mother would throw a fit!'

‘Oh hush about Mother. Surely you have some. Look at my face. I’m like death. I can’t go to dinner like this.’

I shook my head. ‘But I haven’t, Clare,’ I said sadly. And then I brightened and said, ‘Oh look. You can use my pastels if you like.’

She looked at me, incredulous, as I went to my drawing things, still sitting among our unpacked luggage in the corner of the room. We had only just arrived on the morning train. But when I got out my carefully wrapped box of pastel crayons she grabbed them eagerly, searching with her nervous quick fingers through them until finding one of an appropriate rose colour, and began crumbling bits and experimentally patting the dust against her taut cheeks. She looked so pathetic that I disguised my dismay at her rough handling of my prized chalks.

‘No one expects you to look well if you’ve just had influenza,’ I ventured.

She glared at me for an instant and then gave a little scornful laugh. ‘*Influenza*,’ she mocked, returning to the glass.

I looked down at my hands miserably. I hated dishonesty and had no talent for pretence. The prevarication my family indulged defeated me entirely.

Clare had not had influenza. She had lost two stone in weight, was skeletally thin, pale, spotted with eczema, her eyes bloodshot and her hair falling, not from any illness, but because she had been six weeks in Holloway Prison, five of them on hunger strike. In the company of three other women, two of them middle-aged and titled, and the third a twenty-year-old factory girl from Yorkshire, she had smashed several windows in Oxford Street one January afternoon. It had been a calculated act, performed with small hammers carried for the purpose, and in full view of an officer of the law. Arrest, a martyrdom for Women’s Suffrage, had been their intention, and this method of obtaining it was neat and relatively painless, whereas harassing cabinet members in Parliament Square led more often to bruises, wrenched arms, and pulled hair and perhaps no imprisonment at all. I was uneasy with this concept of deliberate law-breaking in pursuit of the Vote but Clare was even now planning her next imprisonment. I feared for her; the starvation was devastating her health. But I felt sorrier for her companion, the little factory girl, Meggie Whyte whom Clare had brought with her to Strathpeffer. Meggie had gone to Holloway too, but she had failed at her hunger strike and seemed miserably guilty about it. Unlike Clare she had not been well-fed all her life, and lacked Clare's stamina as much as her determination. Clare's determination was undoubted; after the first week of her fast they had force-fed her, and she bore still the cuts and bruises about her mouth from what she called their 'instruments of torture'. The battle went on daily between the stomach tube and Clare's furious resistance. They had broken two of her teeth, and she invariably vomited up all they forced inside her. She told it all with calm, cool ironic dispassion, but at night in the hotel room we shared, I heard her sobbing in her sleep.

Of course, I was not meant to know about Clare's imprisonment; no one was. Even the fact that Clare was now a full-time employee at the WSPU headquarters at Clement's Inn was neatly disguised in family circles. Mother and Father maintained that their eldest daughter, having won her history degree from Somerville, was now working as a 'lady typewriter' in London. It was partly true. Clerical work for the Suffrage cause was one of Clare's duties; breaking windows and setting pillar boxes alight were others. And the inevitable consequence of the latter was, as everybody knew, severe influenza.

My poor parents, they really had enough to deal with

without Clare and the Pankhurst style of politics, and I myself could hardly blame them for at least trying to keep the smoke of her fiery world away from their haven in the North. Besides, we were all so very well known in Strathpeffer; there was no escaping the pressure of public curiosity. Staff at the Ben Wyvis Hotel, where we inevitably stayed, knew our every foible and catered to our every whim. The Melroses were an institution at the Strathpeffer Spa. We had been attending regularly, and in Papa's case several times a year, ever since our final return from Ireland and Papa's fateful last return from the East.

We had arrived back at Arradale, that summer of 1907, to find our tall, handsome and indefatigable wanderer, that boisterous man whose big laugh alone had sent children and pets scurrying, reduced to a frail, chair-bound cripple. Somewhere in the wet, unhealthy jungle-forest of the Mazanderan he had done battle with an illness whose very nature we would never define. Mysterious as the dark place in which he had met it, it entered his body like an evil spirit, ravaged it, and departed in arrogance, leaving of that comely youthful man an aged and battered shadow.

I will not forget my first sight of him, sitting in the entrance hall of Arradale, through which he had so often stormed with a clicking of riding-boot heels and a barking of following dogs, now in meek silence, in an old wicker Bath-chair, frail, thin, pathetically eager to reach out to us with stick-arms he could barely lift. As his strength vanished, his affection for us seemed to grow, as if in the past his physical nature had warred against it. Behind his chair, dark, attentive and silent, stood a young man with coffee-coloured skin, lank shining black hair, a huge black moustache, and eyes of a liquid animal brown. Dressed in western clothes, probably cast-offs of Father's as they were suspiciously large, he had the assaulted dignity of a noble family hound dressed up by children in nursery clothes. His name was Hassan Abbas (Father called him, respectfully, Mirza Hassan). He spoke virtually no English, he was in exile from Persia and it was he, out of nothing but pure Islamic compassion, who had brought my father home. Without Mirza Hassan, Father would have died somewhere in the wilds of Mazanderan without our ever hearing. Naturally we were powerfully grateful, though at times I wondered if Father was the same. Sometimes, in certain circumstances, we are really meant to die, and live on only in error.

Of course we tried every doctor in Western Europe who might possibly be expected to offer hope. But none could. They had so little to work on; whatever the culprit microbe, it had made its journey through Father's body and gone its way, burning him, like its bridges, and leaving no footprint, no clue. And you must remember microbes of all sorts were not the vanquished enemies of today. Medical science was young, and anyhow I always suspected that what Father had met called more for the weapons of witchcraft.

It melted the flesh from him; he was skeletal, and remained so, no matter what we managed to feed him. And he could eat little without some evil reaction. Intermittent, mysterious self-consuming fevers attacked and retreated at will. His back remained twisted, and his legs in a strange partial paralysis, so that sometimes he could walk and at others he could not. He who had walked the breadth of Persia would at most now manage the gardens of Arradale House. He regained some strength in his arms. He could write. He could read. His eyes were unaffected, thank God, though he had lost the senses of taste and smell. His mind, isolated in his defeated body, was as sharp, and brutally clear as ever it had been. No wonder he despaired. And yet, in those years of despair, of doctors, of false cheer and self-generated optimisms, he did his life's work: he wrote 'The Gateway', his only full length work, and the book upon which his reputation rests. And though I know it was brilliant, and I know he would never have written it had his health and his wandering feet been left to him, and indeed his name, which is now at least a scholarly footnote, would be nothing but dust; still, I would gladly cast it and him to the winds of anonymity could I have won him his health in exchange.

We had such a pitiful weaponry and in a short time we had exhausted it all and fell back on a defence, disguised in modern jargon, that was yet as old as mythology. Papa began to 'take the waters'. The Strathpeffer Spa in Ross-shire drew its fame from a layer of shale that grazed the surface of the beautiful landscape and cast a sulphurous spell upon the natural wells springing from it. There was an iron spring also, but it was for that sulphur water that those whom medicine had failed resorted there. Others resorted too, those lax and indulgent members of a class with too much time on its hands, who gathered there to see and be seen, to drift languidly among the potted palms and wicker furnishings of the Pump Room, and walk briskly and briefly on the hills, and reward themselves with vast dinners in the many sumptuous hotels. They called it the Harrogate of Scotland, and with its pretty stone buildings, elaborately trimmed with an extravagance of ginger-breading, its magnificent setting in the valley beneath Ben Wyvis, and its air of fashion and style, the name seemed fitting. Whether the waters really did anyone good I cannot say. They were pleasant enough to bathe in, less pleasant to drink, and many claimed cures. Much scientific elaboration was placed upon those mineral springs, as if to hide an older yearning for holy wells and blessed waters that perhaps even Father, in his agnostic heart, might have secretly cherished. Perhaps we should have taken him to Lourdes. Or the Ganges. Or perhaps we should have only had more faith.

But Papa enjoyed Strathpeffer. He enjoyed many things now, that he had seemed in the past to scorn. Most of all, he enjoyed Mother, and she him, in a way that neither had known since their earliest years in Sligo, now so far away. The pathos of his condition opened the gates to her heart that the deaths of her children had closed. Which is not to say that she mothered him; but that she offered him once more all the respect that Victorian marriage demanded as his entitlement, and he struggled manfully to shoulder that burden of duty he had scant strength to bear. And so details of daily life, servants' wages, our behaviour, social engagements, were brought to his study, interrupting his wonderful work, by the way, and she would wait meekly for him to ordain what she was well able to manage without him, and for years indeed had so done. It was the way they both wanted it. But now there was peace between them again, and a sad dignity as each carefully propped the other up, and side by side, leaning one upon the other, they descended towards the grave. Those frail, ravaged years were their best.

Mother's health was, as we later realized, actually worse than his own. The signs were not so apparent, but the seed was there. She had been unwell for years, but since her illness resided in those portions of female anatomy that were in that era as mysterious as Mazanderan, the exact details of her malady were never discussed. She had 'woman's troubles', in the accepted phrase. 'Something had happened' at one of the births, Persephone whispered, and even today I have little idea precisely what they meant. Then, naturally, my wild young imagination provided explanations in frightening plenitude. I do not even know if, other than the 'taking of waters', she received any treatment at all. I cannot imagine that refined, remote, graceful being confessing such intimacies to anyone at all, much less a man, and doctors were almost without exception male. More likely she suffered, bled, weakened and faded in silence, walking with brave, shortened steps about the Spa Gardens, behind Papa's chair, nodding to favoured acquaintances as they passed. Everyone knew them; they had a tragic grandeur that was irresistible.

Youth is so heartless. They, whose time was short, had so much patience, for each other, and even for us. We, with all life before us had so little for them. Clare had her politics, I, my painting. Douglas, far away with his regiment in India, wrote home exactly once a month, each letter a replica of the last, reeking with disinterested duty. They arrived in batches anyhow, and were so alike as to need the dates to differentiate them. Alexander, reading chemistry at Cambridge, wrote when he needed money like any student, and took most of his holidays with friends. Geoffrey spent every waking hour that he shared with my parents in attempting to plumb the limited depths of my father's esoteric version of Anglicanism for any glimmer of faith, and finding none, badgered poor Mother to see to our father's soul. Like every other fool, I suppose he meant well. At least he tried, which is more than the rest of us did.

It was less lack of love than lack of imagination: our parents were our parents, eroded and weathered rocks, but rocks for all that. It was not really in any of our minds that they might actually die. I myself, I must add, worsened things also, by keeping up my campaign for art school, now that Mr Yeats had been taken from me. I had progressed on my own, with some good results, doing some gouache as well as oil, and many soft pencil sketches in the manner, poorly imitated no doubt, of my mentor. Pencil was handy, too, because I could and did carry pencils and a sketch-book anywhere, up on to the high tops with Michael, or around the interesting corners of the Spa which I, being yet at home with my parents, attended as often as they. The rest of the family gathered, as now, less frequently, during term holidays. This was an early Easter, and the Spa Pavilion was snowbound, a spring oasis yet besieged by winter.

We all gathered each evening for dinner in the hotel, although we healthy young people spent the days not in the Spa but out on the hills. Michael and Alexander arrived on the train just before dinner the first night. Michael was reading medicine at Trinity College. The Howies were scarcely more pleased with Michael and his studies than they were with Kate and her social welfare work; medicine was regarded in their circles less a profession than a trade, and Michael, being a gentleman, was expected to have neither. But Michael, in his quieter way, was even harder to control than Kate. He had found his calling at fifteen and nothing would stand in his way.

Clare, of course, was with us already, with her shy, worshipful companion, Meggie Whyte, and Geoffrey, now a youthful curate at St Mary's in Edinburgh, would have to leave us before Holy Week, and therefore had arrived a few days early.

We made a large and eclectic party about our familiar table in the Ben Wyvis's dining room. Father sat at the head in his wicker chair. Mother was at his left and at his right the Persian, Mirza Hassan. In the four years intervening he had learned enough English to serve Papa as a kind of literary secretary, helping in the researching of his book, the categorizing of his elaborate journals, and his correspondence with various scholars of the Persian tongue. As such he was eminently suitable, having his native command of that language and also and most important, being himself a Baha'i, one of the spiritual descendants of the Babi faith which was the central theme of Papa's writing.

At that time I was much in ignorance of Mirza Hassan. I did not fully understand the nature of his exile, nor did I know much about the religious movement that was the cause of it. I confess simple girlish uninterest. May Howie, though younger than me, would by now have known everything there was to learn from our Persian guest, but I lacked her spirituality and her curiosity. What I learned from Mirza Hassan was more immediately practical; since Papa would often call upon my help in his work, either to sketch some artefact or take part in the complex task of collating his notes, I spent much time in their company, and since they invariably spoke in Persian, I struggled to do so too. Sometimes, conversely, Papa would instruct me to go about some improvement of Mirza Hassan's English. Together, we educated each other. I liked him. He was loyal, solemn, gentlemanly and aloof and yet was capable of surprising flashes of humour. He was quite young, but experience had aged him far beyond his actual years and he treated me always as a child, and my father as his contemporary. He loved my father deeply, and loved us all therefore as well, even Geoffrey who regarded him a heathen. Five times a day Mirza Hassan quietly left our presence to pray, retreating to some private corner, where he would kneel and bow, facing the East, and go through the elaborate Islamic ritual which the Baha'i, at least then, still followed. At such times Geoffrey would squirm with distaste as if at an obscenity.

Mother always seated them as far from each other as possible which meant, naturally, Geoffrey was seated a long distance from Papa as well. He sat at the opposite end of the table in his black canonicals, glaring up at Mirza Hassan, the Beloved Disciple at Papa's right hand. Geoffrey of course, despite his solemnity, still glowed with brisk, red-faced health, as indeed did the rest of us, other than Clare. I always felt a kind of guilt, at the Spa, and sensed people looking at us all oddly, wondering perhaps what on earth we were doing there. Clare now lessened the contrast, since she was as wraith-like as Father, and with her bruised mouth and suffering skin looked, if anything, worse. Over my shoulder, I heard a sympathetic Ross-shire voice declare, 'Yes, a terrible pity. Clearly hereditary. No doubt the little plain one will be next.'

The little plain one, had you any doubts, was me. I didn't know whether to laugh or throw my soup. It was harder to laugh at such things these days. I *was* plain, and I was just turned eighteen, long past the age of innocence in such matters. I was also devoted to a young man whose devotion to me had come, in my eyes, to be incomprehensible. At eighteen himself, Michael Howie had the world at his feet. He was well-educated, wealthy, and the heir to a title as well. And he was so handsome, so beautiful indeed, that little Meggie Whyte neglected her dinner to stare at him. He had reached his adult height, which was just on six feet, and possessed a grace that one could not describe without returning to imagery of animals. A cat, a fox, a young deer, a young horse; the grace of all nature's delights: had I not known him, I would have loved him anyhow, I'm sure. So many women did. And this glorious creature, miraculously, loved me, if only because I had entered his life when both of us were yet in that Eden of the heart when sexuality and all its physical vassals have no power. There was never a moment, in his company, that he gave me cause to doubt his devotion. But alone, without that reassurance, I had doubts enough.

Each reunion was a terror or uncertainty until he strode into the room, his quick dark eyes searching it in restless haste until they alighted upon me, and I knew that the incomprehensible was yet the magical truth.

Throughout dinner, Michael told me in whispers of his term at Trinity College. Sandy, who liked women too well, attempted to charm Meggie Whyte away from her visual devotion to Michael. Geoffrey argued with Clare, and Father and Mirza Hassan talked in Persian. Mother sat in peaceful silence, her still-beautiful face only lightly traced with pain, staring out of the tall windows into the darkness where snow was silently burying the flowers of spring.

The next morning I awoke to the unmistakable white light of winter and Michael and Sandy hammering on my door. Clare moaned in her sleep that he should go away, but Sandy shouted joyfully oblivious of her protests, 'Come on, you lazy bunch, there's a foot if there's an inch. We can make the summit by noon if we start right now!'

I shook Clare awake and coaxed Meggie Whyte from the depths of her eiderdown and within an hour we were setting out, packs on our backs and skis on our shoulders, for Ben Wyvis.

Michael and Sandy had discovered this wonderful diversion the previous winter. They were climbing with old companions from their Eton days and one of them had recently returned from Norway with three pairs of Norwegian skis. The boys had persuaded one pair away from him and brought their trophy home to Arradale where, after a brief study, and much searching for wood, they had set about copying them. The original pair were traditional ash-boards, but the boys had to settle for pitch-pine. Still, in a remarkably short time they became quite expert, designing bindings from steel hinges and leather straps, and poles from hazel-wood in lieu of unattainable bamboo. Before the winter was over, all of us were fitted out with skis. We called them 'shee' in those days, and made that do for the plural as well, and that first winter we used not two chest-high poles, but one immensely long one, with which we punted our way across the snow, like gondoliers. Michael and Sandy spent much of their term times tracking down Norwegians and learning more, so by now we were already using twin poles and managing our skis in what was then the modern style. That, however, was not very like what you may imagine it today, since in those days ski-running was an adjunct to climbing only, as was quite natural when the only way to run down a mountain was to climb it first. The boys were climbers foremost, ski-runners second, and the rest of us were camp-followers at best. The route was hard, the weather wild, the mountain formidable, and the pace, set by my brother and beloved cousin, was daunting. Shirkers were abandoned along the way, and complainers thrown in snowdrifts. It was not a sport for the faint of heart.

As always in all the days of my youth, there was a great crowd of us, setting out that morning through the snowy streets of Strathpeffer. Sandy and Michael were in the lead, jostling for position like race horses, a friction essential to their climbing partnership. I followed just far enough behind to avoid the sudden arc of their shouldered skis when they swung about to punch each other. I carried skis as well, as did Clare, walking steadfastly behind me, determined despite her starvation-weakened body to keep the pace. I had begged her not to come with us, for health's sake, but Clare would give in to nothing. Suffering, any suffering, only made her more stubbornly insistent, as no doubt her gaolers had soon discovered. I heard her sharp, pained breathing over my shoulder, but if ever

I slowed my pace to ease hers, she would push on by me to keep in stride with the boys. Meggie Whyte stumbled along girlishly after, with the clumsy step of a city child unused to uneven ground. She was flirtatious in a sad, vulnerable way and sought to win Michael's attention and, failing that, Sandy's. But both boys, I knew well, had no time for anyone but each other when out on the hill. They shut me out too, but I understood. Meggie grew hurt and lagged dejectedly behind, where she was subjected to Geoffrey's ponderous attempts at courtly grace.

'I say,' he puffed occasionally. 'Slow down, old man. The girls can't keep this pace.'

'Speak for yourself,' snapped Clare, as we climbed up the fields below Achterneed, with the snow deeper and lighter as we gained height. Geoffrey said nothing, saving his breath. Geoffrey did not ski; he had refused to ever try; and he walked along with us out of an unwilling sense of duty. He always felt himself our chaperone. He might as well have kept warm by the hotel fire; we hardly needed him. We were adults, we were all more or less related, and moreover, we never listened to Geoffrey anyhow. We did have one attendant to whom we did listen, and he followed far to our rear out of a different kind of duty. Mirza Hassan also accompanied us, and took the hindmost position as a sheepdog trails his flock, his feet patiently shackled by respect. Geoffrey called him 'our bearer' as a lofty silly joke, that I detested. Mirza Hassan nodded, his bushy moustache twitching very slightly, pretending he did not understand. It was his way of avoiding unacceptable conflict, as the same sheepdog turns its white able teeth harmlessly from the prying fingers of a spoiled child.

'We will rest here,' he called forward to the hurrying boys, and settled himself heavily, as if he were weary, on the edge of the stone platform of Achterneed railway station. The boys turned back then, without argument, and Clare flopped down in the snow exhausted and I sat beside her. Mirza Hassan took out his pipe and his Turkish tobacco and began to smoke. He would smoke a pipe and everyone would rest, and no one's pride would be hurt. Geoffrey settled down beside me and waved his hand in the air.

'Phew. Horse dung,' he said, as the smoke curled round us.

'I like it,' I said stubbornly. Meggie Whyte was sitting in the snow beside Clare, stroking her yellow, straw-dry hair.

'It's too far,' she whispered. 'You're too cold.'

'I'm fine,' Clare snapped, sitting up and shaking off Meggie's hand. Meggie shrank into silence. Below us, the valley was already beginning to spread out, dark blue and green, against the white of the snow. More snow fell, and the air grew blue-white. Mirza Hassan sat motionlessly smoking, as the snow made a white cap on his black, black hair, and the boys fidgeted, but still did not argue. Mirza Hassan could outwalk all of us, and then keep going for a day, and a night, and we all knew it. He had guided Father through the Pusht-i-Kuh of Western Persia and alone he had scaled the mighty Throne of Solomon in the Elburz. He declined Michael's offer of skis, though he handled them with shy delight. But he handed them back, shaking his head.

'No. I am not so clever as you. I would only fall, whoosh like an old grandmother, chasing goats.' He laughed against himself enchantingly, and said that in his country, where there was so much snow in the mountains that some of the people remained shut up all winter with their animals, still they had never thought of anything so clever.

'It was the Norwegians thought of them,' Michael said

quickly. 'Not us.' But Mirza Hassan only again shook his head, with the same modesty with which he allowed us to appear to out-pace him. I think it was his modesty that drew me to admire his religion, the way he would preface each explanation with the bowing of his head and the careful phrase, '*we* believe', that emphasis on the pronoun thus expediting any requirement for ourselves, or anyone else, to believe the like. Geoffrey's stolid demanding Christianity appeared churlish in comparison.

Eventually he stood up, stretched himself and waited politely for Michael and Sandy to again take the lead. I looked over my shoulder as we started out again. He was again following with his carefully placed steps, as if there were a thousand miles to go. He made me think of Persephone, shepherding our much younger selves in Sligo. Like herself, he was made older than us by class and experience rather than years.

An old peat road ran down to the fields from the high moorland, and as we joined it we sat down on its low stone wall to fasten on our skis. I was glad; the snow was deep and the weight of the skis on my shoulder was rubbing a bruise through my woollen jacket. Geoffrey sat down on the opposite wall while we fussed a while with bindings and said pompously, 'Highly over-rated, your old ash-boards. Nothing you can do that a fit man can't manage on foot.'

'I'll answer that at the summit,' said Michael as he and Sandy stood up on their skis and started off. I followed after, exhilarated as always by the smooth, silken glide of the skis over the snowy ground, evening out the ruts and holes and making a springing supporting cushion of the snow-laden heather. Michael had spent hours the night before coating them carefully with Speedolin wax.

In a short while, as we mounted higher, we three drew away from the company, with Clare only a short distance behind, and the three walkers, Geoffrey, Meggie Whyte and the patient Mirza Hassan further and further behind. At each rest point we waited for them to catch up, and Geoffrey to maintain loudly he was delayed only by concern for Miss Whyte.

When we had covered half the distance to the summit we stopped just in the lee shelter of a ridge between two burns, to have our luncheon. Packs were opened and the bounty of the hotel kitchens spread about in the snow. Michael helped me unfasten my leather bindings, and stood our skis up in a drift. Then he crossed both pairs of poles and spread his overjacket across them, making a sturdy dry cushion in the deep snow, on which I might sit. Though when I did so, I sank backwards laughing, into the drift. He fetched me out and I found an edge of rock on which to perch, as I shook snow off the folds of my skirt. The skirt, being calf-length, as short as Mother would possibly allow, and woollen, gathered snow like a magnet. The boys, in their tweed knee-breeches, were luckier, but even their woollen stockings were soon coated.

Clare struggled up to join us, and Michael at once found her a place to sit down, and removed her skis and brought her luncheon. I could see her smouldering beneath her polite gratitude, but she had no real argument with Michael who was always thoughtful of her, and she saved her wrath for Geoffrey when he, puffing and panting, eventually arrived.

'The Swiss heat their wine,' Sandy said, passing glasses from a wicker case to all of us, while Michael struggled with cold fingers at the cork. The hotel provided everything; corkscrew, white linen napkins, sturdy glassware, smoked salmon sandwiches, Stilton cheese, cold chicken. It was astounding, and even more astounding, we carried it. As we ate, the wind got up and heavy charcoal clouds rolled intermittently across the face of Ben Wyvis, white and solitary ahead of us. Grey streamers trailed down, obscuring the summit, and snow showers made distant grey screens across one hillside and then another. I sat looking backwards over our ski-tracks curving effortlessly downwards, over hills and dips, down into the valley. Dark patches of forest made a deeper shadow than the cloud shadows sweeping over. Everything was coloured in shades of blue, from the palest ice to the deepest pine blue-green. I got out my sketch-pad and began to hastily draw, thinking I would do the scene in oils when we returned. Michael sat watching me, his dark eyes screwed up against the light, which even in the mist and snow was always bright. He put on his tweed cap and it made a shadow over his face, so I could see just the edge of his newly-shaven jaw, and the two lines of gentle cynicism that edged the corners of his mouth. I loved those lines, as much as I loved the ski-tracks ribboning the hill.

Only Michael, Sandy and I made the summit. We left the others six hundred feet below, sheltering in a shallow corrie. It was Mirza Hassan who persuaded Clare she must stop, and give in to the hill which she was fighting now as if it were her tormentors in prison. She was a pitiful sight as she struggled onward, leaning on the harsh wind, her frail body seeming so light against it as if it would be lifted skyward with each gust. Her face was white, where ours were reddened and sweating, and she stumbled and fell, slipping backwards on the now icy windswept snow. Mirza Hassan put his two hands on her shoulders as she knelt on her skis. He said nothing. He had a gift for calming people like the gift of healing. I had seen him use it often with Father, when frustration and anger welled up in him. Clare knelt in silence and I saw the angry lines of her shoulders soften into submission. Eventually she raised her head.

'You go on,' she whispered. 'We're quite fine here.' They settled down, much to Geoffrey's evident relief. He found a sheltered nook for Meggie Whyte, whose original cheerful disbelief had been supplanted by wide-eyed conviction of our collective insanity. She peered up at Sandy, Michael and me as we adjusted our scarves and hats and took up our poles, peering into the mist and blown snow towards the invisible heights above.

'You're mad, the lot of you. That's what you are, if that's what you call a walk in the country.' She shuddered half in indignation, half in misery, and Geoffrey patted her shoulder with his stiff, commiseratorial gloved hand.

But we were on our way already, the boys exhilarated, and I determined. I was fifteen minutes behind them when we reached the summit. I was panting, breathless, exhausted past the point of pain, plodding rather than skiing, stumbling over the rippling wind-crust, my eyes almost closed against the stinging sleet.

'Isn't it glorious,' cried Michael from the summit cairn, his words thinned to a whisper by the wind. I turned, and below, through ragged curtains of sweeping mist, the white, blue, grey and black snowscape spread out in tantalizing glimpses. Far peaks emerged momentarily and retreated like shy Eastern brides. Clouds rolled and roiled, and bright patches of blue opened, and closed in an instant, glimpses into an un-won better world.

'We must go down to them,' Sandy said, dutiful and sad. 'They've missed so much.'

'Clare *can't* do it,' I answered. 'She isn't well.'

'She's a fool,' he said, and I turned from him. I felt Michael's hands on my shoulders, his gloves frozen and stiff, like Mirza Hassan's upon Clare's. But they did not calm me, but roused some new emotion I had never felt before. I wanted to stand forever, with his height shadowing me, until we were frozen into the icy land we loved.

'I'll remember this all my days,' I whispered. 'Even if I never ever see it again.'

We turned our ski-tips to the descent and ran downward, traversing easily between careful Christiania turns over deep drifts and scoured ice. In moments, our hard-won summit was remote above us again. In five minutes we were once more with our waiting companions sheltering below. Geoffrey greeted us belligerently.

'What took you so long? I was about to come looking for you. Thought you'd got into trouble or something.' He was slapping his gloved hands together in cold annoyance. 'The girls were quite frozen through.'

'We played tennis at the top,' said Michael, helping Clare with her bindings for the descent. She sided with him, to get back at Geoffrey.

'We were fine. He's an old woman. Ignore him,' she said.

But Meggie Whyte burst out in sudden resentful sullenness, 'It's all right for you. You're bred to it. I'm near dying of the cold. If it weren't for Geoffrey rubbing my hands, I'd have frostbite.' She cast him a woeful eye and he beamed with sudden importance and put a protective arm about her small shoulders. Clare lifted her chin with sour disdain.

'Rubbish,' she said.

But I felt sorry and guilty because in my pleasure I'd never thought of the others below. I was glad when Mirza Hassan said quietly, 'Next time, you must not be so long. It is worse for those who wait.'

We all bowed our heads guiltily and nodded our submission, and in repentance waited patiently as Clare and the walkers began their descent ahead of us, leaving them time to gain a lead before we set out. When they were out of hearing we three looked at each other like punished children and suddenly Michael began to grin, whipped his white scarf around backwards to make a clerical collar like Geoffrey's and raised a hand over our heads, 'By the power vested in me by Our Holy Father the Mountain, you are absolved. My children, go in peace.'

'Alleluia!' Sandy shouted and thrusting his poles into the icy snow, jump-turned down into the fall line and swooped away.

'Deo Gratias!' cried Michael, following after. In moments they were far below, care and caution abandoned in headlong descent. Traverses and Christianias were forsaken now for sweeping Telemark turns. I watched from above in envious pleasure that most beautiful of ski-manoeuvres. I knew they had quite forgotten me and I understood completely. Below, their ski-tracks crisscrossed down the snowy hill, as they twisted in and out of each other's path, rising and falling in graceful curves, dropping forward and downward in momentary genuflection, the posture at once bold and submissive. I cheered, waving my ski-poles, knowing they would neither hear, nor see, and then I launched out over the descent myself gliding smoothly and turning neatly but without their courageous style.

They waited for me far below, and I joined them just as the walkers plodded down to meet them. Clare was waiting further below, making her own descent with exhausted caution. Sandy was looking at his pocket-watch and grinning at me. 'Thought you were staying the night,' he said airily.

'Don't tease her,' Michael said. His voice was flat and unhumoured. He did not like me humiliated.

'The snow is too heavy,' I said. 'I couldn't get round at any speed.'

'Telemark,' said Michael.

I shook my head, 'I can't.'

'Of course you can. Keep trying.'

'I can't, Michael. It's my skirt. Even when I get it right, the snow catches my skirt.'

'Oh yes,' Sandy said loftily. 'Excuses always. Girls can't really ski. They haven't the strength.'

'I can so,' I shouted. '*You* try it in a skirt.'

'Fair enough. I'll ski in my kilt tomorrow. *And* I'll Telemark. If women would just do things, rather than moaning . . .'

'It's not half so long,' I cried, getting suddenly furious at his fatuous grin. 'And I *don't* moan.'

'You all moan. Clare moans about the vote. Meggie moans because it's cold, or far, or anything other than laid right at her feet . . . women are the worst moaners in the world . . . thank God they haven't got the vote. Next we'd have them moaning in our Parliament and in our clubs and God knows where else. Women's suffrage, be damned, it'd be men's suffer-age then,' he laughed, pleased with himself, waving his ski-poles in the air.

'You're an ass,' I said coldly.

'And you're a fluff-head,' he replied. 'Shall I carry you down the hill, fluff-head? Poor little thing, quite swooning are we?'

'Don't tease her,' Michael said suddenly.

'Poor little Justina in her poor little skirt. Shall I carry you? Shall I?'

'I said don't,' Michael said and he put his hand on Sandy's shoulder. Sandy looked up, surprised.

'What's this?' he said. Michael was looking at him with an expression on his face quite remote from his normal gentle good nature. He was so rarely angry, but he was angry now. I caught my breath. For just a moment the shadow of James Howie and Hugo Melrose hung over us all.

'I'll try,' I shouted suddenly, to break the spell. They turned to watch and I ski'd uphill, traversing three times, until a smooth slope of untouched white lay below me. I stood for a moment, secure with my skis across the fall line, watching them watching me. I wished they'd turn away, but of course they wouldn't except to fight one another, and so, with that thought to hasten me, I swung my tips around and pushed off with my poles. I let the skis run, gathering speed, gathering my nerve, and then forced myself to make the turn, dropping down on my trailing knee, bending the forward one, lengthening the two skis out into one long line. For a glorious moment, I held it, poles upraised, clear of the snow, the arcing curve sweeping me round. Then the trailing wool of my calf-length skirt, gathering snow like a bride's train, caught up on a deeper drift, dragged across my knee, slowed me and tangled me down. Then I was falling, head over heels, tumbling down amidst a cloud of flung snow, laughing and shouting and furious at once. I ended in a heap, but rolled over quickly, flinging the skis up over my head and bunching my legs, so that I'd swung myself round and on to my feet before Sandy could scramble up and meet me.

'Glorious,' he shouted gleefully. 'I've never seen anything so splendid. You went over three times if you went over once.'

'Oh shut up,' I snapped, but I was giggling. All that tumbling and wallowing in drifts made one silly and submissive. I felt I must apologize for defacing the day. 'I just *can't* do it,' I said, brushing down my offending skirt.

But then he said, 'You were all wrong from the start, anyhow. You'd never have made it, even in breeches. Your bodies are all wrong, I suppose.' And that was not true. I had done it right, for that bare moment. I had felt it and I knew I had.

'Sandy,' I said. 'If I were in trousers I'd ski circles

round you. You may be stronger but I've twice your nerve.' He blinked amazed.

'Balderdash,' he said. 'Poppycock. Female whimpering poppycock.' And just then Michael arrived beside me, and as casually as brushing lint from a collar, leaned over and punched Sandy on the jaw. Unfortunately, Michael was still on his skis. And when Sandy swung back, and he twisted round to avoid the blow, he fell over sideways and tumbled down the hill. Then he was really furious, and divesting himself of his leather bindings, leapt up and lunged at his cousin, and they both went at it, without humour or sense, with all of us shouting for them to stop. Mirza Hassan eventually separated them, and held them apart with his big peasant's hands while Meggie shrieked, Geoffrey lectured, and Clare, who had laboriously ski'd up to see what was keeping us, told them both what she thought of them. They were all too busy arguing to even notice me, as I climbed the hill once more. This time I went much further, to an outcrop of rock, glazed with hoarfrost and providing a sheltered lee, out of sight from those below. I knew exactly what I was going to do, and it took me no time at all.

I slipped at once out of my heavy, double-breasted and full-sleeved tweed walking jacket, and laid it on the snow. Then, as quickly, I undid the waist buttons of my woollen skirt, pulled it over my head and dropped it on top of the coat. In my determination I did not even feel cold. I stood for a moment and then shrugging my shoulders, I discarded my petticoat and chemise and stood there in the snow in my white spencer, long cream flannel knickers and cream woollen stockings. I flung the rest of the garments on top of my little heap, pried loose a piece of icy stone and weighted them with it, and picked up my ski-poles once more. Experimentally I bent one knee and then the other, and knelt down low on my skis. I felt exotically, wonderfully supple and free. 'Deo Gratias,' I whispered. 'Alleluia.' I thrust the poles down hard and shot out from my shelter and down the snowy hill.

The snow was fast now, falling all the while, light and dry. The skis bit down beautifully, throwing up a bow wave of dry crystals blowing over my bare forearms. I gasped with delight, and genuflected to the hill and felt the smooth arc carry me. I wavered, then recovered, jumping up and dropping the alternate knee. The third turn was best, a smooth ripple like silk, and then I had the rhythm, down, low, around, holding hard into the acceleration, ski carving through and then up, and the change of lead ski, and down once more. In my mind I was watching Michael, and my legs were shadowing his descent. I raised my arms clear of the snow on my fifth turn and shouted, 'There,' as I swept past Sandy glimpsing in an instant his dark open mouth. I heard them shouting as I turned again, skiing on down and behind me the rushing wind sound of another ski-runner told me Michael had followed. He was fast and overtook me on my seventh turn, and then we swept down together, nipping close, brushing perilously by, swinging wide apart and reuniting. Ten turns in all, flying like great birds, and then, exhausted and laughing I swung round into the hill and to a slow, gliding halt. Michael flew by me, skidding his skis sideways, throwing up a great wave of snow, like spray. It covered me and I shivered in delight.

'I'm sorry,' he called and ski'd down to stand by my side, our skis opposed and our bodies face to face.

'It was lovely,' I whispered.

'You're lovely,' he said. He hesitated the briefest moment before he wrapped me in his long, tweed-coated arms. We stood in silence, leaning one against the other, our arms about each other, the snow slowly covering us both.

Far far away, up the hill, voices were shouting, but I did not care. Inside I was still whirling, sweeping, bowing down the hillside, and Michael was too. Nothing they above or anyone could say or do would ever matter. I knew Michael and I were each other's for ever. I was the only Snow Queen who would win him away. He kissed me, on my sweaty, snowy tangled hair, as the others came tumbling, stumbling down.

'Justina, Justina,' Geoffrey was shouting, fussily, 'what will Father say?'

'Nothing,' Clare answered for me, 'If no one tells him.' She cast around all of us a sharp and bitter eye of warning which at last settled on me. 'Get your clothing and dress yourself,' she said, her voice clipped. She was not pleased. I nodded, but then I saw Sandy and my remorse was buried in triumph.

'Ten times,' I said. 'Ten times. And I never fell.'

He was silent and then he shrugged, embarrassed and annoyed. 'You'd do anything, wouldn't you?' he said. But he ducked away from Michael as he said it, and he said no more.

Meggie fidgeted behind Geoffrey, staring wide-eyed, and I wondered what she'd say back home in Yorkshire about us all. 'Aren't you cold?' she asked at last, and Michael laughed aloud.

It was Mirza Hassan who brought my clothes down from the rock up on the hill. He held them folded across his arm, as if he were a gentleman's valet, and indeed I suppose he often enough performed that service for our crippled father, and other more intimate services as well. He made no expression as he handed them to me, and he had retreated into the comfortable pretence of linguistic limitation, as often. But as I thanked him I saw deep in his eyes a look of wonderful humour and warmth and he whispered, 'A woman like an eagle, like a swan!'

I behaved myself for the rest of the descent; clothed again modestly, I ski'd modestly as well, and kept well behind the boys who somewhat gingerly resumed their male camaraderie. They talked again as if nothing had happened, and Clare and Meggie did the same, though I caught Meggie staring at me from time to time. Geoffrey stamped stolidly behind me like a gaoler and behind us all Mirza Hassan walked with his tireless mountaineer's stride, looking about at the clearing sky, holding his bandit's head high. We came down off the hill a different way, and found ourselves in the middle of Strathpeffer. The spring sun came out through the snowclouds and quite suddenly it grew warm, and the snow dripped and thawed. Green grass appeared in gardens and we took off our skis and carried them once more. In the centre of the village, across from the Spa Pavilion, a grand new hotel was being built, in anticipation of the even greater popularity of the famous waters. It would be called the Highland Hotel, and we clambered up the snowy ground before it to wander about and observe the builders' progress.

It was a huge stone building, with many floors and towers and a great long veranda along the entire front. Obviously it was planned as much for the socialite as the supplicant, and we laughed and joked about its projected splendour.

'Too posh for you, by far,' Sandy said to Michael. 'No bog Irish allowed.' They were good humoured again and the punches they exchanged were play. We pretended to be guests in the fine new hotel, and Geoffrey suddenly grew bold, crossed the bare wood of the unfinished veranda and bowed to Meggie Whyte.

'Might I have this dance?' She shrieked and giggled and took his hand and they waltzed around in silence until Michael drew a mouth organ from his pack and began to play. He played Irish songs and suddenly I heard the old familiar tune of 'A Nation Once Again', and I remembered *Cathleen ni Houlihan* and that Dublin night so long ago.

'Stop, Michael,' I cried suddenly. 'It's too sad.'

'Not sad at all,' he gasped, between breaths. 'Jolly nice song.' But it was suddenly terribly terribly sad, and I watched in misery I did not understand as Geoffrey, happier and happier, whirled Meggie Whyte around and around the snowy, half-built dance floor at the Highland Hotel.

That night I could hardly sleep for my own happy exhaustion. Each of my muscles ached, and the ache spread through me, warming me, caressing me, as if I was yet in Michael's embrace. When I closed my eyes I was swooping once more, white as a white bird, down the white hill, and always waiting were Michael's dark arms. I tossed and turned in restless, unfathomed pleasure. You may laugh at my innocence if you choose, but I truly did not know what the feeling was that so joyously stirred me. In ignorance and innocence I finally slept. And yet, on that happiest of nights of my youth I dreamt one of my life's most terrifying dreams. And in the weird nature of dreams there was not one thing in it that could possibly explain the sheer, sweat-soaked horror in which I awoke.

The dream was only this: there was, as I mentioned, a railway station at Achterneed, just beyond Strathpeffer, where we had rested on our way. Sometimes we had used that station when coming here from the south, jumping off early to ski, while Mother and Father went on to the Spa. In this dream, we were all, all on the train. And I got off at Achterneed because the snow was perfect, and I stood there with my skis over my shoulders, reaching up to Michael so that he would step down from the train. It was that old kind of train with beautiful wooden coaches, and a long open platform at the end. All the family were gathered on that platform, and in the eerie timeless way of dreams they were gathered without sense or logic. Douglas was there, although he was long away in India. And Persephone was there too, and Geoffrey, of course, and Sandy and Michael. But *Jemmy* was there, and William even, tiny little William, still tiny, though we were grown, holding on to Mother's hand. And Father was standing as straight and strong as when he was young. And then the train began to move and none of them, none of them had joined me in the snow.

I woke crying out,

'They're all going! They're all going!' and my face was soaked in tears.

8

I was in Holloway Prison when Mother died, in March of 1914. The news of her last illness never reached us (Clare was there as well) until after all was over. I have never forgiven myself, or Clare, this set of circumstances which was largely her fault, but undoubtedly mine as well. People who detonate explosives under railway carriages cannot be deemed blameless.

It was in the autumn of the previous year that I at last entered the School of Art at South Kensington. I was nineteen years old, grossly under-educated, and it was by Herculean efforts on the part of my cousins and brothers that I was tutored in a variety of subjects sufficiently to pass the entrance exams. Tutored, or more accurately, primed and stuffed like a monkey with borrowed tricks, soon to be forgotten. No matter; I was there, where I had so longed to be.

Eugenia Howie was the champion and benefactress whose good offices had won the long battle for me. Mother, weak now and uncertain, opposed no one, least of all her sister and soul mate. And Father had from long before found both the Quigley sisters ever irresistible. When Eugenia chose to throw her weight behind May Howie's pleas, and Clare's insistence, my cause was won. That her motives were complex, and not all to my advantage, I chose to ignore. I was in London, studying art, and out in the widening world.

None of it, naturally, was quite what I expected. The School of Art was itself a revelation and not always a happy one. I was an innocent, sheltered throughout my youth, and exposed to the artistic world only through the unique vision of J. B. Yeats. And nothing in Mr Yeats' ebullient and irreverent company in the years of my Dublin apprenticeship in any way prepared me for the fusty routines of conventional study. Where Mr Yeats' criticism had sent me running to my easel with renewed hope and courage, the critiques of my teachers made me lay down my brushes in despair. They fussed and picked, tearing a painting apart on issues of fashion and triviality. It seemed not in any of them to see the whole wood: always they stumbled against a single tree. No doubt some of this, or most of this, was good for me. No doubt I learned. But in half a year my faith was shaken and my artistic vision failing. And worst of all, and for the first time, I met the prejudice of sex in the world of art. In short order I was made to understand that the role of the woman student, as the role of the woman in all my world, was subordinate to that of the man. Our work was prejudged before our brushes touched the canvas, and to this criticism there was no answer. I might change my every style, my every technique. I might throw out my palette and start anew with the colours that won approval. But there was no way ever I might cast my womanhood away or free my work from the offending shade of sex. All politics are born in personal grievance, and my days at the School of Art quickly ripened me for the suffrage harvest of my sister Clare.

Clare and I were closer that year than at any time since our early childhood, and for the first time since before her Oxford days, we were living again under the same roof. Clare had taken rooms the previous year in Callow Street, just off the Fulham Road, with Meggie Whyte who was working now in London and an American girl called Emmie Anderson. Neither Eugenia nor my parents had ever seen Clare's residence, and therefore were quite content to see me lodging there for my student years. Not that there was anything much wrong with it in itself; it was a small house owned by working people, a milliner and his wife, who thus supplemented a modest income.

It was Clare who turned her two unfurnished rooms into a centre of suffragette sedition and occasionally an armoury. I doubt the poor milliner was even aware. The wall above Clare's bed was draped with the purple, white and green of the WSPU, and round her plain table plans for demonstrations were hatched, letters to government ministers drafted, and street weapons were forged out of rope and tar. Through this factory of rebellion I drifted cheerfully, for the first months of my study, less aloof than simply detached. Art totally absorbed me and I viewed the world with a casual disinterest that was almost criminally selfish. Later things changed, and not for the better.

Of my three room-mates, I had most communication with the American, Emmie Anderson. Clare, though my sister, was much my senior, and made older by her single-minded devotion to her cause. Throughout that winter she was only with us half the time, since she was in and out of Holloway with sickening regularity, a victim of the appalling Cat and Mouse Act, that released hunger strikers on licence long enough to salvage their health, only to drag them back within prison walls to complete their sentences. Clare had had so many sentences and releases that it appeared for a time that she would spend much of her remaining life commuting to Holloway.

As always, she thrived on conflict and grew ever more stonily determined, her spirit waxing as her battered physique waned. She must have been very tough simply to have survived, but no one does such violence to their body without retribution. She was permanently underweight, red-eyed, sallow-faced, plagued by a cough, and skin complaints. She was snappy, difficult, and burningly courageous and the courage endowed her with a magnetism that overpowered all her physical infirmities. Among my artist friends were several young men who would call on me at Callow Street and spend their time there gazing upon Clare with the eyes of Adam upon the fatal tree.

But such a Boadicea, a Joan of Arc, was no soul mate for a dreamy artist. Nor was Meggie Whyte, her faithful worshipful factory girl a more likely friend, for though we were of an age more or less, Meggie found it impossible to maintain a friendship that had no elements of subservience. She trailed Clare like a puppy, but wilted in shyness if I attempted to converse. Class stood between us, a barrier erected by neither her nor me, which neither of us could cross. Oddly enough, Geoffrey crossed it, and Geoffrey, from the winter he met her in Strathpeffer, never had ceased deluging her with letters and trinkets, and photographs of himself at various high points of his clerical career. I suppose it was a form of courtship but neither of them seemed the slightest bit aware. And the only words of love Meggie ever spoke were inevitably directed to Clare.

So, of our foursome in Callow Street, it was left to the American stranger, Emmie Anderson, to become the friend of my brief student life, and it was with her that I shared the café teas, the Museum wandering, and the careful walking out with two carefully innocuous young men whose correct antecedents permitted what in later years might be called a date. In those years, modesty and propriety so framed such an event that it was almost impossible for emotion to enter it. We all chose our companions, or had them chosen for us for reasons of calculated safety. Emmie's young man was an earnest young socialist working for the WSPU at Clement's Inn, and mine was a fellow art student, Richard Underwood. They were both as boring as rice puddings, and I daresay they thought much the same of us.

Richard Underwood was quite typical of my fellow students, actually. Hardly the Bohemians I had expected (my appetite whetted by the Stephen's Green studio of JBY), they were a tense and solemn lot, and concerned as much for their futures as bank clerks. It has never in my notice paid anyone to worry much over the future, least of all creative artists. They failed themselves accordingly, seeking a security in their work that undermined it irrevocably, and as companions they failed my expectations. I found more happy communion with Clare's suffragettes. Rebels all, they had in their violent way far more powerful conviction than my students, and art, any art, demands conviction. I suppose it was inevitable that I be drawn into their circle.

Emmie Anderson fascinated me with her slow, endearing accent, and her sprightly fashionable style. She dressed well, even to go into the street to smash windows, and laughed delightedly at the shock of Holloway Wardens over her lacy underwear. She came from some very important New York family, and once in my naïvety I asked if she knew my dear Mr Yeats who now resided in New York. She only laughed, but not unkindly, and said New York was rather large. Actually, for all the deliberate calm of our 'dates', I do imagine her young socialist was quite intrigued. Emmie was pretty in a plump cheerful way, and men did notice her. But we were at that age when youth wins notice regardless of beauty, and even I was noticed, and by more than one. Richard Underwood was quite taken with me until he came to Callow Street and set eyes on Clare. I cared not in the slightest, my joint devotion to Michael Howie and art made me quite oblivious of men. But Richard Underwood had an influence on me, despite that, that would long outlast our friendship of that brief year.

As an artist he was thoroughly mediocre, a natural outcome of his personality. He was a pale, gentle and essentially spiritless soul, better fitted indeed for clerking than for art. I say this not out of meanness but as a necessary truth. He spoke a great deal about style in an airy way, and occasionally asserted himself by loftily criticizing my work. I felt sorry for him and held my tongue. I knew enough already to know how far I surpassed him and how deeply he was aware of it. All this is merely preface to what comes next, and if you will forgive its apparent vanity, you will soon understand its purpose.

Late in January we were given a set piece, a life drawing upon which our first major assessment would be made. It was an important class and we all worked very hard at it, myself with breathless determination, sensing already that as one of only two women in the group, I was swimming up-stream. The ability to judge ourselves is the backbone of artistic skill; Mr Yeats had honed this ability in me, and to a considerable degree I possessed it. When I completed that drawing it was good, and I knew it was good.

I awaited, with the honest confidence that is more satisfying than pride, the judgement of my teachers. Across the studio Richard Underwood, red-faced, with his brown curls dampened with the sweat of concentration, fussed over his board. My heart went to him. Life drawings were not his strong point; he was far happier with his uninspiredly pretty landscapes, and I knew he'd found the class a terrible strain. It was the custom for our work to be judged publicly, before the class, and the experience could be gruelling. He looked up to me and smiled, unhappily, and I smiled back, a moment's encouragement, before the door of the studio opened, admitting two teachers, and the assessment began.

Both of these men were then well known, and later even more so, so I will refrain from mentioning names. They moved among the students with slow and dignified steps, lowering eye-glasses to study a detail, murmuring to each other. At each easel some small personal comment was made, and my fellow students puffed with pride, or blushed with misery accordingly. There was a strong strain of sarcastic humour in the older of these two gentlemen, and he unleashed it briefly on our other woman student, a heavy-set, graceless girl who stood the while nodding miserably as he made mockery of her execution of the model's anatomy.

'Miss Barnes, when we desire a hunchback we will provide you with a hunchback as model. Preferably one with two left thumbs, I should imagine.' She nodded silently as he moved on, and continued nodding like one of those odd children's toys with bobbing heads, as they advanced on down the awe-stricken row of students.

They stood a long, long while before my drawing-board, and eventually I heard what sounded like a small sigh escape from the younger of the two men. I was standing directly behind him, and suddenly realized he was, despite his full beard, not half as old as I imagined. Nor was he the confident master his bearing inferred. He was but a sycophant, aping the great man beside him. That party, with a bristling of his grey beard brought about by a clenching of teeth, suddenly turned from my board and stalked away. Neither of them had spoken a word. The younger man followed, his face lit by curious enquiry, and then the older, the great master, strode across the room and spying the drawing of my beau, Richard Underwood, suddenly seized it, holding it up with a loud, flamboyant, 'Ah, hah.' He held the drawing aloft, his deep-set angry eyes sweeping the room, until he held all our attention. 'Now,' he said, 'we will have a lesson.' He recrossed the room with Richard's drawing in his hands, and then took mine as well and set them both up side by side on an easel in full view of the assembly. They sat beside each other in splendid isolation, and I cringed inside for Richard at the contrast, wishing it had been any drawing but mine set there to humiliate him. So deep was my concern for him, so great my concentration upon his unhappy features that I did not even hear that the teacher's first words were addressed to me. He repeated them, none the kinder for repetition.

'Miss Melrose, explain to the class how your drawing fails in comparison to Mr Underwood's.'

I looked up, wide-eyed, yet certain I had misheard and said, 'Sir?'

'Must I repeat myself yet again?' he roared. 'Have you no ears? Your drawing, Miss Melrose. Recite to the class its inferior qualities.' And when I was yet silent, this time in stunned uncertainty, and growing anger, he bellowed out, his grey beard leaping forward with each word, 'Have you no eyes, woman, either?'

'My drawing?' I whispered.

'The arm, perhaps,' the second teacher muttered in reply. 'Perhaps you should find the arm less well executed.' His voice trembled with his own uncertainty and the fear of angering his superior. Fortunately the elder man was slightly deaf, and had taken a stance at a slight distance surveying the class whose shocked faces were all turned towards me. I could not believe it was happening.

Honesty is a ruthless master. I could not do it. It was not to spare myself humiliation; I rather would have suffered that than inflict the same on poor innocent Richard. But I could not have condemned my drawing before his, had they both been the work of strangers. It was an affront to art itself, a disloyalty to the central reason of my being.

'It's not inferior,' I said.

'What?' hissed the master.

'Oh something, something must be,' pleaded his underling at my side. 'Please, Miss Melrose, you must be reasonable . . . .' He twisted on his small dapper feet back and forth like a child needing the toilet.

'Have you no humility, either?' demanded the master. And then he burst out in a diatribe of passionate ferocity, his arms waving, his words spluttering, spittle clinging to his beard. He verbally shredded my drawing, finding flaws that no one but he could see, contrasting it again and again to Richard's, finding there virtues invisible to all. Even Richard protested, bravely, at one point, but allowed himself to be rapidly over-ruled. And after each raging sentence the master swung his heavy head around like a great bull, his fiery eyes on mine and demanded, 'Is that not so, Miss Melrose? Is that shadow not false, Miss Melrose? Is Mr Underwood's shading not superior, Miss

Melrose?' until only stubborn fury kept me from fleeing from the room. I never knew until that day how stubborn I really was, and how fiercely I could fight, if fight was demanded of me. In the end, he had used all his words, his anger was exhausted, the fires of the eyes quenched. And I had not conceded. He looked at me with infinite coldness and then glanced once round the room. 'The class is finished,' he said and my fellow students scuttled out like a roomful of mice. Richard waited momentarily at the doorway and then fled, and even the underling teacher, with one last pleading glance at me, bolted for the door.

I was alone in the empty studio before my pilloried drawing, and the great man standing glowering yet at the floor.

'Why?' I asked in the silence of the empty room. I had incredible nerve, I realize, but I was so certain that my term at the School of Art was over that I felt remarkably free of all concern. When he looked up, his features were surprisingly calm, almost placid, and he seemed another person.

'Why?' he said. 'Because it was necessary.'

'Necessary?' I whispered.

'Of course. Necessary for you. Necessary for the others.' I watched, uncomprehending and he said, quite reasonably, 'You humiliate them, the young men, that poor calf-eyed boy. You are holding them back.'

'*I* am?' I protested and then flared up in anger, 'Because my work is better than theirs? That is *bad* for them?' He nodded, amazing me, and I cried indignantly, 'Must there be no competition? Must everything be made easy for them?'

'Of course not. But they should not be humiliated by a woman.'

I gasped and shouted, 'Even if the woman is *far* their superior?' and I knew at once he agreed and the knowledge infuriated me further.

'Even so,' he replied calmly. And then he leaned over me, almost threateningly, breathing tobacco breath in my face. '*They* have futures to which they will rise, with encouragement.'

'And I?' I asked, foolishly.

'You? You are a woman. Your future is in the marriage bed. You have no future here.'

I felt quite sick with shock but I shouted suddenly, 'Ridiculous,' as if I was Clare. And I thought of Clare, for courage. He looked at me in excruciating intimacy, his eyes all over my body. No one had ever done anything like this to me, and I felt I could feel his eyes, like rough hands on my naked skin. 'The marriage bed,' he spat. 'Child-bearing will soften your brain. It always does. You will dabble prettily. *They*,' he shrugged towards the mice who had fled, 'will be artists.'

It was raining when I reached Callow Street. Inside I sat at the revolutionary table and wept for an hour on Emmie Anderson's soft shoulder. I was thankful Clare was not there. My troubles, compared to hers, were petty, but my tears, and my humiliation were very real.

The next day Richard Underwood proposed. I think it was a kind of apology, a consolation prize offered for the misery I had endured. I also think he was rather relieved when I refused him. The little episode ended our relationship. We could not go back, and would not go forward; there was no way our friendship could survive either his romantic gesture, or my refusal. Also, I knew that it was the very witness of my humiliation that gave him the Dutch courage to make the gesture. I was made small in his eyes, and thus attainable, and my awareness of the fact rebounded on him, and all his ilk. I had no more London beaus.

My first deliberate action on the part of the suffragettes

occurred a fortnight later. It was mild enough, and at the time I did not connect it with the events just related, but a connection is undeniable. *Radicalized* is the term they use today. By the power of my superiors at the School of Art and of Richard Underwood, I had been radicalized. I was, I suppose, just awaiting my moment, and one Saturday night in February, my moment came.

Clare was out on licence from Holloway; a condition that did not prevent her from appearing, often in disguise, at public gatherings to speak and encourage and enrage. Her licence had run out a week earlier, and she was now in a sort of hiding, emerging recklessly to address some gathering and being whisked away by supporters under the noses of the police. The net was closing in, and she dare not appear too often. Emmie and Meggie Whyte were too well known in their association with Clare to dare public appearances, and our rooms in Callow Street had become a fortress under siege.

We had our own entrance-way, by an outside stairway in the courtyard at the back of the building, and when that Saturday night there was a frantic hammering on our outer door, we all were terrified to open it, expecting to find the police. But it was not the 'Cats' after our 'Mice' but two women, who stumbled in when at last we unbolted the door. Their clothing was dirty and disordered and there was a strong smell of scorched wool about them. One was supporting the other and when the weaker of the pair looked up, wincing painfully against the gaslight, I saw that her face was burnt and blistering and her eyebrows and hair singed and frizzled. Her hands, wrapped in a shawl, were burned piteously. She held them out to me like a hurt child, in dumb misery. They had spilled petrol over themselves, firing a pillarbox, and unwittingly set themselves alight.

Clare, who was as squeamish, oddly, as she was personally brave, turned away in sick horror.

'We must get help,' Meggie whispered. 'We've nothing to deal with this.' She looked at Clare. Clare had her hand over her mouth and with eyes yet averted, waved Meggie away.

'Mrs Higgins,' Emmie Anderson said. 'She's a nurse.' We were like combatants in an underground war. The thought of calling in a doctor was unthinkable even to the burnt victims of their own criminal act. 'Take her to Mrs Higgins, Clare.'

'*I* can't go out,' Clare returned angrily. Shame at her own peculiar weakness enraged her, but she was right. She would be arrested in the street, at once, and the burnt girl with her.

'Meggie . . .' Emmie ventured warily, but Meggie grew almost hysterical, clutching Clare's arm and crying, 'I won't go back there. I won't go to Holloway again. It was the death of me near enough, the once.' She looked wildly around and her eyes, like those of the others, fell on me. Emmie Anderson spoke up bravely and loyally.

'I'll go. If they catch me again, they catch me. Someone must help this girl.' She reached for her hat and coat, and I think I had already decided, but anyhow then Clare spoke in her forceful and determined voice that I rarely could oppose.

'You must go, Justina. They're watching for us. They don't know you. Take them with you. You must go.' She waved us all from her presence, and hastened from ours, into the inner room.

The courage of the poor burnt creature I helped through the little streets of Chelsea impressed me vividly, and like a martyr's wounds it roused in me a spirit to do battle. I did find, eventually, the home of our sympathetic nurse and left the suffering, disfigured girl with her. Her companion fled at the nurse's doorstep, and when I went out to return home I was alone in the still, dark streets of London, with new and fiery thoughts. She had been so brave, never whimpering even, through her awful pain, and thanking me as I left, for my help. The courage alone had ennobled her cause, and her actions, neither of which had ever held my full approval. Violence provides its own sanctity. I had slipped without knowing into a river that was ever rising, as dark and pervasive as the Thames whose embankments I walked that night, and which soon enough would engulf half the world.

If my first act of sedition was also an act of mercy, no such justification could be cast upon my second. Three days later, when Clare suggested I might be of assistance in the delivery of a quantity of petrol to another area of the city, I agreed with surprising readiness. She was delighted and hugged me in one of her rare, rare demonstrations of pleasure. As always, since childhood, I was thrilled. The journey through the streets of London by night became a child's adventure. Other escapades rapidly followed. I was lucky for weeks; I was never caught, and I grew astonishingly bold. Disguising myself once, in Clare's hat and coat to lead the 'Cats' from her trail, I found myself confronted with angry police officers pinning my arms and cursing in disgust at their mistake. I remember laughing in their faces and placing in the arms of one a bunch of hothouse peonies I had bought for the studio.

'You're in with the wrong sort, young lady,' they blustered. I giggled and ran. No one ever imagined I might be up to such tricks on my own; they seemed to assume I lacked the brains. Perhaps I did; I certainly lacked Clare's brutal commitment. Oh, undoubtedly I wanted the Vote, and other freedoms too, but I would get lost in my painting and forget everything soon enough. Nor could I share Clare's sharp distaste for men. But then, I was in love, and to the best of my knowledge, Clare never had been.

I delivered messages, packed gunpowder into tins in basement flats, twisted tarred rope into metal-tipped tawses called 'Saturday Nights' for the women to defend themselves in the streets. I distributed *Votes for Women* among the faithful and chalked notices on corner buildings and kerbstones advising on the locations and times of the suffragettes' great and now customary gatherings. I slipped in and out of Clement's Inn under the eyes of the police with Clare's articles for publication. No one ever stopped me, except one young constable with his mind bent on flirtation rather than the law. I attended street meetings, and listened to speakers, and sat at the foot of the platform sketching Keir Hardie and Mrs Pankhurst. In all that time, although I was aware that the petrol and gunpowder had purposes, and I read in the papers of houses burned and government property demolished, I never actually saw an act of violence, and felt quite oblivious of guilt. Only when Clare and Meggie discussed dispassionately the slashing of paintings in a public museum was my failing conscience aroused. Art was yet inviolable, though property had become negotiable. And I had not even considered the vulnerability of human life. Despite all the violence and damage, the only living things that had suffered were my fellow suffragettes. We had our martyr in Emily Davison, a girl intent with canny wisdom upon the irrefutable argument of self-destruction. And we had other, quieter sufferers in our hunger-strikers whose self-murder, though gradual, was frighteningly real. Some had sickened and died; ignominious deaths of ugly illnesses that no one chose to celebrate. But they died all the same. I watched Clare with fearful eyes, and lied to Mother and Father in my letters home. What else was there to do?

But violence, too, was coming my way, and clothed in deceptive innocence. Late in February a great street demonstration was planned, gathering suffragettes from many places around the country. As was our way, costumes and pageantry played a large part in such events; a kind of natural street theatricality prevailed, as if we felt obliged to give value for money. Not for us the mindless roaring of simple slogans so loved by the rebels of today. We had pennants and banners, colours and robes, children with flowers and horsedrawn tableaux. It was all rather sad in the cold wet February streets, but we were buoyed up with a wonderful camaraderie, massed women together with our few brave, imaginative male supporters. Even Richard Underwood, to his credit, came along, though now to follow like a spaniel at Clare's heels. Clare herself, weak from a further imprisonment and hunger strike, was carried on a sort of litter by six strapping Yorkshire lasses, though thin and frail as she was, I daresay one of them could have carried her alone. Amazingly, she still dressed with care, almost pathetically trimming her hats and pressing her lace collars as if on her way to meet a beau, though Holloway was her most likely suitor. I marched side by side with Meggie Whyte and Emmie Anderson, through the streets of the city to Trafalgar Square.

It was there I saw the ranks of mounted officers awaiting, in the rain. There is always confusion in a crowd; always the danger of panic. I cannot say which happened first, whether the crowd panicked, or indeed the police, or even their horses. But suddenly there was scuffling, shouts from a clutch of ruffian hecklers, and as suddenly, the horses and their riders charged.

A crowd is such a mindless thing; a great dinosaur with ponderous limbs and no brain. It cannot turn, it cannot move, it cannot in any way respond in haste. It sways, moans, swings around in massive disorder, united by its sheer size into one appalling force. It can crush barriers, break fences, burst through barricades; but its strength is also its vulnerability. Like a massed community of insects, marching ants or drone bees, its group success is only at the sacrifice of the individual. Before fences break, limbs break, skulls crush and blood flows. Behind, in its savage innocence, the crowd is often quite unaware.

Two were killed that day; one woman beneath the horses' frightened hoofs, and an East End child of seven, smashed against the railings of a staircase. I saw none of this, and knew it only from the papers the next day, even though I was yards away. All I was aware of was the gay excitement turning in seconds to fear and savagery, as the strong struggled over the weak, and the lucky ran away. I saw Clare's litter overturned and her helpers flee screaming, and in the chaos, Richard Underwood lifting her up and half carrying her away. He was arrested later, but I saw nothing of that.

With my arms linked still through Emmie Anderson's and with Meggie Whyte shrieking and clutching at my coat, I struggled to get away, to find an alley-way, a side-street, some shelter from the turbulent human storm that would not prove a trap. The panicked crowd moved like a river, flowing like water, finding the easiest exit, twisting in small human eddies, breaking like waves against any obstacle at all. In the midst of it, just as my footing was going, I felt a firm strong masculine arm grip my shoulder with a ferocity that assured me its owner was a member of the police. I looked up raging, all my anger at what I was seeing turned upon the hand of the law and saw, to my total astonishment, my brother Geoffrey.

'You stupid little fool,' he shouted, and then he reached out for Meggie, who ran into his arms. As I stared the crowd pushed me and Emmie forward and Geoffrey shoved me into the arms of another man and I saw that man was Sandy. He gripped my collar, like a cat's scruff, and grabbed an amazed Emmie Anderson as well and the two of them ploughed with us thus imprisoned through the turbulence towards the haven of St James's Park.

They did not stop until we arrived in the green cool blessed peace of its comparative emptiness and they yet held on to us. They seemed to think we actually desired to go back, which was rather unlikely. Meek as lambs, we went with them to Callow Street and home. The rest of the afternoon, spent waiting for Clare, was one of the bleakest of my life.

Geoffrey, my pompous and beloved oaf, had developed a sudden strain of forcefulness, concentrating his formerly flaccid views into powerful anger and determination. He had learned much of our activities from Meggie, who foolishly related it all in her letters to him, and had come to London ready to do battle. Sandy informed him of the Trafalgar Square meeting, and our likely participation, and they followed the march, almost catching up with our section when the violence began. Obliged to rescue us, he was now twice as angry and had over us a powerful additional weapon.

'Immoral, indecent, indiscreet; all of which, Justina, is precisely what I expect of you. But stupid! So stupid as well. I honestly believe you *are* quite addled. No doubt that fall really damaged you, and I suppose I must be compassionate, but I do say you *try my patience*.' He looked down at me, with his comical face bearing the wrath of the righteous yet uneasily, but I was not inclined now to laugh. Under his freckles he was bright red, and his Adam's apple, quivering in outrage, set his clerical collar trembling.

'What fall?' asked Emmie curiously.

But I was not about to explain Sligo and Michael's tree

and I shouted back at Geoffrey, 'Be damned with your patience, you stuffy imbecile.' Sandy said with tired displeasure, brushing street dust from his tailored trousers, 'Oh do be quiet, Justina. I've had all I can take.' He sounded forty years old. I grabbed my hat and coat up from where they'd been dropped on a chair and crammed the hat atop my collapsing pile of hair, stuffing curly wisps in under the crown. '*Where* do you think you're going?' Sandy said, with a deliberate yawn.

'Out,' I said and Geoffrey strode across the room, snatched my coat, and clutched at my hat. It tore loose, cascading hair and hair pins over my eyes, pulling at the roots so I cried in pain.

'Sit down, you silly female,' he said, and I turned and jabbed my hat pin hard into his clerical behind. His roar of outrage cloaked the sound of the opening door and he was diving for me with both hands when Clare stepped shakily into the room.

'A family party,' she declared. 'What a positive joy.' She was grinning, pale, battered and joyous on violence, the sweet nectar of her youth. Instantly Geoffrey's anger was deflected from me to herself. He swung around in a comical right angle turn, his two outstretched hands reaching now for her. Somehow she managed to slip out of her coat just in time to drape it across his grasping furious fingers. He stood there like a baffled coatrack and she said, 'Thank you very much Geoffrey, how kind.'

'You harlot!' he spluttered, flinging the coat to the floor.

'What?' asked Clare, tiredly, slipping off her hat.

'Whore. Hussy. Shameless woman.' We all stared and Clare looked up from her hat. Her incomprehension was only matched by her lack of interest.

'Oh be quiet,' she said.

'Tempter of the young. Corrupter of womankind . . .'

He gestured towards myself and Meggie, and raged, 'Your own sister, dragged about the streets . . .'

'Meggie, darling,' said Clare, 'make me a cup of tea.'

Her rationality triumphed momentarily and Sandy, whose distaste for Clare's suffragettes was no greater than his dislike of Geoffrey's Christians, looked immensely relieved and settled in an armchair, expecting normality. Meggie trotted loyally towards the back room where we had primitive cooking facilities, but Geoffrey reached out a lanky, black-sleeved arm and caught her wrist. As always when he touched her, or even looked at her, she softened, changing texture and becoming physically rounder, more pliant. She looked up at him in silence.

'Sit down, Meggie,' he said. She turned, uncertain.

'My tea, Meggie,' said Clare.

Meggie looked at Geoffrey still, and then back to Clare. She blinked like a well-trained dog confused by conflicting commands.

'Over there,' said Geoffrey, directing her towards the chair beside Sandy's.

'*Make my tea*,' said Clare. Her voice was harsh and unlikeable, but abruptly she changed, looked hurt and allowed a little of her true exhaustion to the surface, so that misery bloomed across her pinched starved face. 'Please, Meggie, I'm so tired.'

Meggie wrenched herself free and ran to Clare but Geoffrey swung her back with a word like a ball on an elastic string.

'Stay.' She stayed. I watched amazed as tears trickled down her bewildered, pretty face.

Oh think of yourself, silly, I wanted to cry, but I somehow could not speak, and Sandy swore suddenly and without apology and said, 'Do what you're told.' Poor Meggie. She looked to him, to me, to Clare and to Geoffrey and he reached out one hand, a big strong hand

and laid it on her shoulder, and closed the fingers gently over the fabric of her dress. Will drained out of her, into his gentle hand.

'Meggie is leaving you, Clare,' Geoffrey said.

'No I'm not,' Meggie whimpered, but she stepped back, to slip beneath the bridge of his arm, and shelter there.

'She's coming with me,' he said.

'No. No, I'm not,' Meggie whimpered, her head leaning against his arm. Her eyes were closing, as if she were hypnotized.

Clare stared, shocked and serious. 'She's mine,' she whispered to Geoffrey. 'She's staying with me.' But she sounded weak, and afraid of him.

'Oh no,' he said. 'She belongs to herself. Not you. Don't you, Meggie darling?'

Meggie nodded, her eyes yet closed.

'And she wants to come with me. Don't you, Meggie darling?'

She shook her head, squeezing out fresh tears from her tightly closed eyes and said, 'Yes.'

'You see?' said Geoffrey. He stood very straight and ominous in his stiff black.

'Meggie?' whispered Clare. There was no answer, and she whispered the name again, and then said it aloud and then shouted it, but Meggie would not hear. She stormed and raged, and tore off her gloves and threw them at the girl, but there was still no answer. Then she turned her rage upon Geoffrey and cried all sorts of things from our past, how he'd always hated her and cheated her and stolen her rights from her and none of them made sense. In the end she sank to her knees and cried openly, sobbing on her sore, battered hands before the couple standing silent as carved saints. She looked up and demanded, her face grotesque, 'She's mine. What do you want her for?'

'Yours?' he said. 'What do *you* want her for?' He

paused, watching the shock of discovery grow upon Clare's face. 'I want her,' he said with pompous righteousness, turning to smile down on the numb girl in his arms, '*I* want her for my own dear wife.'

Meggie left us then. She left that same day, with Geoffrey, not taking even her clothes. Sandy, gruff and embarrassed came back for them, not speaking to myself or Clare. The rooms were full of women when he returned, angry, beaten women, and he walked among them like a man among wolves. I hated him then, more than I hated Geoffrey, because Sandy, unlike Geoffrey, was neither gentle nor a fool. And neither of them cared at all what an awful thing they'd done to Clare.

I have said it was Clare's fault that I was in Holloway that spring, and my fault as well. But in truth the fault was more accurately theirs. They had humiliated Clare, they had struck at her when, weak and defeated, she who could fight so splendidly had no fight left. They had taken from her the only one she ever appeared to love, and they had made her cry. Clare, who never wept, wept then, all night in my arms, crying Meggie's name. I do not wish to know, or to have you volunteer for me the rationale the modern world would place upon that tearful night. We were another race, ours another world from yours. We could yet love without corruption. Clare had loved, and lost. And my love for her, rising in response, was suddenly overwhelming and demanded a grand and reckless act.

Then too the pressure of time hurried me; I knew, as no doubt did Clare, that word of our crimes was even now winging towards Arradale. Geoffrey and Alexander had left in grim and unforgiving mood. The only reason I wasn't dragged away, along with the compliant little Meggie, was the ferocity of my hatpin and my teeth. Geoffrey was by then twice bitten, and thrice shy. Sandy washed his gloved hands of me in disgust. No Christian impulse drove him to save me and he would not lower himself to tussle with me in the dust. They left without me, but my sins went with them, straight to the family bosom. I imagined I had a week before forces were mustered to summon me home.

On the third day of my week I found the railway marshalling yards in the East End, with a battered, corrugated iron fence that any fool could get over. The first night, dressed in a black skirt and jacket for invisibility, I only investigated, slipping into the yard, roving about, picking my particular carriage, one long disused and a good safe distance from the sheds where the trainmen worked and sheltered. Safe I say, for both my sake, shielding me from discovery, and theirs, protecting them from harm. We were rebels but not murderers. In those days we seemed able to draw a distinction.

The explosives were the easy part; I had ready access, and the help of shadowy male volunteers with a good knowledge of chemistry. I often regretted Sandy's disdain for us, his Chemistry degree would have proved so useful. As for female volunteers to help in the laying of charges, I had more than I could cope with. At risk of serious disappointment to others, I chose Emmie Anderson, less because of my undoubted trust in her than as a reward for her continuing loyalty to Clare. There was not a doubt in either of our minds that we were doing this only in part for the Cause, and in greater part for Clare.

I only wished she could have been there to watch. What a splendid, flaming cataclysm it made, and how it burned, lighting the sky above the railway yards, silhouetting the trains and the shouting men. What consternation and what delight. Do not ever imagine that only men love the childish pleasure of destruction; this is an unsexed vice. I think we paid for it, too, because we wasted time in our watching and our triumph, exchanging kisses of victory, like debutantes at a ball. We were amateurs. We should have run.

We did, then, run, but a little too late. The streets were filling with people, drawn from the little houses by the noise and flames. And we, two darting female figures, hampered and distinguished by our skirts, went not without notice. 'It's the women. The suffragettes. The bleedin' suffragettes!' We were over the back fences, climbing, scuttling, fleeing like cats, but shouting strangers were everywhere and some came running at our heels.

Our destination was a 'safe house' on St Bartolph Street but we never reached it. The crowd caught us amidst the maze of streets off Petticoat Lane, and jostled us in confusion. Some were hostile, spitting women, and arrogant crude men, pulling at our garments and tearing down our long hair. Others, the majority, were sympathetic but they could do little but scream and shout and tussle with our captors, and into the middle of it, like the master of hounds into his victorious pack, came first one constable and then a half-dozen more. They were big, burly and humourless: there was no flirtation this time. I was frightened, but even more angry. A lifetime of gracious breeding rebelled quite unreasonably at the rough hand of the law.

'Let me go!' I demanded, quite imperiously. They did not listen. They saw no Scottish gentleman's daughter, but a harridan with loosened hair and grubby hands. Another constable grasped Emmie from behind with both big arms about her waist, and when she bit his arm he whirled her about like a top, and struck her face. Blood came to her mouth and her eyes widened in amazement. The crowd howled, anger and approval indistinguishable. We had become a spectacle, a show, an amusement to be shouted about through the streets. When the Black Maria came to take us away, a huge congregation had gathered watching now with the distant eyes of disinterested strangers. What supporters we had had amongst them were gone, slipping away from the presence of the law. I had never before felt so utterly alone.

In the Black Maria, my isolation increased. We were thrust separately into little partitioned compartments and though I could hear Emmie moaning and crying I could not see her and was frantic to know what they'd done to her. That was always the worst of the prison experience; never knowing the fate of others, uncertain of one's own future, cut off entirely from those one loved, those who might worry or fear. I did not even know if anyone would be told of my imprisonment and throughout the hours of police court, and journeys in the hard-seated, clattering vehicle, I was haunted with the terror of being swept away into an isolation no one would penetrate. Would Clare be told? Was she even now searching for me? What of my friends, my parents? Oh, indulgent questions, indeed, for one so obviously guilty; had I thought of them all before? Of course not. But I thought of them now.

Fortunately for both Emmie and myself, no verifiable connection could be drawn between the explosion in the railyards and our presence in Petticoat Lane. It was night, the streets were filled with people and confusion. There were no accurate witnesses. In the end, we were charged with public rowdiness, a crime we were certainly guilty of, but a crime of much lesser weight, and little significance, and sentenced to three weeks in the Third Division. By morning Emmie and I, now quite cut off from each other and alone, were each in a cell in Holloway prison among the ordinary night rabble of the land, drunkards and prostitutes and petty thieves. This was no carefully engineered political sacrifice, but common arrest without dignity or privilege. In the eyes of the wardresses and our fellow prisoners we were but a curiosity, greeted with hostility.

My immediate reaction, after fear and anger, was a kind of exhilaration at being involved in something alien, vivid and real, but the excitement soon faded. I was deathly tired, having slept not at all, and the grey of early morning showed me a surrounding of bitter harshness. My cell itself was so small that even I could have lain full length in only one direction. That direction, paralleling the corridor wall of the enclosure, provided length enough for a fold-down plank bed, upon which a primitive straw-filled mattress was spread at night, and upon which I had shivered throughout the small hours. Blankets were scanty, narrow and filthy, as was everything about the cell other than the stone floor. I was desperately cold. Our clothing had been taken from us, and we had been issued with a ridiculous collection of garments, so ill-fitting and in such bad repair that we might as well have wrapped ourselves in blankets or rags. The prison arrows, so beloved of comedians and cartoonists were less amusing when one wore them. The cloth was harsh and the shoes were as stiff as shoes made of wood. Nothing fitted, nothing felt clean, and the common usage of ancient eating implements, and multi-purpose scrubbing tools made hygiene a distant dream. Somehow my constitution was strong enough to cope, though Emmie rapidly developed dysentery, a hideous experience in this world of slop pails and twice daily visits to a gruesome WC.

At once prison routine enwrapped us, hasty, noisy, dirty and essentially vicious. We were hurried and prodded, shouted at and humiliated from slopping out, to chapel, to worktimes, and mealtimes, and exercise and finally to lights-out at the end of each ghastly day. There is something in the very act of giving orders to the defenceless that arouses the less-than-human in all humanity. The wardresses were women, like ourselves. They were daughters, mothers perhaps, sisters. They had homes, and wore clean underwear and ate at tables. And yet they could so readily turn upon us a sadistic dominance that would shame any keeper of common beasts. These are not new thoughts to you, or indeed now to me, rocking as we are on the teetering edge of this century. But in 1914, to the young woman I was then, they were unthinkable.

We, as common criminals, were in the Third Division, our diet and our treatment the lowest Holloway had to offer. I am glad of that. I saw it all, not just the conditions, but the people themselves, those poor wrecks of humanity trudging out to the exercise yards, sick, corrupt, lost and essentially innocent. No one struggling to raise children in the East End of London in those days went to prison for trivial reasons. No man who steals, no woman who corrupts herself, for bread for children, is guilty of a crime. I was a long way, suddenly, from Arradale Castle and Merrion Square.

It was customary by then to hunger strike for political status, but I had no heart for that, nor was I even certain my motive *was* political, or my cause just. Around me were causes, in the form of syphilitic bodies and starved faces, that claimed a deeper justice than any of mine. I began at last, and quite suddenly, by the powerful force of circumstance, to think. And not before time, you may quite reasonably declare.

There was plenty of time for thought; we were allowed little other diversion, no books, no drawing or writing implements. Upon our arrival we were each given a Bible, a hymn-book and a book on hygiene, ironically enough, along with whatever uncompromising religious tract was currently on hand. Humourless and patronizing, these latter inspired nothing in me but an angry contempt;

contempt for the hypocrisy of staff who could load us with such Christian nonsense in so unchristian a place, and anger directed quite firmly at my brother Geoffrey, who could easily have written any one of them. They had his authentic bumptious voice. I threw them away with the same distaste I felt for the formally printed Morning and Evening prayers that decorated the cards bearing Prison Rules left pointedly in our cells. The religion of the authorities had little appeal just then.

I did read my Holloway Bible, though, in spare moments between scrubbing my cell and doing my prescribed prison work. That was sewing; shirts, if I recall, though mine resembled nothing so much as a shroud. I hated to sew, was terrible at it, and suffered perpetually bloodied fingers, and the wardress's regularly scathing tongue. After, I would sit at the shelf extending from the cell wall that served as a table, reading the Bible and finding as others before me the great comfort it offered the oppressed. At intervals throughout my stay the chaplain would arrive, announced by the sharp voice of the wardress but a moment before. If he found me at my Bible there was lavish praise, as to an obedient child. I grew to detest his visits, with their echoes of Geoffrey, though he was an old and probably a kindly man. I hadn't time for his kindness. I was cold, miserable, intolerant and bitter, worried about my friends and my family, and under those conditions I thought a great deal, and for the first time, about many things.

Foremost, I thought of Clare. My respect for her leapt upwards, to heights approaching worship. That she could endure this, regularly, repetitively, deliberately. And add to it the agonies of the hunger strike and all its ills, surpassed my imagination. And yet she would, and willingly, and was even now quite likely in some other wing of the prison doing so once more.

I doubt anyone who hasn't experienced it can really imagine what imprisonment is like. Leaving aside the physical deprivations and ills, the very loss of freedom and its accompanying total loss of privacy are devastating blows. Surely those who so petulantly insist that further punishments must be heaped upon this basic one before justice is done have never known imprisonment themselves. To lose one's liberty – this is, in itself, a punishment that outstrips in severity all we can imagine of it; and it only gets worse with time. The much-used imagery of a caged bird cannot be avoided . . . the bird, of course, standing in for the soul, winged and barred. The number of times in my short stay in Holloway that I rose to place my hand upon that locked door, forgetting entirely, as if it would open to me! How quickly all spirit, all humour leaves us in such circumstances. I would lie on my straw mat, my eyes closed against the ugliness around me, dreaming of Michael and the snow. But always that rattle would come at the door, the harsh scrape of the peephole flap, the brisk uncaring voice demanding, 'Are you all right, number 7? Are you all right?' The peephole closing before there was time to even answer, but what did they care? There was only one answer that would do. For that, that loss of privacy, was corollary to the same loss of freedom, and both denied one all value and made mockery of anyone's interest in one's fate.

I am getting quite bitter about this and I think I shall stop. Suffice to say, I did not like Holloway. Within its walls I had my first (sadly not last) glimpse of the true darkness that lurks in so many human souls and the social darkness of the land and times in which I lived. Of such experience revolutionaries are born but, no, that did not happen. I was an artist, and as an artist I reached always for the personal, the individual moment, the individual face. Those were the memories I carried from Holloway;

the twelve-year-old prostitute, and her companion in sin of seventy-five, toothless and laughing, almost the only laughing face within the prison. The twenty-year-old mother of three, frantic for the fate of her children, untended by any but casual neighbours while she served her sentence for petty theft. Theirs were the faces I painted; not the cold faces of wardresses. And I was and am now forced to admit, had I been allowed my chalks, my paints, my charcoals within the walls of Holloway, even there I might have grown content. Art builds its own freedom within any prison walls.

On my tenth day at Holloway when the wardress rattled open my door and barked 'Chaplain!' I did not even bother to arise. I was sewing at a sleeve and kept sewing, my eyes down, as the heavy male footsteps entered my cell, hoping they would, of their own, go away. When they didn't I looked up sourly, my usual anger churning inside me, and saw not the white-haired old prison visitor but, red-faced, dog-collared and ridiculous, my brother Geoffrey.

I flung down the shirt, jumped to my feet and cried mindlessly, 'Out, out, out. Get out. I don't want to even *see* you . . .' And how stupid, because from Geoffrey, if I was only silent, I might learn something about the outside world of friends and family so painfully shut away. But I couldn't stop, but raged on and on, senselessly, hysterically I suppose. He, smug-faced and righteous, embodied suddenly the entire prison system, every word of authority, every cell, every lock, every key. And amazingly, as I cried and shouted, he made no move, said no word at all. All his pomposity had vanished, all his archaic condemnations, everything. Only when I had stormed out all my abuse and fell silent out of sheer exhaustion did I see that he was crying, wet childish trails down his freckled cheeks, dripping on to his shaven lip, and down his pimply neck to his stiff white collar. My mouth fell open. I could not believe it . . . what feelings had he that I could have so violently offended?

'Oh stop it, silly,' I said crossly. 'You've no care what I think.'

'She's dead,' he sobbed then. 'She's dead.'

'Clare!' I gasped. But of course it was not Clare. He put his fumbling hands on my prison-clothed shoulders and crumpled up against me like a little boy.

'Mother's dead,' he said. 'She's dead.'

And that was how I learned.

9

Temple House
Ballysodare
15 May 1914

My dearest Justina,

Forgive me if this letter intrudes too quickly upon your grief, but certain matters demand our attention. Foremost is the question of your future. Doubtless your duty towards your father at this time will keep you a while longer at Arradale, but the time will come when you wish to resume a life of your own. I think you must realize, in the light of preceding events, that there will be no question of a return to South Kensington. Your unfortunate sister Clare has made her own bed, and in years to come will be obliged to lie in it. She has chosen to forsake familial guidance and in such a circumstance there is nothing further we can do. Your own case is thankfully different. Your uncle and I choose to believe your previous involvement with your sister's unsavoury activities a mere flaw of youth; an expression of your vulnerability and impressionable nature, which time and guidance will readily remedy. Bearing all this in mind, I would ask you now to consider seriously the proposal I made to you upon the occasion of the funeral at Arradale.

Our lives here are perhaps provincial, compared to the

excitements of London, but we do manage to amuse ourselves, and during the Season, the vice-regal court offers pleasant opportunities for a young girl of presentable demeanour. Nothing, of course, can remain a secret for long in Dublin, but people have been remarkably understanding and I trust even now that your position has not been irrevocably marred. I daresay certain doors are closed to you, but many quite worth entering are open. You have never, and I speak frankly out of kindness, my dear, been our great beauty, but you have your own charms, and a good wardrobe can work wonders. Forgive me if I sound frivolous, but you will understand that our own grief over your darling Mama is also both recent and deep and it is only from the wisdom of superior age that I can assure you that a little pleasure is not out of order and may well heal many scars.

May is quite delighted with the prospect of having you with us once more and poor dear Persephone wept with pleasure when I announced our plans. I do understand your attachment to your artistic dreams (Oh I *do*, my dear, I do) but perhaps they must be held in abeyance a while. There will always be opportunity later, perhaps even as a married woman you might find some acceptable outlet for your talents . . . several of my friends paint and one has even exhibited, in modest fashion. (Her husband was quite enchanted, and bought in all the paintings himself!)

Michael will of course be *charmed* to have his favourite female relative once more among us. He has many young men friends clamouring to meet you, and Miss Young has a most presentable male cousin of her own! I envision a most happy foursome! I confess that the dear Miss Young expressed the slightest shy concern about your advent upon the scene, knowing Michael's great fondness for you (how foolishly imaginative are the little jealousies of youthful lovers!) but Michael *hastened* to assure her that she need have no fears. *Everyone* knows you were but as brother and sister and will always be thus!

So, my dearest lamb, I beg you to consider *seriously* my proposition, knowing with confidence I have already your father's ready accord. Scotland's loss shall be Ireland's gain! All Dublin awaits you! Do write soon with your affirmation so that I might prepare all for your early arrival,

With love and concern,
your devoted aunt,
Eugenia

I put down the letter and returned to my easel without speaking although I knew that Douglas, who had delivered it into my hand, was awaiting my response. On my canvas the face of the child prostitute in Holloway looked back at me, a haunting of my own creation. I dabbed at the thin hair moodily, fiddling, my mind on Eugenia's letter and my eyes, in furtive glances, on Douglas.

I could not accustom myself to his new appearance, the new Douglas returned from four years in India with his regiment. He stretched out, straight as a board, on the little wooden chair in the tower room, leaning against it rather than sitting upon it, as if, even out of uniform, it was impossible for him to bend. I had commandeered the North Tower for my studio and furnished it with only the one chair and my easel and paint table. It wasn't good, I had found, to get too comfortable when I was working; though I had added a deerskin rug on which I sat crosslegged on the pine floor at times, while I thought. Douglas' long legs reached half across the room so his spur-trimmed bootheels rested upon my rug. He seemed impossibly tall, and impossibly dark-skinned, tanned by Indian suns to a very un-Scottish brown against which his eyes, a pale, pale blue in the bald North light, seemed quite unnatural. He was very handsome, and very cold. He made me uneasy, as if he were no longer my brother, and I wished he would go away.

Douglas did not look at me, however, but kept his eyes steadily upon the shiny grey and black back of the Reverend Feathers who walked with stately steps back and forth along a deep stone window ledge. Douglas tapped the ledge, annoyedly, with his swagger stick.

'So, what has she to say?' he said at last

'Eugenia?' I asked mildly, dabbing at my painting, my eyes averted from him. He did not answer. After a while I said briskly, 'She is very good, and very brave. She is frightened, but insists she must have me anyway. It's really very kind,' I added quickly.

'Frightened? Of you? Nonsense. What's there to fear?'

'For Michael,' I said calmly. 'She's frightened for Michael. She feels I shall ruin his chances if I come, and yet she insists I come.' Douglas was silent for a while, tapping the swagger stick, annoying the Reverend Feathers.

'Shall you?' he said.

'Ruin his chances? Of course I shan't.' He shrugged, making one too violent tap of the stick that sent the harassed Reverend Feathers scuttling with flapping wings off the window sill and up to the top of my easel.

'Get off,' I said. 'You'll get paint on your feet,' and he got off and began walking about the floor, pecking at the deerskin.

'Then you'll go,' said Douglas.

'Of course not,' I snapped.

He, watching the crow, said quickly, 'You should let the poor creature go. It's a wild thing. It's cruel to keep it caged.' He shifted his feet sharply and the crow flew to the window ledge.

I glared at him and flung down my brush on my paint table and rushed to the window, flinging up the sash. The Reverend Feathers stood mildly in the open space high above the gardens of Arradale. I shoved him with my hand. 'It's not caged!' I shouted at Douglas. 'Look!' I shoved it again and it swept off the window ledge into the sky with a loud flap of wings. It sank down towards the garden and then caught the air, rose, circled and landed on the ledge. It walked back in. 'See?' I demanded. 'What will fly, will fly. I'm not making it stay. I can't *stop* it staying.'

Then, of course, the tears came. 'I can't stop it loving me,' I wept, frustrated hands covering my face. I looked up at the window where the crow stood patient, solemn and black, cocking its bright eye at me. 'I can't stop him loving me,' I said.

Douglas waited until I calmed. He offered me no comfort. When I was quiet he said, 'Have Michael and Miss Young announced a date?'

I turned my face back to my easel and picked up my brush. 'No,' I said quietly. 'No. They haven't.' He shrugged. Being engaged himself, he thought along marital lines, as if suddenly there were no other courses for anyone in life.

'Nevertheless,' he said briskly, 'Eugenia is undoubtedly right. I see no reason for you not to go.'

'Impossible,' I said. 'I cannot leave Father.' Douglas was thoughtful, rubbing the white ivory top of the swagger stick across his upper lip, ruffling his sun-bleached moustache.

'He wants you to go, you know. Besides, he's got the darky.'

'Don't call him that.'

Douglas laughed. 'No offence, old girl. I've nothing against old Hassan. He's a damned nice darky, actually. Just like this fellow,' he reached a hand out to the Reverend Feathers. 'Eh, darky,' he said and the crow pecked him with his long black beak.

'Damn the sod,' he swore, sucking his finger. 'Sorry, Justina.' The Reverend Feathers cawed once and stepped neatly to the outside of the glass, raising up and stretching his neck to look in at Douglas through the pane. I could not stop laughing. 'Thing's a blasted menace. Verminous too, no doubt. You really ought to get rid of it.'

'Oh I shall,' I lied happily. 'As soon as its wing is better.'

'How much better does it need?' he grumbled. 'Flies well enough.'

'There's flying,' I said softly, reaching out of the window and scratching the crow's shiny head. 'And there's *flying*.' It rubbed against me as kindly as a cat. Michael had found the crow, two days after we buried Mother. He had found it high on Creag nam Bo, with its dislocated wing bent back on itself. Michael fixed the wing with the knowledge vested in him by Trinity College, and gave the crow to me. 'Let it go when it wants to leave,' he said. 'Then it will be ready.' He kissed me over the crow's ruffled, feathery back, and I agreed. I knew already it would leave no sooner than he.

'Hello, Reverend Feathers,' I whispered. 'Hello, your Reverence.'

'That's not funny, you know,' Douglas said. 'Geoffrey's quite put out.'

'Let him be. Silly prig.' I stroked the crow. It strutted up and down the window sill and I began again to laugh, 'Oh I can't help it. He's so like Geoffrey they could be twins.'

'Geoffrey's a good, decent man. He got *you* out of a lot of trouble for a start.' I snatched up my brush and worked in silence. Geoffrey indeed had obtained my early release from Holloway, by virtue of his clerical influence, a favour for which I would have been more than grateful had he not been so insufferably pompous over it. And having his pomposity echoed now by his fiancée and smug associate, Meggie Whyte, did not help. Clare, as well as myself, had suffered the indignity of being escorted north for Mother's funeral by that stuffy and righteous pair.

'Bother Geoffrey,' I muttered angrily, reaching for my palette knife to lift off an unintentioned glob of burnt umber. 'And bother Eugenia as well. I daresay he's put her up to it, anyhow. They all only want me married off, the sooner the better.'

'They all may just be right,' said Douglas with a kick of his spurred heel against the table leg.

'Be damned . . .'

'Justina . . .'

'Be damned,' I said. He was very quiet and reasonable and then he said slowly, 'Of course you needn't go to Ireland if you'd rather not. Good Christ, there are fellows aplenty here . . . why there's a good half-dozen in the regiment I could name right now.' He straightened up, growing animated. 'There's Wilhemina's own brother for a start . . .'

'Douglas,' I said curtly, 'I don't want to marry your fiancée's brother. I don't want to marry *anyone. No one.* Do you understand?'

He sat up straight and laid his swagger stick across his knees. He looked comically like Father and I giggled again. He pretended a smile and then said lightly, 'This is all very modern and admirable, old girl, but a bit impracticable.' He leaned forward suddenly. 'Who's to support you, anyhow? Father's unwell and hardly likely to last long. You can't expect me to, always. I'll have a wife, family, quite enough on my plate without indulging your spinsterhood.' He twirled the stick disconsolately in moody self-pity. I found this most unfair. *He* had never supported me or anyone. I jabbed roughly at the painting, leaving a petulant white smear on my subject's prison bonnet.

'I'll support myself,' I whispered. It was the groundless bold assertion of a child and he took it as exactly that.

'With that?' he gestured towards my easel, laughing lightly. 'Oh, surely.' He stood up, stretched, and dismissed the conversation. 'Well, old girl, promised Father I'd have a word with that old sod Fraser. They really do take advantage, you know, with Mother gone and Father in this fix. After next summer there'll be some shaking up around here. Wilhemina is a positive *genius* with staff.' He smiled cheerily and emptily and waved his hand in a half-salute as he went out, 'Better give that sack of feathers to Cook. Put him on toast and he'll pass for quail, eh?' He was grinning inanely, trying to win my favour. Douglas liked everything tidy, every conversation tied up with a jest like a package in string. I said nothing and he went out, still waving his little salute. I gave him time to get down the tower stairs, and when his bootheels receded into silence I stood my brush in white spirit and went to see Father. The crow went with me, sitting on my head.

I walked through the big rooms and long corridors of Arradale and I felt uneasy in my childhood home. Wilhemina had come to see us here, and I had not liked her. She was a tall, bony handsome woman who gushed over us all and treated my wise, crippled father like an imbecile, pushing his chair about the house and exclaiming over sights to be seen as if she spoke to a child. She clutched and embraced Clare and myself with extravagant affection, proclaiming us her new-found sisters. I thought it ridiculous, but Douglas stood by with worshipful approval on his face, and Alexander made much of Wilhemina whom he clearly thought superior to either of us. She was indeed very beautiful but also a ninny and I did not like to think of her as mistress of Arradale. It was my home from babyhood, and I liked it as it was, but she, who had set foot here but once, would soon rule and change it. Clare and I would henceforth be passing guests.

Father's study was on the ground floor for reasons of access, and now that Mother was gone he slept there in a short, narrow Highland bed that Mirza Hassan had taken apart and brought down from one of the upper rooms. The study was dark, in the back of the house which was half built into the hill, with windows at the bottom of sunken shafts. It was warm in winter though, and cool in summer and its darkness seemed to please Father, who no longer took any interest in the outside world. The landscapes that he sought now were the interior landscapes of memory where he wandered as avidly as once he had wandered the world beyond. The room was piled with books, maps and papers and I was terrified it would go afire and he would be trapped there in his chair and die. There was a lift shaft in Arradale House, and I tried to persuade him to use it and come up into the sunny morning room or the graceful dining room with its western windows and slanting afternoon light. But he had no interest. Sometimes, when we were alone in the house, more or less, with the servants busy with their own affairs, I thought of us as a fairy tale, I in my tower, and he beneath the ground. Mirza Hassan climbed all the stairs a dozen times a day to bring messages, invitations, comments, back and forth, for Father and I were close in our mutual imprisonments. Faithful servant; he was indeed, and in the fairytale I imagine he would have sought, and won, my hand.

I smelled the odd smoke of their pipes far down the corridor as I approached. Usually they smoked Turkish tobacco, but sometimes they mingled it with hashish, to ease Father's pains and to improve their conversation. It never seemed to affect them very much, and in later years I was startled to find this old familiar turning up in the strangest places and causing much furore. When I entered the room Father was resting in his old wicker Bath-chair before the open hearth. There was a woven rug across his twisted legs, and his head rested back against the cane. His eyes were closed as he drew dreamily on the pipe, and he was smiling faintly. His was the face of a dying man, but he had been dying so long, it had grown to seem normal. Mirza Hassan watched, waited, ready to catch the pipe if it should fall, or to catch any last fragment of conversation before Father slept. I thought of Father's sons, my brothers, with disdain.

Mirza Hassan put his finger in front of his lips as I entered, but the crow on my head flapped its wings and suddenly cried its loud, gravelly cry.

'I'm sorry,' I said, as Father woke. Mirza Hassan shook his head, smiled his white, white smile, bushy moustache twitching good-naturedly, and shrugged.

'She never gets any older, does she?' Father said. He was gesturing to me with his lame thin hand, but both Hassan and I knew he was speaking of Mother. Often, in dim light, in dreams and near-waking, he mistook me for her. He had not accepted that she was gone.

'No,' Mirza Hassan said quietly. 'She was born the age she will always be,' and I knew *he* was speaking of me. Father nodded, drugged and baffled, but content. Then quite suddenly he became fully awake and totally rational. He asked me about Eugenia's letter, about Michael, about May and James, about when I would be leaving for Dublin.

'I shan't be going to Dublin, Father,' I said.

He only smiled. He said something to Hassan in Persian, that I did not catch and then he said in English, 'If you could have seen her, on Sligo Quay, walking out on her father's arm, there wasn't a man in the town would not stop to watch. And Eugenia a mirror of her; oh, if only I could be there again to see.'

'Father, I would rather be here. I can paint, and we'll be together.'

'I daresay I'd be wise to send *you* along to watch her, old man. But her father will be there, when the ship puts in. And Mrs Moore. Funny old Mrs Moore.'

'Father, I'm not going.'

'What, Nell?'

'Father, it's Justina.'

'Of course, Nell, of course. It's late surely, she should be in her bed.' He leaned his head back again, and whispered, 'And I in mine.'

I looked and saw he was sleeping. Mirza Hassan smiled at me, cocking his head sideways. He tapped the filled pipe and nodded wisely.

'I can't leave him,' I said.

'Justina,' he said softly, as he rose and reached his hand to my head and the crow stepped calmly on to his fingers. He held it before his eyes and spoke to it in Persian. It bent its head to be rubbed. 'Justina, he is leaving you.'

10

And so I was once more in Dublin, in the beautiful spring of 1914. It was my first return there in five years, and everywhere familiarity was edged with a subtle shadowing of change. The wide Georgian streets were as airy and light, the parks as green, the sea air as soft, but a new mood was upon the city, and in the households of all I knew there.

The greatest change for me was that Mr Yeats was no longer there. He had never returned from New York, where he had gone so lightly so many years before. The Stephen's Green studio was empty, and the circle of friends that had met there dispersed. At first I could not accustom myself to his absence and was certain that I would again glimpse his amiable tall figure through the crowds in a Dublin street, or simply make him materialize by boldly knocking upon his studio door. Once, I passed George Russell in Nassau Street, but he did not know me, grown five years older, and naturally I did not speak.

But even had they all been there, and the studio alive with people, it would have made no difference. Eugenia, who had dreamed of artistic triumph for me, had other dreams now. Art, always an unlikely companion, had proved a fickle seducer. At its doorstep was laid the events of my London winter, even as my artistic yearnings were once blamed upon my disastrous fall from Michael's tree. All such nonsense was now to stop. I was a woman now, and it was time to put away childish things. Eugenia fell fatefully into line with my masters at Art College: there was but one place for me and that was the marriage bed. And this unspoken but determined goal became the *cause célèbre* of all the Howie family that spring. All Eugenia's marvellous energies, and all James Howie's sturdy fortune were directed to this one end. It was both her apology and her memorial to her dead sister. She who had led me astray would see me into the fold before the year of my mother's death was out, turning my mourning crêpe into a wedding veil as swiftly as by a magician's sleight of hand.

I was, as you'll imagine, scarcely *delighted* with all this. But there was little I could do. Nor had I any longer the legions of ready support that had always been my strength in the Howie household. The Howie children were now but flighty partial residents and they all were engaged in battles of their own. Merrion Square was under siege by the twentieth century, and neither Eugenia nor James Howie was liking it at all.

The source of all conflict was the great range of intellectual, spiritual, and social interests of their three offspring, and their insistence on putting the same energies to practical use. It may be difficult, in an era when parents invariably seek achievement as a measure of their children, to understand the misery that such an untidy outflowing of humanitarianism could invoke. But Edwardian Dublin was not a meritocracy. Station, not production, was the Howies' aim. Service to the less fortunate was acceptable, indeed mandatory, but only in its proper place, and not as a *raison d'être* of all life. Thus Kate's tireless social work won no honours at home. Nor did May Howie's desire to serve art and literature that had led her first to the Cuala Industries, and now into a tiny printing house on Abbey St. Nor indeed did Michael's unswerving intention of laying his medical gifts at the feet of Dublin's poor.

How, you may well ask, did such a pair as Eugenia and James, so firmly entrenched in their narrow social bonds, produce such children of changeling politics? How, indeed. Perhaps it was something in the air, for the whole of the world was stirring with new ideas. Perhaps it was Persephone's nursery tales of Irish heroes and finer, holier times. Or Padraic O'Mordha plotting revolution. Or perhaps it was Cathleen ni Houlihan, after all, calling her children to her side. We were all products of a rich and pampered era, and one way or another, we all grew to revolutionary thought. Generous times produce generous natures, and generous natures rarely fail to rebel against the terrible parsimony of the common man's lot. And the lot of poor ordinary people, in Dublin of 1914, was harsh. The strikes and great lockout of 1913 had left a city full of disease and poverty, in crowded tenements that eclipsed in misery even those I had glimpsed in London's East End. May, Kate and Michael had a century's work before them, were they allowed by parents, and fate, to carry it through.

Small wonder that James and Eugenia, armed to do battle against this formidable crew, set upon me instead that spring with such heady fervour. By comparison to their own brood, I was an easy foe, the sole malleable creature about, and I was seized upon in desperation and hastily kneaded and pummelled until I emerged, a brief and unlikely lady of society. Like a mayfly, I spread my wings in the last golden summer of their world.

But let me not diminish Eugenia's achievement. Nor the task before her. Picture the plummeting spirits of my brave aunt confronting, fresh off the steamer at Kingstown, my twenty-year-old gypsy self, surrounded by battered cases of my father's; my easel and paintbox firmly grasped under my right arm; and in my left a giant brass-trimmed parrot cage in which resided, grumpy and bleary-eyed from the journey, a great grey-backed hooded crow. And the whole of me, lest you forget, in full Edwardian mourning, yet, for my mother, as gloomy as the bird. It seemed to have been my fate to turn up on Irish shores at regular intervals draped in black crêpe. Eugenia could hardly hold *that* against me. But the Reverend Feathers was another story, as were the half-dozen Irish urchins I had gathered from the lower decks like the piper of Hamelin, to cluster around his cage while I sketched them one by one. I had had a wonderful journey and was quite delighted with myself. Eugenia looked at me, at my crow, at my luggage, and at my coterie and forced the bravest and most radiant of smiles.

'Oh Justina, darling, this *will* be splendid fun.'

Fun I cannot vouch for; Eugenia was a fine dissembler of emotions. But effort there was in plenty, and expense, and remarkable imaginative courage. Before I had been in Dublin two weeks I had been physically transformed. Eugenia had, with great compassion, divested me at once of my mourning, and proceeded to replace it with a total wardrobe of new, expensive and very beautiful clothing. I was trooped through every ladies' outfitters of Grafton Street, every fashion salon. Costumes for all possible occasions were lavished upon me; dresses and gowns, hats, cloaks, shoes, shawls, parasols, sporting outfits and evening dresses, elaborate accessories for every costume, and in every colour. James Howie trotted happily behind, a perennially open note of credit. Eugenia opened her jewel case to me and laid its bounty at my feet, even those most special items that resided regularly in the family safe. Her generosity was only matched by her determination.

'A Christmas engagement is always nice . . .' she announced at breakfast on the fortnight's anniversary of my arrival. Indeed so, but I hadn't even a suitor, much less a fiancé. This seemed to trouble Eugenia very little, as if the choosing of a husband was as simple as the selection of a gown, and rather secondary.

There was something in this, actually. Leaving aside issues of love, which were not being considered, and issues of alternatives, which like my career in art, were not being considered either, how really did this search for a husband differ from any other of our shopping expeditions? As with gowns, there were certain emporiums only where one looked. The proper house party, like the proper dress salon, would only offer goods of eminently suitable character. As in the matter of clothing, there was a margin, narrow, but definite for personal taste. If one style of gentleman, say the young Guards officer, did not suit, then another, the Galway landowner, for instance, might. It was all terribly reasonable, and had I been in a mood to be reasonable as well, I might indeed have gone along with Eugenia's plans and done quite well for myself, in the parlance of the day. After all, Eugenia loved me, and the line-up of young men she painstakingly gathered for my perusal were, as well as financially and socially secure, really very pleasant, some quite comely as well, and no doubt a good number would have made excellent husbands. But I was not reasonable. On the contrary I was in love, and people in love have little interest in such mundanities.

I must correct a possible mistaken impression. Although I readily admit to having been in love with my cousin Michael, I would not wish you to imagine I ever conceived the possibility of marriage to him. First of all things, he *was* my cousin, and a sort of double cousin at that, considering our mothers were twins, our fathers cousins. My knowledge of genetics was precisely nil, but even I knew that there was something about called 'too close', that precluded union. And if I needed reminding, my brother Geoffrey, always the master of ecclesiastical form, had years ago let me know the church's opinion, should I ever entertain such an incestuous thought. (Geoffrey always imagined I was up to much more than I was.) No. I would never marry Michael Howie. But, with equal firmness I knew that as long as we both lived, I would never love another. And so, naturally, I would not marry. It wasn't such an extraordinary thought, really. Nuns and monks never marry. They have their higher cause, and so did I; theirs being God, and mine a gentle blending of art and my beloved. I knew, naturally, that *Michael* would marry. He was virtually engaged now to Edna Young. But I also knew that his marriage would be duty, and his love for her a husbandly mature bond that would have nothing to do with his love for me.

What a naïve and lovely (or unlovely) picture. But think a moment, before you judge. What artist has ever been happy in marriage? And what better, for the unwed votary of the muse than a perfect spiritual union, forever unsullied by the rough give and take of the physical; a union which, in my case at least, lifted the romantic yearnings of a young girl into a separate high sphere where it would in no way get in the way of the desire to paint. I needed no husband; I had already the perfect husband of my soul.

This, naturally, cut little ice with Eugenia Howie. A woman of passion for some forty years, she was not about to be won over by the brave new cause of platonic love.

'Of course you need a husband,' she responded at once, in precisely the tone she would use to send an errant child back to the nursery for a mackintosh on a rainy day. I balked. Naturally I had not included my feelings about Michael in my argument for the single state, only distilling from it a general, formless commitment to celibacy. This was a relatively easy stance in 1914, when my knowledge of the other-than-celibate state was limited to the point of non-existence.

'You've no idea what you're talking about,' Eugenia concluded firmly and accurately.

'Kate's not married,' I persisted stubbornly.

'Precisely,' said Eugenia. I'd picked a bad example. 'Need we say more?'

'And May?' I pursued, a little desperately.

'May's turn will come next year,' Eugenia replied. I nodded, absorbing that, watching May, sitting across from me at the breakfast table, reading a book. It was evident that May's marriage plans must wait in abeyance on mine.

'May can have my turn,' I blurted. May smiled into her book. She was reading St Augustine. She was my friend and ally and I knew she wouldn't mind.

'May is a year younger,' Eugenia replied and added blithely, 'And with May I anticipate *no* problem.'

I was uncertain whether that reflected upon May's beauty, which was quite in excess of any of mine, and indeed had already won her many suitors whom she brushed off like so many distracting moths; or indeed upon May's compliant nature. If the latter was the case I suspected Eugenia was riding for a fall; May's compliance was like the compliance of water that will so readily be channelled and governed and reshaped to fit any container, and yet will, with the mood upon it, wash cities away to their destruction. That was May.

'You needn't bother about me, Mama. I'm going to take the veil.'

'Oh, hush, darling,' Eugenia murmured. She never listened to May, possibly because she really could not understand half of what she read, thought and said. Eugenia was back within the pages of *Irish Life*, spectacles down upon her nose, reading the Society columns: 'Oh look, here we are,' she exclaimed breathlessly, and adjusting the spectacles began to read aloud.

'". . . Thursday's House Party at the home of Sir William and Lady Cottenham was much enlivened by the charming presence of Miss Justina Melrose, Sir James and Lady Howie's delightful and eccentric niece, recently arrived from Scotland . . ."' Eugenia's voice trailed uncertainly into silence. She lightly tapped her unopened boiled egg with her spoon, and removed her spectacles, laying them atop the folded *Irish Life* beside her place.

'Justina,' she said, 'I don't think eccentric is one of the adjectives we are seeking.'

'It was only the crow, Mama,' May squealed delightedly.

Eugenia cast me a withering look. 'Justina, you are simply not trying,' she said.

I don't suppose I was, actually, though by no means did I deliberately sabotage Eugenia's efforts. Eccentricity was not a thing I sought, though it sometimes sought me. Still, Eugenia persisted bravely, leading me ever onward, with May in attendance, a lady-in-waiting, and herself and Persephone trailing after in their black, like two Spanish duennas. Thus we progressed through the drawing rooms of Rathmines and Terenure, the gardens of Howth, and the pages of *Irish Life*. Eugenia perused its columns like an actress seeking her reviews. And my performance at any event we might have attended was judged accordingly.

It was a peculiarly aimless summer in every way, but this one sole aim of my hoped-for marriage. Our household was listless and feminine; airless and oppressive. James Howie was away in Sligo and would only return for the Horse Show in August which, climaxing the summer season, would also mark the end of our current stay in Dublin. After that we would return for a while to Temple House with James, and undoubtedly continue Eugenia's hunt for a husband for me on that lesser territory, had we not yet succeeded here. In the meanwhile, I shared the house with May and Eugenia and Persephone and the servants. Michael was but a visitor from his rooms at College, and throughout that summer no day arose when Michael was present that Miss Edna Young was not in attendance as well. Eugenia took no chances.

Miss Young was a pleasant young woman of very good family, with a wide mobile strong-featured face, a broad expressive mouth, and hazel eyes that lit into sheer beauty when she was happy, and indeed she was remarkably happy whenever she looked upon Michael. I found to my surprise that I was not jealous of her, but actually grew fond of her, fond of her very devotion to Michael whom I loved, and wishing often that she would not so clearly distrust me. I was no threat to her, or her future, but this obvious fact was one she seemed unable to believe. She would kiss me warmly whenever we met, but often I caught her eyes upon me, when she thought herself unobserved, with a fearful envy in them that was most ironic. She would marry him, share his bed, and bear his children, but she could not forgive me for the childhood he and I had known. Perhaps had she been less jealous of me, I would have been more so of her. Those who envy cloak themselves too readily in the colours of defeat.

But I must be defeated in the end, not she, as Eugenia so often reminded me, placing before me one after another of her charming young men, and I, like some ingrate princess banished each from my sight. There were long summer afternoons I spent alone in my room, looking out over the greenery of Merrion Square, stroking the Reverend Feathers' silken back and dreaming of home and our lost winter hills.

Of course there were reliefs from the round of house parties, theatre evenings, lawn tennis and golf; not every day produced a social occasion. I had my days off, too. And when I did, I would fly at once to my room, gather my paints and easel, and with the Reverend Feathers perched once more upon my hat, flee out of the door, and away by tram or trainline to the seaside towns around Dublin Bay. There, at Sea Point, or Kingstown, or Dalkey, or in high green Howth, or down along the quays of the Liffey, where the great sailing ships berthed, I would set up my easel and paint.

Sometimes Michael would meet me. We would have tea together, and walk along the Quays, or he would sit beside me and watch me sketch. Eugenia never knew about those meetings. Nor did she know that frequently I went with Persephone to Dame Street where Kate lived in rooms by herself, writing tracts against the people at whose tables I dined, and in whose ballrooms I danced. Often Kate questioned me in a sharp, purposeful way about those houses, those people, and in answering I felt a cold sense of betrayal, as if more serious things than I could imagine were being considered. Strange, silent young men slipped in and out of her rooms, and papers and objects changed hands. There was an air of quiet and cold clear thinking that was frightening there, and made me long for those innocent years of the past when revolution was a thing to be argued about loudly in cafés. Violence, like love, grows serious when people cease to speak of it openly.

We met Padraic O'Mordha there. Persephone was yet engaged to be married to him and wore, whenever out of Eugenia's presence, a tiny amethyst and jet ring. It was a Victorian mourning ring, an odd, and appropriate choice for this marriage promise that would never be fulfilled. When Padraic began training with the Dublin Volunteers, Eugenia had insisted that Persephone break the engagement. Dutifully, Persephone had broken it, but only for those hours of her life spent within the Howie household. Deception was so natural a part of Persephone's life that this small ruse seemed to strike her as totally without harm. Nor, I think, did it fool Eugenia. There was such an immense difference between everyone's public and private lives that such hypocrisy was lived with amazing ease by all. Besides, we all knew it was not politics, nor family strife that would forbid Persephone's marriage, but her failing health that made thought of a wedding somehow indecent.

Eugenia took her regularly to the continental resorts, lavished upon her good food and mountain air, nursed her when she was ill, cheered her when she was mournful, called for the priest when she feared for her soul. But Eugenia could not save her. Padraic stood dutifully by, his ring upon her finger and his eyes upon the forbidden beautiful face of Catherine Howie.

Kate encouraged no suitors. Like my sister Clare, with whom she would not speak, and to whom she bore so great a resemblance in spirit, she had no time for men. Like Clare, she lived life in the mind, not the heart, and her joys and triumphs were the clinical victories of ideas.

'Clare's a fool,' she announced gaily to me one day that spring. 'They've sold themselves to Carson, and now Carson has betrayed them. What made her think she'd get justice from an Ulsterman?' She laughed, throwing back her delicate head, her heavy hair seeming to unbalance it. I could not understand her. Clare's defeat, Carson's refusal to honour his promise to guarantee Votes for Women in the North, was no victory for her. It did not bring Irish freedom. It did not defeat Carson.

'Why are you fighting *Clare*?' I asked. 'You have everything in common.' Kate shrugged.

'I have nothing in common with England.'

'She isn't *England*. She's your cousin.'

'My cousins,' said Kate grandly, 'my sisters, my brothers, are starving in the tenements of Dublin. I have no other kin.' Padraic gazed at her with utmost devotion. Leave an Irishman alone with rhetoric and he falls in love. 'Come,' Kate said brightly, 'You come. *I'll* show you *my* Dublin now. You've seen quite enough of Mother's.'

Out in the street she impatiently hailed a jarvey to transport us to the slums and the two of us went off, leaving Padraic restless and unhappy behind with his sad, frail fiancée leaning on his arm.

'Padraic O'Mordha's in love with you,' I said as we clattered away.

'Silly fool,' she laughed gaily, but she was preening as she did so, adjusting her hat, and glancing once over her shoulder, a sly look down the crowded street, before we turned the corner and lost him from sight. I clutched the Reverend Feathers up close to my jacket front, and stroked his wings disconsolately, feeling sad for Persephone and Padraic both.

Kate took me somewhere in the city. Naturally, it was somewhere I had never been before. But Kate had been there, and everyone knew her. The jarvey left us outside a stone archway leading into an inner close, as such an arch might lead into a stableyard. A crumbling square of four-storey buildings faced inward on a dank and dirty cobbled enclosure. In the centre, around a single water-pump, barefoot children played in muddy water pools. At one end of the tenement block great braces of wood held up a decaying gable wall, across the face of which the ruins of phantom rooms were yet marked, with tattered paper, and hearths hanging over emptiness, where another dwelling had collapsed into the street.

'Twenty families use that pump,' Kate said briskly to me. '*And* that,' she added, pointing to a grim little stone hovel, the solitary earth closet, standing resplendent in the cobbled yard. I could smell it, in the June air, from where we stood. Dogs, chickens, children and cats scuffled about the cobbles. Even the smallest of the girls had a borrowed baby slung in a shawl upon her hip, a dirty scabrous baby, drooling and snot-nosed. They all ran to greet Kate, each showing off her little human treasure, a dozen smudge-faced madonnas. I saw Kate take one of those grubby infants in her arms, and even though she held it with the awkwardness of a childless woman, she won my respect.

'Half the men are unemployed. The rest earn less than eighteen shillings in the week. That woman there,' she pointed to a toothless matron, 'was widowed last year. She earns seven shillings charring and supports three children.' The woman nodded, smiling her dark soft smile, quite happy to be so openly discussed, though I felt odd, caught between Kate's humanity and her politics. 'That woman lost two children to typhus,' she continued, pointing to a thin girl surrounded by four children more.

'My little Theresa Mary, the best little angel ever seen on this earth, God rest her soul, and her brother Joseph, ten months on the day he died. There's not a night we're not awake till dawn with weepin' and prayin' for them both.' The children around her nodded and smiled in agreement. The mother looked no older than me and she'd given birth to six. One of the children came boldly up and tugged at my skirt until he won my attention.

'Can I see your bird, please?' he asked. I lowered the Reverend Feathers down to be seen and stroked and at once the whole flock of children were around me, laughing and shouting, gleeful and glorious. Their poverty, their dead brothers and sisters were forgotten.

'One third of the deaths among children in Dublin are caused by living conditions like this,' I heard Kate say. 'One third. It is murder.' But the children were not listening, nor were their mothers who clustered around my grey-backed crow as happily as their little ones. Kate stood alone, her delicate features tense, her eyes on the dirty stone walls of the court.

On the way home, on the empty open deck of a tram, Kate said to me, 'We need guns.'

From that day onwards, I lived in two worlds, two separate cities of Dublin, in which I led two quite separate lives. Oddly, so did Kate, whose savage politics did not prevent her from occasionally, from whim, familial duty, or some private reason of her own, returning briefly to Merrion Square, flitting through her gorgeous wardrobe and emerging from the house once more a lady of Dublin society, bound for one of the elegant homes of the people who she so clearly despised. On such occasions she could flirt, smile, chat gaily and dance like any Edwardian lady, and she left always in her wake a flotsam of entangled male hearts. I think she did it for fun. Her work was hard, and her sense of humour bitterly sharp. She found it quite titillating to dance upon the battlements she would burn.

As for me, my part in her work was modest. I stood and ladled soup out for rows of shuffling men, and distributed used clothing, the cast-offs of Eugenia's acquaintances, to eager hands. Many times I saw some once treasured hat go bobbing off incongruously on a lice-infested head, or even more incongruous, little boys scampering off in girls' skirts, teamed with men's shirts, their poverty so universal that such miserably cobbled together costumes brought no shame. 'Better than trousers,' their mothers would nod. 'There'll be no wearing through at the knees.' More often, I simply watched with my sketch pad, in a quiet corner, recording that strange, miserable and yet fiercely cheerful life, until, once noticed, I would be forced by crowds of pressing faces and eager hands to give up my work for the more popular creation of instant tiny sketches of each child, his pet dog, or chicken or doll.

'That won't fill any stomachs,' Kate declared coolly.

'Neither will guns,' said I.

Michael came with us, sometimes. I think he found it very hard, to be surrounded always by illness and the cause of illness which he could recognize, and yet, being only a student, was not free to treat. Still, he did the few things permitted, he talked to the mothers about clean water, and clean hands, and milk for the children. They smiled eagerly and went back to doing things the way they always had done, and there wasn't money for milk for the children. But they did not mock Michael and had they been able to please him, they would have done, no doubt. The children followed him about, like they followed my crow, drawn to him, as to it, an unspoiled beautiful thing. One whole afternoon, he stood outside the stinking privy, and led each child after its performance there to the pump, to wash its hands. It became a game, and for a week at least the hand-washing did continue.

'Miracles are slow work,' Michael said wryly one night. He was tired and depressed.

'Only for those who wait for them to happen,' said Kate. Weariness had the opposite effect on Kate. It made her excited, flighty, and eager for action. After a day's work in the city, she could sit late into the night, talking and planning and arguing with Padraic O'Mordha and his friends. That evening in early July we sat in an exhausted circle about the stained round table of Kate's threadbare lodgings, arguing that sort of argument that becomes nothing more than a festering sore, picked over and over until no one is sure who has said what, nor how many times. We all should have gone home and to our beds hours before, but no one was willing to leave a scene of such acrimony without some fine cathartic moment to give purpose to it all. And the moment would not come.

'Ah, 'tis but one more English trick,' Padraic muttered, stirring his tea in endless cold circles. 'Home Rule is English trickery and Carson's guns are English trickery. And now they've tricked us again, and there'll be no Irish guns to be the match of them. They're all in Carson's pocket. Asquith, Redmond, all of them. Bastards, the lot of them.' He stared into his tea and Persephone reached her small hand across the table to pat his sleeve, but stopped half-way because Padraic's own hand had closed upon Kate's where hers lay upon the table, and they sat silent together in mutual morbidity. 'There's not a one anywhere we can trust,' he finished.

'Better be done with them all and start again,' said Kate. She shook her head, a familiar impatient gesture. 'Sweep the board clean,' she said.

'Life,' said Michael slowly, 'is not chess, Kate. Clear the board, and you've changed the rules. Who knows what game the people will choose then to play?'

'Not an English one,' said Kate.

'An Irish one then? Will it be different? Irish bosses or English bosses, they'll still be bosses, Kate. Do you think those women in Angle Court will notice if their six shillings wage comes from the pocket of an Englishman or an Irishman? Do you think they care?'

'No bosses,' said Padraic. 'There'll be no bosses. Only the people, ownin' and workin' and doin' it all fer their own selves. A workers' republic. An Irish workers' Republic.'

'I want to go home, Padraic,' Persephone said suddenly. 'It's late, and Justina must be home, and I'm tired.' She was very white, as if she'd just had a coughing fit, only she had not.

'We'll go,' I said, but Kate would not let go of us. She became hospitable, and insisted on making tea for Persephone, until Michael spoke abruptly.

'She needs her bed. Leave her be.'

He was quietly angry, and Kate went quiet too. She was afraid of Michael now, even though she was the oldest. He rose and helped Persephone to her feet. She looked pleadingly at Padraic, and said, 'Are ye comin' now?' But he waved her away and turned back to Kate, his devotion to her clear on his face. I saw emotion conflict there and suddenly he blurted out something he should not have said.

'Ah, ye needn't bother, my darling,' he said. 'We'll have guns fer ye, Kate. We'll have guns.' He got up suddenly, aware that the moment that eluded us all night was in his hands, and our eyes were all on him. He shook his unruly shoulder-length mane of red hair, his eyes almost mischievous with violence and laughed joyfully. 'Jesus, Mary and Joseph, we'll have guns.'

He went out without bidding any of us, even Persephone, farewell, and I heard his laughter down the stairs. There was silence in the room, upon his leaving us. Then Michael said in a slow, careful voice, 'Kate, what is this?' She stood up, busied herself gathering teacups from the table. 'Kate?'

'Nothing a woman would know about,' she said, and I could not fathom, from her prim smile, whether she spoke exactly the truth or some great irony.

'Kate,' Michael said, 'I saw a child die of measles today. If Padraic has guns, and there's fighting with the North, and fighting with Austria and Serbia, and fighting with all the world, children will *still* die of measles in Angle Court.' He suddenly crossed the room, and took her shoulders in his hands, turning her to face him, not with anger but with fierce determination, 'Call on saints, if you must, but not for guns. Bread, milk, clean water. Not for guns.' He looked for a long while into her pale, beautiful eyes, and then slowly shook his head, turning very wearily to me and Persephone.

'You should not be worryin' yerself, Michael,' she said sadly, as we went down the stairs, 'Yerself with yer examinations and all yer studies. Ye've enough to be doing with.' She leaned on his arm, and I noticed from the stairs above that her hair beneath her hat was entirely grey. She was, quite suddenly, old.

'I'm fine,' said Michael, gently. He hailed a jarvey and took us both home.

Persephone went in ahead of us, and Michael and I stood on the doorstep, in the light of the gaslamps.

'Are you coming to the garden party?' I asked.

'Am I coming?' he laughed wryly. 'Lord and Lady Aberdeen and the cream of Dublin . . . do you think I've a *choice*?'

'Miss Young will be there?' I asked casually.

'Oh most certainly.' He was quiet. He reached one hand and touched my chin, turning my head to face him, 'Justina . . .' I turned away.

'Your mother's found me a husband,' I said. There was a very long silence. I was conscious of his hand, yet hovering like a bird's wing, beside my face.

'Who is he?' he asked, without moving.

'Oh, a man. He's quite nice actually, and terribly handsome. And a terribly good family,' I laughed. 'I frankly don't see what he wants with me.'

'Justina . . .'

I laughed again. 'Oh, he probably has a wooden leg, or false teeth, or something that doesn't show. Don't worry. Maybe he gambles . . .'

'His name?'

'Rupert French. It's a Sligo family.'

'I know him,' Michael said. He paused. 'He's a nice bloke, Justina. Rides with the hunt, a good horseman too, no wooden leg,' he laughed gently. 'He's quite the prize, my dear.'

'Oh wonderful,' I said brightly. 'Then everything will be perfect. I'll marry Rupert French and you'll marry Edna Young and everyone will be happy.' He turned me around to face him and we stared at each other in the blurry gaslight. After a long, long while, we fell forward into each other's arms.

On the morning of the garden party, the Reverend Feathers disappeared. He was not in his cage, where he slept at nights, nor in my room. Nor was he in the walled garden where he was free to fly through the open window in May's room. May and I searched everywhere, and when we reported the loss to Eugenia she looked faintly pained and said, 'Of course. He's a wild bird and he's flown away. Now do go to Persephone and prepare. We must leave at two.'

Two was hours away, but the preparation for such an event took hours. Every item of our complex costuming must be checked, re-pressed, combed free of lint, examined for a single loose thread. Each hat underwent personal examination, and shoes, polished and buffed, awaited Eugenia's review like soldiers before the Sergeant Major. The more elaborate the wardrobe, the more the need for perfection: six yards of Belgian lace were of no avail if marred by a gravy spot, nor was an eleven guinea tea-dress about to pass muster with one of its forty buttons astray. There was no excuse for the minutest shabbiness when one had two lady's maids, and eagle-eyed Persephone at one's command. Nor had the concept of casual wear entered our world. We had sports clothing, but it was no more casual than what we wore to a Dublin Castle ball. Hours to dress, hours to do our hair, and no grounds for protest, when everyone knew there was no other claim upon our time.

Still, at twelve-thirty, May and I were yet running about in our dressing gowns amongst the trees and bushes of our little garden, searching for my errant crow.

'Oh surely he's not flown away?' she asked sadly. I shook my head. I could not believe it. He had always been free and never left me. At one-thirty, Eugenia found us and in great fury sent us off to dress. Of course there was no time at all, but somehow we managed to cram ourselves into our tea-dresses, and shoo-ing away our frantic maids, did each other's hair. Persephone slipped in while I was struggling with May's yellow ringlets, and instantly took command of them with her sure, patient hands.

'I never found him,' I said mournfully, staring blankly into the mirror of my dressing table. She had a mouth full of hair-pins and only shook her head. When she had finished May's hair, and re-done mine she turned away from me and said, facing neither of us, 'I'm terribly wrong to be tellin' ye, and me sworn to never speak, but it was the rogue of a coachman, Finnerty, takin' him away down the street this mornin' to let him go.'

'He did what?' May cried.

'It was so's ye not be chancing takin' him with you to Phoenix Park, like ye did to Lord and Lady Cottenham's in the spring. Yer not to be spoilin' yer chances, you see.' She looked at me with dark, tear-wet eyes and I could not be angry at her.

'Where did he take him?' I begged.

She paused, miserable, and said, 'Ah, I'd tell ye if I could, but I'm not knowin' a thing about it.' She looked down, but then brightened, 'But it's one thing I'm sure of, an' that's that the useless Finnerty is the laziest man on God's good earth. It will not be far, wherever.'

'I'll find him,' May said firmly.

'But how?' I cried. I've never been one for tears, but I wept then for my poor Highland crow, lost in Dublin streets.

'I'll get the truth from that sod Finnerty for a start,' cried May, valiant in my defence, 'And I'll find him. Go on, you tell Mother I'm ill . . .'

'She'll never believe me . . .'

'Say I've my visitor. Say it aloud in front of the servants. She'll be too embarrassed to argue.' She grinned wickedly and darted for the door. A minute later I saw her slip out through the garden gate and down the street. I did just what May said and it had precisely the effect she predicted.

'Oh, how inconvenient,' Eugenia whispered, pained and awkward. 'Never mind. This is *your* occasion.' And so I was led forth, to James Howie's chauffeur-driven Hupmobile, with the cowardly Finnerty at the wheel.

Of course my mind was not on the party, nor the Vice-Regal Lodge, nor any of the notable guests. It was not even upon Rupert French who, in spite of Eugenia's plans for us, I had only met twice, and who was naturally a total stranger who meant less to me than my crow. Still, in the subtle, graceful way such things were arranged, I found myself placed firmly in his company for the afternoon. Michael arrived, a little late, with Edna Young and her family, and there too a similar wordless covenant was made so that suddenly we were a foursome, two young couples strolling about the sunny garden, sipping punch, and chatting harmlessly before our elders, who observed us rather as if we were a new arrangement of trinkets on a mantelpiece.

Eugenia watched from a distance, much more beautiful than either Edna or I, and her face was calm with satisfaction.

Rupert French had just seated me at a white iron table and brought to me a bowl of late strawberries and a glass of punch, when I saw May arrive. She looked oddly eccentric and I could not place why until I realized that her charming blue and white tea-dress, and huge white feathered hat, were now teamed with a bright red silk shawl, something very May Morris and totally out of place. I looked anxiously for Eugenia's disapproving presence, but she was not in sight, and then May saw us and hurried towards us, wrapping herself tighter in the shawl.

'Terribly chilly, isn't it,' she said to Edna Young as she swooped down amongst us, in a flurry of red silk.

'Is it?' said Rupert, solicitously.

May blinked, wide blue eyes upon me. 'No. I suppose it isn't,' she said, and somewhat awkwardly began to slide out of the voluminous shawl.

'Let me help,' said Rupert.

'No!' she said, so loudly that he shrank back, faintly terrified. Poor Rupert. He was a terribly nice young man, always trying to do precisely the right thing. He never should have been exposed to any of us.

'May?' said Michael, quizzically. But May shook her head, white hat feathers bobbing, disentangled herself at last from the shawl and thrust it, oddly lumpy, at me.

'Here, hold this for me, Justina,' she said, a note of frantic haste in her voice. 'It's *scratchy*,' she added as explanation. The shawl landed in my hands, heavy, clumpy, and undoubtedly alive.

'Oh May, darling,' I whispered and clutched it to me close. I felt the familiar poking curiosity of the Reverend Feathers' big black beak prod through the silk, against my hand. I could not hide my delight, but dropped my head over the shawl hoping no one would see.

'Oh strawberries, how jolly!' cried May. 'Do run and get me some,' she said to Michael. He jumped up at once, but Rupert was still there, staring at me and May's shawl, and she said impatiently, 'You too.'

'Strawberries?' He blinked. 'Surely Michael . . .'

'I *love* strawberries. I want masses.' He nodded, and stood, looking politely at Edna and me.

'Oh yes, please,' I cried.

'You've not begun those,' said Edna, a little coldly.

'But I shall. Oh, get a whole tray. And more punch. Take Edna to help,' I cried. That was rather stupid, since a lady hardly carried her own strawberries, but Rupert was a little cowed by now, and helped her to her feet obediently.

'Thank God,' said May, when they were gone. 'Stuff him under your cape.' By happy fortune there was a vogue that summer for little capelets of lace, reaching from shoulder nearly to waist, and my tea-dress was thus adorned. I cautiously withdrew the Reverend Feathers from the tangle of May's shawl, and snugged him up under my cape, holding its folds closed with one hand.

'You look like Napoleon,' said May.

'Never mind,' I beamed. 'You're a wonderful darling and I adore you.' I looked up. Rupert and Michael were approaching with an entire silver tray from the buffet, laden with bowls of strawberries. 'Get eating, girl,' I said.

A sleeping crow, though not precisely a viper in one's bosom, is yet an awkward thing, thus placed. Somehow, though, I managed to get through the whole of the afternoon, and was within minutes of the finishing tape before disaster struck.

Rupert French, God help him, was a romantic. I learned that brief, and forgettable fact, late in the afternoon, when he managed to winkle me away from Michael and Edna, from May and Eugenia, and all our party, and find for us a secluded, though utterly proper, corner of garden, alone. He seated me on a stone bench, beneath a lilac bush, and settled himself on the grass at my feet.

My God, I thought, he's going to propose. Remember, now, I'd been through this once with Richard Underwood, and knew the form. Besides, I had been checked out and approved by his family, and he by mine, and the rest was formality. He was, for all his pleasant face and handsome athlete's body, a very shy young man, quite unused to courtship. An arranged marriage, for a boy like Rupert, took a terrible strain out of life. He smiled up at me, and I tried to smile back, while struggling to immobilize an awakening crow.

'Are you cold, my dear?' he asked.

'No,' I said, and then added, 'Yes. Yes I am.'

'Do have my coat,' he offered kindly.

I declined, fearing the slightest physical contact would reveal my feathery deception. He subsided to the grass, a little desperate for conversation and then suddenly blurted out, 'Oh Miss Melrose, you are so very, very pretty.'

'Am I?' I gasped, fighting a claw.

'Oh yes,' he was a little breathless, and having spoken out aroused his ardour. He moved closer.

'Don't,' I cried, and began to giggle suddenly.

'Oh Miss Melrose, really, I shan't . . .' he paused, looking puzzled and faintly hurt. Then a wise, knowing glint crossed his face and he cried out, 'Why, I do think you're *hiding* something.'

'Oh. Oh no. I'm not.'

'Oh yes you are,' he returned.

'No, *really*,' I shook my head wildly, fighting now two claws and a beak, and one flapping wing.

'You are, you are,' he cried flirtatiously. And then he grew quite roguish, in a clumsy boyish way, and actually reached to touch my dress and raise my lace cape to see.

'Come come, Miss Melrose, what have you there?' He grasped my cape firmly and lifted it up. I clutched at my bosom, from which emitted a sudden loud and raucous caw. He dropped his hand and threw himself back, but was pursued at once by a long black beak and a beady-eyed head.

'Oh my God, Miss Melrose!' he shouted, scrambling to his feet.

'A crow,' I whispered encouragingly. 'Just a crow.'

As you may have already guessed, Rupert French did not propose. Eugenia was furious, of course, and any less generous aunt would have washed her hands of me right then. But it was not the Vice-Regal garden party, nor the Reverend Feathers that brought my Dublin summer to a sudden close, but events of a far different, and a far wider world that swept in at the close of July, cutting the golden days short like the shadow of a swift, savage wing.

It was a week later and actually, in the course of that week, the first inklings of a change larger than any of us could imagine had crept in so quietly as to be virtually unnoticed. I had received a letter from home, in Mirza Hassan's hand, dictated by my father. It contained the usual news and the rather startling addition that Douglas' regiment had been placed on a mobilization alert. I read the sentence twice. It seemed so unlikely. Even the dire mutterings of the world press, distorted by our provincial vantage point, had hardly seemed as serious as that. And to tell the truth, I had hardly noticed. Austria and Serbia were squabbling, but someone was always squabbling in those days. It was the squabbles of Ireland that were on all our minds, and on my first reading of Father's letter I actually imagined that Douglas and his regiment were coming to Ulster. When I realized not, I dismissed the matter entirely. So much for my political acumen. But anyhow, the events of the end of that week would surely have eclipsed it. In the world's eyes, they were pitifully insignificant, a footnote to greater history. But the power of history is in direct proportion to one's proximity to it. The world, for all of us, is encompassed by a handful of lives.

I suppose I should have been repentant about my disastrous visit to the Vice-Regal Lodge, but I was not. I was relieved that Rupert French was out of my life, and my relief was augmented by Michael's delight. Together we weathered the grim breakfast at Merrion Square the next morning, as we had weathered such family post-mortems throughout the years.

'I shouldn't laugh,' Eugenia said sharply to her son, when her list of my calumnies was complete. Michael had been quite unable to *stop* laughing. 'If you think you are somehow *helping* your cousin, you are quite mistaken. It is all very well for you, but when she is a bitter old maid of forty, she'll have precisely you to thank.'

'It's not Michael's fault,' I cried. 'Michael had nothing

whatever to do with it.' Eugenia glared. She did not enjoy my defences of Michael.

'There has never been anything,' she said, 'in either of your lives, from the very day you met, that did not involve the other. And in no way has your mutual influence improved either of you in the slightest. You are a disaster together. A disaster.'

'We love each other,' Michael said, and I said, turning upon her two pairs of eyes brimming with outraged innocence. She looked pained, and older than usual, behind her pince-nez.

'Love in itself,' she said, with a look on her face of surprised self-discovery, 'rarely justifies much.'

I'm afraid we became thoroughly rebellious then, and after a certain amount of restrained shouting and argument we left the house. We simply went out, over protests and over commands, Michael carrying my easel and paint-box like in Sligo days of old, in cheerful insurrection. I had rarely felt so free.

We were to meet Kate that evening at her rooms, for a late supper, but until then we had all the summer day to ourselves. We walked the short distance to the railway station at Westland Row and boarded the Dalkey train. As it pulled away from the station we sat side by side in an empty compartment, clutching hands, like two errant, but determined truants from school. I remember that I wore a pale coffee-coloured linen summer suit, with a soft white poet's blouse, tied at my chin with a big black bow. My straw hat had matching black ribbons trailing down my back, that Michael caught in his hand as he sat beside me on the train and twined around his fingers. I can see him still, nervous, young, sun-browned and, as always, a little too thin. He had just finished his examinations and the strain of them yet showed. He wore a high collar and a straw boater tilted forward to shade his eyes. The bright sea light glared off the mud-flats and we both squinted into it to see the shellfish gatherers and their children silhouetted against the sea. I thought of painting Michael and traced in my mind the lines my brush would follow, the shadows of thick lashes, the quirky downward turning of the mouth that mixed laughter and compassion, the dark, adult glint of his shaded eyes.

'I'll paint you,' I said. 'Today.'

'No. Paint yourself. I don't want to look at me.' I laughed. But in the end I painted strangers.

We left the train at Kingstown and walked along the curving seafront, watching the yachts flitting about the bay. We walked a long while, until we reached the round tower at Sandycove. It was just a tower then; James Joyce had not yet made it famous. Below, among the rocks, there was a place set aside for public bathing, neatly segregated by sex, men on one side of an outcrop of stone, women on the other. The water was deep and green. Michael set up my easel and stretched himself out on the rocks, watching the bathers. The women did not really swim of course, but dabbled toes and sunned themselves in costumes that protected almost every inch of them from sun. But the young men swam, and their bodies were quite beautiful, even in their ridiculous long leggings and vests.

'They're lovely, they're lovely,' I kept whispering as I painted. Michael watched quietly. He understood. His studies, too, enabled him to see the human form in abstraction. After a while he slept in the sun, and I was glad, for I thought he needed rest. I painted on, imagining his future. The thought of Edna Young naturally entered, but somehow did not intrude. Something vastly peaceful had overtaken me, like a capitulation to fate, or the divine. I woke Michael only when the light was going, and I had completed my work. I had painted in water colours and had chosen as subject a cluster of male bathers before the silken, blue-green haze of sea and sky. Part of the rock upon which they gathered was included, the rest was emptiness. The whole had a translucence that was almost eerie and I was uncertain myself how it was attained. It was the best work I did all that year and for a few years to come. Of course, it was not fully finished that day, nor would it ever be, since from the moment I cleaned my brushes that afternoon, and put them away, they were not to be touched again for almost a year.

'Is it over already?' said Michael, when he woke. He looked sadly about and got slowly to his feet. The sun was low. When we returned on the train, the sand-flats at Sea Point and Blackrock were fore-shortened, the tide had run in, and driven the children and dogs and shell-gatherers away.

It was hot on the train, and I felt sticky and salty as if the seaside had followed us home, like guilt. We were both very quiet, tired, and subdued. Everything we had run from still waited in the city we had fled. We went to Kate's rooms in Dame Street, but she was not there. Persephone let us in. She was waiting for Padraic and had been waiting for hours. Her hands trembled as she made us tea and she spilled things. Something was wrong and in my naïvety, I thought it something personal, to do with love.

Late in the afternoon there was a sound of running heavy footsteps on the stairs and Padraic burst into the room. He was sweating and dishevelled and joyful. He carried something wrapped in a mackintosh which he held on to even when he grasped Persephone about the waist and swung her in half a circle in the air.

'Oh, let me be,' she panted, displeased. 'It's too old I am for yer nonsense.' He did not listen. He kissed her and kissed me and embraced Michael.

‘’Tis done,’ he cried. ‘’Tis done. And a fine day it’s been.’

‘Where’s my lamb?’ said Persephone, watching him. Padraic looked about us, calming into sense.

‘Kate? Has she not been here?’ He was concerned, but not very. ‘Oh, she’ll be with the others, no doubt,’ he said, but when Michael asked which others, he declined to explain. He turned to me then, still holding his coat-wrapped parcel as slyly as May had carried my crow in her shawl. ‘Will ye be tellin’ me now,’ he said to me, ‘where might I be keepin’ this?’ He was proud, glowing, and he unwrapped the coat with a flourish, and laid a military rifle on Kate’s table amidst our cups of tea.

‘Glory be to God,’ said Persephone. I stood in silence.

Michael lifted the rifle carefully, balancing it in his hands, sighting down the barrel, to the floor. He said, ‘You brought this *here*?’

‘And what else was I to be doin’ wit’ it? With the place alive with British Tommies? Carry it about the streets of Dublin all the night?’

‘Where’s *Kate*?’ Michael said, now urgently.

Padraic shrugged, not liking Michael’s anger. He said, ‘An’ how am I to be knowin’ that? And myself marchin’ to Howth half the day with the Volunteers, to the landing? An’ the rest of the day filled up with outwittin’ the English buggers along the way home. Ah, but we gave them a fair run, an’ not a rifle lost to them.’ He was glowing again, dreamy and drunk on victory. Michael gave up on him and stood glowering at the window, and I sat alone by the rifle laid on Kate’s table, thinking of how we’d lain in the sunshine of Sandycove, while the yacht sailed in across the same sea with guns for Ireland. I did not know what I felt, whether I was angry at them for playing at war, or at myself for not being there as well.

Padraic muttered, ‘They’ll be meetin’ at the O’Connell

Bridge to celebrate. The whole of Dublin will be there.' He sounded like he wanted to be there too, accepting the adulation of the city. Michael picked up his hat and took my arm.

'There'll be trouble,' he said. 'She's no business in the middle of it.'

'And where better?' cried Padraic joyfully. You would have thought that Kate herself was Cathleen ni Houlihan, not a flesh and blood girl he loved.

'She'll get hurt,' I said angrily.

'Not my Kate,' said he.

Padraic picked up the rifle and hid it stupidly under the bed in Kate's room. I stood at the doorway, watching him. Her room was a mess, her stockings and a blouse scattered on the bed. He blushed and muttered as he brushed against them trying to hide his rifle.

'I'll find her,' he said then boldly, as he came back among us. But Michael was too angry to let him go alone, and Persephone was too frantic for Kate's safety. So in the end we all went, Michael and I ridiculous in our seaside costumes, against the evening light of the city, with Padraic the revolutionary at our sides. Persephone was wrapped in a shawl and looked an old, old woman, full of misery.

The O'Connell Bridge was crowded with people, and in Sackville Street groups of young men vied for space with prostitutes and beggars. Young boys and girls ran about in a heady excitement, dodging the trams that clanged and sparked along their ordained paths, converging on Nelson's Pillar where the routes all began. We walked up and down amongst strangers, in an anxious silent foursome. Persephone grew tired, and began to cough, and Padraic was impatient with her, and I with him.

'Let me go alone,' Michael said. 'I'll find her more

quickly alone.' But I thought suddenly he wouldn't be safe, and begged him to stay with us, as if in some mad way, that would be safer.

Padraic kept meeting people he knew and there was an annoying air of smug camaraderie and shouts, pretentiously in Irish, among them. But no one had seen Kate. We went down the other side of Sackville Street, back to the Liffey and came upon a great crowd, running along the quayside into Bachelor's Walk.

It is the nature of humanity to follow a hurrying crowd, as if each led to treasure or the feet of a Messiah. Jostled and confused, we stumbled forward, shouting to each other and others we met. There were more shouts ahead, angry and taunting and the sound of breaking glass. The crowd had formed into an arc, its rear to the river, and before it, half surrounded, a party of British soldiers. I remember thinking how young they looked, and frightened, like children, rosy-cheeked, with toy guns. Stones thrown over their heads smashed windows and thudded on stone walls beyond.

'Yer bastards,' shouted Padraic lustily. 'Yer bloody bastards.'

It was then I saw Kate, at the front of the crowd. She was dressed extraordinarily, in a sort of disguise, a poor woman's dark dress and plaid shawl, and the shawl wrapped up over her head the way such women wore them. But I knew her at once, and the disguise fooled no one, not even the shy young soldier a half-dozen feet away, whom she was so fiercely haranguing. Her beautiful voice, her elegant accent, and even in her obscene shouting, her perfect grammar, all betrayed her. Her face was screwed up into such pinched, sharp lines of unreasoning hatred that all her beauty and youth were vanquished. The young soldier recoiled physically, as if the vicar's daughter had thus assaulted him. Politeness and caste overwhelmed him; even his rifle was held with deference.

'Bastard,' she shrieked. 'Whoreson, son of an English bitch. Go rut on your filthy English mother!'

'Yer bastards. Yer devils!' Padraic shouted gleefully, rushing to her side. I thought of Geoffrey and wondered why sanctimony and evil used the same words.

'Get her out of there, Padraic,' cried Michael. 'There's going to be trouble. Get her away.' The crowd stilled suddenly to Michael's words, as if seeing a new possibility. The soldiers too tensed, and stepped further back, and a new dimension had fallen upon us. Kate crouched in the roadway and took a loosened cobble in her hand. 'Don't throw that,' Michael shouted. But she threw it anyway, with a sharp, sure powerful hand, devoid of mercy. It struck her young soldier in the forehead and he went glassy-blank-eyed and fell to the ground. Cheers and shrieks arose at once and the crowd surged forward and back and in the awful noise of it I did not even hear the firing begin.

Shouts turned to screams, and anger to fear. People began falling, shot, or stumbling or diving down for shelter, and as each fell others stumbled upon them or clustered over them, so panic bred panic, and the soldiers, panicked further, continued to fire. In death's moments, men and women return to their deepest true selves. Husbands shielded wives with their bodies and women ran to save their children. Persephone reached for me, for Michael, for Kate, her arms outspread like the wings of a mother bird, crying little wails of motherhood; we, her chicks to the last. I ran for Michael and Michael ran to shield the children, to aid the fallen, and to stop and stand fearless and outraged in the street, shouting to the soldiers.

'Stop! Stop it! For Christ's sake. There are women and

children!' And Kate, through all of it, stood before the bullets and the terror hurling bricks and rocks in murderous joy.

'Kate!' I cried, 'get down. Get down.' Persephone then leapt upon her to drag her down and Michael, his arms about them both, threw himself into the line of fire in their stead, and all three of them fell.

Quite suddenly the firing stopped. Orders were shouted, the air went half-quiet as the street emptied and only the wounded, the dead, the smoke, and the soldiers remained. Suddenly I could hear again the sound of the trams on Sackville Street, and the hooting of the Guinness barges on the Liffey. The living city grew up around our isolated moment of death. Someone was giving orders in a cool, precise English voice. 'All right now, little Miss, if you've no one here, you just be off to your family. You shouldn't be here amongst all these.'

'I have someone,' I whispered. I looked down at my feet. Kate had vanished and Padraic with her. Against the stone wall, by the river, where Persephone had hauled Michael down to safety so many times, she sat now, her back propped against the wall. Her skirt was splayed out and her booted legs indecently uncovered. Her hat was gone, and her grey hair tumbled loose. Her dead eyes, yet open, stared out across Bachelor's Walk, into an endless space. The whole front of her dress was soaked through with blood and blood was on her mouth and nose and chin. Across her legs, Michael lay, with his arms outstretched and his dark head in her lap, like a child sleeping through a nursery tale. His straw hat, lifted by the wind, blew dustily down the road. I caught it, and held it in my arms, and before the soldiers could bully me away, I crouched on the pavement beside my dead love.

'Michael,' I said. 'It's over. Nothing worse will ever happen now.'

It was July, 1914.

Part Two

11

'In the carpet bazaar,' said Mirza Hassan, 'the rug-weavers worked beneath the great awnings of their tents. The tents were like dark caves, with beautiful rugs on every side and upon the floors. Inside, in the dimness, was the beautiful tea urn, faintly gleaming; the water-pipe, the small cups, all made in brass, enchased with wonderful figures, a great mystery.'

We sat on the snowswept flank of Ben Wyvis in the spring of 1915. Below, the land was mist-shrouded and white, and we talked of these warm eastern places. It was Easter. We had left Father below, in the Pump Room of the Spa with his two attendant nurses. I doubt he was aware we had gone.

'I would sit for hours, watching the rug-makers.'

'Do you miss home, Hassan?'

He stopped speaking, his hands held out before him, palms together, not touching. His eyes were distant. Then he smiled, his sudden, extraordinarily white smile, beneath his thick black moustache, the smile almost a statement in itself. 'Oh, yes.'

I was not really listening. I sat with my knees drawn up, my skirt making a tent over them, and the Reverend Feathers cradled in my arms. Snow fell on his smooth wings.

'Always, I sat before the loom, to watch the picture grow. Leopards, trees, hunters, holy words. Wonderful pictures. Then, one day, I crept round behind the weaver, thinking I would see how this magic was created, surely even more wonderful than the picture before me. And there, what sorrow! What misery! No longer were there shining animals and forests and deep silken colours; but only dull threads and knots and a sombre shadow of the picture I had cherished. I wept with my disappointment and the weavers laughed at this foolish boy.'

I smiled politely and looked down, stroking the wings of the bird. I was accustomed by now to the attempts of friends to divert me. But Hassan leaned forward and touched my arm, a rare moment, charged with great warmth.

'Justina, we make a picture of life, as a carpet. We make it beautiful with the faces of loved ones, the treasures of possessions, and the patterns of our dreams, and we look upon it and are delighted and want no other picture. But we are the weaver and see it from the weaver's side alone. Who knows? Perhaps it is ugly, even evil, behind.' He paused and leaned back against one elbow, in the snow. He was wearing a strange fur hat he had brought from the East, and when he puffed at his pipe he looked like a camel-driver lost in a desert of white. 'But now, Justina,' he said, 'if we do not weave, but let Allah weave, then often the picture is ugly to our eyes, because we do not see from the weaver's side. But Allah sees. Allah sees.' He leaned forward again, the pipe in his left hand, drawing figures on the snow with his right. He showed me an imaginary loom. 'Look, now, here is you, and here am I, and here is Michael . . . a knot, a snare, a tangle . . . but look behind, if you but could, and you would see the tapestry Allah weaves of us all.' He laid his pipe down in the snow, and sat straight, facing me, his legs crossed. He looked suddenly very young. He took my two gloved hands between his own, bare, and heedless of the cold wind. He held them tight, looking into my eyes. 'Let Allah weave, Justina. Let Allah weave.'

I shook my head, and drew my hands away, and wrapped them around the patient crow, who nestled contentedly in the folds of my skirt. I dropped my eyes from those of Mirza Hassan, but he pursued me, unerringly. I clung to the crow even as he lifted him from my hands.

Hassan held the crow up at the level of his face, as if it were a hunter's falcon. He looked carefully at its sleek reptilian face. 'He is at home here,' he said, raising it higher so it could see the wide hill. 'He is savage.'

'He's not savage,' I said.

'He will pluck the eyes from a lamb before its mother's face.' He laughed softly and stroked the crow. 'But he is beautiful all the same. Let him go.'

'He does not want to go,' I said.

'Now. Now he wants to go.'

I shook my head again, fiercely, impatient. But I stood up as I took the crow from his hands, and shook the snow from my skirt. 'Good,' he said encouragingly, standing beside me. I raised the bird high in the air, and then drew him towards me and kissed his head. He was exactly like a tame cat, a true pet. Then with a whimsical shrug I lifted him up and flung him skywards, watching with wonder, as always, at how swiftly his wings caught the air. He flapped, sank, regained height and after his two heavy wing beats suddenly soared. I watched yet, calmly. He had always been free, and was quite accustomed to flight. He flew onwards, circled our heads, and then struck out northwards, along An Cabar and into the mist. Before he vanished I knew already by the sure stroke of his wings that he'd never return.

'See,' said Mirza Hassan, his hand on my shoulder, 'it is good. He does not need you now.'

'He never needed me,' I said. 'He loved me.'

'He loves you still,' he said quietly. 'He does not need to be with you to love you.' I peered restlessly into the mist, striving to see what was beyond my sight. Mirza Hassan put his arms round my shoulders and held me to him. 'Let Allah weave,' he said. I clung to him as if he were my father, and I again a child.

Eventually I said, still leaning against the rough wool tweed of his coat, 'Is Allah our God too? The Christian God?'

'Of course. How can there be two Gods?'

I drew back and stood silently watching the mist roll down from the heights of the hill. I held my hair down against the wind, where it whipped about my face. 'Geoffrey says Muhammadans are pagans.'

'Geoffrey has not read the Koran,' Mirza Hassan said, very gently. 'Never mind, though. Those who persecuted all my family, my parents, my sister, my brothers, all put to death for Allah's sake, they too, those persecutors, read the Koran, just as we did.' He smiled again, looking down at me struggling with the wind in my hair. 'And had they not, I would never have been alone in the Elburz, never have met your Father, never have climbed with him in the Push-t-Kuh, nor brought him home from Mazanderan. Blessed be Allah, the beneficent, the merciful.' I faced him then: he was smiling and gentle.

'I will never be so forgiving,' I said. 'It would be as if I had forgotten him.' I was stubborn, my head downcast, my eyes on the falling hillside below.

'And if you did forget? And will you *not* forget? You will live four times the span of his life. What will your memory be when you are old, older than your father, older than everyone you know?'

'How can I say,' I shouted, angrily. 'And who knows I will be old? Perhaps I will die tomorrow.' I said it with the hopeful fervour of the grieving young.

Mirza Hassan looked, smiling, towards the darkening sky. 'Your crow has flown beyond your sight,' he said. 'Does he vanish from God's sight as well? Does he cease to exist when you cease to see him?' He touched my face with his rough dark-skinned hand. 'Let Allah weave,' he said.

We descended slowly through the snow, at Hassan's pace, I following in the steady, almost plodding steps that could cover fifty miles in a day. I had no skis. I had not ski'd all winter. Nor had I painted, danced, jested or even laughed. I had faithfully done nothing that could be assumed by life to be an affirmation since the day Michael died. I would endure, I would not enjoy. Doubtless, life was quite unaware of my small stoicism. Certainly the world of men was not. But I clung stubbornly to my isolation, assured in myself that one moment's willing acceptance of life would break forever my bond with my dead cousin. I thought no further than that.

But time had passed and the world to which we descended was changed. The war in France was nine months old, as old as my grief. It had weathered its first winter and faced its first spring. Already it was like no other war before. It was becoming, from a small surprising skirmish quixotically born in the summer heat, a colossus, a giant of history. It was becoming, even then, the Great War. And yet I had hardly noticed.

How small and narrow are the confines of human love, human grief. So that even death, most universal of all, as often isolates as it unites. Many, many young girls were grieving that autumn, that winter, that cold early spring. Cousins, brothers, husbands and lovers were squandered already in the ditches of France. I had hardly thought of them. Grief may ennoble; it did not ennoble me.

And yet, in my way, I *was* isolated. For when strangers

saw my mourning black (oh yes, again and for this cause, all these years later, I still cannot even begin to laugh), and rushed with their sympathy, a terrible awkwardness occurred. For Michael had not fallen nobly in France or Flanders. Michael had fallen for no purpose, by grievous foolish error and futile accident, on a British street. In the hysteria of 1914, this undoubted fact could find no tolerance. Patriotism rode the nation like a gorgon. One could not look into her awful face and proclaim that our British soldiers had made so hideous an error. And so an air of complicity was added to the futility of Michael's death.

Faces of compassion turned stony at the mention of Bachelor's Walk. And in the onslaught of the Kaiser's War all was, perhaps relievedly, forgotten. Those who would be remembered seek martyrdom in quiet times.

The times were not quiet. Even Strathpeffer, far in the untouched north, was marked by war. No longer did young people gather at dinner with their elders, or go out in gay parties to walk and ski. They, like my three brothers, were all gone elsewhere, to training camps of the Territorials, or the New Army, or already to the wet cold fields of France. Douglas, two years a Captain in the Seaforths, went to the front in August with the first of the British Expeditionary Force. He had fought on the Marne and at Ypres, returned home for a hurried wedding to his fiancée Wilhemina, and was now at Neuve-Chapelle patching together his decimated company. Geoffrey was there as well, commissioned as a chaplain to our father's old battalion, and Alexander was at a New Army training camp in southern England. We were a military family; there had not even been discussion, but a ready assumption, on all our parts that all who were able would go. I think Father was aware what was happening, where the boys were, though sometimes in confusion he would ask for them, before foggy recollection drove him to embarrassed silence. Time was the most renegade of his faculties; this war of nine months was sometimes telescoped into a fortnight's or even a day's event. On occasions, he could not be convinced why they did not manage home again for tea.

Aside from his professional nurses, and Mirza Hassan, I was Father's only companion. All the social butterflies had flown; the decorative convalescents, the wilting ladies. We were alone, mourning daughter and invalid father: the old Spa days were done. Strathpeffer had found her war duty. Her streets were filled with uniforms, the khaki and tartan of the military, the bright blue of the convalescent soldier, the brave red-crossed white of the nursing volunteers. High above the village square the magnificent new Highland Hotel, built for a future of luxurious indulgence, had opened its doors as a hospital. Its rooms were wards, its halls and corridors echoed to the painful clump of crutches. On the parquet terrace where Meggie and Geoffrey had danced to Michael's harmonica, rows of Bath-chairs promenaded in the brisk air: the blind, the amputees, the shell-shocked, each partnered by a fresh-faced VAD, dancing a new solemn reel.

As always, there were letters waiting upon our return. Even fractious families grow close in wartime. We all wrote to each other, all the time. A paper tracery netted us together, Ireland to England to France. I lifted the neat packet of envelopes from the desk in my hotel room, and sat down on the settle sorting them with one hand, and untying my snowy walking boots with the other. There were two with the military postmark, one from France, one from Buckinghamshire. Douglas and Alexander checking in. The letters were addressed to Father, but were as much for me, since I would read them to him, and attempt to make him understand. There was none from Geoffrey, but mail from the Front was so often delayed, and inclined to arrive in redundant bundles. The London postmark meant Clare; the one from Dublin, May. Kate did not write to me, nor I to her. I was not, like Hassan, a forgiving Baha'i, but at present a most bitter Christian. Despite Geoffrey's counsellings, I doubted I'd ever forgive Kate.

I saved May's letter to last, the bon-bon. Clare's letters were as ever polemics, though now in a new cause. May, even in the midst of war, in the memory of grief, found moments of wit and fun. But I read the boy's letters, always first, skimming the first lines in breathless haste until normality had been established, the permanent fear temporarily held at bay. So often letters from the boys were obituaries of friends.

Douglas wrote of the weather, his horse, a small anecdote about a village behind the lines, a snippet of trench gossip about old friends from the North. Much of it might interest Father in a mildly diverting way. There was no mention of the war. One would not imagine he had just come through a major battle and was even then under sporadic fire. But Douglas had never written about war, which was his profession, any more than a plumber would write about plumbing. Perhaps he assumed Father quite capable of filling in the military details. Perhaps he wished to keep the details to himself. Others did, and more so, every day.

As usual, his letter ended with an admonition to me to see to the health and needs of his 'dearest Wilhemina', as if this same lady were a wilting invalid in dire straits, and not the hale, hearty and determinedly capable young woman living in considerable luxury and surrounded by two dozen servants at Arradale Castle. My ordinary resentment of his elaborated concern for her and his ready dismissal of any problems of mine before her greater cause, was stilled. It is hard for a man to go to war and leave behind a pregnant wife. He clung to me as his immortality.

Douglas had married Wilhemina during a Christmas leave, a year earlier than planned, spurred on by the decent haste of wartime. She at once took Arradale and all of us under her fearsome wing. My tower studio was now a nursery-to-be. Father's study had vanished into new butler's pantries. Father and I were besieged in a wing of the house, strangers, both, to the castle without. Small wonder we fled to Strathpeffer. 'The poor dear does depend upon you so,' wrote the mournful husband from France. Indeed.

Alexander's writing was bright and breezy and he talked much about the war. Everyone could tell at once, even from letters, who had, and had not, seen the Front. I read it sadly. Poor darling, his head still full of pretty faces, and sport. Even his boyish pomposity had come to sound like a charming game.

I hurried through it and laid it down, and fussed a moment with the buttonhook and my dress shoes. Father would be waiting in the dining room for afternoon tea. I looked up before I opened Clare's envelope. Snow was falling steadily beyond the window, and I watched through the bars of the Reverend Feathers' empty cage. It looked inviting and I wished suddenly I was still on the hill and had my skis. The wish surprised me, with its sudden violation of my code. I felt no guilt but a kind of gentle peace.

I read Clare's letter dutifully. 'All is changed,' sang her beautiful script, 'We must move onward to our new destiny.' But nothing had changed. Women's suffrage was subject to Our Glorious War Effort, but the message was the same; the personal is irrelevant and must fall before the principle. The bomber of railway carriages makes shells for France, the virago becomes the VAD. Queen Christabel had decreed and we her faithful lieges . . . there is but one Cause, it is Holy, and it is Ours. Oh, Clare. I laid the letter down upon its face, and opened May's.

Merrion Square
4 April 1915

My *very* dearest Justina,

Darling, if I see one more balaclava or woolly stocking I shall scream . . . why *couldn't* we have fought this war somewhere *hot*! Oh well, they also serve who only sit and knit . . . pity the poor Tommy who gets my last pair, one was twice as long as the other if it was an inch. Oh God, I suppose they'll break them up and give them to amputees . . . one to a big Irish Guard and one to a wee Scots Jock. Oh damn it, darling, I don't know if it's worse to laugh or sit and cry. This can't be *Ireland's* war. And every Irish boy I know is fighting it.

Never mind, I shan't get morbid or political. Do tell, how is Kaiser Bill? Still boldly awaiting Der Tag? Anyhow, we've no fear of Arradale falling, even if all the world does . . . can you imagine storming *her* battlements? Oh don't ever let Douglas see this letter. Or the censor!! Imagine! They'll think you've the old boy stuffed up your jumper!

I saw Mother and Father last week in Sligo. They are not coming to Dublin after all. I doubt they will, this year, at all. If ever. We all retreat, I suppose, in our own ways. Father is reconciled. He is old, but at peace. I never realized before but he is genuinely, modestly, religious. It *does* help. Mother puts on a brave face, but it's only that. Life is over for her, I know.

While I was there, Persephone's sisters came with her family from Donegal to visit her grave. Quite hundreds of them, and scores of little Monogues running about. I hadn't even realized there *were* sisters! And what a rag-tag strange lot, the old women keening over her stone in the old way, under their shawls. Wasn't she always a mystery? How ever did she become what she did, coming up out of that!?

Padraic is not keening. Kate apparently has comforted him quite satisfactorily. (Oh, May, girl, what a sour creature you sound!) But they *are* so flagrant. I wouldn't mind so much if they didn't always hide it so under their unending politics. I daresay they use the Irish colours for a bedsheet. And it would help if they had some discretion, some restraint . . . I honour and respect what they believe, and Ireland's cause is not alien to me . . . but things *were* moving forward before the war, and now it is simply embittering to everyone to hear such talk with everyone's sons and brothers at the Front. Even Maud Gonne is nursing in France, after all, but then France *is* her second country. I beg Kate to hold her tongue, but I think she revels in causing distress, and a black armband is a red rag to a bull for her. Oh enough, she brings out the worst in me.

Dearest, there was something special I had to tell you, and so I've saved it till last. Michael came to see me, a few nights ago. Don't be shocked, dear, it was nothing extraordinary really, just one of those things that happen. It had followed a dream, though it was not itself a dream. I had dreamt we were together in Sligo, you and I and Michael, walking in the hills above Glen Car. I awoke quite suddenly, intensely happy, with the feeling that some hand of great compassion had touched my shoulder. When I sat up, there was a blue light in the room. It made a beautiful shape, like a scroll of wrought iron, like the altar rail in St John's in Sligo. It moved across the room, at the height of a man's head, and just as I grew frightened, it went out of the door. It was so kind. I know he felt my fear. Isn't it strange how even the ones we loved most in life, frighten us in death? It *was* Michael, dear, I know. I knew I could tell you. Who else could I tell?

Be happy darling, and do, do begin again to paint.

Your loving cousin,
as always,
May Howie

I did not begin to paint, not for over half a year. But the next day I went to the big hospital in the Highland Hotel and signed on with the VAD. As an affirmation of life it was unspectacular, but would do. And as I would train, and serve in Strathpeffer, it was probably the largest effort I could make for the war and my country. I could no longer leave Father; his days were ending and I was the last of all the family left to him. It was quite impossible to say, then, whether he, or the war would last the longest; both were uncertain qualities. While both lingered, this would be my life.

I was given basic Red Cross training, but for many months was hardly called upon to use it. Such matters were, in this remote convalescent hospital, essentially in the hands of the professional nurses. We scrubbed and polished, scraped and rubbed: floors, walls, banisters, bedposts, dishes, pots, bedpans. Every furnishing, every vessel of human need was cleaned to distraction, again and yet again, and all by us. Oh, those polished parquet floors, made for dancing, how I came to detest them! My hands were red, blistered and perpetually sore, stiff with scabs and scars. Had I thought then still of my career in art, it would have worried me but, certain that was all behind me, I had little care. And yet, it was there, a year and more from Michael's death, that I did again begin to paint. And my VAD work was directly the cause.

A soldier was brought in off the train one night. He was an officer from an English regiment, the Duke of Wellington's. We knew there was something special about him from the quiet, stealthy way they brought him to us, in the dead of night. He had an entire ambulance reserved for himself, and a room apart on the third floor. The room was kept darkened, with curtains around the bed providing a solitude within solitude. A special directive went out immediately concerning the secretive room and its solitary occupant. No one was to enter without Sister's specific permission. There were to be no visitors, no clergymen, not even orderlies nor VADs to clean and bring meals in the ordinary way. The curtains were never to be opened, and no lighting but one solitary gas mantle shielded in the corner of the room. A pair of older silent trained nurses were assigned to watch over the patient, and all other entrants to the room got no further than the curtained exterior of the inner sanctum.

As for those of us whose duties of cleaning, and serving, brought us even that far, there was a whole new set of rules, but within them lay the clue to the enigma on the third floor.

'No mirrors,' whispered another VAD to me. 'No mirrors, and nothing like a mirror. No metal. Not even a shiny plate.' She paused, and leaned closer, 'It's a monster in there. He hasn't any face.' There are no secrets in hospitals.

One day I was sent by Sister to polish the floor in what had quickly gained the accolade of The Room. I was considered *reliable* (Oh, dear Eugenia, could you but see me now) by the nursing staff quite simply because my ravaged view of life made me immune to flirtation, pranks, any form of fun or youthful good spirits. I was twenty-one, going on fifty. Nothing but work mattered to me, and work itself only as a kind of morphia. Sister didn't mind the reason; what mattered to her was that I could be counted on, like a trustworthy machine.

I was on my knees, scrubbing away at a particularly resistant spill mark when, from the curtained enclosure of the bed behind me, there came a low sound, remarkably like a laugh, but for a certain muffled quality, a legacy of bandages and drainage tubes. Then a voice, bubbly with fluid, but human, spoke with clear if painful humour. 'If floor polish will win this war, we're well in the lead.' I froze, shocked and a little terrified, as one addressed from a coffin. But this next sally was better, 'I do say, if the face is as pretty as what I'm seeing from here, this *will* be a treat.' I was bottom first to the bed, head down like a washerwoman. I gasped, less outrage than amazement, and instinctively turned my head to the voice. There was a quick rustling of curtaining, and the voice, gentler, older, said, 'No, dear, don't turn around. Not yet. There.' The last was a pained, tired gasp. When I turned to face the bed he had managed to draw closed again his curtain peephole, and his invisibility was secure.

I sat back on my haunches, staring at the blank green curtain. Then I said, 'I don't think you should talk any more. You sound tired.'

There was a long, long silence. Then a bubbly whisper. 'Oh my dear, I am.'

He said nothing else that day. I knew already, from the voice alone, a great many things about him. He was English. He was upper class. He was a charmer of ladies. Or he had been. He was incredibly brave. Over the days that followed, I fell a little in love with a man I knew as only a wry, teasing voice.

I doubt the feeling was much reciprocated. He had other things on his mind; foremost, I imagine, his titled English fiancée who waited determinedly in the Ben Wyvis Hotel for the summons to his side that he would not give. I had seen her, at night, when I dined with Father; a great beauty. Still, he went to the trouble to quiz the nursing staff and the other VADs about me; because quite soon he was aware of all sorts of things I had not told him.

Whenever I cleaned the room, or sat beside him in the night, with instructions to call the duty nurse, had he any need, he would talk. Talking was physically difficult. His mouth was shattered; I knew simply from the quality of his voice; and his wounds not healed yet, and still draining. I could smell them, through the curtaining, a sad ghostly accompaniment to his charm. But he made a determined effort. He asked me about my father. He asked me about Ireland. He asked me about my three brothers. He was quite persistent. One day he asked me about art.

I did not answer. There was a sudden awkward silence between us; our first. He was flustered. 'You *are* the artist, aren't you?' he said, uneasily, as one uncertain of his informants. I nodded to myself, my head down over the instrument table I was scrubbing.

'Yes. I was, once . . .' I said slowly.

'Surely one never *stops* being such a thing . . .' he said hastily and he sounded relieved when I said, 'No. I suppose not.'

It was then I realized what he wanted from me, but that day, thankfully, he did not ask. When he did, it was as gracefully casual as if he was requesting another sugar in his tea.

'I say, Nurse, could you do a chap a little service?'

'Of course,' I said, a little warily, because the unspoken was always the loudest thing in that room. He went on in the same pleasant tone.

'They won't let me have a look, you understand. I see their point and all, but I would like to. It would make it easier. One's imagination does rather run riot.' He paused a moment, to catch his breath, and then went on, levelly, 'Of course when my hands are better, I'll be able to do a bit of a recce, but you see . . .'

Of course I hadn't seen, not even his hands, but I knew the state of them. He'd met not only shellburst, but a thing called 'liquid fire' that they used in the trenches and his hands were frightfully burned, and wrapped in bandages yet. I had spoken to the Sister who dressed them, and doubted they'd feel much ever, but I didn't say that. I said only, rather stiffly, 'Now, now. We both know the rules.' I felt hateful saying it.

He paused again, uncertain, as if once more his careful research of me may have failed him. He said quickly, 'It must be you. You're the artist. An artist can look at anything . . . it's like being a doctor.' I shivered, remembering how I had thought once the same, of Michael and

I watching the bathers at Sandycove. Oh surely, we could look sanguine upon beauty, but this?

'Please,' I said, 'I can't bring a mirror . . . I can't possibly.'

'Oh I know, I know,' he said impatiently. 'Frankly, I don't want that. It's too close, too real. That's why a portrait is different, after all, not like a photograph. There's this third element in there, the artist . . .' I realized that he knew about art, had probably studied it, loved it. 'It's like an intercession. Like praying to saints.' I heard exhaustion defeating his courage.

'I'll do it,' I said.

And so, in that strange, strange setting I accepted my first commissioned portrait, not for money, but for an overflowing outpouring of gratitude. We set a date and time, a day we cunningly figured that Sister would be off, and only one trained nurse on duty. In the small hours, while I watched at night, and stood guard against slipped tube or sudden haemorrhage, he would reveal himself to me, and I would do a pencil sketch. All that week I braced myself for this manifestation.

The moment, when it came, was made no easier by the late hour, the silent ghostly hospital filled with sleeping misery, the tense silence in which we sat waiting for danger of interruption to pass.

Finally he said, 'Are you ready?'

'Yes,' I whispered. But I did nothing. Gently he reached a bandaged hand to me, through the slit in the green curtaining.

'Come, dear,' he said, as sweetly as a bridegroom. I stepped forward and drew the curtain away.

At first I did not know where to look, not out of embarrassed dissemblance, but out of confusion. The roadsigns of features were gone, or so grotesquely distorted that the face, as a face, was not recognizable. I was looking upon an object, a prismed cataclysm, where the lines of eye, brow, cheek, chin were reoriented in new, aberrant ways, a horrendous living Cubism. But I kept looking; the alternative was murderously shameful. And as an object, I could just bear to approach this monster whose beautiful bravery had charmed me with words.

'Is it too much, dear?' he whispered, kindly. The voice seemed more distorted now, now that I could see from what it emanated. The area around the mouth was yet bandaged, and a drainage tube was plastered beside the moving gap from which he managed to speak. The nose had healed, leaving a convoluted cavernous undivided nostril. The cheek was simply gone on one side, and skin had healed unnaturally over mal-shaped bone, filling into the dark hollow of the missing eye. Above, his forehead, quite smooth and unlined, was totally untouched. The right side of his face gave clues to what had once been on the left; a partially complete cheek, mottled by burn marks, and calm and magnificent, one fine hazel eye. From the eye alone I could tell quite how stunningly handsome he had been.

'No,' I said honestly. 'It's not too much.' I laid my sketch-pad on my knee, and began to draw. Rarely, rarely, even under the meticulous demanding eye of Mr Yeats, or the laboured pedantry of the School of Art, have I drawn with such care of detail, such searched-for painful accuracy. Again and again, finding one line of my sketch faintly untrue to the alien form before me, I erased hastily and began again. I drew as an architect, an edifice for another world.

When I was done I looked once more at the thing before me, already grown faintly less awful with familiarity and I smiled.

'Oh, a noble act,' he whispered and gently, like an actor slipping into the wings, he let the curtain fall. From the depths of his sanctuary he said, his voice somehow clearer again, 'I think I should like to see your work, my dear. I do hope I can focus properly; my vision is not quite right.'

'Now?' I whispered, my voice shaking.

'I think so, dear. It's late. Someone might yct comc.' I wished fervently that he had chosen to wait, to put off the violent moment until he had rested, slept, made himself stronger. But it would not have been like him to do so.

'Of course,' I said, and I slipped the smooth paper through the curtained entry to his seclusion. I dropped my head into my hands, tears wetting the rough reddened skin. He was silent for an endless long while. At last his voice came again, very distant, but quite calm.

'Oh, my dear, you do have talent. I shall always treasure this.' There was a pause. 'Do tell. Can you find me something I might keep it in? I would hate to have it damaged.'

I jumped up, and whispered, 'Yes. Certainly.' I ran from the room, in a mixture of relief and confusion, and had just found and collected a large brown envelope from Sister's office (quite forbidden, of course) when a horrible realization thrust through my naïvety and I ran headlong up the corridor to my charge. I had left him alone. He, who was never to be alone. And at this cruel moment. Visions of surgical scissors, knives, razors, all possible self-destructive instruments inundated my mind, as I clattered up that silent corridor. I burst into the room, gasping for breath and raced to the curtained bed, flinging aside the curtain in my terror, oblivious to all our previous discretion. He was sitting there, studying yet my awful reproduction of his hideous face. His one eye held a faint hint of humour. He had heard my frantic footsteps.

'My word, dear, there's not a sharp instrument in the room and the window's quite thoroughly locked from without. Did you think I'd not tried all that already?' Then, quite gently, he laughed, patted my hand, and slipped the portrait into the envelope. 'When you're famous, I'll have my secret,' he said. Then he looked squarely in my face and said, 'Oh, I shall manage this, my dear. Quite satisfactorily.'

All the next day I went about my duties in a terror of anticipation, awaiting at any moment the horrible blanched-faced whispering from nurse to nurse that signalled a suicide in the wards. He was as resourceful as he was strong, and I knew, for all his jesting about it, had he the desire, he'd find the tool. But he did not. When I saw him, or rather saw the curtained bed, again that late afternoon, the voice that came from behind the draperies was firm and in control. He gave me a letter for his fiancée, yet waiting fruitlessly. I took it but whispered tentatively, 'Won't you see her . . .?'

He was silent and then said, 'Oh, no, dear. That wouldn't really help. This is best, really.' He paused again, and said, quite rationally, 'Oh, I do know they think I'm being terribly morbid here, on my own, but that's not my reason, you do understand.' I did. He was not morbid. He went on, 'I must let her go, don't you know. She's been wonderful, courageous. But a lifetime of this takes more than courage. No, my dear, that sort of thing is done, for me. All respect to St Paul, but in my particular case, I think it's better to burn.'

I only saw him once more, briefly, to say goodbye. I was taken off that duty for two weeks, and after that time, it was arranged for him to go to London, to a particular hospital ward that specialized in such cases. He was, despite the individual horror of his condition, hardly unique. The effect of modern weaponry was rarely the neat bandaged heads and graceful arms-in-slings beloved of the illustrated magazines. I went to his room to bid him farewell, and behind his blessed screens he took my hand to the wreckage of his mouth and kissed my fingers goodbye.

Within days, and hardly realizing what was happening, I was sketching and even painting again. A week later, I deliberately withdrew *The Sea-Bathers at Sandycove* from my folder where it had languished, and completed the finishing touches. My brush went as readily to the subject as if no time had passed and I sat yet with Michael beside me, on the shore. I completed it, framed it, and sent it to May Howie in Dublin, feeling, as I did so, a chapter of my life draw closed.

When father died, early that November, Douglas was allowed home on a compassionate leave. The end, when it did come, was quite sudden, and followed, as often happens, a surprising rally. The night before, Father was more vividly aware of his surroundings, and of us, than he had been for years. All of that was of course deceptive; sudden references to dead friends, my mother, Michael, and times irrevocably past, belied his startling logic. But a stranger in the room would have regarded him as a man in full control of his faculties. He spoke in Persian with Mirza Hassan for much of the evening, with great excitement. Half the time they talked of mountains, the rest of religion. They talked with great fervour of the one they called The Blessed Beauty, the Prophet of the Baha'is.

It was only when Father had fallen asleep and I was sitting beside his bed with Hassan crouched on the floor beside him, his hand on Father's, that I said, 'Is he one of you?'

'Of course,' said Hassan gently.

'For how long?'

'Years.' I was faintly shaken, though why I should be I really didn't know. But it was odd to know he was dying outside the church he had raised us in.

'He's not a Christian any longer?' I asked uneasily. Mirza Hassan released Father's hand, stood up and walked to the window. He stood looking out on darkness, and said with his back to me, 'In any way that might matter, I'm sure he is yet . . .' He turned and smiled, his smile-statement. 'Do you understand?'

'I think so,' I said. But I was glad that Geoffrey was not there.

In the morning, I was awakened by Hassan at five. It was dark out, and raining. He was standing by my bed, looking down at me sleeping, a privilege no other man had had.

'Justina?'

'Is it morning?'

'Your father is free,' he said.

I met Douglas off the train at Strathpeffer station, on a rainy November day. He climbed wearily down the steps of the last carriage, carrying his own kit bag. He had travelled light, and not bothered even with his batman. He had travelled in haste as well, and had not slept. His face was thin, his eyes shadowed. He tossed the kit down on the station platform and reached to light a cigarette before we had even spoken. Then he leaned forward and kissed my cheek. His fingers around the cigarette were shaking.

'Godawful journey,' he whispered. 'How are you, my dear?' He smiled, a wan chivalrous smile and said, 'I say, you do look fetching in that.' I was in my VAD uniform and cloak.

'Oh, I'm sure,' I said, dryly, but he meant it. He put an arm round my shoulders as we walked to the hotel. I could not remember him ever having been so affectionate. Behind him was the great battle at Loos, which we had celebrated as a victory.

We left the following morning for Arradale. Wilhemina had arranged for the funeral, as indeed she arranged everything. I was grateful; it was a task I could barely face, and her determination, in her advanced pregnancy, was admirable. But of course it was a very Christian funeral and I worried in secret that I was betraying Father by not speaking out. I confided in Mirza Hassan but he only smiled and said, 'Can there be two Gods, Justina?' and I realized I had worried for nothing.

But there was trouble at the funeral, anyhow. Local people at the churchyard had seen Hassan, dark and foreign, and word got out that there was a Turkish spy amongst us. That same evening, a constable was at the door, sent away with some fervour by Douglas. It was ridiculous, but such was the climate of the day. I wondered what would become of Hassan, among hostile strangers now, without Father's patronage.

That evening, we of the younger generation gathered in the drawing room, a little self-consciously filling the roles of our dead parents. Wilhemina succeeded best at this, but then, she had not a childhood's worth of memories to vanquish there. It is most difficult to play the lady and gentleman in the rooms where one indulged one's nursery whims. Clare had travelled up from London for Father's burial, but neither Alexander nor Geoffrey could attend. Eugenia and May had telegrammed their condolences. Eugenia's were terribly formal and distant; death was not an easy subject for her now. But I wondered often after if no memory remained of the dun-coloured stallion that no one could ride, and the wayward chestnut mare.

May's telegram was quite simple:

BEFORE ABRAHAM WAS! ALLELUIA!

'Charming,' murmured Douglas, upon my reading it aloud. It was puzzling, like all his answers to everything.

He seemed immensely mellowed, like an old, old man grown wise with the torments of life. I suppose it was precisely what he was. There seemed no anger left in him, nor any arrogance. Nothing could arouse him beyond his gentle compliance and his mind seemed far, far away. Even Clare brought only a brotherly, thoughtful response, though of course they had long been enemies. Ironically, they now at last stood on the same side of an argument and defended the same cause, at least in logical theory.

But Douglas deflected Clare's praise as smoothly as he eluded any other tributes to his gallantry. 'One does one's job, my dear, that's all.' And though she bridled and seemed dissatisfied, he would go no further, regardless of how often she raised the subject. She was as fervent in support of the fighting in France as once she had been of fighting in the streets, and was constantly finding new ways each of us might support our country. When she suggested quite seriously to Wilhemina that her imminent offspring, if female, might be christened Christabel Britannia, Douglas got up and left the room.

I followed him quietly down the corridor. He was wandering aimlessly, looking in his newly refurbished house, for some place of old memory in which to go to ground. He ended in the old kitchen, where we had shared our nursery teas, and I slipped in behind him and sat down across the table. He looked up, raising his head from his hand.

'Oh, thank God it's you,' he said. 'I don't think I could stand any more.' I sat in silence, and very slowly he began to talk. 'You know,' he said, his tone almost quizzical, 'it isn't at all like what one was brought up to expect.' He sighed, stretched his long legs, furrowing his brow as he struggled with thought. Iconoclasm did not come easy to Douglas. 'I suppose that's why it's so damnably difficult to talk about. I mean, there just isn't any common ground, is there? Clare, Wilhemina, they're wonderful girls. They mean terribly well, I know that. I do *know* that. Only,' he paused again, screwing up his eyes tight, 'only I wish they'd both fucking shut up.' I guess he heard my gasp, involuntary and horrified. He opened his eyes. 'Oh Jesus Christ, Justina. Forgive me.' He reached for me with both arms and I ran into his embrace. Sobbing over my head, he began to talk, at last, great gusts of words, tumbling out in confusion. 'The noise, damn it. The noise is the worst of all. Sometimes I just pray we'll get a bloody Jack Johnson on top of our heads just to shut out the noise forever. If only I could sleep,' he whimpered. 'And the way men *die* out there . . . it isn't just neat bullet-holes and white crosses in the ground, you know. God, what a mess that stuff makes of a man . . . blood, guts, brains, shit . . . all over everything. All over us . . . all over . . . oh, Christ, Justina why am I telling you this?'

'Tell me,' I whispered. 'Tell me.' I was seeing the face of my English officer at Strathpeffer as he spoke and I clung to it, as to a crucifix.

'And the whole God-damned thing is so ludicrous. Ludicrous! They're idiots. Idiots. They tell us to attack for no reason, and retreat for no reason, and march, and kill and die for no reason. There's not a one of our staff officers ever comes to even see . . . it's all gone crazy . . . there's so much lost and nothing ever won . . .'

'But you won at Loos,' I cried stupidly.

'Loos?' he spat. 'Loos was a disaster.'

Saying that seemed to settle something in him, and he did not seem to want to talk further. He sat stony silent, staring at the flags of the floor. When he looked up, his face was its familiar controlled mask, and he even smiled slightly. 'Oh dear, what a night. What a day. I say, how about a cup of tea? There's no one about.'

I smiled and went to the old range, like a child

approaching something forbidden. When we were very small, we would at times creep down to the sleeping kitchen and make meals for ourselves in the night. It was not food at such hours that drew us, but the chance to perform acts forbidden us; acts sacred to the servants. They were more familiar acts now; VADs soon learned to make tea. I found the huge old kettle, as old no doubt as both of us, and put it on the range. After a while it filled the quiet kitchen with steam and I made the tea. While we drank it, he spoke of Geoffrey.

'He would have got leave, you know. Chaplains do. But he wouldn't ask. He said Father didn't need him. Said something about Mirza Hassan, actually, but I didn't understand it. But it wasn't ill-feeling, you know. He just couldn't bear to leave the others . . . one does feel that. And I suppose, being a chaplain . . . I mean being *his* kind of chaplain . . .' he looked up at me with great candour. 'Do you know,' he said, 'he is most incredibly courageous.' He sipped his tea. 'He's never out of the Front Lines. Not like half the Piskies I've known, tucked up in the rear with the Staff, most of them!' He laughed, puzzled. 'And there's Geoffrey, still looking the prize fool, big ears, freckles, just the same . . . up there in the lines, day after day. Never sleeps that I can see. Never stops smiling. Jesus, how can he smile? Spent all one night in front of our wire, in a shell-hole, trying to comfort some poor sod, blown half to bits. Even the stretcher parties couldn't get to him. Not that there was much point. We reckon when there's fifty per cent gone, we leave the rest . . .' he laughed, a gruesome laugh, 'But Geoffrey just stayed there, fire all around, talking and joking with the bastard, giving him water and morphia and holding that mess in his arms. Jesus. It's as if he could hold the whole thing at bay himself, right all the wrongs.

I can hardly fathom it's still him . . . he was always such a twit, you know?'

I nodded, stunned. He looked up at me and smiled. 'If that's what faith does, my dear, I wish I had it,' he said.

Douglas' leave lasted four more days. The birth of his child was due at the end of that week. I saw him looking upon Wilhemina like a longing six-year-old upon his mother, as if she might suddenly produce that miracle early, like a sweetie from an apron pocket. The miracle was not achieved. Douglas went back to the Front without seeing his son who was born three days later. I stayed on with my sister-in-law as long as I could. The baby was fine and strong and the name chosen for it, very deliberately by Douglas, was Hugo. He had told Wilhemina, and told me, and even written it down. Christabel Britannia, or any masculine variants, were not to be entertained.

I returned to Strathpeffer and took up my VAD duties once more. Mirza Hassan came with me. Briefly, he occupied Father's old suite of rooms in the Ben Wyvis Hotel, but only long enough to put in order what remained of Father's already well-ordered papers, send most to his London publisher, and entrust the rest to me. When that task was done, he came to me to tell me he was leaving the country. I was not surprised, though very sad. Father was his only reason to be here, and Father was gone. He had little cause to love Britain, a country that treated him with suspicion and distaste. But he was not bitter, only sorrowful at leaving me. He spoke of going to Palestine, to the shrine of his faith, at Akka, where there was a community. But he and I both doubted he could reach that place in the midst of the war, and he thought, failing that, he would make for America. Though Father's will had made handsome provision for him, he scrupulously used only the barest necessity of that sum, and returned the rest to me. When I said farewell to him at the railway station, it was like saying farewell to my father at his graveside. Like Father, he was going empty-handed as he had come, into a complete unknown. He bowed over my hand as we parted.

'I love you,' I said. He smiled, courteously.

'Let Allah weave,' he said. He stood at attention, his hand raised to his fur hat in salute, as the train pulled away.

12

Douglas was killed in France at Christmas time. He died leading a raiding party on a segment of German trench relinquished the following day. For twenty-four hours, fifty yards of France were ours. It was a death whose purpose and meaning were known only to the mysterious mind of God. We were informed by the dreaded telegram to Arradale, received by Wilhemina. I learned by telephone in the crowded foyer of the Ben Wyvis Hotel. I telegrammed Clare and May. May telegrammed Eugenia and James. Sandy was informed by his regiment, and from Geoffrey we heard nothing at all.

Douglas was buried in France. Wilhemina, in her powerful way, won permission to visit his grave. She did so; returned silent to Arradale, packed her personal possessions and, taking her son and her entourage of staff, retreated to the Kentish home of her parents. For the first time since Justin Quigley's fortune built it there, Arradale Castle stood empty on the lonely shore of Loch Ewe.

After Douglas' death, there were no visitations, no dreams. His departure, like his life, was formal and businesslike. All his affairs were long since in order, his will written, witnessed and signed. Nothing was left to chance, except, I suppose, his poor young life. I hoped, with little reason, that he found some segment of the faith he had envied, to comfort him in his dying hour.

Wilhemina stayed two days in Strathpeffer, on her way south. She was noble in her grief, and my original distaste for her was long forgotten. Austerity suited her; she wore widow's weeds well. The war was changing everyone, and what had once been foolish, attained grandeur, and what had seemed grand, appeared often a frivolity. The marching bands, the music, and the fine speeches grew hollow. But I could not forget the nobility of my brother's widow, mounting the train steps with my brother's fatherless son.

'When it's over . . .' Wilhemina whispered to me, an open vague promise for Arradale.

'Safe journey,' I said, and the train pulled away. She held her baby's hand upon a little handkerchief and they jointly waved goodbye. I turned round on the station platform; it was snowing and the hills were lost in mist. I remembered my dream of trains and snow at Achterneed, and realized that I was, as then, alone in all the North.

My superiors, perhaps conscious of this as well, suggested I take a leave of absence and go to London to stay with my sister Clare, or visit my Irish cousins in Dublin. When I refused that, they offered me a transfer to a London hospital, if I should prefer. At first I declined that as well; I could not see where changing my physical locality would alter the changes that had occurred in my life. Nor was I really lonely. Those whom I mourned could not in this world be replaced. And, that accepted, I was not without friends. I had my work at the hospital, the unending stream of letters to those of my family who remained, and I had my painting.

Word of my late abandoned talent soon got out, and I was kept as busy as I might like with volunteers for sittings. I sketched and painted all my fellow VADs, and there was soon a vogue among my patients for miniature pencil portraits to be sent home to mothers, wives or fiancées. These, of necessity, were done in haste, lest Sister see me busy with anything other than my appropriate duties. It became very good training, as I learned by force to produce a likeness from a handful of lines in a handful of minutes. I also learned to lie; faces thinned by dysentery, eyes hollowed by harrowing sights, were better presented to those back home with a little graceful flattery. It, too, was a useful skill I would be grateful for in future years. In the world of commercial portraiture, it is vital that the artist be capable of totally honest reproduction. It is also vital that she know when and when not to use it.

My days were full, and I was more or less content. The withering reality of other people's miseries is a fine anodyne for one's own. I began to live again, to attend parties, to go walking with friends. One day I went to the storerooms of the Ben Wyvis and looked out our old pairs of skis, left there untouched for years. Mine and Michael's stood yet against a wall, side by side. I took his down, stroked the carefully waxed wood, brushing the dust off, and put them back. Then I lifted my own, and carried them out into the snowy daylight. I ski'd every day I could that late winter, and early spring. Now I wore trousers, loose, knee-length breeches, as voluminous as any skirt, but trousers all the same. Times had changed.

I would perhaps have served out the war there, in my highland retreat, had I not received a letter that spring, quite unexpectedly, from the disfigured English officer whose portrait I had sketched. It came from the 3rd London General Hospital, from what was titled the 'Masks for Facial Disfigurements Department', and was addressed simply to VAD Melrose, Strathpeffer. I opened it with a mixture of astonishment and slight, dishonourable fear. It was not unknown for patients in great distress to fall fatally in love with the first kind nurse they met. Many of my compatriots had had the painful awkwardness of having to reject such sad suitors. I had had two of my own, and did not want a third, particularly not one like this. It was shameful of me, and thoroughly vain. I flattered myself, and did him disservice, quite forgetting his true nature, in the months that had passed.

11 February 1916

My dear Miss Melrose,

Do please forgive my forwardness in writing without an appropriate introduction, but in our way we do have a certain acquaintance, and my purpose, though most friendly, is not frivolous.

I wish firstly to assure you that my recovery progresses at pace, spurred on, no doubt, by the wonderful encouragement I received under your care. It has been my great good fortune to fall into the care of Captain Derwent Wood, a man who in both genius and compassion is equally blessed.

He is a sculptor of the Royal Academy whose talents have, during wartime, been put to use in a most remarkable way. After much care and research, he has succeeded in fashioning, with infinite delicacy, the most wonderfully clever masks to be worn by patients in my situation. I cannot stress enough the marvel of his work. With such a device, I will be able to go out about the business of the world, in a way that otherwise would not have been possible. (Not everyone possesses your beautiful sang-froid.)

The crux of the matter, of which I write, is this: there is an immense amount of work in this department to be done. Derwent Wood is tireless, and heroic, but alas only human, and surely would benefit from assistance, but the work by its very nature requires the highest degree of artistic skill. I thought of you at once.

Forgive my intolerable boldness, but I have already spoken to Derwent Wood myself, on your behalf. I assure you, I would not have done so had I not been so driven by an awareness of the needs of my fellow sufferers, and of your shared concern for them.

Begging you again to forgive this intrusion in the good faith in which it was made,

I am
your faithful servant
Captain (the Hon.) James Hartingdon
Duke of Wellington's

One does not say no to such a letter. Whatever my trepidations regarding the work ahead, most of them founded in a real uncertainty that my skills were up to the mark, there was only one course to take. I approached my superiors at the hospital and received their ready assent. Within a fortnight an exchange of letters between Strathpeffer and the 3rd London General had completed the transaction proposed by James Hartingdon. Another month would see me ensconced as artistic assistant to the Masks for Facial Disfigurements Department, otherwise known as the Tin Noses Shop. I packed my now modest and workaday wardrobe and my easel and paints and made the round of farewells before setting out. I had a week's leave in which to do so, and spent most of it enjoying spring snow on the hill. At last my goodbyes of all sorts completed, I stood my skis against the wall in the storeroom, by Michael's once more, and booked my railway passage south. Then, a day before I was to leave for London, they sent Geoffrey home.

A telegram preceded him; cryptic and unexplanatory. It did little but disturb. There were references to 'his condition', to his need of rest and nothing else. I telegrammed Clare, and received this reply:

SAW G. IN LONDON HOSPITAL. NO WOUND.
USE OWN JUDGEMENT. C.

I was mystified, and angry. If Geoffrey had been in hospital in London I should have known about it. I did not understand what Clare was thinking of. But now, without Douglas nearby, I had only Clare's assessment to go on. Alexander was on the Somme with his own battalion and had not seen Geoffrey for months. I met the appointed train in confusion. When he stepped down from the carriage looking quite normal, and apparently deep in conversation with a young private soldier on whose shoulder his hand lightly rested, I felt, for one cruel moment, a touch of Clare's testy indignation. What was he doing here, delaying my departure? Then he turned his face directly towards me without recognition and I saw at once that he was blind.

They placed him in a ward for shell-shock victims, which was deceptive, and caused confusion in the family. Shell-shock was not well understood, even within the medical services, certainly not by the innocent public. There was a resonance of blast injury in the naming of it that was unfortunate. The uninitiate looked still for signs of physical damage, and failing to find them, retreated into suspicion. Geoffrey's healthy, if thin body and his perfect unblemished eyes baffled everyone. All that was lacking was sight, and that lack, being utterly subjective, was hardly convincing. Judgements ranged from 'hysteria' to 'lack of moral fibre' to, harshest of all, 'plain cowardice'. Geoffrey had a hard time at Strathpeffer. Far from the Front, it was not an enlightened place.

But Geoffrey *was* blind. He could not see, and that fact, real enough, baffled him as much as anyone. At least he had me as an ally, though I guiltily knew that had it not been for Douglas' attestation of his bravery, I might not have believed him either. The doctors and medical staff believed him, I suppose. Still, unable to offer either explanation or cure, they retreated to the comfort of convention, patted his head and suggested a quiet retreat to some country vicarage to recover. Geoffrey knew precisely what they meant.

I had, of course, postponed my departure immediately upon his return, and devoted the next fortnight exclusively to his care. He was not a demanding patient. He was friendly and helpful to everyone around him, insisting on doing most everything for himself; making his own bed, seeing to the needs of others when he could. He had already adapted remarkably to his sightlessness. In the afternoons, he would sit talking with other patients, or allow me to lead him out on to the terrace, where a sudden warm spell provided thin sunlight and light spring breezes. We sat side by side, I surveying the lovely valley and distant blue hills of the Aird, he nodding gently in response to my description. He had changed beyond recognition from the pompous, opinionated boy who had clumsily danced on that same new floor with the suffragette, Meggie Whyte. It was four days before I dared to ask if he'd heard from her.

'Oh, of course, of course,' he said, adding gently, 'Dear soul.' He was silent for a long while. At last he said hesitantly, 'It's hard when they're very young. She *is* very young, you know.' After another silence he told me that Meggie had come to see him in the London hospital, along with Clare. He didn't say much. I gathered there was not much to say. She cried a lot. I had an image of her red-nosed and self pitying, whimpering into a lace handkerchief by his bed. 'Of course it was terribly awkward to talk. One couldn't expect . . .' He trailed off. Meggie had left with Clare and he'd heard from neither since.

At the end of the week, Geoffrey persuaded me that my presence was unnecessary, and I would be of far more use with Derwent Wood in London, as planned. He anticipated already a slow, but sure recovery. 'Oh, it'll sort itself, it's probably just a nervous thing. I've always been prone to nervous things, haven't I? Remember all those rashes and things I'd get when we were children? Poor Mother, chasing after me with lotions . . .' He laughed apologetically. I felt uneasy leaving him, but he insisted, and in the end I agreed. It was only after he had extracted this promise from me, and released me from any responsibility, that he opened his heart and really talked to me. It was the last afternoon before my rescheduled departure. The weather had changed; the day, starting bright, turned sullen, and as evening was falling, snow began to fall with it. We sat yet on the terrace, in coats and scarves.

'We must go in,' I said. 'You'll get chilled.'

He laughed suddenly, a totally new laugh, strong and sardonic and then he said, 'No fear, little sister. I've slept in a mud ditch all winter. I'm past the reach of such things.' He leaned his head back against the headrest of his chair, closed his sightless eyes and whispered, 'I'm past the reach of everything.' He kept that posture, his hands tense on the wicker chair arms, one forefinger lightly tapping a rhythm of recall. Then he said, speaking very slowly, 'I was giving this poor chap communion . . . he was one of my rare few . . . really religious, daily communicant . . . and then a shell came over, went off in the next bay . . . must have been a shell splinter or something came across . . . there was a lot of dust, noise, the usual.' He gulped, and swallowed. 'Then suddenly the dust had cleared, and I was holding the Host in front of this big red hole . . . whole head, gone . . . just . . . oh Jesus.' He lifted one hand and laid it across his blind eyes. 'Damn the bastard.' I waited until he had swallowed back the tears. 'I was all right, you know. I went about laying out the body, anointing it . . . but the next morning, I woke up and it was still dark, and then I realized it wasn't really dark because everyone was moving about, quite normally, and it *was* morning. Only, I was dark. They took me to the MO and he sent me down to the CCS and they sent me to Rouen, and then London, and then here.' He shrugged, becoming more in control and said plaintively, 'I swear I'm not funking it, my dear. I'd do anything to see again, and to go back. But I can't.'

I looked down on him, my heart full of useless compassion. He was, despite his thinness and pallor, still red-headed, freckle-faced, big-eared Geoffrey, a saint in a fool's body. 'It'll be all right, darling,' I said, 'It's only shock. You'll get over it. All of it . . .' I reached to touch his hand and he grasped mine in his. It was cold and sweaty and shook against mine until he grounded both on the chair arm.

'You know,' he said, 'most of the chaps are lucky. They just think it's twaddle . . . there isn't any God or anything. But I know different. I *know* there's a God . . . I know it. He's there, all right. And he hates us. We murdered his Son and now he hates us. He'll have blood from us all.' He paused, drawing a sharp inward breath, whispering in amazement, 'He *hates* . . . and *I hate Him*. Oh Justina, you cannot conceive how much I hate Him!' He gasped and I reached for him, but as my hand brushed his cheek he turned sharply away, burying his blind eyes in the cups of his palms. I heard him whisper very softly, 'Oh, the Innocents. The Innocents.' Or perhaps 'The Innocence!' I could not tell from the sound, and it seemed not to matter anyway.

That was the man I left behind in Strathpeffer that wintry April morning in 1916. I promised him I would return north at my next leave and he assured me he would be recovered long before and would see me in London on his way back to the Front. And so we gaily kissed, and joked and lied, brother and sister together, and parted. I watched him waving blankly into darkness as I walked, case in hand, to the train.

I spent the night in Edinburgh at the North British Hotel, and the next evening was in London, at Clare's flat in Callow Street, where nothing had changed but the colour of the bunting over her bed. I had arranged to stay with Clare at least until I could find a place in a nurses' hostel or a flat of my own. I had doubts about our compatibility for any extended period; so much of our natures and beliefs were beginning to run different ways. But there were financial considerations to be made. Naturally there was no pay involved with my VAD nursing. It was quite rightly assumed that ladies endowed with sufficient leisure time for such work had also sufficient means of support. Gentlemen's daughters, middle-class wives, their own servants, brought in under their wings; we were all what was called of independent means. Which meant, as in my case, that we had always been, and would always be, supported by the wealth of some man. Clare had earned her own living with the WSPU, but she, like myself, had behind her our father's fortune, now transferred to Douglas and, in his will, in measured portion, to ourselves. I had enough to keep me, if not lavishly, without need to worry, for a reasonable number of years, after which it was still assumed I would marry. But my resources were not unlimited; Douglas' judgement had been clear. Too much money, and I might not choose to marry at all, and remain forever a drain upon his estate. That must be preserved, for his wife, and most important, his son. He had guarded carefully against dilution. We were but suckers of the family tree, of uncertain worth. The main root stock must be made secure.

So, in Clare's flat, we two aberrant daughters pooled

our resources and set up camp, for what I imagined would be the duration of the war. There was much talk of a big push in the coming summer that would bring victory and peace. I decided after a day or two that I could tolerate Clare, and she me, for just about that long, and no more.

The mass abandonment of the suffragette cause, and its replacement by an equally virulent patriotism had a destructive effect upon Clare. Her loyalty to Christabel Pankhurst was supreme, and though Miss Pankhurst engendered such devotion in many, many others, it always faintly mystified me regarding Clare. I had thought her a leader; it was years before I realized she was not that, but that equally dangerous thing, an unquestioning second-in-command. But her war work, unlike the Votes for Women campaign, was passive. From being a violent creature, she had become a voyeur of violence, a far less attractive thing. Perhaps she realized, because, as the war progressed, she became depressed and moody, raging against one German atrocity after another, willing to believe the most unbelievable charges about the enemy, while countenancing not one word of reproach against ourselves. Now that conscription, introduced in February, had ended the need of recruitment, her skills of incitement, speech-making, and writing were oddly impotent, and like an engine out of gear she whirred louder and louder into hysterical, and useless fury. I pleaded with her to take up nursing, not because I thought it particularly noble, but because I knew her to be always the better for action. She protested angrily that her talents, that is, her skills of the spoken and written word, were the equal of mine, and her work equivalent to mine in the Tin Noses Shop. That I was repairing, while she was exacerbating, passed her notice. My suggestion ended in a furious row, and a sudden spate of tears from Clare. It was then, too late, I remembered her fear of blood, and helpless shrinking from the sights and sounds of pain, and I was sorry to have brought her to shame.

When I arrived at the Masks for Facial Disfigurements Department, James Hartingdon, had already gone, back out into the world behind his new, superbly painted metal face. A letter arrived shortly after, saying he had found work in a bank some distance from his father's country seat. I wondered if the decision not to go home had been his, or theirs. I found Francis Derwent Wood a marvellous artistic enthusiast, with that sturdy mechanical bent that often marks the sculptor, and sets him off from the painter whose visions are in two dimensions, not three. But he was, also, an excellent painter as well, and it was at his side that I learned to depict in enamels the colours of humanity upon his exquisitely moulded electro-plated masks. Before him, on his workshop table, half cheeks, eye hollows, chins, jaws, brows, were laid out, shining and silver before a row of photographs of the faces, now gone, they were designed to replace. Sometimes, when a photograph was unavailable, I would be sent to the soldier in question to draw freehand an image of the face that had been. Such occasions, far from harrowing, were often full of humour, and I was permanently startled by the immense courage of these poor creatures who would laugh and tease me and insist, 'No, Nurse, my nose was *twice* that long.'

'It *couldn't* be. You'd look like Pinocchio!'

'Now, Nurse, we're none of us to blame for the faces we were born with,' a solemn nod of the head. 'What you lot give us is another matter.' Another solemn glance at my drawing. 'Sorry, Nurse. If I told you the truth of how handsome I was you'd be so wildly in love with me, there'd be no holding you back. A man's his virtue to think of, you know.'

I loved them all. Who would not have done?

The work was immensely involving, and though not every patient managed the cheeriness of 'Pinocchio' they were wonderful partners, all of them, in the reconstruction of their faces, and lives. We had our bad times; we had sudden relapses, and deaths. We had suicides, more than once the result of our chief horror, the necessary, but gruelling first visits of families and fiancées. I saw the best, and the worst of human nature. But there was heroism among the women too, faced with a gargoyle in their marriage bed. Not all fell to whimpering, or broke out in hysterical screams. Some were saints, whose awesome task I could barely countenance. Nor did it help to glamorize; they were mostly very young, innocent girls, whose marriages of a few months must now weather a half-century under gruesome strain. Naturally I sided with my poor, tortured patients, but I could not, could never, condemn the women who fled in terror out of their lives.

Fortunately, such occasions were rare. We were busy, active, full of hope, and in an odd way, the war that was the cause of it all was pushed out of consciousness in our intense, claustrophobic world. So, too, was much else that was occurring on the outside, which might possibly explain why, that third week in April, the arrest of the Irish Nationalist Sir Roger Casement in Ireland, emblazoned across news placards, aroused no bells of alarm.

Ireland was not large in my thoughts that spring. Like most of the rest of Britain, I had found my attention drawn inevitably to Europe and beyond. May Howie's letters from Dublin showed that much the same was occurring there as well. I received one during my second week in London in which she expressed her concern for Geoffrey, described the struggle to get paper supplies for her small publishing house, and added the sad footnote that Rupert French, my erstwhile suitor, had been killed by sniper fire, near Béthune. So, had I become a wife, I would be now a widow, anyhow. It saddened me, and brought back a startlingly clear picture of him, on his knees in Phoenix Park.

Such things were now constant in all our lives. Clare proudly told me upon my arrival that Richard Underwood, my companion of art school days, had made 'the final sacrifice' the week before. As if a man *chose* a bullet through his lungs, of his own free will. Poor Richard and his chocolate box landscapes; he deserved a gentler end. Each letter from Eugenia and James named some Sligo champion, fallen in the fray. It was everywhere, and everyone's purpose was turned towards France, or Salonika or Palestine. Home Rule, agreed to but not granted in 1914, lay in abeyance like Votes for Women. There would be a time for all of that.

Sandy had just arrived home on leave when news of the Easter Rising first came. I remember we were walking from Victoria Station, arm in arm, when we heard two women discussing it. They were Irish women, poor, working class women, and their faces were red with outrage.

'To think o' such a thing, wit' our own boys in France!'

'Ireland's undyin' shame.'

We bought newspapers, and read what we could. Not a lot, in a censored press. But word of it was everywhere, though only as a counterpoint to more serious matters of the War. Alexander stopped in the street to read and dropped the paper in the gutter when he was done.

'Idiots,' he said, but there was less anger than sorrow in his voice.

Of course, we were filled with concern for friends and family in Dublin, and communications were limited. Accounts grew lurid, of fighting in the streets, and half of Dublin in flames. We waited in anxiety to hear. And then, quite surprisingly, in the middle of it, a letter arrived from May, quite as normal.

Merrion Square
1 May 1916

Dearest Justina and Clare,

Well, my loves, the pathriots have had their day. Abbey Street is burned one end to the other, the GPO is in ruins, Sackville Street pretty well gone. I suppose it's proved something, if only that our noble Irish architecture pulverizes quite as readily as French. The talk is it was a gunboat on the Liffey, but I have it on reliable information that it was a fishing-smack. Never mind, the explosives were quite as effective, regardless. There have been a lot of deaths, no one is admitting how many, but a good number must be 'innocent' passers-by. Dubliners *will* know what's going on, and watching the fighting was becoming the new sport. Nobody was ever quite sure who was fighting whom. Kate is safe. I can't say where, because I don't know, Mr Censor, if you're reading this. Padraic has been arrested. Something that should have happened years ago.

As far as I can tell, we do not yet have a Republic, in spite of all. We ourselves have been quite safe, though we have heard the explosions, and at night the sky was red with fires. I am now without employment, as our printing house is a pile of bricks, but we are seeking another site. I daresay when I write again it will all have blown over, more or less.

your loving cousin,
May

I was relieved at least that all I knew were safe, and wept few tears for Padraic, imprisoned or otherwise. I wondered what role Kate had played, and knew that if May knew, she would not have committed such information to writing. In time, no doubt, I would learn. May's next letter was dated 10 May:

Dearest Justina and Clare,

I imagine you will have heard the news. We are all quite devastated. Kilmainham is never out of our minds. The executions go on and on . . . who would have thought it would come to this? They were fools, but surely only fools. I do not understand what our Government is thinking of. There is anger and bitterness everywhere, and bafflement in every house. We did not ask for this, but our hearts go out, unwillingly albeit, to these poor misguided men. Ireland will not rest easy with this.

your loving cousin,
May

I read the letter to Sandy. It was the last day of his leave. He sat in his civilian clothes, by the window of Clare's flat, looking down into the courtyard below. The milliner's wife was hanging out washing in the spring sun.

I was as stunned as May at the remorseless executions of the Rising's leaders. In a world already brimming with death, now we were killing our own.

'Why are they doing this?' I said.

'Treason is treason,' he said. He did not sound convinced.

'It wasn't treason,' I said. 'It was vaudeville.'

'They killed people. Destroyed a large chunk of city,' he mused over a cup of tea. 'Hardly vaudeville.'

'It was *theatre*,' I said again. 'It was all for show. How would they ever have won?'

'Whether they would have won or not is not the point,' he said. 'The lesson is that they don't try again. The Empire has her back to the wall. This summer is the clinch. We've no time for sideshows, vaudeville or not.'

'Would *you* have executed them?' I demanded. He looked at me coolly, his intelligent green eyes unblinking.

'Would I have? Justina, three weeks ago I executed two of my own men for running away under fire. Cowardice. Poor blighters scared half to hell by the noise and all the rest. Turned around and ran. Perfectly normal. Intelligent, even. But not to be allowed, or the rest will follow. A lesson for the rest, my dear. That's all.'

'It's criminal,' I said.
'And the rest of what we're up to is not?'

12 May 1916

Dearest Justina and Clare,

Today, strapped to a chair because he could not even stand, they shot James Connolly. *What is the purpose of this?*

Yours in sorrow,
May

I received one more letter from Ireland that week. I opened it in haste, not noticing the handwriting or the postmark, until I saw that it was not from May.

Easter 1916

My dearest cousin Justina,

Michael is avenged. *Requiescat in Pace.*

Kate

The postmark was Galway. She was on the run; joyous and unrepentant. Later, I learned from May, Padraic joined her there. He had escaped his imprisonment, and like Kate, gone to ground. Two months later, in a Catholic church in County Sligo, they were wed. None of the family was there to see, but she thoughtfully sent each of us, Clare, myself, May, and her mother, a flower for remembrance of her. There were sixteen red roses in her wedding bouquet.

'Sentimental ass,' said Clare. She threw her rose aside. But I held mine, and pictured Kate on her pony on the day we met, bowing down to give her hand of welcome to Clare; the perfect Irish county lady. It was the first of July, 1916, the opening day of the great battle on the Somme. All week, along the whole south coast of England, they heard the guns, and even in London I could feel them, a faint tremble, like an earth tremor, beneath our feet. The china trinkets on Clare's mantel rattled and shook. I was still holding my rose when the knock came at the door. I opened it, and standing on our outside staircase was the milliner's wife and the telegram boy in his uniform.

'Miss Justina Melrose?' he said.

'Oh God, Clare,' I cried. 'It's Alexander.' She came running, but when I opened the envelope I found the cable was from the Highland Hotel hospital in Strathpeffer. Captain the Reverend Geoffrey Melrose was dead.

13

On Christmas Day 1917, my twenty-fourth birthday, I sailed for France. I was taking up a nursing position in the great base hospital at Etaples, and travelled in a party of four other VADs and an older Nursing Sister. The crossing was rough and stormy and made at full steam, as we bucked against an angry wind, in haste against the U-boats. Everyone was sick, except me. Persephone's old reminder of my being a seaman's granddaughter stayed with me, a latent hypnosis. I stood at the rail, watching the angry sea and half looking for the white trail of torpedo wake. In the east the French coast emerged as a blackness against first light. All around us it was still night. I had a vivid awareness of the old phrase, 'the dark hour before the dawn'. The war had become an endless night, and though I did not know, that darkest hour before the day lay yet ahead of us.

The war was three years old. The great Somme offensive had failed. Third Ypres, the awful battle for Passchendaele, had failed. The cost in casualties was so shattering that every household was in some way touched.

Conscription stripped the nation of its youth. Honour and duty, those flags we had followed into the great conflict, fluttered meaninglessly. The implication of choice upon which they had rested was gone.

The London I had left behind was grey and grim. Food was short, and rationed. Zeppelin raids had been supplanted by aeroplane raids. The city was dangerous, and the civilian population tired, testy and frustrated. But I did not leave because of greyness or deprivation. I was going to a greyer, more dangerous place. I left because hatred, once a periphery of civilized life, had grown huge in the national heart, had become, like love, a cure for all ills, for shortages, for fear, for bereavement and disappointment; even for personal ills like the loneliness of loveless women. Clare brooded upon the war like a spider with a webful of flies.

The war paper *Britannia* (once the *Suffragette*), for which she contributed articles, now concentrated all its efforts in a purge of aliens, the foreign-speaking, or sounding, anything remotely connected with the enemy. German shops were closed, along with shops of any suspect name, windows were broken, little German dogs were stoned in the street. The WSPU had transformed itself into The Women's Party, and its aims into an ever fiercer pursuit of the enemy, at home and at the Front. I remembered sadly the old table in Clare's flat around which we had talked of a fine and holy world where women ran the parliaments and made the laws and how, in that gentle, distaff era, there would be no more wars.

The night before I sailed, Clare and Meggie Whyte took me out for a celebration dinner. It was a peace offering from Clare, who well knew why I was going. I had worked for over a year at the Tin Noses Shop and would have continued perhaps, had it not been for Clare. As I had early anticipated, frictions quickly rose between us, but we had managed to get on, no doubt in part because we were rarely together. Clare had taken a job in a munitions factory, the same one in which Meggie had worked for two years, and that, added to her work for *Britannia*, kept her busy and away from the flat for long hours. My day was long as well. We met often for ten minutes and a cup of tea before bedtime, or to share out a scanty supper. We were both too tired, usually, to even talk.

But one evening in November, when the miseries over Passchendaele were at their height, I foolishly mentioned a young patient I had worked with, who had been remarkable for his cheerfulness under awful stress. Half-way through the story, when I spoke the patient's name, Clare froze in horror. It was only then I realized I had neglected to even tell her he was German. I had grown so accustomed to the fact it really had ceased to matter. Of course we nursed German prisoners, and naturally there were some resentments among even ourselves, particularly those recently bereaved, but such touchiness soon vanished. The war was taxing Germany, too, and she was conscripting school children. A miserable sixteen-year-old crying at night for his mother touches any heart.

'Konrad?' Clare whispered.

'Oh Clare. He's a child.'

'You waste your time on the enemy, while our boys . . .'

'Clare, *please*.'

'While Alexander faces death at every hour . . . and Douglas lies in his grave, and Geoffrey . . .'

'Germans didn't kill Geoffrey, Clare.'

She was silent then. The truth about Geoffrey was not to be discussed. She stood up, brushed her skirt down with nervous hands and stalked about the room. At last she said, 'I hope at least you make them wait their turn.'

'Oh, certainly,' I said wearily. 'They're not even allowed to *die* without our permission. I'm going to bed.'

That night I lay awake for hours in my tiny room, thinking of my brothers and all they had gone through, and Alexander alone in France. Suddenly I wanted to be with him, to share the danger he faced somehow for all of us, and to share a measure of what might be our last days together. He was the last of my brothers, and the war had a long way to run. It was as much that as anything that made me apply, the next day, for a transfer to Etaples, no doubt as near Alexander and the Front as I was likely to get. But a good part, too, was a sudden fierce need to get away from Clare. She had become a symbol of all that curdled bitterly in the wounded British heartland. Sometimes I had fearful fantasies, imagining the shells she made shattering the faces of men for me to rebuild, so like some doomed Penelope I wove each day a tapestry for her to destroy. Sometimes I wept at night, thinking about it. I think perhaps I stayed too long at the Tin Noses Shop. Its images have stayed with me for the rest of my life.

Clare and Meggie took me to a genteel restaurant in the West End, the best our limited purses could afford. It was filled with women dining alone, Christmas Eve without their men. Conspicuous by their happiness were the lucky exceptions; a young lady in a hat covered with roses clutching the hands of her fiancé across the table, both unable to believe their good fortune: Christmas, and leave, and still together. Meggie looked upon them and twin tears welled up in her big, sad eyes. Clare saw them, and turned away. Meggie still wore black for Geoffrey, though it was more than a year. Bereavement was so universal that even sympathy was rationed. But mourning was a kind of trophy: better to have loved and lost than never been loved at all.

The meal was skimpy, and bland. It was officially a meatless day. It was also apparently everything-else-less as well. We dined early, since the regulation hours were between six and nine-thirty, and after that it was illegal to serve food. Often, after a late night at the hospital, I had brought home hostel girls who depended on cafés for food and because of the rigid hours had missed both lunch and dinner and were truly starving.

Meggie looked glumly at her plate and glumly about the room, her eyes roving to the happy couple. She said suddenly, 'We'll none of us ever marry now. There'll be none left when the War's done.' Votes for Women seemed a long time ago. Since I had precisely no plans for ever marrying, I was unimpressed.

'Oh, pooh,' I said. 'You'll marry if you want to.'

'We shan't,' she said again and then she looked round tearfully and suddenly wailed, 'Oh, who'll look after me?'

It was extraordinary. She had looked after herself alone for years, and worked in factories since she was fifteen. Clare smiled gently and took Meggie's small hand.

'I'll look after you, lambkins,' she said. Clare was, as often, at her nicest with weak women. I wished she could be the same with men. I looked around the room and was abruptly aware of women, as women, the numbers of women everywhere. Women alone, women with other women, women in the streets in factory clothes, and nursing uniforms, and struggling alone with clusters of children. Meggie was right; the natural balance of our generation was gone; almost all the young men I had known were in their graves. 'How odd,' I thought, as we left the restaurant and walked through cold London streets towards home. Near St Martin-in-the-Fields a chorus of convalescent soldiers in bright blue suits sang carols. They seemed as remote from us as monks. They looked to neither left nor right as we passed, but stood motionless between two VADs. They were like prisoners from an alien country, and I *saw* them as prisoners, held captive by women, patiently enduring. Clare ran forward and dropped coins in a Red Cross-decorated soldier's tin hat laid before them.

'Aren't you going to give something?' she said sharply, but I could not take my eyes from the soldiers who had never moved, but kept singing. It was only as I approached with my coins that I saw each of them was blind. I fumbled the coins from my purse, dropped them, and ran. Like Geoffrey, I had had enough. I left London gladly, in the dark of the next morning and, as the ship ploughed across the Channel, with the consciousness of a turncoat, switching sides.

I stayed in Etaples until the end of January, doing the kind of basic nursing and general dogsbody work I had done at Strathpeffer. It was hard and tedious, but the intensity and pressure of the Tin Noses Shop was gone, and I was relieved. It was almost like a brief, seaside holiday, and I even painted, not portraits but daily scenes of life behind the lines, the hospital trains unloading, the rows of Red Cross ambulances, the quay-sides crowded with leave-takers, and the grim, shuffling rows of the gassed and blinded, bound for the darkness of Blighty.

At the end of January I was moved up to Amiens, to another big stationary hospital, and it was there, one February afternoon that, quite out of the blue, a knock came at the door of the room in which I sat rolling bandages, and Sandy strolled in.

I looked up, speechless. I was so startled to see him there that I almost did not recognize him and the weird thought crossed my mind that he was an illusion, a ghost. He wore a greatcoat over his captain's uniform, and one sleeve was empty, his arm folded over his chest in a linen sling. He grinned at my consternation, stepped closer and peered at me in the dim light of the oil lamp.

'Good God, what's happened to your head?' he asked.

My hands flew up to it in instinctive surprise and I cried, 'Sandy, what are you doing here?' as I, with another quick instinct, whirled about, looking out for Sister.

'Relax,' he said, 'I've cleared it all. Connections.' He grinned again knowingly, but continued to peer at my head. Then I realized the source of his curiosity and said impatiently, 'Oh, silly, I've bobbed my hair, that's all. What's wrong with your arm?' I was suddenly the nurse.

'Nothing,' he said, the usual schoolboy response. 'Scratched it on some barbed wire.'

'Oh, grow up,' I said. 'Let me see.' Anyone who had worked in the gangrene wards knew there simply wasn't any 'nothing' where wounds in this war were concerned. But he kept laughing and staring at my hair and when I tried to see his arm, dodged me and with his good hand whipped off my white cap to better see the damage. He let out a great peal of laughter.

'Good God, Justina, only you . . . only you would *dream* . . .'

'Only me nothing,' I snapped. 'Everyone's bobbing their hair.'

'Oh, *certainly*,' he agreed, though quite disbelievingly. 'But only you would end up looking a positive golliwog!' He howled with laughter again, and ruffled my short tight curls. 'Wog! Wog!'

'Shut up. They'll throw you out.'

'Wog, wog, wog!' I've never seen anyone so amused. Eventually, in swinging to hit him, I missed, and grazed the bad arm. That shut him up. 'Jesus!' he whispered.

'Oh Sandy, I'm so sorry.'

'Not half as sorry as I am.' He sat down on the edge of

a chair, and I fussed round him. 'Some nurse,' he muttered. Then he looked at my hair again and sniggered.

I said, chastened, 'I had to Sandy. It was full of lice.' He smiled.

'I like it,' he said honestly. 'Really, I do.' He smiled again. 'Oh, this War,' he said. 'Imagine Mother . . .?'

I shook my head. She'd never know. 'Is the arm really all right?' I said.

He nodded, serious for an instant, 'It's fine, really. I'm not an idiot. They gave me a few days back here to recuperate, but it wasn't much. I hardly felt it at the time.' That wasn't reassuring. I knew what amazing things men sometimes didn't feel during the pressure of battle, or in shock. 'It was just a damned sniper,' he added, rather as one would talk of a pestering wasp. 'Pity though, any other time I'd have got a week or two in Blighty for it. Nothing doing now.' I knew what he meant. Officers and NCOs were a rare commodity and there was persistent rumour of a big enemy push at any time. Anyone capable of functioning authority hadn't a chance of getting home. In a way, for Sandy it hardly mattered. I was the only 'home' he had left, and I was here.

We had grown very close in the years of the war, and from an unpromising beginning had become good friends. I had never detested him, as I had often detested Geoffrey, but in the past we had little in common and little respect for each other's ideals. But such family idiosyncrasies were luxuries when the family, and all the world, were under such threat. He and James Howie were my only male relatives left. And of all our once great rambling Melrose tribe there was only Sandy, myself, and Clare. We, the two youngest, treated her, our elder sister, rather as a child whose tempers and tempestuousness were to be gently humoured, and ignored. The war had given us a savage maturing; she was a master of ideas, but we were masters of life. And yet neither of us, unlike Clare, had any real interest in the war.

By virtue of survival, Sandy now commanded a company, but he had never been a professional soldier like Father, and Jeremy and Douglas, and he had no interest at all in his career. All that mattered to him was the survival of his men, and after that, that he might survive as well. The outcome of the war held little meaning. The only enemies I had heard him speak of for years were the weather, and the Staff. He lived in a faint, wistful hope of a future civilian life in which he would pursue his interest in chemistry in the sacred stillness of the laboratory, remote from politics and the dealings of the world. I knew he had not believed it would really happen, though, for a very long time.

It was my tacit awareness of his hopelessness that bound us closest. He had no pretence with me. It was only between us that Geoffrey's suicide was ever discussed. And suicide it was, without a doubt. At home, a public conspiracy agreed to accept at face value the hospital verdict, a verdict that any nurse knew to be a lie. 'Died suddenly after a relapse' was a code phrase I recognized at once; a phrase I had used more than once, myself. From the 'wound' that Geoffrey suffered, the only 'relapse' possible was the work of his own hand. I knew what had happened, precisely. They had thought his being a clergyman to be safeguard enough; unlike the mutilated James Hartingdon, he had not been protected from himself. It was a sad, shallow assumption, and it failed.

For Clare I had invented some story of an infection; she was pathetically ready to believe me in all our surface converse. Beneath that I did not probe, and Clare readily fled all unpleasantries. But Sandy knew before I even told him, nor had he the slightest wish to condemn. 'Poor simple sod,' was the strongest comment he made.

And so, that left only us. He looked at me fondly, leaning back in the stick-backed chair. He looked big and tough and capable, and the chair seemed silly and feminine beneath him.

'Oh, my little Wog,' he said. 'Poor Wendell. I hadn't prepared him for anything like this.' He said it, conspiratorially, to himself, and when I said, suspiciously, 'Who's Wendell, then?' he shook his head and said, 'Now, now. None of your business.' Another thought had struck him in the meantime and he said curiously, 'I say, speaking of wogs, have you heard anything of old Mirza Hassan?'

'I don't like that, Sandy,' I said sharply.

'Oh, never mind,' he smiled sweetly. 'Take a jest, eh girl? I did *like* him, you know.'

'He's in New York.'

'You don't say?' he looked up brightly, with deepened interest. 'How amazing. Who'd have thought . . .'

'I had a letter a few weeks ago. Wilhemina sent it on. She gets everything for Arradale. He's working in a restaurant, or something,' I said sadly. 'Cooking Persian food. Of all things.'

'Why not?' Sandy said casually.

'Oh, you,' I snapped back. 'What would you know? He's a *brilliant man*, Sandy.'

'He's a peasant, love. Don't romanticize.'

'He wrote half Father's book. I swear it. I worked with them.'

That silenced him briefly and after a while he said, 'Have you heard from the publisher?'

I shrugged, resignedly. 'Everyone agrees it's absolutely brilliant. But unfortunately, during the present time of national trial . . .' I made a small grimace.

'Short of paper?' he asked mildly.

'Shorter of resolve,' I said. He looked puzzled. 'Babism is pacifist, my dear. *The Gateway* will find no publisher until the bloodletting is done.' I was quite angry. He was sorry he raised the subject and sought to dodge it.

'Ah, New York,' he said, musing, again. 'That *is* a turn-up for the books. I say, I must ask old Wendell to look him up when the Show's over.' He leaned back and grinned.

'All right,' I said, still sharply, 'you're on. So *who's* Wendell, I'm meant to say, right? And *will* I be introduced?'

'Come on, Justina,' he said, a trifle hurt, 'I've not done this to you much.' I relaxed.

'Oh, I'm sorry, Sandy. It's just that practically everybody else *has*.'

'I'm not asking you to marry him, love. Just meet him. That's all.' He paused, tiredly and then said, 'It's just that I want you to have *someone*. There's only me left, you know.' He was gloomy and silent and I was abruptly sorry I had fended his honest attempt to look after me.

Chastened, I said as sweetly as I could, 'Go on then, tell me about him. Have you been friends long? Is he an American, then?' He had spoken of New York, and Americans were suddenly amongst us in growing numbers, vigorous and alien, the new novelty. He looked up wryly, and the smile he gave me was a polite struggle against a growing black mood. These things struck him from time to time and made him bitter.

At last he said, looking down at his mud-splattered riding boots, 'They're so young, these Yanks. Young in the war, I mean, they're full of such spirit,' he smiled again, wistfully. I picked up another long strip of lint and began rolling it neatly. It stuck to my fingers, where scabs and rough patches marked all the old sores and infections I was never rid of. I winced and tugged it free. 'They're *survivors*!' he said fiercely. 'Don't you see?'

Slowly I nodded. I knew just what he meant. I felt

strange and very tired. He sat silent while I worked and outside evening turned the two squares of window a darker and darker blue until they were black. The room, lit only by the smoky lamp, grew dim. The brightest thing in it were the bandages, and his white sling. It glowed, folded across his chest, white and luminous.

Suddenly my sore stinging fingers, the hopeless futile work I did, and the image of his white unnatural arm fused into an eerie union, and I sought and sought for their meaning until it came all at once, breaking over me with bright power. I cried aloud, 'Oh Sandy!'

'What is it?'

'Your arm. Look at your arm!' I stood up, backing away from him. 'They're all gone,' I whispered. 'Jemmy and William and Douglas and Geoffrey . . . and there's only us left; and I'm spinning nettles and you have a swan's wing for an arm. Look!' I flung down the bandages onto my table and stood in horror of them, twisting my fingers against each other. 'Sandy, it's all coming true.' I was crying, wide-eyed, staring at the table and as he rushed to put his arms round me, I shrank away from him. Then Sister came bustling in, in amazement.

'It's all right,' Sandy said abruptly. 'Leave her to me.'

'And I should say *not*,' Sister retorted, and he replied with his sharp scathing anger,

'Good God, woman, I'm her brother.' But I smiled at her, shaking my head and saying,

'No. It's all right. I'm his sister, and he's only a swan.' I looked around. The room had gone hazy, and quite suddenly, began to whirl. I was quite aware, as suddenly, of making no sense at all, and when the onrush of faintness became overwhelming, I relaxed into its safety with gratitude.

* * *

What a novelty it all was to find myself a patient, after so long being a nurse. And what a fraud as well. I *might* have had 'la grippe', certainly not the horrendous demon that would attack us all later that year, but a mild variant. I might have had simply that general disability that always struck me when plagued with what Eugenia called 'my visitor'. More likely I think I had nothing but too much excitement, too much work, too much memory. Whatever the cause, it was all my salvation. Sister was not amused. Sandy's 'connections' had not been with her, or Matron, but with a sympathetic orderly, the brother of an NCO in his company. We would all have been in terrible trouble, having broken a raft of rules all to do with the unforgivable mingling of the sexes, brothers or not. But as it was, a great wave of sympathy surrounded me, lapped over on to Sandy and even on to Wendell Pyke who had, unbeknownst to me, waited outside the hospital gate, all that cold February afternoon, until Sandy emerged.

The next day, tucked up in bed in a corner of the nurses' tented quarters, watched over by Sister's anxious eye, I was treated to a proper visitors' hour. Alexander sailed in, clearly unimpressed by my 'illness' and presented me with a ridiculous trinket, a black velvet pincushion embroidered in pink, 'A Souvenir From the Trenches', which he unwrapped with a flourish and thrust unceremoniously on top of my newly cropped head.

'You're an absolute darling,' I said sourly.

'You're an absolute dramatist. You were *always* an absolute dramatist. Justina Bernhardt Melrose. My God, I'd almost forgotten. You and your swans and Jemmy! And that time in Ireland, and Michael's bloody tree!' He was laughing gleefully, and if my premonitions scared him like they scared me, he never let on. He sat back, smiling smugly. 'I've brought a friend.' I looked up, warily, guessing he was lying.

'Sister wouldn't allow it.'

'Special dispensation for dying VADs. I'm serious, love, you'd better get that thing off your head and smarten up.'

'Alexander,' I cried, snatching the pincushion and throwing it back at him, 'You beast.' I looked around for somewhere to hide, but short of diving beneath the bedclothes there was, of course, nowhere. I hadn't even a hairbrush at hand.

I clawed fingers through my tangled curls and glared at him, horribly conscious of my shabby convalescent state. He ignored me, rising to his feet to greet the man who, ducking to slip beneath the open tent flap, came slowly into the dark interior of my 'ward'. He was quite tall, and moved slowly and deliberately with a straight-backed Sandhurst posture. I saw only silhouette against the bright entrance of the big tent; the nipped-in waist, and narrow-calved officer's silhouette. When he came within the circle of oil lamp light I saw his hair was very fair, quite blond. He had a reserved, compelling presence, and by the way Sandy became suddenly clumsy and nervous as he rose to perform our introduction, I knew that he was the dominant party in their friendship.

'Justina, please meet Wendell Pyke, officer, gentleman and ally,' he grinned nervously. 'Wendell, my sister, Justina Melrose.' Sandy stood back and the officer stepped closer and extended a big, long-fingered hand.

'My dear Miss Melrose,' he said, his flat American accent somehow undoing his own formality, 'I do hope you are recovering?'

'Quite splendidly,' I said, taking his hand and throwing a sour sideways glance at Sandy. I couldn't be sure he'd not told his friend what a fraud I was and I suspected Wendell's concern might be prelude to some joint mockery. But he kept up the pretence, anyhow, and sat cautiously by my bedside, studying me carefully, as if expecting me to expire momentarily. Unnerved, I countered by staring back, while Alexander fidgeted in unaccustomed silence. I remember thinking abruptly, 'I never want to paint you. You're handsome beyond truth, there are only four planes to your face, and your eyes tell me nothing.' They were grey, flat and reserved. The face was firm and angular with a prominent straight nose, solid, slightly heavy chin, and long, clean-shaven upper lip. It was a patrician face, and the voice a patrician voice, despite its colonial accent.

He continued to stare at me and then said quite suddenly, 'You're a very brave little lady, but I think you've had quite enough war. You should go home.' My mouth fell open in amazement and before I answered I glared again at Sandy, who was fading into the shadows beyond the lamplight.

'Oh, really?' I said, 'And should I? And how long have you been here, that you know so much about us all? Ten minutes?'

'Justina,' Sandy implored.

'Yanks!' I snapped. And I looked pointedly over Wendell's head, at the dim heights of the tent. Then above its darkness an aeroplane engine droned. Wendell turned to Sandy and looked up for an instant, warily.

'Should be all right,' Sandy said quietly. 'Hardly imagine one would get through to here . . .' his voice trailed off as he listened and Wendell listened. Others had got through often enough; we'd all been bombed and the week before a tented ward had been damaged and a patient and a nurse killed.

'Perhaps you'd better get under the bed,' I said to them both. Wendell looked slowly towards me and Sandy's eyes were on my face, silently signalling, pleading for me to behave.

Wendell smiled, a big broad, relaxed Yankee smile and

he leaned back and said, 'All right, Miss Melrose, I asked for that. No, you shouldn't go home. And yes, I've been here since October, but that's ten minutes compared to what you all have been through. I'm very sorry if I've offended you, but you're just so damned pretty and sweet sitting there, I don't like to think of you in the middle of this.' He shrugged, and smiled sheepishly, and I liked him for his honesty and dutifully apologized.

Sandy instantly relaxed and returned to my bedside, grinning and pleased with himself. I was aware then how much this introduction meant to him; how much he needed us to like each other. I think then, quite immediately, we did like each other, at least as much of each other that each of us was willing to show. Sandy scurried around and persuaded another VAD to find us tea, and even shortbread, and we sat together enjoying this feast, I with a handsome young male on either side of me, quite the honoured lady. We talked about ourselves and our homes, and Wendell was so interesting to me with his descriptions of New York and America and the sea crossing from Hoboken, that I really did not feel that either Sandy or I had much to offer in competition; we seemed very ordinary, and he very glamorous.

He was a West Point graduate, from a family that, like ours, had a military heritage to fulfil. He had come across with General Pershing's 'First Hundred Thousand' and served, with Captain's rank, in the 42nd Division, The Rainbow Boys. The Pyke family was, I suppose, a colonial equivalent of our own, firmly based in New York's 'Four Hundred'. They possessed a townhouse in the city itself, estates on both the north and south shores of Long Island and land in Virginia expressly for keeping their personal supply of bloodstock. They hunted, played polo, and entertained themselves and their friends much as we did, though really with considerably more money, and panache. They had that way of the American aristocracy of being very British in the eyes of their compatriots, while in our eyes, naturally, remaining uniquely colonial. Oddly, it was that latter factor, which often they, and Wendell in particular, tried to suppress, that we ourselves found most attractive. Sandy and I were never quite happy when Wendell was being *very* British. He was quite capable of doing and saying almost everything the same as we did, but always slightly more perfectly. We felt faintly shabby by contrast, and were not yet aware that our very shabbiness, our worn casualness, was the quality he most sought to imitate; the essence of a truly ancient line.

Of course I did not learn all this over a cup of tea around my convalescent's couch. Twenty minutes was our time limit, before Sister's good nature was over-tried, and my honoured guests suitably disposed of. But naturally, we met again. Naturally, but not with the ease which that implies, since even in 1918, the lives of VADs were much oppressed by stern discipline and vaulting morality. We were simply not permitted to meet with officers, not even in the company of our brothers. (Other ranks were esteemed safe enough; no respectable girl would fall in love beneath the great military-social divide.) However, though innocent we might have been, we were not without cunning and guile, and all manner of clever ruses had been worked out by us and our sisters over the years. The standard method was the 'casual' stroll about the town with a trusted VAD friend, and the 'accidental' meeting with, oh surprise, two gentlemen we happen to know. Then the quick dive into the sanctuary of café or hotel lounge, where the two pairs might risk, amid a crowd of strangers, a temporary transformation into couples.

Sandy had a few more days of his recuperative leave; Wendell was actually stationed just outside Amiens. Wendell had seen some action already and was now training new arrivals of compatriots, fresh from Stateside, enthusiastic and innocent. When Wendell described his own leavetaking from Hoboken, the flags and the cheers and the new snappy songs, it was like looking backwards through time to our own selves in 1914, and our country as excited as his at the beginning of the War.

Two days after our first meeting, Wendell and I were together again. I was already back at work in the ward, and had a few hours free one evening, and in response to a written message from Sandy, and quite without thinking why I was doing it, I coerced a friendly London girl, who shared my duties, into a clandestine tryst. She was quite delighted when she saw Sandy, who was thoroughly presentable, and indeed they got on so famously that I really did have most of an evening alone with Wendell Pyke.

After that a correspondence began, a regular, even lavish exchange of letters and, even more lavish, a trail of small, exquisitely careful gifts began to fall my way. They were perfectly chosen, small treats, items of food, wine, terribly respectable books, nothing personal, indeed each gift for myself with the express intention that I share it happily with my friends. In no time at all I was the most popular VAD on the ward, and the entire hospital had an interest in my new romance.

Romance? When did it become that? I find it impossible to say, and also have always wondered if the subtle shading from friendship into something more was a mere accident of circumstances, the loneliness of war, the unique pressure of our times, or truly reflective of growing emotion. I did always love his letters. They were deep and intelligent and revealed a side of him usually covered up by his military veneer. In that way he was not unlike Douglas, and even more like Father, with that rare blend of soldiering and scholarship. (I know precisely what you Moderns will have to say about that.) He was certainly a sensitive man and once, over the small candlewax-stained tablecloth of a French café, grasped my gloved hands and whispered emotionally, 'I can't believe the courage of you all. If people back home had any idea what you've done, what you've seen . . . all these years . . . by Christ it would stop the singing.'

He was also very impressive. His family were powerful people, who maintained large financial empires, and took part in careers in banking and law, by which they made the empires even larger, and all the while doing so in such a way as to appear to be merely playing at these pursuits. They were graceful people, accustomed to the graceful use of power, and their blood was yet unthinned by the diffidence and eccentricity that marked our grand families in Britain and Ireland, my own included. We were languid beside them. To say I was impressed is insufficient; I was overwhelmed. He was the most pressingly influential man I ever knew and his pursuit of what he wanted was awesome. And, for whatever the reason, he wanted me. He thrust into my life with uniquely American power, through gates obligingly opened by my faintly sycophantic brother, and once there he set up a besieging camp. Diffidence is a frail defence against a determined mind.

But why did he want me? I asked it then, and I've asked it, with bleaker reason perhaps, since. I am not coy by nature, and I have no desire to veil any charms I might have possessed in hypocritical modesty. I willingly accede that in my twenty-fifth year I was not unattractive. I was supple and slender, courtesy of all that floor and bed-pan scrubbing and hauling massively heavy inert bodies about. My skin was no worse than anyone else's in those days of poor food and poor hygiene under canvas in France. My bobbed hair actually suited me very well, much better than its former heavy and formally dressed masses. It was a nice pleasant light brown colour, with curls that were everyone's envy, in spite of Sandy's golliwog taunts. My eyes, well, you can see them today, eyes don't change after all; but they were young and clear and since we were all a bit starved half the time, looked quite amazingly large and filled with that expression alternately defined as innocence and dim-wittedness by various loving family and friends. If you chance to look through my work, there is existent among the War Years' collection, a small watercolour entitled Amputee Ward. The VAD nurse whose face is reflected in the mirror behind the legless soldier is me. Have a look some time. Was I worth the pride of the Shippingham Pykes of New York?

Wendell evidently thought so. It is possible that he fell for bloodlines. We *are* rather up there. But he was too romantic to be so calculating. He was indeed very romantic, not always the blessing in a man it's held up to be. No, I think it was a combination of two factors. The first was a classical situation, the American abroad, and like all travellers wide-eyed, and a little lonely, ready to make impulsive decisions, decisions that would perhaps be different at home. The other factor involved his own inner nature. Wendell was, on the surface, a staid man. And how, or why, you may ask, would I fall for such a man? Simply because I had fallen for the frog and princess story of old, the beauty within the beast, the hidden soul that only the lover's kiss reveals. And he had done precisely the same. Within the beast of my rag-tag and unruly nature lurked no doubt a jewel of a lady, the lady my mother and Eugenia Howie would have made of me, had either had their way. And within Wendell's beast of Yankee aristocracy there also lurked a beauty, a frail spirit of Bohemianism he would do all in his power to suppress. I welcomed it, just as he yearned for the hidden lady buried within myself. And so we fell in love, each of us, with the part of the other that the other would willingly deny; romantic victims, both, of a blackly ironical star.

Witness our ultimate meeting of that brief ten-day courtship, the last occasion of the odd threesome of Sandy, Wendell and I. It was the night before Sandy was due to go back up the line. We were all feeling thoroughly glum about it, and I, in a rebellious mood born out of angry despair, simply broke all the rules and agreed to meet my brother and his American friend for a late supper in one of the better remaining hotels. It was a lovely old building and inside the atmosphere was warm and firelit and we sat late, savouring rare luxury, sipping coffee and brandies. Wendell and Sandy talked most of the night between themselves. They had a closeness that was quite unconnected with me. I was aware that I was a sort of gift from Sandy to Wendell, whose acceptance of the gift was the seal upon their friendship. There is a bond between men in warfare that rises above any bond they might feel with women. I had seen and noted it often before, in others. In 1918, out of sheer ignorance, I failed to reach the conclusion that in the sophistication of today would be inevitable. But ignorance was a wise guide: Wendell was *not* homosexual. And Sandy, all his life, had shown an interest in the opposite sex a little too vigorous for proper containment in the bounds of our stricter morality. But both, faced with misery and death, sought out a man for comfort. We love what we understand. No one who did not know the trenches understood their poor tenants. I was, for both of them, a sweet memory of a sweeter past and nothing more.

Of course when they talked among themselves, they did not talk of the war. They talked of art that night, actually, with a fluency that on Sandy's part amazed me, and on Wendell's put me in awe. I suspected Sandy had learned what he knew mostly from Wendell, but was stunned to hear that he had poked about the ruins of churches seeking out old paintings, and visited the great cathedral at Amiens whenever he was behind the lines. From Wendell nothing surprised me; he was a man of wide talent, wide interest, and his family were far more cultured than mine. The money won by the mundanities of American banking was poured out on the treasures of Old Europe. His father was a great collector and Wendell, at his young age, was already a rival.

For all my years of painting, and my brief tenancy at South Kensington, I was dismally ignorant yet of the great, and lesser, masters, who were surely to be my guides, and like all self-educated people, I was vulnerable to sudden terrible abysses in my knowledge. Listening to my brother and Wendell Pyke, I teetered in miserable silence on the edge of such a crevasse.

Wendell lounged with unaccustomed lazy relaxation, his dining chair pushed back and his legs outstretched towards the fireside near our table. He was smoking one of those long, thin cigars that he much favoured and talking of the painter and writer Wyndham Lewis who had recently been appointed War Artist, attached to the Canadians, and of whom, until this moment, I had never heard.

'Hardly seems much point,' Sandy said. 'The whole thing's been photographed on every side and from the air as well, if anyone's going to ever want to know what it looked like. Which I can't imagine,' he added sourly.

'They will,' Wendell said, 'after it's over. If only to plan the next one.'

'Oh, don't talk of it,' I whispered. 'The only thing that makes this one possibly bearable is knowing it's the last.'

'The last?' Wendell laughed softly, 'Oh, my little angel.'

'What's amusing?' I demanded, angry to be mocked.

'Is that not what we are fighting for? Yourselves as well? Now that you've deigned to join us.'

I think I sounded every bit as scathing as him, but I achieved little. He only laughed again. He said eventually, 'Wars are made in banks and offices, my dear. What you see out here is just for show.' It sounded very impressive, but so does everything truly cynical. 'If the bankers and moneymen want another, they shall have it.'

'Never mind, Justina,' Sandy said, trying to be cheering. 'Next time perhaps *you* can be War Artist.' I shuddered, but Sandy went on gaily, 'Really, she'd do splendidly. You should see her work, Wendell,' he added. 'She's really terribly good.' He smiled at me encouragingly.

'My, my,' I said, a little sharply. His flattery was rare, and would have been welcome, had it not been marred with a trace of condescension.

'Oh don't get miffy,' he returned annoyedly. He was getting a little drunk and wanted everyone happy. 'Really Wendell, you must demand to see . . .'

'So you've said,' Wendell replied coolly. Then he softened and turned to me and said, 'Ah yes, I must certainly.' It was the greatest attention he had ever given my work, and it was said with a perfect blend of politeness and disinterest that ruled the discussion closed. I felt humiliated, like an over-enthusiastic child, and furious at Sandy. This faculty for making me feel younger than I was was one of Wendell's most powerful tools. I determined not to mention my painting to him ever again.

He went on smoothly, ignorant of my anger, and began a monologue on artists in New York, praising Walt Kuhn as of especial interest, and John Sloan, both gentlemen as unfamiliar to me then, as Lewis. Sandy listened, trying to look intelligent, and only looking sleepily drunk. 'Of course,' Wendell said suddenly, perhaps to waken him, 'you do have a point about photography.'

'Have I?' Sandy said dozily, turning his brandy glass to the firelight.

'Yes of course. Take portraiture for instance . . .' He paused, and then continued, 'Of course it's never been my particular fancy. Frankly I'd take half the stuff off our walls at home and throw it out . . . but Mother has a "precious" sort of taste . . .' he laughed gently. 'But conventional portraiture is dying anyhow. Who in today's world has the time, or indeed the interest, in half a dozen excruciatingly boring sittings for, no doubt, a mediocre replica, when a good photographer can produce a superb, and indeed *artistic* likeness in half an hour? In fact there is a good argument for the photograph being actually *more* artistic, being as it is a direct reflection of the true . . .'

'Mr Yeats said photographs were for corpses,' I said. There was an instant silence and Sandy woke up enough to glare at me uncertainly.

'What?' whispered Wendell.

'A photograph was fine for a corpse, but painters paint souls . . .' I trailed off, not certain I had remembered it right, and finding the words on my own tongue lacking the resonance of the same on that of Mr Yeats.

'Jack Yeats?' Wendell asked warily. 'Jack Yeats said that?'

'Not *Jack*,' I said impatiently. 'Mr Yeats. John Butler Yeats.'

Confusion briefly crossed Wendell's face, and a faint unease, as if he had been caught out in error. He looked smaller for it, and petulant. Then he laughed broadly and replied gaily, '*Oh*. The old man. Oh, of course.' He smiled at me, his composure again secure. 'Oh I suppose he might have said something of the sort.' His vagueness surprised me and I pushed with sudden boldness.

'Don't you *know* John Butler Yeats?' I said.

He was taken aback. He took out a new cigar, snipped the end with a little silver tool, and lit it. Then he said, 'I'm *familiar*, of course. He's not my style, naturally. Jack Yeats, there's another story, another story indeed. I have a Jack Yeats I really rather like, though to be honest, I'm not *quite* certain. The Irish fail to hold me. Russell and all those fairies. Child's stuff. Now, even Augustus John . . .'

'But he's in New York,' I said. 'Surely you *must* know him.' Wendell looked at me oddly.

'No, my dear. I'm terribly sorry. I don't.' His voice was very reasonable. I remembered Emmie Anderson telling me that New York was a very big city. But even so, Wendell was in the world of art, and I was quite certain that in that world Mr Yeats must be as famous in New York as he was in Dublin. Wendell blew cigar smoke upwards, a misty veil in the candle light. 'Is he in New York then?' he asked mildly. And then, answering for himself, 'Ah yes. I do recall now. John Quinn used to go on about the old man. Think he was finding him a bit of a nuisance to tell the truth. But that was *years* ago, surely. Hadn't realized he was still around. He's surely not still painting? He must be terribly old.' He looked mildly inquiring, and unhappily I shook my head.

'I don't know,' I said, sadly. Wendell was distressed by my sadness, since he did not understand it, and he attempted to deflect it by chatter.

'Of course I shouldn't be unfair. The Irish have made a definite contribution. In fact I made two trips over myself, with my father, buying. On our way to France of course,' he added. He looked across to Sandy, who was asleep in his chair. I thought he would be angry, but he only smiled indulgently and nodded for me to look too. I glanced across, yet distracted. Wendell said, with another smile, 'Do you know, when Sandy wanted us to meet, I almost refused.'

'Oh?' I said.

'Yes. Do you know why?' I shook my head. 'It was when he told me you were an artist.' He grinned.

'But you like art,' I said stupidly.

'Oh indeed. I *love* art,' he laughed, 'My father always used to say that the only thing wrong with an interest in art was one's incessant need to deal with artists.' He laughed again, and then added, 'Of course, most of the time one generally deals through an agent.' He sat back smoking contentedly.

'I'm supposed to find that amusing, too?' I said warily.

He laughed richly, 'Oh, my dear. Nothing to do with you. You're the girl of my dreams, I assure you. Only it wasn't what I necessarily expected.'

'From an artist?' I said.

'I had no way of knowing,' he explained happily. 'I really was quite afraid you were going to be terribly Washington Square.'

'Oh, really,' I said uneasily, not quite knowing what he meant and suspecting I might be it anyhow. 'And am I not?' He leaned forward and took my hands, before my sleeping brother's wearily innocent face.

'You?' he said. 'You are simply divine. I couldn't care if you painted pumpkins with fairies on them. I'd still adore you.' And right there he leaned over the table and kissed my cheek. I was too shocked to move.

The next morning Alexander came, alone, to see me. He was going up to join his unit by motor lorry, before noon. He looked washed out, and the worse for all that brandy, and was very low. When I teased him about falling asleep he neither laughed nor got angry. He was very serious about everything.

'Stop it,' I said. 'You're making me superstitious. Be yourself.'

'You're always superstitious,' he said, but he was not joking about it any more. 'I suppose we all are,' he added darkly.

'Go on. Get on with you. I'm not talking to you like this.'

'Oh, I'm going. I have to. I've only a few minutes. I came to talk to you about Wendell,' he said, quite urgently. 'I want to know how you feel.'

'About Wendell,' I said cautiously. 'In what way?'

'Justina, don't waste time.'

'For heaven's sake, I can't just say . . .'

'Do you like him? Love him? Will there be something between you?' He stared at me hard, holding my shoulders. I looked around. His voice was rising and I was afraid of making a scene. 'Answer me.'

'He's very nice,' I said.

'Very nice.' He looked quite cold. 'Oh, surely you can do better than that . . . you've had days to think . . .'

'All right. He's *very* nice. I like him very much, and I hope I'll see more of him.'

'Of course you'll see more of him.' He shook his head impatiently. His gas mask and haversack clacked together. 'Will you marry him?' he asked.

'*Marry* him? Sandy, he hasn't . . . I mean it's never remotely come up . . . we just aren't on such terms.'

'He *wants* to. Will you marry him?' He was holding my arms so hard they hurt. I winced and suddenly he released me and turned away, and then turned back and said, passionately, 'Oh Justina, I know it's right . . . he's just right for you. He's artistic, and well-bred, and yes, he's rich, too. He'll look after you always and you'll be happy.

We'll all be happy. He's the best friend I've ever had since Michael and Michael was, well, we were the same blood. He's like a brother. A cousin. Like Michael,' he said at last, breathing the name wearily. 'Oh Justina, it will be just like it was. And after this damnable war, we'll be together, the three of us, and we'll even go skiing. We'll go to Switzerland and ski, the three of us.' He said it wistfully, so sadly that I would not argue and say that Wendell was *not* Michael, and not like Michael either. He wanted it to be so. I was silent. He misread my silence and very gently said, 'Justina. It's all right you know. I mean with Michael. I know it is. He wouldn't mind. He'd be happy, even. I know, you see. Most of the chaps, I mean the ones who've got a girl at home . . . they're all happiest if there's someone in the wings, waiting, just in case they go West. It's not supposed to be like that, but it is.'

I turned away, moving my head slightly in a nod that was neither agreement nor dispute. He whispered, 'Justina?'

Still facing from him I said, 'It's all right. You can go, Sandy. If it happens, I'll marry him.' He embraced me in silence, kissed my cropped hair, and was gone.

14

Merrion Square
9 March 1918

My dearest Justina,

Just received your latest two letters, together, despite variant postmarks, both much mauled by the rites of passage. Bless you for writing about Alexander; I am so relieved to hear he is *really* all right. Sometimes I think I could not bear it if we were to lose anyone else. Dublin seems a perpetual funeral, everyone in black, black armbands everywhere. Last week I was back home and the talk of Sligo is the miserable sadness over Robert Gregory. Poor Lady Gregory, first the nephew, then the son, and such a son! And three little ones left behind. But why am I telling you; you know as well as any what grief war brings . . .

I made the terrible mistake of mentioning, in passing, the name of a male friend, and poor Mother was at once running for the orange blossom. *Then* I had to tell her he was a Jesuit priest! I think she was more shocked by my using his first name in conversation, than by the potential of a blasphemous liaison! Though I hasten to assure you there is nothing of that in it! (As if there would be.) No my dear; Father Joseph McLafferty, SJ, lecturer at University College, poet, scholar, theologian and *not* interested in boring little girls forever begging for books. But he is *so* kind and so brilliant and we have had the most wonderful discussions. What a world of wonders and knowledge there is to explore! And all wrapped away in the silence of libraries! I met him at the printing house, the new one, on Temple Street. (Hopefully quite beyond the range of gunboats on the Liffey.) We are publishing a small volume of his own verse. All quite magnificent, and perhaps with this ecclesiastical blessing upon us, we will be protected from the suspicious eye of the clergy (who are sadly not all Joseph McLafferty) and escape our usual aura of literary original sin.

Well, my dear, I suppose I had better face up to it, and roll out the Big News. *Kate* is *pregnant*. I had better pause while you run for the smelling salts. Well, she really is. I don't know why I find it so surprising, actually. I suppose it was quite to be expected, though *she* protests herself totally taken aback. Do you suppose she possibly didn't know 'The Facts'?! The Pathriot is crowing, naturally. At such times, we all go back to our native selves, and Padraic is now up to his neck in the peat bog, shouting about Sons for Erin. Serves Kate precisely right, I'm afraid, though it's harsh of me to say it.

Clare has been informed and so far her sole comment upon the subject has been a brown envelope with, unaccompanied even by a letter, a birth-control tract by Margaret Sanger. So don't indulge yourself with any delusion that *you're* the only one in the middle of a war!

Seriously, darling, I am so glad you are at least well back, in Amiens. (Though I wish you were in London, I can't help it, I truly do.) The talk here in all the newspapers is of the big German offensive everyone is certain is imminent. And I daresay there's no smoke without fire. After all, spring has arrived, so surely it's time to start killing one another, is it not? Oh darling, what a world. It is not always easy to keep Faith.

Well, regardless, I must fly. I've a stack of proofs to read yet, and it's nearly midnight. Do keep safe, and give my love to Alexander if you are in touch.

Your loving cousin,
May Howie

PS I do understand your reservations, but your friendship with Wendell Pyke can hardly do harm at this point, and doubtless must be a great comfort to both himself, and Alexander, and indeed perhaps even a little to you. I am well aware you are an island, but even islands are connected to other islands deep beneath the sea.

M.

I read May's letter by the light of a smoking oil lamp in a nurses' bell tent, pitched beside the old piggery of an abandoned farm near Dernancourt. The smell of pigs is not readily vanquished. I sniffed wistfully at May's smooth beige vellum, fancying a whiff of talc, or even scent wafting from Ireland, and remembering May's flowery pretty Dublin bedroom as I did. I read the letter again, and laid it down, and turned down the lamp, so that only a dim glow awaited the two VADs not yet in their camp beds, and lay down to sleep on mine. But I could not sleep. May's letter had unsettled me, with its blithe references to intimacies I barely understood, and its disturbing perspective of the war I knew too well.

Kate pregnant; I could scarcely imagine it. That reed thin body, that whip sharp intellect, softening into gentle motherhood? I was a little horrified; it seemed unnatural. Besides, my own ignorance of 'The Facts' surely outstripped Kate's, and I was unsure which troubled me most, the real evidence of Kate's new knowledge, or the verbal assurance of May's. How did she know so much, and why, for that matter, didn't I? I made a firm mental note that I would simply approach someone and ask to have the whole thing, in all its messy detail, put before me. Surely it could not be so much more horrific than anything I had seen and observed in the past two years. But as always, my determination floundered on my own ignorance. Who could I ask? A married Sister? A VAD widow? One of my equals, no doubt my equal in innocence as well? It was impossible. There are some things, if not learned young, that become increasingly difficult to ever learn. Are you finding difficulty believing me? Does it strain your credibility that I had nursed dying men in all intimacy for two years and yet had not the faintest idea how to make love to one? I daresay it does. But you will have to take it from me on trust, because that was the indisputable case.

What a childish silly concern at such a time. I was a quarter-century old, sleeping beneath canvas, at a Casualty Clearing Station a few miles from the massing enemy and I was wrapt in adolescent anxiety about the facts of life. How silly life is. That other concern, more reasonable indeed, came back to me now. May's relief that I was safe in Amiens was no comfort, for I was not in Amiens at all any longer, and those rumours in far-off newspapers took on frightening reality when, on a still night, sniper fire from the tense uneasy front line could be heard. In this, as in those intimate matters, we, who were much concerned, were held in thorough ignorance. How often we turned to the Home Front newspapers to learn what was happening all around us.

What was *happening* all around us, unfortunately, looked very like chaos. But that was the way of things. There was great tension that spring: the war, from the beginning, was seasonal, bound by the elements to summer action and winter lying-low. Each spring before had brought an offensive, French or British. This spring was different. We were fairly sure there would be no action on our side; America had joined the war a year before, but we were yet waiting for the great bulk of her troops to arrive. An army was easier to raise than to transport; soldiers were more quickly summoned than supplies. As yet both shipping, and weaponry lagged behind Yankee patriotism; but not forever. For once, we were content to play the old enemy game of solidity and defence. Time was on our side. When the Americans came we could win; numbers would decide for us. We knew it, and so, of course, did the Germans. If they were to win, they must win soon. Tense and aware we awaited attack.

All along the Front preparations were made to resist. The medical services made their own arrangements. Beds were emptied as much as possible for coming casualties, supplies increased, and avenues of evacuation explored. Front line units were pulled back, Casualty Clearing Stations shipped out unnecessary and vulnerable personnel. Everywhere everything was made ready for the possibility of sudden retrenchment. Everywhere, that was, but where I was. In our sector, down near the 'tail' of the British segment, behind the thinly held lines of the Fifth Army, no such arrangements were made. Someone had got into their head the idea that we just might advance instead, and thus prepared for both contingencies by holding just where we were. There were no evacuations, no sites chosen for retreat. Our hospitals remained where they were and some of us even moved up. Thus, two weeks before, I had been sent up with a party of nurses to Denancourt, within ready reach of the Front Line. I went happily enough, trusting in my superiors, and taking lightly the grumbles of the seasoned veterans, ambulance drivers, and orderlies who took a more sceptical, masculine interest in strategy. We nurses did our jobs, more terrified of Matron or Sister than the Germans. And I was used to everyone's grumbling. Alexander grumbled all the time; all soldiers did. He was with the 51st division, on the Northern flank of the Flesquières Salient. Before he left he had grumbled about the Salient itself, and why they didn't pull back and shorten the line, much lengthened recently by the addition of yet another long segment formerly held by the French. It stretched now right down below the River Oise, and Alexander said it was too thinly held by far.

That much I knew from my patients. They came back edgy and fearful from this new line, unnerved by a whole new system of defence, quite different from the old threefold trench lines with which they were so familiar. They were nervous and distrustful and again and again voiced quietly the soldier's darkest fear, 'They're set to abandon us out in this Forward Zone. We're the Forlorn Hope.' The new front was manned by redoubts and strongpoints, with no sure line of retreat. No wonder they felt threatened, though it was a fear as old as the war, that one's own group were the sacrificial lambs. And of course they all were. Lambs of God who bore away the sins of the world, into the mud of France. Have mercy on them.

Finally I slept, fitfully, for a handful of hours. In the black of the night I was stunned awake by a brutal onslaught of thunderous noise, an instantaneous explosion of sound that struck the bell-tent like a huge gust of wind. The tent flaps blew open, fluttering out into a night suddenly alight with white flickering fire. I leapt up, certain we'd been blown up, but the noise continued, endlessly, and the tent yet stood, and I flung on my clothing and shoes, in wordless panic, beside my companion in the tent, both of us stumbling over each other in the eerie wavering light. I found my apron, and tied it half on, and I remember clutching up May's letter and thrusting it in my pocket as a talisman. It would travel a long, strange way with me. Outside, the whole line of the sky in the direction of the Front was lit with continuous fire, and the drumming of it resounded through everything one touched; the ground, the tin walls of the huts, even the great stucco walls of the abandoned farmhouse; like unending earthquake. I felt panic rising, and fought against a great yearning to scream and run about like a terrified child. In the stableyards, horses were galloping and stumbling into one another, and men were shouting, trying to capture them. Somewhere a dog was barking hysterically, a sound as thin as a bird cry in the tumultuous night.

I staggered over the rough ground to the main farmhouse which housed the ward in which I worked, and reached it just as a shell struck the road. It crashed into a standing supply wagon with a great fiery thud and roman candle fountains of flame. Shards of wood showered by me, splintering into the stone walls of the building, and I ran for the shelter of the front door. Inside, with the horrendous noise pounding against walls, windows and ceilings, there was yet the measured calm of the hospital, nurses hastening by in rustling linen, whispered commands, silent murmurings. I saw by the dim light a clock on the wall reading 4:45. The German bombardment was five minutes old. It would go on for five hours.

Long before it finished we were preparing to evacuate, a hideous business of moving wounded, frightened men in near darkness to the safest, most sheltered corners to await transport. All the while the noise was continuous, and we worked in fear of gas shells, and for some time both staff and patients struggled against the suffocating protection of gas masks, while the evacuation continued. When the bombardment stopped, in the grey light of a fog-wrapped morning, we knew the attack had begun.

Between us and the advancing enemy were only the scattered fortifications of the Forward Zone, and the sturdier, but shell-pounded lines of the Battle Zone, in which the main fighting must occur. We did not know then, but already the Germans were slipping, unseen in the mist, between those forward defences. In the eerie light of the ravaged morning, long lines of ambulances began rolling westward, and we hastened about the wards, collecting the walking wounded, and organizing them into an order of retreat. In a quiet dark corner, three beds were yet occupied, their silent tenants the grievously ill and dying, impossible to move. I sat amongst them as the sound of vehicles made a continuous clatter beyond the shuttered windows, engines raspy in the cold, damp air. A boy of eighteen with a gangrenous leg and a raging fever held my hand as the bombardment recommenced. Now the shells were falling far back, on our lines of supply, leaving the front lines safe for the advancing infantry. I listened to the shrieking and whistling as they passed over our heads and wondered when the Germans would arrive.

While I sat there, one of the three hopeless cases quietly died, without a whisper or word of complaint. Then two orderlies came and took the second away, a place having been found for him in an ambulance, where he might take his chances like the rest. He moaned and cried whenever they moved him the slightest bit and I wished they would leave him to die in peace. The room seemed empty then, a strange quiet in the midst of chaos. The thunder of the thousands of guns had become so persistent that one fancied one was not hearing it. Hearing had *become* the guns, a mesmerizing background as involuntary as the pounding of one's heart.

'We're moving out now, Nurse,' a quiet voice said. I looked up and met the sad brown eyes of a Canadian ambulance driver. He looked straight at me as if the boy in the bed whose hand clutched mine were already dead. 'Come on, please,' he said. I looked from him to my patient and back, my mouth wide with innocent surprise.

'*He's* here,' I said, dumbly.

'He'd never make it, Nurse,' he said very softly, doubtless hoping the boy would not hear, should he be conscious at all. 'Honestly, it's kinder. It would hurt him terribly.'

'I'm not to *leave* him, am I?' I whispered, still the meek and obedient VAD.

The Canadian stepped closer. He was a big, rangy man, with an aura of open country about him. He leaned over the bed, with one hand on my shoulder, the other on the boy's pulse.

'Ma'am,' he said with sorrowful respect, 'he's leaving us faster than we'll leave him.' My head came up, and I must have looked quite shocked, because he patted my shoulder with his big kind hand. But I shook it off, my mind leaping back to Arradale and Mirza Hassan and my father.

'No,' I said, suddenly. 'No. I shan't go.'

He paused for a moment, considering. He was a placid, pacific man, but I think he was about to simply pick me up and carry me bodily to his waiting vehicle, but his intentions, whatever, were shattered by a sudden huge explosion as a shell crashed into the now empty ward beyond, bringing down roof and walls and blackening the air with dust, smoke and the reek of cordite. I had flung myself instinctively across my poor patient, and was crouched there, yet shielding him, when the Canadian staggered up from the floor. His forehead was cut, and his eyes were hardened and serious.

'Nurse, I've four men and another VAD waiting outside. I can't wait. You've got to come now.' I peered through the dust at the face of the boy on the bed. He was awake, looking about in bewilderment for me, until his hand again found mine. I could not leave him.

'No,' I said. The Canadian looked at me with as much respect as the fleeting instant would allow, and left the room. I huddled down by the bed, waiting for the next shell, living from instant to instant. I don't know how long we were alone there, but suddenly the Canadian reappeared. He stumbled into the dusty room, blinking against the darkness after the light outside. He had something in his hand and when he located me in the murk he crossed quickly to my side and thrust what he carried into my hand. I grasped it instinctively, then looked up stunned. It was a service revolver and I said, almost angrily, 'I don't want this. I'm not going to kill Germans.' He looked at me pityingly.

'No, Ma'am,' he said. 'That's for him,' he gestured to my patient, 'when they get here. And for yourself.'

He nodded curtly and stepped towards the door, but I shouted after him, 'Nonsense!' He looked back, a little amazed at my anger, and I said, 'So we'll be taken prisoner. What of it? It's surely no worse than dying. They're not *animals*, you know.' I was remembering the German children I'd nursed in London and was bitter at his slander of them.

'Ma'am . . .' he said awkwardly, and paused in ludicrous embarrassment.

'A fate worse than death?' I snapped. 'Oh, *really*.'

He looked at me steadily and said with withering accuracy, 'Begging your pardon, Ma'am, but I reckon you're in no position to know.' He touched his cap, solemnly, and retreated out of the door. I heard the roar of an engine, and the clatter of a vehicle driven in haste out of the ruined farmyard. My anger with him was tempered by compassion; the road he travelled was, if anything, more dangerous than the wrecked building in which I sheltered, now alone.

After he had gone, an eerie stillness settled about the old farmhouse. The bombardment had eased as the barrage crept forward deeper into our lines, and no shells fell any longer. Only the thunder of the firing persisted, and that too lessened. In the distance I could hear rifle fire, and the rattling bursts of a machine gun, and knew an infantry battle was going on somewhere out in the mist. The dust had settled within the small room where my patient and I remained. It had been the kitchen of the old farmhouse, and at one end was a large, empty unadorned fireplace, with terracotta hearth and black pot hooks yet hanging. It was very primitive and there was no water in the building, only a handpump outside. I wished I had water, to bathe the dying boy's sweat-soaked face, but I daren't venture out into the mist. I had the eerie feeling of presences out there, just beyond my sight. Yet there was no sound of any living thing. The horses had all been taken, and the dog was silenced, and even the stray cats that hung about for food scraps had, in the way of cats, vanished at once when the bombardment began. The boy in the bed awoke again and said that he was cold. I took off my cloak and put it over him and after a while, when that seemed insufficient, ventured as far as the bombed, smoking ruins of the main ward, once the long dining room of the house, for more blankets. As I returned to the old kitchen, with a stack of red blankets in my arms, I saw the shadows of a figure slip past the shuttered window, breaking the bars of light that fell across the floor.

'Nurse?' my patient said, feeling blindly about with one hand, for me.

'Shh,' I whispered. I crossed the room quickly, trying not to pass too close to the window, and bent over the bed, spreading out three of the blankets across him. He thanked me very politely, and I took my handkerchief and wiped sweat from his forehead, and prayed he would go to sleep and not make any more sound. All the while I listened frantically to hear, above the endless din of the guns, the more personal threat of footsteps without. A long while passed, and I relaxed a little, certain that the passing stranger, whether friend or foe, was long gone. Then the boy awoke again, moaned and thrashed about in confusion and delirium and, licking dry lips, asked me for water. I touched his face and whispered gently, 'Later.' But there is no later for the thirst of the dying. He looked at me in desperate agony, some last trace of noble courage warring with unbearable need. He said at last, 'Oh please. Please.'

'Yes,' I said. 'Yes, of course.'

I tucked the blankets up closer around him, since he was still shaking with cold and then, steeling myself, I approached the bolted kitchen door. With my hand on the latch, I remembered the pistol given me by the Canadian ambulance driver. For a moment I resisted its temptation but a clatter of none-too-distant firing overcame my courage, and my pride. I went back to the table in the centre of the room, where I had laid it disdainfully down, and took it now in both my hands. I stood looking down at it in the dim light, quickly assessing how I would use it. I was not as innocent in such matters as one might imagine. I had never fired a pistol, but like any other child of the Scottish Establishment, male or female, I knew how to shoot. The pistol in one hand, and an earthenware jug in the other, I crossed the room, slipped the bolt, and stepped out into the clammy day. The fog had thinned, and sun was filtering through, and it seemed strange and eerie, after the long hours huddled in near darkness, to find nothing more than the farmyard, much the same except for two shell holes where the hen run had been, and a total absence of any living thing. Our bell tent yet stood as I'd left it in the night, tent flaps flicking gently in the light wind. Cautiously I crossed the cobbled yard to the solitary pump that served house and stable.

The heavy cast iron handle required two hands, and I laid the pistol and the jug down on the kerbstone that surrounded the horse-trough, and pumped vigorously up and down until the water, with a hoarse rasp, began to flow. The rasp disguised the first footfall, but as I released the handle and turned to lift the jug I heard the quick thud of steps, spun about, glimpsed a running figure, and in an instant dived for the pistol, raised it wildly, and fired. The crack of the shot slammed back and forth across the cobbled court and the figure disappeared in a flurry of movement behind a stone wall. I stood dumbfounded and horrified. The echoes faded, and there was no further sound, and in horrible remorse, I called, 'Hello?' and then stupidly, 'Have I shot you?'

The realization that I had probably killed someone so shook me that I quite forgot where I was standing, and indeed forgot that the someone was quite likely an enemy soldier. I felt I must approach and see what I had done; perhaps he was wounded, and suffering. I crept forward towards the wall, all my concentration upon it, leaving the water jug sitting by the pump. In my shock and ignorance, I never even imagined treachery. But there was none. When I reached the wall there was nothing at all. Not even any blood. The stone boundary continued quite some distance, to the wall of a cowshed, which formed part of the court. Beyond it was a maze of old stone buildings and new tin huts, and my bewildered eyes searched them, and returned to the bare cobbles at my feet, and I wondered if I had imagined everything.

I was about to return to my water jug when a voice

said, quite clearly, 'Stay where you are, please, and put down the gun.'

Instead I whirled about, and stared. The voice was so like that of my Canadian that I was certain it was him, come back for me.

A man dived at once behind the shelter of the water trough, having crept right up behind me while I searched for him. It was not my Canadian. I had a glimpse of both face and figure and saw not the big rangy driver in RAMC uniform, but a man of middle height, wearing, amazingly, civilian clothes. 'Who are you?' I cried, my voice shrill with uncertainty.

'Put that gun down and I'll tell you.'

It was the wrong thing to say. I raised the pistol menacingly towards his minimal hiding place and said,

'No. You say.'

'Miss, you're going to kill somebody.'

'Quite likely,' I said, and he ducked down at the new tone of my voice. His own became patiently cajoling.

'Now come on, before you shoot your own finger off or something.'

He lifted his head, on which he wore a rather ridiculous wide-brimmed hat, pinned up at one side, like Teddy Roosevelt's. I could see a glint of eyes beneath it, as if he were assessing me, my determination, and the distance between us. He was going to rush me, I knew, and I said sharply,

'If I can drop a stag at fifty yards, I can drop you there. So don't move.'

He flopped back down and then, after a moment, said in a voice of plaintive misery, 'Goddammit. In the middle of a pigsty in the middle of this bitch of a war, what do I meet? Goddam Annie Oakley.' And then he began to laugh. I stood silently amazed, and slowly he stood up, and strolled towards me, perfectly casual, and reached his hand out for the gun, saying as he did, 'Go on. Shoot me. I'm tired of living anyhow.' He was grinning, a big wide grin that lit up his tired dirty face with beguiling charm. Then his hand touched my shoulder, and he took the gun and laid it down and wrapped his two arms around me and we stood clutched together in the cobbled yard, he laughing, and I sobbing until two quick cracks of rifle fire froze us both.

'Jesus Christ,' he said. 'Where?'

'In here,' I whispered. I snatched up the water jug and he grabbed the pistol, and I led him, running, for the shelter of the kitchen door. He flung me through and bolted the door behind him and ran at once to the shuttered window. For a long while he stood silently peering out through the slats and then I saw his tense shoulders relax and he turned to me. He saw the man on the bed then, and his face registered brief surprise.

'Alive?' I nodded. 'There still a *hospital* here?' he asked.

'No. Just me. And him.' I turned to the boy then and filled a cup with water and tried to help him drink it. But he could no longer swallow and I only wet his lips again and again, until he seemed satisfied. The man came over and stood beside us and looked down at the boy. His nose wrinkled at the stench of gangrene. I think he understood at once why we were there.

'They're just over that sunken road,' he said, and gestured beyond the blank walls of the kitchen. He did not need to explain who. He looked at the boy again, and at me, and took a deep breath. 'I'll get you out of here, Nurse, if you want. I've an artillery horse tied up in the barn. I was just coming for water when I saw you.'

'What about him?' I said. I knew what the answer must be but I hoped for some miracle. The man put his hand on my head. He still held the service revolver in his other.

'You just go outside, Nurse, and bring that horse,' he said.

I looked up at him. His face was still and expressionless, a hard, lined outdoorsman's face, beneath light brown hair and stubbled with light brown beard. He was handsome, and his mouth was gentle. I looked at the revolver, held easily in an accustomed hand. 'Go get the horse, Nurse,' he said again. I stared.

'You're going to shoot him,' I said.

He looked straight into my eyes. His own were blue-green, very fine, with small hazel lights. Their beauty fixed itself upon me with great incongruity. 'Yes,' he said. 'I am.' His honesty, my fear, and the hopeless state of the boy on the bed combined to almost win me. But civilization is a stronger master than often we suppose. I turned away.

'You go then,' I said. 'Get your horse. We were fine here before you came.'

'Not for long,' he said coolly.

'I don't care,' I returned at once. 'He's my patient and I'll stay with him.'

'Very noble,' he said, but not quite with the sarcasm the words might imply. 'And very useless. He's got an hour left, maybe two, and pretty miserable hours at that. Then he'll be dead anyhow.'

'God forbid I spend my last two hours with strangers who want me dead,' I cried. He sighed, seeming old, and wise.

'I don't want *anyone* dead. Not anyone in this whole damned war in this whole damned continent. But when the Germans come, and they will come, Madam, you'll be damned little use to him. *He'll* die with a bayonet in his gut, listening to six Jagers raping you on the floor. If it were me, I'd rather be shot.' He looked grim and miserable, and from him I believed what I would not believe from my Canadian. But I said hastily, fighting terror, 'You're trying to frighten me into running, and I won't. So just go.'

'I'm trying to save your life,' he said. Then he sighed again, and sat down heavily on the wooden bench by the empty hearth. He took out a packet of cigarettes and slowly lit one as if he had all the time in the world.

'Aren't you going?' I said. He looked at me wearily from beneath the tilted brim of his hat.

'Do those shutters latch?' he said.

At dusk, the boy died. In the late afternoon he had grown hysterical with pain, and we ransacked the cupboards of the ruined hospital and found more morphia and gave him so much that mind and body were separated. After that he was quite gentle and happy and convinced that he and I were courting at some dance he recalled from the past. He died sweetly, holding my hand and whispering, 'Oh that was lovely, dear, do let's dance again.'

I covered him with the red hospital blanket and sat down. The man was sitting by the shuttered window, looking away. The moon had risen, full and hazy, and bars of moonlight came through the shutters and strengthened as the light failed. I felt very alone with the stranger in his odd civilian clothes, and vulnerable in a way I had not felt while the boy still lived. The man turned towards me. He had removed his hat. His hair was long and Bohemian.

'You did that beautifully,' he said. I think he smiled. He added quietly, 'When I'm dying, I hope you're there.' I imagined that the possibility was quite real, considering our situation.

'Are you a spy?' I said. His head came up, in a gesture of amazement.

'What?'

'You're not in uniform.' He laughed again, running one hand across his forehead, brushing back long messy hair.

'Oh,' he said. 'Oh, I see.' His accent was broad and flat, like Wendell Pyke's. He was an American. 'No, nothing so daring as that.' Then he did something comical. He reached inside his jacket and drew out something small and white, and handed it to me. It was sheer habit because there was no light to read. As I stared blankly into the dimness he laughed at himself and said, 'Jack Redpath, *New York Herald*.'

'You're a journalist?' I said.

'That's right.' I turned the card around in my fingers, feeling its stiff edges. I said, 'If the Germans come, they'll think you're a spy. They'll shoot you.'

'Thanks very much. Now what can I say to cheer *you* up?'

'You shouldn't have stayed.'

'You shouldn't have either.' He reached out his hand, hesitantly, 'Miss . . .'

'Melrose,' I said, looking away. 'Justina Melrose.'

'Justina Melrose,' he smiled, 'the Rose of No Man's Land.'

'Soppy song,' I said. But I took his hand. We shook hands solemnly and I sat down then, on one of the empty beds. 'What shall we do?' I said. I was frightened. My purpose in remaining behind was over now, and what courage it had begotten was gone. 'Can we get back?' I gestured vaguely towards the west.

'Not tonight,' he said. 'God knows where anyone is. We might be overrun already. Maybe not. But either side will shoot us in the dark. We'll see what morning brings.'

'Germans,' I said, 'more than likely.' I shivered. 'I'm sorry you stayed,' I whispered.

'You make me feel so welcome,' he said wryly and

when I laughed he added, ‘I don’t know about you, Florence Nightingale, but I’d love a drink.’

He grinned hopefully and I nodded, indicating the doorway through to the ruined ward.

‘Where we found the morphia. There’s some brandy behind a box of dressings.’

‘Wonderful,’ he said. He groped his way out of the room, clambering over the wreckage in the hallway and I heard him blundering about cheerfully in the rubble. He was back in a short while with a dark shape clutched under each arm.

He poured the brandy into tin cups and handed one to me. It was warming and wonderful, the first nourishment I had had all day. Jack Redpath filled my tin cup twice more. Exhausted and hungry, I was quite soon thoroughly drunk. My head was whirling and when I tried to stand, I had to give it up. He peered at me in the slatted moonlight and laughed delightedly.

‘Oh, I must sleep,’ I mumbled.

His laugh was louder. ‘Yes, I reckon you better.’

I stood up, and stumbled awkwardly against him, and he put a brotherly arm about me and escorted me to one of the two empty beds. I remember lying down and I remember the good gentle feeling of his hands carefully smoothing blankets over me. I heard him say, just before I slept, ‘Oh damn, Jack, what a time for a sense of honour.’

I was puzzling over it when I fell asleep. I had slept for only half an hour and was at the deepest, dark level of unconsciousness when I felt the same hands on my shoulders shaking me brutally awake.

‘Up, up,’ he shouted, and when I did not instantly respond, he dragged me up, and hauled me stumbling and protesting from the bed, and down to the floor and underneath the metal frame, and held me clutched there in his arms and then the first explosion told me at once where I was, and why and what was happening. The last of the window glass crashed and tinkled on to the tile floor.

'Round two,' said Jack.

The British had staged a counter-attack and for two hours an infantry battle raged around our refuge. Small arms fire came from all sides, and for a while a trench mortar was trained upon the main wing of the building, further demolishing it. It was clear that both friend and enemy regarded the building as an objective. Our presence there was both unknown and irrelevant.

'Oh God,' I whispered against Jack Redpath's rough woollen shirt-front. 'Let our side take it.'

'Let *somebody* take it before they both blast it to hell.' He tightened his arms around me and said, whimsically, 'Jesus, what a waste.'

'What?' My voice was shaking with confusion and fear.

'Shh,' he said, but I struggled and cried.

'Oh, let me go. Let me out. I'd rather die out there than trapped . . .' But he held me tighter and whispered gently that we were safe, that the building would not fall, we would not be trapped. His voice was mesmerizing, and my panic subsided into exhaustion. I relaxed against the pressure of his arms.

He said quietly, 'Shall I tell you a story?' an extraordinary thing to say, and like a small child I whispered back, 'Oh, please. Please do.' And so he began a long, wonderful story about the small town in Ohio where he had spent his boyhood and in the midst of it I fell asleep. Around us the firing continued, but I slept anyhow, secure, and comforted, and for the first time in my life, in the arms of a man.

I was not in his arms when I awoke. He was lying with his back to me, facing the doorway, his whole body tense, and I heard a heavy clunk as he shifted the service revolver in his hand.

'What is it?'

'They're at the door.'

'Who?' I whispered stupidly.

'They haven't said.'

I heard a thudding and crashing and the bolt jiggling and a mutter of voices, unidentifiable in the din. Then the door splintered and fell inwards, letting in moonlight that was at once blotted by dark shapes. Something heavy was dragged into the doorway; there were shouts and commands, to my joy, in English. I opened my mouth to cry out, but Jack anticipated and his hand clamped across my face. Then the firing began again, from within our tiny refuge, and no one at all could speak. They had mounted a Vickers Maxim in the doorway. We were a stronghold.

I cannot say how long it went on. We were deafened, shattered by it, echoing from the stone walls, and from the constant return of fire. The room was clogged with dust and fumes and cries of pain cut through the clatter of the firing. Then, quite suddenly, it all stopped. The gun was still. Outside, firing continued, but seemed faint and far away by contrast and an illusion of stillness fell upon the room. Jack raised his head and peered out, and then wriggled from beneath the bed. I followed. The air was still clouded with dust, but in the moonlight pouring through the splintered shutters, I could see nothing but dark, still shapes and a spidery outline of the machine gun, abandoned in the door.

Our defenders were dead or dying. It was time for the *coup de grâce*, the sudden assault, the grenade to still all opposition. 'They'll rush us,' said Jack. We stood side by side in the moonlight, among the scattered dead. We were both non combatants. We had both come to the War with uncertainty that had grown into distrust. But neither of us bore martyrs' blood. We ran, together, for the gun.

Its owners had made a barricade of the broken door and we crouched behind its poor shelter, and Jack positioned himself behind the Maxim, his legs stretched out on either side, knees raised and his hands finding the traversing handles with ease. He flung the end of the feedbelt at me, and shouted, 'Come on, girl,' as if this was something we'd done together for years. He glanced once over the barricade, ducked his head and pressed down on the trigger with both thumbs and my last thought before the clatter and smoke drowned all thought was that he had done this somewhere before. Clumsily I fed the belt towards the gun while he swung the barrel back and forth, raking the dark courtyard again and again. If fire was returned, I was unaware, concentrating utterly on the feedbelt in my hands. I never looked and I never thought. The act itself became its only end. Then the gun jammed, Jack cursed softly, and it was done.

'Get down,' he shouted, and he pulled me down, away from the door and huddled with me against the sturdy stone wall, and we waited for the end. *Then* I thought. Then I had terrible leisure to think, because the stillness dragged on and we waited in unbearable tension for the final retaliation that still did not come. Aware then of what we had done, I felt ravaged by our own violence; compromised. All I could think of was Michael dying a martyr in Bachelor's Walk. I would die a murderer. I put my head on Jack Redpath's shoulder and I wept.

But we did not die. We sat there until the dawn, and, with the grey light, realized we had been saved. No attack came and outside there was silence. The fighting had moved away and when we looked out over the cobbled yard, we saw only dark awkward shapes in German *feld grau*. Some of them, surely, we had killed. I wish I could say we acted nobly, and checked for wounded and offered aid, but we did none of those things. Jack went out to the stable and found the artillery horse had survived, and brought it through to the courtyard. While he watered it, I gathered scraps of food and medicines and the Webley revolver. Then we mounted the horse, bareback and together, and rode west.

At first the land seemed deserted, but for the distant sound of artillery, but in a short while we came upon a roadway and on it we met a party of Gordon Highlanders, a small group, cut off from their unit, moving westward as well. They were exhausted and dirty, their kilts caked in dried trench mud, and they took little interest in us. From them we learned that the main body of the Fifth Army was falling back; they didn't know how far. Lost, and without their officers, they seemed stunned, more refugees than soldiers, with that dull lack of curiosity I associated with German prisoners of war. For a while we rode beside them, but then went on. Twice more we met isolated bands of men, straggling back towards Amiens, and when we reached the main road to the town, we came upon an artillery unit, disciplined and orderly, but also in retreat. It was evident that something massive had happened, a major battle, and it had gone against us. We were falling back, retreating. The eyes of the men we passed told us everything: exhaustion, pain, fear, and something new that I had not seen before, defeat. The Germans had done what, in four years, we could never do; they had broken through. The rigid trench lines were in disarray, the fighting was mobile and fluid once more, like at the very beginning. And as at the very beginning, we were on the run. *We're going to lose the War*, I thought for the very first time.

We reached Amiens by evening, on roads clogged with the retreat. Lines of ambulances crept slowly through the cluttered streets, and Jack and I followed them, walking now because the horse had gone lame and we'd left him at a village a few miles up the line. Amiens was full of rumours; that the Germans were just outside the town, that they had broken apart the French and British lines, that they were marching on Paris. When we reached the big stationary hospital it was overflowing with wounded straight from the field. It had become a casualty clearing station, virtually, and it, too, was evacuating. The building had once been a beautiful private home, and its gardens were filled with casualties, lying everywhere. I looked around at the chaos and misery, and for one bitter moment I wanted only to run. Jack Redpath stood with his arm about my shoulder, more or less holding me up.

'I'll find a room,' he said gently. 'There'll be plenty of work left in the morning.' I felt a great surge of gratitude but I shook my head. I was supposed, after all, to be a nurse, and nurses were, as we all knew, tireless.

'No. I'll stay here.' I started to ask where he would go, but before I could speak, a sharp commanding female voice snapped, 'Melrose? Is that you, Melrose?' I looked up and there, bleary-eyed, her apron blood-spattered, was the same Sister who had attended my fainting spell during Alexander's visit weeks before.

'Yes, Sister,' I gulped, wriggling out from under Jack Redpath's kindly arm.

She glanced for one long moment at me, and at him. Then she said, 'Another brother, I've no doubt, Melrose. I shan't ask where you've been. Have an hour's rest, and a wash and take over from Nurse Forsyth in the Gas Ward. We're moving out tonight.' She turned away, but turned back again and her eyes settled on Jack. 'We're hard pushed for orderlies,' she said. 'Perhaps your brother would care to help?'

* * *

We left Amiens by road, I riding in an ambulance packed with gas victims, coughing and gasping for breath. I did not know Jack Redpath was with us until we reached Abbeville, where I glimpsed him, briefly, helping to haul free another vehicle that had slipped into a ditch. He looked up and waved cheerily, and then we went by. I wondered how long he would stay with us.

At Etaples, he was there ahead of me, unloading stretcher cases into the big base hospital. It, too, was crammed with casualties and more poured in by road and rail all the while. Many were still bloody and dirt-encrusted, straight from the fighting. At the quayside, hospital ships were taking the overspill to England. Everywhere the atmosphere was grim, misery and suffering compounded by the shock of defeat. We had not the resilience any more to rescue optimism. We scurried about, not meeting each other's eyes.

That night, for the first time in three days, I slept in a real bed. It was the bed of another VAD, but she was on night duty. I undressed and washed gratefully and fell into the bed and thought about Sandy in the Flesquières Salient but I was too tired even to worry. Belatedly, I thought of Wendell Pyke and realized I had not thought of him for days. I felt guilty, and was unsure why. In the morning, the VAD whose bed I slept in shook me for a full half minute before I awoke. As I did, I heard myself saying, as in a dream, 'Jack?'

The German attack had begun on the twenty-first of March. By the fifth of April, they had overrun the old Somme battlefields, taken the famed ruined city of Albert, and were but eight miles from Amiens. But there, at last, they were stopped. In the days that followed the news cautiously began to turn. We were holding, we were no longer retreating, the Channel ports were safe. Hope began to rise, the awful pressure on the hospitals eased slightly, and in the relative calm we all looked about ourselves and took stock. I received word from Sandy that he was safe, and that he thought Wendell's Americans would have missed the fighting. Then Wendell wrote to say he was glad someone had the sense to pull us out of Amiens before things got rough, and that he still doubted the wisdom of sending women so near the Front. I decided already I would not tell him about the farmyard at Dernancourt.

Jack Redpath stayed on in Etaples for two more weeks. The night before he left for Paris he took me out to dinner in an old hotel overlooking the seafront. It was a sad, battered, lonely place, after four years of wartime meetings and farewells. There was a little band, playing old French songs and modern vaudeville numbers, and making them all sound alike. Jack asked me questions about my home and family and I told him about Arradale, and Dublin and Father and my brothers and Clare. He had no brothers or sisters of his own, he said, and his parents were dead. His father had been an elder of the Scottish Presbyterian church, in Ohio, but Jack had no religion at all. He thought the world had outgrown it. I found that hard to argue. We were both very sad all through the meal, and I knew it was because he was going away and had not asked if he would see me again. I think I knew already why, and almost wished he would not tell me, though I knew he must. After we had coffee, he ordered liqueurs and he sat gazing into my eyes as if he were in love with me. At last he began.

'I was seventeen years old. Her name was Ellen Merryweather, and she was seventeen too, and I think it was the name I fell in love with. It made me think of circus ponies prancing, it had such a happy ring. I was going to be a great writer, and she was going to be a great actress and naturally no one would understand us in Ohio. So we hopped a freight and we came in on it to Hoboken and we looked across the river and saw New York, just sitting waiting for us. And Ellen said, "I can't go to New York a sinful woman," and so in Hoboken I married her. Nobody gave a damn how old we were, and I daresay I looked old enough. I *was* old enough in one way, sure enough, because Ellen was pregnant. So she ended up working in the back of a candy shop, and I got a job sweeping the floor in the press office, and that's how our marriage began. The funny thing was I married her before we knew she was pregnant, and she lost the baby anyway. But we were married by then and, my dear lady, to my everlasting sorrow, we are married now.' He put his hands together, like a supplicant and his eyes were full of sad warmth. 'Would God that it were otherwise, Justina Bride Melrose. The best things in life come always a little too late.'

And so, on a rainy night on the quayside of Etaples, we said goodbye.

15

Etaples
12 November 1918

Dear, dear May,

How sweet it was when the bells of peace were ringing! I cannot describe how wonderful we all felt, even those of us on the Ward who could not get out to celebrate. Everyone is filled with joy and there was dancing in the streets and almost an hysteria. Two of the girls went out for a short while and came back in tears! Total strangers had kissed them in the middle of the street! I wasn't off until late, but then dear Wendell, who is quite recovered now, arrived with three bottles of champagne and we all drank a toast to the Peace. We partied quite late and of course I was up early again this morning so I am feeling ragged as you'll well imagine.

Sadly, there is no end to the work, nor worse, to the misery, even though peace has come. We are as busy as ever. Of course men are still coming in with wounds, and trenchfoot and dysentery and all the rest, even now, but worst of all is the influenza. We have been as busy with influenza cases as we ever were with wounded at the height of the battles. And it is so sad, when they have survived so much, to see them dying of this wretched thing. It's so terribly, terribly fast. They come in, big tough young men, complaining of a headcold or something and in a day or two, they're dead. Wendell was really terribly fortunate. Still, now that there is no more fighting, those who do recover can at least hope to go home.

Regarding home, and in answer to your question, no, I don't yet know where I shall go. Wilhemina has returned to Arradale, and of course she has asked me to come to stay, but I don't think I shall. It's so full of memories and we're all so changed . . . Do thank your dear kind Mama for her sweet offer; though actually, should I come back to Ireland, I fear I'd be far more suited to Dublin and your own company, than to Ballysodare. Poor Eugenia, I haven't even told her I've bobbed my hair!

I searched everywhere for a christening gift for Eithne Maire. (So Padraic can whistle for his Sons of Ireland!) At last I came upon a rosary of tiny pearls in one of the little religious shops. The Padre blessed it for me. I still can't imagine Kate Catholic. *Or* a mother! What a pity James won't have her home. Eugenia must long to see the baby. Speaking of presents, do you know Douglas' little boy shall soon be three! Wilhemina says he's very like Douglas, too, though Clare thinks he favours Father. I promised Wilhemina I'd do a little portrait, when next I see them.

I imagine by the time this reaches you, you will have completed your Retreat. I am utterly fascinated, and I would have said quite amazed, were it not for the fact that nothing you do any longer surprises me. But the *Carmelites* of all orders! Oh, a braver girl you are than me!

I hope to see Sandy at the end of the week. I think he'll be back in England by Christmas, or just after. I was thinking it would be lovely if all of us could spend this Christmas together, somewhere, perhaps Dublin, perhaps Arradale, if we could persuade your good parents to venture forth from Temple House just once! Of course I don't imagine Clare will come if Kate is to be there, and I know Padraic can't possibly appear too publicly, even now. But still, it would be lovely if even *some* of us could be together again once more. There are so few of us left, after all.

Who would have imagined, four years ago, that it would come to this? Ah well, I must not get morbid. I will of course convey your love to Sandy. I am quite overjoyed with the prospect of seeing him, alive and well and the war done at last. These have not been easy times. Still, better times no doubt lie ahead,

All my love,
Justina

PS. *Of course* Wendell has asked! (Am I not the greatest prize of the Western Front?) I said no. It's far too soon, anyhow.

J.

The night before Alexander arrived in Etaples, Wendell and I dined together in the best and most expensive hotel he could find. I went openly to meet him, even though he had been until recently a patient in my own ward, and thus set among the Untouchables where VADs were concerned. But the war was over and the worst they could do in retaliation was send me home, and we were all going home anyway. I felt quite smug about it all.

Wendell had been two weeks in the influenza ward. He had been sent down from a Casualty Clearing Station, nearer the Front, with a dozen other Americans, all suffering the same. They all looked and seemed so much healthier and stronger than the rest of us but they fell ill as quickly. Wendell got off rather lightly, but he was quite sick anyhow. It really was a ferocious illness, nothing at all like any flu I've seen since. But though I nursed hundreds with it, I never had even a headcold. I must have been simply immune. Wendell and I thought ourselves terribly lucky to end up together in the same ward. All my romantic VAD compatriots insisted it was 'fate' and I must accept his proposal. I think they had their minds firmly on those marvellous gifts that kept coming our way.

Wendell did make life luxuriant and exciting, even in those circumstances, and the dinner we had that night was rather different from the one I had shared a rainy evening half a year before with Jack Redpath. There was no wartime seediness about this dining-room; it seemed as immune to the war as I to the Spanish flu. There was good food, and good wine, and flowers on the table. I don't know where any of them came from but by then I had learned that no strictures ever fully apply to those who have enough money. There is a certain fraud to all but the truest of famines.

I felt guilty sitting there, but Wendell laughed when I said so.

'Saint Justina. Isn't this hairshirt martyrdom enough?' He plucked playfully at the sleeve of my VAD uniform. 'I'll bet you're dying to burn that thing and get yourself into a pretty frock.' Wendell was buoyant, cheerful with the febrile cheerfulness of the convalescent, and filled with the cocky delight all the Americans felt in their victories. It was reasonable; they had done everyone proud, and were eager to be in the forward line of garrison divisions moving on into German territory in triumph. I imagine we would have been the same had the war ended three years before. As it was, all we wanted was to go home. Wendell was studying me with visible affection, over his wine glass.

'Well, my girl,' he said suddenly, 'I'll want an answer, you know. You've no excuses left. No war. No lofty duties . . .' He smiled wryly. I must have looked terribly glum because he said, rather hurt, 'Well, don't you *want* to marry me?'

'Of course I do,' I said distantly. 'Of course.'

He looked exasperated, 'But not yet.'

'It's so *soon*, Wendell. The War's only just finished.'

He lifted his blunt chin and turned away from me in a

gesture of annoyance. 'What then, a Peace Treaty?' He turned back and looked at me coolly. 'I must say, I admire your aplomb. How *old* are you?' he said.

'Twenty-five. Almost,' I added ingenuously.

'*Almost* . . . My God, Justina, you sound like a little kid.' He flicked a small crumb off the table. 'You know, most women *your* age are taking years off, not adding them on . . .'

I blinked, baffled. The four years of the War were a timeless hiatus. All our common lives, the natural order of our days, being disrupted, we felt as if no true years were passing, and now with the war ended, we would begin just where we had left off before. Like princesses in a tower, we had slept, and would wake ever youthful. It never occurred that someone might think we'd grown old.

'But why?' I asked stupidly, as that realization grew.

'Oh really, my dear.'

'Are you saying I'm too *old* to marry?'

'No dear. I'm not. I'm saying you're too old to stall. So am *I*,' he added impatiently. 'Damn it, girl, if we want to raise a family we can't . . .' But he stopped because I had got up to leave. 'Oh come on, darling, you *know* I don't mean it that way.' Even at such a moment he could succeed in making me feel myself the one at fault. I sat down. He grew gentler.

'Come dear,' he cajoled, still as if to a small child. 'You tell me what *you'd* like to happen . . . what do *you* really want?'

'Me?' I felt stunned. I had not had the leisure to think of such things for years. At first I could not even answer. Then suddenly I did know, quite precisely, and when I spoke my mind felt far away, in a dream, 'I want to sit by a lovely summery shore, by a green, gentle sea, and watch sea-bathers, and paint . . .' and then I drew a breath and words tumbled out like a child's Christmas list, 'And I want to go walking again, on the hill at Arradale and I want to ski in the winter at Strathpeffer, and ride, on an old longcar, back to back, to Strandhill . . . and I want to paint again, oh, I want to paint . . .' My hands were outstretched as if I could grasp the picture before my mind within them, and Wendell clasped them in his own.

In one of his sudden moments of vigorous emotion he whispered, 'Oh, you dear child. You shall. You shall do all those things. Every one. And you shall do them as my own sweet, darling wife!'

How could I tell him I wanted them not tomorrow, but yesterday, and not with him but with Michael Howie? So I closed my eyes and shook my head as if shaking tears away, and he took my silence for concession and was content.

The next afternoon Alexander came in by train to Etaples. His was one of the lucky battalions marked for an early return to Blighty. For them the war was ending with the Armistice; the claiming of the prize would be left gladly to others. Dusk was falling when I went to meet the train, and there was snow in the wind, and I was excited by it, in a childish way. I had gone to the station with another girl who was meeting her fiancé. We both clasped our arms about ourselves against the cold, and shuffled our feet and giggled together as we waited, for the simple joy of the war being over. We had lived so long with it that neither of us could quite believe that its threat no longer overhung the heads we loved. That joy came tumbling back from time to time, like the morning memory of a wonderful evening that comes with wakening, a happiness preceding its own definition. Jane, the other VAD, and I hardly knew each other well but we felt like sisters now, joined by the common blood of survival. She decided as we waited that we must all go together for tea and cakes, something lavish to celebrate, and I, without thinking, agreed.

I was sorry I had as soon as I saw Sandy step down from the train. He looked tired, with that special tiredness the war could breed, the way Douglas had looked on his first, and last Christmas leave, as if he carried the whole responsibility for everything himself, like Christ. He turned to look for me and could not disguise his dismay that I was not alone. But before I could do or say anything that might end any obligation he had slipped too readily into the accustomed politeness of our upbringing, greeting Jane with a kiss, shaking hands with her fiancé whom he had only met once before, and kissing me, too, with the cheery formality demanded by being 'in company'.

'We don't have to stay,' I whispered as he patiently followed Jane's lead to her tea shop.

'Of course we shall,' he murmured. 'Too delighted.' The words were meaningless. His forehead was lined with pain, and eyes squinted shut against the gentle light within the café.

'What's wrong?' I said.

'Nothing, dear. Just this damnable headache from the train.' I knew then, right away, and was wild to get him away from there, out of that noisy, draughty place, but there was nothing I could do. Jane chattered on and her fiancé boomed loudly about some trivial nonsense involving a sergeant-major. I could see Sandy wince with each reverberating word. He took two sips from his tea and put it aside. He ate nothing. I could stand no more and I got up, reaching for my coat, and turning to the surprised cheerful faces of our friends muttered, 'We must go. Terribly sorry. There's some business we must do before the shops close.'

They were closed already, but I did not bother even finding a better excuse, but grasped Sandy's arm and hauled him to his feet. He looked confused, but did not protest, and I led him hastily out into the street. The wind was blowing, snowy and cold off the sea and he breathed great gasps of it, and said, 'Oh bless you. It was so stuffy in there, I couldn't bear it.'

'You should have said,' I returned quickly, but I did not wait for his reply, but took his elbow and steered him in the direction of the hospital. I was determined that he see Sister, or someone, at once, but did not know how I would arrange it. To my concern for his welfare he protested his need to get out to the big training camp beyond the town where the rest of his battalion were assembling. I knew how stubborn he could be, too, but fell back on his own weakness of good manners.

'I can't possibly walk back alone, Sandy. The streets are quite wild, these days.'

He looked at me as if I had gone mad, but obediently stayed by my side. He was walking like a drunk man, with a swaying stagger of which he was quite unaware. He became peevishly obstreperous outside the ward, and refused to wait for me to find Sister, and I was searching my mind for some pretext by which I would detain him when he arranged it all himself by collapsing in the corridor. I remember him reaching out one hand to steady himself against the wall and saying with vast self-annoyance, 'Oh Christ, Justina, I'm going to do a bloody Bernhardt.' And then he just fell.

Two orderlies picked him up and carried him into the influenza ward. They were very matter of fact, because they were doing that sort of thing all the time. People were dropping quite suddenly just anywhere, on trains, in the streets, anywhere. They put him in the one empty bed, on which, that morning, I had assisted in laying out the body of an Australian sergeant who had died at dawn. It was all rather depressing, and I had to be as matter-of-fact as everyone else, because that was what was expected. But late that evening I shut myself in a broom cupboard and sat down on a metal mop-pail and wept for two sustained minutes. Then I dried my eyes, scurried through to the dispensary to wash them, and went about my business. No heroism, just no choice.

Sandy just went straight downhill. I think he was simply too tired to fight anything. He'd used all the strength even a young man has in those four years. There are limits; he had passed them. Of course I was with him all the time, and of course he had excellent care, not just from me, but from everyone in the ward. And from all my friends there among the nursing staff and the doctors I received assurance that he had every good chance. And yet, from the moment I knew he had the influenza, from the moment indeed that he spoke of his headache, a surety locked around me that he was doomed. It was as if I was waiting for this, for one more black gesture from the demon of the war, one last word to be spoken.

'He's going to die,' I said to Wendell, very calmly.

He held my hand. His own was shaking oddly. He said that Sandy was not going to die; there was no reason for him to, and his sound, persuasive logic gave me hope. Wendell was still 'staying in' in the Convalescent Home attached to the main hospital, and he came to see Sandy every day. Sometimes Sandy knew he was there, sometimes not. He suffered a great deal; they all did. There were terrible headaches, terrible backaches and continuous, strength-sapping fever. It was an unpretty illness of incontinence, sweat-soaked sheets, and humiliation. Once, when I cleaned him up, he moaned, 'Oh, not *you*,' a small protest against indignity in a small sad voice. Mostly he was too delirious to know who was there, or to care.

He woke one night from such a delirium, calm and

preternaturally cheerful and saw me and Wendell sitting there, and he grinned suddenly and said, 'What now, Cassandra? The war's over. Wendell's here. You're here. I'm here. So much for you and your silly damned swans.' He grinned, and waved one hand, a triumphant flippant little wave, and still smiling went back to sleep. And that was the end of it. He died a few hours later, without waking again. Farewell Arradale, and all my youth.

I was very, very bitter. I was bitter for a long time. I was bitter with everyone around me, the nurses and VADs, the doctors, Wendell, myself, everyone who had not saved Sandy. I was bitter also with God, in Whom I had taken to having very little belief at that time anyhow, and with Whom I was intensely angry then, and perhaps remain so just a little, even today, over Alexander's death. It seemed simply so totally unfair, and although I was never so foolish as to expect any magical protection for me and mine that I would define as 'justice' I was still reasonable and rational and all reason and rationality told me that this was one death too many. It was the war being *over*, of course, that made it such a deliberate slap in the face. Of course other people lost brothers, and lovers after the Armistice, days after, weeks after, even years after, as a result, direct or indirect of the War. But I daresay a good number of them also felt slapped in the face. Eighteen years before when I waited with Clare in the walled garden of Arradale, I had in the world five fine brothers, a splendid father, a handsome, gentlemanly uncle, and my beautiful cousin; eight knights to be my champions throughout my life. Now there was but one old, sad man in Ballysodare, even at this moment awaiting one more shock of bereavement. If the great weaver of patterns found some splendid symmetry in sweeping away each and every one of these lovely creatures, I could not fathom it, nor can I today. When I see the other side of that tapestry, it had better be good.

Of course Wendell was there to comfort me, but Wendell proved a sad comforter, and I ended instead comforting him. It surprised me, because I had thought him a strong man, but his strength was the physical strength of a powerful body, and the social strength of a commanding mind. It was not a spiritual strength. Death requires deeper things.

He was absolutely shattered. I suppose it was in part because of his being, as Sandy had said, 'young' in the war. He had not time to form many deep friendships, and his own Division was formed of young Americans from all across their wide continent. There were not the villages serving together, as in the British New Army battalions, or the tight regimental companionship of our old regular army. He was among strangers, and the deaths around him had been strangers' deaths, until now. Sandy was the first person he had loved who had died in the war. He was experiencing at its very end what we had all experienced at the very beginning. He must have felt terribly alone.

Some days later, when Sandy was already lying in the crowded cemetery of Etaples, we walked along the brown winter strand, and a more forbidding seascape I have never known. The cold Channel waters slipped in and out upon stony shingle, and grey sleet strafed our faces. Wendell kept talking about Sandy in the disconnected way of the grieving, laughing suddenly about little anecdotes, rallying into humour, collapsing into black misery. He had one hand companionably on my shoulder and squeezed it tightly each time a new thought came to him. He was telling me about Sandy as if Sandy had been his brother, not mine. I listened, nodded, agreed. We came to a stony jetty broken down into little more than a heap of weed-and-mussel strewn rock. The winter light broke out of clouds and fell upon the rock pools with sudden stirring beauty.

Wendell stopped. He pointed towards the shining water and said, 'That, you see. He would have loved that sort of thing. He had an artist's eye, a true artist's . . . oh God, Justina, I just can't stand it.' He fumbled for me, and muttered, 'Oh please, please, I'm so alone.' He held me in his arms and wept upon my wet shoulders. 'Oh I love you, I love you,' he said desperately. And it was there, by that cold, bleak sea, we agreed to marry. I was not sure, even then, that it was me, or Sandy's ghost, he wished to wed.

But, if why he asked was subject to debate, surely much more so was, why did I agree? I have been asked that many times since, by Clare, by May, by many others, friend and otherwise, and as many times, by myself. I am afraid there is no easy answer. Clearly it was Sandy's wish, expressed to me almost a year before, and agreed to then, but that was not all, and after all that time and with the War ended, I felt only lightly bound by my pledge. I suppose a good part of it was love and loneliness, both Wendell's and mine. We were the classic bits of flotsam on an angry sea, the lost ships in the night seeking sanctuary. And we were both so isolated. Had any of his formidable kinsmen been to hand, I doubt there would have been any proposal. Good sense, that great Yankee substitute for wisdom, would have overridden passion. And had any of my dwindling family been at my side; had Clare with her cynical tongue, or May with her wise good humour been there to counsel me, perhaps I would have said no. But there was no one for either of us, and though I wrote to both Clare and May, and to Eugenia as well, it was only to inform them of my engagement, not in any way to seek counsel in advance. Yet there was one person whose judgement I did seek; so greatly did I value it that I boldly poured all my personal miseries and doubts into a letter to a man who could only be called a stranger, and sent it, like a foolish schoolgirl, chasing after him. But if Jack Redpath received this missive in Paris, which, after so many months of no contact, was as unlikely as his even still being in that city, he did not make any haste to reply. After a few days, embarrassed and humiliated, I prayed it would vanish in the chaos of the war's end, and never be seen.

And so our plans were made. I would complete my duties, and he his, and when the time came for the lauded return to Hoboken, if not by Christmas then perhaps not much after, he would seek a brief leave. We would marry in London and sail together to New York.

Then, and so quickly, what had been a momentous private decision became a public fact. Parties were given in our honour, everyone congratulated us. My ever romantic companions on the ward were overwhelmed with delight. It was the fairy-tale end to a complex, but fairy-tale story. As is the way of such things, the momentum of events quite swept us along, pleasurably enough, and doubt was jettisoned, unnecessary cargo. Soon I was thoroughly enjoying myself and answering Clare's stunned, cold displeased letter with wicked fun. I was waiting, a little uneasily, for the Margaret Sanger tract in the brown envelope that I was sure would follow, and oh yes, was still floundering around in my ignorance, too mortified to find anyone to tell me 'what every girl needs to know'.

And then, just before I was to cross the Channel, my last day at the hospital completed, and my farewells ended, two letters arrived. One was from May in Dublin, and the other from Jack Redpath in Paris. I sat looking at it in silence. It had arrived amidst my new gaiety like the Ancient Mariner at the wedding feast. I remembered with chagrin the emotions, now so inappropriate, I had poured into my own letter, and was afraid to open his, much less read his reply. I steeled myself, and slit open the battered envelope, but at once was relieved to find what appeared in no way to be an answer at all. There were two sheets of paper, and on the upper one, without any salutation was a brief manuscript:

HIS LAST GIRL

Oh shall we dance?
I'm feeling rather flighty,
With the morphia in my head.
I've another girl in Blighty,
But will it matter, when I'm dead?
Oh do let's dance!
You really are so pretty,
And I swear I'll never tell.
Oh such a dashed pity,
My leg's all shot to hell,
But oh, let's dance!
I know the Boche are coming,
And the boys have all gone on,
And the wretched guns keep drumming,
And my knee is carrion,
Still please let's dance!
And when you meet some happy year,
With luckier lads than I,
In my silence I will hear,
And be blessed where I lie,
When you dance.

Carefully, I lifted the script and set it aside, and found beneath it a briefer letter.

Dear Justina,

Marriage cures a broken heart the way an alligator cures a broken leg.

Love,
Jack

I stared at the paper, unsure whether I was meant to laugh or cry. 'Oh May,' I whispered, opening her letter, 'please help.' But hers was briefer even than Jack's.

Merrion Square
23 December 1918

Dear, dear Justina,
Don't.

Love always, and ever more,
May

Part Three

16

18, Gramercy Park South
20 September 1920

May Darling,

Well, my dear, my little one is born at last, a lovely baby girl. Dark eyes and hair like Mama, a perfect beauty, and now I have a lovely family, 'one of each'. All's quite well now, indeed I'm positively thriving, but I confess to having had quite a miserable time. Nothing so bad as the first, thank God (Mrs Pyke assured me in measured whispers that 'the others' are always easier) but still rather a trial. Of course it would be the hottest day of the summer (even in *September*!). The weather is terrible. New York at its worst; the heat unrelenting and the air thick like steam. The grass in the park is all withered brown. Why *do* I choose to have my babies in the summer? Not, I suppose, that one *chooses* that, or anything about it really. The Lying In Hospital was airless and I was quite out of my head with the gas, imagining myself with Michael on Ben Wyvis in the cold, cold snow. Isn't it strange how the past yet clings?

We have agreed on Eleanor Clare. I don't suppose Clare will be much impressed, but I *was* pleased to remember Mama. Quite fortuitously there is an Eleanor amongst the Shippingham aunts and there's a funny little conspiracy about to infer that *she* and not Mama is the namesake. Oh they *are* comic! I shall call her Ellie anyhow, not Nell. Only Mama could be Nell.

Little Wendell is quite taken with his new sister. He's really been terribly good, though quite mystified, poor pet. Just a baby himself, and now this intruder!

Still he seems such a big boy beside the new arrival. Have I said, he is walking already for over a month! I must tell you, the most extraordinary occurrence rather marred my homecoming. We were all in the drawing room, and Wendell had champagne sent up for a family celebration and in the middle little Wendell toddled in, so he was allowed to stay. Then he wanted his little shirt off, and who could blame him, in this awful heat and so of course I took it off for him. Pandemonium! Mrs Pyke looked as if a grown man had exposed his most private regions. I honestly thought she would faint. She went icily silent; Wendell *père* was furious with me; the whole event quite ruined. Now can you imagine? A baby of a single year? Oh, sometimes May, I do get angry.

But I must stop saying these things; it seems disloyal, doesn't it? After all, they *are* Wendell's family, and if I begin carping at everything, I'll end up just like Clare. She at least has met her match in Mrs Pyke. Like poles of a magnet they repelled so violently that they almost swung round to attract. Throughout the whole three weeks of her visit in July, I lived half in terror of a terrible explosion, half in hysterical mirth. Do you not think that people who Believe in Causes are all remarkably alike? Whether it be Propriety or Revolution, the passions are the same. Of course the family were not to be impressed with her journalistic successes or her politics. (Journalism is a *trade*, my dear!) And of the latter I too have my reservations. As if the War were not enough to teach us that reason and forgiveness are the *only* way. Still she rages on. Now it is Reparations, and Making the Germans Pay. Actually, I think Mrs Pyke rather agreed about that, but for her determination not to agree with Clare about anything. I was sorriest for poor Meggie, dragged along into the middle of it. They do make a comic pair now, Clare so stern in her tweeds, still more beautiful than anyone, and Meggie dressing up her homeliness with more frivolity every day. Like a wolfhound and a poodle in tandem.

Still it was good to see them both; a touch of home, even the arguments! And we did have fun together. We all had a day out at Coney Island, even Wendell, and myself hugely awkward at seven months. (Wendell's Mama thoroughly shocked at my appearing enceinte – albeit wrapped up like a Turk in all that heat!) Clare built sand castles for little Wendell with the determination of a Napoleon. She was really quite sweet with him. She talks to tiny children precisely as if they were adults, and do you know they seem to rather like it!

You see, with even *Clare* managing to be remotely maternal, on occasion, I do find it ever more difficult to understand Kate. Of course I know you are a most loving aunt, and happy to care for little Eithne, and no doubt your dear Mama is simply overjoyed, but it really hardly seems right that she is so much away from her own parents. I cannot understand Kate, and dread to think what will happen should she 'fall' again. But I confess to being mystified; they are such dear creatures, how can one not like them? Of course I know there is that other child of theirs, Holy Ireland, whose birth they must attend (and a hard labour it is proving, is it not?). I wish we knew more what Padraic was really up to, or maybe it is best that we do not. Perhaps for that reason, Eithne *is* better away from them. How bad is it, May? Please tell me. We hear such confused stories and I worry so, over you, and your parents, and all of our friends . . . it is hard to think of such violence in the gentle fields of our childhood.

Dear May, it made me so sad to think you even hesitated to tell me of your conversion to Catholicism. Of course I was a little stunned, but I was never opposed. Please don't think I am against such things. The War did shake any faith I had, but it was a weak faith no doubt and I am not about to be superior about it doing so. The War turned as many to God as it turned away . . . in that way it was simply like all the rest of life. And of course I feel no different about you, how could I? Imagine though, you and Kate both, now, but how different you are! *Catholic* it must be to house you both. I'm sorry your Mama was so aggrieved, but I suppose we must expect it, and in time, no doubt, she will forgive. Poor soul, her world has changed beyond imagining, has it not?

I am so glad you were able to see early copies of *The Gateway*. I have written to the publisher to thank him personally, and of course I now have several copies of my own. It *is* a magnificent effort, though I cannot help being sad thinking of the years it took to see print, and most of all, that Father never saw it, nor had any cause for hope. What saddens me even more is Mirza Hassan. How I wish I could contact him somehow, so that he might see it. I always thought of it as half his book. (And I know Father did the same.) The most frustrating part is that I actually have an address; an old one, from during the War, but still it might prove a beginning – but I told Wendell about it and as soon as he saw the district he forbade me to go there. I am such a coward, May. Part of me yearns to simply go anyhow, but I dare not. Were it Wendell alone, perhaps I might, but they are such a fortress when they are together. I cannot face the wrath of all of them. But to think of Hassan and I here in the same city, perhaps but half a mile apart, with no contact after all these years! I won't go on about it, it makes me miserable.

I do get lonely among them sometimes. How I would love to see you all again. Wendell speaks vaguely of a 'European tour' but it is hard to know with Wendell what really to believe. And he is genuinely terribly busy. Besides, I doubt he would intend to bring the children, and I could not bear to be separated from them by such a distance, and for so long a while. How did our mothers ever manage, being so much apart from us? Wendell presses me to make much more use of the nanny, but I simply refuse. I am quite adamant and so, alas, is he. We are both very stubborn. Not always the best thing.

Oh, May. Life is a tangle, isn't it? How little we know of it when we are young. And how little we know of a man on our wedding day. Still, I have much to be cheerful over; I've my two lovely children. And I have my painting; though I confess a pang of guilt when you asked what I have done. Precious little, I fear. It isn't really the babies, though. There is something in the atmosphere. I have never needed lavish praise. (Look how I fended South Kensington!) But there must be *some* receptiveness, beyond that awful condescending head-patting in which they indulge. 'Oh do meet our dear clever Justina. She *paints*, don't you, dear?' They don't mind, you see, as long as things are kept in their proper place; my babies in the nursery and my painting much the same. I did manage to do some nice pieces in August, on Long Island, water colours of the Great South Bay shore, and a small portrait of an old clam fisherman. I trundled off each morning with my easel, hugely pregnant and by that time no one cared what I did as long as I stayed out of sight!

I must go, darling. We're meant to be lunching out and Wendell detests our host but is going for some business reason and consequently will be in a hideous mood. The last thing needed is for me to be late. I'm *always* late. How can one be otherwise, if the baby is fretting, or whatever. But of course that sets off the entire thing about the nanny again, so the best course is to be *on time, punc*tual, my dear, if one is organized properly one is *never* late. Understood?

Oh, understood.

Love in adversity
Justina

Theresa knocked at the door, two sharp raps of insolent respectfulness, and I slipped the letter under the blotter before I answered. She came in languorously, carrying my luncheon frock over her arm, slightly extended, like an accusation, and I lacked the courage to do anything but hastily dress. Theresa was my personal maid, provided for me like all the rest of the staff, and the house itself and all its furnishings, by the particular choice of Mrs Shippingham Pyke. The family townhouse stood three doors down on the same side of the Park. Our own, virtually identical, had been selected for Wendell and his yet unchosen future wife years before. Sometimes I sensed the ghosts of other prospective brides moving among these same chintzes and mahogany, phantom sisters of my own. I suspect almost all of them would have rooted more readily there than I.

'Of course Justina is *born* to this life,' Mrs Pyke was fond of saying, even while despairing of me. My genealogy was her armour against the faint dismay of her friends at Wendell's marriage. We had wed in London, without awaiting the family blessing. Thus Wendell, doubting my acceptability, sought to forestall opposition with a *fait accompli*. It was a mistake. Unwittingly we had deprived the family of a great social spectacle; the public blending of their bloodlines with those of the Melroses of Arradale. We had discarded our best card. We arrived in New York in January of 1919 already a couple, a hasty wartime match, returning soldier and VAD bride, a youthful folly. The image was disastrously wrong. On my first evening in the family home Wendell's father, a solid, heavy-shouldered man, drank port all evening, hardly speaking. When he drew me aside, into the library, he was on the edge of sullen drunkenness, though his speech was clipped and assured. He found us a corner where no other guests might come and leaned against a mantelpiece, staring down at me.

'I'm a blunt man, Justina,' he said. 'I was not consulted

over this match and I'm not pleased with it, but since it's made, I'll back my son, and his choice. We should manage to get on quite satisfactorily, if we meet each other's expectations. If not, I have the wherewithal to undo it. I just wish you to understand that.' I said nothing. There was nothing to say. Then he smiled lamely and said with awful patronizing good humour, 'There, there, that's a good girl. Now it's said it can be forgotten. Come through and join Mrs Pyke and Wendell's sisters. My, my, that's a pretty dress.' He went off, absently, in a soft cloud of Havana smoke.

I had been married for three weeks on the occasion of that conversation, but its cynicism left me strangely unmoved. I suppose I expected little more from the father, having already, I fear, lost my innocence regarding the son. I am not, I hastily add, referring to physical matters. That side of my marriage, which I shall not detail, was precisely as one might expect in such a union, the fruit of my ignorance and his impatient youth. Great lovers are not created overnight. Like geisha, they are trained and my training was pitifully slight. But these are after all, simple natural matters, managed by the most ignorant of peoples, and were that all that troubled us, no doubt we would have found a way to happiness. That Wendell was a romantic, and a physical man, I surely realized, and was ready, and happy, despite my appalling lack of knowledge, to accommodate. What I had not known, and could not accept, was that Wendell was also a rake.

I found out within days of our wedding, a foolish silly incident at the house of friends in Scotland, no doubt brought on by frustration on his part with our blundering marriage bed. I forgave that first, abortive indiscretion out of embarrassment and disbelief, blotting it quite out of my mind as if it had never occurred. The next occasion was aboard the *Carpathia* as we sailed for America, a much more serious event that I could neither forgive nor forget. This was no matter of housemaid's apron strings, but an evening liaison with a titled lady, the culmination of Wendell's voyage-long infatuation with her conversation and her daring. She was older than me and far more sophisticated, one of a type that grew prevalent in those years after the War, drowning memories in champagne and flirtation. I suppose it was quite the feather in her cap, seducing a man on his honeymoon. But in truth there was no honeymoon, no romantic spell of devotion, nor even an honourable interval of fidelity. From the night of our first fumbling consummation, Wendell's interest in me died. He bore a sad love-curse, by which romance and reality were almost always irreconcilable. His moment of victory was invariably his moment of defeat.

Looking back, I feel pity for him, but then I was too hurt and young to feel anything but misery. But how then, knowing the man, could I have not seen it all in advance? Well, how could I have done? Such matters were never discussed. We talked of family, and houses, and the raising of children, the entertainment of friends, those public sides of a marriage that would indeed remain to be dealt with when frail passions were past. And as for passions, in those weeks before our marriage Wendell's devotion to me met its romantic and unconsummated height . . . no woman ever took his notice.

Nor had he the telling cynicism of the true philanderer. Had he been that, it would have been easier. But Wendell was a pure romantic. Most of his liaisons were actually innocent, in that they were defections of the heart alone. Some were clearly otherwise. But each, at its beginning, was marked by a boyish ingenuousness that was almost charming in naivety. For Wendell romantic love was born afresh every day. He lived in a permanent recurrent hope, only deflated occasionally by the reality of consummation. I had known that side of him, honourable, courtly, given to moments of extraordinary intensity of love, and it was most compelling. Perhaps because of that I could never hate the women who fell for him, but felt sorry for each in her turn.

And their turns passed, with a slow, sad grace, in a rhythm I had come, in two years, to know well. It began always in an innocence. The beloved was much on his mind, her name much on his tongue. My opinion would be sought. If she were a servant, her position would be improved, if a lady, her acquaintance would be furthered and often, at dinners arranged for that purpose, I would be the trapped and unwilling accomplice of my own deception. Lest I portray him as needlessly cruel, let me add that at this time no thought of seduction had crossed his mind; he was simply drawn, like the mythical moth, to the flame. Only always it was I, and occasionally she, who was burned.

Theresa was his present fancy. I knew because, having been but a backdrop to our lives, a usefulness in starched black and white, she became suddenly a topic of much interest. Comments were passed upon her capability, a reference made to her Irish immigrant family, her fresh 'old country' complexion praised. How fond she was of children! How they all loved her below stairs! From a cypher she had become St Theresa, practically overnight. I suppose I should laugh, because it was pathetic and funny, but it was also humiliating. The girl was sharp-witted and not blind. Her wages had been raised, her duties lightened, and she knew why. When the master dallies, the mistress is judged a fool.

It is not my nature to order servants about unreasonably, but in the case of Theresa, even the mildest co-operation had become a matter of her whim. Strangely, I had once liked the girl immensely, perhaps because her black-haired, blue-eyed Irish beauty reminded me so of Persephone. But that was all over now, and our present unease was not helped by Wendell's insistence, out of a perversity I do not yet understand, upon throwing her constantly in my company. I could barely leave the house without Theresa being attached to me out of some pretence. Then Wendell would beam happily, at mistress and servant in cheerful companionship, the perfect domestic scene.

I saw her watching me, over my shoulder, as I glanced in the mirror to adjust the brim of my hat. Her face was smooth and impassive, the sweet-turned mouth gentle in a perpetual smile, yet I was certain of her scorn and wondered if it were real, or a fiction of my own humiliated imagination. Then the baby wailed her thin new-lamb wail in the nursery and I turned to run to her.

'Mr Pyke is waiting below,' Theresa reminded, calmly.

'Ellie's crying,' I protested. 'My baby's crying.'

'Isn't Nanny there?' she asked, eyes widening in innocence. I stopped. Of course Nanny was there. Theresa was holding out my little silk jacket, and reluctantly I shrugged into its cool interior. Wendell was standing silently at the foot of the main stairs, tapping one tan glove against the other with abrupt controlled little flicks.

'Ellie was crying,' I said, as he helped me into the car. He settled himself beside me, his hat on his knees and the September sun through the car window lighting his boyish blond hair. He tapped on the glass and the car was driven away.

'Aren't babies always crying?' he said mildly. The sun flickered painfully behind his silhouette and I looked down into the dark, hot interior of the car. 'Nanny is quite capable. You undermine her authority by not trusting her.'

'I trust her. Of course I trust her.'

'Then let her do her job.'

'My baby is *my* job,' I blurted stupidly.

'No, Madam.' Suddenly he was angry in his rare, deep cold way. 'Your job is being my wife. Pity you are so little aware.' I turned and looked out of the window. I thought of the two big beds, and the two big rooms, in which we slept separately.

'I'm sorry,' I said. 'She's so little still. In another week I'll be fine, I promise. She'll be a proper horror like her brother and I'll be glad to turn her over to anyone!' I laughed as gaily as I could and glanced across at him, under wet lashes. But he softened, and smiled, and relaxed enough to reach one hand to take mine.

'Of course you won't,' he said 'You'll coddle her and spoil her because she's my little girl,' and added with small-boy wistfulness, 'but sometimes I'd like a little of you to myself.'

I pulled back from him and heard my own voice go cold. 'You have as much of me as you want, I think,' I said.

'Justina, don't be difficult.'

'How is that difficult?' I said. 'It's simple truth.'

He straightened in his seat, and then abruptly slammed shut the little glass window between us and the chauffeur. It was hotter than ever then, within the closed car.

'How like you,' he said. 'Truth, truth. You and your sanctimonious Bohemian honesty. Let us have pure truth. Be damned to grace and dignity. Justina the free spirit. Never mind your duties, your place, *my* place, indeed.' He flung an angry hand towards the red-brick frontages of Washington Square North, as if I had personally assaulted their autumnal dignity.

'I can't discuss things when you're like this,' I protested.

'You can't discuss things ever,' he shouted. 'All you

can do is drift about in paint-spotted aprons and hide in the nursery when anyone comes. I should get a blasted gypsy wagon and drive you off into the sylvan splendour like damned Augustus John.'

'Well, that would be perfect,' I said smiling as sweetly as I might. 'He keeps two women, too.'

His face went pale and his mouth dropped open. Any other man might have slapped me, but Wendell could never do that. 'Justina, you *stun* me with your crudery,' he muttered at last, but somehow I had ceased to care.

Something still and peaceful within me had taken root, and it blossomed now, fed by his anger. *You do not own me* it said, and comforted by it, I turned away, my eyes on the tall trees of the Square that reminded me in a sad distant way of Stephen's Green. And it was at that memoried, prophetic moment that I saw him, as if all my lonely longing for the past had conjured him out of thin air. And indeed he strode as light as a ghost, down the shady pathway, a tall brisk-stepped angular old man with his white beard trimmed short for the summer heat and a black, loosened neck-tie flapping.

'Oh!' I cried and then in expanding delight, 'Oh! Oh look!' I grasped Wendell's sleeve, my annoyance with him as forgotten as his own anger with me. I hardly felt his stiff tug to be free. 'Oh look, look!' and I leaned forward and rapped furiously on the glass door until the chauffeur obediently slowed his vehicle and turned towards the kerb.

'What are you doing, for God's sake?' Wendell spluttered, slamming the little window open. 'We're late already.' He leaned forward and ordered, 'Drive on, man. Drive on.'

The chauffeur half turned over his shoulder just as I burst out, 'But it's Mr Yeats! It's Mr Yeats!' I was holding both Wendell's arms, shaking him and laughing delightedly. But the car rolled on and I suddenly realized we were not stopping, that Mr Yeats was dwindling behind me, down a bench-lined pathway in Washington Square and this miraculous moment was vanishing with him.

'Who?' Wendell said, removing my hands curtly and turning up his cuff to observe the military-style wristwatch he still wore. I whirled about on the seat like a child, staring out through the narrow back window. 'Justina, you'll ruin your frock,' he snapped.

'Oh damn my frock,' I cried. I was peering back, and begging, 'Oh please, *please* stop,' in the helpless voice of a child. Then suddenly I was aware of the most vivid of memories, so vivid that I was again my fourteen-year-old self, skirts raised and hat askew, running through the streets of Dublin, after my vanishing artist. It was as if Mr Yeats had been snatched out of my world by the hand of time, only to be deposited here utterly unchanged, a dozen years later, in Washington Square. I felt if I could but reach out and touch his coat, I would at once be freed to follow him back into the life I had lost, all those years before, in Ireland. Memories came tumbling back, one on top of the other, of people and places, and most of all of the person I had been and the artist I had dreamed of being. Then suddenly I was myself once more, a grown unhappy woman, sitting in the back of a big, hot motorcar before a house on Waverly Place. Mr Yeats was gone. The trees of the Square were a green smudge behind us. Beside me my husband sat cold and unimpressed by my childish tears.

'When you're quite done, we'll go in,' he said, and I knew that the past was an irrecoverable thing, vanishing like an old man down a crowded city street, glimpsed ever smaller, and harder to identify until it was utterly gone. There was no going back; life went merely forward into what was duller, harsher, plainer and harder to bear. It was a bitter, maturing moment.

'All right,' I said. I opened my small bag, removed a silk handkerchief and neatly blotted my eyes. That was easier to do in our era when no one made up. I did not ask him how I looked. 'We'll go in now.' And so we did, as if nothing extraordinary had happened, and the whole event vanished from Wendell's awareness, swallowed up by his vast lack of interest in anything about myself that did not directly apply to him. But something had changed forever in me.

A woman is a bride as long as she is in love, and a wife as long as she obeys. A woman neither obedient, nor in love, is as restless as a chestnut mare. So why did I remain? A simple question; and there is, of course, a straight and simple answer: because there was nowhere to go. But there was much more to it than that, there always is.

Fledglings teeter on the edge of the nest out of a double ignorance. The nest is cramped, but tolerably comfortable; they do not know it will grow too small. And they do not know they can fly. Once they have discovered both truths, usually by accident, they leap, blissfully unaware that had they not done, they would simply have been pushed.

My nest was more than tolerably comfortable. Aside from his one chilling flaw, Wendell was not a bad husband. He was gracefully generous; the gifts of our courtship continued to shower down upon me, though now both their expense and their intimacy increased by virtue of our married state. Indeed, were clothing and jewellery the *raison d'être* of my life (as for some women they are), my marriage would have been blessed. He was fair, and remarkably tolerant regarding my own family, at least the little of it he had experienced. He welcomed my difficult sister under his roof with a true brother's loyalty. As far as possible he was just in his judgements between his parents and myself. I qualify merely because the climate of parental mastery and filial duty in which he had grown was so powerful and long-standing that it would be quite unrealistic to expect him to be other than subject to it. It had, too, its rewards of a sort. Wendell was an only son, and his three charming sisters were as subject to him as I had been to Douglas. Uncomfortably, I found myself in quite the regal position Wilhemina held at Arradale; my wishes superseded theirs and during the summer months on Long Island, it was I, not even the eldest of them, who presided over the table of what had been their childhood retreat. They accepted my presence with touching humility and I liked them very much. They were the balm of my uneasy existence, though I saw little of them. The eldest, Mary, was the wife of a Boston man. The second, Phyllis, studied at Sarah Lawrence College, and the youngest and sweetest was an invalid, crippled by polio at ten. Her name was, appropriately, Grace, and often during the first two summers of my marriage, we shared long afternoons under the shade trees of The Grey House, that huge and rambling wooden 'cottage' on the shore of the Great South Bay, where all generations of Pykes came to escape the oppressive New York heat. She read, in her wicker invalid's chair, much like Father's at Arradale, and I painted and in her cheerful company I quite forgot the less happy side of my life.

Wendell was often away, involved with business affairs, over which he made much weary lamentation, exactly as his father did, but without which he was sadly lost. He did adore his son, though the child's tears and small miseries and even his small pleasures soon bored him. Still, he tried valiantly to play with him, and devoted summer afternoons to us, with great fuss and demonstration. But they were tense and restless times and even sailing his little ketch on the bay, he could not let half an hour pass without looking at his watch. Sometimes, observing him, I thought of Sandy in his grave at Etaples, and wondered what Wendell was hurrying for.

Sandy's memory still haunted him. The only occasion on which he ever opposed his mother was the choosing of our first child's name. Alexander was his fervent preference, hotly argued. But in the end, and significantly, he lost, and yet a third Wendell Shippingham Pyke was christened at the Church of the Ascension, Fifth Avenue. As if by apology, young Wendell came into the world with features so remarkably like my brother's, that he seemed more Sandy's child than mine, and though I called him Wendell aloud, in my heart he was Alexander.

And he, of course, was the surest answer to the question I have posed. Scarcely had the first glimmer of future unhappiness appeared in my marriage, than I discovered myself pregnant. There was no going back, no altering the future, and in circumstances like that one blindly makes the best of things and is a fool to do otherwise. Besides, the Pykes were delighted that Wendell would have an heir, and Wendell himself was touchingly proud of me, as if I were the first woman in the world to produce a child. Despite our sophistications, in these ancient matters of wedding, and childbearing, we are no different from the simplest of peoples. Our most complex customs find their parallel in an Afghan Village. A child confirms a marriage. But a woman with neither father nor brothers has little power, even over that child. I had come, like Ruth after Boaz, without kith, without kin, into a foreign land. His people would be my people, and his gods . . . well, that was another matter. But were my marriage to alter now, it would be by their decision, and on their terms. Alone, I would not fly.

And so I went into the house on Waverly Place, at my husband's side, and dined there with my husband's friends. I smiled and was charming to the man whose manners he despised, but whose co-operation in business he required, and did all that was expected of me, quite unaware that by the end of that day, I would no longer be alone. My brief glimpse of Mr Yeats seemed like the frustrating half-memory of a dream. I even came to fancy that it was an error, a mistaken identity, that he had never been there at all. It was easier to believe that, than that I had found him, to no avail.

After luncheon, a small party of us went on together to a gallery on 8th Street where an exhibition of a group called 'Adirondack Primitives' had engaged Wendell's interest. He had visited it twice, and earmarked two paintings for purchase. I believe he wanted some response from his friends, because it was a new field to him, and his confidence was lacking. I liked the gallery; it was bright and cheery and busy with an odd mix of people. Half were like Wendell and his friends, serious and faintly disapproving of the other half, who were colourful and eccentric by contrast. Those were the artists and their supporters; a modest enough community, hardly to be distinguished by their dress or style from any more staid professions. And yet there were differences, an outlandish coat, a gypsy shawl, a flowing Byronic necktie, small enough gestures of defiance, but sufficient in a more ordered world to signal the presence of rebellious spirits. Wendell and his luncheon companions stepped among them like determined berry-pickers, after the fruit but wary of the thorns. I was admittedly drawn to the opposition; they seemed so brave, with their faintly shabby clothes and hopeful eyes. I liked their paintings too, mountain and farmyard scenes enlivened by bright, unreal primaries. I went round by myself, admiring each in turn, while Wendell and his friends carefully dissected the two he was considering, in technical terms I did not understand.

Twice I eluded the too-enthusiastic conversation of a young man in a long grey coat, knowing that Wendell was watching. I escaped eventually, only to be overwhelmed by a jolly mannish woman, wearing a stalker's cap. Again I was aware of Wendell's eyes upon me. I knew from experience that any interest I might express in such people would result in a scathing and self-assured attack on 'that intolerable woman' or 'that ridiculous young fool'. Such judgements were proffered for my own protection; Wendell bore a conviction that my foreign birth deprived me of any social sense whatever. 'I *know* these people,' he invariably responded. 'Trust me, my dear.' Having little choice, I trusted, and kept silent at such gatherings, for safety's sake.

But as I did just that, there appeared from an inner room a lady I had not seen before. She was tall and thin, and distinguished by a wonderful head of light brown hair, piled up in a soft, old-fashioned dressing, just as my mother had worn hers. It was unusual; half the women of the company wore bobbed hair, and she was not old, though, like most of Wendell's acquaintances, she was older than me. She wore a dress of soft lavender silk, and three strings of pearls, and looked softly, dewily elegant, as if one observed her through a mist of gauze.

'And who is this charming creature?' she asked sweetly, as she took my arm at the elbow. 'Is this possibly the young Mrs Pyke?' The question was oblique, and yet there was no one to answer but myself, and so I nodded, and said I was.

'How delightful. And you are an artist too,' she added, though it was something I had long since ceased to claim. Someone had told her, however, and she then turned her lovely misty smile upon me, and I looked behind her gold-framed lenses and saw, magnified by their convex planes, huge myopic and endearing blue eyes, peering into my own. Quite suddenly I had an overwhelming desire to fling myself on to her lace draped shoulder and weep. People of great compassion affect me like emotional magnets. 'Why, you poor thing,' she whispered, no doubt because that great wave of misery showed on my face.

I blinked back embarrassing, ridiculous tears, sniffed and whimpered in explanation, 'I'm so sorry; I've just had a baby.'

She nodded with great wisdom. Then she turned abruptly, and even as she slipped her arm gently through mine, called with sharp authority across the room, 'Wendell, dear, your young wife is very tired. I am taking her across for tea. You will be for ever making up your mind, anyhow, won't you?' She said it in such a way that it was apparent that Wendell would be 'for ever' whether he chose to or not. I had never heard anyone address him like that and was wickedly thrilled by it, particularly because he made no protest. Then I was led grandly to the door of the gallery while he watched as a man in a spell.

Once out in the stifling heat of 8th Street the lady turned to me and said gaily, 'Oh they *will* go *on* so!' She was humorous and sweet, but uncompromising. 'I love art, my dear, but in the end a painting is something to hang upon a wall . . . not a way to God. I can't abide making a religion of it!'

I laughed, delighted, the words were like a splash of bright sea water, washing everything clean. I walked happily beside her, crossing to the north side of the street and turning left, towards Sixth Avenue.

The avenue was noisy and busy, smelling of strange foods and filled with the sort of people, foreign and

European, that I rarely saw. I was hardly ever out on foot in the city, except for my daily excursions, trailed by Theresa, to the locked confines of Gramercy Park. I felt wild, and reckless, merely being away from Wendell's oppressive chauffeured car. I did not know where we were going, and as we turned up the avenue, under the shadow of the elevated railroad, I became fearful that I would be too long away.

'Is it far?' I asked timidly. 'Wendell will want to leave as soon as he's bought his paintings.' I think she laughed. The rocketing clatter of a train drowned all sound. When it had passed, she was smiling in a gentle, contented way.

'He shan't buy a thing until we're back,' she said.

'How do you know?' I asked.

'Because it's my gallery.' She giggled like a schoolgirl, and clutched my arm.

The house was on 10th Street, between Sixth and Fifth Avenues, just down from the Church of the Ascension which I attended most Sundays with the Pykes. It was a three-storey brick-fronted structure with ivy-smothered walls and a short flight of steps leading up to the front door. Black wrought iron railings framed the little well below the stairs and rimmed the steps. The door was black painted, and trimmed with a brass knob and a knocker in the form of a lion's head. On either side were pots of red and pink geraniums. We climbed the steps together and the lady spent a long while searching for her key, and then, giving up, bent down and fished a spare one delicately out of a hiding place in one of the flower-pots. 'I lose them all,' she said absently, as she did. Beside the bell-pull, I saw a small brass plate on which was engraved simply 'Dobbs'.

The door let in to a modest entrance hall, from which a white-painted stairway adorned with a Persian runner curved upwards to the first floor. To the right a panelled door led through to a long, lovely drawing-room with a bow-window fronting the street. There was a grey marble fireplace, the hearth filled with flowers, in the centre of the gable wall, and aside from a few plain chairs and a large refectory table doing service as a desk, the room was barely furnished at all. The walls were white painted and hung all about with paintings, which made the room like a homey version of the bright gallery we had just left. The effect was enhanced by the polished wood floor which, but for one brilliant primitive carpet, was quite bare. In the bow of the window, among myriad bushy green conservatory plants, was one long dilapidated sofa draped in an eastern fringed shawl in which two large tabby-striped cats nestled securely.

'Do pardon the shambles,' said the lady mildly, shifting one cat for me, as if it had been a cushion, and offering the space it had occupied. 'Please be comfortable . . .'

'Oh, I shall,' I cried, delightedly. 'It is so *very* lovely.'

She laughed richly. 'Not quite Gramercy Park?'

'Not quite,' I said, and a picture of the overstuffed, over-plush, fiercely formal drawing room of my own home bustled across my mind like a pompous matron. The lady adjusted her gold-rimmed eyeglasses, and tickled the ears of the cat who, cushion-like, had never unfolded throughout its displacement. She smiled a secret smile. I had an eerie feeling she knew all my thoughts.

'Not being married, you see,' she said, 'I can have everything just as I like. It's a terrible indulgence.' She straightened and looked down at me where I sat between her cats. 'I must introduce myself, my dear. I'm Millie Dobbs.' She held out one white gloved hand, and I extended mine.

'Justina Pyke,' I said, feeling very shy. She was a little formidable, no matter how nice.

'Has Wendell mentioned me?' she asked.

I was flustered, and she peered at me curiously, but was quite unruffled when I mumbled, 'No . . . I'm afraid I can't recall . . .'

'Thought not.' Her smile turned to a grin of girlish mischief, as when she had spoken of her gallery. 'He likes to forget about me,' she said, and before my imagination could leap to reasons why, she again forestalled my thoughts, saying, 'I am his adviser in art, my dear. I tell him what to buy. Naturally he'd rather believe he does it all himself, so I am best far in the background.'

'How rude of him,' I said.

'Oh, not at all. They're all the same. None of us are happy around our mentors. Myself included, I assure you.' It was gracefully said, though I sensed untrue, but its purpose was achieved and Wendell's dignity emerged only lightly tweaked. 'Do speak to Peter and Paul,' she added, slipping her gloves from long fingers, 'and I shall make us a lovely glass of tea.'

Peter and Paul were both on my lap when she returned, an interlocking heap of grey and black stripes. I thought of the Reverend Feathers who I had not remembered for years.

'Do you like them?' Millie Dobbs said, when she returned. She was carrying an Indian inlaid wood tray, upon which sat two tall glasses of tea, set into silver filigree holders. The tea was served Russian-style, black, with slices of lemon. She set the tray down on a low table before me.

'I love them,' I said, adding illogically, 'They remind me of a crow I once kept.'

She raised her eyebrows but said only, 'How endearing,' and I was left to figure whether she were charmed by the keeping of a crow, or its resemblance to her cats. She crossed the room to her desk and absently removed her hat and laid it down on top of a pile of books. The gesture, with its old-fashioned use of hat-pins, reminded me again of my mother. Everything about her spoke wealth, grace and taste, all softened with Bohemian charm.

I said, 'Thank you, Miss Dobbs,' as I lifted my glass of tea.

'Oh do call me Millie, my dear, and I shall call you Justina. Such a pretty name.' She sat down at the far end of the sofa and studied me carefully through the wide distorting lenses of her eyeglasses. She said slowly, 'Wendell is a dear boy, but always in such a hurry.' She paused. It was odd to hear her call him a boy, herself being hardly *much* older. But it was neither inappropriate, nor patronizing, just a plain statement of facts. She added, a little more harshly, 'All the Pykes are in a terrible hurry. They are a generation or two behind some of the rest of us, and are forever trying to catch up. A pity, really.' She smiled sadly.

'Do you know them?' I asked in a small voice. 'I mean really know them?'

She nodded.

It was all I needed. She had forced a tiny gentle wedge into the doorway of my discontent, and through that sliver of an opening all my unvoiced unhappiness came tumbling tearfully out. Two whole years of the almost unthinkable, always unspeakable, finally found words.

I sat for half an hour, cuddling the two great soft patient cats, and quietly crying as I told this stranger all that was wrong with my marriage, all my most private miseries. It was a terrifying divulgence in the narrow social world in which we all moved. And yet I trusted her completely, and none of it appeared to surprise her in the least. She nodded patiently as I spoke of their rigid daily lives, their endless rules and regulations, their discussions of family matters, as dry and solemn and loveless as a parliamentary committee, and the sad disdain in which they held the painting that had once been my life's dearest delight. But I told her more, too, things I had never thought to tell anyone, about my marriage bed, and Wendell's defection from it, and the procession of fleeting romances by which he betrayed me.

'If it weren't for my babies,' I heard myself gasping, 'if it weren't for them . . .'

'What then? What, if it weren't for them?' She was smiling wisely and I blinked in amazement.

'I don't know,' I whispered. Without even realizing, by the simple fact of her presence, she had led me further along the path of revolt than I had ever dreamed to step. But it was not Millie Dobbs alone. My true rebellion had begun before I met her, that morning in Washington Square. If Millie Dobbs and I combined to form a chemistry of insurrection, the all unwitting catalyst was Mr Yeats. Regardless, the alchemy was done. Out of the lead of my marriage a new bright gold was born. I looked up, my eyes flitting in triumph from one lovely object to another around the cool peaceful room.

'I shall leave him,' I said.

'Of course you won't,' said Millie Dobbs.

And of course I didn't. All the necessities of my marriage yet remained, unchanged by any meteor of intuition. But the light of that moment infused my daily existence with a new warmth. I had found at last a companion of my heart, a soul-mate like May or Michael, someone before whom I might again become my own natural self; flawed, irreverent, but honest. My exile was ended.

Thenceforward, I visited Millie Dobbs every week. Her invitation came immediately upon that first afternoon, as we walked back to the gallery on 8th Street where I imagined Wendell waiting with growing impatience.

'I simply must see more of you,' she said firmly. 'Fridays at two?' she added in such a way that the matter appeared already settled. But I was certain Wendell would not allow such a thing; he had never encouraged friends of my own. My companions were invariably, if subtly, chosen by him from among his female relatives and the wives of his friends. I was ashamed to confess this common, but humiliating domestic arrangement, and said only,

'I'm afraid Wendell is terribly busy.'

Millie said at once, 'I'm quite sure he is. But it's *you* I'm asking.' She paused just a moment and added, 'Don't worry, my dear. Wendell will be delighted.' She said it drily and I must have looked disbelieving because she explained then with a wry grimace, 'Justina, dear. Two generations ago, when all New York ever thought about took place among a half dozen families within a half mile of here,' she gestured vaguely so that her gloved fingers drew a celestial orbit centring on 8th Street, 'the Pykes made a remarkable triumph. One of their number married one of ours. It was their crowning achievement and henceforth we are bound in fond familial embrace. *Any* Pyke will always go willingly to the house of any Dobbs, for we were in the sandbox first.' She sighed, 'But never mind. It serves our purposes perfectly just now.'

I have to admit that even coming from the extraordinarily convincing tongue of Millie Dobbs, this assertion struck me as doubtful. Perhaps I did not fully understand either the family into which I had married, or the city from which they had sprung.

New York was changing. It was a city of dust and clamour. Everywhere there were new construction sites, great holes in the ground from which huge new buildings, twenty and thirty storeys high, and more, were springing up. Miracles but a decade ago, they were already commonplace, and would soon be obsolete. Their shadows, alien and long reaching, stretched over old squares and parks, and darkened the staid and placid rows of brownstones and the cobbles that seemed yet to echo the sound of carriage wheels. Elevated trains thundered, automobiles crowded streets, trolleys were mechanized. The patient dray horses plodded through the heat on their last few rounds, before motor traffic vanquished them all. These new and noisy streets were filled with a new and noisy humanity; an ever wider mix of nations and races. New foods, new clothing, new faces invaded and changed familiar places. Over the genteel murmurs of the 'four hundred' arose the babel of the 'four million'.

No wonder Mrs Pyke retreated each afternoon within the gates of Gramercy Park, or passed in smooth remoteness through her city's busy streets, shut up in her husband's long black car. The city of her youth had vanished. It lay forlorn like a ghost beneath the new, vigorous and alien New York that I met in 1919, just as that post-war city now lies, in turn, buried beneath a fantasy of glass and steel. But those whose time is passing cling ever closer to times that are past. Mrs Pyke and her sisters and cousins found far more of interest in the marriages of their ancestors and the bloodlines of their heirs, than in Treaties in Versailles or the clamour of workers in Union Square.

'Why, Justina,' she exclaimed with a visible, if surprised triumph. 'How delightful. Of course you must go, my dear. And yes, *do* go alone. I can see Millie *any* time, after all.'

At once all aids were at my disposal, and Nanny's hours arranged to suit, as well as the dinner hour of the family. This, normally beginning at one, was actually put forward to twelve, so that my appointment in West Tenth Street not be inconvenienced. As it was customary for the senior

Pykes to join us for alternate Friday luncheons, this was virtually miraculous. Indeed, any wedge of invention parting the deep rooted tradition that governed our intertwined households was astounding. Until this happy meeting with Millie Dobbs, my daily life, except for those brief, and hardly informal, interludes on Long Island, was so rigid that at any time of any day for two whole years I could tell precisely what I would be doing.

Like a holy liturgy, our weeks unfolded. Sundays always with the family, first at church, then an interminable luncheon, either at our house or the parental domain, then a long stiff gathering in one or the other drawing room, with nanny and fretting babies in attendance. Three evenings a week Wendell and I dined with friends. On Thursday mornings I was 'At Home'. On Tuesdays Mrs Pyke was 'At Home'. Most other mornings were occupied with letter writing and interminable telephone calls from Mrs Pyke, in which the social complexities of the days ahead would be discussed with all the serious consideration of an army strategy. On Saturday evenings we attended the theatre in season, or entertained at home.

Not all of these occasions were a trial or even dull though their sheer repetitiveness, the familiar round of the same, well-worn faces, spiced stiffly with the occasional deliberate 'someone new' (who was invariably so like the others as to fade into the pattern at once), did not inspire excitement. Even then, conversation, had it been allowed free rein, and not bent to the snaffle of 'propriety', might have bred its own interest. But this was a world in which social intercourse was a duty, not a pleasure, and friends a vague burden to be borne. To one raised as I was, in the give and take of our rambunctious family, dipped early into the happy maelstrom of Dublin, and indulged with a flare for rebellion, this measured, tideless life was sadly alien.

But then, like Moses parting the waters, came Millie Dobbs. On that first Friday, I left 18 Gramercy Park South with real trepidation. In the intervening week so very much fuss had been made about my social conquest, so much excitement generated, that I really forgot the person I had met, her image overwhelmed by that of the social paragon the Pykes so clearly regarded her. Overhearing my mother-in-law confiding *sotto voce* to a friend, 'Whatever interest would Millie Dobbs have in the plain little thing?' did not enrich my confidence. But the Friday came, and I summoned the courage to go, and the courage as well to turn down the offer of the chauffeured car which had been provided. Alone, and on foot, I would enter the Promised Land.

As long ago in Dublin, the sudden feeling of being free, out once more in the streets of a city without attendant or guardian filled me with terror and delight. My steps literally lightened as I left the autumny trees of the Park behind, until I was almost running southward down Irving Place. How silly and childish I sound, twenty-six years old, a married woman and mother of two, frisking in my brief freedom like a schoolgirl. But marriage of the kind I made does not add to maturity, but indeed detracts. All my young experience, my years in London, the terrible times of the war, were undone, so far behind me that I could hardly imagine myself having lived them. As I turned down 17th Street and crossed Union Square, I thought of Jack Redpath and the farmhouse in France. What would he have thought could he see me now? I felt diminished and ashamed.

More slowly I walked south again on University Place. My mind was full of the past, now that I was free of the physical bonds of the present, and I remembered London and the School of Art, and chalking notices in the streets for the suffragettes. A well-dressed lady walking two big black poodles nodded politely as I passed, and I nodded back at the faintly familiar face. A friend of the Pykes no doubt; Old New York was not yet dead.

I had a horribly seditious desire to turn and run after her, clutch her by her little fur wrapped shoulders and declare, 'I dynamited a railway carriage when I was young, and was sent to Holloway!' I might even have done it, but for a conviction that the only response it would draw would be one more gracious absent-minded nod.

At the corner of Fifth Avenue and Tenth Street, outside the entrance of the Church of the Ascension, Millie Dobbs was waiting for me. She wore a flowered dress and a black shawl and a little straw hat trimmed with a russet ribbon. She seemed the prettiest, calmest, most peaceful person I had ever seen.

'Oh, Miss Dobbs,' I gasped an outburst of sheer gratitude for her existence.

'*Millie*, my dear. Now do slip in here,' she gestured towards the dark entrance of the church. 'Let's have a look at La Farge, shall we?' She led me in, and we moved slowly through the shadowy interior towards the great mural of the Ascension behind the altar until, with eyes gradually adjusting to the cool gloom, we stood before it. We remained in silence until at last Millie turned to go and I followed. Out in the street she squinted at the bright sun through her gold-framed lenses and smiled happily.

'There. That was nice, wasn't it?' she said, as if we had shared something trivial and intimate, like a glass of tea. I managed to nod eagerly, and agree. Not for years had I known anyone who could commence a conversation with an issue of true depth; no one, indeed, since Mr Yeats. We talked about religious painting as we walked up Tenth Street.

Thus began my wonderful Fridays, a cycle of adventure

and escape, born that autumn afternoon in 1920, that would open to me doorways, and widen horizons, much as Stephen's Green had done for my fourteen-year-old self. And just as my childhood was shed in the studio of J.B. Yeats, so, in the household of Millie Dobbs, was the childhood of my marriage left behind.

How can I describe her to you? She was a lady. She was an artist. She was a patron in the old dignified sense of the word. She painted well, and with great humility, and had neither illusion nor false modesty about her ability. 'Educated amateur, my dear. Good eye, reasonable technique, limited imagination.' So she summed up herself, squinting sideways at some project of her own, exactly as she would at some stranger's work she was assessing for purchase. I always disagreed, not just because I worshipped her, but because I loved Millie's paintings, her strange dreamy mystical images that sprang from somewhere far deeper than imagination. I remembered Mr Yeats' friend, George Russell, whose style and modesty Millie's recalled. But she would not concede; judgement of art was her profession, and she was businesslike and unsentimental in that regard.

Her profession was also her pleasure; the gallery in 8th Street was an amusement and an opportunity to forward the efforts of others. Millie had no need of employment. Her wealth was family wealth, old money, but money all the same. She had no ambitions, except for her friends, but for her friends she was a shrewd tigress. Every struggling spirit in the Village was regarded as her charge; artists, writers, actors, all had sought refuge with her, and she befriended them all and supported many.

Of course, by the nature of Bohemians, she was likely to be 'taken' on occasion, and no doubt this did happen. 'A few dollars for the rent' begged from the ever-generous Millie Dobbs surely crossed more than one bar counter.

But on the whole Millie was a shrewd judge, and she had that crusty good sense of the Yankee New Englanders from whom she sprang. Spongers and abusers of privilege were invariably found out before long.

'That man has had his due,' she would occasionally announce, as the only explanation for the rejection of some hopeful, and I would come to realize that the party in question had overstepped, and was now firmly beyond the pale.

But for the rest, the generosity remained; Millie's doors were ever open. Often some tired young man, or pale frightened young woman, newly evicted from a Village attic, would be in residence for days, even weeks, while new lodgings were being found. Always penniless, these quiet, grateful lodgers crept in and out like thankful mice, and left, upon their departure, some pathetic artistic crumb, a little painting, a few pages of manuscript, a clumsy poetic tribute. Millie had an old camphor-wood seaman's chest in which all these offerings were carefully stored. Once I teased her about her sentiment and she laughed sharply.

'Sentiment? Nonsense. One of those young men will be the next Henry James. Don't ask me which, I'm no prophet. But something in there,' she gestured to the camphor trunk, 'will be worth its weight in gold. Even geniuses must start somewhere.'

On that first Friday visit, the house seemed as empty as it had done the previous week but for, far upstairs, the faint erratic sound of typing, betraying the presence of some mysterious lodger. The creative struggle went on throughout my visit, interrupted, but not ended, by periods of long painful silence. Every now and then a sudden flurry of thunderous tapping broke out, wayward inspiration made concrete. Millie served me tea, again, and no reference was made to the house's other occupant.

We talked about painting; what I had done, where I had studied, what I hoped to do next. Millie, unlike Wendell, had indeed heard of Mr Yeats, though they had never met. I almost told her of seeing him in the Square, but stopped short in shyness. She chided me gently for not bringing with me the portfolio I had promised to show her. I pretended to have forgotten it, but the truth was that I was ashamed.

All the previous afternoon I had sat in my bedroom, with my little son clambering curiously about, playing with my chalks, and scribbling happily on some paper I had given him, while I sorted and assessed what work I had in my possession. Most of my past efforts were yet across the Atlantic, some at Arradale in the loft, some with Clare, and the rest with May. She, my most faithful devotee, had hung all the walls of the Merrion Square house with my paintings. I think her affection for me rather outweighed her good taste.

But what remained to show Millie Dobbs, being mostly my 'American collection', post-marriage and post-babies, was so pathetically scanty, and of such a shabby quality, that I lost my nerve. If she regarded *herself* as a dabbling amateur, what would she think of me? But Millie was not easy to fool. My forgetfulness did not impress her.

'It is unwise to be your only judge, my dear,' she said gently. 'All creative people have judgements like the tides. When they are happy, they are convinced of their genius; sad, and they despair of a smidgin of talent. We collectors serve our purpose, if only as rocks upon which the tides may wash. We go neither up nor down, but stay much the same. Show me your work, Justina.' I turned away.

'I can't paint there,' I said, hating myself. It sounded so childish and self-indulgent. 'I don't know why. I just can't.'

'In that case,' she said brusquely, clearing away the tea things, 'you must paint here.'

'What?' I whispered.

She smiled her wise smile. 'An artist must *live*,' she said.

Like everything else Millie set her mind to, it was promptly accomplished. If the Pykes had any objection they scarcely had time to voice it. The following day, Saturday, a large car arrived at the door of 18 Gramercy Park, and from its depth Millie Dobbs emerged. She swept in, unannounced, but instantly welcomed by Wendell's mother who had stopped by for coffee two hours before and was yet firmly ensconced. After the required trivialities, performed with perfect breeding, Millie announced, gaily, 'Your charming daughter-in-law has agreed to indulge my fascination with art. She shall be painting at my studio, for my edification, each Friday afternoon. Isn't she kind? And oh, could I beg a little favour? I would so like if someone from the house might bring her few things round?'

On the Friday after, I was deposited on the doorstep of Millie Dobbs' house by Wendell's car, clutching my easels and paintbox, like one more lost Village mouse. She welcomed me in out of the stormy October day, with open arms, a prodigal daughter returned at last home.

Millie Dobbs' studio was at the top of the house, a long bare room stretching from end to end, with ceiling slanting low under the eaves. Facing the street a large window let in north light and at the opposite end another overlooked the small garden. The floor was unfinished wood, partly covered with two squares of linoleum, and the unadorned walls were painted white. Canvases were stacked about the room, and a large table stood in the centre, carrying jars filled with brushes, and a tray of chalks. In the centre of the room a black Franklin stove provided heat on winter afternoons. Like every artist's studio I have ever entered, it filled me with a wonderful sense of peace. Reverently I laid my paintbox on the table and stood looking down at its smooth mahogany surface. The paints had long been replenished, many, many times, and the oils and brushes as well, but the box itself, battered and worn, was the one James Howie had given me twenty years before, that Michael had carried about the Irish countryside.

Quite suddenly, I was crying. Then I looked up from the paintbox and through a wet blur I saw a face. It was a face in a drawing propped on Millie's easel, a dark man with black hair, portrayed in charcoal before a background of mystical birds. No. It was not Michael. As I've said, the visions were done. It was Mirza Hassan.

17

'Prophecy is the most alarming grace. All that is humble in man, all that is respectful, rebels against its audacity. What man dare make so extravagant a claim, that God has chosen him from all humanity to bear his Word? Surely here is the Pride that went before the Fall. Here inspiration and madness meet. And yet, prophets have arisen in every age and through them have come the wisdoms that guide the world. Without honour in their own countries, without honour in their own ages, they are yet the holy ones of history. Only Time, the wise judge, divides the lunatic from the inspired.

'But what of those to whom no time is given? What of the men who walked with the Christ, who spoke with the Buddha, who followed Muhammad upon the Flight? We who watch through the dark glass of centuries might envy them, to whom revelation was immediate: how sure must have seemed the path to heaven with the Christ by one's side. Yet Judas betrayed, and Peter denied his Lord. Those whose lives span the chasm where two Ages meet, face terrible choices. Nor have all the fortune of Saul, struck blind by the Light of Faith. For many the road to Damascus is a road to Hell. No. Do not envy, but pity the man born in an era of prophecy; his faith will know a fierce testing.

'The man of the modern era stands back from such questions with a fastidious relief: they are questions of the past. They do not concern him. Another age, innocent of science, unfettered by rationality, jousted with God's knights. But the tournament is over. The age of prophets is done. But has reason truly silenced the voice of God?

'Herein I propose to present a startling thesis, and forthwith I step out upon a dangerous track: the narrow path that lies between Inspiration and Blasphemy. For I would propose to you that the age of miracles has not ended with those simpler innocent times, and that the era of prophecy is yet with us. I would propose to you that our own century too has known a Prophet, that his Word is among us, and spreading among the quiet faithful as the word of each of the prophets was spread. What I will expound to you is either the greatest of Truths or the greatest of Heresies. Once more a voice has cried in the wilderness; once more a Prophet has arisen in the East. Stand now in the shoes of the Sanhedrin, for our age too must face the double-edged Sword of Revelation.'

Hugo Melrose
introduction to *The Gateway* 1915

The Friday of the following week was crisp and blue and gold, and Millie and I forsook the car and walked to Washington Street. It was a long walk, almost to the foot of Manhattan, and we made it longer by wandering in and out amongst the little streets of the Village along the way. As we walked she drew my attention to buildings, trees, garments, faces, always evoking the brilliant undeniable colours of New York. She was attempting to retrain my eye and my palette, both, in her opinion, too fettered by the softened lights of the Old World.

'Look,' she said. 'Brown and blue, like fresh ploughed earth.' The face of a Negro child. Or, 'There, kindergarten colours!' An ailanthus dripped yellow leaves before a red store front; behind it the blue, blue sky of a November

New York. In November in Arradale, the trees were dreamy russet, wrapped in a gauze of mist, and the sky was the colour of smoke. I nodded, eager to learn, grasping her words like a handful of sweets. Millie had arranged that I begin a course at Cooper Union in the winter, a series of life classes to improve my anatomical drawing. She was very serious about my career. More serious, I fear, than I.

'How long have you known him?' I asked. I felt shy, and clutched the book I was carrying closer to me. It was a copy of *The Gateway*, with its beautiful blue and gold cover. I had brought two with me from Gramercy Park, one for Millie and one for Mirza Hassan.

'Almost four years. Since before he was married.'

'It's hard to think of him as married.'

'Oh, very married indeed. And a father of two.' I laughed.

'Oh, imagine! I can't get used to it. He was always so solitary.'

'Well, he's hardly solitary now,' Millie said. 'Fatima, and the little ones, and all Fatima's family, of which there are hundreds. And then the Coffee House, which must be the centre of all the Persians in New York, and Syrians and Lebanese as well. There are quite a few Baha'i amongst them. They have not had an easy time at home. And of course, like all immigrants, they brought nothing and had little English. So scholars bake pastries, and holy men mend shoes. Not a bad thing, I suppose. Emigration brings a great humbling; we who have been mighty are mighty no more. By the rivers of Babylon we weep, remembering Sion.'

'He had nothing even in Scotland. He wore Father's cast-off clothes.'

'He had three dollars, and not even a winter coat when the Baha'is brought him to me. He stayed less than a month, ate scarcely anything, and thanked me profusely every day. He took no money. He worked as a labourer, on a site down in Wall Street, to raise the rent for a room of his own. He brought me flowers on the day he left. Within a year, he was running the bakery, and within two he owned the lease. Then the Coffee House . . . but by that time he was married and Fatima's father helped. They are remarkable people, the Persians. Once they ruled the world.' Millie took my arm as we crossed Canal Street. I felt six years old.

'Oh, my dear, let's have some chestnuts,' she cried gleefully, having spotted a chestnut vendor pushing his little cart down West Broadway. We ran to catch him up, and she purchased two paper cones of hot, roasted chestnuts. Their smell filled the air with wintry warmth. We took off our gloves to eat them, messily and incongruously, as we walked up the street.

'Oh, look at us,' I laughed.

'Nobody cares,' she said briskly, flicking charcoal from her fingers and licking them neatly. 'This is where the *people* live.' The street was crowded with working people and their children, and no one noticed us. I loved it there, and looked with envy at the funny little apartment windows with bright curtains, and potted plants decorating fire escapes. I imagined living there, amongst the noise and colour. I glanced across at Millie in her elegant suit so at home anywhere. I thought of the exiles bringing Mirza Hassan to her door.

'But you're not Persian . . .' I said.

'So how am I Baha'i?'

I nodded. She was always a jump ahead.

She peered at me through her thick lenses. 'Are you Galilean?' she asked.

'Of course not!' I laughed.

'So how are you Christian?' she said. I blinked. 'Christ was Galilean,' she reminded.

'I was *born* Christian,' I said stupidly.

'If we all stayed what we were born we'd still be worshipping trees,' Millie said mildly, adding, 'Not that that's all such a bad thing.' She took my arm again and we continued down West Broadway and crossed to Trinity Place.

'I was raised in New England,' Millie said, 'I lived in my grandfather's house because my father was, of all things, a missionary. He went off for months, even years, but we never went with him. Once, I complained when he was about to leave and he chastised me for not caring about those innocent souls he was pledged to save. I asked him what would happen to the souls he *didn't* reach . . . after all, he could hardly reach them *all*. With infinite sorrow he assured me they must go to hell. He didn't like it any better than I did, but he believed it. I was fourteen. I stopped believing at once. What kind of God could play such a game . . . hide-and-seek in the clouds, and death for the children who cannot find him? Preposterous. But,' she paused, 'to be without God is preposterous, too.'

'Is it?' I said tartly.

'Of course it is. It was not *God* I should have questioned but my father's mistaken image of him. *He* would have *some* of humanity condemned to destruction; I, in my atheism, would condemn all.'

'If there's no God, there's no hell,' I said stubbornly.

'Oh, really? And what of the Somme and Passchendaele?' That silenced me. Millie patted my hand. 'In 1912 I was approached by a young friend with a most startling proposition. Not only was there a God, not only had He intervened in human affairs in years gone by, but He was indeed doing so today. His Prophet had walked the earth even in my lifetime, and his Prophet's son, moreover, was coming to New York. "Ridiculous," was my immediate response. And of course such claims were not precisely new; I had been living in the Village for some years and I was quite accustomed to Village vagaries. Prophets, like poets, might be found in every bar. But she was a *good* friend, and so, quite reluctantly, and rather grumpily, I went along to see.'

'And what did you see?' I said, breathlessly, I suppose, because she made a wry smile.

'An old man with a beard; a coterie of faithful women . . . what did you think?' She laughed her sharp, New England laugh.

'You're teasing me,' I said.

'Of course, dear. Religion is much too important to take seriously.' She slowed and stopped at the corner of Rector Street. She said, 'He was Abdul Baha, the eldest son of Bahá'u'lláh, considered by the Baha'i to have been God made manifest amongst us. Not just *their* God, but everyone's God, Christian, Jew, Muhammadan, Buddhist. He who had spoken so many times before was speaking now to our age.' She paused and said mildly, 'Outrageous, really, when you think of it.' Her eyes were far away, preoccupied behind her blurring lenses, and suddenly her face became animated with excited recollection. 'It was as if,' she said, pausing between words, 'as if I was among the earliest of Christians, following their Lord, their convictions as certain as the light of the sun, their faith as serene.'

'My father said that once,' I remembered suddenly, 'only he was talking of the persecutions. He said it was like the days of the catacombs.'

'How strange. What he found in the East has found you in the West.'

'I never listened to him,' I said. 'I took notes, and made drawings, but I hardly noticed what it was all about.'

Millie smiled. She slipped her gloved hand through my arm again and we walked once more. After a while she said, 'So many gifts of our childhood mean nothing until borne to us in a stranger's hands. *My* father's faith, so presumptively rejected, returned to me when I became Baha'i.'

The Coffee House was on Washington Street, on the block below Rector Street, in a three-storey red-brick building with a green awning at the front. On the upper floors were apartments, with windowsills filled with plants. On either side of the Coffee House, shops and cafés were clustered, each distinctly Eastern in origin and in goods. This was the Syrian quarter of New York, and like every other district of the city it began abruptly, continued on both sides of the street with passionate self-absorption, a flowering of silks, brasses, pottery, strange foods, beautiful confectionaries, and ended with equal abruptness. Shish kebab turned on spits in windows, and filled the air with spices and the scent of roasting lamb. Pastries, dripping with honey, were stacked in bakery displays, and everywhere the scent of vague sweet spices, and pervasive tobaccos evoked a bazaar in the desert. But New York was here too, dirty cobbled streets, and seagulls sweeping in from the river to snatch the leavings of vegetable carts, and beyond, the far hooting of tugboats in the harbour. Children, dark-skinned and shiny-haired, ran about, shouting in half a dozen languages, occasion ally breaking startlingly into the American English of their schools.

'What do you think?' asked Millie.

'Oh, it's wonderful,' I cried. We had stopped in front of the building. Cedars of Lebanon Coffee House was written across one plate-glass window, and beneath, words in Eastern script presumably said the same. In the window were trays of pastries and a carved and painted Persian horse.

'Is this it?' I asked nervously. Millie nodded. I hesitated, and just as I reached to open the door, two tiny children carrying a puppy burst out, to a jangling of brass bells, and leaving the entrance open wide. Cautiously, I stepped within. The interior was dim, lit only by the dusty bars of sunlight creeping through the half-curtained windows. The air was filled with the smoke of pipes and cigarettes and a low mutter of male voices speaking softly in foreign tongues. Clusters of men sat around small round tables on which herds of tiny coffee cups betrayed long afternoons of talk. At one end of the room was a counter on which more pastries were displayed and beside which was a huge brass coffee urn. The scent of coffee, richly inviting, permeated the room. A woman, dark, and looking more eastern than the men because she yet dressed in the loose dark garment of her native land, was drawing coffee from the urn. She was heavy and middle-aged, and smiled all the while as she filled cups and set them on a wide brass tray for a young girl, dressed in an American skirt and blouse, to carry to the tables. The young girl was very beautiful, with long, curling black hair, and long earrings. She looked up, seeing me, and Millie behind me, smiled shyly, and ran into the kitchen at the back.

He came out from the kitchen wearing a white apron, carefully drying his hands on a towel which he laid aside as he entered the room. He looked prosperous, a little older and a little heavier, his hair slightly grey, and his moustache maturely luxuriant, and he walked with the same steady, unhurried peasant's tread that had mounted the Throne of Solomon.

'Hassan . . .' I whispered. He peered in polite, curious

silence, then extended his arms wide and smiled his white, exotic and familiar smile.

'Praise be to God,' he shouted. 'My little swan.'

I crossed the room running, and among strangers in a strange land we embraced.

I suppose I spent as much time with Mirza Hassan and Fatima in the months that followed as I did with Millie Dobbs. It was a wonderful winter. New York was cold and snowy, and often blizzards raged down the wide avenues, and drifted banks knee deep around lamp-posts and storefronts. Traffic slowed, and stopped, but it was no trouble to me. I would pull on fur-lined boots, and stride out through the storms as happily as long before in Strathpeffer. Just once or twice I longed for my skis, though there wasn't a hill worth thinking of in all Manhattan. Mrs Pyke declared me mad, and became seriously flustered when, on occasion, I even took Wendell, wrapped in a woolly suit and encased in sheepskin, in the stroller. But she didn't stop me because always behind me was Millie, who on occasion would send me home from my visit in her own car, as a kind of reassurance. But I was a child of the North, and found days like that fun, and my son, quick to learn, soon found them the same. I painted at Millie's studio, with Wendell playing with the cats on the floor beside the warm, friendly black stove. Or we sat for long lazy afternoons in the warmth of the coffee house on Washington Street, and Hassan's two little girls played with my son, and we adults, Hassan and myself, Fatima and her mother and father and three tall handsome brothers talked while I sketched them. Outside, wind and sleet blew by and the streets were empty, but within all was colour and laughter, as the old men stood around and watched my drawings grow beneath my fingers. I usually worked in charcoal and pencil because they were quick and easy to transport. Fatima begged me to bring Ellie as well, but I dared not; there was just so far I might go with the Pykes. I knew where I must stop, or so I thought.

These episodes grew longer and longer, without my really noticing until, by March, three or even four afternoons a week I spent far from the refinements of Gramercy Park. One of those was devoted to my life class at Cooper Union, where, in a freezing bare room, I, with a cluster of earnest young students, mostly from the immigrant population, worked studiously portraying the blue and goose-fleshed torso of some brave young mannequin. One or two of those young men were friends I had met through Millie, poets and writers and fellow artists eking out a grim living by posing in the chilly nude. My naivety obviously was long behind me, but even had it not been, these clinical sessions hardly touched my sensibilities. It was only when Wendell, coming upon a sketch and recoiling with actual horror, protested, that I even stopped to think about their remote sexual implications.

'Good heavens,' I said in my best brisk VAD voice. 'I've seen more of that in the wards, after all. I saw more of *you* there, *and* before we were married, too.'

'No comparison,' Wendell muttered, embarrassed by the memory of ourselves as patient and nurse. 'And besides, it was hardly *frivolous*. Those men were ill.'

'So will these be, unless someone puts some heating in that place,' I returned sharply. 'And it's not *frivolous*,' I added angrily. 'It's art.'

'Always the first excuse of the voyeur,' he said. He actually *said* that. I walked out. I fully expected my class to be forbidden but, oddly, that didn't happen. I suspect he feared a confrontation with the dry humour of Millie Dobbs.

I forgot about that incident then though it arose in time

to haunt me. And it was not until early spring that my defections from the family home, and my resolute insistence upon engaging my child in my life rather than leaving him utterly to the care of paid staff, brought us to impasse.

One afternoon in March, 1921, I sat in my favourite chair, with my back to the window, and the light on my easel. My subject was an old man from Teheran, whose beard curled in blue white wisps almost to his waist. He posed solemnly, hands on his knees and eyes fixed upon the far side of the room, in deep contemplation. He looked as if he should carry a sword. He never uttered a word as I worked, though all his friends gathered to watch and make comments and tease. While I painted Hassan and Fatima sat on either side and we talked about Baha'i. Everyone in the room soon became involved, eager as schoolchildren to help my understanding. Often my questions were translated and the entire party joined in formulating the answer. I felt honoured.

Fatima spoke rarely, but with great eloquence, surprising in a girl of such youth and flirtatious beauty, and whenever she spoke her husband paused and turned appreciatively to listen. I envied her that loyal companionship and I envied them both their marriage, filled with life, and tolerance, and laughter. Each time I went there I left more reluctantly for the cool, bloodless confines of my home. At eighteen months, Wendell seemed quite of the same opinion, running off to hide in the kitchens with Mirza Hassan's daughters, Khadija and Aiysha, whenever it was time to leave. His attachment to them, particularly to the eldest, Khadija, was touching and often he wept for them as we made our way home, and arrived at Gramercy Park blotched with tears. If his father saw, I was scolded for over-tiring him and of course I did not argue. Nor did I mention where we had been. Having not done so at the time of my first visit to Washington Street,

I found it increasingly difficult to open the subject, until eventually it became impossible. My husband assumed always I was with Millie Dobbs; if not with his approval, at least with his acquiescence; and I did not disillusion him. It was foolish, in its telling precedent of tacit dishonesty, but I took the easiest course, a common, female error.

Wendell climbed on my knee and for a while I painted around him, laughing in my heart at the sages of South Kensington. 'Let them try this,' I thought.

'Can I take him out?' Khadija asked, politely, her great black eyes, womanly at three years old, full of motherly commiseration.

'Oh, please,' I said, heaving him down on to his fat legs. They toddled off, and Fatima called without even looking, 'Hold his hand.'

Solemn as a nanny, Khadija led Wendell out into the sunshine beyond the door. I watched his blond head bobbing beside her black, oriental curls and thought suddenly of myself and Michael Howie. Warmed by the image, I worked on, and Fatima's mother came from the kitchen, holding a lump of dough which she rolled and stretched in her hands as she watched me. Mirza Hassan sat, a king amidst his court, in the midst of the coffee house.

'Was the Bab the Baptist?' I asked him, swirling cerulean blue into the grey on my palette, seeking the blue-white of the old man's beard. 'My father seems to be saying so.'

Hassan nodded thoughtfully, and after long silence he said, 'The Christian mind seeks Christian imagery. But we too awaited a restorer of the faith.'

'A Messiah.'

Hassan smiled cannily, 'He Who Arises. The Qa'im.'

He smiled again. 'But consider the Bab the Baptist; Bahá'u'lláh the fulfilment, if you would like.'

'The Christ?'

'He Whom God Will Make Manifest.' He laughed his soft slow laugh.

'You would make a good Jesuit,' I said. He shrugged, still smiling.

'From the shell of Judaism came Christianity,' he said. 'From the shell of Islam, Babism, and from Babism, came Baha'i. God's Word is a phoenix, ever arising.' He joined his two tough, brown hands together, so that palms and fingers formed the wings of a bird, flapping upwards. Fatima shrieked girlish laughter, her jewelled fingers over her face.

'Your phoenix flies like a fat pigeon,' she made wings of her own hands, still laughing. 'Flap, flap,' she teased, dodging her husband. 'Flap, flap.' She danced around him and he clasped her hands in his own and wrestled her playfully, until suddenly Fatima's mother slapped her own two floury hands together in two sharp claps of disapproval. The room went silent, and I turned, and saw why. A man, tall, alien, and angry, was standing in the door.

I stared in silence for a long, long while, and then laid my brush down on the table. 'Hello, Wendell,' I said.

'Justina.' His voice was a comic mix of husbandly outrage and boyish hurt. At his speaking of my name, Hassan, who had watched uncertainly, stepped forward to welcome him into the room, his broad hands both held out at waist level. Wendell ignored him, as if he were an importuning beggar, and that dismissal filled me with anger. I stood up, abruptly, before the anger would find words, and turning my back to Wendell and the door, I walked through to the kitchen with my brushes and palette.

I went directly to the deep ceramic sink in the scullery

at the back of the kitchen, and carefully scraped the palette clean with my broad knife and then, laying both down, began work on the brushes. I wondered in a fey, foolish whimsy how long it would take for Wendell's anger to surmount his fastidiousness sufficient for him to enter the humble kitchen behind me. As I waited for his footsteps my eyes fell on the back door, open to the spring sunshine, leading out to the cobbled alley and beyond, the anonymous streets of New York. A great impulse arose to run through that door and away, an impulse extinguished at once by the thought of my little son, playing in the street somewhere, with Khadija, and Ellie in her ruffled crib at home.

The steps came then, slowly, and I stood very still, not turning, carefully working the feathery tip of one sable filbert around and around my soapy palm. The steps stopped just inside the kitchen.

'Justina.' I did not answer. 'Justina, my car is waiting at the front.' For an instant I thought he would simply turn on those words, and await my following, but he lacked that confidence. I ran water over the brush, until the stream dribbling off it was satisfyingly clear. I shook it and laid it on the edge of the sink. Then very slowly I turned round and stood facing him, my hands behind me, steadying myself on the cool ceramic.

'What right have you to come following me?' I said. I looked as coolly as I could straight into his shallow blue eyes. He was immaculately dressed, much out of place amidst the floury tables and dull walls of the bakery. He looked very handsome, very remote and unlikeable, his handsomeness like that of a too-perfect article of furniture that repels the touch.

He stared back until I dropped my eyes and then he said, 'Following you? Madam, what makes you imagine I have time to follow you? I assure you I have better and more interesting things to do.' I shrugged.

'All right then, why are you here?' I said boldly.

'I am *here*, Justina, because I have been severely let down by my wife.' He spoke as if his wife was not me, but some other, unworthy party, known to us both. 'My *wife*,' he continued, 'who has been given extraordinary elements of liberty, and much indulgence, in return only for a modicum of sense and reasonableness that any dimwit could be assumed to hold, but of which she is, apparently, quite devoid.' He looked carefully round the kitchen, and I knew he was looking for Wendell, as if I were hiding him somewhere, and I was terrified that he would ask where he was. But all he said was, 'We're dining with John Quinn tonight.'

'I know that. I would have been back in plenty of time. I always am,' I added with the self-conscious justice of the reformed. My predilection for being late I had scrupulously overcome, lest my brief escapes be curtailed. But that was not the issue today. Wendell went on as if I had not spoken.

'Since I had a wish to possibly purchase that Brancusi of Quinn's, I naturally chose to consult with a knowledgeable party, in advance of seeing it, and therefore called this afternoon upon Millie Dobbs.'

'Oh, I see,' I said quietly.

'No, Madam, you don't see at all.' He sounded sad, as if he pitied me. He looked slowly round the café kitchen, assessing it with a faint wry smile, as if it were a shabby and worthless lover in whose embrace he had discovered me. 'The issue is trust, Justina,' he said patiently. 'Trust. You have betrayed my trust.'

'I!' I exclaimed, stunned by the irony of his evident hurt. '*I* have!'

He nodded sagely, his face barely registering emotion,

but for a twitching set of lines at the corners of his petulant mouth.

'There must be nothing but total honesty between husband and wife,' he said. I stood open-mouthed, not believing what I was hearing. 'You see, otherwise elements of suspicion might enter, and there is no poison greater in marriage than suspicion.' I realized then that the capable, respected, dignified man to whom I was married was in one small channel of his life simply insane. Insanity cut through his quite ordinary soul like a volcanic intrusion, leaving normality undisturbed on either side, but seething, itself, with madness, a madness centred on one concept only, that of fidelity. He had so wildly lied to the whole world, that now he had accomplished the difficult task of truly lying to himself. In that moment in the coffee house of Mirza Hassan, our true roles reversed in his mind; he was the faithful spouse, I, the harlot. He would never see us otherwise, and neither, indeed, would much of the outside world.

'Wendell,' I said patiently. 'All I have done is come, a few afternoons, to this pleasant, social place, to meet an old friend of my father's and his very respectable wife and family. We talk, and I paint. Nothing could be more innocent.'

'Innocence is not the point!' he shouted. 'You have lied to me.'

'I never lied. I never said I didn't come here. You never asked where I went.'

'You said you were with Millie.'

'I was. Millie brought me here.' I said it triumphantly, sure the old magic would work, but he only smiled coldly.

'I know that,' he said. 'Millie told me everything. Millie doesn't lie.'

'In that case Millie will have made very clear the totally acceptable motivations that bring me here.'

'Millie,' said Wendell, 'is an old maid. What would she know?' *Oh far more than you ever will.* But I spoke in the silence of my heart, knowing my defeat. Wendell grasped victory with the cool dismissal that was his greatest strength, summing up like the lawyer he was, 'When you say you're with Miss Dobbs, I expect you to be with Miss Dobbs. Not,' he glanced once more with distaste about his surroundings, 'roaming the streets.' Defeat bred foolhardiness.

I shouted, 'I'm not a child. Don't talk to me like that. I'm not a child.'

'You're hardly a woman,' he said.

I turned from him and gathered my brushes. I felt suddenly old, and strong. I lifted my palette and stepped carefully across the room, avoiding coming too close to him as I did so. As I passed him I looked once across and said clearly, 'My womanhood is not defined by you.' I felt dignity descend on me like a shielding cloak from which he visibly stood back. Respect welled briefly in his hurt young eyes, but in that moment there was a happy clatter of childish shoes in the café behind and Wendell's voice shouting, 'Mama, Mama, look!'

They burst into the room, hand in hand, my blond baby son and his dark baby mistress. Oblivious of everything, they rushed to me, right by Wendell's father without even seeing him. Khadija's face glowed with pink outdoor cheeks and her comical maternal pride, as Wendell carefully handed me a grubby paper bag. I crouched down, and he clambered on to my skirt as I opened it. Inside, pink, white and hazed with sugar, nestled a cluster of Turkish delight.

'Lady give Wendell some,' he announced, plunging a small fist into the bag. He had just withdrawn one pink square and was about to place it in his mouth when it, and the paper bag, were snatched suddenly away, and I looked up astonished to see my husband glaring down at us in wordless rage. He scrunched the bag of candies into a ball and hurled it into the sink. Wendell stared at his father in deep silence. Khadija, with a slow dignity, stepped carefully back, across the room, until she was hiding behind the leg of a table.

'Why did you do that?' I whispered. Wendell grabbed my arm above the elbow with one hand and swept our son up with the other. Without speaking he dragged me to my feet and spun me about and hauled me stumbling and protesting to the door. Stiff and silent he marched me out through the Coffee House while the old men looked on in amazement.

'My paints,' I mumbled, 'I must have my paints.'

He did not stop. My face reddened with the effort of fighting him and the humiliation of being seen thus before my friends. Fatima shrank against her mother, who waved floury hands in dismay. Mirza Hassan watched me in misery, unable to intervene, and unable to turn away. One by one the old men lowered their heads. A woman's misbehaviour was her husband's affair. But Hassan stared after, even as I was bundled into the back of our big car before his door, and my last image of the Coffee House on Washington Street was of his kind, patient, astonished face. The car swept away, turned a corner, and another, and turned uptown, for home. Wendell had never spoken. Our little son, his amazement decreased, began in an uncertain way to cry, for his sweets, for Khadija, for normality. I reached an arm to pull him on to my knee, but his father's big hand prevented me.

'Don't be ridiculous,' I said sharply, but the hand remained, thrust between me and my baby, like a barrier. 'What are you doing?'

Wendell leaned back against the leather car seat. He held our weeping son closer and said in a clipped cold voice, 'To mingle with street people and Bohemians is your foolish privilege when all is said and done. I may discourage, but I will not forbid. But I will not have my son's health and morals endangered amidst immigrant rabble. If you have not the sense to protect him, then I must.'

'What do you mean?' I said irritably, trying again to reach my crying child. Wendell's grip tightened until my arm hurt.

'I shall remove him from your care.'

Sheer disbelief enabled me to get through the rest of that day, and the dinner party at John Quinn's apartment that night. My natural optimism, my faith in his good sense outweighing his moments of fanatical rigidity, carried me with the hopeful, though no way assured, conviction that he would soften from such a fierce dictate. I did not then really comprehend the dangers of my situation, and, by a stroke of fortune, I was spared that evening and for some time to come, from the repercussions of my 'sins'. For that evening, at the table of our art collector host, my husband fell in love. I saw it happen. In an abstract way, I even found it beautiful, for the moment in which one human being is bewitched by another is quite enchanting. And, having seen it, or variations of it, before, I was not even terribly concerned. I judged this fancy to be like the others. In a perverse way, I even welcomed it. Wendell was always at his best when at the dawn of a romance; young, wistful, sweet, generous. His adoration for his beloved washed over on to all around him, even me. If I but listened patiently to his psalm of her praises, he would be again my kind, good friend. If it sounds a queer bargain, perhaps you'd like to think of a better one I might have made. Besides, it was not only Wendell who began a liaison that night, though mine was rather more innocent.

John Quinn maintained a grand and spacious apartment on the top floor of 58 Central Park West. Although we had dined with him twice before, both occasions had been in restaurants, once at Delmonico's and once at the Hotel Lafayette, and always there had been a sizeable crowd present. Conversation had turned on legal matters and fine art and Wendell had dominated it. In his company I had the illusion of meeting dozens of people of note as if in a silent film; his own opinions and ideas so pervaded the gathering that strangers became a mere optical glass by which Wendell was enlarged, and illuminated. Occasionally he would declare someone 'fascinating', which I came to understand meant they had agreed with him, or 'an absolute bore', which meant they had not. His judgement on Quinn was more reserved; he respected Quinn the lawyer who had much influence and power in the city, and he envied Quinn the collector of art and manuscripts for both his collections and his knowledge. But Wendell did not allow himself friends; and he dredged up Quinn's Irish background with inappropriate scorn, as if he had stumbled out of the Kerry bog a moment before.

It was hardly the case. He was an attractive, elegant, gentlemanly man, who greeted us at the door with grace and dignity. He was very kind to me, the way a handsome bachelor is to a woman he is not really interested in, as if in apology for his lack of interest. Besides, he was aware of my painting, through Millie Dobbs, whose opinion he clearly respected, and had twice attempted to ask about it, and was each time cut short by Wendell. I prudently held my tongue.

John Quinn took my arm and led me down a long, long corridor, lined floor to ceiling with books. The drawing room overlooked Central Park, dim and lush in the spring dusk, and rimmed by the soft lights of the city. It was a beautiful setting. My host led me about, introducing me to the other dinner guests, while Wendell watched, half proud and half annoyed. Each room in the house served as a gallery, every available patch of wall bearing a painting, some English, some Irish, mostly French. Sculptures were set in lighted corners and I noticed one bedroom that we passed was stacked with paintings covered in dust-sheets, like the store-room of a museum. I had never in my life seen so many beautiful things in one small place. I could not suppress my delight, and though I feared Wendell's disapproval, our host warmed to my pleasure in his collection and spent a long time describing one and another painting, how it came into his possession, who the artist was, what would be his place in history.

I stopped before one small painting of a young girl and sighed, laughing, 'It makes me want to give up entirely.'

I looked up. John Quinn was looking down at me quizzically, standing very close. I remember thinking he looked tired and vaguely ill, which, I learned sadly later, was much the truth. He said softly, 'You like my little Gwen John?'

'I love it.' He stood back, admiring it with satisfaction. 'So do I. You can't imagine the difficulty I have getting her paintings. She's as modest as she's marvellous; nothing is good enough to please her.'

'She's wonderful,' I said. He nodded.

'Oh yes. Your husband's been after that for a year, but he won't get it.' He laughed, conspiratorially, and I laughed back. Then he said suddenly, 'I wonder though, if he were living with the woman, would he even look at her work?' My eyes met his; they were pale, and sharply aware. I was amazed at his insight, and a little frightened.

'Oh, none of us have honour in our own countries,' I

said, trying to be light, but he just looked sadly down and then quietly turned his fine aristocratic head away.

When we came back into the drawing room, Wendell had forgotten me. He was standing by the dark drapery of one of the windows overlooking the park, talking to a beautiful tall woman in black. His face told it all, sweet and softened, filled with delicate wonderment. *Oh my poor dear*, I thought. Because in the strange way of such things, I still loved him, and his vulnerability at such a moment could break the heart.

She was seated next to him at dinner. Whether it was his luck, or some clever rearrangement of his own doing, I never knew nor cared. It did not matter. The course of such things was inevitable once begun; he would have sought her and found her anywhere. Her name was Margaret de Quincey. She was thirty-one years old, the daughter of a Philadelphia banker, and a widow for a year. Her reputation was impeccable, and indeed she had only just ventured forth into society after her bereavement. The marriage, childless and passionate, had been a love match, and her mourning black was genuine. There is nothing I can possibly say against her, and nothing I wish to say. The flower is not responsible for the hand that plucks, nor the hare for the hound that pursues.

Dinner was very formal, ten guests all in evening dress arranged about a long table, candlelight, and the hushed footsteps of the French couple who cooked and served the meal. John Quinn at the head of his table in wing collar and black tie looked the Victorian paterfamilias presiding over his 'family' of artists and writers.

Ireland was the subject of the dinner conversation; the Sinn Feiners raising havoc in the Irish countryside, and James Joyce raising havoc in the American courts. John Quinn was embroiled in the long defence of the *Little Review* publication of *Ulysses* and didn't want to talk about it. But everyone else did; the rich and refined are as fascinated by prurience as the man in the street, and word was out that Joyce was 'racy'. No one, naturally, admitted to that interest; much talk flew about of artistic merit and great experiments. Quinn looked sour and changed the subject, to no avail.

The man beside me, small and dark with a pixie-sharp face and a huge brown moustache, was apparently a writer. He talked to me about *Dubliners*, which I had not read. He seemed convinced that my Irish connections must give me unique insight into Joyce, but whenever he spoke of Ireland a picture rose in my mind of the mossy limestone walls of Temple House, and Eugenia Howie in a great feathered hat; a country where no Ulysses had wandered. My eyes turned again to Wendell and the beautiful woman in black.

'Mrs de Quincey is making a conquest,' my writer proclaimed with a theatrical wink.

'Yes,' I said, 'my husband.' That ended our converse for the night.

Mr Quinn's companion, the lovely Mrs Foster, served as hostess, and after dinner led the ladies from the room. I found myself in the drawing room, suddenly face to face with Margaret de Quincey. Close up, she was even more charming, rosy-cheeked and sweet as a milkmaid, her red-brown hair dressed beautifully with a head-band of pearls. She smiled warmly, and caught my hand. 'Your husband has been so kind to me. I was quite afraid to come here at all, alone, the way I must do everything now, but he made me so at ease. How lucky you are to have married such a man!' Her face was wistful but without a trace of jealousy. She was a truly fine woman, which of course made everything that much worse.

When the gentlemen rejoined us, Wendell rushed to my side with an elaborate display of husbandly affection, but his eyes were on Mrs de Quincey. 'I see you've met my wife,' he said gladly. 'Justina, we must have Mrs de Quincey to dinner. She's quite the bravest woman I've ever met.'

I nodded, and said, 'Of course.'

He put his arm about my shoulders and gave me a little hug. His *bonhomie* was that of a child whose precious new toy brings forth a flood of good behaviour in gratitude. I left them alone together and wandered from the room.

I followed the long corridor, glancing distractedly at the hundreds of books. In the entrance foyer I set my demitasse down on a little table. I hoped Mr Quinn's French manservant would appear and that I might ask him to send for our car, and relay my excuses to the company. Wendell would be angry, but his anger, softened by his new conquest, would be manageable. I wanted my home and my children and nothing more. But no one appeared and I had not the nerve to seek anyone, and so I stood before a pair of Nathanial Hone landscapes, dreaming of Ireland and the past. The doorbell rang, but no one came even then, and it rang again. Impulsively I crossed to the front door. After-dinner guests were customary on such evenings, and I assumed one such would be waiting without. I unlatched the door and swung it open. In the shadows of the elevator foyer, a tall, sparse figure was standing, an old man, wearing a dark overcoat, carrying a cane and a hat. He wore eyeglasses, down on the bridge of his long nose, and his hair and beard and moustache were white. His eyes were deep-set and expressive and the eyebrows, startlingly dark in contrast to the white hair, were turned quizzically downwards into a furrow of thought as he tried to place my much-changed face.

'Now I shall have it in a moment, so you mustn't be telling me,' he protested in a fine Irish voice.

'Hello, Mr Yeats,' I said.

18

'He is a practical man,' said Mr Yeats. He raised his pencil from the paper, and thoughtfully prodded the bridge of his eyeglasses with its blunt end. 'A lawyer. A logical man. He lacks imagination.' He lowered the pencil and made several quick, sure strokes on the paper, looked up again and said, 'Without imagination there is no love. He does not know how to love, though he is the best and most generous friend.'

I made a little twitch of my chin to indicate understanding. I was sitting to Mr Yeats, hands on knees, on a straight wooden chair, in his room at Petipas. He was talking about John Quinn, the art collector and his faithful patron, but he was talking of Wendell as well, in a sort of code, for me.

The code was necessitated by the presence of Theresa sullenly fanning herself against the heat in a corner of the small, cluttered room. Her pretty pink mouth formed a perpetual pout of resentment; a resentment that I shared, but did not express, because she was the price of my freedom.

It was October of 1921. Ellie was a year old, and Wendell two and two months. It was six months since my meeting with Mr Yeats at John Quinn's on the night Wendell fell in love with Margaret de Quincey. Our re-acquaintance, and their romance, were exactly of an age, and the former had been quietly blessed by the latter. The disastrous clash that threatened our marriage that night was avoided, or at least averted, by Wendell's sudden new obsession. Out of apology perhaps, or in a plea for condonement, his condemnations were forgotten. My visits to Millie continued unhindered, as did my classes at Cooper Union. I was allowed, also, certain evenings to attend meetings of Millie's Baha'i community, at which I could again see Mirza Hassan and Fatima, though I never dared return to Washington Street. But on none of these occasions could I bring my children, nor could I ever escape the chaperonage of Theresa.

Her attachment to me, always under the guise of companionship, or practicality, always with a cheerful casualness that disguised Wendell's unbudging determination, was now of complex purpose. She was, of course, a spy. Wendell's distrust of me was not lessened by his current lack of interest. I was no longer his love, but I was still his wife, the 'mother of his children,' a phrase, with its reduction of my role to breeding dam, that I grew to hate. Whatever his behaviour, mine must be impeccable, and seen to be impeccable. And in Theresa he was assured of the most grudging of witnesses; for all the public conviviality of our companionship, she hated me, and would have happily seen me in the street.

Her hatred was ironic, because I was no longer her rival, nor she mine. Wendell's love for her, like his love for me, was long dead, eclipsed by his new fervour. As Mrs de Quincey's powers waxed, Theresa's had waned, and from the role of confident seductress she had faded to that of discarded paramour. It showed in her manner, and it showed in her face. She gained weight, and her perfect clean features were coarsened by a doubled chin and thickened jowl lines. I knew what she would look like in ten years' time; rough and easy, like a Dublin street woman. With the hardening of the face, had come a hardening in the voice, a bitterness under the sweet smile, and she alternately poured attentions upon Wendell or bombarded him with complaints. He was heartily sick of her and would have dismissed her had he not feared the scandal she might raise. Instead he coupled her to me; securing his freedom at the deliberate expense of mine. I took no comfort in his dilemma, or her misery. Nothing is sadder than the death of infatuation.

She sat now, knees apart, toes together, an overweight schoolgirl, seething in boredom. 'Ma'am, I'll die of the heat, I shall,' she moaned, fanning herself with a rolled up scrap of paper.

'Why not go for a walk, until Mr Yeats is done?' I suggested as mildly as possible. 'You've half an hour at least.' She looked at me suspiciously, and at the painter.

'You won't be running off anywhere, Ma'am?' she mumbled. Theresa wasn't a diplomat.

'To Paris. To Rome. To the Orient,' said Mr Yeats, waving his pencil gleefully. 'To the wonders of Byzantium.'

'Yes, Ma'am,' Theresa said stiffly. She could not comprehend Mr Yeats, but knowing he was Irish made her uneasy. The Irish in New York were always expecting someone to be telling everyone back home what they were really up to. 'I'll be back in twenty minutes,' she said sternly, and stood up, stretching herself vulgarly, her large bosom bouncing into place, her too-tight skirt sticking sweatily around her wide buttocks. *Oh Wendell*, I thought sadly, *How hath Troy fallen!*

The door closed behind her and we heard her footsteps, plodding heavily down the steep stairs. The house was very quiet in the middle of the afternoon, its occupants out about their business, and the kitchens still. The Petipas boarding house had been Mr Yeats' home for twelve years, almost all the time that had lapsed since our unexpected farewell at Stephen's Green. He had come to

New York by chance, and stayed on by apparent accident. He was quite old now and on all sides family and friends urged him homewards to Dublin, and indeed one of the first things he told me that spring was how fortunate it was that we had met before he made his departure. But it was autumn now and that departure, set for one date after another, had somehow never come. Of course I had come late to the scene, but John Quinn assured me in a moment of frayed temper that the return of the Yeats patriarch had grown mythical over the many years, like the advent of a messiah, an event beyond plausibility and time. Poor Mr Quinn; he tried so hard to organize chaotic lives as rigidly as his own, quite oblivious that chaos is the food of artists, though the destruction of other men.

Chaos reigned happily in the little bedroom and studio of the Irish painter, a pleasant arena of art, dominated by an arresting and unfinished self-portrait in oils upon which he had worked for years. Books and clothing and the accoutrements of his trade were scattered about happily, amidst piles of papers, stacked canvases, jars and bottles, old cigars, new newspapers, cups of tea purloined from the kitchens. Mr Yeats long ante-dated the present owners of Petipas, an Italian couple who had come but recently, and therefore he was comfortably above any law they might set. The Breton sisters whose name yet lingered had left two years before; Mr Yeats showed me sketches of them and recalled them as fond tyrants. But the Petipas Restaurant remained long after. It occupied a four-storey brownstone on West 29th Street, the building being yet there when I passed a year or two ago, though no longer a public establishment.

From being a minor boarding house with good French cuisine, it had grown into a gathering place of the arts, by virtue of the splendid conversation to be found at its table. Presiding there, wine glass and cigar to hand, and sketch book always ready was that master of talkers, John Butler Yeats, who long ago had enchanted the dinner guests of Temple House. He had found the perfect venue, with just the right blending of American shirt-sleeve ease, and Breton old-country formality, where the young were adventuresome enough to seek his company, respectful enough to listen, and intelligent enough to contribute. In the summer evenings, dinner was served in the walled backyard, under a striped awning, from a long table covered in white cloth and cheered by bottles of illicit wine. Artists and writers gathered happily; projects were planned, abandoned, replanned, strokes of genius came and went with the empty wine bottles into the dark. Moths fluttered about the candlelight, and the sticky sultry New York night wrapped itself comfortably around the evening like a dark soft cat. In the winter the company moved indoors to the big dining room, cosy against frigid nights. It was a place of dreams and through it flitted some remarkable people. I met John Sloan there, and Dolly his wife, and Padraic Colum, and Jack London, and the poet Khalil Gibran. I brought Millie Dobbs, who loved it as much as I, and who became at once a regular. I did not, of course, bring Wendell. I had been to dinner there, with Millie, three nights before, and I had agreed to sit to Mr Yeats, on the turn-about agreement that he would sit to me. That prospect amused him greatly. 'Now when you are very, very famous, someone, in perusing your collection one day, shall proclaim, "Who is that white-bearded old man who looks like Abraham?" and another will answer, "But that is John Butler Yeats!" and I shall have my immortality!'

'Heaven help you,' I said, 'if your immortality rests on me!'

I had been working steadily now, for almost a year,

since the day I met Millie Dobbs, and I had done portraits of Wendell's sisters that had actually pleased their unaffectionate father, a definite triumph. At present I was working on a less appealing task. Wendell, with an insensitivity quite extraordinary even for him, had hit upon the idea that I must portray Mrs Margaret de Quincey in oils. Again, perversity comes to mind, and I suppose some modern Freudian might work up a telling insight into his motives; but frankly I'll do without it. I agreed to the portrait because to refuse would be churlish to Mrs de Quincey, without cause. In the public eye (and Wendell had made his suggestion of the portrait in a public situation before half a dozen mutual friends) she was no more than an unfortunate widow who we, as a couple, had befriended. To comply to his request was natural; to refuse was to cast up questions that must be forever suppressed. And so, a week previously, in the drawing room of 18 Gramercy Park, we had our first sitting, and it had not gone well.

'Creation requires love,' said Mr Yeats. 'The artist must love his subject before he can do it justice.'

'Surely not,' I said, a little stiffly, his words having tugged a personal thread. 'Anyhow, it's not possible. You can't possibly love everyone who sits to you; they might be total strangers. And they might be quite despicable.'

Mr Yeats nodded solemnly. 'They might,' he agreed, his voice mild. 'But there is always *something* lovable in a human creature. The artist must seek that something; it is that he must strive to paint.'

I was quiet for a while, letting the soft sound of his pencil make the conversation. Then I said, defensively, 'She's really quite lovely. I do like her immensely. So it *can't* be that. The face is difficult, that's all.'

Mr Yeats worked on behind a small enigmatic smile. He said thoughtfully, 'Whenever I find myself with nothing but praise for someone, I usually find a feeling rather the opposite in my private self.'

'I do like her. She is charming.'

'Even though she is using her charm upon your husband?' I turned angrily away.

'Justina.'

'How did you know that?' I asked sharply. 'Who has been talking about us?'

'You have, my dear.' He smiled gently. 'This isn't Dublin,' he said, 'where all is talk and very little happens. In New York things happen all the time, and no one is meant to talk of them, and all is kept secret from those most concerned.'

'Oh, yes,' I said suddenly, resisting the urge of tears. 'Oh, yes, it is like that.' He nodded wisely again, tilting his long head and sighting down his pencil tip at me.

'Ah, Justina, we are out of place. We are not Americans. We shall both return.' But I knew he did not mean it at all.

Theresa returned, however, sweaty and fractious, announcing that it was twice as hot outside and we were late, Ma'am, anyhow. I acquiesced. Mutual talk was half the pleasure of our sittings, and Mr Yeats and I were both in agreement that talk in the presence of Theresa was sadly subdued.

As I was leaving, he said, 'If you were to come to dinner tomorrow night, with Miss Dobbs, a most promising table would truly be complete.'

'Oh, I couldn't possibly,' I said wistfully, feeling Theresa's suspicious eyes upon me.

'Ah, a pity,' said Mr Yeats, but as I placed my hat on my head and took up my gloves he mused contentedly, 'Of course the best thing about Petipas is that there is always room at the table for one or two more, even at the shortest notice.' I suppressed a giggle.

'How fortunate,' I said, ignoring Theresa.

'Fortunate, indeed,' said Mr Yeats.

It was not often that I dined at Petipas, perhaps four times in as many months. Invitations had arisen, and mostly been passed up; I dared not press Wendell too far. Of course our social calendar was full, but there were certainly more frequent opportunities; those many, many evenings I spent alone, the children asleep in the nursery and Wendell at work late, or at his club, or simply 'engaged'. He never felt the need to tell me where he went, and I certainly never asked. That he met in secret with Margaret de Quincey was beyond doubt. Her gentle shyness with me following certain evenings told all. I did not presume for a moment anything remotely improper occurred. She was quite above such behaviour, and Wendell would not have desired her otherwise. Nobility was her greatest charm, and in six months he had placed her on a pedestal of such dizzying height that he himself was awed to approach. Such humility had hardly been a feature of previous *amours* and a wiser woman than I would have seen this exclusivity for the danger it was. I was merely baffled, torn between belief in his protestations of innocence and reluctant condemnation. Always Margaret's sweet unpaintable face rose before my doubts in saintly recrimination.

'He's such a *good* man,' she confided in me. 'So like my husband. What would I have done without him? Without both of you!' she added in kind haste.

Over the summer she was so much in our company that I came to regard her as a sort of sister-in-law. She even joined us for our August retreat to the Grey House on Long Island. There she sat with sweet patience, beside myself and the crippled Grace, for long summer afternoons beneath the shade trees. Wendell, invigorated by her presence, played boisterously with his children, swinging the baby in the garden hammock, and taking his son on expeditions to the creek for minnows and crabs. At the day's end they would return, with treasures and trinkets to be shown for my approval, and for Margaret's as if she were as much their mother as I. They were pleasant days, often enough. We three women made a good company, and as Wendell was intolerably unhappy any day on which he might not see Margaret, these weeks in her constant presence were a boon to us both. He relaxed and became again boyish and generous and full of love for all. As Theresa was the price of my freedom, so was Margaret the price of peace, and we existed through the hot sultry days in an innocent ménage-à-trois.

Of course I was miserable inside; what woman would not have been? But I confided in no one, not even May Howie whose letters followed me everywhere like the most faithful friends. But May was intuitive as always, and at the end of August she wrote to suggest I spend the following summer in Ireland with her. My whole heart leapt at the thought, and a warm flow of homesickness enveloped me, but I hid the letter away. It would take all of the winter at least for me to gather nerve enough to make such a request.

The only other person who seemed aware of my odd plight was the frail invalid, Grace Pyke, whose physically stunted life granted her in youth the perceptions of an aged observer. Once as she read, and I sat sketching her thin serious face, she looked up suddenly from her book and said abruptly, 'The family have always spoiled Wendell. They have made him think himself a Super Man, above the lot of ordinary men. So nothing ordinary can ever seem good enough for him, and he must quest forever after the Holy Grail.'

'Perhaps he'll find it,' I said, laughing, wishing to make light of it.

'No,' she answered earnestly. 'He never shall. It is not possible. But I fear he imagines he has.' She looked down at her book, resting on her blanketed braced stick legs. She seemed to gather strength, as if she would suddenly, miraculously stand. She looked up and her eyes met mine. 'Leave him, Justina. Take your children to Ireland and don't bring them back.'

I stared, stunned. 'Grace . . .' I whispered. She spun her chair round with her strong slim hands upon the wheels, and hurriedly wheeled herself away. Shaken by her very solemnity, I did seriously consider what she said. But there was no way I could do such a thing, even had I truly wished it, and I did not. I could not conceive what she in her wisdom foresaw.

When I returned from Twenty-Ninth Street, with Theresa, Wendell was already home. He was in the nursery playing with his son, while Nanny, somewhat disapproving of his presence, bathed Ellie. He was in a strange mood, sentimental, and even affectionate. He complimented me on how well I looked, and his every gesture towards me was kind. But the kindness was solemn, like kindness at a funeral. I wondered if he had bad news to convey to me, and worried for a moment or two, before it was evident that nothing was amiss. When I asked lightly if I might possibly attend the dinner at Petipas, he seemed only too glad to grant my request, as if he were seeking some gesture in my favour he might make. Mystified, but grateful, I accepted his good nature, and declined only the offer of his car, since Millie Dobbs would provide hers.

The following day, his mood was unchanged, and more startling, the night between had seen a remarkable event. He had come to my bedroom, in the dark hours of the morning, and requested my marital favours. I had responded, since it never occurred to me that I might refuse, and though I could hardly enjoy the experience, touched as it was by the same sentimental melancholy, it had left me with an odd remembered warmth. Naturally, neither of us raised the subject over breakfast, with the children and their nanny present. But he kissed me as he left for his office, and wished me a pleasant evening, since he was planning a late return that would preclude our meeting before I went out.

I walked in the park with the children in the afternoon. It was a day turned suddenly crisp and clear, as autumn descended from Canada, catching the summer city unawares. The air was crystalline and the sky a deep blue and splashes of fall colours touched the trees. I felt extraordinarily happy, as most New Yorkers do when the heat of the summer flees the city, and the best days of the year lie just ahead. As I walked I dreamed of Dublin and Arradale, and taking my babies to see May, and James and Eugenia, and Wilhemina and all my family. I returned late, refreshed and happy, and went up to my room, while Nanny prepared the children for their evening meal. I dressed quickly, in a black suit and white blouse with a big silk bow, and was about to return to the nursery when I saw something extraordinary lying on my bedside table. It was a jeweller's box that I had never seen before, and since it was clearly placed there for my eyes, I lifted and opened it. Inside, resting against white silk, was a Byzantine cross set with garnets and pearls, an antique and obviously a treasure. With it, in Wendell's tight precise hand, was a tiny note:

My dear wife,

I have loved you more than you've ever imagined,

Wendell

I lifted the jewelled cross and then set it back down with a sudden shiver. It seemed like a gift from the grave. I left it lying there in its bed of white silk, and hurried away, upstairs to the nursery, to spend the bedtime hour with my children. They were asleep when Millie's car called at the door.

Autumn had driven the diners of Petipas in from the awning-covered yard of summer evenings, to the long front dining room and its open fire. The room was warm and cheery with the fire's glow, a cluster of candles and the light from the open kitchen shining through. When we entered, a large and animated crowd of men and women were gathered already about the longest table, before the fire. The table was spread with a white cloth and amply laden with wine bottles in gentle rejection of the Volstead Act.

At the table's head sat Mr Yeats, wine glass at hand, and sketch-pad at his elbow, discussing Mark Twain with the writer Van Wyck Brooks. The gentlemen all rose as we entered, and Millie waved a deprecating hand lest conversation be interrupted while we found places. I sat beside Dolly Sloan, the wife of the painter, while Millie went round the table and seated herself between the dancer, Clare Reynolds, and John Sloan. There were ten people around the table, one or two of them strangers, the rest acquaintances and friends. The moment I sat down I felt happy and alive and young, the way I once had felt in Dublin with Michael and Kate and Padraic and May. I could listen contentedly for hours. That evening the subject of debate was the value of the sketch, and Mr Yeats argued persuasively that whereas the sketch as a substitute for a finished work had no value to him, the finished work must, in its expression of immediacy, achieve in finality the nature of a sketch. He went on to maintain that the self-portrait on his easel upstairs on which he had laboured for eleven years would, upon completion, be a sketch.

Throughout the meal I pondered on that, while Mrs Sloan sipped too avidly at the unprohibited wine, and the rest of the party grew merry. At the end I looked up to Mr Yeats and said, '*Life* is like that. When we are young we see clearly all we will do, all we will achieve, all we will love, in a few quick pure lines. And then the older and older we get, we fuss and we fuss and we add colour and shading, and we scrape off, and paint over, and every day we grow further and further from the vision that was once so clear.'

He studied me sadly, over the rims of his glasses. I thought he looked suddenly really old, and rather ill. He had suffered influenza through September and I wondered if he'd not fully recovered.

He said, without his usual humour, 'Everything is clear when we are young. It is easy to be certain of everything. The older one gets the harder it becomes, until at last, adrift in uncertainty, we are punished with the sure convictions of our children, just as in youth we tormented our elders with our proud and certain truths.'

I thought of Clare and myself causing misery at Arradale, so sure of our duty to proclaim our holy faiths. Marriage and children had undone all my certainties; only Clare, husbandless and childless, had kept her anger pure.

'What, shall the sins of the sons be visited upon the fathers, then?' cried a cheery voice down the table. I looked at the young man who had spoken; he was fair-haired and round-cheeked, a boy of nineteen or twenty, who would one day be a famous critic. He seemed barely a child to me, and I was shaken to remember that Michael had died at an age no greater than his. Thinking of it, I felt hugely old, the way I had felt at the end of the war.

I was glad when the party broke up from the table, and we all wandered out with our cordials into the sheltered yard behind the building. The night was brilliant with stars, even over the bright city, and the air smelled of woodsmoke and dead leaves. We began a game that we had played before, when dining outside, watching the lights come on in the windows of surrounding buildings and making up stories about them. Mr Yeats had created the game and it became a vehicle for an unending debate on the relation of truth to fiction, romanticism to reality.

Millie and I each chose a window and invented characters to occupy them, elaborating ever more marvellous tales in giggling rivalry. While we stood there, a man came into the yard. It was not unusual. Friends and strangers gathered there, late and early. I hardly noticed him. It was only when Millie went off to converse with Dolly Sloan, that he approached. I realized he had been listening to our stories because as he stepped behind me, and before I might turn, he began to speak. His voice was flat and dry, with a midwestern accent, dimly familiar. He began at once creating a story of his own about our two windows.

'Behind that pale curtain lives a young woman. She is far, far from home and lonely and each evening she lights her lamp and sits writing verses to a man she met years ago in a foreign place. Each night she writes, and cries over her writing, and then just before she extinguishes her lamp and goes to her lonely bed, she crumples all the papers and throws them on to her fire.

'Now, just beside her, only one room away, but in the building backing upon hers, lives that very man. Only a wall separates them, at night, but each day they go about their lives in different streets, and never meet. He, now, is an artist, and he sketches by *his* lamp and sketches her face again and again all evening, and casts *his* efforts upon *his* fire.' His voice was faintly humorous, mocking his own little melodrama, and then he touched my arm from behind, and something powerful and warm flowed upwards from his touch.

'Look up,' he said. Obediently, I did. Above the rooftops the smoke from the two chimneys mingled in one pale, starry stream. I stood very, very still. The voice had stirred me with its familiarity but the touch of his hand upon my arm brought me to excited certainty.

'It's you, isn't it?' I said.

'Justina Melrose, the Rose of No Man's Land.'

I turned very slowly. He wore a long belted raincoat, and a black beret, and he had grown a thick beard. His eyes were exactly the same, fine and green, and crow's-footed at their corners when he smiled.

'Oh, Jack,' I cried and I flung myself into his arms.

And that was how I met Jack Redpath again, at the Petipas Restaurant in New York. I wrapped my arms around his neck, and clung on to him, as to a piece of miraculous fortune that I dare not let go. He seemed happy enough with the bargain, crossing his hands on the small of my back, and getting comfortable, with his bearded chin against my cheek. Its tickle reminded me sagely of my unwarranted intimacy and I jumped suddenly back.

'I was just beginning to like that,' he protested sadly.

'What are you *doing* here, Jack?' I cried. 'Where did you come from?'

He laughed lightly at my frantic amazement.

'I *live* here, remember?'

'At Petipas?' I said, wide-eyed.

'In New York. West 20th Street, actually. It's not very far.'

'Why haven't I seen you?' I cried. 'All these months . . .'

'It's a big city,' he said. And indeed, it was.

I smiled sheepishly, holding his hands in both of mine,

'Oh Jack, somehow I'm always a little girl from the country, with you.'

'What could be better?' He raised my hands, and kissed my fingertips. His eyes fell on Wendell's broad band of wedding gold, and he shrugged resignedly. 'So you said yes to the alligator?' he said.

'I'm afraid so.'

'How's your leg?'

'I've still got most of it.'

'But not all?'

'Not all.' We stood a long while in silence looking into each other's eyes.

'I think we should talk,' Jack said, at last

We sat outside at a little table in the corner of the yard. It was cold, and Jack went in and got my fur jacket from Mme Jais, and we remained there, even when all the company had gone back to the cheer and warmth of the fire. We talked for hours, exchanging our private histories since the day we parted in the midst of a war not yet won. Jack's war went on long after mine; as I prepared for my London wedding, he was following the advance to the Rhine. He entered the Rhineland just behind the British Army of Occupation and witnessed the Union Jack hoisted over the Hotel Monopol in Cologne. Then, by car, rail, or on foot, throughout the Armistice period, he criss-crossed Europe with a notebook and an observant eye. Among ruined cities, defeated soldiery, returning prisoners and wandering refugees he gathered stories to wire home, ending up at last at the Peace Conference in Versailles. Even then he did not return, but stayed on until April of 1920 in Paris.

'I always knew you'd do that,' I said.

'What, stay on?'

'I thought you'd never go back at all, somehow.'

I stopped, embarrassed. 'Of course, with your wife waiting . . .' I added quickly.

'Oh, I didn't come back for her.' He smiled his honest, disarming smile. I looked down at my wine glass. 'I came back,' Jack went on, 'for two reasons. Two reasons, from two places. The first was an orphanage in the Rhineland. I went along with some American soldiers delivering food. It was a seedy place run by a bunch of Catholic nuns. Fifty children, fathers all dead heroes, mothers God knows where. Nothing special, just a lot of dirty, hungry kids; not starving, just hungry, not naked, just ragged; but anyhow it was Christmas Eve, so I wrote a bit about them and sent it off to a magazine that used to take features on the war. Got it back a few months later, in Paris, a bit dog-eared, and with a reminder: "Our readers have sacrificed much in a war against Germany. Write about French orphans, please." I was busy with the Conference then, and all the talk was of the new League of Nations, "to promote International Co-operation and International Peace". I walked out of it all, that day, found a pretty French mam'selle and spent half the next week drunk, and the rest of it in bed.' He looked up suddenly. 'Beg your pardon, Ma'am, but that's what I did.'

I tried not to blush and I looked away at the lights of the building at the back of the yard and said, 'And what was the second reason?'

'That was in the spring of the next year. I decided I had to see all the places where all of it happened. I knew I was going to spend the rest of my life hearing about and talking about the Somme and the Marne and Passchendaele and Loos, and I'd only seen half of them, and then hiding behind a parapet, through a cloud of cordite darkly. So I spent that spring walking the old battlefields, watching the farmers clearing the wire and the old shells away; a gingery business too; watching the land go back to being farmland from being hell. It was somewhere near Fricourt. I got to talking with a farmer, a big old man in a black smock. He'd been ploughing. His team were standing yet in harness, just unhitched from the plough. I remember thinking how good it was to see plough horses again. I'm a farm boy, remember,' he grinned suddenly. 'And all the horses I'd seen in years were hitched to guns.' He drank from his wine, and filled the glass again and filled mine. 'The field was sown in barley, just coming up, green and soft. I asked, just to be sociable, how it would be. He laughed. I can see him yet, laughing, in his black smock, just two or three teeth in his mouth, and a grizzly grey beard, dirty red bandanna around his neck. He seemed to know something I should know. Then he pointed to the field and said, "Bon. Très bon," and still laughing, he pointed over my shoulder to a little wood. There, there were half a dozen make-shift crosses, war graves, waiting to be tidied up, or moved. He pointed to the field then, and shrugged, and then, in case I'd not taken his point, he stepped quite casually in among his green barley, and leaned over after half a dozen steps, lifted something and tossed it to me. It was a human thigh bone. The whole field was just a boneyard. It was one of the old battlefields. I could see then the line of the trenches, still showing underneath, where he'd filled them. Fertilizer. Human fertilizer. God's highest creation dunging the fields. "Bon. Très bon."'

'He laughed?' I whispered.

'What else? Cry?' Jack shrugged, and downed his wine. 'I wrote that one up, too. Another reject. Too much for our readers' sensibilities.'

'And then?' I half-smiled.

'Oh, you guessed it. Another mam'selle. Another

week-long drunk. Only this one lasted three weeks and still didn't do the trick. So I went to England, and then took a boat home. But even in New York that barley field wouldn't leave me alone. I had a ghost to lay, and the only exorcism I have ever known is words. I wrote the stories again, as fiction. I sent one to the *New Yorker* and one to *Collier's*, and in half a year they were both in print. So our readers' sensibilities can relish in fantasy what they won't tolerate in fact.'

'That's very cynical,' I said.

'Yes,' said Jack. 'So am I.' Then he smiled again and apologized. 'Oh I'm sure it's only half true,' he said. 'Besides, a whole new career has blossomed as a result, and I'd be a hypocrite if I pretended I wasn't enjoying it. So from Jack Redpath, journalist, I have become Jack Redpath, writer of short stories, and the only casualty in sight is truth.' He laughed.

'And poet, surely, too,' I said. He was silent. 'I liked it,' I added then. He nodded.

'Tell me about the alligator.'

I laughed. 'I don't really think of Wendell as an alligator,' I said.

'What's he like?'

I shrugged, 'He's serious. Very formal. Very hard-working. A good father. He's a very good father. Oh Jack, I've two lovely children, you know, a little boy of two and Ellie, my baby girl . . . they're quite the most beautiful children.'

He smiled. 'When you ask a woman about her husband and she tells you instead about her children, there's generally something wrong with the marriage.' He looked very wise, like a sage, with his beard and black beret and he was far too near the truth.

I said abruptly, 'I don't want to talk about it, Jack.' He

looked so chastened that I laughed. 'Anyhow your marriage wasn't perfect either that I recall.'

'No,' he said. 'It wasn't.' He paused and just as I caught the significance of the past tense, he said, 'She died of influenza in March 1920, while I was drinking myself stupid in Paris. They couldn't even find me through the agency. I never heard until I got off the boat in New York.'

'Oh, Jack.'

'Oh, please. Don't offer sympathy. Sympathy is hardly what I deserve.'

He sat drawing wet lines on the table with his finger in spilled wine and I said foolishly, 'Surely it wasn't your fault . . . what could you have done?'

'What? What could I have done? Lived decently, treated her right, stayed with her, stopped drinking . . . that's something for a start . . . and maybe taken her back to Ohio and made a decent job of what I'd begun, instead of ditching her here with my disillusionments . . . as if she'd never had any disillusioning of her own. Oh forget it, it's nothing to do with you.'

'I'm sorry,' I muttered miserably. The door from the back room of Petipas opened discreetly and I heard Millie's refined apologetic voice.

'I'm *terribly* sorry to interrupt, Justina, but I'm afraid my car *is* at the door.'

'I'm just coming,' I murmured, rising awkwardly from the little table, avoiding Jack's eyes. For a moment he let me go, but then he looked up suddenly, and caught my wrist. His hand was big and rough, as if he still lived an outdoor, woodsman's life.

'No, please. I'm sorry about that. Please don't go.'

I shrugged, and pulled my hand free, 'It's all right, Jack. But I do *have* to go. Miss Dobbs is waiting.'

He looked up to the lighted doorway where her graceful, slope-shouldered, deferent figure was outlined by the soft light.

'Millie, I've met an old friend from the war,' I said hastily. 'This is Jack Redpath . . .'

I heard her soft laugh. 'Oh, I know Jack,' she said.

'I'll take Mrs Pyke home, Miss Dobbs, if you wouldn't mind,' Jack said.

'Surely, Mr Redpath,' she laughed again, 'if that's what she would like.' There was the faintest question, framed in light amusement. Jack looked at me.

I nodded. 'Yes. I should like that.' The door gently closed and we were left alone in the dark.

'How do you know Millie?' I said. He laughed.

'The formidable Miss Dobbs. Patron saint of bad writers and drunken journalists. I was introduced by the local dying poet in my neighbourhood bar; she got him out of some kind of a jam. She fed me and Ellen our whole first winter in New York.' He grinned, and pulled his black beret down over one eye. 'That was 1907. Whenever I'm feeling successful and pleased with myself, I manage to run into Millie. It cuts me down to size.' He stood up. 'If I'm going to take you home, I'd better do something about it . . . you don't mind if we walk?'

'I should love it,' I said. We rose together and went back into the restaurant, through the back room and by the kitchen. In the long dining room, Mr Yeats and John Sloan were sitting alone at the corner of the table. Everyone else had gone, and around them a litter of glasses and a tray full of cigar butts recorded a fine evening. A bottle of Vermouth sat between them and each was sketching the other as they talked. When I called out to them, Mr Yeats, who had grown quite deaf, seemed not to hear, and so I left without a goodbye.

We walked down Seventh Avenue to Twenty-Third Street, and turned across town. The streets were quiet. I was unused to being out at night, beyond the cocooning shelter of a motorcar and felt a little afraid. But Jack was as comfortable in the darkened city as a cat. Overhead dim stars emerged between flying white clouds in the narrow channels of sky above the buildings. A cold wind blew in off the river. I walked close beside Jack in the comforting shelter of his shoulder. He talked about a story he was writing about the war. I remembered walking beside him on the road to Amiens. It seemed a thousand years ago.

The square of buildings around Gramercy Park was dim and remote, and the windows of number 18 were darkened except for those upstairs. I felt uneasy, as if I had stayed out far too late. 'Surely it's only eleven?' I said. Jack peered at his wristwatch beneath a streetlamp.

'Ten past twelve, little lady. Shall I call your pumpkin?'

'Oh, Jack,' I whispered. He glanced across at me, and smiled a small, curious smile. 'I've never been so late,' I said.

'Then it's about time you were,' he said. 'This town only wakes up at the witching hour.' He was looking up solemnly at the tall, narrow brownstone with its imposing curve of iron railings surmounting the wide sweep of stairs. 'You've done all right,' he said. It was a dry observation, without malice.

'That wasn't my reason, Jack.' He smiled again, wryly. 'If I thought it were, I wouldn't be here,' he said. He put his hands on my shoulders and for a terrifying moment I thought he was about to kiss me, there on my own front steps. But he didn't, of course. He looked solemnly down and said, 'Whatever the reasons, the thing's done. *Plus ça change, plus c'est la même chose.*' He shrugged, adjusted his black beret and walked away.

Theresa answered the door. I was surprised. It was late, and there was no reason for her to be awaiting my return.

'Isn't Mr Pyke at home?' I said, as I entered.

'Yes, Ma'am,' she said. Her voice was low, and she turned her face away. For a moment I suspected the old foolishness, and felt a sharp pang of disgusted anger, but there was something more than embarrassment in her reticence. It was less sullen than frightened. I imagined Wendell upstairs in a rage at my lateness, and had Theresa been a friend and not an enemy I would have begged advance warning. Instead, I gave her my jacket, rather stiffly, and walked, head high, as calmly as I could manage, up the stairs. Actually, it was not Wendell's nature to give way to rages; ice was his weapon, not fire.

He was not in the drawing room, nor in his study. I continued up the second flight, until I saw the light from my bedroom washing softly out from the door left partially ajar. When I entered he was sitting on the edge of my bed, his head drooping into his palms.

'Wendell?' I whispered. He did not move. I stepped closer. 'Wendell, are you all right?' Still, he did not answer, and I began nervously to explain myself.

'I'm terribly sorry to be late. I met an old friend, a person I knew during the war, Jack Redpath; and naturally we wished to talk . . .'

He still did not move. Panicky ideas swept through my head. *He had telephoned Millie and found I had stayed on alone. He had looked out of the window and seen me with Jack . . .*

'I walked home with him,' I said boldly, my instinct for truth quite unswerving. 'It was pleasant and we could talk more . . . Wendell, what is *wrong*?'

He looked up then. I was struck incongruously by the very handsomeness of his features, how boyishly beautiful he remained, even in his thirties.

He smiled. 'Did you have a nice time, then, my dear? How lovely.' His voice was preoccupied and dreamy.

'Yes,' I said, quite loudly, wondering if he'd actually heard me. When he still did not move I turned away and removed my hat, and laid it on my dressing table. I saw myself in the mirror, and behind me Wendell watching me with the same preoccupied gentle smile. 'I'll go and see the children now,' I said.

Suddenly, he became animated. He straightened and said, 'No. Come and sit down. I want to talk.'

'All right, as soon as I've seen the babies.' I turned to leave the room and he jumped up.

'No,' he said.

'Wendell, I want to see the children.'

'No. You can't.'

'I *can't*?' I said, amazed. '*Why* can't I?'

He paused just a few seconds and in those few seconds I became suddenly wildly afraid. I turned again to the door and he bounded across the room and caught my arm.

'Let me go, Wendell. I want to go to the nursery. I want to see my babies.'

'They're not there,' he said.

I felt sick. 'What?' I whispered. I was fighting him, struggling to be free, my only thought those two little beds upstairs. 'Not there?' I gasped. 'What do you mean? Why aren't they in bed? It's after midnight.'

'Sit down, Justina.'

'I want my babies.' I broke free and ran from him bounding ahead of him, up the stairs. The nursery was dark. I ran in, with only the light from the landing, and saw at once that the two beds were empty. I switched on a light, and rushed about the room like a dumb animal, pawing at bedclothes and curtains, as if my children might be hidden away somewhere.

'Justina,' Wendell said. I looked back at the doorway. He was standing just outside.

'Where are my babies?' I cried. 'What have you done to them?'

He blinked, stunned by my panic and said, his voice filled again with its dominating calm, 'Good God, Justina, they're quite *safe*. There's nothing to get hysterical about.'

'Where *are* they?' I screamed.

'At the Grey House.'

'*What*?' I stared at him, and round the empty room and back at him. 'Are you *teasing*?' I had a brief burst of hopeful anger, that he'd made up some terrible, pointless game.

'Of course not,' he said flatly. 'My mother has taken them to Long Island. That's all.'

'In the middle of the night?'

'No. Just after you left. You've been away a long while. I sent them in the car. They telephoned their safe arrival a short while ago. They're settling perfectly satisfactorily.' A numb relief warmed me faintly from within. I felt my balled fists relax, and a soft release of tears. I could not imagine what ugly foolishness he was indulging, but I believed him that my babies were safe. I was shaking all over, with fear, relief from fear, and something more, the vision of a monster that had surfaced in my panic. In those moments I had thought him capable of anything. I turned away. I could not look at him.

'Justina,' he said.

'I want my children back,' I whispered. 'Send the car back at once. I want my children here.'

'Justina, I wish you to listen to me.'

'When you've done what I've said.'

'No, dear. You listen. And then you'll do what I will say. *Then*, the children will come home.'

I flung my head up and glared at him. 'What despicable game are you playing?' I said.

'Sit down, Justina.' He stood very calmly in the doorway and I knew I must do what he said, or he would stand there forever. I sat down, on Wendell's little low bed. He crossed the room and crouched on his haunches in front of me. I turned my face away, but he reached out and caught my two hands. I was drawn to look at him, as children are drawn to the images of their nightmares. He was smiling gently. He looked loving and caring, the way he had looked on the distant day I had met him in France, as he sat by my hospital bed and worried about my vulnerability in the war. 'Justina,' he said, 'please listen.'

'Bring my babies back,' I begged.

'Justina.' I was quiet, listening at last. 'Justina, I wish you to grant me a divorce.'

19

Somerville
Oxford
13 December 1924

My dear Justina,

Received your letter of 23 November at the close of Michaelmas; much involved in preparations, days spent in the Bodleian, quite unable to reply. Do hope you received the small parcel. I instructed Meggie most carefully upon its dispatch, but she is such a muzzy-headed little fool one never knows what will happen.

I was most impressed with the latest Redpath effort; the man has remarkable talent, well deserving of the name he is earning. There is a *vibrance* about these colonials . . . This is not however to imply any approval on my part of a social connection. People of this breed are invariably difficult, but I will leave you to your own judgement, such as that is . . .

May passed through on her way from Dublin back to Paris. She informs me that Uncle James is no better and no more reconciled to his loss, and this two years and more after Eugenia's death. I doubt he will make any recovery. Perhaps had he been yet at Ballysodare . . . but with that all gone . . . whenever I think of it I get such an urge to shoot Padraic O'Mordha, that I quite bitterly resent the Free Staters beating me to it. May he *not* rest in peace. Eithne is a pleasant enough child; biddable and quiet and capable of quite adult conversation. Wise for her years, but what child would not be, under the circumstances. Cathleen ni Houlihan still lying low in Sligo, as well she might. She's a noose around her neck, our dear cousin.

Wilhemina asks after you. She is well, though lonely, with Hugo away at his prep school in Perth. I saw him during the long vacation: a perfect miniature Douglas, steeped in solemnity at nine years old.

Regarding your present situation: I respect your courage (or is it stubbornness?) but I again *urge* you to consider my offer. (Or Wilhemina's.) There is absolutely no point in your staying on in New York. By your own admission, your social life is limited by lack of both time and funds, your relations with the Pykes non-existent, and your financial situation precarious. As to your living quarters, I acknowledge that the war prepared you well for roughing it, but what is acceptable as a temporary measure is demeaning in a permanent arrangement. No doubt it reeks of Bohemian charm but four flights of stairs and a leaking roof . . . you are not a child any longer, Justina. You have a birthday coming very soon and if I am closing on forty, then *you* are past thirty. Time to plan the future.

Hesitant as I am to raise a painful topic, I feel I must speak out as I fear very much you are unhealthily deluding yourself regarding the children. You must face reality. They are gone from your life until they are adults, by which time they will have grown into strangers. However good a friend you have in Grace Pyke (and she sounds indeed noble) the woman is a frail invalid and, as a sole link to your children, hardly a rock to build upon. Anyhow, seeing them on so uneven a basis will only upset you, and, dare I say it? upset *them* further. A clean break is your only hope of any happiness ever again.

From work upon my thesis I can assure you that history reveals you in fine company. Women have been thus abused, betrayed and callously discarded throughout the ages. This is cold comfort, I know. You have been bitterly wronged. But these were the issues we fought for, those days before the war. The vote was only a talisman. And now with talisman in hand, our work is just beginning. Come home, and make some measure of good of your misfortune. It will be like the old days, the three of us, together again.

Yours with much concern,
Clare

I folded Clare's letter back into its envelope and laid it, a little selfconsciously, on the small pine mantel of the little fireplace of my room. Jack was by the window, studying the painting on my easel, deliberately not intruding on my privacy. I crouched by the black slate hearth, and warmed my hands over the brave little flame. I wanted to put more wood on, but dared not; I bought my firewood nightly in small expensive bundles, sold by the street vendors, and even in cold December, I rationed it carefully. After a decent interval, Jack looked up from the painting and spoke casually.

'How's Clare?'

'Very Clare,' I said. He laughed. 'She thought well of your story,' I added.

Jack nodded sagaciously. 'The approval of an Oxford don!'

'Oh, hardly a don. But she *is* rather brilliant.' I laughed, 'Hard to believe, I know, but we have our academic side. It's your misfortune you've met the dunce.'

'I like the dunce.'

'Just as well,' I said. 'She's not getting any wiser with the years.'

'But more beautiful by the hour.'

I turned away. There was an awkward moment of silence, and then Jack also turned away and busied himself with the little Christmas tree he had bought from a grocer in Sheridan Square, and carried up my four flights of stairs. He set it up in a corner of the room, to the side of the fireplace, in a bucket of sand he had also carried up the stairs. Its piney scent filled the room, achingly nostalgic of better times and places.

'It's lovely, Jack,' I said, trying not to cry.

The night before, he had taught me how to make popcorn with hard kernels of yellow maize in a frying pan, and we had sat for hours stringing the white fluffy stuff on long threads, jewelled with bright cranberries. He was as patient as an eager child, threading his needle through the crumbling kernels and telling me about his Grandmother in Ohio teaching him tree-trimming, long ago. I told him about the cedar chest filled with blown glass and hand-painted ornaments that the servants brought solemnly down from the attics of Arradale each Christmas Eve, while Clare and I and the boys waited breathlessly for the reappearance of all our old favourites, and the wondrous crystal Christmas star that was always last out of the chest, and first away.

'The tree stood from floor to ceiling,' I marvelled aloud, 'and the ceilings were fifteen feet high.'

'That's some house,' said Jack.

'It was just home,' I said. 'You know what it's like when you're a child. Normality is defined by what you know most intimately, castle or cabin.'

'I used to watch my Mom and Dad sitting on the front porch in the summer, with the dog asleep under Dad's chair, and Mom mending, or shelling peas, or knitting; her hands always working, Dad's hands always still. And I'd try to imagine other children, all over the world, in African huts, and desert tents, with their Moms and Dads, just like mine, talking about neighbours and the newspaper, only they'd be Negro or Chinese or God knew what.' He laughed aloud, straightening up to pin the silver paper star to the top of our tree. 'Oh the innocence of it all!'

'It must be true, underneath,' I said doubtfully. 'There must be some root point where we're all the same.'

'Brotherhood of man?' Jack smiled, stringing white

ropes of popcorn pearls about the piney branches. 'I think we settled that one for good and all round about nineteen-sixteen.' He grimaced, struggling with the tree.

'Harsh thoughts for Christmas.'

'Well,' said Jack, looking once round my threadbare room, 'I've seen better Christmases, all in all.'

I think he was more angry for me than I was for myself. When we finished with the tree I went through to my little kitchen and made us coffee and with the smell of it blending with the pine scent, we sat around the fire watching my little sticks burn to white ash. The tree was mysterious, like a wood spirit. I wished I could afford candles, or electric lights to make it cheerier. My eyes went unwillingly to my two carefully wrapped gifts for Ellie and Wendell sitting in lonely isolation on my table. I had not placed them under my little fir. The children would never see them there. Grace Pyke, God bless her, would deliver them to the massive, glittering tree at 18 Gramercy Park.

Jack set his cup down and got up and wandered across to my easel again. The painting was a near-finished portrait of an eighteen-year-old, commissioned by his wealthy grandmother.

'It's good, Justina,' Jack said.

I laughed. 'It'll be better when I'm paid. *If* I'm paid.'

'Good Christ,' Jack said, 'if the de Laats don't have money, there's none left in the city.'

'Oh they *have* it,' I said mildly. 'That's half the problem.' He looked blank. I said, 'When you have *some* money, you're quite aware of it, and quite aware that not everyone has as much. But when you have *that* much money, it's like being a child in Arradale Castle. Money is so much the norm that its lack is incomprehensible. Never thought of. Mrs de Laat came by, after the second sitting.' I paused. 'That was the arrangement, you see. I'd be paid half after the second sitting.'

'Didn't she like it?' Jack asked, uncertainly.

'Oh, she loved it. She oozed and enthused all over the room. She stayed for an hour. Drank tea, and ate up half a dozen little sandwiches that I had *hoped* might be left over for my supper.' I laughed, remembering. '"Why, Mrs Pyke, these are quite scrumptious . . . who does for you . . . oh, I suppose you do for yourself?" Can you imagine, Jack, she was honestly looking about for some cupboard in which I kept three footmen, a cook and a maid.' I threw my head back, laughing gaily at the single attic room that had been my home for almost a year.

'What about the money,' said Jack, unamused by Mrs de Laat.

'Well, she never mentioned it. And then when it was time for her to go . . .'

'You just *let* her go?'

'Oh no. I'm far too mercenary for that. Or too hard-pressed, anyhow. I said, something about, "Oh, will Mrs Thompson," – that's the boy's mother – "will Mrs Thompson be settling with me?" She looked quite blank, and then she suddenly twigged it. "Oh! My dear, I quite forgot! There's some kind of a fee, I suppose?" She seemed a little disappointed, as if the whole delicious experience of being in a real artist's studio had been soiled. However, I pointed out that there was indeed a fee, and she rallied magnificently, and rummaged about in a huge tapestry handall, that she carried everywhere, and after a great deal of time looked up at me like a little child. "Oh, my dear, I don't have any money at all. Would it be all right if my husband were to write a cheque?" I agreed it would be wonderful, particularly if he did it soon!' I laughed again.

'And has he?'

'Oh no. Of course not.' I was still giggling.

'It's not *funny*, Justina,' Jack said. 'What gives these

blasted people the audacity . . .' I stood up and walked to his side, taking his arm, gently, with my hand at his elbow. He was quite rigid with anger.

'No audacity. Just ignorance. That's all. An innocence of the ways of the world. Someone else's world. I saw it all, long ago, in my Uncle's house.' I turned away from him, at the thought of that dear ludicrous place forever gone.

'What will you do in the meanwhile?'

'I'll get by. There's a little put away. And they *will* pay. Next year,' I laughed gaily again, 'like their tailors.'

'And you're not expected to eat until next year?'

'Millie won't let me starve. I can borrow from Millie.' He was staring at our brave, sad little Christmas tree.

He said, 'Justina, I just got two hundred dollars from *Story Magazine*. I don't *need* it.'

'Goodnight, Jack.'

'Why the hell not? Why from Millie, and not from me?' I wouldn't answer. Eventually he grabbed me roughly by both shoulders, kissed my forehead and stamped off to the door. I felt sorry. He'd been so kind bringing me the tree. I called after him, as he started down the stairs.

'Happy Christmas, Jack.' I was leaning over the rails, watching him down the dark stairwell.

He stopped and grinned. 'Oh, you'll see me before that.' His angers were brief.

'Will I, Jack?'

'You will. Tomorrow. And the day after. And the one after that. And every damned day of your goddamn life, until you learn how to say yes.' He touched his forefinger to his bristly forelock of sandy hair, nodded brusquely and stamped down the stairs. I went in and shut the door and stood leaning against it. As always, when I'd sent him away, I was sorry that he was gone.

* * *

That Christmas of 1924 was the second I spent away from my husband and children, and the first I celebrated entirely alone in my attic studio flat in Gay Street. I had moved there in January from West Tenth, where, for most of the previous year I had lived by the kind charity of Millie Dobbs to whom I fled from Gramercy Park, the night Wendell took my children away. I never slept under his roof again.

So it was at Millie's house on that pretty Greenwich Village street that I awoke the next day, alone in a single bed, to a brilliant autumn morning and the contemplation of my suddenly altered future. That Wendell wished for this freedom, so that he might marry Margaret de Quincey was small secret to the world. But no one, no one at all, ever imagined he would divorce me. It was simply not done. Rare in any circles, unheard of in our own; it was the unseekable solution, the inconceivable response, the Excalibur for which he might never put out his hand. The courage of his iconoclasm awed me.

That same morning, Mrs Pyke arrived. Tearful and puffy-eyed, she swept me into her lacy, lemony bosom, commiserating and bemoaning my fate, and the fate of all women, and the perfidy of her son, and all men. Afterwards, a more formal meeting with both the elder Pykes took place in Millie's house, Millie herself looking on with disgruntled cynicism, like one of her own striped cats. Wendell's father expressed his sympathy, his concern over the children, his desire to spare his family and mine (who was there left to care?) from disgrace, and, more ominously, the difficulties that might fall my way, should the matter come to public notice. Already, the word 'co-operation' crept frequently into our converse.

Within a week, a week in which Wendell's two older sisters and their husbands had both called, commiserated, discussed and planned, a sort of strategy had been formulated. First, an attempt at reconciliation should be made. All of us, I believe, sensed the futility of that, but some duty must be shown towards the honourable institution of marriage. (The question of approaching Mrs de Quincey was considered and rejected; she was yet considered by all an innocent party in need of protection.) Then, a final plea to 'see sense' was to be placed before Wendell and, that failing, I was, regretfully, to remove myself to Ireland, to the company of my cousins, to sit out the extended period required for the necessary legalities. Naturally I would be granted ample financial resources and the children too should be provided for while in my company and while spending 'brief vacations' in America with their grandparents. It all sounded thoroughly reasonable.

Once I got over my shock, a strange excitement replaced it. Curiosity, not fear, filled me with imaginings, as if I stood at the threshold of a slowly opening door, one I had perceived closed forever. I was hardly a wounded lover, after all, those betrayals having been long past. The thought of Wendell leaving my life left no deep pain. I had no wish to cling to a husband who neither loved nor wanted me. I wanted only my children and I saw, somewhere ahead, a peaceful world without Wendell, a world of my children and I, in some small private place, warmed and sheltered by work and love. I was living in a fantasy, but one in which I was subtly indulged.

Families have no morals. The most primitive of human foundations, they are rooted in an era older than religion, and it is from that savage past their loyalty springs. The Pykes did not love each other particularly, and Wendell was truly out of favour for his defection, but with one saintly exception they closed ranks round him with a secrecy and purpose I could not dream to penetrate.

Every counsel they gave me, couched in kind words and apparent compassion, every scrap of advice, was intended only to further their ends. They led me, all that winter, like a blinkered donkey after the carrot of my children. And like a donkey I followed in patient plodding innocence, believing every word.

Two people put an end to their elaborate plans, and an end to my childish little dream. The first was my cousin Kate O'Mordha, and the second, Wendell's frail crippled sister, Grace Pyke. Two more different women one could not imagine, working in tandem by the hand of fate, with the breadth of the Atlantic between them.

I was out of touch with Irish affairs that winter, partly because of the sudden change in my circumstances, which concentrated all my thoughts on my own concerns, but more for a sadder reason. I had lost my Irish companion, my mentor and my guide. At the beginning of February 1922, John Butler Yeats died in his room at the Petipas boarding house, watched over by the eleven-year self-portrait that sought to be a sketch. Wrapped in my own miseries, I did not even hear until days afterwards. But he was gone, to a further land than Ireland, and I would not see him again.

Thus the Anglo-Irish Treaty and the birth of the Irish Free State were distant news items in the American papers, punctuated occasionally by the more vivid descriptive letters of May Howie. She and her parents supported the Treaty and she wrote with anger of those diehard republicans, Padraic and Kate prominent among them, whose stubborn resistance engendered civil war. Violence was all around. Houses were burned and blown up and shootings and gun battles as common as in the days of the Black and Tans.

'We are a *useless* country,' May wrote. 'How can we

determine our future when we cannot agree what future we want?'

I worried over her, and my uncle and aunt and little niece but, preoccupied with my own troubles, I felt removed from theirs. May's telegram came in a week of lawyers and wrangling and exhaustion and eclipsed it all.

11 June 1922

DARLING MOTHER DIED YESTERDAY STOP LETTER TO FOLLOW STOP MAY

The letter came fast on the heels of the telegram, as if the vehemence of May's anger had speeded it across the Atlantic.

Merrion Square
18 June 1922

Dearest Justina,

I think now I have calmed enough to write, but I must write quickly, before it all overwhelms me again, and what should be a letter of explanation and condolence becomes a diatribe.

I have done with my sister Kate. I wish never to see her, to speak with her, to hear from her again. If, like the Jews Father Antony tells me about, I could sit in mourning for her and treat her afterwards as one dead, I would do so. She has broken the tie of blood that bound us, and I am her kin no longer. May merciful God forgive me these words, but I will not retract.

Last week, Kate came home. Father and Mother had just returned to Temple House from staying with me in Dublin, and she was awaiting them when they arrived. She was alone; thin, drawn, beautiful. Kate the unerring dramatist. She proclaimed a conversion, a true change of heart. Violence and all its consequences were evil. She wanted no more of it, no more of the struggle. Padraic, in response to her courageous stance, had deserted her. Alone, abandoned and weary, she wanted only the comforts of her family, the love of her daughter, and the hope of a new life. She was throwing herself upon the mercy of her father and begging sanctuary. What father could refuse?

Naturally, they took her in. She did indeed seem changed, older and sadder, wearied out with struggle, and longing to see her daughter, who was, thankfully, with me in Dublin. Mother telephoned and begged me to join them for a reunion, which by blessed good fortune, I was unable through work to attend.

It lasted for three days. On the fourth, Father, while standing at his dressing room window, looked out to see the house surrounded by armed men, hiding behind the walls. Of course he alerted Kate, who, I am told, replied quite calmly, 'Yes, Father, I know,' and immediately ran off down the stairs. Father followed her to the cellars in time to meet Padraic and six strangers, all armed and masked, coming up out of the wine cellar. Padraic thanked Father for his unwitting hospitality and sent his men about the house to take positions at the windows. They were Republican fugitives, all of them.

Outside, a call came for surrender, and after arguing fruitlessly with Kate, Father, with great dignity and no small courage, gathered Mother up, dashed with her to the coach house, and got her into that same old 1910 Lancaster and drove her sedately down the driveway, waving a white handkerchief for protection. Oh, dear Father, it would all have been so funny, had it ended differently, after all.

But Padraic was in the window of that little bedroom they shut you in when you fell out of the tree, and he began screaming and shouting abuse at the Free Staters and calling them traitors and threatening to blow up the house (they'd filled the wine cellar with explosives, so well he might have done). And someone, somewhere, fired a shot. Then it started from every window, and all the walls, and Father, who was always a terrible driver, opened the throttle full and careened down the long drive, and missed the bend at the bottom and went straight into the wall, and Mother was thrown, right up against the big plano tree, and when he reached her she was already dead. And that was the end of the whole pointless exercise. Padraic and his men all surrendered and came out meek as lambs, hands in the air. And Kate sneaked out the back and got on Father's big hunter and rode away, jumping the garden wall (six feet!) and off to the Ox mountains and her freedom.

The Free Staters were terribly good to Father, and all the Republicans were terribly sorry; everyone forgot all their arguments in their remorse. They even apologized when they blew up the explosives and set the house ablaze, though for what purpose other than a sheer mania of destruction, I cannot imagine.

Yesterday, a death notice appeared in the *Irish Times* (so calculating, our clever Kate, just the paper to most offend):

Lady Eugenia Howie
Martyred for Ireland
11 June 1922

Poor Mother how she would have cringed.

But she is in the churchyard of St John's at Sligo, now, and Temple House a roofless ruin of fire-blacked stone. Father is with me in Dublin, and I doubt he will ever return.

So that is how it happened, and this where it all led to, all our bright dreams.

Yours in sorrow,
May

I was stunned by Eugenia's death, almost beyond reason. She was not *my* mother, but my aunt, an aunt whom I had not seen for years, and with whom I had often been in conflict. But she was my mother's sister, her twin and her shadow, a last link to a rapidly receding past. In her lace and flowery hats; antiquated and wonderful and worn to the day of her death; she was the embodiment of all the lost grace and beauty of my childhood world. For me, the Edwardian era ended not in 1910, but in 1922 in the flames of Temple House. How I mourned that old limestone mansion, Michael's home and the home of my artistic self.

I fled to Mirza Hassan for consolation, just as I had done over the death of Eugenia's son. I went alone to Washington Street and the Cedars of Lebanon Coffee House. Wendell's dictates hardly applied now. I took the letter with me and we sat together reading it over, and drinking strong bitter coffee, and talking endlessly about the past. Hassan was the only person in New York to whom the names and places I spoke of could have any meaning. Our talk was full of laughter; laughter evokes the dead as readily as tears. I left him in the late afternoon, sad but at peace.

When I returned to Millie Dobbs' house, Mrs Pyke was awaiting me. She greeted me with funereal solemnity that informed me at once she had learned of May's letter and my loss. She was full of sympathy and horror at the barbarous ways of places other than New York. She professed no matter more important to her than aiding me in my distress. 'You must put forward your departure date,' she said. I shook my head.

'We were sailing in August, anyhow,' I said. 'May will understand. If anything, it will be better. She will have had time to come to terms, and to settle Uncle James in Dublin . . . and the children will cheer them both so.'

Mrs Pyke paused. I can still see her, her puffy eyes opening in orchestrated amazement, her fat white hand raising dramatically to rest upon her tailored bosom.

'The children, my dear? The children? Surely you can't mean . . .'

'But our passages are booked,' I said nervously. 'We're to sail in August.'

'To the middle of a *war*, Justina? My dear child!' She waited for me to recover sense and reconsider.

'Well, hardly *that*,' I said. 'Certainly not in Dublin, anyhow. It was only an incident, after all . . .'

'Your aunt's brutal *murder* only an incident?'

'It wasn't murder,' I said quickly. 'It was really only an accident . . . here.' I got out May's letter from my purse and thrust it towards her. 'Read it yourself.' She turned away, her left hand shielding her eyes as if I had placed the bloody evidence of an atrocity before her.

'Unthinkable,' she said. 'The children cannot possibly travel to such a place. Why, I wouldn't sleep the whole time you were away, just thinking of them among such hooligans.' She patted grandmotherly tears from her eyes with a discreet handkerchief. My shock and disappointment must have showed clearly. She softened her face into a small trembly smile, and said admiringly, 'Oh, you are a brave little soul, aren't you? But don't worry, my dear. *You* can still go. After all, you're a modern independent woman, and who am I to stand in your way? I shall worry terribly, but naturally you have a duty to your family in Ireland.' She patted my arm conspiratorially, 'We women live lives of duty, every one of us. Never mind. We will simply put your departure forward. You can sail next week, and I shall be happy to continue to care for the babies in the meanwhile. Do you know, it's really rejuvenating me, and it *is* best to shield them from all this adult nastiness, isn't it?' She patted my hand again, 'There now, all fixed. Not a disaster, just a little change of plans. It will all work out fine in the end, don't worry. They'll be perfectly safe and happy with me.'

As if to enforce her point, news came within the week of Padraic O'Mordha's execution at the hands of the Irish Free State. On that grim note, I wrote to May of my change of plans. I had rebooked my passage, and was in the midst of packing a limited wardrobe for the voyage, when Grace Pyke came to call. That was in itself a remarkable thing, since it is not easy for a woman whose mobility is limited to a wheelchair or a few halting steps on metal crutches, to pay social visits. But this occasion had a more pressing purpose.

I was alone in Millie's house, when the Pyke family car drew up before the brick steps. I watched from my bedroom window, waiting for Mrs Pyke to emerge with her bustling dignity on to the pavement. Instead, when the chauffeur stepped round to open the passenger door, there was a long pause, and then the slow, awkward progress of Grace's thin, spindly figure dragging itself upright. The chauffeur was a kind Italian man, who hovered about, ready to catch her if she fell. Grace always appeared so light as to be blown away by the first breath of wind, but she was stronger than anyone imagined. The driver followed behind her as she made her determined way to the door and I rushed downstairs.

She was waiting, a little breathless, on the step. She leaned forward and kissed my cheek, balancing awkwardly on her crutches. She gave me a big smile, conspiratorial and triumphant. 'About half an hour,' she said to the chauffeur as she hoisted herself up the final step and made her way inside. He stood watching like a father until the door closed. I sensed he was her ally, and her visit, undoubtedly secret, would go undisclosed. I followed behind as she swung herself along between her crutches, her braced legs sliding forward with a fish slither and a clatter of steel against the floor. Her shoulders were broad and muscular. I knew I must make no effort to help. Grace's heaviest burden was not her disability but her family's cloying, wounding protection of her.

'There,' she said, heaving herself down into a chair. 'Not so bad, really.'

'Will you have tea?' I said hopefully. She looked wistful, her eyes drifting around Millie's lovely room. 'Oh, I'd love to, dear, but I mustn't. It gets awkward. My stupid bladder, you know.' She shrugged, taking off her gloves with a sharp disdainful action, as if divesting herself of the pains of the flesh. 'Never mind, I've only come to tell you something and I mustn't be away long, or they'll guess, and then they'll badger poor Francisco for the truth and he'll be forced to lie.' She laid the gloves on her knee. 'This isn't going to be nice, dear. Perhaps you should sit down.'

I sat, my eyes on her thin, commanding face. I thought of the life she might have led but for that brief summer illness long ago. 'What is it?' I asked fearfully.

'It's about the family,' she said. She looked down at her hands on her flat, formless lap. Her legs drifted sideways, unrelated to her. 'Don't believe a word they say to you. They are unctuous, self-interested liars.' She looked up, and smiled brightly. 'There now, that wasn't difficult either.'

'What do you mean?' I whispered. 'About what?'

Her smile was gone. 'They are manipulating you. They have planned it from the start. They have only one end, and only one interest, their own. When they are finished, Wendell will be married to Mrs de Quincey, and the children will be theirs. They will cut you out of their lives without a thought. They will make it impossible for you even to see your children, much less have them for your own.'

'But that's not possible,' I gasped, disbelief warring with terror. 'It can't be.'

'Why not?' she asked sharply. 'Simply not cricket?' Her mouth softened at once into her warm smile. 'Now come on, don't get upset. I didn't come here to make you unhappy, I came here to help you.'

But I was upset. I whispered, 'But they promised. Wendell should have his freedom, and when it's all over, I shall have the children.'

She leaned back in her chair and looked at me carefully. It was hard to imagine she was years younger than I.

'Their only grandchildren, their only heirs? Oh Justina, use your head.'

I was, then, using it, and thinking all the thoughts I should have thought months ago, and each one but increased my terror. 'My babies,' I cried. 'They can't keep my babies.'

She looked at me with deep sadness. 'I'm very afraid that they can. But at least we can try to stop them, you and I.'

* * *

And so we did. In the months that followed, when I had perhaps cause to regret our action, I was comforted by the knowledge that everything Grace Pyke had said of her family proved to be true. Once I ceased to be the compliant dupe they had trained to follow unquestioningly behind their lead, they too ceased to play their role. Compassion vanished, replaced by ruthless family loyalty and a brutal disregard for anyone beyond that rigid pale. Even Grace, family though she was, was treated like an enemy. Of course she, too, had showed true colours and they could never quite forgive the transformation of their pathetic little invalid into a woman of rebellious power. They suspected her role when I announced my refusal to go to Ireland at all. They were correct; Grace had seen at once that getting me outside the country was entirely too useful to their cause. Arguments arose but I stood firm. I wrote May again, explaining my situation, and received her full support. I would not leave New York without my children, which meant, naturally, I would not leave New York.

Had Grace's part not yet been evident, her next move was certain exposure. She hired a lawyer to advise us and, if necessary, to fight for my children through the courts. The reaction was swift, a message from Wendell's father frightening in its brevity;

Petition filed. Do not defend.

But by then it was already too late. We were too far along our new path to turn aside. And on the surface, my position was strong. That I had left the family home to take up residence with Millie Dobbs was not in my favour and could be represented as desertion, but, beyond that, Wendell had no case. He, not I, had begun a liaison outside of marriage and, discreet as he was, there were rumours about. I had been a correct and faithful wife. The best he could hope for was an amicable separation with all my rights retained. But Wendell wanted much more. It was only when the case reached the divorce court, late in 1922, that I fully realized how much he wanted, and how far he was prepared to go to gain it. The full meaning of his father's threatening letter unfolded before me.

Grace was in hospital with an indefinable infection when our case came to court in November. And so I found myself alone, but for my hopelessly outclassed lawyer and the faithful Millie Dobbs, facing a petition for divorce on the grounds of adultery. Named as co-respondent was the Persian immigrant owner of the Cedars of Lebanon café, Mirza Hassan Abbas. It was wildly, comically ridiculous, but for the fact that it was happening to me and its consequence would be disaster.

Few truths are really self-evident. Surety of our own justice is merely the consequence of our intimate knowledge of ourselves. Knowing our own souls we are convinced of our natural innocence. But to a stranger, a judge, we are but a cipher potentially guilty of the vilest act. Often I have looked back at my divorce through a stranger's eyes and seen the judgement grow clear.

Picture it: see before you the plaintiff – blond, Anglo-Saxon, innocent; husband, provider and father. Scion of a fine New York family, he stands bewildered, his American honesty baffled by the wiles of foreigners. And the defendants? Scottish lady sunk to Bohemian cellars, mysterious eastern stranger from her past: it was the stuff of a thousand bad novelettes. And a judge indulging in a ready xenophobia was willing to believe it all.

Remember where we were. It was 1922. America's most recent experience with foreigners, in the trenches of France, had not endeared them to her. Isolationism, nation-as-hurt-child, was thriving. Sacco and Vanzetti languished in prison: this was not a good place in which to be exotic. And once a lie has made fertile the ground, all further lies root readily. A Greenwich Village address becomes Babylon; artistic eccentricity, depravity. My sketch-book nudes appeared in court, its subjects no longer shivering paid models in my Cooper Union class, but companions of lewd revelry. That perfume of devilishness some artists cultivate can, in proper circumstance, suffocate. When that sketch-book went about the courtroom, Wendell's case was quite probably won. But he was a methodical man and left nothing to chance. He had saved until last his final thrust, his *coup de grâce.* I saw Theresa O'Malley walk into the court, and I knew I was lost.

For some people, truth is not only self-evident, but simply non-existent. Theresa was one of those people. Like the story-spinning Persephone, she existed in a nebula of fact and fantasy, fluid and ever-changing. Truth was what served well at the moment, nothing more. What she hoped to gain; what Wendell had perhaps promised her; I can only guess. Perhaps it was simply vengeance for those days of humiliation when she slipped from the role of mistress, and I remained wife.

She sat a winning actress, blushing, resisting, allowing halting words to be drawn from her; the convent girl thrown innocently amongst Bohemian squalor. She lied and lied, inventing totally fictitious occasions, elaborating true ones until the Cedars of Lebanon Coffee House, quiet rendezvous of bearded old men, became a den of sin. Lurid tales of drink and men, and my children unsupervised in the street, flowed in a river of regretful confession from her sweet-turned mouth. From time to time she cast across the room sad glances of apology for her errant mistress. I sat in rigid silence listening to her betrayal. She broke into tears at the end and was helped away, but I remained dry-eyed, and unmoved, as the brazen whore they thought I was.

And so I lost. I lost the divorce case, my home, my husband and my children. To award custody of children to the father and not the mother was most unusual in those days, but everyone agreed the circumstances were extraordinary. My right of access was denied; I was regarded a dangerous influence on my daughter and son.

There was, of course, a terrific row for a while in the newspapers, and any hopes the Pykes had of keeping it all quiet were dashed. But they weathered it; families like that always do. Wendell took the children away for a long quiet rest in New England. Margaret de Quincey joined them to be of comfort. Such was her character that even then I was certain her comforts came to an end at the bedroom door.

And what of her, then, this Margaret de Quincey; was she the innocent I believed her or the scheming devil behind it all? (As Millie Dobbs, for one, was quite positive.) I chose to believe the former, and I think it was so. Her grief at my grief seemed real, so too her deep disappointment in me for having failed Wendell, whom she adored. And, adoring him, she could not be expected to doubt his word on the matter of my calumnies. Perhaps I was protecting my pride in my own judgement. More, though, I was protecting my sanity. That woman would raise my son and daughter; I wanted her to be a saint.

And Wendell, my husband and father of my children; an evil man, a liar? No; but a man fatally won by his own myth, enthralled with the image of his fateful love of Margaret thwarted by my presence until all wrong in the affair shifted itself from his shoulders to mine. Their love was perfect; only two perfect beings might possess it. The Super Man had found the Grail. All fairy-tales must have an evil witch, and the role fell to me. I saw him stand in a court of law and weep over my deception of him. His tears were, incredibly, real.

And Theresa, the linchpin of his case? She was dismissed from service on the day the court ruled in Wendell's favour, and I never saw her again.

So I went back then, to Millie Dobbs' home on Tenth Street in a state of total numb despair, and there, with no choice about the matter, began to pick up the remnants of my ruined life. All I had left was all I had brought to my marriage in the first place, myself, and my painting, and both had been soundly rejected. But they were mine, and falling back upon them, I found an extraordinary thing had happened.

Art is a rare metal, forged in fire. I painted now day and night, escaping into work as grieving people do, and a remarkable change began to occur. I, who had failed miserably at the business of life, found suddenly that at the business of art I could do no wrong. I painted as I had not painted before. My brushwork was sure, certain, and strong. All trace of youth and, dare I say it, all trace of girlishness, of hesitancy, of *femininity* retreated from my work. Colours leapt out for me, lines showed their sure paths. I commenced at once upon a portrait of the convalescent Grace Pyke that thrilled me shamelessly with its powerful grasp of her life-under-siege fragility. When I finished it I wanted to sing. Millie Dobbs, being more practical, hung it in her gallery and sold it on my behalf for a stunning sum of money. She handed me my proceeds one winter night along with my evening glass of tea, and 'the scales fell from my eyes'. I looked down at the neat stack of bills and knew a security I had not known since I left my father's house. No man would ever keep me again.

The Pykes, I must add, were not barbarians, and I had not been left to starve. Family pride would not have permitted that. But I had sent back each one of their dutiful cheques and no longer even opened the envelopes. I did this with Millie Dobbs' cheerful approval; necessary and proper considering that if Wendell's family was not supporting me, somebody, for the meantime, had to be, and that somebody for most of a year was Millie Dobbs. A career as a portrait artist is not easily established, though Millie's wide connections certainly eased the way. I would pay it all back, I vowed, and of course she never let me at all.

But by the end of that year I was able to, had she allowed, and able also to find myself rented accommodation of my own, and live for the first time ever a totally adult life, independent of every living thing. There was a lot of joy in that, I will admit, and a lot of joy in my life, in spite of all. No artist who is working well is ever entirely unhappy though, contrarily, no woman who has borne children is ever entirely complete in their absence. What joy I had was the delight of a caged thing, under the shadow of bars. I lived in a prison guarded by ghost-warders; my two missing babies growing older, without me. Their faces haunted me wherever I turned; I glimpsed them in imagination a dozen times a day in the street, in the subway, in shops, in the faces of the children of strangers. Had I truly not been able to see them at all, I think I would have gone mad.

Fortunately for me, for all of us, I had still my powerful ally, with her indisputable entrée into the fortress of the enemy. Grace Pyke saw my children whenever she chose; they lived yet in their father's house at 18 Gramercy Park, or with their grandmother in her town house, or on Long Island. Grace could not be denied access to them, in any fashion, and Grace, by deceit, courage and trickery, won blessed, if infrequent, access for me.

I will never know quite how she did this. There may

have been elements of compliance even from Wendell's mother. She was a ruthless woman, where her son's interests were concerned, but she was not utterly heartless. Nor did she in any way believe the horror stories of the divorce court. Like Theresa, she used truth as a flexible tool. Now, with no need to persecute me, she had no real desire to do so. Perhaps she turned a blind eye. Or perhaps Grace's loyal following among the servants of the house provided her shield. In any event, as week passed week, days would arise when, often without warning the family car, driven by the kind and noble Francisco, would arrive, and out would tumble my little boy and girl, and behind them, dragging her rag-doll legs, their dear and devoted 'Auntie Grace'. These were the days I lived for, for two whole years.

It was early in 1924 that I found the attic flat in a narrow brick house in the middle of the pretty crescent of Gay Street. It was charming, run-down, and cheap, and after a week of vigorous cleaning and an assault upon the cockroaches, it was habitable. Only *just* habitable with its four flights of rickety stairs and damp patches of peeling ceiling after each day of rain, and Millie, who had not lived in a bell-tent during the war, was faintly appalled. But I painted all the walls with gallons of white emulsion, and Fatima Abbas found me cheap and beautiful bedspreads, block-printed with Persian horses and warriors and I covered my tattered Salvation Army sofa and chair with two, and hung the third like a medieval tapestry over the hearth. Cheap dhurries from the same Washington Street shop covered the uneven floors and the garret window, stripped of curtains, threw good, if not perfect light, on my easel. When I was done I was insufferably proud of it all; it wasn't exactly Arradale Castle, but unlike even that lofty place, it was mine.

Two nights after I moved myself and my belongings

from Tenth Street, I was sitting peacefully alone by the ashes of my little fire, when there was a sharp knocking at the door. I answered with trepidation, wondering if the rent was due already. But it was not my Greek landlord, but Jack Redpath, with a bundle of firewood on one arm, and a bunch of hot-house roses on the other. 'Welcome home,' he said, stepping inside as casually as if he called every day.

What was extraordinary was that I had not seen him once since that fated October night when he re-entered my life at Petipas. Admittedly, in the turbulent weeks that followed, I hardly noticed. Even meeting him faded like a brief, restless dream, and I gave him little thought. That he gave much to me I only learned, much later, from Millie Dobbs, our mutual confidante. Sad and helpless, he watched my miseries from afar, wisely aware that a connection of my name and his would only add fuel to the fires in which I burned. He was famed already in Village circles, half for his writing and half for another talent entirely. It was not my affair; I heard his name from time to time, and tales of his exploits, but they did not concern me. To me he was just a friend, as honest and faithful as Millie Dobbs.

From that day onward, he was my steady companion; supporter, confidant, critic and brother. Our friendship was kind and platonic and if at that time he wished it otherwise he had the wisdom and grace to keep that wish to himself. I was certainly unready for romance.

Often, he brought friends; fellow writers, painters, actors, dreamers all. We drank tea, late into the night and talked of everything. The talk was frank and free. I learned things I had never known before about men and women, their minds, and their bodies. Though I was older in years, and in some kinds of experience, than almost all of them, in certain of these matters I felt startlingly naïve.

Some of these young people were remarkably free with their lives, even by the standards of half a century on. But, cut free from the bonds of a society that had dismissed me, I listened with wide-eyed curiosity and felt no inclination to condemn. In that way I was my father's daughter, gifted with the same boundless curiosity that led him to foreign lands and companions and a foreign faith.

Of that foreign faith I also learned more in those curious years. Adversity fuelled my faith; not the fierce troubling of violence and war that often merely embitters, but the slow adversity of loneliness and deprivation that made me think. In the angry times of the war, when loss piled upon loss, I would willingly have spat in the face of God. But in the quiet nights, thinking of my children, I began to seek Him. Perhaps it was age. The headlong stampede of youth was over; there were years ahead for which I must find purpose. Each month I met with Millie's Baha'i community, and wondered if my purpose might lie there.

I liked their placidity, the calm certainties they offered but never forced on me. I liked their friendly gatherings in ordinary places, the implication that God was abroad in the world, not shut up in Gothic arches. The twenties were passing, and the world moving further from the War. Once more, arguments and boundary disputes and national prides and recriminations filled all the papers. Nothing had been learned. My heart, like many hearts, yearned for a new order, a fresh revelation. People turned many ways; to leaders, to loves, to faiths. I turned to the new nationless nation of Baha'i.

I took Jack Redpath with me. He wasn't impressed. He had left God behind in the ditches of France, discarded like the butt of a cigarette. He was not going back to find Him. But he made no effort to stop me. Unlike Wendell he was happy to allow me a mind equal to his own. He escorted me to Millie's door on those occasions, and left me there, and while my strange assortment of artists, working men, society ladies and Persian immigrants pondered the message of a prophet, Jack went to a favourite hang-out on Fourth Street and drank rye whiskey until we were done. If the meditations had been long, he was often in a more elevated state than I, when the time came to go home.

In spite of his reputation, Jack was not a drunkard. He could, however, do great justice to a wide variety of spirits of the unreligious kind, and I was not unaccustomed to his arrival, burly and bleary-eyed, at my door at three in the morning, his black beret over one eye and his beard frosted with snow. His intentions were totally honourable; my Gay Street flat being less than half the distance back to his own refuge on West Twentieth Street, he found me a convenient haven on cold winter nights. He slept on the Salvation Army sofa, under my winter coat, and I slept in my own bed with nothing more seductive than my small tiger cat. A friendship of this nature is often very rich, and in some ways sweeter than an affair.

Jack worried about me, convinced (with some reason) that my struggling career could not provide an adequate income. His own was flourishing. The serious fiction that appeared to accolades in *Harper's, The Dial, Scribner's*, and *The Atlantic*, was shrewdly augmented with a steady flow of Westerns and mysteries aimed at the lesser heights of *Detective Story* and *Ace-High Magazine*. He made good money, and since, aside from occasional drinking bouts and feeding the neighbourhood cats, he had precisely nothing to do with it, he saw no reason not to give it to me. I, however, fresh from my disastrous marriage saw reasons in plenty. He quickly learned I was totally serious, and not to be persuaded, or charmed.

Gifts, however, could not be refused. And gifts of food and particularly firewood, accompanied him on every visit. I think he really expected to find me freezing or fading away *à la Bohème* in my garret. In truth, my blessedly robust health was better than ever, and if at times I worked at my easel wearing two jumpers, heavy woollen stockings, my winter coat, scarf, hat and woollen gloves with the fingers cut out, it did no permanent harm.

That first Christmas in Gay Street, my thirty-first birthday, Jack brought, in addition to the tree, a beautiful fresh chicken from a market near the waterfront, a sack of potatoes, greens, coffee and apples, and two fish-heads for the cat. The last was only fair since the cat itself was a gift from an earlier visit. Gratefully, I cooked Christmas dinner and we sat down to it together, two stray waifs playing husband and wife. It was a sweet and happy Christmas, though every glance at the popcorn-decorated tree aroused an image of Ellie and Wendell beneath their own tree at Gramercy Park, with another woman's hands undoing the ribbons of the presents I had wrapped.

On Boxing Day, which had no special significance to New Yorkers, Grace brought the children to me. Wrapped in my good, fur-collared coat, I met them down in the street. Grace could never mount the steep, perilous stairs to my attic. It made us both sad that she would never see my home, and I made sketches of it to compensate. I was waiting on the sidewalk when the car arrived. They were very late; I had waited half an hour in the cold, dry winter wind.

'Oh, I'm so terribly sorry,' Grace whispered, as Francisco held the door open for me. 'There was trouble at home. I almost couldn't get them away.' I climbed in beside her, not imagining what the trouble might have been, but thinking only of the horrible emptiness I would have felt if they had not arrived. Twice in the past that had happened, and I had turned after a bleak hour and wearily climbed the steps back to my flat.

'Never mind,' I said happily, 'we're all here now.' Grace looked tired, and the children sat huddled over to one side of the car, quite miserable. I reached my arms out to them and Ellie, with a glance at her brother, scrambled across Grace's metal-bound legs for a kiss. She retreated almost at once. Wendell reached solemnly and shook my hand.

'Merry Christmas,' he said very properly and added, quickly, 'and thank-you-very-much for my present.' I heard in his voice my own, in childhood, parroting bored gratitude to uninteresting adults.

'Did you like the big ladder?' I said encouragingly.

He stared back with five-year-old candour, and blinked once.

Grace leaned over hurriedly. 'The big, big ladder on Mommy's fire engine?'

Wendell blinked again. He had forgotten my present, lost among the mountains of family gifts.

'*I* liked the ladder,' Ellie lied sweetly. I hugged her, and her brother as well, who shrugged predictably away. She curled against me in her red velvet Christmas coat, a bonny, dark, rosy-faced treasure, sucking her thumb, as Francisco drove us uptown to Schraffts. Sleepily she stroked the fur collar of my coat, as if it were a cat. She mumbled around her thumb, 'Margaret's coat is furry *all* over.' Grace and I looked at each other and gently laughed.

I looked across to Wendell sitting as far from me as he could in his grandfather's car. His profile was identical to my brother Sandy's. He wore a blue suit with long trousers, a miniature of one of his father's; very American. I did not like small boys in suits. My brothers had all worn kilts, which suit children far better.

He cheered up during lunch. Food always made him happy, and there wasn't anything really wrong, no deep misery or jealousy or hatred of me. Only the understandable annoyance of a small boy snatched away from his toys on the day after Christmas for a drive around the city with a grown-up lady who was nine parts a stranger. He had lived but five years and two of them in my absence. What *could* I mean to him?

'I *liked* my lunch,' he said purposefully, as we left the restaurant, a moment of mature apology and concern that brought me to tears. While I ran to the powder room to dab at red eyes, Grace shepherded Ellie and Wendell back into the car. Outside it was snowing gently, soft purposeful flakes that promised a fine fall. I thought, watching the lights of the city come on, warm and mysterious through the blue-grey light, *If I could take these two little ones home for one night to Gay Street I'd ask nothing more of man or God*. It was a lie, of course, and God, or whatever, probably being quite aware, I was not given the chance.

Ellie, the ever-loving, snuggled against me dreamily all the way home. Just as we turned into Christopher Street, she murmured, in her thumb-mumbly voice, 'Margaret will be our *new* Mommy now.' Beside me I heard Grace sigh.

She got out of the car, with difficulty, and very deliberately, as I kissed the children goodbye. She was standing, propped on her crutches by the lamp-post in front of my house when I joined her on the pavement.

'They're going to marry,' she said quietly. 'I should have told you.'

I nodded, stiffly. But of course, I always knew they would.

'When?'

'Not for a long while. When they're sure the scandal's over. It must seem a quite *separate* event.' She sagged heavily on her crutches, her head turned sideways against the blowing snow. 'Forgive me. I kept putting it off.' She glanced at the closed windows of the car where my children, lost in their private world, played a hand-clap game, oblivious of me. 'What a bitch of a way to learn,' she said, and hobbled to Francisco's waiting door.

20

7 Rue Zacharie
3 July 1926

'Dearest Justina,

Your letter was awaiting me when I returned from London, a most agreeable welcome, after a bleak time. London is dismal; wet, smoky, and filled with discontent. The Strike was a symptom only of a deeper malaise. I think only now are people waking up to what the war cost them all, and how little was gained. Whenever one passes through Victoria there are limbless beggars and I think how bravely they once went through that 'Gate of Goodbyes' and I want to weep.

'In Paris, too, times are not good. There is less money about except in the hands of the few who always have money. Everyone's business suffers, including our own. Revolutionaries talk of communism in the cafés, but that is nothing new. The butcher complains, and the shoemaker next door complains, and the local Magdalene, when I meet her at the market, also complains. Our printer demands payment in advance. Still, I had a most pleasant and profitable luncheon with Miss Weaver in London, and came home bounding with hope. She too is interested in the Redpath poems . . .'

Jack stopped reading and raised his hand, finger and thumb forming a circle of success. He grinned. I nodded from my paint table, and squeezed out a snake of pigment on to my palette.

'Go on,' I said. 'Perhaps she says more.'

He read on

'I must say, in reading the proofs, I am struck again by their quality, and their passion. In particular, 'My Lady', which I could not fail to realize was written to you . . .'

There was a moment of silence from Jack. I felt his eyes on me and did not look up, but carefully wiped my fingers on a paint-stained rag. He read on, a trace of self-mockery in his voice.

'Oh Justina, it does make me sad to think of you in New York, alone, with this special friend no longer there. I do wish you'd reconsider and come, too.'

'Oh my friend, May,' said Jack, before continuing.

'Anyhow, I trust you will give Mr Redpath my regards. If he will be so kind as to call on me upon his arrival in Paris, I will be delighted to discuss his future plans. A novel is, of course, the logical next step and the War the obvious subject. Enough time has passed now for our views to clarify.

'Thank you so much for sending the catalogue for 'Faces of Strangers'. How lovely to see your name in such official print. I only wish I could see the paintings myself. Perhaps Miss Dobbs' gallery would consider a travelling exhibition!? Do write as soon as you're able and let me know the extent (huge no doubt!) of your success. I have sent the catalogue home to Papa. I know it will thrill him. After all it *was* he who started you upon this path, all those years ago!

'We spoke of that, when I was in Ireland with Eithne, during the winter. It was a strange visit, full of *déjà vu*. I took Eithne to Ballysodare to see her father's grave. It was a pleasant place, a pretty churchyard, quite moving, though Kate has the grave covered with Republican paraphernalia . . ah well, no doubt Padraic delights in it. He was as bad as she, and twice as romantic. Eithne wept, little pet. She remembers him very fondly; he *was* always sweet with her. I was quite moved myself. Somehow I cannot stay angry with Padraic. He was one of those "bewildered" by that "excess of love". Too much heart, too little head. Kate is precisely the opposite.

'I did see her, you know, in spite of my vows. (Our good Lord must laugh a great deal over my fearsome vows.) I cannot stay angry. Not even with her. I think of Mother and how sad she was when we fought and I know I must forgive. We met and kissed over Padraic's grave; Eithne between us. Kate will have relished the symbolism, no doubt. She is not changed. Partition inflames her. She spends her days writing tracts against the Free State. History, and Ireland, are moving past her. She remains quite beautiful.

'In Dublin we went to the theatre, Kate, Eithne, and I; to the Abbey, which, like Ireland, has outlasted many enemies. Again there were echoes of the past. The play was *The Plough and the Stars*, Sean O'Casey's newest, and there had already been trouble over it, like the *Playboy* Riots, before the war. Yeats was there. (Do you remember when you all saw *Cathleen ni Houlihan* and it ended in a great row and Kate being shipped off to school in England?) He made a splendid speech. He looked very grand, white-haired and fierce. Maud Gonne was in the audience, dressed in black, like an old keening woman. I recognized her even before Kate pointed her out to me; she's remarkably tall, very distinctive. The audience howled the play down, like they did with Synge, and the *gardai* were called out. Nothing in Ireland ever really changes.

'Eithne loved the whole thing; howling audience, thundering poet, *gardai*, all of it. Later we met some people and they were talking (quite fondly) of the old *Playboy* days, and Eithne was listening wide-eyed, and an old woman asked her if she had seen Maud Gonne and when she answered yes, told us *she* had seen Miss Gonne as a young girl and Eithne was her image. Let us *hope* the resemblance is only skin deep!!!

'She is a pretty thing, however, and when I see her off to school with the Sisters, in her blue smock and little wooden shoes, I am quite ridiculously proud. She has become too dear to me, considering the circumstances. My Irish visit was haunted by the fear that Kate might demand her back and, newly reconciled, I could not argue, even had I the right. Fortunately Kate's mother instinct remains unstirred. At times like these, I think of you and my heart aches. I do so fear for you now, with their marriage imminent. Even Grace will lose her influence if Wendell's new wife so decrees. Oh dearest, forgive me being a Cassandra, but I see only sorrow ahead for you in New York. Please reconsider . . . I have a funny little flat, but there's plenty of room and Paris is full of artists and writers; just the place for you. I *know* you could be happy here.

With much love,
May

'PS. In answer to your question about the matter of Bahá'u'lláh: Dearest, it is not for me to judge who are, and who are not the holy men of God. (This is why we think it wise perhaps to leave such decisions to Holy Church.) But my heart tells me without question that if one truly seeks God one cannot possibly offend Him. Does a parent take offence if their child's baby tongue misforms his name? The man or woman true to conscience is true to Christ. M.'

'A wise lady,' said Jack Redpath, as he laid the letter down.

'You'll enjoy her,' I said.

'So would you.' There was another silence in which I deliberately did not look at him and did not answer. I lifted my palette from the table and returned to the easel restlessly wiping painty fingers down the front of my smock. He sat where I had placed him, to my left, in the clear light of the curtainless window. I was working at my fourth attempt at his portrait.

'I can never get you right,' I said. 'Mr Yeats said creation requires love, but somehow, when there's too *much* of that, it becomes difficult again.' I looked quickly up, and back to my canvas, so that I would not meet his eyes. He looked frustrated and confused.

'Justina . . .'

'I can't paint the children, either. I get so *angry* with myself. I do so want good portraits of them, of all . . .'

my voice broke and I fiddled with my brush, looking down at the paint dribbled floor.

'Justina, you can't keep on like this.'

'They're my babies. I can't leave them.'

'For three or four glimpses of them a year, you'll spend your whole life like this?'

'Sit still, please,' I said sharply, returning to work with clinical determination. 'You're the worst sitter ever.' I fussed at the canvas, making it worse. I worked messily until I could again sound calm and controlled and I said, 'As long as I've hope, any hope . . . it's what I live on, Jack.'

'But there isn't any hope. There never really was, and any there might have been is over now that he's married the bitch.'

'She's not a bitch. She's not, Jack.' He looked heavenward, his mouth tight and exasperated. 'She's not. She's a wonderful woman. She's terribly good to them, and they love her.'

'Few stepmothers are wicked at the beginning of the tale.'

'Don't say that. She'll never be wicked.'

'No,' he agreed amiably enough. 'But she'll be a damn sight more self-assured. A ring on a woman's finger works wonderful transformations.'

I laughed suddenly, looking down at the gold band on my paint-smeared hand. 'Not in my case, I'm afraid.' I shrugged.

'You don't believe in divorce, do you?'

I shrugged again. I put down my brush and thrust my hands into the deep pockets of my smock. 'No. I don't suppose I do. It's strange; I never really felt married to him, but I feel no *less* married now. Poor Wendell, I'm making a bigamist of him.' I laughed gaily.

'No. He's doing that fine by himself.' He looked up to

the door through to the kitchen on which I had taped the *Times* review of my 'Faces of Strangers' exhibition. He laughed, nodding towards it, 'They must have been hopping mad at that.'

'It was just coincidence,' I said. 'Bad luck. I didn't suspect that it would even get a mention.'

'Oh, I was sure of it. If I hadn't been, I'd have seen to it. I'm owed some favours yet.'

'To please me, or to spite them?'

'Both.' He grinned, unrepentant. 'Only I'd have made sure it reached print on the *very day* of the wedding, not just two days before. *And* I'd have put it on to the Wedding Page. Rimmed in black.' He threw his head back, laughing gleefully.

'Oh, sit still,' I said. I adjusted the difficult shadow beside the nose. 'I'm not like you. I don't *want* to embarrass them. If I could vanish completely, the way they'd like, I'd be happy to. But I have to live. Still, I do use my maiden name. Most people won't even know who I am. Or care. *Their* set won't read that anyhow.'

'Oh yes they will.'

I giggled, thinking. 'Oh, I suppose. Actually, one of Mrs Pyke's friends came to see it. She was quite taken with everything, but she acted as if she was committing treason, skulking in with a big-brimmed hat and a veil, almost a disguise. She bought that little one you liked of the Negro child on the stoop. I was rather touched, actually. When she went out she said that I must come and see her some time, in spite of everything. It was kind.'

'Will you?'

'Of course not, Jack. She didn't *mean* it. But it was kind that she *said* it, that's all.'

'Blasted hypocrites,' said Jack. I smiled and did not argue. We all bear swords for those we love, that we would not bear for ourselves. Jack glowered. 'Well, she's got herself a little masterpiece, anyhow. It will earn her a fortune some day, when you've starved to death.'

'Wishful thinking, Jack Redpath,' I laughed. 'I'm not doing so bad as that. And Millie's seeing me later about another commission. Something terribly rushed and hush-hush; very mysterious. It's all to be done in one sitting. No doubt someone fabulously rich and important. You wait now, when you come back from Paris all New York will be at my feet. I'll be more famous even than you.' I dabbed at the tip of his nose with my brush, but he just reared back, faintly annoyed. There was no cheering him.

'Ma'am, that won't be difficult,' he said. 'I reckon a year in Paris will be just about long enough for the New York literati to forget they ever heard of me.' He scuffed the sole of one boot against the floor. He wore workman's boots that he bought down at the waterfront. He looked half artist and half longshoreman.

'Jack, no one is making you go,' I said gently.

'I have to go,' he snapped. Then he leaned back in his chair, nodding to the easel, 'Do you mind?'

'No. I'm done. For today.' He looked guilty.

'I'm sorry. I haven't been much help.'

'It doesn't matter.'

'Justina, I have to see it all again. I know that. I've been away from it, and that was good, because it all settled, and compacted, and seeped into me, like ground-water. But now it's all down there and I have to go back to tap the spring, and make it flow.'

'I think that's pretension, Jack,' I said.

He didn't get angry, but considered it carefully and returned, 'No. It's not. You couldn't paint in Wendell's house.' I shook my head. 'It's like that. No one here knows what it was like. I have to be among people who know, who saw the things I saw. People who know I'm not lying about half of it. Then I can write it all down so hard and sharp, and untrammelled that all of them, *all* of them will *know* it's damn well true.' He stopped suddenly. His fists were clenched. I believed him.

'I understand,' I said.

He relaxed and reached for his cigarettes. He stopped in the middle and looked up into my eyes. I stood still, by my table where I was cleaning my brushes. The portrait watched me with the same thwarted hope.

'Please come with me,' he said. I turned my back on him and looked out of the window and heard the chair scrape and the thud of his boots as he got to his feet.

'Oh, damn you to hell,' he said. I turned round and faced him and his anger and shook my head. I smiled gently.

'Go on, Jack. Go and get drunk. It would do you the world of good. Or find a woman.' He stood up, wiry, and bristling like a scruffy fighting dog.

'I don't want any damn woman, Justina.' He went out and slammed the door, and this time I did not follow to the stairs.

Slowly I walked across the room, and then stood looking down from the open window, where the electric fan buzzed rhythmically, like a trapped fly. I watched his plaid shirt until he reached the corner of Christopher Street. I leaned on my hands, out of the window, feeling sullen July like animal breath on my face. Then I drew myself back into the stifling room, straightened, wiped sweat from my forehead with the back of my hand, and retied the cotton scarf that held back my hair. It was eleven in the morning, and the heat of the day was only beginning.

I tidied the studio, watered the parched geraniums on the fire escape outside the kitchen window, and fed my little striped cat. Then I washed, for the third time that day, in an attempt to rid myself of the city's sticky heat, and dressed, to go out to see Millie. I wore a cotton shirt-waist, with long sleeves buttoned at the wrist, and a cotton skirt which, though short, stopping just below my knees, was dark and of a heavy weave. I wore as well a full-length underslip, silk stockings, white cotton gloves and a little straw hat. A ridiculous amount of clothing for New York's summer, but so far from my girlhood's imprisonment in yards of fabric that I felt, by contrast, quite airy and free.

Outside the air was thick and grey, curdled with ugly odours, fumes from motorcars and trucks, stench of ashcans and rotting vegetables, horse-dung, factory chimneys, river-wharfs. The sun, hazed and dreary, drove pedestrians to the shady sides of streets. I walked languidly, dreaming of Scotland and Sligo and cool, fresh green fields. I thought of the Gray House on Long Island, where I had spent earlier summers and was glad that Ellie and Wendell would soon be there, playing on the wide, maple-shaded lawns, or splashing in the bright waters of the Bay. But their summer oasis meant a desert of their absence, in New York, for me.

I crossed Sixth Avenue, lingering under the cool shadow of the elevated railway. The turrets of the Jefferson Market Court stood out gaudily against the flat white sky. Tenth Street made a pretty contrast, with its vine-covered frontages and ailanthus trees. Millie Dobbs, in a wispy tulle dress and wide-brimmed straw hat, sat, imperturbably incongruous, like a slum child, on her own frontstep. She had spread a Persian prayer rug over the stone and settled upon it, sipping from a tall glass of iced tea, and cooling herself with a wide Chinese fan. She beckoned me to join her.

'I'm having a picnic,' she said. She poured tea for me, also, from a jug perched on the low window-sill, and settled down on the step once more. We sat talking, like Scottish fish-wives.

'How is my picture coming?' she asked, looking at me over the rims of her glasses. She meant my portrait of Jack, which was for her collection.

'Not very well,' I said.

She said nothing, but her head, weighted with its piled mass of soft brown hair, tilted back questioningly.

'I can't get him right. I think I know him too well,' I said quickly.

She sipped her tea and said, 'You've had a row.'

I nodded, feeling miserable.

'Paris?' she asked.

I nodded again.

'Ah, well.'

'He's very angry with me.'

'Well, he'd better get over that,' she said sharply.

I felt from her tone that he might have to answer to her and I said quickly, in his defence, 'Oh, I'm sure he will.'

'And will you?'

'Of course.'

She shrugged. She poured more tea, and adjusted her hat and looked across the street to where one of her more eccentric neighbours, an old Armenian sculptor, was strolling in a long white robe with a large black cat on a lead.

'It's not unreasonable to be in love, Justina,' she said.

'What do you mean?' I asked suspiciously. 'Who are you talking about? Jack? Or me?'

'Anyone who happens to be in love, my dear. Come, let's go inside, and I'll find that address.'

In her drawing room, she sat at her plain pine desk and held up a pad of paper by the telephone on which she had written a name. She studied it for a long while, probably deciphering her erratic, spidery hand. She said at last, 'Justina, I don't know what to make of this.'

'Can't you read it?' I said ingenuously.

She laughed. 'Oh yes. It's not that. I wish I *knew* this woman,' she said.

'I thought you did.'

'No, dear. Friend of a friend of a friend . . . that sort of thing. I don't know even how they tracked me down, but someone of them had heard of you. Anyhow, they know what they want: very specific. One sitting, two hours, no longer, three o'clock tomorrow. You are to arrive alone and they even specify how you are to *dress*, if you can imagine. 'Plainly dressed.' The woman was very clear about it. That wasn't Mrs Draper, herself, mind, but some relative. *Terribly* secretive.'

'Perhaps they have nosy neighbours and they're afraid I might prove outlandish . . . some people are rather put off by artists.' Millie shook her head briskly.

'No. No, frankly, I don't understand this one. They haven't even specified who you're to paint, though I did press that, I mean you have a right to *know*, and they intimated it was a child. That was all.'

'Well, I'll soon find out,' I said lightly. I had other things on my mind, Jack foremost of them, and it didn't seem that important.

'It's all so queer and mysterious,' Millie said suddenly. 'Perhaps we'd better pass this one by.'

'Nonsense,' I said, with the courage of impecuniosity.

She looked up and smiled and then, a little reluctantly, handed me the paper. It was a Fifth Avenue address. I studied it, and then folded it and put it inside my handbag. 'I had better be going,' I said, glancing at the clock on the marble mantel.

'Are they coming today?' Millie asked.

'I hope so. Grace sent me a note yesterday. She wanted me to see them before the family left for the country.'

Millie stood up. 'Ah, good,' she said. 'Wait here.' She went out of the room, and came back carrying a tiny parcel wrapped in tissue paper. 'Fatima brought this to me. It's for Wendell. Khadija made it, look, it's quite lovely.' She handed me the wrapped object and I turned back the tissue paper and found a small leather purse, carefully stitched with bright wool and decorated in an eastern style with embroidery and beads. 'She made it herself,' said Millie. 'Isn't she clever?'

I turned the tiny, detailed thing around in my hands. 'It must have taken her hours.'

'Isn't it sweet?' Millie said. 'She still remembers him.'

I felt sad then, but I put the purse back in its tissue wrapping, and put it, also, into my bag. I imagined her sitting in a corner of the Cedars of Lebanon café, stitching carefully like a peasant woman, in her devotion to my son.

I stopped at a café on Greenwich Avenue before I went home, and had a roll and iced coffee for my lunch. I sat at a little table on the pavement, under an awning. Two old Jewish men, dressed in black, sat at the next table, arguing about Trotsky. Automatically, I drew out my notepad and began to sketch them. I laughed at myself, silently, seeing myself in the shadow of Mr Yeats. Yet it was from such street sketches that my 'Faces of Strangers' exhibition had grown. I sat a long time at the table, sketching and sipping my coffee, aware of myself as a city dweller, at home in the heat and the crowds.

It was two o'clock when I reached home. Grace and the children were to come at three. I went down to the street early and waited for the long black car. It did not arrive, and the heat grew oppressive until I felt dizzy with it, but I waited still. At four o'clock I gave up and climbed the stairs to my flat. I felt weary and chillingly empty inside. They would go to the country now and I would not see them until September. The length of time seemed too long to physically bear. I went to my easel to work, and scraped away at the frustrated portrait of Jack Redpath, removing layers of paint, and tediously beginning again from my initial sketch. I made some progress and felt less awful, and at five had just gone to the window to invite my cat back down from his afternoon sleep on the mansard roof, when I saw the car arrive.

I dropped the startled cat on the floor and threw off my smock and ran eagerly down the stairs. Wendell and Ellie were just scrambling out of the car when I reached the street. They did not rush to me, but stood back, half looking over their shoulders, their faces brimming with mystery.

'What is it, darlings?' I said. Ellie put her fat finger to her lips as if I too must guard the secret, and she reached back and took the gloved hand of the woman who emerged from the car. The woman moved easily, with cool liquid poise that Grace Pyke in her metal braces would never know. Her face was shielded by her stylish cloche hat until she raised her head, her eyes meeting mine, and extended her free hand with a sweet, tremulous smile.

'Hello, Justina dear,' she said. It was Margaret de Quincey Pyke. I stood in silence for a long bewildered moment, and Wendell stepped back from me and took Margaret's other hand, so that my children flanked her, like a queen's attendants.

'Where's Grace? Why hasn't Grace come?' I asked, numbly. It was a stupid question, its answer so apparent. But she made no comment other than another sweet smile.

'Aren't you going to ask me up to your apartment?' she

said. 'I'm dying to see it.' She was so calm, pleasant, even radiant in her benevolence that I stopped feeling like a criminal caught out, and began to respond quite normally.

'Of course,' I said. 'Of course I am.' And then to the children I said, 'Come, let's show Margaret where I live.'

'Mommy,' said Ellie with exquisite ambiguity. I looked warily at Margaret but she was yet smiling beneath her cloche hat.

Upstairs, she wandered about, coolly elegant in the stuffy heat of my attic rooms, making me feel dowdy and shabby in my plain skirt and blouse. Her body formed graceful arcs whenever she stopped, leaning gently backwards, to admire something. She was long-sighted actually, and it gave her an air of faint, delicate reserve. The children pulled her by one hand and then the other, showing her favourite objects and their very familiarity with my home spoke loudly. But she said nothing, other than small gracious comments on my taste.

'You do awfully well,' she said honestly, her eyes meeting mine. 'I know it must be difficult . . . I could never, never achieve . . . but then, you *are* an artist.' She had stopped at the easel. Shyly, like a schoolgirl venturing into secretive adult territory. 'Is this your man friend?' she asked.

'That,' I said sharply, 'is the writer Jack Redpath. I am painting his portrait. For a fee.'

The large, honest brown eyes met mine. 'Oh please, I didn't mean to offend,' she said. Then she touched the canvas, dreamily. 'It must be exciting to live in this world.'

'I don't live here for excitement,' I said. 'That's not why people become artists.'

Again she looked wide eyed and apologetic. 'I *have* offended you,' she said. 'I'm so clumsy. I'm sorry, Justina, I really am.'

'Why have you come here?' I said.

She turned her head quickly away. 'Yes,' she said tiredly, 'we *must* discuss that.'

She crossed the room and sat down on my Salvation Army couch, her gloved hands one upon the other on her knees. The children came to her side, carrying my striped cat between them. She smiled, patted the cat, and said to me, 'Before we talk, do you think the children might have some milk, and cookies maybe, if you have some, in the kitchen?' Her eyes were urgent.

I nodded, rose and led Wendell and Ellie through, found them milk and the drop scones I had baked in anticipation of their visit, and sat them down at my small scrubbed table. I put the cat on a third chair, beside them, knowing that diversion would engage them entirely. I went back to my studio, and pointedly shut the door. Margaret sighed.

'You do know, Justina, that these visits must end.'

They were the words I had expected since she stepped from the car, yet when they came, I did not accept them.

'No,' I breathed, and then in a louder, more desperate voice, 'No, why should they?' She looked at me pityingly and I grew angry, 'I'm their mother,' I cried, 'I have a right . . .'

'You've no rights, Justina.' Her voice was gentle but uncompromising, and she added carefully, 'The agreement *was* wise, dear, whether or not it was fair. This uncertainty is bad for children. They come home confused and unhappy from these visits. Hasn't Grace ever told you?'

I shook my head.

'How long have you known?' I said. 'I thought . . .'

'That it was secret? Oh, it was, Justina. No one ever talked about it, but of course we all knew. The children told me, you see. They never lie to me.'

I was stunned, and deeply, irrationally hurt.

She said, 'Wendell and I are married now, and they are old enough to understand. They want a normal Mommy and Daddy like other children. They cannot have that, as long as they come here to see you.'

I sat on the edge of my battered armchair, twisted the hot sticky cuff of my blouse in my fingers.

She said, 'Please try to understand.' And the awful thing was that I did understand. Everything she said was essentially logical and true. I felt myself drifting into numb, helpless agreement. Then she said, 'Please, please realize that everything I do, *everything* is for the sake of the children, and you, who love them as much as I, can only put their welfare . . .'

'As much!' I cried, 'as much! How can you even imagine . . .' and then I could not for a moment longer bear her wide, innocent eyes, her honesty, or her pity. 'You bitch!' I said and I jumped up and grabbed her two thin wrists and jerked her to her feet and slapped her once and then again, and again, across her beautiful, elegant face. Her head jerked back with each slap but she made no effort to avoid my blows and as suddenly as my anger began, it stopped in grievous remorse. 'Oh God,' I said.

She stood silent and brave as a martyr. Tears slipped down her smooth tanned cheeks, and I knew they were for me. I heard a noise and the cat scuttered by and I saw that the kitchen door was open and the children were watching me. Wendell laughed, an awkward, nervous laugh and Ellie tried an uncertain grin, gave it up, and began to cry.

Margaret stepped back, seeing them there, and said with a bright, deliberate smile, 'It's all right, darlings, Mommy and Justina are just being silly. See, we're friends again.' She leaned forward and kissed my cheek and as she did, she said quietly, 'I'll leave you alone with them.

Take as long as you like.' She lifted her purse, smiled brightly at the children and looking once, sadly, about my little room, she went out of the door.

The door closed behind her and I saw Ellie's eyes upon it uneasily. Her security was no longer vested in me. I said hastily, 'It's all right, sweetheart. She's waiting downstairs for you.' An awkward silence fell. I felt I was speaking to a stranger's children.

At last, Ellie said, 'Wendell spilled his milk and the cat drank it.'

'Oh, that's all right,' I said, but she was argumentative.

'He spilled it on purpose.'

'I didn't,' he cried. 'She pushed into me.' And then they began to fight, oblivious of my presence. I sorted them out with a promise of more milk, for them, and the cat, and having arranged that, in the kitchen, stood leaning against the ice box, watching them gulp from their glasses in that drowning-man way of small children. Like a drowning man myself, I was aware of every detail, every sound, with the heightened awareness of the condemned, and consciously memorized every nuance, the beading of milk on the soft down of Wendell's lip, the habitual twisting of one dark curl about her finger that Ellie maintained while she drank. I studied them, freezing their images in my mind, trying not to imagine how long it would be until, if ever, I saw them again. Once, only once, the bold lawless thought arose that I would grasp them and flee, down the fire escape at my kitchen window, into the hot city beyond. But one does not run when there is nowhere to go. Small pampered children cannot become gypsies in an instant. They need toys and clothes, food and books and their own familiar beds. And so I simply played with them, using our last minutes as I would have chosen to use all the years, in ordinary domestic peace.

They themselves brought it to an end. Wendell, dutiful and proper, said, 'I think we should go. Francisco will be tired of waiting.' I was certain he had centred his concern on the chauffeur rather than his stepmother out of a diplomatic kindness to me.

Ellie was no diplomat. 'I want Mommy,' she said.

'Of course,' I answered smoothly. Wendell's small sturdy hand brushed against my arm and held itself there, steadying and protective. I thought suddenly, *You're more man than your father already*, but I said only, 'But just wait one moment. I've something for Wendell.' When I returned with the little tissue-paper-wrapped package Millie had given me, he looked politely eager, as if the gaining of gifts was already beneath him. Ellie looked wistful and I realized miserably that I had nothing to give her at all. I thought wildly, while I handed the package to her brother. She was looking around, sure that her gift must be somewhere. I said, 'It isn't from me, you understand. It's from Khadija, Wendell, do you remember her?' I was sure he would not, but he nodded.

'I remember her.' He opened the parcel and looked carefully at it. Once he turned it over. I could see him trying to make it into something other than what it was. He said finally, 'It's a girl's thing. It's a purse.'

'Oh, not really,' I said. 'Boys can use purses.'

He looked uncertain.

'Besides, Khadija *made* it. For you.' That made him think and when I added, 'Of course, if you don't like it, you can give it to Ellie,' he suddenly put it in his pocket.

Ellie looked longingly at it. 'It's a girl's thing,' she prompted him.

'Khadija made it for *me*,' he said.

Her eyes blinked once and then she turned hopefully to me. My mind went blank. There was nothing in my flat but rude essentials. Suddenly a wild thought struck me and I strode boldly to my paint table and lifted, from my jam-jar full of brushes, my best sable filbert.

'Would you like Mommy's brush to paint with?' I said.

Her eyes were on it at once and her two hands reaching. Carefully I laid it across her palms. She closed her fingers about it, and carried it horizontally, like a holy offering, before her. I smiled, knowing I was an idiot. Brushes of that sort, expensive and fine, were not for children and I could ill afford to replace it.

'Mommy's brush,' she whispered, and bearing her trophy before her, followed her brother to the door.

I don't remember what I did for the hour or so after they left; nothing very much, I don't suppose. I probably dabbled at my easel. I undoubtedly washed the milk glasses, and put away the uneaten scones, and put the cat's saucer back in its place on the floor. I did not cry. I didn't see any point in it; no real tragedy had occurred. No one had died. Nothing had really changed that I would be aware of for weeks, even months. I had not seen the children often in the past years. As for the children themselves, they would hardly notice. A gap in our acquaintance would lengthen, stretch out, and blend imperceptibly into a permanent state of affairs. By the time they realized what had happened, they would have forgotten me. I loved them enough to be comforted by that thought.

After all, I reminded myself, they *were* happy. They loved their father, they loved Margaret, even their grandmother, despite a certain stiffness, could be counted on to amuse them pleasantly. Their home was comfortable; their nanny well chosen. They had the country to look forward to at vacation time. They were not in any way deprived, or neglected. It is not necessary for children to have the love of any *specific* person, after all.

I was totally calm, more aware of the suffocating heat

of my flat than anything else, and that led me to conclude logically that the best thing to be done with the remainder of the daylight was to go out to the park and sit in the shade of a tree. I was, I realize, quite irrationally rational. I suspect this is what is meant by shock. The only intrusion on my calm was the recurrent and illogical thought of my mother; her memory and her image would not leave my mind. But I supposed it was seeing Ellie, who resembled her greatly, that caused that, and I paid it little mind.

I did not stop walking when I reached the park but continued, without thinking really, down West Broadway. I was not conscious of going anywhere in particular, nor particularly conscious of where I was, or the fact that it was getting dark. I remember wandering through Chinatown and Little Italy, where there was a festival of some kind going on. No one paid me any attention. Cities are good that way. You can walk through them with tears all over your face and not draw a glance. It was deep dusk when I reached the doorway of the Cedars of Lebanon Coffee House. I had not chosen to go there, my steps had simply led me there, as if my feet sought a refuge my mind had not requested.

Hassan was standing in the doorway, smoking his pipe, watching the life of the street. People seemed to live in the street much more in those days; the only escape from the oppressive heat was outdoors, and children's playgrounds were the pavement and the cobbles. He was looking downtown, towards the Battery, his eyes distant as if he looked at mountains. I was standing beside him before he noticed me. I must have looked devastated, because he said nothing at all, but touched my arm lightly and led me inside, through the café, to the kitchen.

I sat at the bakery table, and told him what had happened. He smoked his pipe thoughtfully, filling the air with exotic scent. He looked dreamy and unaware but when I said suddenly, 'I'm at the end of the road,' he replied at once.

'No. Your journey is only just beginning.'

'I've lost everything,' I said. 'I have nothing.'

'Those with nothing, God clothes in freedom,' said Hassan.

'I am sick of it,' I cried, slamming a fist on the floury table. 'I am sick of riddles and I am sick of a God who talks in riddles.' Hassan smiled. He took my two hands gently in his.

'"The most manifest of the manifest and the most hidden of the hidden. There is no God but Thee."'

'I think,' I said, 'I would rather do without.'

'Undoubtedly,' he said, patting my hands, 'but you haven't that choice.'

I stayed that night at Washington Street. Fatima made a bed for me, in Khadija and Aiysha's little room. They awoke surprised, but not disturbed to find me sleeping there. 'Have you brought Wendell?' was the first thing that Khadija said. I shook my head.

'Wendell's gone away,' I said. 'But I gave him your gift.'

She absorbed that solemnly and then gave a placid oriental smile, like her father's.

'He'll come back,' she said.

'Will he?' I asked whimsically. Her confidence was unshakable, however.

'Of course,' she said. 'He has to marry me.'

At breakfast, I remembered my appointment at the Fifth Avenue address of Millie's mysterious client. Until that moment it had totally slipped my mind. I felt dizzy and light-headed, the way one does when one has talked too long and late, and must awake to face the New York heat. Outside, even in early morning, the sky was white and the pavements steamy. My eyes ached from crying in the darkness. But I drank coffee with Fatima and her mother and ate the sweet pastries that Hassan had baked before dawn. I wondered if he had slept at all, and felt guilty before his cheerful broad, moustached face. After breakfast I took the subway back to the Village, and returned to my airless apartment, buying a fish-head along the way, to feed my poor abandoned cat.

I opened windows and laid out my brushes, minus the missing filbert, and prepared a canvas, finding in those methodical duties surprising peace. I washed myself all over, and yearned for a proper bath; a luxury my little flat could not provide. Then I dressed, modestly, in the plainest garments I possessed, a navy skirt and pale blue shirt and small blue beret. I glanced in the mirror and saw a French schoolgirl. That should do, I thought. A faint interest began to grow upon me, regarding my unusual clients, and I spent the subway journey uptown imagining explanations for their secrecy.

The address, when I reached it, was almost a disappointment. A plain, bland, brick-fronted structure rose up, ten storeys from the pavement, with nothing to decorate it other than a bit of carved stonework over the solid oak doors, and, far above for only the birds to see, some Grecian nonsense of cornices near the sky. Nothing whatever revealed that within its walls some of New York's wealthiest citizens resided, in considerable splendour.

I entered, feeling altogether *too* plain now, gauche as a country girl, and stammered the name I had been given to the uniformed doorman. He glanced unappreciatively at my easel and canvas and paintbox, but apparently someone was expecting me, because he directed me without argument to a bank of lifts. I stood waiting for a cage to arrive, rejoicing in the dank coolness of the lobby.

The floors were marble, the walls wood-panelled, the lift-cage itself ornate with brass. I was whisked upwards, eight floors, and came out on a sumptuous landing, with Chinese carpets under foot, and gilt-framed mirrors on the walls. With definite reluctance, I rang the bell.

There was a long, long silence before faint footsteps indicated I had indeed been heard. Another silence followed, and at last, just as I was agonizing over the choice of ringing again or fleeing the place, the door was slowly opened by a maid in full uniform, with a sad, sallow face. I gave my name and was ushered in, shown a delicate chair on which to sit and left alone.

Half an hour passed and then a door opened at the end of the vestibule in which I sat, and two figures came slowly into the room. Both were women, one older, grey haired, and the other young, fair, and veiled in black. The older woman supported the younger as if she were an invalid and together, with halting steps, they crossed the room. They reached me and I was surprised that it was the younger woman who spoke.

'Miss Melrose,' she whispered, in a voice scratchy with recent tears, 'thank you so much for coming. Such short notice. But there was no other way. Will you come?' She motioned with one listless hand that I was to follow her, and she detached herself from her supporter and made her way, shakily, towards the door. I glanced at the older woman, who nodded encouragement, and I gathered my easel and paintbox and followed. As I brushed past the grey-haired woman, she said softly, 'Isn't she brave,' as if I should understand at once, and certainly agree. I made a sound of acknowledgement, feeling as if I were in a strange gnostic dream where secret knowledge was the privilege of a rare priesthood.

I remember a long corridor, so dimly lighted that the colour of the brocade paper was not clear. I had an impression of gas-lamps, though I doubt that. Few places in New York yet retained those. The woman paused so suddenly at the end of the corridor that I almost stumbled into her. I was conscious of my breathing, loud and awkward, and tried to stifle it.

'Please,' she said, 'just a moment, while I get myself ready. There.' And she opened the door. The room within was in almost total darkness. Heavy draperies were drawn tight across the windows, so that even the white summer light was vanquished. After a moment, my eyes adjusted and I saw dim outlines; a few pieces of furniture, and at the far end, a pale, unidentifiable shape. The woman walked slowly into the room, and stopped by that distant whiteness. She said, sadly, 'I suppose you will need light.'

In other circumstances I might have laughed at the absurdity of it, but here I only said as practically as I could, 'Well, yes. If I'm to paint, I will.' I think she nodded. Then my curiosity, spiked by a touch of actual fear, grew suddenly demanding. 'If you don't mind, could you tell me who . . .'

But she silenced me with a quick shake of her head and crossed the room to the tall windows. One by one she drew the draperies aside, solemn as a temple virgin. Light, in broad wide beams, entered the room and lit first the doorway where I stood, then a chair, a chesterfield sofa, a wood-panelled wall, and then, finally, the long pale shape at the end of the room.

I approached with cautious reverence, as the veiled lady returned to stand beside it, where she had stood before. A trestle or a table, completely clothed in white, lace-edged satin, stood like an altar before her. On it, white and glistening, was a tiny, beautiful casket in which, clothed in the unmistakable stillness of death, rested a tiny child. Though the lady leaned over, her black veil trailing like Persephone's hair once trailed over William,

I had no inclination to imagine it as a boat. My only inclination was to run.

I must have turned, because I felt hands, gently restraining, on my shoulders and the older woman's voice saying, 'When I saw your exhibition, I knew you were a woman of great courage. I knew you would be afraid of nothing.'

Oh would that it were so! Unable to flee, I managed at last to find words.

'Oh, the poor little angel,' I whispered.

'My baby,' said the veiled woman. She lifted the veil off her face. She was very young, shy, blonde, very lovely. She said, 'Isn't she beautiful?' As if the infant was cradled in her carriage, not her coffin. I stepped forward and made myself look down at the dead baby.

'Oh yes,' I said. 'She is beautiful.'

'Matthew thinks she's quite like me, do you think so?' She smiled shyly, again the proud young mother.

'Yes. Yes she is like you,' I said.

She smiled again, satisfied. I saw her eyes were red-rimmed, as mine had been that morning. She said, very practically, 'I said to Matthew again and again that we should have her portrait done. Of course I didn't *know* this would happen, but she was always a sickly baby. Then when she took this awful croup . . .' She looked up suddenly, and said quickly, 'You mustn't worry, you know, there was nothing contagious or dangerous. Not scarlet fever or anything . . . do you have children?' I nodded. 'I do understand. I would worry too. But she's quite, quite safe, aren't you, darling?' She leaned over the coffin, cooing and then abruptly closed her eyes and turned her face from me.

I said, very carefully, 'Do you want a portrait?'

She kept her eyes closed but nodded vigorously, her

lower lip clenched in her teeth. The older woman stepped to her side.

'Come, Daphne,' she said gently. The young mother allowed herself to be led away but she stopped in the doorway and lifted her head. She looked straight into my eyes with terrible desperation.

'Oh please, make her *very* pretty,' she said.

It was the hardest charge of my entire career. Nothing before it, nothing after it, ever matched it. All afternoon, in that airless silent room, I worked with that tiny cold corpse for company. I worked with meticulous care, so that every line of the soft cheek, the feathering of eyelashes, the translucent, delicate nostrils, be perfectly recorded. But beyond that, I must do more. I must capture in that tiny perfect face the holy spirit of life that had fled. I must transform that stillest of sleeps into the ordinary sleep that children take, so that the infant in my portrait would appear about to awake before each watcher's gaze. I must turn back death; a formidable task.

And then, as I worked, a strange thing began to happen. I became, very gradually, aware of being no longer alone. No one had entered. Nor had my tiny companion stirred. A ghost was with me, I knew. I worked on. I was not afraid. People are only afraid of the supernatural in anticipation and in recollection. In its presence there is often a remarkable peace. I thought at first it was the ghost of the baby I painted, but the formless thing that communicated to me with no words was not a child. It was a woman. I painted on, finding the soft colours I sought, working the cheek, the one small curled hand, the soft wisp of downy dead hair, as if for that silent watcher's approval. When I was done, I knew quite suddenly who was there. I laid down my brush, and stepped back. The infant on my canvas was surrounded in lace and satin, the bedding of her cradle, not the dressings of her grave. She dreamed sweetly and would soon wake. She was perfect. She was alive. I felt behind me the wave of approval I had longed for on the Christmas of my seventh year. I stood the canvas to dry, propped against a wall.

'Thank you, Mother,' I said. 'I like it too.'

As I left that dark, cool apartment and went down through its dim lobby out on to the sudden brilliance of the hot afternoon street, I felt I was rising upwards from a mausoleum, from a grave, out of the underworld, into the world of living men. Elation struck me; the eerie elation born of Nell Melrose's visit, the triumph of my painting, the delight of being alive. I clambered on to a bus and paid my fare and settled back on the dirty seat breathing in the smells of fumes and human sweat with earthy joy. All the way back to the Village I was filled with excitement and adventure as if each street I passed led somewhere wonderful, and the most wonderful of all lay far ahead. At the corner of Twentieth Street and Seventh Avenue I got off, and began to walk deliberately west. It was a hot, silly thing to do, in the sticky afternoon, carting my heavy folding easel, and James Howie's mahogany paintbox, but I had not far to go.

Jack Redpath lived on the north side of West Twentieth Street, on the block between Eighth and Ninth Avenues, in a funny little house set behind another so that it was reached by a door in a wall, like a garden door. It had a tiny garden, a rare thing, and his being the ground floor apartment, he had the use of it. When I first knew him in New York, he had lived there with a mistress, a chorus line dancer from Kentucky. But she moved on, in the manner of many mistresses, and he lived there, now, alone. I visited him once, at his invitation, in the safe company of Millie Dobbs. I had never, until this day, gone there alone.

Outside the plain door in the tall brick wall I stopped, and set my easel down, leaning it on the door-jamb. There was a painted brass knob and I turned it, finding it open. This was another New York not yet under lock and key. Besides, Jack Redpath's little flat though now, if it still exists, no doubt a precious urban jewel, was then a genteel slum. And he had nothing in it worth stealing anyhow. Even when he was earning a great deal of money, he had almost no possessions though he managed to go through the money just the same. My entry made easy, I still hesitated. My hand dropped from the knob and it clicked back into place. Shyness overwhelmed me. I was still in awe of Jack even though he professed his devotion to me regularly. I did, then, an odd, childish thing. I set my paintbox down in the street and I stood up on tiptoes, so that I might peer through a narrow, splintered crack near the top of the battered old door. Through it, framed in my blurred loophole, I saw green and gold of garden, a stucco wall, and a small straight-backed chair. A yellow and white cat slept on the chair, undisturbed in the late afternoon sun. There was no sign of Jack.

I stood back from the door, lifted my paintbox and easel again, and let myself in to the garden. As I closed the door behind me, I called, 'Hello?' in a voice too quiet to awaken even the cat. I walked carefully up the paved path, between two wiry old wisteria bushes and under the shadow of the garden' solitary frondy ailanthus tree. There were old, clay flowerpots, some empty, some filled with weeds, and a large stone urn, also overgrown, in shady corners of the narrow strip of greenery. Someone, certainly not Jack, had once gardened avidly here. As I passed the wooden chair, the cat rolled over on its back, and curled its forepaws in feline delight. I paused to tickle it. On the patio stones, a newspaper and an empty coffee cup sat abandoned. *He likes to live alone*, I thought suddenly.

It was strange to recognize that intimate fact about someone I had known for so many years. Our homes, if we have homes, are our great betrayers. The door to the apartment stood open, and I called hesitantly, 'Jack?' and again got no answer. Reluctantly, I stepped into the cool shadows within. It was a cramped one-room place, with a minute kitchen and bathroom at the back; the garden was its only charm. The entrance-way was a tiny vestibule which, in winter, held firewood, and now was occupied only by a solitary coathook on which hung Jack's trench-coat and his black beret. Inside the gentle tapping of his old black typewriter sounded as dreamy as the buzz of the garden bees. I stood for a long while, savouring that thoughtful, peaceful sound. Then, setting down my burdens by the coathook, I stepped quietly into the room.

He sat with his back to me, before the typewriter on his broad, black desk. His hands were resting on the keys and his head was tilted backward in thought. It seemed wrong to interrupt and so I stood watching, thinking how often he had watched me at my work, and remembering how he had watched over me at the farmhouse at Dernancourt. His fingers stiffened and reached for the keys, charged with the private excitement of creative thought, and then suddenly the thought metamorphosed into an awareness of my presence and he spun round in his chair.

'Justina?' he said warily.

'The door was open,' I apologized. It was only then that I remembered that we had parted in anger. I said, 'I was on my way back from my appointment . . .'

'Oh, please, please come in,' he said hastily, and he stood up and crossed the room to where I hovered at the door. Circumspectly, he kissed my cheek. 'You look twelve years old,' he said.

'I was supposed to be plain, remember?'

'Oh, the mysterious sitter,' he laughed. 'Well, who was it? Calvin Coolidge?' He laughed again.

'No,' I said.

'John D. Rockefeller?'

I shook my head, turning aside.

'I know. Valentino. *Ze Great Lover*,' he murmured, nuzzling my cheek. 'No wonder he wanted you alone . . .'

'No,' I said suddenly, drawing back so sharply that he looked hurt. 'No. It was no one famous. It was a baby, actually.'

He peered at me. 'What's wrong, Justina,' he said quietly.

'She was dead. She had died and before she was buried, her mother wanted a portrait. So I painted it. That's all.'

'Oh, Jesus Christ.'

'No really, Jack. There was nothing awful about it. I was glad. It was a lovely portrait and her mother was very happy . . .'

Emotions are such aberrant things. Why does kindness feed grief, and grief in turn feed passion? The moment his arms circled my shoulders, and he pulled me up against his rough cotton shirt, I began to cry, not just for the baby, but for my own children lost to me. And as I wept, and he stroked my back, and drew from me all that had happened between Margaret and myself and Wendell and Ellie, my misery transmuted to desire. I became aware suddenly of his embrace; the surprising spare bony lightness of his body in my arms. He began to kiss me and I did not resist.

I remember standing alone, perfectly in control, in the centre of his tiny room while he carefully left me, and closed, and locked the door. Then, one by one, he pulled down the buff battered blinds, so that the room grew dimmer and dimmer until it seemed almost dark. He came back to me and gently lifted my childish blue beret from my head and laid it on his papers on the desk. Then he led me to his roughly-made bed, in the innermost corner of the room and we sat down side by side. Until that moment I had never imagined that one could make love in the afternoon.

Across half a century, one image remains; my blue French schoolgirl clothes scattered with his garments on the floor. It was that, not his nakedness, nor mine, that told me what I had done; what I had become. All my scruples, all my upbringing, had vanished into ether. Nor could I plead ignorance, or passion. There is always time, in the fumbling clumsiness of buttons and buckles and ties, to say no. What is lacking is usually the will. I lay against his sweaty shoulder and thought, *I am a divorcée in a stranger's bed*. He kissed my curly damp hair.

'Justina Melrose, the Rose of No Man's Land,' he whispered, laughing.

I held him closer. 'I never knew it could be a *pleasure*,' I said.

He sat up and stared at me in amazement. Then he turned and slammed his big fist into the pillow.

'Jack?' I cried.

'I'm going to break that guy's neck,' he said.

But it didn't seem important any more to either of us, and we both laughed together, and stretched and yawned and in the dusky afternoon light, we went to sleep.

And so I became Jack Redpath's mistress one sultry July afternoon. There is nothing other that I need tell you. Like a few others before me, I had come to New York an innocent; and I left it, seven years later, a woman of the world.

Part Four

21

Jack Redpath was a born gypsy. Like a true Christian, he was in the world, but not of the world, and its material charms meant nothing to him. In all the years I knew him his possessions would not have filled a single small room. Amongst them, the largest and most valuable item, his old Royal typewriter, was simply the tool of his trade. Beyond that, he had sufficient garments to cover his proverbial nakedness, a few books, which he changed regularly for others, and a well-worn dictionary. Everything else in his apartment, cooking utensils, crockery, furnishings, was borrowed or purchased casually, second-hand. When we left New York in the fall of 1926, he simply closed the door and left everything behind.

I confess that I was, myself, far more tainted with worldly goods, so that when I became Jack's companion a certain adjustment was necessary. This I managed in a manner to which I, and my long-suffering friends, had grown accustomed over the years. I might appear as untrammelled a free spirit as Jack, but material possessions were not so much discarded as hidden away, like dark secrets, in the attics and storerooms of two continents. May Howie was custodian of my pre-war paintings, some ancient clothing, many of my letters. Wilhemina, at Arradale, suffered my earliest collections, as well as a trunk with letters and mementoes of my mother and father. Clare no doubt had a few odds and ends left behind in the Callow Street flat, now transferred with her to Oxford. And to the best of my knowledge my old pitch-pine skis *still* stand against a dusty wall in the forgotten cellars of the Ben Wyvis Hotel. So now, as I departed New York, Millie Dobbs became the chagrined inheritor of stacks of canvases, cases of letters and drawings, trinkets made by my children, and, on the day before I bade her farewell, my dear grey-striped cat. (Jack's feline companions, two or three, borrowed and exchangeable like his books, were expected to be free spirits like himself. They parted without formal good-byes.) And so, though gypsy I became, it was only with the able help of a full supporting cast of box-rooms and attics. I hate confessing this; I would far rather have been as splendidly liberated as Jack. Though I assure you, as one who has attempted to chronicle his extravagant life, a little signpost along the way might have helped. The only Redpath letters in existence are those I scrupulously preserved.

Still, in 1926, no one was famous or important and we lived from day to day. When we sailed on the White Star liner *Majestic*, bound for Southampton, we took into our rather sumptuous stateroom, before the disbelieving eyes of our cabin steward, one typewriter case, one easel and paintbox, and one army kitbag, between us. And for the next ten years we possessed little else. 'Those who have nothing, God clothes in freedom.' Mirza Hassan, pastry baker and visionary, was quite correct and correct, too, in his prophecy that my journeys were just beginning. For the decade that followed that sailing, I seldom spent more than six months in any one place, and those places were as far and disparate as a river barge on the Seine and a mudwalled shepherd's hut in Persia. We had, indeed, nothing. I would say 'nothing but each other' as the convention holds, but it would be untrue. I never possessed Jack, nor he me. We were two solitary planets spinning in parallel course; perfect companions. Those ten years were the happiest decade of my life.

I cannot possibly chronicle it all, but I will tell you of the places and people that mattered, and those things we did that had lasting effect. The rest seems strangely inviolate. Sorrow must be catalogued so that we may understand it. Happiness is sufficient unto itself.

At the quayside at Southampton, I set foot on British soil for the first time since 1919. Ships and quays brim with nostalgia for those of us whose childhoods were punctuated by journeys by sea. But aside from dim memories of Liverpool and Sligo, the occasion aroused little emotion. England was never my home; like any other born to the Celtic fringes of the kingdom, I held her a begrudged stranger. I was most aware of a greyness about everything; how poor and shabby and rundown the docklands and their inhabitants looked. Suddenly the Great War, so far back in my memory, seemed like yesterday. I was consciously aware of moving backwards, into the past.

Our first port of call, after Southampton, was Oxford, where Clare was expecting us and preparing a welcome. After a night in a London hotel (no more charmed than the cabin steward with our eccentric luggage) and the journey up by train, I had resumed my Britishness and felt surprisingly at home. Very little had changed. Skirts were shorter, hats smaller, motorcars slightly more prevalent, but in most respects this was the country I had left, an uncertain war-bride, at Wendell Pyke's side. The one greatest difference was that the uniforms that had filled the streets were gone, and the 'brave boys in khaki' had vanished into the anonymity of civilian dress and civilian jobs and, as was evident on street corners in Southampton and the capital, civilian unemployment as well.

Somehow, I expected to find Clare as unchanged as the nation, and I approached our reunion with trepidation. I did not know Oxford, and Jack and I were both a little awed by it, as if we had no place in so seriously academic a place. Artists and scholars make uneasy companions. Eventually we found Somerville College and were directed by the porter to Clare's rooms, and I remember mounting the stairs and stiffening my courage to face the onslaught of polemics that awaited me in the old days of the WSPU. But then the door swung open and, framed in lovely wainscotting the colour of honey, stood a fine, dignified woman of forty years, greeting me gently with my father's wise smile.

'Justina, darling, you're still as pretty as a child.' She embraced me, kissed me, and held her hand out to Jack.

'Mr Redpath, this is an extraordinary honour. I read everything you write.' I think that really shook Jack. He wasn't overtly modest about his talents, but the idea that *any* effort of his might have seen the bright light of an Oxford day quite overwhelmed him. We all have our Rubicons.

She seated us comfortably in her study and then disappeared into a back room where I could hear voices. She had promised tea, and I imagined there was a kitchen, and possibly a servant to whom she was giving instructions. I stood up, and walked about the room, which was very attractive, wood-panelled throughout and the walls lined with tall bookcases. Books were everywhere, on her writing desk, on the tables, on the floor. The window, of leaded small panes, looked out over green lawns. It was a very beautiful and very peaceful place and I was glad that Clare had found such a refuge. Jack watched me as I wandered around, touching lightly her possessions, as if I might re-establish our sisterhood by physical contact. She seemed a stranger; a remote, kind, but awesome stranger, and it was odd to find these little family mementoes, photographs of May and the Howies, a faded sketch of Alexander which must have been my work though I could not remember it and, most haunting, an old picture of all the family, lined up before the pump-house at Strathpeffer, visitants from an Edwardian past that seemed hardly to be our own. I smiled shyly at Jack.

'I told you we had our academic side.'

He grinned. 'How's the dunce?' he said.

Clare came back into the room, and behind her came not a servant, but Meggie Whyte. She had put on a stone at least in weight and was as plump and pink-cheeked as a Yorkshire farmer's wife. She was carrying a tea-tray and trying very hard to blend into the furniture, to be merely a hired retainer, of no import. But of course I greeted her as the companion she had once been, and reluctantly she allowed herself to be introduced to Jack, and we all had tea together and during that time Meggie relaxed back into her old self and became jolly and almost flirtatious once more. I looked from Clare to Meggie and back to Clare. She was gently aloof, watching her round little companion's bursts of giggly laughter with kind tolerance. She was beautiful, her fair hair greying and drawn into a smooth classic bun; her tweed suit the perfect matching grey. Clare aged well, and Meggie badly, and yet they seemed a mellow pair.

After tea, Clare sent Meggie out with Jack to show him the Colleges and we had half an hour alone. As soon as the door closed behind them I realized why

'You can't possibly think of marrying him,' she said. Suddenly, the old Clare was back.

'That's a relief,' I said. She raised her eyebrows. I smiled slyly, feeling unfairly mischievous. 'I was so sure you were going to say I *had* to.'

There was an icy pause. 'Justina, I'm not a prude.'

I shook my head, laughing and unable to suppress my delight.

She said, 'He's a charming man and a brilliant writer, and he'd make a terrible husband.'

'I quite agree,' I said gaily.

She grew red and angry because I wouldn't oppose her. 'What precisely are your intentions?' she asked.

'Thoroughly dishonourable,' I answered cheerfully. 'Just like his.'

Clare stood up, left the tea table, and walked to her desk where she sat down, very deliberately. I imagined she was treating me as a recalcitrant student, without even realizing.

'That is all very well for a man,' she said sternly.

I looked up, amazement widening my eyes. 'What?'

'That sort of behaviour. *That*,' I saw she was excruciatingly embarrassed. '*Men* can, but you . . . why, what will become of you? Supposing he leaves . . .'

'Leaves?' I said sharply. 'Do you mean like my husband left?' That silenced her. She looked sorry, as if she had unwittingly offended me, and I hastened to set her at ease. 'Clare, he is a wonderful friend, and we are very, very happy. What more can possibly matter?'

She looked away. Then she cast me a knowing glance and said quickly, 'Supposing you fall?'

I blinked, unused to the coyness and then realizing what she meant I said, 'Pregnant?' I laughed aloud. 'Oh, Clare.' Then I sighed and said very slowly, 'I've had my children. There won't be any more.' I said it with such authority that she acquiesced.

It was Jack who had shown me that there need not always be babies; a knowledge that until then I had not possessed. I said to Clare, 'Outside of marriage a woman is as free as a man.'

She looked uncomprehending. Feminism, like her Margaret Sanger tracts, was an abstraction in Clare's life, which she would never need to put into practice. Like the war years, it seemed far behind her; an adolescent love affair she would rather forget. For the rest of the half-hour she tried to convince me that I must stay with her, or go to Arradale with Wilhemina, or even Dublin with poor Uncle James. She, the great fighter for the rights of woman, would have me bend my life to the conventions and strictures of our times, like any Edwardian maiden aunt.

I listened politely. I was gaily happy for the first time in years; I was in love. It seemed wrong to use my good fortune as a means of her humiliation, and so I tried as well as I could to agree without surrender. In the end she gave up on me and my stubbornness. ('You were *always* stubborn, Justina, from the day you were born.') and announced that she would await my return from Paris in defeat. On that note we parted, though she hid her displeasure with me as soon as Jack and Meggie re-entered her rooms. Meggie dashed about, cleaning up the tea things, being busy and humble, and demonstrably of another world. Later, Jack and I, hands held between us, descended the stairs.

'Clare is a very fine woman,' he said, 'but her little lover has a heart of gold.'

We returned to London that same night, though not to a hotel, but to the townhouse Wilhemina maintained in Bryanston Square. She had journeyed down especially to meet us, and opened the house up early for the season. Even her little son Hugo, removed from school for the occasion, would be there. Poor Jack was running the full gauntlet of Melroses and their heirs.

This stay was pleasanter than our brief meeting with Clare. Wilhemina was my sister-in-law, not my sister, and whatever she might have thought of my situation (and she could not have thought well of it), her own impeccable breeding prevented the slightest reference to it. Unlike Clare, she felt neither duty, nor right, to interfere. We were treated royally, wined and dined and introduced to all her impeccable friends, and at night given two pointedly separate rooms with an equally pointed interconnecting door. Such was the proper *laissez-faire* of the British aristocracy.

My greatest pleasure in our three-day stay was re-meeting my nephew Hugo, grown in the years of my absence from a shy four-year-old to a self-assured young gentleman at school. He was tall for his age, sandy-haired and brown eyed and, beneath the polished reserve so typical of public school children, a likeable imaginative child, visibly straining for release from the burdensome restrictions of his role as the Arradale heir. Fatherless children; those whose fathers have held positions of dignity; carry a bitter weight. Watching him in stiff collar and tie greeting his mother's guests I longed to take him by the hand and run with him to some place of air, and sky and hills where he might yet be a child.

We sat talking late one night, sharing stories of the castle that was both our homes. Through him I saw not just my brother Douglas brought alive again, but all my brothers, and my youthful self as well. When we parted, he kissed me with glorious awkwardness and begged to come and see me in France.

Three mornings later we took the boat train to Dover and the Channel crossing. It was here, in the familiar railway stations and ferry terminals, that the memories of the War came rushing back, in a great swamping deluge so that people and sights I had not seen since 1918 became realer and more immediate than the actuality of business travellers and tourists in which we moved. Khaki-clad ghosts crowded around, kitbags and rifles and rucksacks borne patiently in haunted procession. Again and again I glimpsed faces, young faces, and thought them to be those of familiar friends, now grown far older, or dead. Jack felt it too, and we wondered if all our generation were besieged by spirits, or if our long absence had bereft us alone of the natural healing of time. On the crossing we stood at the ship's rail and teased each other each time we caught ourselves looking for torpedo wash in the gentle autumn sea.

But there was none, nor were there troopships at the quayside in France, nor hospitals, nor hospital ships, nor the long sad lines of walking wounded. Warm French sunshine lit a coastline confident in peace. I remembered the rockpools at Etaples and the sullen sky under which Wendell Pyke had wept for my brother and proposed. Those times, and he, my husband, as well, seemed as dead and gone as Sandy Melrose, buried in the past.

We landed at Calais and, travelling inland by train, came to Paris on a rainy October evening, entering the city by the Gare du Nord. The date of my first arrival in Paris quite eludes me; I am lucky to have the year right, and that only by deduction. But it was autumn; damp, misty and cold; and our taxi-driver drove wildly and erratically down the Boulevard de Sebastopol while Jack tried in insufficient French to make clear to him our destination.

That was the tiny Rue Zacharie in the tangle of little streets that lie around the lovely Gothic church in St Séverin. This centre of obscurity, a stone's throw from the quays and opposite Notre Dame, was where my cousin May Howie had come to live some four years before. And it was to May, the baby of our family who had proved its greatest strength, that I went so happily that rainy autumn in the company of my love. She, whose pestering attentions had been the bane of my childhood, was now the one adult creature on whom I would most rely.

May Howie ran a publishing house from her flat in the Rue Zacharie. Or, more precisely, from the ramshackle and indefinable storeroom, home once of animals or some obscure machinery, that lay below it. Therein she maintained a typewriter, a polite young French assistant called Marie Bujold, and a thundering and ancient printing press. That creation, which she always referred to by the Christian name of Alphonse (after, I assume, the manufacturer, a certain Alphonse Gautier whose name, writ bold in cast iron, decorated the machine) served only for small editions of limited interest; verse, pamphlets, and occasional runs of an intermittent literary magazine. Larger efforts demanded the co-operation of a French printer of greater stature. Both the printing house, and the little magazine bore the title, The Fishing Cat after a neighbouring street whose name translated accordingly. There was no connection I know other than May's having been charmed by the image, which she extended with a letterhead logo of abstracted cat swiping forever with its paw at an equally abstracted carp.

May's publications were primarily verse and prose fiction, a careful personal selection of what she held to be a true reflection of the best new work in English. It was not the ultimate vanguard, where the brilliant and ridiculous often ride side by side, but the solid rank and file of serious literature. She published many fine people, including some whose daring of public mores and conventional linguistic restraints kept them otherwise muzzled, but it was never their outrageousness that inspired her. She had the cool eye of a confessor; she had seen it all before and could ignore some surface offensiveness to get at the worth beneath. Her judgement was excellent, and there was nothing that she published that need cause an honest heart shame. But the Ireland she had departed after her mother's death was not always noted for honest hearts. May came to Paris for many reasons, but an escape of literary oppression was surely one of them. Another was Eithne, her niece who at the age of eight might as well have been her daughter, and whom May subtly shielded, throughout her childhood, from the woman whose daughter she was.

That night, as we crossed the dark Seine, on to the Île de la Cité, I embraced Jack, in the dim confines of the taxi, quite out of character for me, schooled from infancy to avoid public display. But Jack, always rather exhibitionist, readily returned my embrace, and we kissed on the Pont au Change, and our driver, who had been grumpy, softened into charm.

'Look,' Jack said, as we again crossed the Seine, and I turned over my shoulder and saw the great Cathedral I had heard of all my life. Then we were in the Place St Michel, stopped still in the street, our taxi driver blocking all traffic without a care. He grew expansive and coaxed Jack's French along until we had made clear to him our destination. Later Jack told me he thought we were honeymooners and, presented with romance, a Frenchman always grows generous. I suppose we appeared so. I remember I wore a plaid woollen suit with a little brown velvet collar and a brown cloche hat, which would have passed for a 'going-away' suit of suitably provincial taste. I look back and see us very young, though in my mind at the time I regarded us both as old.

Our driver wound his way carefully down the narrow Rue de la Huchette and dropped us at the corner of the Rue Zacharie. Jack paid him, and probably over-tipped him, because he smiled gloriously under his little film-star moustache, and he shouted something gaily as he drove away. I suspect it had some reference to bed.

We followed our directions and found ourselves standing in a sylvanly quiet cobbled street, with shuttered shop fronts and the lights of one small café shining out on the rain. Before us was a narrow stuccoed building, with a broad double coachdoor and a narrower entranceway beside it, and on the first floor above, gently lighted windows behind a tiny iron balcony. There was a bell of the old pull kind, and in the light of a gas street-lamp I read, 'The Fishing Cat'. I pulled the brass knob and somewhere a pretty chime rang and in a moment there was a clatter of footsteps and a rattle of ancient latches behind the door. Then it opened and standing before me was a slender child in a blue smock, with red hair bound in a braid down her back, and the face of an Irish queen. She extended one small, confident hand.

'Cousin Justina? Monsieur Redpath? Do come in. Aunt May will be ready presently.' The accent was a delightful mix of Irish and French.

'Eithne?' I said.

'Eithne Maire O'Mordha,' she said firmly. She shook my hand and turned to Jack.

'How do you do?' he said solemnly. His eyes were full of laughter but he shook hands with great refinement. She looked so tiny next to him, and so in control. 'Aunt May is having difficulties with Alphonse,' she said, with a faintly cryptic smile.

Her cheeks were very red, and her narrow oval face, lit by that smile, glowed mysteriously. She wore the common blue cotton smock of French schoolchildren, thick white stockings and wooden clogs. The smock had a broad white collar tied with a black velvet ribbon that matched the ribbon binding her hair. A holy medal dangled from a heavy silver chain around her neck, and her fingers entwined it casually as she assessed us. Then, having concluded us apparently satisfactory, she led us through the door and into a tiny vestibule from which stairs led up to the first floor, and from which a planked door let into a room at the left. Beyond the door a steady rumbling and clanking emerged, broken by an occasional loud bang and a sharp exclamation in an angry and female voice. Eithne Maire O'Mordha carefully opened the door and poked her small head through into the room beyond. '*Chérie*?'

'Curse this devilish contrivance and curse old Gautier as well! What is it?'

'*C'est la cousine*.'

There was a silence, and then a muffled, 'Oh, good heavens!'

In an instant a figure emerged, clad in green overalls and smudged from head to foot in printer's ink and oil. Only the blond curls frothing over a red bandanna revealed the figure of my cousin May. Her small fingers opened slowly and dropped the spanner she was holding with a clang on the stone floor. Then she cried, 'Darlings!' and clutched me at once in an inky embrace. 'Oh, forgive me, I was *struggling* with the disreputable Alphonse,' she gestured towards the printing shop beyond the open door. Then she kissed me and kissed Jack as well, whom she had never seen before. Remembering that, perhaps, she drew back, and begged forgiveness, 'But it is so lovely, darlings,' and then kissed him again, and Jack, being a gentleman, kissed her back. Eithne Maire O'Mordha stood like a little metronome, eyes shifting solemnly from one to the other, and back to me.

May's flat, at the top of the stairs, was pretty and feminine with lace curtains at the windows, and flowered chintz furnishings and seemed at the moment quite out of keeping with its overall-clad owner. But May, I remembered, had always liked delicate things about her, the sweet scents and gentle textures of another era. May seated us on a low chaise before the hearth on which sat a pale-blue enamelled stove. She opened the stove door and riddled the fire and sent out a pleasant glow. Then, while we warmed ourselves, she disappeared into a bedroom to change. Eithne Maire O'Mordha sat solemnly on a footstool watching us. I smiled at her, and she smiled back and enquired candidly if Jack were my *mari (non)* or, if not that, my *amant (oui)* and seeming quite satisfied with the answer, amused herself by dragging a small sleeping terrier out of its bed by the hearth and showing it off to us. Jack rubbed the dog's ears to the delight of it and its mistress and I looked about the room. There were two walls of bookshelves, and the remaining walls, clad in delicately flowered paper, were hung with clusters of pictures; some photographs, but mostly paintings, and almost all of those, my own. I looked upon those early, Irish efforts with a clinical assessment and was surprised to find a good many holding up well. One or two I would have happily burned, however, and more than that number showed signs of physical decay, the result of my unschooled technique. Over the tiled hearth with its enamelled stove hung *Seabathers at Sandycove*, still better than anything else in the room, and much I had done after. To see it there was to meet an old friend in a strange city; I was filled with warmth and I took Jack's hand a felt serene and safe.

May came back into the room after a surprisingly short time, dressed now in a black skirt and flowing white blouse, tied at the chin with a soft black bow. Coupled with a neat bolero jacket and a wide-brimmed hat, that outfit comprised her daily uniform, except when she was assaulting Alphonse. Her fair hair was cropped at chin-length, and centre-parted, so that it fell in two thick clumps over her ears, with pleasant naivety. She looked older, her small sweet face highlighted with sharp inquisitive lines about mouth and eyes. She sat on the footstool beside Eithne, gathering her braided hair in her hands. She looked up to me, and to Jack.

'Well, Mr Redpath,' she said, 'will you speak for a generation?'

We stayed with May above The Fishing Cat printing press for three weeks, until early November when we found accommodation of our own. It was I who found our flat, in the Rue St Julien off the Rue Galande, three floors up and overlooking the walled churchyard of St Julien-le-Pauvre. It was a small and primitive establishment, but it was cheap, and since we intended staying only part of that winter in Paris, it seemed foolish to spend more. While I was finding it, Jack spent the days with May, planning out the structure of the book he had come there to write. In those three weeks, May Howie, with her sharp insight and natural editor's instinct, turned Jack gently and surely in the direction he must take, and the Jack Redpath that the world would know was born under the sign of The Fishing Cat.

The little flat comprised a single large room, containing a humble version of the enamelled stove that heated May's establishment, and a brass bedstead. There was an alcove with a gas-ring and oven, which with a deep ceramic sink and a wooden pantry-cupboard amounted to a kitchen. Sanitary facilities were a grim horror in the back court. I had not lived like this since war time and was not enchanted to resume such deprivations, but the conditions, if primitive, were fairly typical, at least within the financial limits I had set. A bathroom, likewise, was beyond expectations; the public baths, clinical and depressing, would have to do. Having made my arrangements in my stumbling French, with Mme Desmonde, the *concierge*, I set about the bleak room with scrub-brush and soap. I swept all the floors, bought cheap cotton rugs to partially cover them, polished the old brass bedstead, and flung out the mattress for fear of vermin, replacing it at painful expense. Cleaned and polished, the room had the barren air of a convent school dormitory; so much for *la vie Parisienne*.

But in its favour were blue window-boxes before its two windows that promised spring bulbs, and a view down into the sheltered green of St Julien-le-Pauvre's enclosing walls. Jack, on first seeing my creation, grinned gaily and ruefully and kissed my forehead. 'St Justina-la-pauvre,' he said. But we were very happy there.

Having approved of our new dwelling place, Jack brought home a stack of roughcut wood from a sawmill with which he constructed a solid, unmovable work table. He placed his old typewriter on top of it and was instantly at work, oblivious to any other practicalities of life. He did ensure that the cast-iron stove was working, and went out each morning at dawn and returned with a day's supply of fuel, wire-bound bundles of wood and a small sack of little pressed coaldust briquettes. Beyond that he left domestic arrangements to me; not because he expected a woman to do such things, but because he, alone, would not have thought to do them at all. He was accustomed to a bachelor existence, where laundry was the occasional shirt washed out in the kitchen sink, and food was something to be sought in bars and cafeterias when the day's work was done.

That was all very well in New York, with a more or less steady income from the short stories and newspaper articles, but here our situation was changed. Cafés, charming and companionable, were indeed a temptation against which we struggled all winter; how lovely always to leave the severe little room and find laughter and talk, wine and food, and warmth one was not paying for, as well. But cafés were expensive and our resources were scanty.

We had brought with us to Paris a modest sum of money, our joint combined fortunes, which, though clearly not enough to provide for an entire year, was still obliged to carry us a long way, since at present we had no income at all. The novel Jack started that winter was an orphan child; conceived under May Howie's influence, but without a financial backing, which she simply could not provide. There was neither commission nor any guarantee of publication. We had set out on a year-long gamble that would require very careful management were we not to end in destitution.

My immediate contribution was to learn in weeks the life-long skills of the French housewife; to shop with austerity and cook with ingenuity and waste not the tiniest scrap. Eithne Maire O'Mordha was my surprising guide and mentor. With a wicker basket over her arm and my hand firmly clutched in hers, she led me about the streets, from fishmonger to grocer to baker to butcher, examining all with a sharp, cynical eye, sniffing at cheese, squeezing cabbages, prodding the stiff feet of chickens hanging in feathered splendour in the poultry markets. From time to time she would step out into the street to assure me that Monsieur the Baker was a cheat and a liar or, conversely, that Mme the Poulterer could be trusted with one's life. In this way I soon built up a chain of suppliers who provided the necessities of life, all of great value, and at minimal cost. At home, I learned to cook all this bounty with growing culinary talent, remarkable considering that I never entered a kitchen with serious intent until I was a woman of twenty years.

Acknowledging too, man's need for higher bread, Eithne Maire introduced me to vendors of loftier wares; an art supply shop in the Place St Michel, where I could renew my charcoals, and paper, and dwindling tubes of oils, a stationer for Jack's typing paper (which he went through with lusty extravagance) and the second-hand bookstalls along the quays where for a very modest fee a wide range of reading in a variety of languages might be obtained. We even found a newspaper vendor who sold foreign language papers so that, when nostalgia struck us, we might read of our two native lands. Seeking perhaps another nostalgia, Eithne Maire regularly led me within the walls of St Séverin or St Julien, our neighbour, where I stood, faintly uneasy, while she, head veiled, went about lighting the candles for secret, eight-year-old needs.

Domestic achievements aside, my own career suffered an unsettlement in our move across the sea. Unlike Jack, I needed connections if I were to gain work, contacts through whom I might find commissions. But in Paris I knew no one other than May, whose social acquaintances were fellow writers and artists, with neither the funds to afford a portrait nor the self-importance to desire one. Millie Dobbs, with her deft business mind and her circle of society ladies, was far away. Of course she had not abandoned me, but wrote regularly with suggestions and encouragement and was already planning an exhibition of my Parisian efforts, upon my return, which at that time we still expected to be within the year. But none of that solved the problem of immediate financial need.

Still, I worked steadily, finding in the act of painting itself, the confidence to go on. Each afternoon, while Jack wrote, I took my easel and paints out into the city. I worked along the quays, wrapped against the damp cold, with the mournful persistent crying of crows and the tall trees for companionship. I painted buildings, animals, children, the barges on the Seine and their curtained windows and pots of homely geraniums. I went to the great markets of Les Halles, across the river, and painted fishes and fruits and the tough faces of farmers coming in from the country. I walked great distances with charcoals and sketchpad, making quick impressions of my new city to paint in the relative warmth of home. But wherever I went, it was faces that drew me, that made me halt among children in the Jardin du Luxembourg, or convivial artists on the Boul' Mich', take out my notebook and sketch. And it was in doing that, that I came upon a brief and lucrative new career.

Paris of 1926 was once more a city of tourists. The post-war years were ending. The after-shock of the great conflict had faded. Heroes lived on in dull jobs, limping from old wounds and hiding maimed faces by habit. Life resumed a normality of petty travail, politics descended to familiar corruption, economic, not military details dominated life. Rising inflation was beginning its acid corrosion of values, sapping a nation's strength and making good people lose heart under the guilty weight of their own apparent fecklessness. Though by merciful heaven we did not know it, the pre-war years had begun.

Into this impoverished world came the visitors from abroad; primarily, and most extravagantly, Americans, a lively young crowd, some of them men who had met France first as combatants on her soil, and were now returning for a peacetime glimpse, dragging in tow loud-voiced children and mid-western wives. They filled the boulevards and swamped the good expensive hotels that offered luxuries unbelievable in the Rue St Julien. They came to shop, to view art treasures and ecclesiastical wonders from their schooldays, and to venture into the famed and saucy night life of Paris, always more glamorous in legend than reality.

Winter was not their favourite time, the Parisian winter being particularly dreary, but even in winter they would turn up in the cafés of the Boulevard St Michel and the Rue Mouffetard, looking about them with their placid smiles and their good-natured curiosity, drinking their *apéritifs* and hoping to see *life*.

I was soon aware of them. If I sat down to sketch a child, or an old man sipping *café au lait* in the morning, I would find those placid smiles and curious eyes upon me. Fingers, discreetly shielded, pointed so that the mid-western wives and the restless children might take note. The sharp, twanging voices grew still. I was on stage.

Now at first I found this disconcerting; in spite of repeated charges by family and friends, I am not naturally extroverted. Moreover, I was rather aware of a lie going on; an artist I might be, but not a *French* artist, not that embodiment of the foreign and Bohemian that they sought. Solidly British, and wed to one American, and now in liaison with another, as a touch of Parisian colour

I was a sham. My initial honesty, when approached by one kindly and sun-browned lady, demanded I confess all. But two things stopped me; one, my respect for the human need of romance, and the other, my respect for our own need of money. So the lady from Peoria, or Des Moines, or Wilkes-Barre, went away happy with her Parisian portrait, and I went happily home to Jack with a handful of *francs*. We discussed it all very solemnly, and judiciously decided that the needs of our case absolved any sin of prostitution. As we celebrated in our favourite café, I remembered my ill-gained half-crown in Dublin long ago, and our tea with Persephone at the Shelbourne Hotel.

I was never, as it turned out, reduced to chalking pavements, though I have no doubt that I would have done it, had the need arisen. I had very little sense of propriety or shame; and I had massive faith in Jack. The pages of manuscript slowly piling up beside his typewriter were worthy enough Cause for me. Of course, I had to play my game carefully; my French was always terrible and still is; I am no linguist. So I countered that difficulty by more or less becoming a mute. I looked faintly uncomprehending at requests in English (genuinely uncomprehending at any in French) and managed in a form of sign language to communicate my willingness to sketch, and my price, which varied according to the café and its clientele. The general impression among the native population was that I was something outlandish, possibly White Russian, but the Americans, modestly unconfident of their own linguistic skills, passed me with flying colours. Mlle La Bohème featured no doubt in photograph albums from sea to shining sea.

Fortunately for me I possessed a gift for the quick sketch, honed by Mr Yeats, a ready collusion of hand and eye that produces a sure likeness in minutes. It is not a necessary ability for an artist, but an extremely useful one, and even years later, when through a widening circle of acquaintances I had gained a good clientele for proper portraiture, I still kept this little skill in my bag of tricks, insurance against a rainy day.

Rainy days there were many, by the way. Days when café windows steamed, when the little stove in our flat burned low and drearily under an inclement wind, when Eithne Maire came in with her school cape dripping and her red pigtail curling in ringlets at its end.

She had become my frequent companion. In spite of being eight years old she was a better friend than many adults, having the rare grace of speaking only when she had something intelligent to say. Often she did have things to say, however, having lived in a hothouse adult world all her life, forced like rhubarb into an early maturity. May treated her straightforwardly as another adult, having that honest way with children that many lively, childless women possess. She had neither the inclination, nor the time, to enforce a parental code of superior and inferior roles. Eithne, when not at school, or out doing the shopping, spent her time in the printshop reading proofs of works that solemn judges might forbid her own mother to see.

My arrival gave her yet another outlet for her ideas and her energies. On Saturday afternoons, after her morning at school with the Sisters, she joined me, following behind with my paintbox, and sat beside me as I painted, watching with sharp critical eyes. Or if I was sketching in cafés, she charmed the tourists so readily that often they begged that she be included in their sketch as a sort of talisman of Paris (the little Irish fraud). I did enjoy painting and sketching her; she had a remarkable face and an even more remarkable presence, so that upon entering any room she could create a silence of admiration.

She asked me about my children, in whom she was greatly interested, because by her reckoning they were her second cousins (I suppose they were) and she felt a proprietary affection for them. When I told her how I had to leave them behind in New York, she actually cried. Then she said she would be my daughter in Paris if that would help. I did not tell her that nothing would help, and in the end, anyhow, I was wrong. She became as close, indeed, as any daughter, before we split forever, and when we did I grieved over it with a mother's pain.

But that was long in the future, that cold wet winter, while I sketched in cafés and Jack Redpath wrote the long first draft of *The Virgin of the Somme*.

Midway through the winter, we left Paris for the north and the old battlefields of the Pas de Calais. We spent several weeks there: an eerie, sad time. Though some places had been extensively rebuilt, others lay yet in ruins, and in others the war had become a natural feature of the landscape. We found hay stored in the remnants of dugouts, pigs penned in with duck-boarding, and in a field near Béthune, an abandoned wheel-less Red Cross ambulance served as a chicken coop. The lines of the trenches were often clearly visible on the bare winter fields, zig zagging like some ancient hieroglyphic, under a heavy grey sky. There were bones everywhere.

At Easter Eithne joined us at St Omer, where we were then staying. She came bearing a list of suggestions from May on Jack's latest segment of manuscript, and sat at night in our small hotel, explaining them to Jack in her clear, concise voice. 'Perhaps you should write it,' he said, not entirely facetiously.

'No. I am only a parrot,' was her reply. But a very *clever* parrot, I thought.

From St Omer we travelled seaward, to Boulogne, where we met Hugo Melrose off the boat from Folkestone. He had deluged me with letters since our meeting in the autumn and begged politely to be allowed the promised visit to France. I was happy to accede, particularly while Eithne was with us. I had developed a sense of family in recent years; most of us do as we grow older; and I wanted these children to meet.

They made a funny pair, miniature Scottish gentleman and risqué young woman of the world, but they amused each other, and us, and I took them together on a pilgrimage to the graves of my two brothers buried in France. Sandy lay at Etaples, and I knew the place well, but Hugo's father, Douglas, had died near Lens and was buried nearby in a place I'd never seen. We went first to Etaples, to the military cemetery, now forbiddingly tidy and formal, rows of anonymous crosses that made a foolishness, somehow, of individual love. We found the one bare white cross, distinguished by his name and rank. Jack stood back with the children while I laid the flowers I had bought that morning on Sandy's grave. Sandy was mine, alone, a private grief.

At Lens, it was different. Hugo had brought with him a weight of thoughtful mourning for the father he had never known. He was old enough to assess his state, and his fatherless childhood, once a normality, now seemed a deprivation. I think meeting me sparked his awareness; I gave living proof that there had indeed once been a Melrose family, beyond his stiff scholastic Aunt Clare.

'What was he like?' Hugo asked, standing hands clasped behind him, beside Douglas' groomed military turf. His eyes stared blankly over the white monument into an incomprehensible past that to me was simply yesterday. I read the name, slowly, in silence, to buy time.

Captain Douglas Guthrie Melrose
Seaforth Highlanders

'Very proper,' I said slowly. 'Very decent and brave.' Hugo watched me carefully. I tried to forget the bombast and pomposity I had resented as a girl, and remembered the tired, doomed young man in the kitchens of Arradale.

'Did you like him?' Hugo asked, with gruelling honesty. I thought for a while.

'Yes. In the end, I liked him. I liked him very much.'

We walked round all the graveyard together. (There were so *many* graveyards, beside every roadside in that northern corner of France, clusters of headstones, gathered there like the rubble farmers heap up to clear the fields.) We held hands, all four of us, like a family; widower, and aunt, and fatherless children. We talked about the war, and why Jack was writing a book about it, and why I had sought out an eastern faith of pacifism, and why there must be no such war again. I wanted so to instil in these young minds something of what had happened in those quiet fields where my generation died.

But they were, for all their funny sophistications, children yet. I saw them grow restless, and we let them go, and they ran and shouted among the deserted headstones like a little boy and girl, while Jack and I sat alone on the perimeter wall.

'Do you think it's all right?' I said, watching them.

'Oh, let children play on *my* grave, when I lie dead,' said Jack. 'Only spare me the marching bands.' I smiled. We kissed, in the spring sunshine.

'I wish they were ours,' he said.

'They are.' I turned round on the wall, watching them. Jack lit a cigarette, and sat smoking it contentedly. For a while I didn't think about the war, or the past, or the present either and the fact that we were running out of money.

Eventually, I said, 'Wendell told me once that the war was all made by bankers and moneymen for their own purposes, and when it suited them, we'd have another.' I hoped he'd deny it. He stubbed out his cigarette irreverently on some Tommy's stone, and stood up, looking for the children, far off, framed against a lowering sky.

'He's probably right,' he said.

When we returned to Paris, with the book yet unfinished, our financial situation became desperate. I went back to my tourists in Montparnasse, but there was only the bones of a living to be made that way. Jack renewed old newspaper contacts, and did brief articles for the English language *Paris Tribune* and eventually was driven to lay the book aside and concentrate once more on the short stories that had always earned his bread. He found new markets; May published a trilogy of Ohio stories, in *The Fishing Cat*, and a longer effort about a military chaplain, on leave in London during the war, appeared in Ezra Pound's new *Exile* review. But those efforts took time and a great deal of work, as much as the novel itself. He would work all night on a story or an article, with frightening intensity, and then go out for firewood, come back, drink coffee and begin again, picking disconsolately at his manuscript, too tired to work and too tired to leave it alone. I knew it could not go on. Then, just when I had reconciled myself to the necessity of fleeing France in defeat, I found my footing at last.

It was Gertrude Stein who launched my career in Paris, though assuredly not deliberately. She had no great interest in me, though Jack was another matter. That was, I believe, the usual way of things. Jack bumped into her at Sylvia Beach's bookshop on the Rue de L'Odéon. We were regular visitors to Shakespeare and Company, making frequent use of the lending library, to which May Howie had introduced us, and vouched for our reliability. Miss Beach was a kind, hard-working American woman of about Clare's age, as sharply intelligent, though sweeter natured than Clare. She shepherded many lost artistic sheep, and understood artists' weaknesses and desires. From the day of our first visit, she made sure to always have at least one copy of each of Jack's two small volumes of verse on her shelves. He, in his honesty, doubted anyone ever opened either of them, in all the years we went there, but their presence was a gentle encouragement, a reminder in bad times that his belief in himself as a writer was not unfounded. I used to touch those two volumes for luck whenever I passed by the shelf. Shakespeare and Company was a sort of clearing house for the arts, particularly amongst the expatriate Americans of that day, many of whom used it as a convenient mailing address. Famous people from many countries passed through its doors, and rubbed shoulders among crowded shelves, and we met many, and a few even became friends. Miss Stein did not become a friend, but she was, even accidentally, a wonderful help.

Miss Beach introduced Miss Stein and Jack, as he was busy and edging his way around her solid self, and after a few words of explanation, she became quite ebullient. She was genuinely interested; she had read one of those two slim volumes of verse and a few of his stories. Besides, she liked young American writers with great promise, and I believe by then she had fallen out with Hemingway. Perhaps Jack appeared a replacement. In any event, we were invited for luncheon one Sunday in the spring.

We walked, on a lovely morning, through the Jardin du Luxembourg to her apartment on the Rue de Fleurus. The apartment was full of people when we arrived and, though some left, a good number joined us for a lunch which was quite proper and formal, surprising me. Miss Stein, immensely heavy and rather short, was very American, and not at all in the way of the Shippingham Pykes. I expected her to scorn conventions, and I suppose, aside from the luncheon, she did. She dressed oddly in flowing robes and wore her thick, rather wonderfull hair piled up like a peasant woman's. Her voice was gravelly and masculine and quite appealing, and she made jokes and dominated everyone's conversation, like a man. Her companion, Miss Toklas, was quite different, tall and angular and not at all raucous. She reminded me of Wendell's eldest sister, and I imagined her background was similar. Miss Stein revelled in her American ways, and unlike some other expatriates I met, made no attempt to be French.

She was quite taken with Jack. He had the proper combination of ability and humility to cast an aura of brilliance that would not outshine her own. She kept him beside her throughout the afternoon, solicitously enquiring of his opinion on all matters literary. Of course she was equally famed for her knowledge of art, and her apartment was hung with a masterly collection. Her one comment to me that I recall was on that theme: 'No,' (after some thought) 'I don't think there *will* be any great women artists.' With that, I was dismissed. Actually, I know she intended no harm, and might possibly not have even meant what she said; she liked creating argument, like flower arrangements. She was, like my sister Clare, what we called a 'stirrer'.

I wasn't much offended. In fact, I was relieved to be ushered out of her commanding and exhausting presence. I found myself in a room with Miss Toklas and two English society ladies discussing the weather. Reticent by nature, they indulged in the familiar exile's volubility that comes on all of us when we meet compatriots abroad. They were a generation older than me, and pleasantly indulgent on a sunny spring afternoon, drawing from me details of my past and my family and we were soon discussing Strathpeffer's Spa that they in their youth had also attended. By afternoon's end they had learned a lot about my past and enough of my present to know I was an artist, living with a struggling writer, and we were poor as church mice. I happily related our circumstances; our poverty was transitory and chosen and held no shame.

'Well, my dear,' the elder of the two ladies, a bony woman with iron grey marcelled waves, stood up, removing a notebook from her handbag, 'we shall have to do something, shan't we?' On the spot she offered me a commission to paint each of her three grandchildren, resident in Paris where her son lived with his French wife. I was to set the price, at whatever I chose.

It was, of course, an act of charity, but I was hardly about to stand on pride. It was a godsend; and it opened the door to so much more. Within weeks, I was approached by another lady, equally elegant, but French this time. She too had grandchildren and was not to be outdone. An Italian princess followed and a Russian émigré. I had become that wondrous thing, an object of fashion. 'That dear little thing who paints so sweetly.' Laugh if you please; it paid the bills.

The afternoon with Gertrude Stein was a turning point. I was working in portraiture once more. There was, albeit, an element of prostitution here as well; sentimental French *mamans* saw their children in a sugary light that vied with my natural realism. I consciously curbed my style and introduced chocolate box mannerisms that were not my own. (Alas for dear Richard Underwood, dead in the trenches. He would have excelled!) But these were minor adjustments, and if one is to live from the arts, rather than, like Miss Stein, drift lofty above them, there will be compromise.

Compromise or not, I was in work, and we had money, again, and always, for the rest of our years. Jack was able to return full time to his book, and we were even able to travel, and take pleasures, days out in the country, and occasional restaurant meals. When you have been poor, little pleasures, cups of coffee in cafés, or a Sunday outside the city, become very special and I never again lost my delight in such simple joys.

Having money, being once more free to take time from work and go out into the city and beyond, we began to have a social life, something we had lacked, but not really missed since we had first arrived in Paris. We went out to museums and galleries, went to the races, picnicked in the Bois de Boulogne, met with friends. Our friends were May's friends, at first; a healthy variety of students, artists, keepers of shops and hotels. There was nothing particularly Bohemian about her circle, though their politics were generally to the left, but in the mild, despairing way of unpolitical people. Occasionally, a fiery old Russian would come in to our favourite café in the Place St Michel, and rave about Stalin's betrayal of the revolution. He was colourful, but did not touch us deeply. Many of us who were young in the Great War sought our salvations beyond politics. I suppose I was one of them; I never trusted a politician or a general after the Somme.

I found, in Paris, a Baha'i community, like the one I had known in New York. They were the same gentle mix from all walks of life; one or two Persians in exile, the rest Europeans seeking a new peace. I went most weeks to read and talk with them, and at home, in privacy, I made the daily obligatory prayers. Sometimes I forgot. I was never a one for ritual; even the modest ritual of Baha'i. Jack, as always, found his spiritual sustenance over the old-fashioned zinc bar of a local hostelry.

I would find him afterwards, pleasantly mellow, over a stack of saucers, conversing with working men about working men's interests. It was not, perhaps, as people have later pictured Paris between the wars, the literary Paris of genius and revelry. There was, of course, a great deal of genius about (and a lot of nonsense as well) but it was about in bright secret pockets where serious people were working. It was *not* logically enough, making itself noisy in cafés.

Which is not to say that we knew no writers, or artists, or names that were then, or are now, famous. Of course we knew them; our world of foreign guests on Paris' generous doorstep was small and intertwined. But Jack was not a chatty writer; when he was working he did not want to talk about it; talk of work made him uneasy and unhappy, shaking his confidence which was mercurial and prone to great dives. The only writers he enjoyed were those who were really working also. You could tell them because they were alternatively ebullient or glum and never spoke about writing at all. They talked about the rent or the price of milk, or the vagaries of the *cocotte* of the previous night. That, in truth, was *la vie parisienne.*

Lest you find us totally boring, I will admit that Jack

did occasionally go off drinking with the likes of Robert McAlmon and Dan Steinberg, and on one occasion, he and Steinberg vanished for two whole days. They had fallen asleep after a session on a Seine barge (Jack was very fond of the barge folk; fellow gypsies) and were miles downriver of the city when their host and drinking companion remembered to wake them. They turned up, bleary and ragged, late on the third night, having made their way back to Paris more or less on foot. I was moderately, though not overtly, worried. Jack had a feline survival instinct and I expected he'd be all right.

Those occasions were all uniquely masculine; or attended by a different sort of woman than myself. I never cared for women who drank in public, and would not be one of them. Jack and I understood each other over that; and over a few other things that were the inevitable consequence of wine and the company of some of the women we knew in those days. Jack was in love with me, and in his heart he was always faithful; but tomcats are not lapdogs and never become so.

I did not much care for McAlmon; perhaps I did not know him well enough. Steinberg seemed a harmless drunk, but again, I hardly knew him. They were Jack's circle more than mine. And though he did, a few times, go back to Miss Stein's apartment on the Rue de Fleurus, I did not accompany him, which suited everybody best.

I suppose the most eminent, and the most enigmatic of our Parisian geniuses was Joyce, who we would occasionally glimpse in Miss Beach's bookshop, peering painfully at a book or magazine, an anachronistic, formal figure, very proper, old-fashioned Irish. He reminded me of a Trinity College lecturer who used to call on Eugenia and James for tea, and it was impossible to connect him with his extraordinary and puzzling writing. May gave us

Ulysses as a present. Jack spent all one night reading bits of it, staring, turning it over and looking at the cover, reading more and saying from time to time, 'Jesus *Christ*.' I never knew if that were awe or despair. It didn't stop him from getting thoroughly drunk with Joyce one evening, just the same.

There were others too; some I only recognized later, in their famous years, as earnest youngsters I had known in Paris. But they were the background to our lives, which like those of most people were made up of work, and modest play, and mundane details of shopping and cleaning and dealing with the *concierge*, who never accepted Jack's propensity for typing through the night. If we lived in a remarkable age, we were not aware at the time. The truth is, when one is in the centre of extraordinary events, they become ordinary. It is not the moments of genius one recognizes but little common-life things; Joyce singing quietly to himself amidst the shelves of Shakespeare and Company, or Hemingway sitting at a café table feeding pieces of brie cheese to the café cat.

I liked Hemingway; a big, clumsy man for whom, on first meeting, I felt an instant affection, which nothing in future years could abrogate. When I met him, he and his wife were no longer living together and there was a romantic involvement with another woman and he was unhappy. He made me think of Wendell when the first bright edge had dulled from a new romance. But I liked him better than Wendell; his sins were heated and awkward, not cold and precise. He didn't talk about any of that, naturally; nor did he talk about writing. He talked about skiing in the Austrian alps, desperately, as if skiing were a kind of salvation. We drank white wine and Jack listened because we were not talking about writing. We shared notes on bindings and argued about the best woods for skis and I told him how Michael and Sandy had made skis for all of us when there was nowhere to buy them closer than Norway. Some time in the late evening, while the café owner was rattling the metal shutters down, we all agreed we would ski together in Austria when another winter came.

We did, too, though not in Austria and not with Hemingway. We must have seen him again, but that night we talked about snow was the one occasion I remember clearly. Not long after, he left Paris, as many of that set were doing. Times were changing, and for us too. In the autumn of that year, a year from our arrival, Jack finished the final draft of his book about the war. Another year, almost, would pass before it would see print, but that was the last year of the life we had known, because upon the publication of *The Virgin of the Somme*, Jack Redpath met the entrancer called Fame.

That was the autumn we were meant to return to New York, but in the end we never did so. When the time came, we had little reason to go back. Jack had given up his apartment, as I had done with mine. He had no family and my family-by-marriage had no wish to see me, nor would they relent on the matter of my children. As for the children themselves, I had accepted that by then they had quite forgotten me, though this did not turn out to be the case. Of course I wrote regularly to them. I wrote every week of every year, fifty-two letters sent out into a void from which I expected no reply. I doubted even that my letters ever reached their destination, but ended, rather, in Margaret Pyke's wastebasket, their seals unbroken. Still, as an attempt to avoid such censorship, I framed my letters with great care, keeping them light and cheerful and as innocently impersonal as the letters of a school friend. Sometimes I enclosed extravagant little notes from Eithne (she felt very romantic about those New York waifs). Always, I signed merely 'Justina', making no claims that might give offence.

As for my friends in New York, I was in constant touch with Millie Dobbs, and from time to time sent paintings, which she displayed in her gallery to sell, or very often, bought herself. I used to wonder if she really cared for them or if they were destined for residency in the camphor-wood trunk. Mirza Hassan also wrote, weekly in quiet times, less often when business was rushed. He had bought another coffee house, and installed his brother-in-law, Mohammed, as manager. He told me about Khadija, and the American ways she was learning at school, and how much he missed the mountains of Scotland, and the greater mountains of his faraway home. He said I would visit Persia to find peace, which is just one of the prophetic things he would say, when there was no reason to imagine them coming true. It was his gift. His letters were affectionate, fatherly and wistful. I think he realized already I would never come back.

The third friend of my New York days with whom I never lost touch was Wendell's crippled sister, Grace Pyke. She wrote often, and promised she would come and visit me some time, which was a kind of dream in which we both indulged. She sent me photographs of the children, and detailed reports of their growth and progress; very honest, both the good and the bad told fairly; and half her return addresses were hospitals or convalescent homes.

As I have said before, I am of a generation where the written word was valid basis for relationship; letters and diaries bound us to our friends and our own pasts. We kept records of our lives, as second nature. Our hopes, loves and memories were all committed to paper, for our eyes, and those of the future. Thus we could be friends for life with an ocean between us; loving those we might never see again in the flesh, spiritual companions like the saints. It took effort and discipline, neither quality today much in vogue. But I ask you, what will you people do for history in years to come, when no one writes letters, or keeps a diary, and manuscripts vanish into baleful green-eyed gods?

So it was with regret, but no great sorrow, that we turned our backs on the New World that autumn, and set down our shallow roots in the Old. For if we had little reason to go, we had good reason to stay. May Howie was full of hopes for Jack's book, and involved herself at once in arranging New York and London publication. But such things took time, and in the meanwhile, our major income was my own. (I had, by then, developed a definite reputation for portraiture, but in Paris, not New York.) And when two particularly good commissions, plus a quick detective story for an American magazine, gave us an unexpected surplus, we indulged ourselves in an autumn journey to the Pyrenees.

It was a wonderful interlude. I had not been in mountain country for many years and I had not realized how much I had missed it. We stayed in the high garrison town of Mont Louis in the old province of the Cerdagne. We had travelled by rail, and electric railway, and at last like peasants, with packs on our backs from the station, for there was no way upwards but on foot or horse-cart. Jack had come to write, and I to paint, and I knew we could not have found a better place.

We stayed in an old plain mountain inn, frequented by *alpinistes*, with bare wooden floors, and old-fashioned fire-places, ablaze in the cold autumn nights. The tariff was remarkably reasonable. So much so that we stayed extra weeks, and even sent fare back for Eithne to join us during her autumn holiday.

The Pyrenean hill towns were extraordinarily primitive, in those not so *very* distant years. Few roads, few 'conveniences', a peasant life of harsh farming lived in a rich cultural isolation that had not yet met the self-conscious debasement of tourism. We were kindly welcomed and gracefully tolerated as a cheering piece of foreign colour. Around us men tended sheep and cattle, and women washed their linens at dawn in a pool below the windows of the inn. Peasant costumes were worn naturally, tattered and mended, the quiet bond of an old people. It was, of course, an artist's paradise, and though I have never been drawn to reproduce landscape (no matter how much I have loved it) I revelled in the smaller scenery of gabled village houses, working women with their laundry baskets, and spinning wheels, dogs, children, chickens, rough and endearing mule carts. There was so much to paint always; church processions, woodsmen working with ox-drawn logging wagons, lines of white Pyrenean cattle following their cowherds to the fields. I worked daily, in watercolour and in oils, carefully crating my finished paintings to be borne on a mulecart down the valley when the time came to return.

In the wooden-shuttered room at the inn, overlooking the village *place*, Jack worked peacefully unaware. His mind was not in the Pyrenees, but far off in Ohio. He was writing a new book, about his boyhood romance with Ellen Merryweather whose name he had loved and with whom he had ridden a freight train to New York. It was to be called *American Dreamers*, and in that ancient European setting he brought those uniquely American happenings to life. I think we would have stayed forever had the money not run out.

But before that occurred, Eithne came to stay. She came bounding off the train at la Cabanasse, in a grey striped smock and a wide-brimmed straw hat, trailing red ribbons. Her hair was plaited in two long red braids, bouncing on her shoulders. Over one arm she carried a wicker basket containing her clothing, a bread roll, some sausage and a bottle of wine; a rather grown-up selection, I thought at the time. She carried as well a buckled folder in which resided a long list of amendments and corrections for *The Virgin of the Somme*, to be dealt with by Jack.

'New York thinks you are wonderful,' she informed him, and added primly, 'London is not so certain.'

I took her basket and he lifted her on to the mulecart that had brought us down from Mont Louis. She was wearing wooden sabots, like the peasant children and but for her bright hair might have been one of them. For a fortnight she went everywhere with me, and everyone assumed she was our daughter, just as they assumed (and were not disillusioned) that we were husband and wife. They called us *les Américains,* because of Jack, and because Americans were much more exciting than *les Ecossais*. So Eithne became *la petite Américaine* or more often *la belle Américaine*, both to her annoyance, because she liked at the time to think of herself as French, and though she would admit to Irish she was *not* either British or a colonial. Like many stylish children, Eithne was something of a snob.

Jack and I took her up into the high mountains, foothills of the towering Carlitte. I had bought her alpine boots, and boys' corduroy trousers like those I wore myself, and she ran ahead through high meadows, tumbling in the autumn flowers like a puppy. I liked watching her revel in that masculine freedom I had been denied at her age. When the going got rough Jack carried her on his back.

He was tough and tireless, and skilful with campfires and forest shelters. We slept in mountain huts, when we could, because it was late autumn and bitterly cold at night, and each morning in the clear air snow lay dusted on the ground. We slept snuggled together, all three of us, in innocent warmth.

When we came down again, into the town, shepherd boys along the way turned to watch with respectful silence. Their eyes were on Eithne, with a haunting devotion, as if she were a holy statue to be carried through the streets. Jack walked behind with me, his arm across my shoulders. We were sun-browned and windswept and happy. He said, watching Eithne's red braids bouncing on her blue shirt, 'She does not know. She does not even imagine. What havoc she'll wreak!'

When we left Mont Louis, our host and hostess at the inn kissed us both on both cheeks, and together lifted Eithne on to the seat of the mulecart that would take us, our minimal luggage, and my crates of paintings down the valley to the rail station. We drank toasts of farewell in the wintry air, and I looked longingly back at the white tops of the mountains as we rode down the steep rough road.

'We'll come back in the winter,' Jack said.

'Oh, splendid,' I whispered, leaning back in the mule-cart, my eyes closed. 'We'll take Eithne again, and Hugo as well, if Wilhemina will let him come, and we'll ski. We'll all ski.' I was joyfully excited thinking of it, and the beautiful snowfields that would cover the meadows and forests where we had climbed. But though we did come back, and we did ski, it was not this winter, but another, over a year later, in 1929, and we stayed in the busy centre of *les sports d'hiver* at Font-Romeu.

When we arrived back at our little flat on the Rue St Julien winter was there, awaiting us, not the beautiful sun and snow winter of the Pyrenees, but the Parisian winter of rain, and cold, and smoking recalcitrant fires. It was damp in the flat, and musty smelling and rats had got into the kitchen and gnawed things. I hated it suddenly, and hated the city and I daresay Jack felt the same, because he stamped around getting in my way as I tidied up, and grumbling about the book, and May Howie's caustic editing, and everything else. We snapped at each other and argued for half a day, as if we had left our love behind in the high mountains, and then, quite suddenly, realizing what we were doing, burst out laughing, and made up over a bottle of wine.

That night, as we lay in each other's arms, he suddenly whispered, 'I love you so much. I wish I had met *you* when I was seventeen.'

'We'd have hated each other,' I said, laughing comfortably against his shoulder, my face against the hollow of his throat. But he didn't laugh.

'We'd have had so many more years,' he said. He said it with such a weight of misery, as if we were to part forever in the morning, that the words became terrible, and, after he had gone to sleep, I wept in the darkness, unable to get them from my mind.

But, of course, we did not part in the morning, for any more than the few minutes required to get firewood and fresh eggs and milk, and by mid-morning, when May came in, Jack was working, and I was stretching a canvas, and both of us had forgotten what was said.

May looked very pretty and very proper, in her 'business' suit, the black bolero jacket and black skirt, and the white blouse with its big floppy black silk bow. She stood in the middle of the room, holding aloft an envelope, with a transatlantic postmark, and that tired look of a thing that's come a long way. It was open, but she handed it to Jack, even though it was addressed to her. He looked at her, uneasily, with the betraying nervousness that never left him when he was aware of his work under judgement. But she just stood smiling her wry, sharp smile.

'Well, *I've* read it, so *you* might as well.' It took an impossibly long time for him to fumble out the letter, unfold it, read it, maddeningly expressionless while he did.

'Oh Jack, please . . .' I cried, unable to bear the tension.

But he suddenly flung it up in the air, and grabbed May, hugging her and swinging her around in a joyous circle, until he set her down in the middle of the room, and boldly kissed her mouth. She drew back, a little astonished, and slightly ruffled, like a cat that had been too presumptuously handled.

I burst out laughing at her sudden loss of dignity, and at his equally sudden affection towards a woman whose editorial judgements he had been cursing all the day before.

'Well, I'm glad you're pleased,' she said primly, straightening her bow, and he responded by laughing and swinging her around the room again. By then, realizing it was the only way I was to learn anything, I collected the letter from the floor and read that B. W. Huebsch of New York was to publish *The Virgin of the Somme.*

So taken were we all with this joyous news that we were half-way through a bottle of celebratory wine when May, looking shocked, suddenly exclaimed, 'Oh Justina, how could I have forgotten. There was a letter last week for you.' She ran out at once, without finishing her wine, and returned a few minutes later from her own flat on the Rue Zacharie.

The letter, with a New York postmark, like Jack's, was addressed neatly and correctly, in a gracefully inked female hand. I think I knew at once that that unfamiliar writing was that of Margaret Pyke, and I tore open the envelope in a panic. I had always dreaded such a letter, assuming as I must that Wendell or his wife would only communicate with me on an issue of great seriousness. And such an issue could only mean my children.

I read the first lines without drawing a breath, and then suddenly relaxed, a little astonished, and much relieved, sitting down, and slowly unfolding the other pages tucked within the first. There were two letters. The first was, indeed, from Margaret Pyke. It was brief and formal and astounding.

My dearest Justina,

Eleanor has greatly appreciated your many letters over the year. I think they give her, at present, a source of happiness that is otherwise absent. I do not wish to go into detail, but there have been difficult matters at home, concerning myself and Eleanor's father. In the light of these unfortunate events, and ensuing tensions, I have decided that it would perhaps be wise to allow Eleanor to begin a correspondence. Naturally this should be limited by discretion. Forgive this intrusion, but, as I always tried to make clear, my *only* concern is the welfare of the children themselves.

Yours with sincerity,
Margaret Pyke

Still pondering that, I carefully spread out the second sheet on my knee. It was printed, in a young child's awkward, deliberate hand, and ran the full length of the page.

18 Gramercy Park
3 November 1927

Dear Justina,

Mommy said I can write to you now. I'm glad because I like all your letters so much and I was always afraid you would stop writing them because I didn't answer. Daddy said I was too little to write letters. Daddy always says I am too little for everything. Wendell says so too, but he's *always* bossing me.

I go to school. I like it very much, except when the big girls take all the chairs first at lunch. I got a gold star in English and a silver star in Art. I should have gotten a *gold* star in Art, but the teacher is grouchy and makes us draw stupid things like bananas and apples, all day. At home I paint horses. On Saturday I ride a horse in Central Park. Do you have a horse in Paris?

Wendell goes to school too. He hates his school. The boys all fight. Sometimes he cries but I don't tell Mommy because he says he'll hit me.

I still have your brush. It's my favourite brush even though it's not very hairy any more. I keep it in my special box. Please give my love to Eithne Maire O'Mordha.

Love,
Ellie Clare Pyke

PS Here are two pictures I painted. The dog's name is Ned. The boy's name is Wendell.

I read the letter twice, laughing happily as I did so. Then I handed it, with a smile, to Jack, and I unfolded the two paintings she had stuffed into the envelope with the letter.

I laid them carefully on my knee, one on top of the other, and gently smoothed out the cruel creases of their long journey. It always touched me so how children will struggle for hours over a drawing and then fold it in brutal innocence. The top painting, undoubtedly her favourite since she had placed it in the choice position, was of the family poodle, a small, lively black creature that had been in the house when I first arrived, and was bearing up remarkably under the onslaught of many canine years. Ellie had painted him on a red rug, with his red tongue lolling happily; a difficult pose, strikingly well executed by a hand that was hard to imagine as that of a child.

'Oh Jack, look,' I whispered, lifting the painting so that he might see it. Then I saw underneath, her second, less favoured offering, and I was struck silent, in awe. The single most amazing feature was, I suppose, its simple maturity. It was so much older, so much more powerful, more confident, than the words of the letter that it seemed impossible that both were the work of the same hand. This, then, must be the feature of prodigy; a single vaulting leap forward of intelligence and ability, in one narrow field, so that a mere child, gauche and ordinary in every other aspect, carries, like a high banner, one beautiful adult talent.

On the creased and battered paper spread out on my skirt was a face; the face of my son, and haunted by the mystery of family resemblance, the face also of my brother Sandy, Sandy as a child, the companion of my girlhood. And all drawn by a hand that did not exist in this world until he was gone from it. How could she so beautifully portray what she had never seen? I shook my head silently and handed the second painting to Jack, and to May.

'Oh dear God, it's so like Sandy,' she said.

'It's Wendell,' I answered. I stood up and left them exclaiming over it, and walked to the window and looked out and down into the green of the churchyard of St Julien-le-Pauvre. I stood silent, remembering. Temple House and the high bedroom in which I was imprisoned, until my uncle brought his wonderful gift. Was this then what James Howie saw there, thirty years before?

22

Merrion Square
3 January 1933

Dear Justina,

I have no greater pleasure than in sending you this, the first copy off the presses of *A Pyrenean Autumn*. I think you will agree the quality of production is superb and the colour reproduction excellent. I must apologize for not sending it sooner, it has been in my hands since London, but the past week has been hectic.

Father's tests were completed yesterday. It is, as we expected, a cancer. We are not telling him, though I imagine he knows well enough. He is old and ready to leave. I will stay here now until the time comes.

There is much enthusiasm in New York; the combination of Jack's name (and skill of course!) and your lovely illustrations has proved magical. (Though one prim lady in a house that shall be nameless informed me that the whole would be more palatable if you and the gentleman were actually married! Can you imagine?) Still, against such stern odds, I yet have hopes of a good publication. I have contacted Miss Dobbs about the possibility of a simultaneous exhibition on the lines of that upcoming in London. Oh, we are well on our way, my little ones.

I spoke to Kate, briefly, by telephone when we received the news about Father. She is still playing the peasant in Sligo, so the telephone was a borrowed one and our conversation difficult. She is always full of mystery and portent. Yes, she would come if 'they' could be guaranteed to leave her alone. She imagines herself the centre of conspiracy and plot, but I suspect de Valera has other things to worry over, more important than Kate O'Mordha and her three milk cows.

I have informed the Sisters of the situation, so that I might take Eithne from her school in time to bid her grandfather safe journey. I think there is no terrible hurry; those as old as Father resist this illness sternly; it is the young that it burns up like a flame. When the time comes, I will be most glad of your company, but I have no wish to interfere unnecessarily either with your work, or Jack's. Perhaps when you are in London for the exhibition, we will know more accurately.

Please tell Jack that my curiosity is boundless and as his 'agent' I surely am entitled to see just a few early pages?

I must go, darling. I hear Papa calling, thumping his old stick against the banister like a shillelagh . . . he's apt to come rumbling down the corridor in that chair in another moment, and his driving is as bad as ever, poor dear!

Give my best love to Eithne (I do *hope* she's not too much trouble to you), and if you are writing to Ellie, please let her know that both I, and Papa, *adored* her Christmas drawings and they are all framed and hung in pride of place (second only to her mother's!) Oh, I do *wish* those fools would allow that child some training! If only Grace were still there . . .

Love to all
May Howie

PS: Regards to Mme Desmonde, Coco, Mlle the Magdalene, Marie and my beloved Alphonse. M.

The book itself was wrapped separately, within the package that had contained May's letter, and I paused, looking down on the smooth brown paper. I felt I should wait for Jack, but he'd gone walking along the quays to think, and might be back soon, but might as well end up in a cheerful café and not be back for a very long while. I shrugged and, a little guiltily, tore open the paper. I could not resist. The dust-jacket was pale green and decorated with a small pen and ink sketch of my favourite view of Mont Louis, looking down from the high meadows, on to the citadel. Underneath was printed in slender, graceful lettering:

A Pyrenean Autumn
Essays on a Mountain Journey
by

Jack Redpath
with illustrations in colour by
Justina Bride Melrose
Constable and Company Ltd

I looked upon it lovingly as it lay in its brown paper on my knee, like an infant in its shawl. I traced my finger from his name printed there, to mine, feeling sentimental and foolish. People speak of a book as being like a child to an author, and although I have often dismissed the comparison I did know what they meant. This was the fruit of our union, and the only child our love would know.

That Jack and I should be now launching ourselves as author and illustrator of a travel book was not something we would ever have thought of on our own, and hardly in the natural course of either of our careers. The project, from conception to final publication, was entirely the invention of May Howie, and proved, like so many products of her agile mind, an excellent choice. By the time of its appearance, in January of 1933, Jack had two major novels in print. The first, the war novel he had come to Paris to write, appeared in 1928 in London, as *The Virgin of the Somme*, and half a year later, in New York. It had been reprinted seven times, in both countries, by the time Jack's second offering was published in 1930. That was, of course, *American Dreamers*, a lovely book which I adored, preferring it to the first, actually. I have always found it difficult to read about the war. Oddly, reading *American Dreamers* also brought the war to mind, for me, but only because its rich detail of his childhood in Ohio echoed the stories he told as we lay under fire in the farmhouse of Dernancourt. Reading his work opened a window to his youth, and curiously a window to his first marriage, which he never discussed. I found myself half jealous over the young stranger who had courted Ellen Merryweather (Mary Holloway in the book), but then, perhaps I was beguiled by fiction. After all, if Ellen Merryweather was as enchanting as he portrayed her, why then, did he drink?

Having produced these two extremely disparate books, Jack fell into a sudden trough of despair. Critical acclaim is a two-edged sword. Both his previous works had been well received, both had earned money. From a little known short-story writer, with an audience of the New York literati, he had blossomed into that wondrous thing, the 'first novelist'. Never mind that he'd earned his living from the written word for years, he was, in the literary world, a bride. With the second novel the marriage was consummated; he was a proven writer, not a single-book phenomenon. But the honeymoon ended there. Words like 'great promise', once so flattering, now burgeoned threat. With what might the promise be fulfilled?

Jack's confidence, never strong, began to fail. He had no answer to that question. Like many creative people, he was not fully in control of the talent he possessed. It drove him; he did not direct it, and had little idea where it was headed. He struggled with themes, rejected them, re-engaged them, and floundered. He had grown afraid of his own power. It was a sad and difficult time. We went off to Font-Romeu, in February of 1931, and spent weeks there skiing and climbing and Jack did no work at all. He became instead fanatically involved in improving his skill on his skis, as if that was all that mattered. He got terribly good. I had been his teacher, once, as Michael had been mine, but now he far surpassed me. I would have enjoyed it all more had there been paper in his typewriter, or indeed were the typewriter upon his desk in our rooms, not lying in its case on the floor. I was at a loss; I daren't question, nor attempt to direct him. On the subject of writing, we were strangers.

As happened more times in my life than I could ever be entitled to, my rescue (and Jack's) came in the form of my cousin May. Having the sensitivity to know that something was wrong, and the sagacity not to mention it, May sent us instead, in the fourth week of our absence, a message of casual suggestion. 'A friend' (May was a mistress of the creation of fictitious and useful 'friends') had been admiring my collection of oils and watercolours of Mont Louis, made during our first autumn journey there in 1927, and residing, like much of my *oeuvre* in stacked heaps in May's accommodating printing house. 'Would they not make a splendid foundation for a book?' questioned the encouraging friend. 'Of course a text would be necessary?' (The friend was apparently unaware of Jack.) Prompted by these observations May had spoken casually with acquaintances and colleagues, and, as easily as a plum falling from a tree, what should appear but a publishing house eager for just such a book. Of course, May knew, we were *far* too busy, but wouldn't it be fun? The rest of her letter dealt with the pregnancy of Coco her wire-haired terrier, and books were not mentioned again. Oh, the tongue of the Irish. I left the letter lying around our rooms for three days before Jack noticed it, read it, and leapt upon the idea like Coco upon a rat.

We returned to Paris a fortnight later, with three of the episodic essays already complete. It was Jack's salvation; work that was virtually journalism, that asked nothing of him that he doubted he could do, and let his tired mind rest.

The project, once begun, expanded healthily. I sorted drawings and paintings; we spent long nights reminiscing over our first Pyrenean adventure, reminding Eithne, now a much more grown up young lady, of her childish idyll there. It was a good time, Jack worked steadily, I myself glimpsed the new world of the illustrator, and we were very happy. I owed it all to May and was intensely grateful, knowing that this proposition did not, as she maintained, fall into her lap, but that she had worked hard for it, gone out doggedly and made it happen, while we disported ourselves in the snow.

On the day of its completion, Jack rolled the final sheet from his typewriter, and without a pause, slipped a fresh sheet in and began the opening passages of *I Dreamed I saw Joe Hill.* He was cured. In this, his third novel, he returned again to boyhood scenes, and to the Pennsylvania coal mines where, for a brief spell of political youth, he had worked with the radical IWW. It was his broadest and most demanding canvas and he set about it with confidence and command. But it was very hard work, and he had, now, been with it almost a year. He was difficult, moody, and occasionally drunk. I slipped in and out of his workroom bringing coffee and fresh ashtrays, and not speaking a word. I cooked for us, and cleaned for us, and when there was time, I painted. My feminist granddaughter would have been appalled, but feminism meant different things to us then. Besides, I loved him dearly and believed in him utterly. For two beyond the bonds of holy matrimony, I think we did rather well.

I was still sitting holding the book when Eithne came in from school. We were staying in May's flat, in the Rue Zacharie, while she was in Ireland, since there was hardly room in our own for Eithne, Coco, and the business of The Fishing Cat which I was meant to be overseeing. She came in with the comfortable casualness of a child in her own home, flinging down her books on the table and her cloak in a heap on the floor. She saw May's envelope on the table and cried at once, 'Oh, a letter from Ellie at last.' I shook my head.

'No. It was from May. And there's this.' I lifted the book and showed it to her, and she sprang upon it with a delighted cry, that just missed covering her disappointment. Her attachment, at great distance, to my daughter and son was genuine and Ellie's increasingly long silences deeply distressed her, though I doubted as much as they distressed me.

'Oh, it's come,' she cried. 'It's beautiful.' She hugged and kissed me. 'Oh, Jack will be *so* happy.' She said the last in a shy breathless voice.

Eithne was fifteen and tremulously romantic, and I knew she was enamoured of Jack. She had grown tongue-tied in his presence and would no longer let him treat her as a daughter. It was an innocently hurtful defection, and I could not convince him that its cause was the flattery of a new kind of love. They walked funny awkward circles around each other, in painful silence.

I made her tea while she pored over the book, and when I came into May's pretty front room with the tray, she rose and took it from me and set the tea things out on the table for me. Then she hugged me and kissed me again and said again, 'It's a beautiful book. The most beautiful ever.' I saw us in the mirror above May's writing desk, startled, as always that her reflection was taller than mine.

Taller, slimmer, infinitely more beautiful; I gave the reflection a rueful smile. Somehow, I had not realized until I saw us standing together, that her womanhood could only be won at the price of my ageing. At Christmas I had passed my fortieth birthday; I was growing old. We all were. May, Kate, Clare; Clare was forty-seven. Even

Jack was growing grey, and in the way of men, more handsome for it. I was not grey yet, but I was changed. There were lines on my face, and little stubborn sags beneath my eyes and under my chin. When we are young we are sometimes enamoured with the vision of ourselves grown old, our faces taut and distinguished, pared down from youthful naïvety into sharp true lines of experience. The reality is different. The lines of age fall in all the wrong places. Flesh sags and weakens, the body, however well used, becomes lumpen and heavy. Age flatters no one, certainly no woman. It did not much distress me. I had never been a beauty like Kate or Clare and I had almost always been happier than either of them.

Eithne was a beauty. Neither Clare nor Kate, in the bloom of their youth could have matched her. Her beauty came not from Quigley or Howie lines, but from that handsome rogue Padraic, her father. Time and again, I would look upon her and see his irksome irresistible face, all fire and mischief. Eleven years dead and gone from our lives; he had left us, yet, an inheritance.

She was tall, like he was, and moved with the same theatrical grace. Her face was long and narrow, her eyes darkly brown, the mouth sensual and restless. Her red hair, no longer in girlish plaits, was yet worn long, and wound about her head like that of her passionate mother; an anachronism that suited her exquisitely. As you might imagine, she was not without admirers.

Chief among them at present was Jean-Michel Bujold, the son of May's assistant in the printing house, the widowed Marie. He was seventeen, a dark, intense lad with the unnerving habit of watching Eithne as she moved about the room, the way a cat watches a bird. I did not like him, and was glad that she rejected his attentions. Her reasons were purely political: 'Oh, he is *very* handsome. But a communist, an atheist! I can't possibly marry him.' Dear Eithne, yet then the good convent girl. I wondered often what the future would hold for her. Not Jean-Michel, that was certain. I could not imagine her married. I envisioned her in the theatre like her father. Eithne, however, had determined to be a writer, like Jack. She spent long hours alone, dreamily closeted with notebook and pencil, and when she was not writing, she was reading. She read avidly, and the most extraordinary books. She read all of Jack's, of course, in manuscript form, and her criticism, schooled by May no doubt, was sharp and direct. Only lately, in her new romanticism, she had lost that wise cutting edge.

'I shall read it again and again,' she whispered, turning the book over and over in her hands.

'Oh, it's hardly worth that,' I said. But she sat smiling at the green dust-jacket.

Then she looked up and, seeing May's letter, she said, 'Isn't it strange that we've not heard from Ellie?'

'Oh, not really,' I said, as calmly as I could.

'Supposing something has happened?' she pursued, unnerving me.

'*What* could have happened?' I said, and made myself noisily busy, raking out the fire in the stove. Eithne sat looking with wide eyes at the wall.

'Well, something might have happened!' There was a faint vicarious excitement in her voice. At times she was still very young. 'Perhaps she's been kidnapped!'

'Eithne!'

'Sorry.' There was a pause, her eyes downcast, and then, with urgency, 'But just suppose she was . . . I mean she hasn't written for weeks! She might be anywhere, or even . . .' Large and theatrical tears were welling in those huge brown eyes. I was never sure with Eithne; the depths of her were quite unplumbed. The Lindbergh kidnapping had caught her exotic imagination and for a while she walked in her sleep, or woke screaming with nightmares about men come to snatch her away.

'I think more likely,' I said, 'she's just a very lazy little girl.' I straightened up from the stove, my hand against my stiff back, my eyes on the painting over the tiled hearth, *Seabathers at Sandycove*, and stood like that until Eithne got the message and left the subject alone. The truth was that Ellie was *not* a lazy little girl, only a very unhappy one. Her long silences terrified me in ways Eithne could not imagine.

For five years, since the arrival of her first, childish letter, and her two wonderful paintings, I had been in constant correspondence with my daughter Ellie Pyke. Once the parental ban on our communication was lifted, I was the happy recipient of a heady flood of letters. She was an open, loving generous child who felt happiness, and sorrow, acutely. She had no restraint. Everything that happened in her life, from the loss of a favourite marble to the death of a relative, was poured with equal passion into her weekly recitals. I became a sort of long distance diary; I often wondered how she pictured me, or really *who* she thought me to be. It didn't matter. I was a ready ear and a faithful voice, and glad enough to be both. Through those letters I gained a doorway into her life. In the written word I watched her growing up, and with the written word I made, cautiously enough, to guide her, and even more cautiously, her brother as well.

Wendell also wrote, monthly, short, precisely scripted letters of formal duty. Not that anyone *told* him to write; permission was granted both my children, but hardly encouragement. The duty he felt, like all the disciplines of his life, came from within. He knew fully who I was, and in his careful apportionment of rights, apportioned me a share of his time. I make him sound cold, which is unfair. He was not cold, but he was cautious. Both he and his sister had seen already much misery caused by love. Her response was to plunge into the full stream of her emotions; swim or drown, it did not matter. His was to hover always longingly on the bank. He had been touched, like my brother Douglas and his solemn young son Hugo, with that dank Melrose reserve. He would serve and respect, with honour and justice. He would give generously of time, labour, whatever material possessions were his. But he would give scantily of love.

Wendell's restraints were made up doubly by Ellie's headstrong revelations. Nothing, no matter how private, was too private to be told to me. I learned things I was never meant to know. Ellie's letters were uncensored and, moreover, surely unread. I respected Margaret Pyke for allowing my daughter that honourable freedom, even as I pitied her. My husband had not changed, and his liaisons grew uglier and more foolish as he grew older. Nor had he the sense or discretion to keep his behaviour secret from his little girl. She was a wise child, getting to know her own father. In the last year, things had grown markedly worse. Ellie's letters were filled with the misery of a child in a tottering home; fear, guilt, fantasies of escape. Twice she begged me to send her fare so that she might run away to Paris to live with me. These were not easy letters to read, and harder still to answer. But answer I must. I was her lifeline. I knew that, even before Grace Pyke wrote to tell me.

Grace's letter, the last I ever received from her, arrived in September. It was less a letter than a will and testament, containing, as it did, things meant to be read by a survivor, when the hand that had written them was dead.

It was sent from a convalescent home in Saratoga Springs, New York, which was where she died, a handful of days later. I have it still.

My very dear Justina,

This is going to be a bit tricky. My jailers have forbidden me to read or write letters and I've been obliged to beg these sheets of paper from a fellow inmate. (Forgive the revolting design; beggars can't be choosy.) I'm meant to be 'saving my strength'. For *what*? in the name of God. Oh dearest, I am so angry with it all. Sometimes I could weep for trying so hard to breathe . . . They all come up solemnly at the weekends and cluck their tongues in the corner. They say I must *try* harder. That I've 'lost the will to live'. Such nonsense. I've lost the *ability*.

Never mind, darling. I watch the birds, and the squirrels. It is a very pretty place. I would not have chosen any other.

I don't honestly think I'll be able to write again. So what needs to be said must be said now. Please forgive me that I have not the time to temper the truth with a few compassionate lies. That is a luxury that is beyond us both.

As you are likely aware, things are all wrong between my brother and Margaret. He is incorrigible; a coarse, selfish man who yet thinks himself a gentleman. I have lost all pity for him. He merely disgusts me. As for herself, though she reaps where she sowed, I am sorry. She was fooled, and she was not the first. She has been good to the children, and heroic to him. I wish her happiness and doubt she will see it. But they are adults and must make their own way. It is the children that are my concern. They are very, very unhappy. Oh dearest, those are the hardest words I have ever written. I write them now because you are strong, and only you, and your strength can save them. I have tried and failed and now I must leave them anyhow.

Wendell gives me most hope. He is a fine boy, with all the best instincts. It is remarkable how resilient is decency in a child. He will bear scars, but will, I think, survive them, and rise above all of this. Keep writing to him. He is proud of you in a secret shy way. You touch the deepest, best part of him, just as you did with his father.

Ellie is very much otherwise. She is a very difficult child, rebellious, angry, tearful, even violent. I worry about her all the time. If only, only I could have persuaded them to let her study art; there, alone, lies her happiness, and an outlet for all those troubled passions. If only I could get her to you. She is a bird in a cage, as you were when you were here. But unlike you she has never known freedom. She batters her wings against nothing and does not even comprehend the *purpose* of air.

Oh Justina, forgive me this terrible legacy. But I could not leave without you knowing, though it will be a terrible impotent knowledge. It is for the love of them.

There now, I've done it. It wasn't even that tiring. I shall make this ready to mail, and then I shall sit here, by the lake, until they come for us, and if I am lucky, they won't come until very, very late. I think of you both often, my two wild birds.

All my love
Grace Pyke

The formal announcement of her death arrived a few days later. A few more days passed and I received an anguished letter from Ellie.

I hate God. I hate Him. He took away my Auntie Grace. I prayed and prayed and he took her anyhow.

Her awful faith in a malevolent deity reminded me of Geoffrey Melrose, and though I answered with an attempt to ease her bitter mind, I doubt I succeeded any better than with him. Since that letter, in September, I had heard nothing at all.

When I turned round, Eithne was still sitting at the kitchen table, thoughtfully removing and then re-siting the hairpins that secured her long red braid. All the while her eyes were on May's letter, with unrestrained curiosity. She slipped the last hairpin into place, checked the result with two quick pats of the coiled hair, and said, 'Is May coming home?' She still looked pointedly at the letter and I put it in the pocket of my smock.

'No. Not yet.' I thrust both hands into my pockets and

leaned thoughtfully against the table. 'I think we'll all go to Ireland, after London,' I said, casually. Eithne nodded, knowingly adult.

'Grandfather's dying,' she said.

The exhibition of my drawings and paintings of the Pyrenees opened in London in the last week of January, to coincide with the publication of *A Pyrenean Autumn*. It was my first one-woman show, and Millie Dobbs, my patron and friend, came from New York to attend. She arrived on the *Mauretania*, a fortnight before we came over from Paris, to oversee the arrangement of the work I had shipped in advance. When we reached London, she was well ensconced at Claridges, and we went at once to see her there.

She was quite unchanged. The faint lines that had been about her eyes and mouth when we met had neither deepened nor grown in number. The soft brown hair, still worn in an old fashioned bun, faded so imperceptibly into grey that I cannot ever recall the change. Her wide blue short-sighted eyes remained as dewy as a girl's, and her smile endured; wise, cynical and loving, all at once.

When she opened the door of her suite of rooms she was wearing a gauzy, lacy dress decorated with strings of pearls, the textures and colours as luminous as the sea. She peered just for a moment through her thick lenses at Jack and me standing there and then, recognizing us, extended her lacy arms to us both

'Jack darling, didn't I always *say* you'd be famous,' she said, kissing his cheek, rather primly, as if the words were a reproof for his ever doubting her prediction. She turned to me, 'And my little dreamer, haven't you shown them all.' She was as proud of me as a mother. She said, 'Come in, come in. I'll order tea. This is a *wonderful* hotel and they do a marvellous tea.' She seemed immensely at home there and the staff all seemed to know her intimately, as if she had stayed many times. She turned back into the room, but just as we made to follow her, she suddenly stopped. 'You do know that I've brought a friend?' she said. For a wild moment, I thought she meant a man, and was for some reason quite resentful. But as we entered the sitting room of the suite, a strange young girl rose to greet us.

She was quite tall, and slender, like Eithne, and she appeared about Eithne's age, if not a little older. But her skin was as dark creamy brown as Eithne's was rosy-fair, and her hair was black and worn parted in the centre and drawn back in a shining braid that flicked a glossy tail about her hips. Her eyes were so dark that pupil and iris mingled in one black pool. She reached a confident hand to welcome us, and said in a clear American voice, 'Hello, how nice to see you again.' I stood bewildered.

'You remember Khadija, surely?' said Millie Dobbs.

It was Khadija Abbas, Hassan's eldest daughter, who I had last seen as a placid eight-year-old playing in her father's bakery on Washington Street.

Time, and the benefits of her father's increasing wealth, had transformed that Eastern child into a well-schooled young American lady, preparing to study sciences at Barnard; the epitome of the immigrant dream. Still, despite her perfect American English, her expensive Western clothes, her modern female confidence, something yet clung to her of that other world. When she laughed, I heard Fatima's quick joyous laughter about the coffee house, and when she was silent I saw in her eyes her father's mountain serenity, and just occasionally, when mischievous, she would flash her father's white brigand's smile.

But she was rarely mischievous. Her placidity remained, and her gentleness, the same child who had so kindly tended my little son. I was not surprised that Millie had chosen this peaceful creature as a travelling companion; she seemed to invest even the impersonal hotel room with a soothing incense. While we talked, she, having excused herself, sat at a Chippendale writing desk in the corner, in pretty concentration over some schoolbooks.

Later, when she had left the room, I said to Millie, 'Ellie stopped writing to me after Grace died. I haven't heard for months.'

Millie glanced once to the door of Khadija's bedroom, and then, satisfied we were not to be overheard, said sharply, 'The marriage is on the rocks. I told Wendell off properly when I saw him last, which he well deserved. I don't expect to be hearing from him again.' She softened, briefly, 'I'm sorry, dear. But I've very little time for that man.' She paused and then said, 'Wendell's with his grandmother in New York. Margaret's taken Ellie away to Maine.'

'I see.' I nodded, absorbing it, aware of Jack's gentle inquisitive eyes on my face. The breakdown of Wendell's second marriage gave me no joy. Looking back, it was utterly predictable, and yet I had not predicted it. Like Wendell himself, I had fallen prey to his vision of his perfect love. But I was relieved about Ellie, if only because I now understood her silence.

Jack and I stayed in London a fortnight, until the middle of February. We stayed, with Eithne, at the house of my sister-in-law Wilhemina, in Bryanston Square. Wilhemina's house, like that of the Father in Heaven, had many rooms, and Wilhemina was an extraordinarily proficient hostess, with a great network of family, friends, children of friends, and god-children, so there was invariably *someone* staying. People wandered through corridors, bumping into strangers, and in the midst, Wilhemina moved regally, ordering and organizing like the director of some vast mysterious play. In this mélange, the addition of one young American was hardly noticeable, so Khadija Abbas came to stay a few days with us in Bryanston Square, as a companion for Eithne. My nephew, Hugo, now in his final year at Eton, and preparing to read Classics at Oxford, came up to London at half-term to see us, and promptly fell sweetly and hopelessly in love, with not one girl, but two, courting them simultaneously with offers of his escort about London.

At the end of the fortnight, just before we were to leave for Dublin, Clare arrived from Oxford with Meggie Whyte. Her arrival sparked a predictable day of conflict, which ended with a proper Irish barney in Wilhemina's perfect drawing room. As always with arguments with Clare, it was difficult to define where the personal ended and the political began, because she used them as equal expressions of her ire.

That she was angry with something was evident from the moment of her arrival, tight-lipped and severe in charcoal-grey, bare-headed, her greying bun unravelling in the February wind. Behind her, cheeks reddened in the cold, an absurd hat of velvet and artificial cherries topping her cropped hair, Meggie fluttered about apologetically, like the mistress of a particularly difficult dog. I assumed, self-consciously, that Clare was angry with me. Not because of my successes, which she genuinely applauded, but because I was as happy as I was with Jack Redpath, and had proved her a poor prophet. She greeted us stiffly, like one with a mouthful of swallowed words. But she said nothing about that, and when, as we gathered in the drawing room to await the young people's return, she launched her attack, it was not on Jack or myself, but on our long-dead father instead.

We had learned through his London publisher that *The Gateway* was to be reprinted. I was surprised. It was a scholarly, but obscure work, now relegated to esoteric library shelves. But it seemed that the death of Abdul Baha, a decade earlier, and the emergence of a new receptiveness for the unifying, pacific ideals of Baha'i had generated new interest. Clare had been approached to write a new introduction, and somewhat to everyone's embarrassment, had flatly refused.

'Muzzy-headed mysticism,' she snapped. 'Whenever life gets difficult, and serious decisions must be made, some fool romantic runs off to the East and comes back with a message for Humanity. They may reprint it if they like, but they'll not add my good name to Father's bad one.'

'That's hardly fair,' I said angrily. 'It's a splendid book.'

'It's a blueprint for capitulation. A lot of pacifist rubbish.'

'That's only a tiny part of it,' I said. 'Besides, Father was an historian, he wasn't political. And he wrote it twenty years ago, before the War, or anything. He never knew what was to come. That wasn't his reason for writing it.'

'Possibly not,' said Clare coolly, 'but it will be everyone's reason for reading it. Whether he would like it or not, our dear Papa is at last in tune with the times.' She smiled and swallowed her sherry.

'Why are you so cynical?' I asked. 'Do you *want* another war?' I felt mean-spirited, but I could not forget her rabid patriotism of 1914. She smiled again.

'No, Justina. But in spite of your League of Nations,

and in spite of your Abdul Bahas and your Dick Sheppards, peace is a luxury that we won't long afford.'

'That's not fair,' Meggie Whyte, pink and determined, a dumpy little figure in tweed suit and lacy jabot, glared at Clare with quite definite fury.

'Oh, shut up, Meggie,' Clare said in a bored voice as if the argument was old and tiresome.

'I will *not* shut up,' said Meggie. I couldn't believe it. I had never heard her stand up to Clare. The whole room went quiet and even Wilhemina, who tended to drift about on the externals of our conversations until she could say something civilized, like 'Oh, do let's eat,' or 'Another sherry, anyone?' was drawn into attentive silence.

'No,' Jack suddenly said, 'why should you?'

She smiled a grateful little flustered smile in return.

'Oh, what would *you* know?' Clare snapped. 'You're just a damned Bolshevik, anyhow.' That had been Clare's assessment of Jack since she read *The Virgin of the Somme*.

'Yes, Ma'am,' he said, touching his forelock and grinning. He teased her the way Padraic O'Mordha had teased her as a girl.

'Don't you call Jack names,' said Meggie. Clare turned round, her finely-drawn mouth gone slack, imperious as a queen before a rebellious populace. Hugo came in with Khadija and Eithne, all self-consciously dressed in very adult clothes. They stood politely listening.

'Oh, spare me your infatuated loyalties,' said Clare.

'And spare me your condescension,' snapped Meggie. 'I don't care what you say, or how many degrees you've got. You're wrong. War is stupid. It was stupid last time and it'll be twice as stupid if we go and do it again. *Some* of us can learn from our mistakes!' Clare set down her sherry glass. She walked to the fireplace and pretended to adjust the coals with long brass tongs. Then she straightened and leaned against the marble mantel in a man's pose.

She said, for all of us, 'If you'll just bear with us. Meggie has fallen into the charmed ring of the holy Dick Sheppard and his faithful apostles. We will now have ten minutes on Christian forgiveness and loving our neighbourly blackshirts.'

'Dick Sheppard isn't a Fascist,' Meggie said, 'nor a fool. He's a good man. A bit too good for this world.'

Clare smiled. She looked at Meggie with a mixture of love and scorn.

'The trouble with men too good for this world is, they still insist on knocking about in it, until they and their cuckoo ideas have wrought havoc. What do you know about the world, Meggie?'

Meggie was quiet, and then, still sitting where Wilhemina had placed her, still too unsure of herself to even stand, she looked up and said, 'I know if there hadn't been the War, I would have been married to Geoffrey Melrose. I know that.'

'Oh, glorious,' Clare laughed and then whirled upon her bitterly. 'And what would that have made you? A vicar's wife?' She turned and shrugged in disgust. But Meggie was unmoved, sitting dreamily, looking into the past.

'I should have *liked* that. To be a vicar's wife,' she said. 'Then I'd have lived among folk that looked up to me, and not like here, where they all look down on me instead.' She folded her plump hands, as unbudging as the Yorkshire hills. I wanted to cheer.

Clare said, embarrassed, 'Nonsense, lambkins. No one looks down on you.' But Meggie only smiled.

'Of course they do. They're just too well bred to say.' She was remarkably composed. She turned back to Clare. 'Alright, you've looked after me and I cook and clean and keep house for you. But maybe I'd rather have done it for a man.' She smiled dreamily, and Clare turned her back on us and left the room. Wilhemina was flustered and called us in to dinner, and the children, watching wide-eyed, accepted the invitation to food as an invitation to normality.

But throughout dinner, and until Clare left, with Meggie placidly beside her, the argument batted around the long table, about Fascists and Bolsheviks, about the War and about God. And all the while Hugo and Eithne and Khadija looked on with their smooth young faces calm and distant, certain it had nothing to do with them.

On the fourteenth of February Millie arranged a farewell reception for us at the Soho gallery displaying my work. It was quite the occasion, attended by notables of the world of art and of literature, and I felt distinctly out of place. But Jack was soon surrounded by a clamour of admiring women, and cheerfully signed autographs while I faded gratefully out of sight. Millie and I drank a quiet glass of champagne and toasted our success. The exhibition had been well attended and *A Pyrenean Autumn* well reviewed. I had much to be happy for, as we prepared to leave the gallery for the last time.

The invited guests had all departed and Jack had gone for my coat. Just as he returned, there was an unseemly scuffle as a gallery official intercepted a man attempting to enter, turned him roughly round and shoved him hastily out of the door. It was a sad moment. Even with his back to us, the man had the unmistakable look of the unemployed; the street-weary clothing and scuffed shoes, and the dreary apologetic hopelessness of the bent shoulders, and bowed head. London, and all the big cities, were full of such men in those days. And even though he had come in obviously by mistake, I was ashamed to see him thrust so heartlessly back out into the rain. Suddenly I wanted only to leave the place, where my paintings of sun-browned children, and gentle mountain villages seemed a mockery. I quickly said my goodbyes and went out on Jack Redpath's arm.

'Did you see that?' I said. He nodded.

'Poor bastard, probably just trying to get warm.' He turned his collar up as the wind hit us. 'Bitch of a town,' he said. We turned down the street, and then suddenly, the man was right there. He had waited for us in the cold. He stood with his head turned away, and his hatbrim, dripping water, covering his face, but then suddenly he looked up and as he spoke my name, 'Miss Melrose?' I saw why the gallery official had turned him so hastily away.

I was looking upon a monster. He had only one eye, and below the forehead the whole left side of his face was gone, replaced by a stretched, puckered wilderness of skin. His nose collapsed below the bridge to a puffy knob pierced by twisted nostrils. His mouth was virtually lipless, and wet with drool. I cried out, and instantly he turned away, the collar of his battered army greatcoat flung up to hide his face. It was Jack who stopped him, reaching out one compassionate hand.

'Please, do you know Miss Melrose?' he said.

The man kept his head turned away. From the side, I could see the rain making adventurous rivulets down the strange valleys of his face. 'Oh, no. Terribly sorry. I was mistaken. So sorry to have troubled you.' He moved slightly, as if he would go, but politely awaited the release of Jack's hand. The voice was cultured, English and upper class. An officer's voice, I thought, and I knew who stood before me.

'It's Captain Hartingdon, isn't it?' I whispered. And, as my mind flashed back to my brave, wonderful patient in the Strathpeffer hospital, I prayed he would say no.

'Oh, how charming of you to recall, after all these years.' I stepped in front of him and made myself look upon his face. The wet mouth twisted and I knew he was smiling. The one hazel eye was fine and wise. If one looked only upon that eye, and listened only to that beautiful voice, emerging so incongruously from its brutal prison, it was just bearable, and no more. My eyes drifted away, on to the sodden shoulders of his ancient coat. I thought of Derwent Wood's beautiful mask. Had he abandoned it in the cruel realism of despair? Or had it simply worn out, as fragile and impermanent as peace? I saw that he carried under one arm a square wooden box, the sort that converted into a tray to be hung around the neck so that the owner might sell matches, or small trinkets, to earn his keep. On London's railway stations and streetcorners such vendors were a familiar sight; war veterans, blind, limbless and maimed. 'I was so delighted when I saw notice of the exhibition,' he said eagerly. 'I've looked for your name ever since the war. Quite certain I would see it one day. I've still got your portrait, don't you know!' He made a little sound, a laugh. 'Felt quite chuffed watching all the brouhaha. Quite chuffed.' He smiled again. 'I know my painters,' he said.

It was Jack who said, 'Will you come in with us and see the paintings?' He held out his hand tentatively, but Captain Hartingdon made his sad twisted smile.

'Thanks so much,' he said. 'Terribly kind and all. But it *is* late. I'll come back another day. See it all properly at my leisure. It wouldn't do to rush it, after all.' He stepped back and Jack let him go. He looked at me, and I made myself look up into his face. The one beautiful eye was full of compassion. 'A true pleasure meeting you again, Miss Melrose, a true pleasure.' He bowed his monstrous face over my hand. 'Quite brings everything back.' He turned and walked slowly away through the rain. I put my face against Jack's shoulder and I wept.

23

'Ireland's Eye,' I said to Jack, as we leaned together on the ferry's rail. The little island was just visible through rain and blowing snow, the headland of Howth wrapped in blue cloud. Then I could see the Martello tower at Sandycove, and the long, low shape of the Yacht Club, dark against the shoreline of old Kingstown. After twenty years, I was in Ireland once more.

It looked remarkably unchanged. Yachts bobbed in the ruffled waters of the harbour, gulls wheeled and motor-cars and horse-wagons crowded to meet the ferry. We rode the same railway, beside the waters of Dublin Bay, that I rode a distant summer day, on my last journey with Michael. Only Padraic O'Mordha's beautiful grown daughter, riding beside me, gave visible evidence of the passage of time.

We took a taxi-cab from the railway station into the centre of Dublin, so that we might buy flowers and fruit to bring to May. There were new buildings to replace those destroyed by the gunboat, and over Trinity College, the tricolour flag of rebellion rode a legitimate wind. But there were beggars in the streets as always, shawl-wrapped women with babies on their hips, and the fruit vendors sang the same ancient songs. Empire had been vanquished; the shouters in the streets were now the government. But in Merrion Square, where the old Georgian houses looked down peacefully on the quiet green, and barren trees bent gently in the same sea-borne Dublin light, James Howie's townhouse stood serene.

The cabbie dropped us before the door and, as I stood there while Jack paid him and shouldered our old army kitbag, I became for a moment my twenty-year-old self, dressed in mourning for my mother, clutching my grey-backed hooded crow. *They'll all be there,* I thought, *Eugenia and James, Kate, May . . . Michael . . .* But, of course they were not. Only May was there to let us in, and two remained of the once voluminous staff. It was not poverty that had reduced their numbers, but practicality. An old dying man in his bed had few demands.

James was asleep when we arrived, and May led us into the drawing room, where she had prepared a tea. Inside the house seemed worn and tired, smaller than I had remembered it, the room shabbier and rather dark, as if the loss of Eugenia's radiant presence had been a literal loss of light.

Jack wandered around, looking at all my old paintings, so faithfully hung there by May. I followed him, telling him about the people and places they represented. I saw him stepping as tentatively into my childhood and youth, as I had into his through the doorway of *American Dreamers*.

'This was your cousin?' he said, before an old portrait of Michael at seventeen.

I said only, 'Yes,' and turned aside. For me the paintings were like a forgotten diary, brought suddenly to light, revealing glimpses into a past grown so remote that it seemed a different world.

Later, James awoke, grumpy like a child who had slept too long in the afternoon, and risen hot and unhappy from his bed. He banged against the bedstead with his stick, shouting in his grand Irish voice, 'May? May? Where are you, girl?'

She smiled ruefully, jumped up from her tea, and ran to his side. He slept now in a room just down the corridor from the drawing room; a little study that Eugenia had used for her correspondence. A bed, large and ungainly, had been crammed in its narrow confines, and James and his chair were imprisoned there, amidst Eugenia's flowery wallpaper, and draperies of pink and mauve chintz.

May told us to wait until she had got him up, and into his chair, with the help of the hired nurse. She, a fat, cheerful soul, called Mrs Dooley, stamped through from her own room, muttering to herself. Her sleeves were rolled up, and her arms, pink and shining, were as powerful as a man's. I heard her hearty grunts, and jolly encouragements from behind the closed door, as she levered James Howie into his chair. Then we were called in, and I entered, holding tight to Jack's hand.

The room was dim and stuffy; a coal fire burned smokily in the grate, and the windows were tightly closed against the winter wind. It smelled badly, of sickness, and medicines, and urine; the old familiar smells of the hospital wards. James was sitting in a clinical metal wheelchair, with his back to the many-paned, rain-streaked window, so that though I could see his outline, I could not at first make out his face. The hired nurse was leaning over him, tucking a blue blanket around his knees, with stolid force. Her hands, broad and calloused, were the hands of a peasant woman.

'An' will ye be all right now, Sir James. Or will I be bringin' yet another bottle?' she shouted, as if James were deaf, and he shook his head and covered his ears.

'He'll be fine, Mrs Dooley,' said May.

'It won't do for him to be wetting another blanket,' Mrs Dooley pursued, still shouting. 'And wasn't it himself soaked through twice yesterday . . .' But May smiled and shook her head, and the fat nurse waddled happily out.

When the door closed behind her, James said querulously, 'May, that woman is *unseemly*. You *must* find another. What would your mother say?' May patted his hand on the arm of the wheelchair.

'She's kind, Papa,' she said, 'and besides, they're all like that.' She turned to us and back to him, 'Don't you want to see who's here?'

Very slowly, he raised his head, and peered into the dimness, to where we stood. My eyes had grown accustomed to the light, and I could see his face now, and the first awareness I had was of his reluctance. He did not really want to see us at all, or indeed to see anyone. Like the weary infant that wants only his mother, he now wanted only May. But he said obediently, 'Of course I do. Now, let me see; is it little Justina come back at last?'

'Hello, Uncle James,' I said, and I stepped forward, still holding Jack's hand.

'And this is your husband?' said James.

'Yes,' Jack said, at once. It was the only occasion we ever lied about that. I wondered if James thought Jack was Wendell, or if he were aware of any, or all, of what had happened to me since we last met. There is a kind of senile confusion that masks itself so well that only those most intimate with the afflicted person comprehend any disability. James peered up at me. His face had lost all familiarity.

'You've aged,' he said. I laughed.

'So have you.' He grunted something, and I brought Eithne forward, my arm about her shoulders. 'Hasn't she grown?'

'What? Who's that?' he demanded, suspiciously.

'It's Eithne, Grandpa,' she said patiently, 'Kate's daughter.' She came closer and kissed his cheek, her young nose wrinkling against the smell.

'Ah, you'll not be getting around me that way, girl,' he said, and his face crinkled up in a toothless smile. I think he was talking to Kate. He caught Eithne's wrist, and held her near him, and though she was uncomfortable, she stayed obediently until he let her go.

May pushed her father's chair through into the big, cold drawing-room and we all gathered around it. He brightened under the attention, and became quite garrulous. We talked of common things he could have shared with anyone, gossip, the newspapers which he yet avidly read, politics. He had a wicked, vicarious delight in the miseries and strife all around, smugly aware he was leaving it all behind. I wondered if it mattered to him that we had come, and were his family, or if strangers would have done as well.

Jack lit a fire for May in the cavernous drawing room fireplace, and I sat on a small stool, by James Howie's knee. He patted my hand, as he expressed some point, as if I was a small child. I tried to imagine him as he had once been, but was defeated by the decrepit husk before me, the face so shrunken that the skull showed beneath the skin, false teeth permanently exiled to a glass by his bedside. James Howie of Ballysodare as toothless as a Sligo pedlar, an old man of the roads. After a while, his nurse returned to hustle him protesting off to his bed.

How little he belonged to this world of dissension and fighting, and the grey, hungry lines of the unemployed; he who had courted the daughter of a Yankee seaman on Sligo quay. Far, far away now, the dun-coloured stallion and the white-footed chestnut mare. In all of those last weeks in Dublin, the name of Eugenia Howie never crossed his lips.

We stayed on at Merrion Square, and so indeed did James. After the first week, I wondered if our timing had been wrong, and thought of leaving for a while, to ease the burden on the beleaguered household staff. But May said, 'A week. Two. Maybe even four. But no more. It's only stubbornness keeping him here, you know.'

And so we remained. It was odd waking up in the bedroom where I'd slept as a girl, with Jack Redpath beside me. I felt I had brought him, like a bridegroom, to my home, for this house was as familiar to me as Arradale and far less changed. Jack set up his typewriter in a corner of the bedroom and returned to his work. I spent my time doing charcoal studies of May, and Eithne, and of Mrs Dooley, James's warm and mannerless nurse.

'Who would be wanting a picture of that woman?' he demanded. 'Is it not bad enough having to look upon the real thing?'

'More's the pity, Sir,' she said, 'we can't all be beauties like you.'

At the end of our second week, Kate came home. It was eight o'clock on a rainy, stormy evening, and the doorbell rang, long and stridently. May was busy seeing James into his bed for the night, so I went to answer it. When I opened the door I thought no one was there, and suspected children of pranks. But then I saw a slim, dark figure in a long coat and the sort of broad-brimmed hat that fishermen wear, standing rigid against the lamp-post outside the house.

'Can I help you?' I called, uneasily, and the figure, with a quick turn of its head, suddenly leapt away from the post, and bolted up the stone steps to the door.

'Quickly,' a female voice cried, 'see that I'm not followed, and then bolt the door.'

'What?' I cried, but she was gone, like a deer into brushwood, into the shelter of the house. I started to follow, and then, feeling quite ridiculous, leaned out of the door, and peered into the rainy darkness in either direction. There was absolutely no one in sight; small surprise on such a night.

I closed the door and, in an embarrassed afterthought, drew the bolt across, before I made my way to the drawing room. Jack was there, and May and Mrs Dooley, and I said querulously, 'I'm sorry, but I've just let some woman in; and I haven't even seen where she's gone.' But she was there, by the grey velvet draperies of Eugenia's drawing room, peering out through a slit into the street.

'Did you bolt the door?' she cried, looking up to me and then I saw it was Kate. She was wearing a long shapeless mackintosh, of man's design and sizing, and as she addressed me she removed from her head the broad-brimmed sou'wester hat. She was stark and thin, and her large blue eyes, that had once seemed passionate, seemed now wild and insane. Her black hair was braided and wrapped round and round her head and she looked like one of those paintings of Celtic heroines, fashionable when we were young. 'Why, it's you, Justina,' she said. She had not known me either. I was silent. We had not spoken for twenty years, and between us lay the chasm of Michael Howie's death. She gave a stiff little smile but at once her mind was on her own immediate need. 'Did you see anyone?' she demanded.

May, who had been silent, suddenly stepped forward, collected Kate's wet coat and hat, and said quietly, 'And who would she be seeing?'

The question was the sort of rational challenge one puts to hysterical children and Kate responded defensively.

'They're following me.'

'Who?' May said, handing the coat to the one maid, '*Who's* following you?' Kate roiled under the questioning.

'How am I to know? Are they telling me, now, who they've put to tail me?' She broke away, and ran to the window, where she claimed she had heard a noise. Then we were all made to put out the lights, and sit listening in darkness, while Kate dashed about securing doors and windows. Eventually she returned to the drawing room and there we all remained, for almost half an hour, until eventually May sprang up with an exasperated cry of 'Nonsense,' and began putting lights on, and unlocking doors over Kate's angry protest.

'Do you not care for the life of your own sister?'

'No one's going to hurt you, Kate.'

'No one? I've enemies enough to see me to hell twice over. I'm a marked woman!'

'Oh, who'd want you?' said May. Her voice never rose in volume nor lost any of its sweetness of pitch.

Kate sat down in a corner and refused to speak to anyone. It was Jack who coaxed her out, with the offer of a brandy and the assurance that if anyone came to the door, he would handle them himself while she made good her escape. He was play-acting, but it suited her perfectly. I had no idea if there was anything to all this other than her dramatic imagination. But I was mostly concerned for Eithne, whose return from an evening with young friends was imminent, and who, with her own volatile spirit, would be better spared such scenes as we'd just witnessed.

When the doorbell rang again, I knew it would be her, but once again Kate insisted on the entire performance, lights out, and positions of hiding and menace assumed. Jack, with the fire-poker in hand, advanced bravely to the door.

'Don't *hit* anyone,' I cried. 'It *might* be the *gardai*.' But it was Eithne, after all. She came in, rather delighted with the vision of us all skulking in the dark. Then her eyes fell upon her mother. She cast me a quick, uncertain look, and when I said nothing, turned to Jack, almost wistfully, but her eyes were drawn back to Kate. Kate smiled her beautiful smile and held out her hands in welcome, and I felt Eithne slip from us. She gave a small ecstatic cry and rushed into Kate's arms. Mother and daughter embraced lovingly and lavishly, stroking each other's face and hair, kissing, weeping. The years of their separation were nothing. The years of May's loving, and ours, were nothing as well. Forget all they'll teach you about nurture and environment. What's borne in the blood breeds true.

In spite of Kate's forebodings, no one came to the door, and no one took any notice of her and after a few days she began to go about the city as if there was nothing to fear. She took Eithne with her always, and I worried about where she might be taking her, and whom she might be meeting, but there was nothing whatever I could do. Jack comforted me with the assurance that all of it was drama and dreams in Kate's crazy head and, perhaps because I wanted to, I believed it was true.

It was a strange interlude, as we waited for James Howie to die. Each day, at one o'clock, we gathered round the oval cherrywood table, where Eugenia had sat in mornings past, planning schedules and seeking me a husband in the pages of *Irish Life*. When we were all seated, James would come gliding smoothly in, helmed by his rowdy Dublin nurse. Once docked at the head of the table, he signalled for the meal to commence. He reminded me of my own father at Strathpeffer Spa, ruling us from his invalid's chair. Frequently the conversation grew argumentative. Politics, banned from polite tables, was the meat of the Howie board. Kate had much to say; the de Valera government, the partition of Ireland, the rankle of the Treaty Ports, all felt her tongue. In another era, James would have sent her from his table. But now he sat upon the remote plateau of his illness, secure above all, tossing crumbs of dissent down amongst us to amuse himself.

He had become enamoured of Ioin O'Duffy's blueshirts and talked fondly of Mussolini. Jack and I were only briefly shocked. Poor gentleman Fascist, bewildered by the chaos of our day; his wife murdered and his home burned; who could blame him seeking a surer order?

Kate, who had no more time for Fascists than she had for de Valera, was outraged. But James had turned the tables on her, in his second childhood he could posture and tease, infuriating her middle age as once her youth had so offended his. He would giggle gleefully as she ranted, and behind the befuddlement of his eyes I saw a gay revenge.

Most of those luncheons ended in fights. Though James had to be careful; too offensive a stance would ruffle the Republican sentiments of his nurse, and he'd find himself trundled away on medical pretence, before the sweet. That was what happened at the last of those luncheons together. Kate had worked herself into such a fury screaming what should be done to O'Duffy and his kind that James actually ordered her to leave. Of course she did not go, and he started hammering the table with his pudding spoon, and Mrs Dooley raised anchor and piloted him away. The last we heard of him, as he made the corridor, was a plaintive cry. 'I want my trifle. There's trifle. I want my trifle.' And so he departed into the dusk of his little room.

We sat in embarrassed silence. Shame descended upon everyone except, naturally Kate, who had caused it all. I looked about the table and saw an aged shadow of our revolutionary youth. The sun, glinting through dust-streaked windows, fell in one ruddy winter shaft on Eithne Maire's glowing hair. It singled her out, leaving us to the shadows we deserved, as if she were all there was worth shining upon. I thought of her, and of Khadija, and my son and my daughter, and wondered, would they do better with their world than we had with ours?

Kate and her father did not speak all the rest of that day. Nor were they speaking on the morning that followed. She clung to Ireland Martyred, and he to his lost sherry trifle. And so they did not speak again, and that afternoon he died, suddenly, after a few bewildered gasps for breath and moans of intolerable pain.

So, as it had always been between them, it was finished. Kate refused to view her father's corpse but we, touched by the old superstition, insisted that she must. In the end, she came, holding Eithne's hand, and gave her final cold kiss to her father's cold face.

Mrs Dooley, the Dublin nurse, sat in a corner and wept, 'Oh Jesus, Mary and Joseph, the good soul is gone.'

James Howie was buried beside Eugenia in the churchyard of St John's at Sligo. We all travelled together by train to the West, and stayed at the Clarence Hotel. But Kate went off to her hill farm in the wilds beyond Glencar and took Eithne with her. The funeral was well attended.

Crowds of people came, country strangers, from James Howie's own world. We, who were family, felt like trespassers among them.

Kate did not attend the church, but appeared suddenly at the graveside, dressed in black with a thick black veil. Eithne was with her, and on either side of them walked a tall young man in protective silence. Kate threw down her handful of dirt upon her father's coffin and then all four of them vanished into the crowd. Later Eithne came alone to the hotel on Wine Street, full of excitement and refusing to say where she'd been.

After the funeral we gathered in May's hotel room and drank sherry and toasted James Howie's voyage. May was serene, happy for her father free of an unkind world. It was I who suffered an illogical grief, just as I had done over Eugenia. All that had been grand and beautiful in my youth had come remorselessly to dust, as blackened by time as the fallen stones of Temple House. My grief had begun before James had died; before we came to Ireland at all. It had begun in the Soho street where we left James Hartingdon in the rain, and since then it had grown wider and deeper, over the weeks in Dublin, until it encompassed not just the maimed soldier and my dying uncle, but everyone, living or dead, that I had known in the world. I was grieving for three generations, my parents', my own, my children's, each born in innocence, each doomed to violent ends. Cassandra-like I foresaw, but could not prevent. I was forty years old, and like James Howie himself, I had had enough of this world.

'Oh, May,' I whispered, as we sat looking out over the busy little Sligo street, 'what was it all for?'

'For the Glory of God,' she said without a pause. She smiled at me, and turned away from the window and flopped down girlishly into a chair, lifting her feet to a footstool and leaning back luxuriantly. She raised her hands, palms upward, and ran her fingers up through her thick clumps of yellow hair. It was a gesture of surprising sensuality. I saw it take Jack's eye. She smiled at us both again.

'Well, my dears, it's over, anyway. And now,' she paused, thinking, 'now, I suppose, I'm free. Yes. Now I'm really free.' She smiled again, toying with her hair, her face pensive. She said slowly, 'You know, the trouble with being the youngest is that you end by going straight from girlhood to middle age.' She looked across at Jack, assessing him, I could see, not for himself, but for the very concept of manhood, the bodily concept that she had for so many years denied. She shrugged suddenly, and jumped up from the chair.

'Oh, let's go out. Let's go anywhere, outside in the air, away from all these stuffy rooms. Let's go walking like we used to do.' She reached for my hand, 'Come, hurry, there's a *few* hours yet before it's dark.'

We went out, then, the three of us, and though we begged Eithne to join us, she moaned adolescent preoccupation and clung morosely to her chair. But just as we reached the street, she came running after. It was a dry, sunny day in late February, and we used every one of the hours of daylight left. We walked out of the town towards Strandhill, and then began climbing the grassy sides of the blunt round hill called Knocknarea, that Persephone had told me was the grave-site of a queen. I had climbed it often with Michael, and now I climbed it with Jack, our linked hands swinging between us. Eithne forgot her lofty age and ran around us in leggy freedom, and when we reached the heathery upper slopes she abandoned all pretence of maturity and let Jack chase and tease her as on the meadows of the Pyrenees. He caught her and they tumbled together on the spongy ground, her bright hair flashing like the coat of a wild thing.

May stood laughing delighting in their freedom. She was gay and full of excitement, a great-upwelling of relief after all the days of her patience. She was full of ideas and plans for us and talked about Jack's new book, and what we would do after. She had a grand new plan for us, sparked by the unimagined success of my father's *The Gateway*. We, too, should journey to the East, to Persia, as my father had, and in words and pictures explore the land and the faith he had found there. She had mentioned it before, and we had vaguely considered it, but suddenly on Knocknarea the idea leapt out to me, and I became transfixed with it. Her excitement was contagious, but there was more than that. I wanted to run, to travel, to put distance between me and the world I had always known, as if the act of travelling was a saving act in itself. If we could only keep moving, I thought we might keep free of the world and its murderous course. Like children fleeing into a Garden, we would flee to the timeless East.

On the top of the hill was a cairn; a mighty cairn, of hundreds and hundreds of great stones. When Michael and I had climbed here, we stood on this great mound, scaring ourselves with tales of the royal bones that lay below. I had imagined them rising up out of caverns in the stones, swords in hands, mounted on white skeletal horses. I could only stand there if I held Michael's hand.

Now I climbed the cairn alone. I knew there was nothing to fear. That fierce Irish Queen would not threaten us. Like all who had laid their bones in the earth, she would be glad to be free of our world. I sat down on the top and looked out over Sligo Bay to Ben Bulben. In a little while Jack Redpath came and sat by my side. Below us, May and Eithne were already wandering downwards, hand in hand, to the green patchwork fields below. Jack put his arms round my shoulders and rested his cheek on my hair.

We walked downwards, and the dusk met us half-way down, and when we reached our hotel in Wine Street it was dark. We went together to May's room, full of laughter, and the fresh, cold blessing of the winter air. The room was darkened and we entered it noisily and it was only when May lit the lamp that we saw the figure sitting there. She sat so still, so haughty and unmoving in her mourning black that she might have been Queen Maeve. But it was Kate, her face solemn.

She said, 'Have you heard?'

Behind me, I heard May sigh. So, we had come back to this, the secrets and conspiracies, the dramas of Kate's private war. May said, tiredly, reluctant to surrender the innocence of Knocknarea, 'Oh whatever, Kate, can't it wait until tomorrow.' Kate shrugged; she looked smug with her knowledge and disdainful of us.

Jack said suddenly, 'What's happened, Kate?'

'It's in all the news.' And then she got up as if she'd not tell us at all. She walked to the door, and turned round. 'They've burned the Reichstag,' she said.

24

We left Paris for Tehran in the dead of winter, an unlikely time to set out on such a journey, but Jack's work on *I Dreamed I Saw Joe Hill* had dragged on until late in the autumn, long after we had planned to be away. Though logic demanded we wait until spring, Jack was exhausted and restless and we both felt the need of a radical change.

Besides, the political situation in Europe, and all the world, was daily more disturbing, and there was a feeling about that if one wanted to do things, the time to do them was now.

And so, on a rainy January morning, we boarded the old Orient Express, bound through Switzerland to Trieste and Belgrade and Istanbul. It was a beautiful journey, in comfort and luxury, but that soon came to an end. The next leg from Istanbul to the Turkish Black Sea port of Trebizonde, was aboard a dreary coal-burning freighter, whose few passengers were an unloved imposition, tolerated, but hardly welcomed. We made landfall late in the day, and after interminable difficulties with our passports and searches of our scanty luggage, made our way to a plain but adequate hotel. From there, we set out overland to the Persian frontier in the company of a Scottish mining engineer and a British major. Our mode of transport, an ancient motorcar belonging to the engineer, had all the versatile toughness of the dawn of the motoring era, but even so was quite nearly defeated by roads laid down by the slow feet of camels and mules.

In Tabriz, we parted company with the mining engineer, but managed, through the inventive offices of our British major, to make contact with another party, travelling on to Teheran in a motor lorry, legacy of the British presence during the War. Our Persian driver mastered several languages, English and French among them, and was so hospitable and voluble that there was not a village, nor hill, nor roadside *caravanserai* that we passed whose history was not given to us in full. Upon our arrival in Teheran he insisted on personally escorting us to the house of Charles Rudsworth, our host.

Charles Rudsworth was an Anglican missionary who had known my brother Geoffrey at the Episcopal College in Edinburgh, before the war. Since Geoffrey's death, he had maintained a continuous, if distant, communication with both myself and my sister Clare. For a while his occasional letters came from a small Scottish parish, near Kirkcaldy, later, missionary work had led him to India and the Sudan, and finally, for the past six years, Teheran. Dutifully he had written, with the quiet compassion of a man who takes on all responsibilities for life. And dutifully, I had written back, assuring him of my continued survival, and never expecting to see him again. But when May Howie's plans turned our concerns to the East, Charles Rudsworth came at once to mind. I wrote to him and he replied instantly with the sort of all-encompassing invitation that suggested a lifetime home in Persia, if we so chose. He was a good religious man, of little imagination, bravely dedicated to the uplifting of a people whose own spirituality remained a mystery he had no desire to penetrate.

With his wife, Sarah, he maintained a comfortable home in the northern quarter of the city, amongst wealthier Persians and almost all of the European residents. The house was unimpressive from without, plain, blank walled, and flat roofed. Within, it was much more welcoming, built about a courtyard, entered through arched doorways, in which was a tiny jewel of a garden. Like much of the architecture of the land, it presented a bleak, private exterior about a secret oasis, revealing a desert mentality. But despite its Eastern framework, it was a European home, furnished in western fashion with tables and chairs and sofas, and once inside we might have been in the Home Counties. Self-conscious oriental additions, a wealth of the beautiful native rugs, and a traditional samovar, displayed but unused, paid lip-service to assimilation. We were in the land of the Raj, and I admit, in those early weeks, to have been glad of it. That gentle English retreat was a great comfort after a day battering against the closed door of the East. Later, those same familiar comforts grew into an annoyance, until at last Jack piled chairs and tables and desks into an exiled corner of our room, and entertained his Persian guests squatting on his heels on the carpeted floor.

The Rudsworths showed us one Persia; we in time found another. But that discovery would have been impossible without their gentle sheltering at the beginning, and so I must record the gratitude that remains with me, along with my first glimpse of Charles Rudsworth's cheerful bland face, beaming from his arched doorway, as we stumbled from our lorry through a heavy January snowfall into his English oasis.

That snowfall, coming at the end of our last day of travel, and nearly bringing our progress to a total halt just beyond the gates of the city, was to me the greatest amazement. For no reason I can fathom, I had never imagined the Persian capital to experience such a winter. And so it was the final touch of wonder to come into that city with its domes and minarets and Eastern gardens blanketed in white. And then, in the morning, to arise and see, through the clear mountain air, the great snowfields of the Elburz against a blue winter sky.

'I could stay here forever,' I said to Jack, and in one way or another, we almost did.

It had been our plan to remain a month, perhaps two, in Teheran, visiting the bazaars, the gardens and mosques and monuments, observing the city and its people. I would sketch, and Jack would make notes and then we would move on, to the south, the holy city of Qom, to Isfahan, and eventually to Shiraz. In each of those places we hoped to find a welcome, since not only had we our kind hosts' network of English acquaintances, but also a list of names and addresses provided by Mirza Hassan, the homes of Baha'i families, friends and relatives of his own who he had informed of our coming.

But the East was not to be easily won. We found the city at once more inviting, and more forbidding than we had ever imagined, and both invitation, and resistance, took much of our time. We were free enough, of course, to move about the city at will, and each day we went out, on foot, exploring the gracious boulevards and squares of the wealthy northern quarter, and the closer, more tangled streets amidst the bazaars where more ordinary people lived. I spent days sketching under the arched beautiful roof of the carpet bazaar, and could never get enough of its profusion of colour. Jack often left me, to browse about, watching the elaborate transactions over those wonderful Persian treasures. He had a gift for meeting people; part curiosity, part natural friendliness, part some deep appeal of his own that made people wish to talk to him. He had also a real facility for language, and in a very short time was lifting phrases out of the Farsi or Turkish dialects and using them with ease. Often, when I had finished painting, I would seek him out and find him at the back of some market stall, in a circle of merchants, balancing easily as they did on his heels, talking in a laughable mix of English, Persian and French. The talk would die on my approach; women did not partake of this society.

We would walk together back through the city and Jack would tell me of their conversations, which were extraordinarily lofty; the Persians were great debaters, masters of philosophical thought. No discourse seemed possible that did not deal directly with the message of God and the role of man in the universe. Religion was everywhere, not compartmented neatly as so often in Western life, but permeating everything. The structure of society was the structure of Islam.

'God is the whole purpose of their lives,' Jack said. He was reverent. It was extraordinary, and a little frightening. He had always been so comfortably atheistical, so free of metaphysics. The rock of his cynicism had anchored my faith. Now he was casting free the anchor and setting us both adrift. I became aware within weeks that Jack had largely forgotten why we had come there at all. The book, writing, our purpose, were all submerged. He read the Koran, sitting cross-legged on the floor of our room. Just as when he ski'd for weeks in the Pyrenees, his work untouched, he threw himself into this study with unswerving devotion, leaving it only to venture into the city and find devout and holy men with whom he might talk. He had forsaken the wonders of Persia for the deeper mystery of Islam. Long before we left Teheran, Jack's journey had become an interior journey of the soul. Perhaps because of this I felt at times a division, almost a discord, develop between us, and in a new isolation I retreated to my work, the letters of my children, and the pleasant cheery company of the Rudsworths.

The months slipped by. Spring came, and the strange barren gardens within the city grew greener. With their rows of poplar trees and their little captured streams of running water, they seemed to echo the Koran, and were pleasant places to wander. I set up my easel within their walls and painted. In the market places I sketched Persian merchants, and Turkish and Armenian travellers, and the roguish black-haired muleteers who came in with the caravans. I was tolerated, a foreign curiosity, and some of the bolder young men even posed proudly in their ragged costumes, for portraits. It was a totally male world, its women hidden, or slipping in dark veiled secrecy about the bazaars. I longed to see them, to know how they lived, to glimpse the faces hinted by those sudden flashes of dark eyes within the *chador*. But they were as secretive as their courtyard gardens, shut away from the outside world.

Outside the city, to the north, were larger, more beautiful gardens, and beyond always the magnificent snowy heights of the Elburz. Never long out of sight, they overhung the city like a whispered promise, and I would look up through the clear mountain air and pledge we would go up into them, once, at least, before we left for home.

Home seemed far away. Letters came, erratically, and so late that their news seemed unreal, eclipsed by passing time. Clare wrote, cranky dire warnings about the air, food, and water of foreign lands. May sent cheerful news from Paris of the successes of Jack's latest book, a triumph that seemed, in his new obsession, to barely interest him. The best letters were from my children, whose father's defection from their lives opened a doorway to me. Margaret did not interfere, and in some sheltered courtyard of the heart I cherished an unacceptable dream that they would return to me.

Ellie wrote me constantly, intense, impatient letters, demanding my advice on questions of technique and materials; her dedication to her painting was total, obliterating all other interest, academic or personal. I was frightened by it. Wendell too, freed from his father's commanding presence, reached out to me.

25

Patchin Place
30 March 1934

Dear Justina,

I hope this reaches you before you leave Teheran. Khadija Abbas thinks you may have gone on to Qom, but Miss Dobbs said I should send it to the Reverend Rudsworth, anyhow, because you will surely be back there some time. Persia sounded very exciting in your last letter. It is hard, living in modern New York, to imagine a place where people still ride on camels, and there are no railroads. I wish I could go there too.

You will see from my letter that we've changed our address. We're in Patchin Place in Greenwich Village, near where you used to stay. I like it very much, especially because it's closer to Washington Street and I can see Khadija when she gets home from her classes. Grandma doesn't approve of Patchin Place. She thinks Mother has 'gone Bohemian' as she puts it, 'like Justina'. Isn't that funny? She said it to my Aunt Phyllis. 'Wendell's wives *do* seem to go Bohemian eventually. *It's puzzling.*' I was standing behind the dining room door with Ellie and we both laughed so much that Grandma heard and we got in trouble. I'm *glad* Mother has *gone Bohemian.* She's much, much more fun. She's almost like you.

Ellie's in trouble again. She failed Algebra, Latin, Geography and Chemistry at school, and Mrs Watkins, the Principal, said she may have to leave. Everybody was very upset except Ellie who says she *might* fail History as well if they don't let her start art classes again. I told you Mother made her stop them because she used a bad word at her Algebra teacher. I'm sorry for Ellie. Mother thinks she's spoiled, and so does Grandma, but they don't understand. Ellie used the bad word because the teacher tore up her drawing of him she did in class. And he only tore it up because it looked just like him; even the wart under his nose. All the kids said so. Ellie isn't spoiled. She just likes painting more than she likes people. If they leave her alone she paints all day and cleans up everything, and makes her own supper and cleans up that. But they won't leave her alone. When I grow up I'm going to have my own house with a room in it for Ellie to paint as long as she likes.

I've got to go to college first, though. Father wants me to go to Harvard, like he did, but I want to go to Columbia, so I'll be near Khadija, still. Father wants me to study law, and, I guess I will, unless I think of something better. Law's all right, I guess, only I don't want to always do what *he* wants. He's stupid, though. All I'll ever do, if I learn law, is use it against him one day. The Romans knew better than that. They never let the barbarians in their armies learn as much as themselves. I'm not saying I'm a barbarian, just that my father doesn't know as much as the Romans.

He comes to see us every week, on Sundays, at Grandma's house in Gramercy Park. It's boring because whatever I want to do with Ellie, or my friends from school, or Khadija, I still have to sit around with him on every Sunday. He brings me presents, silly things that little boys play with. He always forgets how old I am. He talks about sports and hunting like he was in a play about a boy and his father. All the time, Miss Potter is downstairs, sitting waiting in the car. I saw her, out of my window, all wrapped up in a fur coat in the middle of a really warm day. My father keeps looking at his watch and I know he can't wait until he can get away with Miss Potter and go to a party or something. I really hate him then.

I did try to like him better, after what you said in your last letter, but it didn't work. My mother still cries by herself at night, when she thinks I'm asleep, and I can't forgive him. Could you? Life is very unfair. I don't mean to me; I'm not feeling sorry for myself because of my father, or anything. I don't miss him at all, and I'm happy with my mother and I love my sister, and our house. But it isn't fair that she's alone, and Miss Potter rides around in my father's car. And nothing else is fair either. Khadija and I go walking together every Saturday and last week we walked down on the East Side, where everyone's poor, and we passed a family who were just evicted, sitting out on the sidewalk on top of their chairs, and tables and beds. The children were all playing around like it was fun to live in the street but the mother just sat on the arm of a chair crying like a little girl and everyone walked by and paid no attention. Khadija and I thought it was awful and Khadija went and bought apples and gave them to the children but then we had to go home because it was getting late. Then at night I sat up in my room, and it was warm and nice and Mother was busy in the kitchen and Ellie was reading a book on the floor and all I could think of was the evicted family on the sidewalk in the dark, with their apples all gone. I was ashamed. Khadija and I made a pledge and when she's a doctor and I'm a lawyer, we're going to make things different. You see, New York really is like ancient Rome, only the barbarians are the Caesars here.

Please give my regards to Jack and Khadija sends her love as well,

sincerely yours,
Wendell Pyke

When I received this letter, the third from Wendell since my coming to Persia, in late May of 1934, Jack and I had been living in the Persian capital for nearly five months.

We had become so settled there, working and studying amidst strangers, that it occurred to me to think that we might never return. It was a not unpleasant thought. A stealthy peace crept over me, and a comforting remoteness from the world I had known, as if I had died there and been reborn here, and nothing of that world existed any longer for me. This is what the East does. It casts us into a different plane and removes all our responsibility. No wonder Westerners seek it, and have always done so. How ironic, though, this should happen to us in a land where those in power were striving as frenetically to gain the wealths and machineries of the West, as we were striving to flee them.

It was, in the end, those western incursions that drove us from Teheran. Our journey, or Jack's at least, had become a pilgrimage, and the real Persia he sought lay in the distant southern cities and the far villages, remote from the eager, westernizing capital. We would go south, Jack determined, where the West had not yet come.

Just before we left I did a portrait of Sarah Rudsworth and her husband, in as English and country-drawing-room a style as I could manage, and presented it to her, along with a pencil sketch of Jack, as a sign of our gratitude. She was ridiculously grateful. It was only after I had left Teheran, riding beside Jack on the long benches of a strange open omnibus, that I began to understand the measure of her affection for us as a measure of her loneliness.

In those days the old walls of the city, once locked each evening at each of its twelve gates, still stood, almost intact. And so when one left Teheran, it was like leaving a city of medieval Europe to set out into the wild lands surrounding. And in truth, outside the capital, the countryside was ancient. Roads were poor. There was as yet no railway. Remote settlements, though linked by telegraph, were still reached largely on foot or on the backs of horses. There were some motor vehicles, like the peculiar charabanc upon which we journeyed to Qom, or the occasional car, often in the hands of foreigners, British or Russian, or American. But the people travelled largely the way they had travelled for centuries. And since we had come there to observe not only the land, but its people, we soon chose to travel the same, on horseback, our luggage loaded upon mules, at the tedious pace of the ancients, stopping at *caravanserais* as old as the Magi.

In Qom we stayed at the household of a prominent merchant whose name had been given me by Mirza Hassan, in a letter from New York.

The Baha'i community of Persia encompassed the spiritual descendants of the Babis my father had met, studied and eventually become one with, in the early years of the century. Even then, the teachings and prophecies of the Bab were slipping beneath the new revelations of Bahá'u'lláh, and by the time I reached Persia, the first had been eclipsed by the second and most of the Babis had become Baha'i, much as the followers of the baptist John became the followers of Christ. And it is to those early Christians that my mind always turns, in recalling the Persian Baha'is. I felt among them that I sat and talked and ate and laughed with Peter and Paul, Thomas, and John, and Mary the Magdalene.They had swept the cobwebs of tradition away. Gone were the veils, the submissions, the guarded courtyard life. The women of Baha'i, like the women of early Christianity, were equal partners with their men, in the spreading of the new Word. It was like dawn after dark to be with them in that Islamic land.

But like the early Christians they had borne the yoke of persecution. Jack understood. 'They are heretics,' he said.

'But they are so gentle, so innocent,' I cried.

'They are to Islam as the first Christians to Judaism; heretics and blasphemers. Open your eyes.' He sounded quite harsh.

'You can't believe that,' I said. He rocked back on his heels, crouched on the carpeted floor of our room. He was silent and thoughtful, and since he had taken to wearing a Persian loose shirt, and letting his beard go much untrimmed, he looked like a *charvardar*, a muleteer.

'I don't know what I believe,' he said. He was cradling his copy of the Koran, in English, that Charles Rudsworth had given him as a sort of trinket and which was now as dog-eared and worn as that of any holy man. 'If it is false, it is a fierce heresy, and not only the Persians have rewarded heretics with fire. If it is true, it is a revelation that must turn the world on its head, as surely, and no doubt as quietly, as did that of Christ. It is so large I cannot encompass it. It terrifies me.'

We stayed on for several days at Qom, among the blue-tiled domes of mosque and minarets, and in that holy city people were kind and tolerant of us. Jack stood outside the mosque he could not enter, and I sketched him standing there, and made the drawing into a caricature, with a shepherd's staff in his hand, and a turban on his head. I entitled it Moses and the Promised Land. I left the drawing on top of his books and he laughed with delight when he found it. Even in our most thrawn and determined moments of opposition, we never forgot how to laugh. We were lucky, that way, I suppose, for it protected our love and our sanity. Still, it was not in Qom, but Isfahan, that Jack met his own holy man.

We travelled there slowly, on horseback, sometimes stopping for two or three days at a likely village or *caravanserai*, to study and to sketch. When we eventually arrived at our destination, we were dusty and travel-worn, and I was very ready for the comforts of the home of our European host.

He was James Cowdry, a geologist, who with his Quaker wife had lived in Persia for many years. Both were acquaintances of Charles Rudsworth in Teheran and, like him, lived amidst a circle of Europeans of differing backgrounds and philosophies, whose common exile in an alien land over-rode divisions that at home would have seemed insurmountable. We were entertained lavishly, and, as in Tehcran, had to struggle against that hospitality lest we never accomplish what we had come for at all.

Among that circle was a German engineer and his

deeply disgruntled wife, a French importer of carpets and brasswork, an altruistic English doctor, growing desperate with the frustrations of practising Western medicine in the East, an Oxford graduate studying Persian poetry, and an old Scottish mountaineer named Andrew Sinclair. He, grey-haired and weather-worn, was working his way slowly towards the Himalayas by climbing anything in his way. He had been fifteen years on this up-and-down journey, and was deliciously cynical about every human institution, having long ago given his affections to rock and snow. He, alone of that company, was free of the faintly martyred lamentation for their life among the infidel that marked the rest, and I liked him best of all.

It was early summer when we came to Isfahan; the bazaars full of fresh fruits, and berries and vegetables, the city's many gardens lush and beautiful. There was much for me to paint, and I was quite happy, though the entertainments of our well-meaning host often intervened. Days were taken up with long outdoor luncheons, leisurely games of tennis, and garden tea-parties. A new female face much enchanted the distaff side of the European community and I was greatly in demand. Persia was a man's land, even for foreigners. Like all such places where men go seeking adventure, or fortune, or ideals, women are likely to be there only by the accident of marriage. Theirs was a sad lonely exile, far from family, writing wistful letters to children in distant boarding schools. For all their servants and tea-parties, they were living in a purdah hardly less restrictive than that of their Muslim sisters behind the veil. They welcomed me eagerly, for news and talk of home. All except the German engineer's wife, who looked at me as if I was mad, sat back in her chair and closed her eyes and said, 'I would give anything, *anything* to be in Berlin. Why would anyone come here who has no need?'

'Justina is interested in the people,' Mrs Cowdry said meekly, on my behalf. The German wife opened her eyes, and then closed them in a slight wince as the far-off sound of the muezzin calling to prayer broke into the quiet English peace.

She whispered, 'Barbarians.'

Jack, who had been sitting reading, got up and left the room. It did not pass without notice, and with a hasty apology to my hostess, I got up and followed him. I knew he found the German woman intolerable, which was unlike him. He had few dislikes, and was usually able to forgive any woman almost anything. But he was different these days; his reading and studying had made him preoccupied and restless and inclined to sudden fits of temper. The bland disinterest in their surroundings displayed by our European friends angered him. I myself was amused by it, and perhaps a little condescending. I did not understand then that their careful distancing provided a protection that those of us like Jack and myself did not have.

I found Jack alone in the courtyard garden staring moodily into the small pool of water that was its centrepiece.

'Shall we leave?' I said, meaning Isfahan.

'I'm sorry,' he said. 'They're such idiots, but they're so kind to us.' He reached for my hand. 'I'll go back and apologize.' I shrugged.

'They're not really idiots,' I said.

'Oh yes,' a voice said behind me. 'That's a fair description. Yes. Idiots. I like that.' I looked up and so did Jack. Andrew Sinclair was standing in the shadows by the arched doorway. 'Mind if I join you?' he said. He came shambling in like a long-boned hunting dog. 'Yes. Idiots.' He smiled. 'The trouble is they eat wrong.'

Jack, who had looked rather amused, now looked silently puzzled. 'Eat wrong?' he said.

'Yes. That's it. They come here, where the climate's all different, the soil, the air, altitude, everything. And they still try to eat like they were at home. Roasting big slabs of meat, steaming great sloppy puddings. And they dress wrong. Collars and ties and all that nonsense. And they import their whiskies, and mix them with the water, as if they were in London. All wrong. They're rejecting the land, you see, and eventually, it gets enough, and rejects them as well. They come all wrapped in a shell. Where the only way one *should* come is naked.' He sat down on the edge of the pool and dabbled his long bony fingers in the water.

'Those who have nothing God clothes in freedom,' I said suddenly. He looked up, his pale blue eyes quizzical in a face that was surprisingly young for all its weathered lines.

'Yes. I like that,' he said.

'Did you come naked?' Jack asked suddenly. Andrew Sinclair grinned, a lopsided attractive grin, showing crooked, strong white teeth like a dog's.

'No. But I'm naked now.' He stood up. 'Naked to the bone.' He looked faintly grim. 'Fancy a little ramble tomorrow?' he said.

It was a moment before I realized it was an invitation, and I wasn't sure to what, but I said quickly, 'Yes. Yes that would be nice.' Jack didn't argue, for which I was glad. I wanted him out of doors and away from his books. Andrew Sinclair seemed a healthy alternative which under the circumstances proved a glorious joke.

Isfahan was a beautiful city, built at the edge of a

desert, below a range of rough and jagged mountains, an oasis jewel of domes, minarets and gardens.

But it was not in the city that Andrew Sinclair intended to ramble, but up on the harsh barren hills above. He arrived at dawn, with a pack on his back, and a snug-fitting dark cap on his head, and led us out through the still city, across one of the bridges that span the river, and into the countryside.

Andrew Sinclair's ramble took all day, a rough and exhilarating climb up on to barren rocky heights from which we could look down upon all Isfahan, spread below like the Persian garden of myth; the blue of the river, the gleaming domes and tiled minarets, the soft rows of green trees amidst the pale buildings. We pressed on at a hard pace. Only when we stopped for lunch, a Persian lunch of nuts and fruit and yoghurt, did we have any conversation. Then he reminisced about the Scottish hills where he had climbed as a boy, listing off their beautiful familiar names like a litany of forgotten saints.

Towards evening, we reached the outskirts of the city once more. I thought we would return directly, but Andrew Sinclair suddenly detoured into a little village just across the river from the city. He slipped the pack from his back and approached the street door of a tiny, mud-brick house. He disappeared within, and then came out in a moment for us, and led us into the dark interior.

The house consisted of two rooms, the first, where our host greeted us, barely large enough to contain our small company, and the second, interior room, where no doubt he slept. It had no furnishings, other than the few worn, poor quality carpets spread on the plain dirt floor. In the centre of the room was a charcoal brazier of some cheap tarnished metal, and around the walls, in niches cut into the brick, were small possessions, cups and plates, books, a water-pipe. The walls were decorated with many pictures, all religious; depictions of Muslim saints, the Caliph Ali, the Virgin Mary and the Christ Child. Their style was primitive and colourful, and but for the eastern costuming and some unfamiliar faces, they might have been the holy pictures on the walls of an Irish cabin.

Our host was a small man, of middle age, very black haired and black eyed, with a wispy beard and handsome, sharp features. His smile showed excellent teeth, white and perfect. He had not been expecting us, but welcomed us as if he had. Andrew Sinclair introduced him to us as Mirza Yusuf Ja'far.

He was a dervish, a holy man of one of the Sufi orders. I had heard of such beings, mystics who studied and chanted and danced in pursuit of oneness with God. They lived often in poverty, and I had seen some begging in the bazaars. Still, not all I had heard had been good, and I entered with some caution and took the place offered me on a rug beside the brazier.

'God is good that you should find my door,' he said, giving an air of portent to our arrival. He spoke the good English of an educated man, jarringly at odds with his rough white woollen rags. He went through to his inner room and came back with trays of delicacies, fruits and pistachio nuts, and tea. He brought wine also, which though proscribed by Islam, was still quite often served. We settled to these temptations, enjoying them after the hard work of our climb. For a while Andrew Sinclair and Mirza Yusuf talked casually of the trivialities common to good friends. But then, quite suddenly, our host stopped, set down his wine glass and began to sing, or chant, a long, beautiful poem.

Such an innovation in the midst of conversation, though

odd in a Western drawing room, seemed quite natural there and I listened with pleasure to his high, sing-song voice, which incongruously recalled old men of Western Scotland I had known who would, also without warning, burst out suddenly in Gaelic song. When he was finished, he smiled self-consciously at our praise, and then gave us a translation, quickly and spontaneously made, of great charm.

The talk and singing went on late into the night. I was very sleepy, from the long day and no doubt from the pleasant wine, to the company of which our host had added a bottle of the distilled spirit called *arak*. I had consumed none of that, though Jack and Andrew Sinclair, talking excitedly, had had much. In the end I withdrew from the small circle as politely as I could and lay down in a corner of the room with my head on Jack's backpack and went to sleep. It was no doubt terrible manners, but no one seemed to mind, or even to notice, and thus I missed much of the conversation and awoke some time later, with the room dim, lit by oil-lamps and the glow of the charcoal.

Mirza Yusuf was sitting very silent, cross-legged on his carpet, his hands on his knees and his eyes lifted heavenwards and closed but for small slits. He appeared to be meditating, as indeed did Jack and the mountain-climber, but the room was scented with a strange dreamy odour and I saw Andrew Sinclair lean forward, holding a long pipe in his hand, lift a coal from the glowing brazier with small tongs, touch it momentarily to the pipe bowl, draw heavily upon the pipe and hand it to Jack. They were smoking opium.

We were not innocents: Jack had indulged in hashish, my father's fancy, on our travels, and occasionally at home in New York. But it was not opium. And Jack was not Persian. Even there, only a few used it to no ill effect, and they were rarely Westerners. Andrew Sinclair, thirled to the hills with an even more powerful addiction, maintained that delicate detachment. But Jack had no such protection.

After a while he became aware that I had awakened, and offered the pipe to me. I must have looked angry, because he averted his eyes. And in a short while he spoke to the mountaineer and together they decided it was time to leave. We returned home late, beneath a starry mysterious sky, and were let in by servants to a darkened house. I was deeply disturbed, and in the morning neither of us told the Cowdrys where we had been. I knew it was only a beginning.

Jack returned to the company of Mirza Yusuf frequently thereafter. Sometimes they met in the mud-brick village house, sometimes in the bachelor home of Andrew Sinclair. I did not go with him. I doubt my presence was missed, or even desired, but had it been, I would have acted no differently. Jack was an adult; I could neither judge nor condemn. But neither would I grant the approval of my companionship. I do not wish to infer that these meetings were occasions of debauchery, or that Jack had descended into some opium den. They used it rarely. They read, studied, listened to the songs of the Sufi holy man, argued deep into the metaphysical centre of the night. The opium was a tool, not an entertainment. But they did use it.

We stayed many weeks. As in Teheran, the pace of life, slow and monotonous for Europeans, seemed to beg us to remain, and our hosts displayed the same lonely generosity. I wished it were otherwise. I wanted desperately to have some reason to leave that would not seem contrived and would be yet compelling enough to draw

Jack away from the vortex in which he was descending. And yet, in that time, turning lazily on the edge of that dangerous spiral, he was also happy, inquisitive and excited. He came home with volumes of the Sufi dervish's dusty books, poring over them with Mirza Yusuf's translations at his side. His mastery of the language increased every day. And something else occurred. He began, at last, to write, something he had not done since we had set foot at the Black Sea port of Trebizonde.

Of course he had worked; he had taken notes, and scribbled short passages in his chaotic notebook, and begun brief, intensely personal essays of impressions and daily events. But that was not writing. Here, sitting cross-legged on the floor, ignoring our hosts' carefully imported western furniture, he wrote, in his scrawling hand, the beginnings of a book. That it was not the book we had come there to prepare seemed hardly important. He was writing, and I held a conviction, perhaps wilful fantasy, that as long as he wrote, he would survive.

But then, on the last day of July, something occurred beyond my scope and outwith my power that at last contrived to call us homewards. I received a letter from Teheran, from Sarah Rudsworth, and enclosed within its folds, its seal unbroken, was another, addressed to me. It bore an American postmark, and was dated many weeks before.

Patchin Place
29 May 1934

My dear Justina,

I am bringing the children to Europe. I wish them to see the Continent, and more particularly, I wish them to see you. Wendell has made his usual objections, which I have chosen to ignore.

We shall arrive in Paris on the fourth of September, and I trust this will be convenient.

Yours very sincerely
Margaret de Quincey Pyke

I ran through the house with the letter in my hand. Jack was not there, but I knew where I would find him.

On the outskirts of the city, there was a cluster of private gardens, some tended regularly by their owners and used for entertainment and relaxation, others long abandoned and fallen into dereliction. Jack and I had discovered one such, some weeks earlier, and often, when the weather was hot, we would retreat to its cool privacy. Almost every afternoon, he took his notebooks there and worked, either beneath the one tall shade tree, or in the tiny wood-framed summer house.

The garden was surrounded by a wall of mud brick, dusty and unappetizing from without. I entered through the gate and made my way through the overgrown tangle of pink and white roses, so old and gnarled that their blossoms were as simple as wild flowers, tumbling in lavish untrimmed sprays to the ground. There was a path, all but vanished in a thicket of young poplar saplings, and one tall tree, a kind of willow, I think, that drooped over the little stream of water that ran politely from garden to garden.

Jack sat cross-legged on a small prayer rug, spread out beneath the tree, an earthenware bottle of wine beside him, cooling in the stream. He was writing in his notebook and did not hear me come, until I stood beside him.

My delight must have shown on my face, because he said at once, 'What is it?' He jumped up, when I told him, and embraced me happily. 'How wonderful for you. How wonderful.' His pleasure in mine was so complete. I did not want to speak. I stepped back, still holding his arms, studying his face. He looked much aged from when I first met him, but still handsome. He looked well; as if nothing he found here could possibly harm him.

I said reluctantly, 'Do you understand that I must go, almost at once?'

'Yes. Of course I understand.' He paused carefully; Jack never made promises he could not honour. Then he said, 'Do you want me to come with you?' I looked down at the stream, to the little pool by our feet, formed with careful deliberation by some forgotten artisan. I could see our reflections, blurred as ghosts in our pale summer clothes.

'Are you ready to leave?'

He smiled, wistfully, 'No. Not yet.'

I reached up and kissed him. 'Then stay. I'll go by myself.' He shook his head. 'I'll be fine. I'm always fine alone.'

'No,' he said, shaking his head again, not wishing to face either choice.

I felt brief hope, and said cautiously, 'I could wait perhaps a week.'

He looked away from me, through the tangle of rose-trees to the city and mountains beyond. 'I don't think it's a question of weeks.'

'No,' I said. 'I didn't think it was.'

It is easy to say, 'I will love, I will not covet,' until one reaches a moment like this. This is the test, and in it, all the dark side of the human heart comes rushing to the fore; the jealousies, the possessiveness, the recriminations that make a bondage of love, from the blessing it is meant to be. I am proud of us. There were no harsh words, and no tears. We took from each other the freedom we had wordlessly promised a day long ago in New York, and silently loosed our silent wedding bonds. He had found what he sought in life and it was not me.

I walked from that paradise garden, back alone into the dusty city. As I walked I imagined him grown old in this place, one of those gentle, contentedly lost beings who find a small forgotten niche far from everything that bred them, in which to live out their lives. He would become a curiosity, an enigma, like Andrew Sinclair, perhaps, though without his restless quest. If the opium did not win, he might be quite happy there.

Four days later I left Isfahan. Jack had found me an escort in the Oxford scholar who studied Persian poetry and was returning now to England. As we drove in his ancient Ford motorcar at a snail's pace through the cramped streets, Jack rode beside me, perched on the door, his feet on the running board. On the long many-arched bridge across the River Zaindeh, he jumped down into the dust of the road. He caught my hand, and released it, in silence.

'Goodbye, Jack,' I said.

We drove on across the bridge and, looking back, I saw him standing there, watching me as if all he possessed was riding there with me, and yet he would not come. A *charvardar* rode out on to the bridge, leading a string of laden mules, and I lost him in their midst.

We remained a week in Teheran, before continuing to Istanbul. I carefully crated what remained there of my paintings, most of which I had sent on earlier to Paris. These last I saw safely shipped homewards; and I wrote to Margaret Pyke, assuring her I would be in Paris to meet her. Then, in a round of faintly awkward social engagements, I made my farewells.

As we rode out of the city, on the road to Tabriz, I looked up to the slopes of the Elburz that I had promised myself. They remained beyond my reach. Their white tops were the last things I remembered of Teheran. I would never forget them, because I had not achieved them. It is those things that elude our grasp that remain with us and are ours forever.

At Trebizonde, my scholar sold his Ford motorcar and we took passage on the steamer for Istanbul. On board, we were taken for a returning missionary and his wife, which amused me greatly, and totally mortified my companion. I think he was glad to be rid of me when at last he safely delivered me and my luggage to my hotel in the Turkish seaport. There, we parted company. He was to remain a further fortnight, visiting friends at the University, and I was to depart almost at once, for Paris.

I left Istanbul on a steamy August morning; seven months to the day of my arrival there with Jack; as we had come, on the Orient Express.

The train was cool and clean, its beautiful furnishings making me feel I was already home, back in Europe where I belonged. I sat on the edge of my berth, idly tracing the polished wood panelling of the carriage wall with my hand. I thought of Jack in the shade of the poplars in the garden in Isfahan. I could picture everything about him, his dusty canvas hat casting a shade over his forehead, the outdoorsman's weathered brown skin, the lines beside his mouth and around his eyes. I could see his notebook, with its faded red cover and the scrawling script I was never allowed to read. I could hear the sound of the little stream washing around his earthenware bottle of wine, and could taste the musty sweetness of it, as he held it up to my lips.

Just before the train pulled out, I got up and left my berth and wandered down the corridors, passing through the dining car with its white-clothed tables set with silver and flowers for luncheon, and entered the smoking salon at the rear of the train. It was wood-panelled and carpeted with Persian rugs and furnished with chintz and brocade arm chairs. Two were occupied by ageing gentlemen with white moustaches and cigars; diplomats or army officers returning from the East. They looked up and nodded politely, as I walked slowly down the length of the carriage. At its far end there was an open platform, roofed over and surrounded by railings, where passengers might take the air. It was separated from the interior salon by a lovely door with windows of engraved glass. Through it, the little platform looked faintly hazy, like something from another time or a dream. The wheels gave their first backward, then forward, jerk, and I remembered Strathpeffer and the station at Achterneed. Then they began to roll, and steam shushed out and clouded my already clouded picture, and just as it wavered and cleared I saw the man running, pushing, battering his way through the crowds. He stumbled into a cluster of old men in turbans, parting them in a flurry of shouting and upraised fists, leapt right over a small scurrying dog, and kept running, racing the train. He was sun-browned, bearded, his canvas hat flying loose from a string about his throat, a pack on his back, and a holdall swinging free from one hand as he ran. Someone in the station cheered. He reached up for the railing, missed, ran three more strides, caught it and swung himself up the steps. The whistle shrilled and the train pulled away. He stood, laughing, leaning luxuriantly against the railings, and I flung open the door, ran onto the platform and into his arms.

26

No coercion: Faith, we must believe.
Gabriel announces morning Eve reprieved.
Her will ceded, His Will her glory seeds.
No concession: a most uncreditable creed,
His plough upon unfertile fields
A penchant for unlikely yields;
Elizabeth through measured age,
She, through measureless Innocence;
Conception of the unconceived. She will assume
God fleshed and feeble in a mortal womb.
Starfall into stable, unstable world
Whirled to deepest gravity; Faith and finite
Fused. Infinity unused to earth
Stoops to the fold of human arms,
In human form entombed,
Three span three His measured days,
The Three-In-One undone,
The unseparable gone separate ways.
No coercion: Faith, we must believe.
No concession: A most uncreditable creed.
Each soul in starry solitude makes, once, the virgin tryst;
Thus mother with thee, Mary, all, thy child Christ.

'Annunciation' from *A Persian Garden*, Jack Redpath, 1937.

In August of 1934, when Jack and I returned from Persia, we did not go back to the flat on the Rue St Julien. It had been shut up and empty, and needed airing, but more than that, it seemed restrictive and small after our wanderings. I think, given a choice, Jack would have pitched a tent somewhere and lived in that; he was growing ever more nomadic. But the choice not being there, we stayed temporarily with May and searched around for something more suitable until Jack secured a Seine houseboat, the *Suzanne*, from one of his friends among the bargemen. It seemed to suit him ideally, as if he wished less and less connection with the earth on which he lived. That he might untether it and float away at will delighted him, though it left me with the strange feeling that I might never be sure of where I would awake in the morning. However, the potential of freedom seemed sufficient, and Jack never attempted the actuality; so we remained pleasantly moored by the Quai St Michel, bound yet to reality by two strands of hemp.

When Margaret Pyke arrived in Paris, our arrangements were not yet complete and we were yet staying in the Rue Zacharie with May. It was there I received her message and an invitation to meet at her hotel near the Place Vendôme. Alone, and wildly nervous, I ventured across the river to the citadels of the Right Bank. I felt a sparrow among peacocks in my plain skirt and blouse and my little felt beret, and the hotel, rich and disapproving, filled me with dismay. I had a terrible fear that the children would be ashamed of me; it was the first time ever in my life that I regretted the way I looked and dressed. I was almost thankful that they were not with Margaret when she greeted me at the door of her suite.

'I thought we would talk alone, for a little while,' she said, inviting me in. I nodded, blushing and awkward. She wore a stylish dress of white linen, belted casually about the hips. She had aged and her face was ravaged and rather tragic. She was still a handsome woman, but all that was left of the great beauty she had been were her luminous brimming eyes, from which, as she leaned to kiss me, tears began at once to fall. Quite suddenly we embraced, remembering that we had once been friends.

She had ordered tea, and she began to pour it with

fumbling hands. I wanted to help, but I could not make myself move towards her. I stood back as she faced me, handed me the cup, and then gazed in silence, her jewelled hands knotted together. She broke them apart and raised them, in two fists, pressed either side of her head, as if fighting a terrible pain. She closed her eyes and when she opened them again they were calm, looking straight into mine. 'It was all lies, wasn't it?' she said.

Slowly, I nodded my head.

'Yes,' I said. 'Yes, it was.' She sighed.

'I am devastated with shame.' She turned away. After a long while she said, 'I left him when I realized.' Again, I nodded, though she did not see. She had done what I had dared not do. But then, she had the resources. And she had allies. Mrs Pyke, and Wendell's surviving sisters had all been on her side. One divorce was grudgingly countenanced; a second, never. I almost felt pity for Wendell with the strength of that family turned against him forever.

'Would you like to see the children now?' Margaret said.

I could not speak. I tried to make some gesture of affirmation, but I could do nothing but stand there. I was shaking. Margaret crossed the room and disappeared through a door on the other side. I can still see that door, white, gilt-trimmed, with an oval decorative panel. I stood frozen, staring at it, and slowly it opened. She had sent them in to me alone, honouring our privacy just as she had done on the day she took them away.

They came in together, a young man and woman of fifteen and fourteen, these two who had once been my babies. They were both so grown, Wendell was as tall as my brother Sandy, and looked so like him with his soft straight hair and intelligent, cautious green eyes, that looking at him was like looking at a ghost. How eerie, I thought, as they stood there. Sandy was the cause of my marriage, and out of its ashes I saw Sandy reborn. 'Wendell?' I whispered.

'Hello, Justina,' he said. His voice was a man's voice. He hung back by the door, lanky, wary, his long awkward arm about his sister's shoulders. He was terrified, but his first thought was her protection. Ellie tucked herself in under that arm, dark and flighty as a blackbird. Her eyes flickered to me then to the floor, then up to Wendell, and suddenly, like a fledgling from a nest she burst forth from her shelter. 'Oh!' she cried and ran into my arms. She was as warm as a little child in my embrace.

Margaret stayed three weeks in Paris. The children spent every day with me. She brought them to me early and collected them late, and dealt with me with every generosity. It is easy to say that she assuaged a guilty conscience; there are other, less courageous ways of doing that. She had made one terrible mistake, made it honestly, and repented it totally. Now she did everything to amend. I cannot say I ever loved Margaret Pyke, but I am scrupulously bound to forgive her. At the end of the three weeks, when the time came for her to take the children away, she brought them to me for one last time. By then Jack and I were living on the houseboat, but I was working in the studio on the Rue St Julien, and it was to that dingy, familiar place that she brought them. It was an awkward parting. She had promised me they would return each summer, and I believed her. But summer was a year away; children grow and change, and so do families. Who knew what voice would speak for them then? I waited for them in the studio like I had so many years ago waited in my flat on Gay Street. When they came through the door, Wendell was carrying flowers, gold and russet chrysanthemums. He had bought them himself. I think I cried. We shared a glass of wine and talked of the future. Ellie stood twisting her black curls about one finger like her baby self.

Then it was time for them to go. Margaret stepped back and turned her elegant head aside. Wendell shook my hand and bent to brush my cheek with a dry, fumbling kiss. Ellie stood unmoving, her eyes devouring me, great huge confused dark eyes. And then, as they turned, she suddenly came alive, tugged free from her brother's guardian arm and dashed to me, throwing her arms about my waist. 'Oh Justina!' she cried, 'I want to be an artist. I want to be an artist, too!'

And that was how it was decided, in one flash of certainty, what her future would be. She had seen what she wanted and had grasped for it, and nothing would stand in her way. I don't think she would have left my side if Margaret had chosen to physically drag her away, but that was not Margaret's way. She stood there in that shabby room, looking around with a mother's protective wariness.

'Ellie, is this what you want?'

Ellie's whole passionate young body spoke for her. She clung to me and begged, 'Let me stay. Please let me stay. I'll be good. I'll clean up my room. I'll wash dishes. I won't bother Jack. Please let me stay and be an artist with you.'

So Ellie Pyke stayed behind when her brother and Margaret left Paris for New York. I found her a tutor in French and I enrolled her in the same school that Eithne had attended. I doubt the Pykes would have approved but it was window-dressing anyway. Her real education was with me. For the next three years she worked at my side in my studio, so like my young self in that of Mr Yeats.

Silent, always listening, always watching, always painting, and her talent was leagues ahead of my own. We are all proud in our own ways, but never so proud as when our children outreach us. It was a sweet, sweet time, the answer to prayers and the resolution of dreams.

Each summer, Wendell joined us too. But he was not like Ellie. Love did not come easily to him. He kept tight his ties to his American family, and never released himself from his own cautious reserve. Wendell built careful bridges to us, where Ellie closed her eyes and jumped. And though he did love me, it was in the manner of an adolescent boy with the first older woman who stirs his heart. He never felt himself my son. But Ellie, flinging herself passionately into our lives, cried out to be my daughter; mine, and Jack's. He called her his blessing, my blackbird daughter who ran to fill the emptiness Eithne had left behind. Eithne was cruel in the way only youth can be cruel, escaping her own infatuation with Jack by transmuting it to anger. He who had been once her father, later her idol, became her chief opponent in a cold, endless argument of politics and world-sorrow. It was an argument he could not win, since she had chosen to cast him as champion of all she opposed. She never listened to a word he said. When she had reduced him to misery, she would leave, bitterly self-satisfied, and Ellie would run and throw her arms about his neck and cry, '*I* love you, Jack,' as I had run once to shield James Howie from Kate.

'The blessing of my old age,' he said, kissing her shining curls. He was jesting but she took him quite seriously. I suppose he seemed quite old enough to her. He was forty-seven.

In October of 1936, Jack published *Caravanserai*, a travel history of our Persian journey. As before, I provided the illustrations, and the finished book was a graceful, attractive production. But times had changed since *A Pyrenean Autumn*. *Caravanserai* appeared in London in the year that began with the death of George V, saw Hitler occupy the Rhineland, Mussolini conquer Abyssinia, and insurrection erupt in Spain. In the October week of its publication Fascists and anti-Fascists were fighting in the London streets. The impressions of two wanderers in Persia fell like a single drop of water into a desert of indifference.

Jack and I were no longer political people. Like many of our generation, we held a bone-deep determination that there must never be another war, and from it sprang our only overt political act: we had both signed Dick Sheppard's Peace Pledge, at the request of Meggie Whyte. But renouncing war was one thing, avoiding it another. It became increasingly impossible not to feel the tug of violence. If we closed our eyes, and turned our backs it was because we had experienced the unthinkable and could not countenance it again. But we were increasingly alone. Critics informed Jack that his next work should be topical. He replied with *A Persian Garden*.

This, undoubtedly his most beautiful work, contrived as well to be his most obscure, his most personal, and his most resoundingly out of tune with the times. (Jack was nothing if not bloody-minded.) It was a collection of twenty-five poems, not a prose word amongst them. Mystical, on occasion incomprehensible, they were poems of revelation, signposts on an inward journey towards faith. Significantly, despite their Eastern inspiration and Sufi influences, they were essentially Christian in theme. They had their real roots in the white-painted midwestern churches Jack shunned as a boy. He had gone a long way to find himself back there again.

They could be, and have been, read in many ways. Some people still see many of them as love poems (with myself as object), and of course they were not. And while I am correcting illusions, I must point out that in spite of what became a fashionable viewpoint, these were not opium dreams. Jack was no Coleridge, and most of these verses were written at home in Paris, in full sobriety. It was not from the opium that the poems sprang, but from the strength by which he resisted it.

But that made little difference to the task before May. She drew me aside after reading the manuscript and said, 'You know I would do *anything* in my power for Jack, but what can I do with these?' It was not that Jack was a bad poet. He was not. (Nor was he the great poet that was later claimed.) He was merely, in 1936, the victim of spectacularly awful timing. *A Persian Garden* celebrated God and peace in a world renouncing both; it was an idea whose time had gone, and would not return for a generation. That it was published at all was due solely to the extraordinary fortitude of May Howie. After a year of unstinting effort she had found an imaginatively compliant house and *A Persian Garden* achieved print at last in April of 1937, the precise day that the Condor Legion devastated the little Basque town of Guernica in Republican Spain.

In late May, a London reviewer spared these few words:

It happens every year or so. I call it Epiphany Time. A writer, often a good writer, who has hitherto shown and fulfilled promise in some sound element, say the writing of good, serious politically aware novels, suddenly, for no good reason that I can think of, SEES GOD. At once, out of the window fly logic, wit, social awareness, characterization, indeed, as in this case, even the art form itself. So what do we have from the ever surprising Mr Redpath, after three splendid novels and two books of passable essays? We have this, a volume of unhinged verse, *à la* Omar Khayyám. Let me set the record straight. I am delighted that Mr Redpath had a lovely time up the garden path in Persia. Nothing could please me more. But must we read about it? Who, in these times, needs this self-indulgent nonsense, and from one whom we could rightly expect to lead us into the serious issues of today.

But no; Mr Redpath has FOUND GOD. Now, I have nothing against God. Not a bad writer himself, judging from his one published work, but oh please, my tender novelists, my budding poets, spare us your intimacies with the Almighty. I find them frankly embarrassing. Enough said; perhaps the difficulty is generational. Mr Redpath is not in the first bloom of youth. But I would think he was not yet too old to feel his blood stirred by a just cause. We will hope that having got this diversion out of his system he will return his considerable talents to something of significance, and not again ask us to sing his nursery rhymes while Europe burns.

Miss Melrose's drawings are pretty but hardly relevant.

I include this in its entirety to give you some idea of the effect, upon the careers of artists, of fashion. *A Persian Garden*, the one work by which Jack's name is still known by a generation who never heard of his novels, vanished without a trace in the tumult of our times. Revived in 1964, it has never again been out of print, and has travelled across the world in countless backpacks and the hip pockets of numberless pairs of denim blue jeans. Had Jack been alive, he'd have died laughing.

At the time, however, he merely taped that blessedly awful review up in a prominent place in the houseboat on the Seine and left it there for everyone to read. That was how he handled such things.

Tattered and yellowed, it was still there in the late

summer of that year. Ellie kept asking me to take it down. She was devotedly protective of Jack.

'I don't want Auntie Clare to see it,' she said.

'Oh Clare won't be impressed by that. She makes up her own mind about things.' I looked up and smiled encouragingly. She was painting as she talked, her easel set up on the stern deck of the houseboat. She looked away, towards the quayside and the horse-chestnut trees spreading their deep late summer shadow over the edge of the river.

'I don't want her to laugh at Jack,' she said stubbornly.

'He won't mind, poppet,' I said. After all the things Clare had called Jack over the years, a little laughter would come as a refreshment.

'Writers thrive on adversity,' Wendell said, over my shoulder. We were sitting back to back on a long bench on the cabin roof. He was leaning against me, bonily awkward, his sharp shoulder blades pressed against my own. Wendell was unused to physical affection, and when he craved it, he had to find it in some unusual, joking way. We spent a lot of time in mock fistfights and wrestling matches. He jostled me, trying to turn me off the bench.

'Stop it,' I said, giggling, struggling to hold on to the stack of papers on my knees. I added, 'They don't, you know. Nor do artists. That's a myth the world puts about to justify not paying us enough.'

'I still wish you'd take it down,' said Ellie.

'I can't,' I said honestly. 'That's for Jack to do.'

She looked puzzled. She did not understand. She wrinkled her nose, and rubbed it with a painty hand. Ellie always had red or blue spots on her somewhere, in those days. She was a comical child, and her wide dark eyes, always surprised by something, and her smooth, faintly oriental face reflecting every emotion that passed behind it. Her rat's nest tangle of shiny black curls, forever uncombed, was tied up in a knotted silk kerchief. She looked a gypsy. She should have *been* Jack's child.

'Did you *know* any of these people?' Wendell asked. He was reading Hemingway's *Fiesta*, self-consciously experiencing Paris.

'I knew some of them,' I said. Before he could ask anything more, I added, 'Nothing is ever *quite* the way it reads in books.' Those times seemed now a very long while ago.

I leaned comfortably against my son's young strong back, drawing my knees up on the bench. I was wearing loose trousers and found them wonderfully comfortable and free. I liked getting up in the morning and dressing with the same simplicity as Jack. I turned over another page and laid it on the deck, weighting it carefully with a blue glazed tile we had brought back from Qom. I liked the smell of the houseboat, a peculiar boat smell of hot, weathered paint. It was pretty, decorated with pots of red and salmon-pink geraniums and two tabby cats, one grey and one orange, who moved in uninvited and stayed with us ever afterwards. From where I sat I could see men fishing in the shadows of the bridges, and beyond the bridges, the spires of Notre Dame. 'The best view and the worst sanitation in Paris,' said Jack of our home. The waters of the Seine, oily and murky, slipped by under the shadows of leaves. I had rarely been happier.

I finished a dozen more pages and laid them beneath the blue tile. I was reading proofs for Jack. His American publisher was bringing out a collection of his short stories. We suspected it was an apology to his loyal readership for *A Persian Garden*. No matter; the money would be nice. But he was busy with a new novel, and I took over what small tasks I could. The episode in Persia had taken something from him; his energies were diminished. He no longer drank much, or caroused with friends, and if he worked too hard he paid for it. He seemed older, and sometimes I worried about his health. But he was happy enough. The new novel was a love story, set during the war, private and personal. Jack wasn't giving his critics an inch. He worked in our old flat above St Julien-le-Pauvre. I used it also as a studio. I was kept busy. Society ladies and government officials sat to me. At present I was working on a portrait of a minor politician, a M. Hubert, whose long-nosed face, and woolly white curls won from my children the name of Monsieur the Sheep.

I was a little sorry that Clare was coming. Her visits once or twice a year, were always disrupting. In the past, Jack had enjoyed them, amusing himself in teasing her, but that devilish side of him was gone now. He would rather have no argument with anyone. Still, she felt a duty to my children; lost lambs in my untrustworthy care, and fulfilled it conscientiously. We would take her out to dinner and ply her with wine which sometimes made her amiable. Wendell would enjoy sparring with her, anyhow; his wits were as sharp as hers. I had promised them dinner at the Brasserie Lipp. It was not a place we frequented, but the children had read about it, and found it exciting. It was the summer of the children; Eithne and Hugo and Jean-Michel and my pair of prodigals who were lost and now were found. I will always remember it that way.

Eithne no longer wore a blue smock, nor read school books to nuns. She wore tight black jerseys that showed her body off, and read Marx and Lenin with Jean-Michel the printer's son. She did not mind now his being a communist, having become one herself. But she would still not marry him. Christian marriage was obsolete; 'a bourgeois indulgence,' she dismissed it, though she fancied a revolutionary wedding in Republican Spain.

Beleaguered Spain was her *cause célèbre* that troubled summer. She was not alone, but I mistrusted her motives. I knew her too well, and I knew her mother, Kate. She was another who must give her love to a nation, rather than a man, no matter what the cost in human hearts. To Spain, and to the Party, she gave all the devotion that once she had given the Church. Oh, my little lighter of candles; it had to go somewhere, I suppose.

At least it did not go to Jean-Michel. I was pleased about that. I disliked him intensely. He had all the humourless pomposity of youth certain of its righteousness. A dark sly contemptuous young man, he scorned what he saw as our frivolity, in dismissive ignorance of our past. Eithne I could forgive; there was something pure and innocent in the fire of her beliefs. There was nothing innocent about Jean-Michel.

In the spring, May had dismissed him from his job at The Fishing Cat. She had found him printing tracts for the Party. 'On my expensive paper,' she declared, outraged. It was not that she was unsympathetic to the cause: a large black-lettered sign demanding ARMS FOR SPAIN filled her window. She would have given them the paper had they asked. But they did not ask.

'Property is bourgeois,' defended Eithne.

'A revolution founded on theft will breed nothing but thieves,' said May. But she did not forbid Eithne seeing Jean-Michel. Authoritarianism was not her style. They met after work (he had found a job in the fruit markets at Les Halles) and went together about the bookshops and cafés near the Sorbonne where the students gathered. They dressed self-consciously like labourers, and talked a great deal, and collected money for Medical Aid for

Spain. During the University holidays, my nephew Hugo Melrose sometimes joined them. He stayed with us, or with May, so that he might be near Eithne. He had no liking for her politics, but could not free himself from the fascination she worked upon him. Naturally enough, he detested Jean-Michel. They made a noisy contentious assembly, wandering about the city, as Kate and Clare and May and Padraic had wandered Dublin. Sometimes Ellie trailed after them, just as I had done there, watching, always watching, and never quite a part of things. Once they kept her out very late and Jack went looking for them, and snatched her away, in an angry scene with Jean-Michel that nearly ended in a physical fight.

In other years, Wendell had been part of that, as enchanted with Eithne O'Mordha as any other. But this year he had come with a love of his own. Khadija Abbas accompanied him to France. They were devoted friends, possibly even lovers, but I doubted that; his youthful awkwardness and her cultural chastity made it unlikely. There were a few years between them too, and she who had mothered him in infancy was motherly yet. It was a pretty friendship, and its prettiness irked Eithne. She was no longer the innocent, blithely charming shepherd boys in the Pyrenees. She knew her powers now, and like other proud beautiful women accustomed to flocks of admirers, was made distressed and resentful by any sheep beyond the fold. I saw her set out to win him and it chilled my soul.

The Pykes all blamed her for Wendell's involvement with the Party, but Eithne did not make a Communist of him. That happened in New York, before he came to see us that year. Khadija told me about it, sadly, 'It began with his caring so. He always cared. Poor people, men without jobs, little children and old people in the streets;

it made him cry when he was a child, and when he was older it made him angry. Once he stopped a man selling apples in the street and gave him his own coat.

'I think it made him hate himself, for not being poor. And I know it made him hate his family. But it was all from caring, from something good. Then we met a friend I had known at school. A beautiful girl whose family were as rich as his. She'd given all her money away to the Communists and now she was happy. She took us with her to meet with them. There was a restaurant on Fourteenth Street, where they all met; the Academy. We sat around tables and drank coffee and they all talked about the Revolution. I laughed, because they sounded like little boys and girls, but that made them angry.' She had smiled suddenly, that white smile, like her father's, and dropped her smoky lashes down over her eyes. 'Wendell got angry too,' she said with a shrug.

'And you?' I asked.

'Oh, me. I am not political. I look and I never see right and wrong. I see people. I see the little boys and girls, posing with their Russian caps, and I find them funny. And then I see also the old men who sit in the shadows and listen and make suggestions so cleverly that the boys and girls think they have thought of them themselves. That I do not find funny. But then, it is too late. Then it is all "Comrade" and clenched fists, and marching in the streets.' She sighed, leaning her smooth brown cheek on the back of her hand. 'But I love him so,' she said.

Wendell came to Paris that summer carrying his Party card.

Jack thought it did not matter. They were young and full of passion, and he thought as well they were possibly right. I was less comforted. All my life I had lived among people who gave ideas precedence over human life; I had not seen any good come of it yet. Nor had I Jack's capacity to divorce myself from the world, and let it roll relentlessly by. And even for Jack that grew difficult. Of all the causes that had troubled our times, Spain was the most difficult to ignore. If one's conscience allowed it, the likelihood was that one's friends would not.

In June of that year, Jack received a letter, a questionnaire, composed by leading lights of the literary world and sent to every writer of note publishing in the British Isles. It was about Spain and it was quite unequivocal. After a brief introduction of the cause, it demanded simply:

> Are you for, or against, the legal government and the people of Republican Spain?
>
> Are you for, or against, Franco and Fascism?

Jack read it carefully and looked up at me with a wry smile. 'Tell me, sir,' he said, 'when did you stop beating your wife?' He sat looking at it for a long while, thinking. Then he folded it neatly and put it under the cats' water dish. He was not one to be intellectually press-ganged.

I doubt the instigators of this graceful piece of moral blackmail were particularly distressed by Jack's failure to answer. There were bigger fish about to be hooked, and whatever stature he had had in the literary world as a leader of thought (*I Dreamed I Saw Joe Hill* won him a brief glory among the Bolsheviks) was effectively eroded by *A Persian Garden*. But the children were another matter.

Eithne castigated Jack over what he called 'Nancy Cunard's little question'. It had no effect. He was not afraid of her. Baffled, and a little over-confident, she tried charm. But her powers as a seductress could hardly win a man who had loved her as a child. That angered her, and he knew it, and occasionally teased her in cynical fun. He was stronger than she imagined, and I enjoyed watching her learn that surprising fact. Once, I was tempted to tell her of the machine gun at Dernancourt that Jack handled with brutal expertise. But I did not. That darkness was ours to wrestle with; she would have darknesses of her own.

Even now, after six weeks, she would grasp any opportunity to raise the subject, in the hope of shaming him into a change of heart. If it were Eithne alone, and the unlovely Jean-Michel, I would not have cared. But Wendell too laid the question before us, solemnly, with the reasoned courtesy of youth when proud of its rational powers. He fought with the head, not the heart, but neither head nor heart won Jack.

When Wendell straightened slightly on our bench and half-turned, and addressed me with his thoughtful caution, I was afraid he was going to talk about Jack and Spain. But he said only, 'Justina, when I was young, we came to see you once and you and Mother . . . Margaret . . . had a fight. You slapped her.' I laughed, sitting up, and swung my legs down from the bench.

'Do you remember that?'

'What were you fighting about?'

'About you. Who loved you most. Like little children, we were fighting about that.' I paused, looking down at my feet in leather sandals. 'That was the last time I saw you, before Margaret brought you to Paris.' Wendell was quiet, thinking about it, and I sat in silence for a while. Then I turned to him, 'Sandy . . .'

'I'm Wendell,' he giggled. I was forever calling him that.

'Wendell . . . I don't mind that you call her Mother.

She's been that to you. I would have loved to have been, but I wasn't there.' He reached his big, bumbly hand along the bench, not looking at me, until his fingers found mine.

'I love you,' he said. He stood up, his back to me. It was I who was cautious then.

'Are you going?' I said quietly.

'Yes.' He did not turn to face me. 'I promised to meet Eithne.'

'Clare should be here soon,' I said casually, while the fingers of my left hand drew a tight circle on the grey bench.

'Yeah. Well, I'll see her tonight,' he said quickly. I stared down at my invisible circle. I was aware of Ellie, having stopped painting, watching us.

'Where's Khadija?' I said mildly. He turned around then and gave me a big, self-assured smile.

'She's gone out with Hugo,' he said, '*again*. They've taken a picnic to the Bois.' He laughed. 'Maybe I'd better be jealous.' He was being a little superior and reminded me, for an annoying moment, of his father.

I said, 'Be kinder to her, Wendell.' He was at once stiffly angry and defensive.

'This isn't romantic, Justina. There's a big rally tonight in the Place St Michel. Eithne wanted me to help prepare.'

'That's not romantic?' I said, smiling a little.

'You don't understand.'

I stood up and walked across the cabin roof until we stood side by side. I said, 'Let me see. First, there'll be a long speech by a solemn little man from the Party. Then, a young girl from the Republic will talk in a beautiful sad accent about her dead parents and brothers and comrades. Then a group of young people from the University will recite ‘On Guard for Spain’ and someone will hold up a flag, and people will throw money and shout “*Salud*” and a recruiter will come for the International Brigades and everyone will sing Spanish songs. You see, I understand very well.’

He turned around suddenly. ‘Why must you laugh at all we believe in?’

‘I’m not laughing, Wendell. I’m only telling you that I’ve been there before.’ He looked serious and old.

‘A road is not used up by one person walking on it,’ he said. He looked at me solemnly and turned away, ‘I’ve got to go.’ I watched as he jumped down on to the flat deck at the rear of the houseboat where Ellie was sitting by her easel. He touched her shoulder as he passed her and then he jumped across to the steps up to the quay. ‘I’ll meet you,’ he said and he waved.

I nodded and called after him, ‘*Salud.*’ He did not answer. I sat down on the bench again and Ellie came up and sat at my feet and put her head on my knees, the black curls tumbling from their kerchief. I stroked each curl.

‘I don’t want Wendell to fight for Spain,’ she said. My hand stopped, frozen on her shining hair.

Clare arrived an hour later. It was late afternoon and the shadows were long. I saw her walking up the Quai St Michel, under the tall trees. She had come alone, without Meggie. She carried an armful of flowers and was looking about herself curiously as she walked. She looked almost pretty, in a severe, tailored way. I smiled and stood up and waved. She was still my sister and I loved her yet.

‘Clare!’ She looked up and held up the flowers in one hand.

‘Ahoy, the *Suzanne*,’ she cried gaily. I ran down to help

her across our little gangplank. We kissed on the open deck and Ellie came running and embraced her aunt, with sun-browned arms. Clare looked pleased and embarrassed. 'Haven't you grown again,' she said.

Ellie nodded, encouragingly. Her generous spirit ran to ease Clare's lifelong awkwardness with children. 'Did you have a nice trip?' she asked. Clare looked surprised to find anyone interested. She smiled drily.

'Oh, the Channel was choppy, and the French trains are perfectly ghastly, but what does one expect, after all?' I saw Ellie trying not to giggle.

I made tea while Clare opened a parcel of little gifts for us, and when we sat down together in the sunshine she said, gesturing towards my loose trousers, 'Look at you. What would Mother say?' Her face was very severe but her eyes were merry.

'Oh, Mother has been spared a lot, I think,' I said looking down. Clare began to laugh, richly.

'Oh, can you imagine what *any* of them would say? Mother, or Father, or James or Eugenia. Good heavens, look at us. Me and my books, and you and your paints. And Jack. *Sic transit* Arradale.' She laughed again, sipping her tea.

'Father would understand,' I said quietly.

'Oh, Father,' she said, subtly annoyed. She was quiet for a moment and then said, 'You know, I was back there last month.'

'Arradale?' I said.

'Yes. I'd forgotten quite how lovely it is. I really had. I had a week there with Wilhemina.' She paused, thinking, looking at Ellie who sat silently listening, taking in everything. She said, 'I was looking at the old cottages by the sea-garden. It would be nice to live there.' She paused again. 'Perhaps I shall, when I retire.'

'Retire?' I said, incredulously. She laughed.

'I'll be sixty in ten years,' she said. 'We're none of us chickens, you know.' I leaned back against the cabin wall, my fingers playing with the leaves of a lemon geranium. The sweet scent filled the air. I stretched my arms, as sun browned as Ellie's, and yawned.

'Speak for yourself,' I said, laughing.

She looked at me, shrewdly acerbic, and said, 'Where's Jack?'

'At the flat,' I said, 'working.'

'He's not,' she said. 'I went there first.' Her eyes were sharp.

I stretched my arms again. 'Then he's with May.'

She was quiet. She sipped her tea and put the cup down on its saucer with a delicate clink. 'Don't you ever mind how much time he spends with her?' she said. I felt Ellie's eyes move from her face to mine.

'They work together.'

'That doesn't answer my question,' Clare said. I looked up, and sighed. She did not change. The moments of warmth all must be paid for eventually.

'We're too old for that sort of thing,' I said. 'Don't you remember? You just told me.'

'Too old to fall in love?' she laughed drily.

'No. Too old to fight about it. I love Jack, and May loves Jack. And Jack loves us both. And I love May.' I met her eyes stubbornly.

'How tidy,' said Clare.

Later, she was apologetic. She always was after her sharper moments. She talked about the family, our one bond, to obliquely make amends. She said, 'I saw Wilhemina again in London. She shuttles back and forth from Scotland like a demented pigeon. Poor old Kaiser

Bill. We should have got her to marry again. It would have kept her from brooding so.' She looked across the river to where the late sun was touching the stone spires of Notre Dame. 'She's quite frantic about the European situation, you know.'

'Can you blame her?' I said, 'with Hugo at that age?' Clare shrugged.

'Wearing the wheels off the Highland Line won't help.'

'It feels good to keep moving,' I said.

Clare looked impatient. 'Far better to get down to doing something practical.'

'Like Meggie?' I suggested perversely.

She hooted with laughter. 'Meggie? What's Meggie ever done?' Her voice was brittle. 'That little fluffhead. The only thing that meant anything to her all year was the Abdication. "Oh, the poor, poor Prince of Wales,"' she mimicked, adding coldly, 'That kind can never rise above their beginnings.'

'Not if you don't let them,' I said quietly. For all her feminism, Clare was as pompous a Victorian patriarch as Geoffrey. Then I said, 'What about the Peace Pledge Union?'

'Oh, that,' she dismissed. 'Dangerous dimwits. Romantics imagining themselves politicians. They're about as political as that cat.' She prodded our resident ginger tom with an annoyed toe and he got up haughtily and walked away.

'On the contrary,' I said. 'He's quite political. He knows what he wants and he comes and takes it. He's as political as Hitler or Mussolini.' She looked angry and I said quickly to deflect her, 'What's the news from Ireland?' She relaxed into her usual cynicism.

'Oh, Kate's involved in *something*, God knows what. Our wonderful family is at it again. I suppose we shall hear eventually, when the shell splinters settle. I can always tell when something's afoot. She gets abominably cheerful. She was across in London in June, happy as a schoolgirl. Mind, she's not very pleased with Eithne.'

I knew that. There was a rift between mother and daughter over Spain. Kate yearned for the Republican cause, and repudiated the Irish Fascists fighting with Franco. But the burning of churches and murders of priests were another thing. She had become Catholic in Padraic's mould, all reverence and superstition. She had not the Jesuitical detachment of May. I laughed softly, 'Only our family,' I said, 'has schisms rather than rows.'

Clare was calmer now. She had another cup of tea and admired Ellie's paintings and talked about *A Persian Garden* which, perversely enough, she had chosen to like. She decided she would return to her hotel and ready herself for dinner, which in her case meant changing from one severe tweed suit to another, equally severe. She got up to leave, but remained for a moment looking across the Seine to the Île de la Cité. She said suddenly, 'You know, Justina, this is thoroughly charming, but it's not a place to be when winter comes.' Solemnly, she bade me good afternoon and walked away through the lengthening shadows on the quay.

In the Brasserie Lipp we took up two tables, drawn together, even before Eithne and Wendell joined us. They were late, and Khadija kept looking up to the door whenever it opened with her large soft eyes full of uncertainty. Hugo sat beside her, pretending he was not doing the same. Jack sat at the head of the two tables, and I at the foot, and now and then our eyes would meet. After the sunny afternoon, there was thunder and rain, and the cascades streaming down the darkened windows brought to mind a far and different café, and myself and Jack Redpath dining alone, on the edge of goodbye. It was nineteen years ago, that farewell in Etaples, nineteen good years I had not imagined to have. *That would be enough,* I thought. *We could not complain.* But of course, for people in love with each other, there is no such thing as enough.

Ellie sat at Jack's left, with her chair moved round so she could lean against his arm. She looked around the room with candid curiosity. I suspected she was looking for famous people. She seemed unaware that more than one in the crowded café was looking at Jack, who was a little famous himself. It was dark; we were dining late, and the rain had driven people in, making the room steamy and hot. Clare looked restless and uncomfortable in her stiff grey suit, on Jack's right. He was talking to her, and I could tell from the soft lines about his eyes that he was being sweet and charming, though I could not hear what was said. Clare regarded him distrustfully, only occasionally allowing herself a brief, stifled laugh.

'Shall we wait for the children?' I said to May. We had kept places not only for Wendell and Eithne but for Jean-Michel as well.

'If they haven't the manners to be here, I don't see why we should,' she said tartly. She seemed tense, as if more was going on than I knew about. I signalled to Jack who called the *garçon,* and when we were half-way through ordering, Eithne, Jean-Michel and Wendell came in, loud and laughing, from the rain. They had not dressed, but wore their mock-workers' clothes with aggressive belligerence, hoping to see disapproval. I think we disappointed them. I even offered Jean-Michel a place beside me, though he ducked away from it like an untrustworthy dog. Eithne and Wendell sat side by side, exchanging quick private smiles. He did not speak to Khadija, and I saw the wet sparkle of her lashes as she quickly turned away. More than one old order was falling about our table that night.

Our three revolutionaries were so secretively aloof that I half expected them to refuse to join us. But youth being generally as hungry as it is rebellious, they made that concession. As long as Jack was paying, even Jean-Michel would share our board. He ate hurriedly, with slovenly greed, not hiding his dislike of us. Still it was not he, but Eithne, who challenged the peace of our evening.

'What do *you* think of the fighting in Spain?' she demanded of Clare, even as our spoons reached out for our soup.

'Unfortunate,' said Clare. She sipped calmly.

I saw Jack begin to grin. Eithne looked baffled. Jack broke off a piece of bread, leaned back in his chair and said to Clare, 'I believe what Eithne means to ask is "are you for or against the legal government and the people of Republican Spain?"' Clare surprisingly began also to grin.

'Do you mean, "are you for or against Franco and Fascism?"'

'You got one too?' said Jack.

'Hardly. But there have been a few about. Tell me, what did you answer?'

'When has Jack *ever* answered a letter?' said May, mildly.

'Ah,' said Clare, 'I see.' She turned to Eithne. She said, 'Young lady, if this is an attempt to align me against Mr Redpath, you are making an error. Whatever my opinion, he's entitled to one of his own. That's called democracy. We used to think fondly of it when I was young.'

'Am I hearing this?' said Jack. Clare took another sip of her soup and then turned sharply about.

'Don't *you* get smug. I'm not on *your* side, either.'

'Sorry, Ma'am,' said Jack. He touched his forelock.

'I don't find you amusing,' said Clare.

'You miss the point, Aunt Clare,' said Wendell. She looked at him in astonishment, but he continued, 'Jack's opinion isn't like my opinion, or even your opinion. He's a public figure. He hasn't got a private opinion any more. He has set himself up as a leader of thought and he *owes* us . . .'

'I've *what*?' said Jack. He looked at Wendell through slitted eyes. He was really angry, a rare, disconcerting event.

Wendell looked uneasy. He glanced to me for encouragement but I turned away. Still, he said determinedly, 'Writers are leaders of the people's thought.'

Jack looked down. He lifted the linen napkin from his knees and crumpled it up as if he were about to leave the table. I half started up to restrain him. But then he said slowly, 'Writers, Wendell, are paid dreamers. The people's pacifier. What, in the ability to make fanciful stories, qualifies me to pronounce on truth?' He studied Wendell's earnest face and shrugged, exasperated. 'Look,' he said, 'we're not preachers. We've no moral advantage because we spin words well.' He looked round the table wearily, 'There are few things uglier than writers become righteous; locked into their own myth, growing gross on their own fantasies like a leach gorged on blood . . . we've no wisdom for you. We're your court jesters. We're *clowns*.' I saw his eyes go to Eithne, imploring her to believe him. She deflected his words as blankly as a mirror.

'Young people read your work,' she said stubbornly. 'You owe it to them to make a statement.'

'Owe it to them?' Jack shouted. '*Owe* it? Who wrote *that* contract? They give me money and I give them what they pay for, my talent and my hard work. And they get it cheap.'

'Aren't we modest,' said Clare.

'Humility is honesty,' he snapped. He turned back to Wendell, 'What makes them presume for a couple of dollars they get my soul as well?'

Wendell said, 'A man cannot speak without speaking for his generation.'

'Oh, yes, he can. Right here, I speak for me, for this one solitary individual, nobody's partisan. One man. The whole damned world can fuck itself for all I care, just leave me alone with my work,' he paused, breathing hard, and then said more softly, 'and my love.' He looked up to me and then around the table: 'I'm sorry, ladies.'

Clare accepted his apology with a small incline of her head. 'So cry the oppressed millions. What makes you a special case?' she said.

Jean-Michel tilted his chair back from the table and gave his shoulders a ripply little shrug. 'What do you expect? He's just a selfish little bourgeois, after all.'

Jack leaned back in his chair and smiled, his tough lean face quite happy, 'Where I came from, little boy, that was an achievement.'

There was a silence, and then suddenly Khadija Abbas spoke. 'Jack is right, Wendell,' she said. Her voice was soft and commanding, and we stilled to listen to her, as in youth we had listened to her father. 'It is only as an individual that we have any meaning; only from individuals is anything achieved. We make a small space around us better, for a small space of time, and then we are gone. That is all God asks.' Hugo Melrose, sitting beside her, watched quietly, with a new respect.

'Fortunately,' said Eithne, 'the Party asked a little

more.' I saw Jack stiffen to reply, but Clare suddenly intervened, her bony hand upon his sleeve.

'All right, children,' she said, to all of us. 'Jack and Justina have kindly taken us to dinner. Let's all enjoy our meal.' She smiled with cool control. 'Any chance of a spot more of that delightful wine, Mr Redpath?' That would have ended it, then. Jack called for more wine. Our second course was served, and we ate, and chatted, but Jack was very quiet and it was Jack in the end who would not let it rest. We had finished the meal with a lovely brie and were praising it happily, even Jean-Michel briefly appreciative, when he spoke quietly to Clare.

'Tell me, what *do* you think?' She looked up and raised her thin eyebrows.

'Serious?'

'Of course.' They seemed suddenly the only two adults in the room. She spread brie on a piece of crusty bread and then left it untouched on her plate.

'I'm not so much of an idiot to imagine much good coming out of either side winning. But I assure you a great deal of bad will come from the wrong side losing.' Jack sighed and nodded. 'We'll face Fascism somewhere,' she said, 'I suppose we might as well gird our loins and get on with it.' She briskly dusted crumbs from her hands. Jack stared down at the white, wine-stained cloth. Clare was quite cheerful, looking about the table, her eyes falling first on me, then May and then once more on Jack, 'You know, chickens, you were right last time. This time you're wrong. We were all of us betrayed once by war. This time we'll be betrayed by peace.'

Wendell said eagerly, 'You see. Aunt Clare knows. It's different now. This time it's *right* to fight.' His face was shining with honest certainty.

Jack studied him in silence. At last he said, very slowly,

'It's so *easy,* Wendell, to be fashionably violent. When you've seen war, come back and tell me *then* it's right.'

I said, 'All this evil sprang from the last war! What might come from another?' Clare smiled gently.

'I think we're going to have to find out.'

'You have no children,' I said.

'If I *had* children,' she answered sharply, 'I'd be on the barricades in Spain.' She looked down the long table. 'Bless you, Jack,' she said, 'it was a lovely evening.' She shrugged her sharp, angular shoulders. 'It's over, little ones. The age of innocence is done.'

The rain and thunder had stopped when we went out. The night was steamy with mist. Jack had called for a cab to take Clare back to her hotel, but I said I would walk with Ellie and meet him on the *Suzanne*. We all said goodnight. Hugo and Khadija and May went out ahead of us and Eithne and Jean-Michel went off to the rally for Spain, but Wendell said he would escort me home first. He had a gentlemanly propriety, taught by his father, that was not a bad thing. We walked slowly up the Boulevard St Germain and turned towards the river on the Rue Danton. It was a hot, dark night, and the café terraces were filling up with people now the rain had stopped. There was a moist, dripping tension everywhere, as if everyone knew the storm was done. Wendell walked beside me, and Ellie slipped back behind us, like a small child, as she always did if Wendell was there. Wendell said, 'Jack's wrong, you know. I'm not fashionably violent. I'm not violent at all.'

'I don't think he meant that.'

'It's because we *love* the world, we love people . . .'

'I know.'

'I love you.' He fumbled his hand on my shoulder, bent

down and kissed me as shyly as he would kiss a girl. He drew back and we walked a few more steps. As we entered the Place St André he said, 'Will you tell Jack. Will you tell Jack I love him too.'

'He knows that.'

'But please,' Wendell said urgently, 'please tell him anyhow.'

'I'll tell him,' I said.

In the Place St Michel there was a great crowd of people grouped round a makeshift podium on a vegetable wagon. Around it young people held up flags, the flag of the Spanish Republic, the French tricolour, and the red flag of revolution. They were singing the *Internationale*. It frightened me; all crowds frightened me since that long ago Votes for Women procession that ended in bloodshed in Trafalgar Square. I drew Ellie nearer me. Eithne and Jean-Michel would be there ahead of us, but of course we could not see them.

'Do you want to join them?' I said to Wendell, but he said no, he would take me home first. As we left the *place* the singing changed. I could not hear the words but the tune was the American song Red River Valley. It sounded haunting and strange in the old French streets.

Wendell helped me down the stone steps in the darkness, though I knew them very well. He took Ellie's arm as she crossed to the boat. But he did not cross with us. He stood on the quayside looking down. 'Well, goodnight,' I said, but he remained looking and looking. At last he turned and walked hurriedly back the way we came.

He did not come home that night, nor the morning after. That was not unusual; often he would stay with May, if they remained late there, talking into the night. Sometimes he stayed with Jean-Michel who still lived with his widowed mother. Jack was also late back, and I was in bed and almost asleep when I felt, rather than heard him come aboard the *Suzanne*. Even a houseboat has the living awareness of any waterborne vessel and shivers alertly at the step of a human foot. I listened contentedly as he moved about the galley, feeding cats and making coffee and eventually settling with his notebook to write. He often wrote half the night while I slept. Sometimes I dreamt things of which he wrote; we were that close.

By afternoon, Wendell had still not returned. Jack woke after having slept to noon, and offered to go out about their haunts, looking for them. But it proved unnecessary. Hugo and Khadija arrived just before one o'clock. Hugo was serious and adult, and Khadija had been crying. Hugo took Jack aside, very British and proper; the men must deal with matters of portent. They talked for a few moments and then Jack came to me and put his hands on my shoulders, looking down into my eyes. He looked weary.

'They've gone out to Spain,' he said. 'Wendell and Eithne both. She's going to nurse. He's joined the International Brigades.' He waited, leaning over me until I had absorbed the shock and then said quietly, 'I'll go after them. I'll bring him back.'

I could see him doing that, too, whatever the circumstances, but I shook my head. 'You know we can't do that.' Numbly I asked Hugo, 'How did you learn?'

'From Jean-Michel. He made all the arrangements.'

'Hasn't he gone?' I asked. Hugo shook his head. No, of course he had not gone. He had work to do in Paris for the Party. By summer of 1937, they saw which way the wind was blowing. They would send no one so valuable to them. But they sent my beautiful son.

A fortnight later I received a letter from Barcelona. It

was from Eithne. She could tell me little. Wendell had been sent to join a unit on the Aragon front after a single week of training. She was angry because she could not go too. Nursing was a guise; she wished to fight 'at the shoulder of her man' like the women of Spain. She promised she would write again when she had news and warned it might not be for a long while.

She did write, several times more. But there was censorship and she could give me no details of times or places, only that Wendell was alive and well and doing what he had come to do. She wrote about the starving, battered city and the brave confusion of experiment under the new order. Beneath the rhetoric, I felt the nudge of reality fighting through. Once, surprising me, she wrote:

> . . . Last night I was very tired, and tired of being hungry and tired of being *glad* that I was hungry because it made me one with the people, and when walking through the streets I came upon one of the many, many ruined churches and I went inside and stood where the wind swept in through the broken windows and the birds roosted on the shattered altar and suddenly I wept. And as much as I hated myself and as much as I knew the Church had been a viper, sucking the blood from the people, I still wept. And then, in what had been the Lady chapel, I found some broken candles and I smoothed one off until it would stand and I set it up on the stone floor and lit it with the matches for my cigarettes, and I prayed for Wendell. I said an Ave. I said it in Irish the way my mother taught me. Then I felt absolutely foolish and silly, and I walked away and left my candle burning on the ground.

Of course it had fallen to us to inform the family in New York. Their response was understandable. They blamed us for our irresponsibility, and our dangerous politics. I imagine they had Jack's published works in mind, though I sincerely doubt they had read them. Wendell, my husband, did not write to me direct. But his mother did, conveying his anger, and even Margaret was hard pressed to preserve her stubborn fairness towards me. I was sorry, but I could not much care; all my caring was with my son in Spain.

Then, in late October, two months after he left Paris, I received a letter at last from Wendell himself. It had been taken out by an English lad, returning from Spain, and was uncensored by any hand.

Aragon
15 October 1937

Dear Justina,

I hope by now you have had time to understand why I went and the way I went. I know it was cruel and unfair, but I was afraid that if I said anything at all, Jack would try to stop me, or you would cry, and I could not have faced that.

I have been here now a long while. I am not even sure how long, only that time stretches out and I feel that New York and Paris exist only in another world, and that I have never really lived in either. Life during war is so day by day, that the friends of a week are dearer somehow than those I have loved for a lifetime. That sounds terrible but if you were here you would understand.

I have many good friends. My unit is very mixed. There are many Spanish now, making up the numbers of the International Brigades, and among the dozen that I work with directly, eight are Spanish. I wish I knew the language and could speak to them, other than the basics that we manage, just to get by. I try thinking in Latin and translating, with guesses, but it doesn't work well. Still, they do everything to help me. They are so grateful to us and so *naturally* kind. The people are very honest and innocent and trusting and eager to learn things. The people alone are very good. I wish their leaders were more like them.

Of course everything is very unorganized *because* of the new freedom. They do not like to give orders or to take them and yesterday, before we went out to take a little grove of olive trees that the Fascists were holding, we had a discussion like a committee meeting, first. In the end, some of the Spanish who were anarchists decided not to go, so we went without them, though we missed their guns, because we have so few. Still we did manage. It is all *fair,* but not very military.

I have become accustomed to war, as much as one does. I have been under fire several times, some worse than others. And I have shot at people and probably killed them. In the confusion you are hardly aware. It comes very naturally. But I hate the aerial bombing, because there is nothing you can do but take it. And the nights are getting cold now and often it is difficult to sleep, in the cold, in the open, and I lie and think. That is when I get lonely, and homesick. Tell Ellie I think of her a lot, and when I can't sleep, or I'm frightened, I think of all the paintings she's done since she was little and I try to picture them and put them in order in my mind, and it helps me sleep. Sometimes I think about New York, and Columbia, where I should have been starting classes. It's funny, I picture it like our school classroom, and what it was like when someone was at home, sick, their chair and desk empty, and I imagine this sort of empty chair and desk in Columbia, and that's me. My other self. If I do get back, I don't think I'll study law. It is too much like politics and all the stuff the Party gave us. When you are in the middle of things, it makes no real sense. I think I will study art history, or literature. Something beautiful.

The Party was right about one thing, the way people are all brothers, underneath. I am among coal miners and shipyard workers, and writers and actors, and aristocrats' sons, and they are all the same, needing to eat, and drink and keep warm at night, and not get shot in the daytime. I love them.

Please tell Jack for me that I have seen war now and I still think we are right. And perhaps if I see more, but not too much more, I will think the same. But I really don't blame him for thinking different. I really don't. And could you please write to Margaret, and tell her what I have said. I know you will be able to make her understand. I try and try to write, but I cannot. She is not like you. I can never tell her the deepest things in my heart.

I miss Eithne. She is working with orphans in Barcelona and wishes she were here, but I am glad she is not. Some of the Spanish women in the militias carry guns, but I don't like it and I would hate to see a woman shot. I know it's not what the Party teaches, and not what she wants me to believe, but I still want to think I can protect her yet. I love her so much. That is the heart of it all, if you could understand. When you were young, there must have been someone you loved as much as I love Eithne and something you believed in that meant even more. The beauty of our love is that we lay it aside for Spain.

I must end this, because my comrade is waiting to take it with him. It is night now, and I am writing by a candle, and above the branches of the trees, the stars are crisp and mountain clear. Spain is very beautiful and very sad. Madrid has not fallen. Madrid will not fall. *Salud*.

Your loving son,

Wendell

27

Do not remember
Spain and the Spanish sun.
Do not remember
The cause. The cause is done.
Do not remember
The boy who was not my son.
But remember Teruel
And remember I did not go.
Remember Teruel
Spain and the Spanish snow.

Jack Redpath
February 1938

My son Wendell was killed in January of 1938 in the battle for the Spanish city of Teruel. He was wounded by machine-gun fire, during a skirmish in a blizzard, and died that night of exposure and shock, lying on the snowy ground. His comrades buried him in the field and returned his belongings to me; some letters, a few boyish trinkets purchased in Spain, and two books, tattered almost beyond recognition: a Baha'i prayerbook given him by Khadija Abbas and Jack Redpath's *A Persian Garden*. The first I returned to Khadija as a remnant of his fidelity; the second is with me yet. Such are the legacies of dreamers.

I do not know who was the more stricken, myself, or Ellie, or Jack. But we were together and, entwined in groping, wordless grief, we were comforted. Others were less fortunate: Margaret, the splintered Pyke family, my lost, miserable, playboy husband.

He wrote to me, during that time of mourning. When I received his letter I braced myself for the recrimination that seemed, in the guilt of my grief, to be just punishment. But there was none there. Instead, there were rambling pages, an incoherent tangle of memories; our marriage, the war in which we met, my brother Sandy Melrose, whom our son had recalled to him as well. Amidst all were confessions of past sins, forswearing of future ones, and, incredibly, a plea for understanding and my return to him, so that we might 'assuage our mutual grieving by starting over again'. This was one of the few letters of my lifetime that I neither answered, nor kept.

Six weeks later Eithne O'Mordha returned to Paris. It was the middle of March. In Austria, Hitler was successfully achieving *Anschluss*. We hung over radios with the punch-drunk disbelief in which we rocked, again and again, throughout that year. The newspapers were full of pictures of German soldiers and blond-plaited girls of robust innocence welcoming them with flowers and Nazi flags. Our pacifist aloofness was gone. We rushed with all the others for the latest edition of the papers, and in the cafés the talk shifted from lamentation over the politics within France, to the threat of the politics without. May's helper, Marie, mother of the Communist Jean-Michel, wept on my shoulder over her fears of a new war. I comforted her; mothers of sons, at such times, know no divisions.

I had just left Marie in the printshop of The Fishing Cat, and gone upstairs with May, when there were footsteps on the stairs, and without knocking or announcing herself, Eithne quietly stepped into the room. Until that moment we believed her to still be in Spain. Since Wendell's death we had had only one contact with her, a pathetically grandiose letter in which she proclaimed my son 'her holy martyr for Spain', and promised to fight on to the end for his memory. The girl who walked into May Howie's flat seemed scarcely capable of such naïve bravado.

Experience is meant to age, but on the very young its visual effect is the opposite. Sophistication and its accompanying pretensions are vanquished. Without them the adventurer becomes a schoolgirl, the woman dissolves into child. She closed the door behind her and stood in front of it, hands at her sides, eyes welling with tears, as she would at ten, or twelve, when the Sisters had chastised her for failing an examination. She wore no provocative black jersey, no militia-woman's baggy trousers. She was dressed as for school in a navy skirt and a white blouse, and a tan mackintosh, her thick red hair plaited innocuously in a pigtail down her back.

'May,' she whispered uncertainly, 'Justina?' We said nothing, too stunned to reply and she continued in a feeble voice, 'I've come home.' She crumpled a little, as if she expected one of us to embrace her. But I could not bring myself even to approach her, and only eventually did May, with visible reluctance, step forward and extend dutiful arms. Eithne flew sobbing into their shelter. May stood very stiff, holding her almost at arm's length, as the girl sobbed wetly against her sleeve. 'He's dead, he's dead,' she cried, as if she had only just learned.

'We know that, Eithne,' I said. Enough time had passed for me to be dry-eyed, and, without the compassion of tears, bitter as well.

'You blame me, don't you?' she said. Her voice had yet that little-girl tone, self-pitying, ready to fly to its own defence.

'Yes,' I said. 'I blame you.' May looked at me but made no comment.

'You don't understand,' she said. I did not even answer that. But she went on. '*He* didn't blame me,' she said urgently. I think I actually laughed.

'I should think not. He was dead.'

'But, no,' she said, grasping her argument with eager haste. 'He never blamed me. And he *did* know, you see. After a little while it was very obvious. He knew it was hopeless and he would probably die, but he didn't blame me, or anyone. He was *happy* to die for the people of Spain.'

'Ridiculous,' I said coldly. 'No one of eighteen is happy to die for any reason at all. He was trapped. All men who die in wars are trapped. By foolish ideas, and cynical governments, and twisted, romanticizing women. You trapped him.'

She began to cry and at last, whimpering into her hands, resorted to platitude, 'He died gloriously for Spain and for freedom and you should be proud instead of denigrating his memory.'

I could have struck her. Memory was all I would have of my only son for the rest of my days. I preserved it scrupulously.

I turned away, but she clutched at me with her hands,

pleading for my forgiveness. I sighed, 'I saw men die for three years, Eithne. During the War. I saw it all the time. It was always the same. Fear and pain and confusion. Unless they were lucky and the morphia took all sense out of their heads. There are no partisans among the dying. All they loved and all they fought for is quite forgotten. All that's left is the human individual, alone in its misery.'

She stared at me, yearning and hopeless, her red hair, worked free of the tight bonds of her plait, frizzing to an orange halo. The deep brown eyes filled up with all Padraic O'Mordha's crazy ungoverned passion. 'Oh please, Justina, I *loved* him. And I love you, too.' My child of the Pyrenees, my surrogate daughter.

I turned my back and went out of the door and left her there with May. She would not believe my rejection, but tried twice more to win me. But I could not relent. I wanted to. I could not do it. Then she turned in desperation to Jack. He refused to see her. A few days later she left Paris for Ireland.

Eithne was not the only one to be leaving Paris. Already a trickle of exile had begun; the far-sighted, some who felt themselves most threatened, others whose roots were elsewhere, or whose ties to the French capital were weak. A few of our own friends slipped away. A Jewish musician, a gently effeminate young dancer, one or two of the rich fast set whose shoulders we occasionally brushed. They, of course, had many homes, and a dozen places to go as amusing as Paris. For the others it was not so easy; jobs and visas must be found, and with them, a haven. Our musician chanced upon a Hollywood band leader and went to play saxophone in California. The poor young dancer, wilting in terror over the fate of Lorca in Spain, fell conveniently in love with a New York choreographer, and came one night to bid us a blushing bridal farewell. But for most, threatened or not, there was no Prince Charming, and nowhere reasonable to go. A future that might never happen seemed little cause to abandon a satisfactory present, though a ripple of unease ran through all of us with each stirring of the awakening German juggernaut.

As for ourselves, it never occurred to us that we might leave. May had lived now in Paris for sixteen years; Jack and I for twelve. It was our home. I watched the beginning of that sad exodus with only curiosity, never imagining it might one day swallow us. As always, as one lives through history, it is nowhere near so obvious as through the sharp glass of hindsight. There was confusion, and a great deal of pessimism in the country all around us; a succession of governments, scandal, disillusionment. The people seemed dispirited and hopeless, like a man sliding slowly towards a cliff, unable to help himself. As often happens when leadership fails, we turned inwards to our personal lives, away from the larger world. For Jack and myself, that insularity and blinkered despair was heightened, and perhaps justified, by Wendell's death.

Neither of us could get over it. I worked in desultory joyless fashion, doing portraits for money that satisfied my clients merely because they were not informed enough to be particular. I had been painting for many, many years and was thoroughly professional; my craftsmanship stood by me, even if inspiration failed. But I would gladly have burned my work of that year. Jack was worse than me. Work was his escape from sorrows, as it often is with writers, and he refused to allow himself that release. He was tortured by a guilt I could not understand. But it stood firmly in his way and from January to late summer, he did no work on the book at all. He did write; articles, a few poems, a serious and very fine essay for the *New York Times* on the state of things in France. But they were brief moments, trivialities compared with the book, and nothing that would intrude on the numbness through which we both moved that year. Thus, just as a quarter of a century earlier, as the world approached calamity, I marched to the muffled distant drum of private grief.

Ellie was our salvation. Ellie had wept and grieved. Ellie had grown angry, and shouted and blamed everyone, Wendell himself included, for what had happened. And Ellie had thrown herself back into her painting and as the months passed emerged healed. She was young, and in her youth she was stronger than us both. She grew closer than ever to Jack and was so sensitive to his moods that sometimes she would come home from her wanderings without warning, go wordlessly to his side, and embrace him, stroking his greying hair with her delicate paint-stained hands, her black curls tumbling over his face. Always it was at times that I knew he was close to despair.

She finished school that spring, and though I considered sending her on to study art, in the end, I decided not. Partly, I was yet affected by my experiences at South Kensington, but there was more to it than old prejudices. I was not so disillusioned as to believe all art schools useless, or even any of them still cast in the Victorian mould I remembered. But Ellie was an instinctive painter, working naturally from something deep within. Craftsmanship and draughtsmanship I could teach her myself. And there was nothing else I would attempt to teach. She painted as a wild bird sang, and if caged by conventions might be ruined. There was no one other than myself that I could trust to allow her such freedom. So Ellie stayed yet with us, happily free of the restraints of education, and when I look back on all my family, it can hardly be denied that those of us who knew the brightest successes, myself, Ellie, May, indeed Jack, had no education to speak of at all.

Ellie entered a period of landscape painting, turning quite definitely away from the human faces that had always been dearest to my heart. She spent her days in the countryside, in small villages just beyond the suburbs, painting and sketching houses, and farmland. Occasionally she went further afield, travelling with a pack on her back, in the company of school friends. They cycled and hiked and slept in the open, throughout the warm summer. In August we took her as usual to Mont Louis in the Pyrenees, to the old inn where we had so often stayed. Our hosts adored her, and having known Eithne as our daughter, had added Ellie to our number, as her sister. Our implied marriage had become an institution there; the only place where I was ever known as Mme Redpath. Ellie was enraptured with the alpine meadows and high peaks which satisfied something in her artistic soul that I had never sought; the holy grandeur of the natural world.

As always, the mountains refreshed us, body and spirit. I began to work again, with the love of my subject that Mr Yeats had demanded as the prerequisite of good painting. A young Pyrenean boy, meticulously rendered, filled most of my working days. I came back somehow absolved of the sin of survival beyond the lifetime of my child, and Jack at last began again to write. We were sorry to leave, each knowing without ever voicing our conviction that we would come back to a world full of fear.

The Czechoslovak crisis was nearing its climax when we arrived back in Paris once more. Newspaper headlines glared from kiosks in the Gare D'Austerlitz as, sunburned and healthy, we stepped down from the train. Our packs were full of dried alpine flowers, and the scent of the mountain winds lingered in our clothes. Never have I so wanted to flee from reality as in that moment of return.

In September, there was real talk of war. The fate of the Sudetenland was scrabbled over in the papers, and French soldiers were called up to their units. I worried about Ellie though I did not worry about Jack or myself. A letter from Wilhemina, balanced delicately between indignation and hysteria, deepened my concern. London was preparing for war; she had seen anti-aircraft guns set up on London Bridge, and in Hyde Park they were digging air raid trenches. She was on the verge of closing the house and retreating to Arradale. 'To think,' she stormed in ink smudged and blotted with emotion, 'they are actually doing it again!' I wasn't sure they were, but it was beginning to look that way.

Briefly, I considered sending Ellie to Margaret and the safety of New York. But her protests were so anguished, and outside the beguiling Parisian summer seemed so safe and eternal that I had little heart for it. Then Munich came. The matter was settled. We would not, that autumn, have a war. At times like those, we live in cloistered moments; an autumn without a war is no small thing.

Looking back, I see too readily how we must appear: how foolish, how naïve, indeed, how abominably selfish. Like Russian travellers on the Steppe, we wrapped ourselves in our furs and did not look behind to where we had thrown the baby out into the snow. It all looked so different, then. Even appeasement meant a different thing, and peace in our time was yet a phrase from church. We did not know, then, that the wolves were everywhere.

A false security; but a security all the same. The talk of war retreated. The city relaxed into its own vivid life, like an exhaled breath. We met our friends again, we worked, we looked forward to the winter, which the first cold winds, and the first yellowed leaves drifting on the Seine, promised near. We planned our winter holiday in Font-Romeu and I bought Ellie red woollen trousers and jacket and new boots for her skis. I was happy and in my rather stupid way, rather oblivious of all the concerns that had threatened us in the summer. Which was why, I imagine, Clare's letter came as such a shock. She wrote it in October, just after Chamberlain's return from Munich, and apparently laid it aside to reconsider, because it was not posted until early November. This was no snap judgement, but the fruit of deep thought. I received it on the sort of late autumn day when the rain never ceased, but kept up a rattling thunder against the wooden roof of the *Suzanne*, seeming to dare our snug shelter within with deliberate malice. Water washed down the decks and blurred the small windows, and I looked up from time to time from the red jumper I was knitting for Ellie (yes, I could knit, quite nicely, though I couldn't sew to save my life) just to be sure we were not awash and sinking. Jack was sitting with his feet up by the charcoal stove writing in his notebook. He always wrote long-hand first, pages and pages, before he would raise a sort of necessary courage to approach his desk and typewriter in the flat in the Rue St Julien. Long-hand was a shadowy half-way house of uncommitment, from which he could retreat easily, crumpling sheets into the fire, with no loss of face.

Ellie had gone out into the downpour to collect our post, which we still had delivered to The Fishing Cat because we were so often away. She came in drenched through, her coat dripping and her hair in spidery tendrils, and handed me three letters; one from Millie Dobbs, one from Jack's publisher in New York, and the third, its delicate inked address almost obscured by waterstains, from Clare.

'What have we done?' I asked Jack, nervously. Clare wrote for two reasons only: Christmas and admonitions. I slit the envelope and unfolded her letter. She wrote like Father, in a script as antiquely graceful as calligraphy.

Somerville
4 October 1938

Dear Justina and Jack,

I do not intend to take no for an answer, so don't argue. I have had discussions with Wilhemina and with friends in Oxford. Arradale is at your disposal, as is Bryanstone Square, for as long as you may need to find accommodation more to your taste. Or, if you prefer, I know of a perfectly reasonable rented property here in Oxford which will tax neither your financial situation, nor your Bohemian inclinations. You may live like a pair of tinkers here as well as anywhere, but in Merry England or unmerry Scotland it's going to be.

Winter's coming, chickens. Time to 'raise anchor', unless Jack intends piloting HMS *Suzanne* right across the Channel some day, which I could just about see him doing.

If you consider me alarmist, take account of your pretty young daughter and all those damned jackboots stamping over Europe.

Looking forward to your affirmative reply,

Your loving sister,
Clare

'What I like,' Jack said sweetly, staring into the fire, 'is that word "taste". That's so Clare. That's so very Clare.'

'It's *all* very Clare,' I said. I toyed with the letter, my eyes avoiding the corner of the room in which Ellie sat, very wet and a little pale. I wished half-way through I had not chosen to read the thing aloud, but once started I could hardly stop midway. 'Do you think there's any sense in it?' I said casually. Jack looked up at me, and at Ellie watching him.

'Of course not,' he said with fatherly care.

And of course we did not leave. That would have been too sensible, too logical, and too lucky. We chose instead to conclude that Clare, in her ivory tower, was out of touch with our real world, and consequently slightly hysterical. This was remarkably stupid of us both; Clare had many flaws, but hysteria was rarely one of them. And Clare, amidst the dreaming spires and sharp intellects of Oxford, had better contacts with those who would know of such things, than ever we did. We chose to ignore her because we did not want her to be right. It was as simple and as foolish as that. At the time both Jack and I were more concerned with the prospect of Clare herself descending in fury to enforce her will, than with Hitler doing the same. So I wrote a long, reasonable letter setting out all the points in favour of remaining in Paris and swearing dutifully that the moment events turned contrary, we would hie ourselves across the Channel to safety. Clare responded with two sentences:

This time, the sky *is* falling, Chicken Little. Reconsider.

But she left it at that. I think she had finally decided we were adults. And so, from the autumn that had not brought war, we turned to winter and a last year's grace in the world of ordinary sorrows and joys.

At the end of January, Jack finished the book. It had been a long, difficult effort, traversed by Wendell's death, and we both rejoiced that it was done. But before he presented it to May, he gave it to me to read, something he had not done before. He had shown May nothing of this work. I surmised uncertainty from this deviation, and approached the manuscript with trepidation.

I need not have done; not if quality were the only issue at stake. Jack had written three much acclaimed novels and I knew from the first page that this was their equal. I also knew that once more he had chosen contentious ground. Not the same argued ground. Jack never did that. Each of his works was different. He was quite impossible to classify. But the mystic dreamer of *A Persian Garden* was gone. *That Sweet Homeland* was to it, as winter to summer, a story for a dark time when all that is green lies hidden in the ground. This time no one could say he was not true to our day.

Though the story began in the Great War, and the title came from a Great War song familiar from every nurses' concert party, it was an ironic title and an ironic book, far removed from the sad compassion of *The Virgin of the Somme*.

It was a spare, dark deceptive story in which love itself became a metaphor of hate, the one as destructive as the other. It was also a political allegory of nations as trapped by history as his lovers by desire. And that was its inevitable downfall.

We brought it to May, nervously, as parents bring a disagreeable child of untrustworthy manners. She took it wordlessly and read it in a night. We returned for a conference the next day. Jack wanted me with him; his confidence was slight.

May sat behind her desk wearing gold-rimmed reading glasses that I was sure she retained for occasions when she wished to be formidable. It was hard for May to be formidable, as sweetly blonde as she was, but she managed.

She laid her hand on the pile of typescript on her desk and said nothing.

'What's wrong?' he asked. May looked at him warily.

'This is another anti-war book, Jack.'

'It's not about the war. It's about love. Or what passes for love in most people's hearts. Anyone can see that.'

'All they'll see, Jack,' May said, 'is that you've made a hero out of a German.'

'For Christ's sake,' said Jack. 'He's not a *Nazi*!'

'Oh, you innocent,' said May.

'Well, what about Remarque,' Jack pursued. 'What about *All Quiet on the Western Front*?'

'That was years ago. We're on the merry-go-round again. The *Nazis* understand. They've banned him.'

'Is that where we're heading?'

'Oh, I doubt it. I'll *try*, Jack.' She paused, considering. 'What do I do if they say, "make him an Englishman"?'

'Burn it.'

'Jack?'

'I said burn it. I've had enough.'

'You don't mean that,' I said hurriedly.

'Oh, don't I?' He got up, nodded to May and walked out. I heard the stamp of his boots down the stairs, reminding me of Gay Street and the way he would walk out on me. The door slammed, down below. I looked up.

'Oh, May,' I whispered.

'He'll get over it,' she said. She stacked the papers briskly. 'It's brilliant, of course. Quite brilliant. But it's just jolly well time he learned to toe the line.' Quite suddenly I relaxed. It had all seemed so important a moment ago, and now it seemed not to matter.

‘Oh no,’ I said proudly, ‘not Jack.’ She raised one eyebrow, delicately cynical.

‘Well, I hope the painting pays well, my dear,’ she said.

We did not argue. We both loved him, in our own ways. What went on between May and Jack was their own business. I would not interfere. She had more or less made his career, and had earned some rights in the matter.

May made tea. We drank it slowly. She riffled through the pages of Jack’s book, reading snatches, and I watched her. She was just a year younger than me, but I could not think of her as being, like myself, middle-aged. She still looked impossibly youthful, the same pert little face that had been mistaken throughout her adolescence for a child’s. She still wore her hair in a short, thick bob, and there was no grey in it at all. She raised her gold-rimmed glasses off her nose.

‘He’s *such* a talented man, Justina. But he’s unruly. He’s *intellectually* unruly.’

‘He’s free.’

‘Call it what you will,’ she said, with a shrug. She paused, tidying the papers again. ‘Yeats is dead. Have you heard?’

‘I read it in the paper yesterday.’ She removed her glasses entirely, and rubbed at them with her sleeve.

‘I kept thinking of you and the old man in Dublin . . .’ suddenly she laughed. ‘Oh, do you remember poor Father and *Cathleen ni Houlihan*?’ We both laughed. But then May said, ‘Do you know, I dare say *Cathleen ni Houlihan* got Michael killed. If you think of it.’

‘Oh, May,’ I said, not liking to remember, ‘it was only a play.’ I thought of the drawing room in Howth that Michael and I had illicitly entered, and the tall man in black, charming all the ladies with beautiful words. 'I can't imagine,' I said, 'he ever intended any harm.'

May Howie was precisely right about *That Sweet Homeland*. No one wanted to touch it. But Jack refused to change it and she kept trying anyhow. Jack spent the spring and summer of 1939 writing Western stories for the pulp magazines. He was still very good at them. He refused to use the pseudonym by which he had previously disguised his commercial efforts, but published as Jack Redpath, for all to see. May handed him his cheques (they were quite reasonable) without comment. They were playing a sort of game, and I think they both rather enjoyed it.

What Jack did not enjoy was the unwise remark by a casual acquaintance who had seen *That Sweet Homeland*, that the author had 'Fascist leanings'. It was hardly a serious accusation, in that it was flung about with indiscriminate stupidity in those days. In another year Jack would have laughed. But he had not laughed about much since Wendell died in Spain, and this particular issue of literary criticism was settled by a fist fight in a Paris gutter. I patched up the damage without comment. The world was turning darker. We were a long way from a garden in Isfahan.

In June of that year Mirza Hassan Abbas died in New York. He had been ill for a short while with a heart condition and collapsed climbing stairs; my mountaineer who had conquered the Throne of Solomon. Khadija wrote me a brief, brave letter. She was immersed in examinations at the end of the second year of her medical course, but promised to see me in the summer when she came to stay in London with Wilhemina and Hugo Melrose. She was as dutiful as a daughter-in-law, and such, in a happier world, she might have been. A following letter from Millie Dobbs affirmed that Hassan's daughters would know no financial difficulties. The penniless exile at her door had died an immensely wealthy man.

Some weeks later I received a parcel from New York containing an exquisite prayer rug, in beautiful shades of silk. He had left it to me in his will. I unrolled it carefully in my narrow bedroom aboard the *Suzanne*, thinking of our winter in Strathpeffer. The colours, blues and dark greens and charcoal greys reminded me of the winter hills and I wondered if that was why he had chosen it for me. I knelt on it, remembering Hassan's white smile.

I was a poor student of ritual, and when I chose to pray it was usually without formality. Body postures could not seem significant to me, and I resented the need of a *quiblih*, a direction in which one must face God.

'If God is everywhere, that is irrelevant,' I had said to Hassan.

He said, 'A child whose mother has gone out watches the doorway through which she has gone. We turn to the place of the last manifestation.'

'Supposing the child's mother returns through the back door?'

'He usually does that,' Hassan agreed.

But this time I wished it to be right. I knelt, I faced East to Akka, and I made the obligatory prayer. Then, when it was finished, I made one private prayer of my own for the man whose life had wound through mine like one jewel-toned thread in a tapestry. Then I stood up, and rolled the prayer rug and thought, *He is gone now and we are alone*. As if acknowledging his passage, our world tumbled onward into war.

By the summer of 1939 we all knew it was inevitable.

Last year had been a dress rehearsal. Now the curtain was going up. Bohemia and Moravia were occupied in March; Czechoslovakia was gone. In April, in Spain, Franco announced the end of the Republic for which my son had died. Hitler was sizing up Poland. Europe was falling like a house of cards, and in England and France stunned governments were feeling their backs to the wall. So were we all.

And yet, when Chamberlain offered the Polish guarantee, committing us to war as certainly as the old treaties of 1911, I felt only a weary sort of relief. There is a time when peace, no matter how dearly sought, becomes a burden.

One summer evening Jack and I sat down with a bottle of wine and made a reckoning of our future. Our period of grace, granted earlier by Clare, was at an end. We had had two severe letters charging us with either blind stupidity, reckless irresponsibility, or a combination of both. Ellie was her chief concern, as she was our own. We no longer dismissed Clare's warnings as hysteria, but nor were we quite ready to capitulate.

We had few material ties. The battered river-barge *Suzanne* was, like our studio, merely leased. Her cramped limited accommodation had precluded collecting possessions. We could leave as we had come with an easel and an army kitbag. But we did not want to leave. France had been good to us. We had friends, we had familiar haunts, beloved streets, endearing bookshops. We had had thirteen good years. It seemed churlish to flee.

If that sounds remarkably naïve, you must remember that I had weathered one war in France already, and had no reason to expect I could not weather another. Like everyone else we envisioned an event like the last; trenches and intransigence and years of attrition. It had been awful and we dreaded it, most of all for the young who would fight it. But we did not imagine ourselves participants. Paris had escaped before, with no Maginot Line to protect her. Paris would no doubt endure.

May was not leaving. She had lived in France so long she could not conceive of going elsewhere, any more than could her French assistant Marie. In the end, we decided the same. We called Ellie in and placed our decision before her, offering her the choice of remaining with us, or returning to America or England. I suppose I was foolish to even doubt that she would choose to remain. That decided, we felt strangely elated. We toasted each other, and toasted France, and awaited what the future might bring.

It brought, almost immediately, a furious letter from Clare, and the announcement that she would arrive at summer's end.

'If we're lucky,' said Jack, 'Hitler will get here first.'

But it was not Hitler who thwarted Clare's plans, but our irreformable cousin Kate.

From our European viewpoint, the troubles of Ireland seemed not only distant, but anachronistic and a little petty. They seemed to have achieved so much of what was wanted. They had divested themselves of the influence of the Crown. They had claimed the Irish name of Eire, and won back the Treaty Ports. If they were not a republic yet, the difference seemed academic and temporary. Faced with our larger troubles, I was impatient with theirs. The British presence in the Six Counties undoubtedly rankled, but since the twenties we had trusted that a temporary measure, one day to be resolved. At times I recalled James Howie's gentlemanly disdain for the industrious and graceless Ulsterman and wondered what the fuss was over. But then James had never wanted a republic anyhow.

Those who did had lately been setting bombs off on the British mainland, a tedious measure, which nevertheless won headlines, even in the foreign press, when on a day in August an explosion in Coventry left five dead bodies in the rubble of an English street. One year on, and such sights would be commonplace; but not in 1939, and not from an enemy within. There was outrage in Britain, an outrage I blithely shared. In Eire, the de Valera government was rounding up suspects, and I was glad. Whatever the cause, whatever my past ties, I had no heart for such aimless brutality. I honestly never thought of Kate the whole while. I had been convinced for years that her role in the movement was a fantasy. I think May felt much the same; she was as shocked as I was when Clare's letter came.

Shelbourne Hotel
Dublin
Eire

My dear May,

You are probably unaware that Kate has been arrested in connection with the Coventry affair. I was informed, myself, two days ago, by a friend in Whitehall and I came here at once. I am not at all sure that there is anything I can do (or even that there is anything I *want* to do), but as you will no doubt agree, there is the matter of family . . .

I do not know of the degree, if any, of her actual involvement in this despicable business. Her 'defence' is laughable, her response to any question being 'Up the Republic!' and that insane smile that once was so beautiful. She is quite happy to be judged guilty, and, I assure you, reckless with it. The Eire government is not in a playful mood and executions are not impossible. But Kate would take credit for the Crucifixion if she imagined it would advance Ireland's cause.

There is no question but that she is *morally* responsible since she cheers and delights in any British death, regardless how hideous. 'Pity it wasn't five hundred' has been her only expression of remorse. At times I wonder what I'm doing here, except that someone must look after her. She hasn't the brains to look after herself.

I came here confident of convincing them of Kate's instability . . . let us face it, family or not, and as unpleasant as it may be to acknowledge, our wild sweet Catherine is crackers. Unfortunately, in Ireland, Kate's variety of craziness is considered perfectly normal.

She had been threatening a hunger strike, but I told her not to bother, as she will fail. I know, having been there, it takes a steadier head than hers. Whatever the outcome, you may be comforted that her situation is not overly unpleasant. It's not a patch on Holloway, and I survived that. Besides, I deeply suspect that Kate will survive not only this, but all the other slings and arrows she can get outrageous fortune to toss her way. She'll survive us all.

I have no word from Eithne and Kate insists she does not know where she is. I do not know if this is good news or bad. I will keep you informed presently.

your devoted cousin,
Clare Melrose

Clare's efforts were to no avail. Rightly or wrongly, Kate O'Mordha was convicted of conspiracy. She, who had thrown the first stone in Bachelor's Walk, had won her martyrdom at last. On the eve of the Second World War, she was a prisoner in an Irish jail. Any sorrow, or indeed any satisfaction, I might have felt over this was abrogated by my deeper concern for Eithne, of whom we had still no word. But even that uncertainty was overshadowed by the rush of other uncertainties around us, and I had little time to worry over it.

World events, hitherto an uneasy background of speculation, suddenly bullied to the forefront of our lives.The political and the personal became one. Wilhemina wrote to tell us that Hugo had joined the RAF, and that Khadija Abbas would not be seeing us in Paris, nor would she return to New York. She was staying on in London 'to look after me,' Wilhemina explained. But she no longer spoke of leaving Bryanston Square. Instead, she was instructing her servants to pile sandbags round the door, and taping her windows against blast.

'It's really happening, isn't it?' I said to Jack. He shrugged and put Wilhemina's letter aside.

'It could blow over yet,' he said. But the next day he came aboard the *Suzanne* with the newspaper folded under his arm, sat down at our kitchen table, and laid it down in front of me. Headlines proclaimed the Nazi-Soviet non-aggression pact. He looked up at me and smiled sadly, 'That's it, sweetheart,' he said.

That evening, Jack and I sat alone at the stern of the *Suzanne*, watching the lights of the city reflecting on the river, and the traffic moving across the bridges. It was a warm, gentle night. Ellie had gone out with a school friend to the cinema to see Garbo in *Ninotchka*. I sat stroking our tomcat, who had settled on my knees, and Jack was smoking a cigarette, with one arm casually across the painted tiller of the boat, as if he were about to pilot us away. We were deliberately not talking, because there was only one thing to talk about. I leaned my head against his shoulder, letting love speak in gestures. There was a shout from the quay above, 'Hello, the *Suzanne*!' and I sat up primly, at once. The voice was young and familiar. I looked up, and by the light of street-lamps saw that it was Jean-Michel. Jack looked up as well. I felt him tense with annoyance, but he said nothing.

'Monsieur Redpath,' Jean-Michel said, with unlikely deference, 'may we talk?' Jack was silent for a moment, but then said courteously, 'Of course.'

He looked at me and shrugged. Jean-Michel made his way down the stone steps, unsteadily, his hand fumbling against the stone wall. He stumbled once, and Jack reached a hand to help him aboard lest he fall in the river. He kissed both my cheeks, and I smelled cheap wine. He shook Jack's hand. Jack looked bemused, but nodded to me, and I went below and brought up a bottle of wine for the three of us. Why drunks inspire all of us to drink I cannot tell you, but I poured three glasses. Jean-Michel was being very formal and polite, as if he were suddenly his own long-dead father. He drank our health. We drank his. He finished his glass. I refilled it. He sipped once more from the replenished glass and set it down precariously on the bench.

'Monsieur Redpath,' he said.

'I've been Jack, or worse, to you for six years, Jean. Why don't we go back to Jack.'

'*Alors* . . . Jack. You are a wise man.' Jack raised an eyebrow.

'*I've* always thought so,' he said. 'But this is the first I've heard it from you.'

'Ah, well. Sometimes it is not convenient to acknowledge some things.'

Jack looked serious. He said, 'People whose opinions are determined by convenience are not worth listening to.'

Jean-Michel took that without argument. He was remarkably compliant, perhaps the result of the wine. He said, 'You have seen the papers?'

'I imagine you're referring to the latest bit of heroism from Moscow?'

Jean-Michel folded his arms and looked at his feet. I thought he was going to get angry, but instead he muttered plaintively, 'I don't understand it. I don't understand.' Jack laughed gleefully, but Jean-Michel was very solemn, 'I cannot see how this is the right thing. All day I have thought about it, and thought of every way it might be of true benefit and still I do not understand.'

'You're not supposed to,' said Jack.

'*Pardon*?'

'Yours not to reason why, Comrade,' Jack was laughing so hard he spilled his wine. Jean-Michel stared tragically into his glass. Jack got up, still laughing, mopped up the spilled wine with a dishcloth and refilled his glass and mine. He threw the wet cloth at Jean-Michel, and it draped like a monk's hood over his head. 'Come on, kid,' he said, 'let's get drunk.' They sat out under the blurry stars half the night, and got very drunk indeed. I left them at one o'clock when Ellie came home, and she and I crept off to bed, while Jack and Jean-Michel, arms about each other's shoulders, sang the *Marseillaise*.

In the morning, Jack was asleep, fully dressed, on the bed beside me. Jean-Michel was nowhere in sight. I was worried that he might have fallen overboard and drowned, and Jack's bleary insistence that he couldn't remember such a thing happening was little reassurance. A day later a visit from Marie put my mind at ease, at least in that quarter. Jean-Michel had not drowned in the Seine. Jean-Michel had joined the army. Whatever Stalin was doing, Jean-Michel would fight for France.

So, too, would so many more. In those last few days of peace, a sudden hectic desperation set upon everyone. The reserves were mobilized, recruiting offices received volunteers. Cellars and Métro stations became shelters, labelled with the numbers they might protect, and a big notice board appeared in the Place St Michel informing us all of the correct routes by which to evacuate Paris. Not that anyone seemed about to do that. Aside from the

Mobilization notices and the surprising sight of less than happy neighbours appearing in uniform, there was little visible change. Some shops were closed (though more were yet closed for the August holidays) but the crowds remained in the boulevards and on the café terraces. Gas masks in cylindrical cases blossomed, slung over self-conscious shoulders, but they seemed more props in a play than serious accoutrements of war. We did not have them, anyhow, since foreigners were not provided for. But then, on an afternoon at the end of August, a black government car appeared on the Quai St Michel, and from it emerged my woolly-haired government official, Monsieur the Sheep, with a supply for ourselves and for May. 'In gratitude for his portrait,' he said. He always remembered us, for which, one day, I would be grateful indeed.

On that same afternoon, I received a letter from Eithne O'Mordha at last, and in reading it, I quite forgot everything else. True to her dramatic potential, she managed, if but briefly, to upstage Hitler's war.

The Convent of the Order of St Clare
Inchmara
County Mayo

My dear, dear Justina,

Please do not be shocked by my address. I am not a nun yet, and not even a novice until tomorrow. But I wanted to write to you, once more, while I am still Eithne, as I was when we were all together. Even if I am allowed to write later, it will not be the same.

I so much want you to truly understand why I am doing this, and I think it will help if you know that I have thought of it for many years, even sometimes in those years with Jean-Michel, even sometimes in Spain. I want you to realize that in no way do I imagine this to be reparation for Wendell's death. Even I am not so foolish or romantic as that. Had he lived, I might yet have done this. Believe me when I tell you that that which brings me here is the same as that which brought us both to Spain.

I have written to Mother. What she has done she has done bravely by the justice of her own lights. I cannot condemn her; she has never for an instant relinquished the vision by which she lived. Few can say the same. I pray that God will be merciful to her, for the world will not.

As for myself, I am a little frightened, but I have no doubts. I have prepared myself carefully, with the wonderful guidance of the good sisters. At times I think this is the only course I could ever have taken, since I was a little child in Paris with May. It is May's doing, you see; she gave me such freedom that even the most extraordinary possibilities seemed quite within my reach.

I have written to her separately, and have sent her some things. I am giving away all my possessions, of course. I enclose a small piece of jewellery that I want you to have. It was my grandmother's mourning brooch that she wore for my Uncle Michael. I know it will mean something special to you.

I have enclosed nothing for Jack but my heart . . . he will be now, as he always was, the only man who ever possessed it. Forgive me, and may Wendell forgive me, but it was true. I know he will not believe me, but ask him for me, would I lie at a time like this? May God bless you both,

your loving cousin,
Eithne

I gave the letter to Jack, and as he sat reading it I unwrapped the tissue paper about the brooch that she had enclosed within her letter. It was small and light in my hands. When it lay revealed on the pale blue tissue, I remembered it from a photograph of Eugenia during the war, pinned to the high collar of her old-fashioned black dress. It was one of those late Victorian peculiarities, already out of date when Eugenia had it made, a wreath of fine gold, set with jet, enclosing a delicate spindle upon which, tightly wound and as black as the jet, were a few strands of Michael Howie's hair. I closed my fingers in a fist about the brooch and held it there until the hair grew warm from the touch of my hand. I looked up from it when I heard Jack lay the letter down.

It lay face up, across his knees. He leaned back in his chair and closed his eyes. For a long, long while, he said nothing. Then suddenly he grasped the letter and crushed it into a ball in his hand. 'Oh yes,' he said. 'She'd lie. The little bitch would lie to the face of God.' He flung the letter on the floor and for a moment put his face in his hands. But then he straightened, and leaned back again, with his eyes closed. He sat utterly still. Tears ran down his lined cheeks, glistening on his beard. He made no attempt to wipe them, or hide them from me. It was the only time, in twenty years, that I saw him cry.

28

That was on the Thursday. On the Friday, Poland was invaded, and by five o'clock on the Sunday, we were at war. It is extraordinary to think that on the sort of sunny weekend that one can lose entirely in casual play, such a thing can happen and the entire world can irrevocably change. Like a sudden death, it leaves one with the certainty that a tiny jump backward in time is all that is needed to undo the thing, if only one could find the way. But no one found the way in 1939.

On the Saturday Ellie and I went for a long, long walk, down the crowded boulevards, and across on to the Right Bank. We visited the Louvre to see our favourite paintings before they were spirited away to some shelter. As I recall, almost everything was still there. We wandered peacefully up the Champs-Elysées, among crowds of shoppers, and sipped *café crème* on a *terrasse* and savoured summer and normality. It was evening when we returned to our own quarter, and the shadows of the trees were soft and dreamy. We knew we were saying goodbye to something, but we were not certain what it was, or what would follow. I found myself wishing for just one more week of peace, as the dying wish for one more day. There were so many places, so many nooks and crannies of a city, that I wanted to visit one last time, so many kind moments I would like to repeat. But they slipped from me, with the last light of the day, and the last sleepy cries of the rooks above in the horse chestnut trees.

The next day, Sunday, was very different. We clung very close together, hardly letting each other out of our sight. We wanted to be together when the war began. We sat in May's flat, Jack, myself, Ellie and May, all trying to work at something, all failing. The radio was on all day, and we listened and waited. Eventually Ellie grew restless and wanted to go out in the streets and see if anything was happening, but Jack forbade it. He was gruff and unreasonable but Ellie did not argue. We were all as jumpy as cats.

At five o'clock, when the news came, we just sat in silence. Suddenly we did not know what to do. Then May got up abruptly and switched the radio off, and went back to the pile of proofs upon which she was working. Jack and I looked at each other. Ellie watched us. He suddenly smiled whimsically. 'You know,' he said, 'I was in this city, not half a mile from here, on the day they signed the Armistice. I heard the bells begin to ring, and I ran down into the courtyard where the *concierge*, an old grey woman from Normandy, was washing clothes. I greeted her, and I think I even kissed her. She didn't mind that, but when I said, "Aren't you going to celebrate, the war's over?" she just shrugged and thumped away at her washboard. "For the time being," she said. "For the time being."' Jack stood up and picked up his beret from the table and pulled it on roughly over his greying hair. 'Damn the old cow,' he said. He turned to the door.

'Where are you going?' I said, trying to sound calm.

'To work,' he said. He looked over his shoulder as if to Hitler and his army. 'It's a long way from Poland. I don't think they'll get here tonight.' I sat down again when he left, across the table from May.

'Shall I help you?' I said. She looked up over her gold-rimmed glasses and nodded, sliding a stack of proofs my way. We had paid our dues to history. Outside, the evening darkened to night and May got up and dutifully pulled her new thick curtains over tape-latticed windows. The blackout had begun.

Jack had not returned when the first sirens sounded. I looked up, stunned.

'Is that *real*?' Ellie jumped out of her chair.

'Where's Jack?' she cried. May said nothing. She stood up, stacked her proof sheets, tucked them under her arm, picked up her coat and went to the door.

'Come, *chérie*,' she said to Ellie. 'It's the cellar two doors down. Number eight.' She smiled brightly as the siren wailed.

'I must find Jack,' I mumbled. I grabbed my coat and hat and ran out of the door and down the stairs. 'Stay with May, darling,' I called back to Ellie. I think May shouted for me to stop, but I did not wait to hear.

Outside the familiar quarter was pitch-black and alien, like a place I had never been. I ran stumbling through the narrow streets, dodging other dark figures, running as I was, shouting to each other. It was not panic, but it was new, and strange and no one knew quite what to do. Some people were simply walking, looking up to the sky, too curious, or too disbelieving to seek shelter. I ran on, clutching my coat about me, tripping over kerbs and cobblestones in the darkness, praying Jack would be still at the studio where I might find him. It was a foolish hope in the chaos of the darkened city, and yet, just beside the dim walls of St Julien-le-Pauvre, we stumbled literally into each other's arms. He had been running to find me. We embraced in the street, with the strange siren wailing, and French voices shouting to take shelter. I did not care, now. I did not mind what was to happen, if we were not apart. I imagined somehow that if we loved each other enough, we would be allowed to die together. We make these foolish bargains with God.

We stayed that night with May and Ellie, and a dozen of her neighbours, in the shelter of a deep cellar off the Rue Zacharie. It was an ancient place, dark and mysterious as the catacombs, supported by great stone arches, older by far than the buildings above. I imagined it would all fall on our heads when the first bomb dropped but Jack said no, it was stronger than anything we would build today. It was hot and sticky, and strangely companionable, as people talked with a friendliness that they never would have displayed above in the street. Someone had one of those little accordions the French play so sweetly, and there was singing. Ellie slept with her head on my knees and I leaned against Jack's shoulder and in the night I dreamed we were once more at Dernancourt, waiting to die.

But we did not die. There was no air raid, no bombs. Nor was there the next night, nor the night after. Nor was there an attack upon our frontiers, nor the rumble of the great guns, nor the streams of refugees. There was nothing. There was no war.

There was war on the radio, and war in the newspapers.

As spectators, we watched Poland's swift, bloody fall. But then it was over, and we awaited our turn, and nothing happened. September passed, and October. French and German soldiery faced each other good-naturedly across the Maginot and Siegfried lines. A barrage of propaganda, printed signs, persuasive leaflets, patriotic or insulting songs, was the only real exchange of fire. Far from expecting it to be 'over by Christmas' as last time, by Christmas we were still waiting for it to start.

Not that we were in any great hurry. The Americans called it the Phoney War, this *drôle de guerre* in which nothing ever happened. They sounded disappointed in us, as if they had expected something more. But we were quite happy for it to remain that way. Faint hopes were aroused, rumours of peace, of negotiation, of settling it all with words, even now. The scattered bones of Poland should have told us otherwise, but the human mind has brief capacity for horror. Survivors forget, or do not survive, and already we were forgetting. The blackout grew casual. Those who had fled to the countryside returned. As autumn slipped easily into that cold, extraordinary winter, we slipped as naturally back into our ordinary lives. Bit by bit, our small personal concerns began again to outweigh the larger concerns of the world. In this selfishness the human spirit knows its best and its worst moments; the small people living their small lives in spite of all.

If we were *not* after all to die in an air raid, or be overrun by Germans, the necessity of earning our living resumed its former importance. And it was not quite so easy as it had been. Jack's career was in the same whimsical limbo it had entered after the failures of *That Sweet Homeland*. He was writing poetry for pleasure, and Western and detective short stories for what money they would bring. That, however, involved American markets and although a fair degree of communications persisted between New World and Old, the existence of a declared sea war which, unlike that on land, was actually happening, certainly slowed things down. And we had the cheerful prospect ahead of blockades and isolation, and no markets at all. Jack turned back to journalism, by invitation, actually, of the *New York Herald-Tribune*, to whom he wired a weekly article on the progress of the non-war. They were good pieces, some of his best writing, but they earned no fortune. He enjoyed writing them, though, as he enjoyed the verse which earned nothing at all. He seemed to have few regrets over his novelist's career, as if that were a part of his life belonging to another person entirely. I had the strange feeling of moving backward in time, so that the man I lived with now was the same Jack Redpath I had met at Dernancourt, carefree, unattached, unknown. He was very happy.

Looking ahead, I could see the possibility of my work, rather than Jack's, becoming our major means of support. I had no feelings about this one way or the other; neither of us ever cared who earned our bread. For creative people it is always so much a matter of luck. But I, too, was having difficulties. Portraiture is an art for stable times. No one anticipating air raids and invasion puts good money into anything so perishable. Nor do we record ourselves for a vanishing history. Life was yet comfortable, there were neither shortages nor rationing. But we were, in that bleak winter, balanced precariously on the edge of catastrophe. One does not sell trinkets to a nation under siege.

I did, surprisingly enough, get two commissions in spite of all, both from dragonish ladies of the French aristocracy who were not altering their lives one inch for any Teutonic upstart. But though they paid well, they were isolated instances, not enough to keep us going for long.

In New York, the blessedly faithful Millie Dobbs, intuiting our situation, dug deep into the camphor-wood trunk and staged a small one-woman show on my behalf. The money, cabled in January, was very welcome. In our usual feckless way we used it for a winter holiday; a last winter's skiing in the Pyrenees.

We stayed in Mont Louis, in the little mountain inn; no more the Grand Hotel at Font-Romeu, haven of our headier days. But the skiing was as good, the price of the hills only the strength of our legs. We ski'd adventurously, high up where the snow lay deep in the windswept cols. The danger of the times was infectious. We were alone, just the three of us, without even a mountain guide, but Jack was very sure of himself by then. Once, we climbed beyond the Col de la Perche and looked out across the mountains of Andorra and into Spain. Jack took off his skis and scrambled up a rocky outcrop, glistening with ice, and stood for a long while gazing out across the snowfields. I imagined he was thinking of Wendell and I left him undisturbed. When he came down he said, 'If you were careful, you could run down from here, all the way into Spain.'

It was harder than ever to return to Paris, and we stayed on extra days and returned almost penniless. The day afterwards, in the grim light of reality that follows a holiday, I assessed our situation and decided it was time to take things seriously in hand. I took my sketchbook and a warm coat and went out to one of the more popular cafés of Montparnasse. The coat was very useful, for though there was a thin blue sky and pale winter sunlight, it was quite exceptionally cold. I felt toughened, however, by the Pyrenean snows, and I found myself a place on the terrace beside the charcoal brazier and ordered a *café crème* and began nonchalantly to sketch. There were no tourists, of course, any more, but four handsome British officers on leave soon gathered and by noon I had sketched each of them and been paid handsomely and invited to join them for lunch. I declined, of course, but I was quite elated. It was so simple, like Jack's short stories. We were two of a kind, I'm afraid, liking our freedom a little too much.

I bought a newspaper and cigarettes for Jack and rode home on the Métro, and read the headlines about the Finnish campaign before going up once more into the cold. It had been a strange winter, with snow even in Paris, and sometimes in the mornings our river-barge was rimmed in with a delicate fretwork of ice.

May was with Jack when I boarded the *Suzanne*. They were sitting across from each other at the kitchen table, Jack's notebook between them. May looked serious and Jack looked sullen and I knew at once they were talking about work. But he looked up when I came in, glad of an interruption. I showed them the fruits of my morning, and Jack laughed and kissed me, but May looked unamused.

She said sharply, 'Oh don't say you're reduced to that.'

'Reduced?' I said, surprised. 'I don't see it like that, May.' I wasn't angry, only curious at her reaction.

'That's *student's* work, Justina. Ellie should be doing that, not you.' I shrugged.

'Ellie's a landscape artist,' I said. I still did not understand, but Jack spoke suddenly.

'Never mind, sweetheart.' He looked coolly at May, 'She's talking to me, anyhow. Apparently I'm not keeping you in the style to which you're accustomed.' He laughed, with no humour.

'Oh Jack,' May said, 'we're not talking about money.'

'Then what's been the point of this damned morning,' he said. May looked up to me for help, but I couldn't help, not knowing the argument. She picked up his notebook and turned pages idly. He did nothing and I watched, intrigued. May could take liberties that I could not; I was never allowed to look at his work. May was reading, her interest caught in spite of herself. She shook her head suddenly, and laid the notebook down. 'Oh Jack,' she said.

'What's wrong?'

'Nothing. There's nothing . . . and *that's* what's wrong. All your beautiful prose, oh really, Jack, do you imagine that any of the fools who read that will even *see* that you never put a foot wrong? It's so wasted. It's pearls before swine.'

'Swine,' said Jack, 'eat anything.' He paused, 'I kind of like swine. They're friendly.' May fingered the notebook. I saw the corners of her mouth crook in her defeated smile. When she looked up she was no longer angry, though her face was passionate.

'How long is this to go on? You have *work* to do. You're a serious writer, Jack. You have serious things to say.' Jack smiled.

'I'm a story-teller,' he said. 'That's all I've ever been. That's all I have to say.' She started to protest but he caught her two pretty hands and held them, and shook his head, 'It's all over, May.' He said it with a finality that ended argument.

The spring that followed that winter was as beautiful as the winter had been harsh. The air softened and sweetened, a perfect blue sky arched over the roofs and tree-tops. Trees blossomed along the boulevards and the water beside the *Suzanne* was rimmed with soft green pollen dust, where a few weeks before had been ice. The rooks came to their restless nests above us. It was impossible in such a spring to even remember we were living in a country at war. It was a spring of lovers, of flowers, of children in gardens and musicians in the streets. Ellie, in a pink blouse and a dirndl skirt, worked at her easel in the Jardin du Luxembourg. Jack and I lazed in the sun on the roof of our river-barge and forgot that we were middle-aged. It was a spring of dreams, that spring of the blitzkrieg.

How could we, children of the trenches, all have forgotten that with spring comes war? We had had eight months to ready ourselves, and when it came, it came with such ferocity that we were not ready at all. One May day we drifted in gentle insouciance, the next we huddled in tense clusters beside radios, besieged the newspaper kiosks and read and reread the bleak headlines with disbelief. The Stukas screamed in over Northern France and the panzers breached the borders of the Low Countries. The names of towns and rivers, familiar from the last war, leapt out in black print. A monster, thought dead, had arisen to life. It was the nightmare of our youth returned, only this time, what had taken years was happening in days. The Low Countries reeled. The news was chaotic, ever-changing, unable to keep the pace, and augmented by wild rumour. But the panzers moved faster even than rumour, through roads jammed with refugees.

Every day we awoke to new disasters; the Germans were through the Ardennes, they had crossed the Meuse. Belgium was teetering; Holland was overrun. Rotterdam held out and was bombed into rubble and dust. The news was of scores of thousands dead, a city in utter ruins in a day. This was a new kind of war. May's assistant, Marie, came running in with the newspaper. Her face was blotched with tears. She was hysterical. 'Look, look what will become of us!' she cried. Jean-Michel was somewhere on the Belgian frontier where all the fighting was, and she could bear no more. Jack sat with her, holding her in his arms until she calmed, and May led her away to rest.

When we were alone, he said to me, 'For Jean-Michel and for all of us, it will be over soon enough. They'll be in Paris before the month is through.' I didn't believe him, then. It still sounded so fantastical. The city was yet calm, and unchanged. The beautiful days were as beautiful. The newspapers and the radio seemed evil spirits from another world. But on the twentieth of May, when the Germans reached Amiens, I believed. Amiens, my magic talisman; Amiens where once we found safety, where the tide turned and the danger passed; Amiens had fallen and the Germans pressed on to the sea.

The next day May Howie sent word that I was to come and see her. I fancied I knew the reason already, and I was arming myself for my defence, even as I walked through the summery streets. She was awaiting me, upstairs in her flat on the Rue Zacharie. She was wearing her formidable glasses.

But she made tea first, while I stood looking out through the criss-crossed tape of the windows, at a mosaic of street below. We sat on the flowered chintz chairs in her pretty sitting room, drinking the tea. May said, 'There's something we need to talk about.'

'We're not going,' I said.

'I know, dear.' She was disarmingly quiet. I looked up surprised.

'Then what?'

'I want you to marry Jack.'

'*What*?'

'Nothing very elaborate. Just a civil ceremony. It shouldn't take long to arrange. If you'd like, I'll see to any details . . .' she spoke smoothly, with unruffled logic.

'May, what are you talking about? I've lived with Jack since 1926 and you've never *mentioned* marriage before.'

'Don't be difficult, Justina. I'm trying to help. You love the man, don't you?'

'Of course I do.'

'Then why *not* marry him, for heaven's sake? What's the harm in being his wife?'

'If I'd wanted to marry, I would have done something about it years ago,' I bridled. 'What lack is there in what we have? What is there possibly to gain in being his wife?' She looked almost amused by my stupidity.

'The rights and protections of a neutral country, dear. I am Irish. Jack is American. Neither of our countries is at war with the Reich. Yours, unfortunately, is.'

'Oh, my God,' I said slowly. 'I never thought.'

'Yes. I didn't imagine you would.'

'Do you think it will help?' I said in a small voice. I was hearing, for the first time, I think, the distant sound of jackboots on Parisian streets. She looked down wearily at her hands crossed in her lap.

'I don't know, darling. You'll still be British, of course. But it *might* help. In the confusion. It might help.' She looked at me anxiously, and I thought for a long while. At last, I shook my head. 'Oh, Justina,' she whispered, 'why *not*?'

I said slowly, 'It would be dishonourable. Like a surrender. To do for Hitler what we never did for God.'

'Justina,' she said urgently, 'God wouldn't ask you to risk your life over a detail.'

That frightened me but I said, 'It's not a detail. I won't buy my safety with Jack's name.'

She sat silent, staring at me in frustration. At last she said, 'I don't suppose there's any point in my approaching Jack.'

'I shouldn't think so,' I said. I laughed. 'Even if he found the nerve to propose, I'd only turn him down.' I laughed again, and May gave up. Clare was right. My stubbornness is my fatal flaw. And so it was that Jack and I remained in Paris, bound yet in our unhallowed union, to witness the fall of France.

It began with the refugees. For some time we had seen them, first the Belgians, then French country people, from the departments near the fighting, making their way through Paris to the south. Then, in the last days of May, their numbers rapidly grew so what had been an occasional sight became a regularity; cars, lorries, even horse-drawn wagons, loaded with families, children, old people, a kaleidoscope of belongings piled up on roof-tops and running boards, all winding their way through narrow streets and down the long boulevards. One morning, when I went out to buy coffee (only to find the familiar grocer's shop on the Boul'mich' closed and silent, its metal shutters down and its proprietor gone) an entire procession passed, as if all one little French village had decamped and set out together. There were two farm lorries and several old motorcars, all laden with the hastily-gathered and rudely-mixed necessities of life; farm tools, bedsteads, bedding, boxes and cartons of clothing and utensils. Dogs ran barking beside or perched gloriously on the piles of furnishings. Children rode in the open, under the hot June sky, wearing their winter coats over their summer clothes, and hugging parcels of spare garments. There is something brutally indecent in the plight of a refugee; this bundling of clothing out of attics and wardrobes, the bald exposure of intimate furnishings. They seemed to feel it, to avert humiliated eyes. Behind the second lorry a little herd of exhausted cattle and two nanny goats plodded patiently on, leaving their manure on the city cobbles. And at the rear, separated from the forward column by a suitable emptiness of road, came a long black motorcar, polished and shining, a uniformed chauffeur at the wheel, and in the back seat an ancient couple, he in high stiff collar and top hat, she, haughtily lean as a hawk, in tailored grey suit; the village *seigneur* and his lady. I had not realized I was staring until she turned, and through the thick glass met my eyes with such indignity, that I turned away in shame. And yet, we watched these processions with detachment, as if all were inhabitants of another universe.

But around us the city began quietly to die. Day by day more shops were closed, blank metal eyes on the stilling streets. Wooden shutters were drawn over the windows of abandoned apartments. Our neighbours in the Rue St Julien left for the safety of their cousins in the country, leaving a small black cat to cry piteously on the window-ledge outside our studio. On the river, the barge-folk, nomads anyhow, loosed their moorings and slipped away. And yet, in much of Paris, so much went on as before. People were leaving, but for those who remained the normal pleasures continued. The cinemas were still showing pictures, the theatres yet played. On the terraces of the remaining cafés people gathered and talked and they did not always talk of the war. We seemed gripped in a sort of mass delusion in which every indisputable signal of inevitable disaster was simply ignored.

At the beginning of June, bombs fell on Paris itself. News spread of damage and casualties and wherever people gathered there was anger and indignation, but not even then was there real fear. But then one morning, I heard on May's radio the name of a place that the Germans had reached and realized that it was a village just beyond the suburbs of the city, where Ellie had cycled often with friends. And that night, as she and Jack and I sat out in the warm blacked-out night, watching the old familiar shapes of bridges and cathedral in new darkness, and waiting for sirens, he suddenly said, 'Can you smell it?'

'What?' I sniffed the air. There was a faint sweet scent.

'Woodsmoke,' he said. 'Fires outside the city. They must be near.'

Ellie went and sat down by his feet and leaned against his knees, a small dim shape in the darkness. He sat for a long while, stroking her hair, and none of us spoke.

The next morning the streets were crowded with cars leaving the city. Along the kerbs, others were parked, while their owners loaded them with belongings. I watched a woman carefully pile three potted geraniums on to the heap of boxes on her luggage rack, weeping all the while. There was a terrible sad incongruity about what people chose to take, or leave behind. Some streets were quite deserted now, but for the pathetic sight of abandoned pets. All morning a small grey poodle ran back and forth along the Quai St Michel, tongue lolling, eyes turned with hope on each passer-by. Eventually Jack took it aboard the *Suzanne* and fed it and gave it water. But in the afternoon, it ran away.

When I went out to buy bread I passed our favourite café as the proprietor was taking in all the tables from the pavement and stacking the chairs in silent dark heaps. He told me he was hoping to go to his sister in Lyons. I went on, feeling the air of panic rising in the city, fighting the powerful desire to succumb to it. We are not unlike sheep, who run when other sheep run. It is an instinct hard to resist.

When I returned to the Quai St Michel, an unfamiliar dark maroon Citroën motorcar was parked by the quayside, near the *Suzanne*. As I climbed down the stone steps I heard voices speaking in French, Jack's voice, and that of a stranger, I thought. But when I went inside I saw that our visitor was no stranger, but Monsieur Hubert, the kind-hearted civil servant whom Ellie had called Monsieur the Sheep. He sat now at our modest table, sharing a bottle of wine with Jack. Ellie was not there. Jack had sent her out with a message for May. Monsieur Hubert stood up when I entered, and bowed over my hand. 'Madame Redpath,' he said. He was a man of proprieties. He remained standing until I sat down beside Jack. Then he said, 'I am attempting to present a matter of some urgency and I fear I am failing,' he laughed gently, his tangle of woolly white hair tumbling over a sweat beaded forehead. 'This weather,' he said.

'What matter?' I asked. I looked at Jack. He looked guarded.

'The matter of your safety,' he said.

I looked down at the plain table on which the wine glasses made damp rings. When I looked up, I said, 'That is very kind, but there are many more others whose safety is also at risk.'

He shrugged, tilting the side of his hand one way and the other. 'There are risks and there are risks.'

'I don't think ours are greater than anyone else's,' I said.

'But that is my point, Madame,' he said. He leaned forward, glanced once at Jack, and took my hands. Do you know, I suspect he was a little in love with me, as surprising as that might seem. It would explain much of what followed. 'You see, I am trying and trying to explain to Monsieur Redpath, but he is a *child*. He sees no reason. But he is in danger, and with him, naturally, *you* are in danger and your daughter as well.'

'Because we are foreign?' I asked, ingenuously. 'But Jack is American, and America is neutral.'

'*Mais non, Madame*,' he shrugged and shook his woolly curls. 'That is trivia. But your husband, Madame, he is a radical, a Bolshevik . . .'

'A *what*?' said Jack.

'*Monsieur*, please, do not take offence. But you have a reputation. You write of labour unions, and insurrections. You write of mutiny in wartime. Your books are well known and they mark you as a radical, whatever you may say. They will be your executioner,' he paused, releasing my hand and turning from me, 'and hers,' he said under his breath. Jack shook his head and raised his hands in exasperation.

'For Christ's sake, they're *fiction*. They're stories, fairy-tales. I'm not a politician,' he said, and echoing what he had said to May, 'I'm a story-teller. Nothing more.'

Monsieur Hubert folded his fat, pale hands on our table. He smiled sweetly. 'Believe me, Monsieur Redpath, *I* understand. I do understand. But,' he shrugged angrily, indicating our advancing enemy, 'these people are not masters of nuance.' He sat back, and closed his eyes, as if he were thinking, or marshalling strength. When he opened them he looked at us both with determination. 'Now, I wish no more of this nonsense. You will take your dear lady, and her daughter, and you will go.'

Monsieur the Sheep was a remarkable man. I don't think any one else ever talked to Jack that way and got away with it. I've often imagined that Jack would have refused entrance to heaven itself, if summarily ordered to go there. But this time he only said, very quietly, 'I don't think that's any longer possible. The Channel Ports are closed, and all the roads north.'

'Then go south,' said M. Hubert. He paused, 'I do not say this lightly. The roads are jammed and dangerous, but for you and Mme Redpath, I think it is yet safer than to remain. But you must go now.'

'But how?' I said stupidly. 'Are there still trains? Can we get on them?'

'My car is outside. You may have it.' We just stared. 'I won't be needing it now,' he said with another little shrug.

'But what of yourself?' Jack said. 'What of your family? Are you to stay, while we go to safety?' M. Hubert smiled. He reached both his hands across the table and took again one of mine and, now, one of Jack's.

'*Mes enfants*,' he said. 'I have no family. I have only myself. As for you, you have been dear guests of France, but you have other homes. Myself, Paris is my only home. There is nowhere other I would go.' He stood up. 'Now, if there is to be *any* safety, you must hurry. All necessary papers, and an explanation in my hand, are within the car; if you are stopped, you must give my name. I have put four tins of petrol in the boot. It is all I could obtain.' He held his arms out wide, and embraced us both, kissing us solemnly on each cheek. 'Goodbye, children,' he said. Then he mounted the little step on to the after deck, and stepped clumsily across to the stone stairs. On the quayside, he waved once and then turned and walked away, across the Quai St Michel, a stubby, comical little Frenchman with a mass of woolly white hair. And while Jack and I were loading our handful of belongings and necessities and preparing ourselves for our flight, he returned to his fashionable apartment on the Rue d'Auteuil, and shot himself dead.

Of course I did not learn that until years after, like so many things about those frenetic, fateful days. Swept suddenly from the placid routine of the ordinary into the powerful immediacy of survival, we lived, like everyone, moment to moment in the shell of our own lives. That day in June on which we rose, as always, from the gentle familiarity of our own bed, saw us, by evening sleeping in a roadside ditch. In between was all the frenzy of an unthought-of farewell, as we cut adrift in an afternoon from the life of a decade.

As soon as M. Hubert left us, while Jack was ransacking the *Suzanne* for what we must take, I ran through the streets to The Fishing Cat seeking Ellie and May. I found them in the printshop, May in her overalls, cursing and struggling with Alphonse, Ellie offering timid and tentative help. May sat down on a heavy wooden bench stacked with rolls of paper, while I told her of M. Hubert's visit. Ellie watched, toying with a spanner, her eyes darkening with fear.

May said, when I had finished, 'You are going?'

I nodded slowly. 'Yes.'

May put her head in her hands. 'Oh, thank God.' She looked up and gave a small smile. 'You know, I thought you might be bone-headed enough to ignore even that.'

'No. I'm terrified, May. He made it sound so threatening.'

'Good for him. Threatening is precisely what it is. I have been trying to get that through to Monsieur the Genius for weeks. You know, for an intelligent man, he can be quite stupendously thick.'

'Jack says you must come with us,' I said. She looked up and laughed.

'Oh does he?' She laughed again, incredulously. 'Jack Redpath giving *me* orders? Oh, I thought he'd know better than that.'

'But, May,' I said.

'Oh, nonsense, dear. It's nothing to do with me. *I'm* not the revolutionary. Just a little old maid running a printshop . . . with noble little neutral Ireland to protect me. I shan't have any worries.' She brushed her hands together, rubbing the greasy dust from one to the other. 'No, my loves. I'll just keep my head down, and ride it through. There's nothing here anyone is going to care much about. A few silly books of verse. Nothing more.' She stood up. 'Come, I will see you off, and look after your things, and as soon as it's over you can come back. More than likely, you'll find us all quite unchanged.' She made it sound like a summer holiday. And before she would come down to the quay to bid us farewell, she insisted on going upstairs to her apartment, and changing from her overalls into her street dress, of skirt and bolero jacket and little straw hat.

While she did, I went with Ellie to our studio on the Rue St Julien, and gathered up every paper on Jack's desk, his typewriter in its case and my mahogany paintbox from Sligo. The easel, too awkward to carry, I left behind, with an unfinished portrait of two little French sisters watching forlornly as I closed the door.

May walked with us back to the Quai St Michel. Jack was waiting beside the maroon Citroën. It was already packed and ready. He took the paintbox and sheaf of papers from me and the typewriter from May and put them on the back seat. Then he turned to her and said, 'Get your things, May. You're coming with us.' He looked determined, but she just laughed, the sort of gay, unruffleable laugh by which she always deflected her mother's admonishments. 'I'm not leaving you here,' Jack said.

'Oh, don't be dramatic, darling. It doesn't suit. *I've* nothing to fear. Not half as much as I might driving in that thing, with you.' She laughed again. 'Go on, Jack, you're wasting time.' Had she been anyone else, I think he would have just put her in the car, without argument. But no one did such things to May Howie, and after all these years, Jack remained slightly in awe of her. He looked at me for help, but I could not help. Defeated, he turned away, and gathered up our itinerant tomcat and sat forlornly on the front wing of the car, quietly rubbing its orange ears, while I went aboard the *Suzanne*. Down below, I sat down at the table where we ate and Jack wrote in the silent hours of the night. I looked all around, at the painted cupboards and the wicker chairs, grasping a memory that I might hold forever; that cramped, narrow, waterborne home, dearer to me than Arradale.

When I came back up on deck, Ellie was holding the tomcat. His slyer, calico mate was, as always in times of stress, nowhere in sight. 'Is he coming?' Ellie asked hopefully. Jack took him, tweaked his ears and handed him to May.

'He's a Parisian,' he said. 'Hold Paris for us, Cat.' He stood looking down at May. He reached almost shyly to hold her, his big hands on her delicate upper arms.

'Goodbye, Sweetheart,' he said. She stared up at him, almost angrily.

'Be what you're meant to be,' she said fiercely. She turned away from his kiss. She embraced Ellie, and then me, and we clung together. Jack cranked the engine and it started roughly. He helped Ellie into the back seat, and held the front door open for me. I climbed in, and he went around to the other side, and got behind the wheel.

May held the cat, sagging patiently, under one arm. She clutched my hands through the open window, and I held hers until the car pulled away on the rough cobbles of the quayside. Jack saluted her briskly, like a soldier. She stood quietly watching us go and I turned over my shoulder for a final glimpse. I'll always remember how pretty she looked, with her tufts of blond hair peeking out beneath the gay straw hat.

The journey was a nightmare. The drive out of Paris took hours and hours, the beautiful tree-shaded boulevards now crammed with a motley circus of vehicles and people of every sort. We had joined that pathetic parade, we were now, as they, refugees. Jack was remarkable; he drove cleverly and well, finding us short-cuts through the narrow streets he had so often walked, but never driven before. He had never owned a motorcar, and rarely drove one, but he was one of those people who learn skills easily, and having learned, never forget them. Nor were all his skills as innocuous as this.

I did not question. As two decades before, on the road from Dernancourt, I had trusted instinctively to his ability and judgement, I trusted now. Jack gave to much of the world the impression of being an innocent dreamer, but there was a lot more to the man than that; I had seen it before, and I knew.

Outside the city at last, we were swallowed up in a great procession making its way blindly south and east, aimlessly, routelessly, driven only by the need to escape the advancing armies closing in from north and west. I don't believe that the greater mass of those peoples even had a destination in mind. It was a mindless flight. And it moved at the pace of the slowest, the farm-wagons, horse-drawn, the push-carts, and babies' prams loaded high with household goods, the stumbling pace of walking children.

There was no way for anyone, motorcar or not, to go faster. Jack coaxed along the unhappy heated engine, and cheerily gave rides to fellow travellers on the broad running boards. For a while an entire farm family travelled with us, their ageing great-grandmother in our back seat with Ellie, their two strong sons flanking the car like an honour guard. When we stopped at the roadside for supper we were treated to fresh fruit and cheese they had brought from their home. After supper, we all moved on, driving as far as we could in darkness, headlamps switched off for safety. Over our heads, the distant rumble of aeroplane engines continued even after dark, Stuka bombers roving the country like wolves.

That night, Jack insisted that we sleep far away from the car, in the shelter of a grassy ditch, beside a hedgerow. I obeyed, but grudgingly. I could not imagine that anyone, German or otherwise, would deliberately attack this vast civilian convoy. Still, our farm family followed Jack's lead, and I was kept awake half the night by the vigorous snoring of their big grey-moustached patriarch. We set out again, before dawn, the next day.

Our destination was Mont Louis in the Pyrenees where we had friends and could expect shelter. But though we had travelled that way often, in the swift comfort of the railway, it seemed now an impossible distance, at this pace. Cut off from newspapers and radio, in the chaos of the roads, we moved in an eerie limbo. I experienced an uncanny *déjà vu*, casting me back to the battlefields of the first War, in which Jack and I, young strangers, fled together from an unseen foe. All around us was the same confusion, the same air of fear and of defeat. *There is no escape*, I thought. *What is meant to be will be, in God's terrible patient time*.

At noon of the second day, we came upon a small

convoy of French soldiers, being shunted from one arena to another, in the confusion of the collapsing order. They were hopelessly entangled in the traffic jam we created, and we stopped and waited patiently as, up ahead at a village crossroads, a local *gendarme* comically assisted in their rescue. We had all climbed from the car, cooling ourselves in the gentle summer breeze, sharing a bottle of wine with our farmer-patriarch. There was a brief air of holiday, of frivolity, as along the endless line of refugees others climbed down from their vehicles to talk, and eat, and even to sing. Children played on the dusty verge, and the black clad great-grandmother emerged stoically from the back of our Citroën to milk the family goat.

'How can they move an army through this?' Jack said, with a hopeless laugh. We heard a sound then, of engines, and first imagined the convoy of motor-lorries was coming through, but then we recognized the familiar aerial drone. Down the procession of families and stalled vehicles a wave of attention stilled songs, talk and laughter. The droning changed pitch and rose to a whining shriek.

'Will it be . . .' I started to ask, but Jack had my arm and Ellie's and was running with us, dragging us roughly with him, stumbling and protesting, so that we were fifty yards from the road when the first bombs struck. Jack flung me down, in the shelter of a vineyard wall, threw Ellie down beside me and lay across us both while the earth rocked and shook with explosions. It went on and on, deafening and terrifying, each wave of detonations preceded by the awful evil banshee shriek of the descending Stuka bombers.

'Why us? Why us?' I heard Ellie crying. But it was not us, but the French army convoy that the bombers sought, and destroyed. We were chance unfortunates, accidents of fate. When the bombers veered off, satiated, and the world grew quiet, but for the shrieks of children and barking of dogs and cries of frantic livestock, we still lay, for long minutes, until we were certain it was over. Slowly, Jack released the grip in which he held us both, climbed to his feet and looked across to the roadside. Smoke and flames arose from the distant crossroads. There was a burning stench I recognized from another war, of explosives and rubber and flesh.

'Did they kill people?' Ellie asked, shakily, like a small child. She was white, shocked; I took my jacket off and put it round her shoulders. We walked slowly back to the roadside where our maroon Citroën stood unharmed. Beside it, the grey-moustached farmer glared upwards into the now quiet sky.

'Pigs,' he said. 'Shitting pigs.' He spat, thick spittle, on to the ground.

The rest of the procession clambered cautiously back from hiding places in the surrounding fields. They were all just standing there, full in the open, watching the fires, when the fighters came. They came in low, just brushing the tops of the tall roadside poplars, so low that I could see the pilots' faces, see that they were looking right at us, when the firing began. This time, there wasn't even time to run.

'They can *see* us,' I cried, bewildered, before Jack hauled me down in the scant shelter of the drainage ditch beside the road. 'Ellie!' I cried.

'I have her,' Jack shouted. 'Stay down,' and I did, praying that he was not lying. I could not see, or hear anything, but the cries all around and the intense, personal spattering of machine-gun fire, rattling with perfect precision down the road. The fighters veered off; we raised our heads, seeking better shelter, but could only wriggle deeper into the ditch before they returned. I heard a shriek so compelling and so near that I could not but look, and raised my head to see a young mother run panicked out into the dusty road, her little girl and boy stumbling beside her, holding her skirt. The machine guns swept the road again, taking them down, one, two, three, like targets in a fairground.

Beside me, I heard Jack gasp. And then suddenly he scrambled to his feet, and jumped up out of the ditch and stood on the edge of the road, silhouetted against the sky, waving a fist at the planes and shouting, 'You bastards, you goddam bastards. There's women and children!' As if that mattered to those people. But my mind leapt a quarter of a century to Bachelor's Walk.

'No!' I cried, and started up after him, but the big farmer was before me, clambering heavily erect. He mounted the road, took Jack's arm with one huge hand and threw him casually into the ditch. Then we all lay flat as the fighters took their final run. When the drone of their engines faded into silence, we hesitantly raised our heads, looked around and then stood up. A cluster of people formed round the bodies of the woman and her children in the road. Ellio watched, crying and holding my hand. Somewhere a wounded horse was shrieking an un-animal cry. Jack had calmed down and he turned to thank the old farmer. The big man shrugged, brushing dust from his dirty cotton smock.

'*Mon ami*,' he said, 'it is a long road, and I cannot drive that thing.' He nodded to the Citroën, and gave another little shrug.

Before we left that place, in the miraculously mobile, though bullet-pocked car, Jack and the farmer took a pistol and a rifle from the dead bodies of soldiers by the burnt lorries. Afterwards, when the bombers came, they crouched at the roadside and fired back. It happened several times during that long journey, and each time they were bolder, staying longer in the open, until they could see the pilots' faces for a target. I hated it, because it was useless and terribly dangerous, but they persisted. It changed them. They laughed and joked, and seemed proud of themselves, as if they had won back a touch of honour for poor France. By the time we parted company in Montauban, the old man and Jack were like father and son.

We had, by then, long since left the car behind, mired in a ditch, its rear axle broken. Beside it, amidst the wild flowers at the side of a hayfield, where we had unloaded them to lighten the trapped car, lay Jack's old Royal typewriter and the mahogany paintbox James Howie had given me in Temple House. Repositories of memories and tools of our trades, they were yet not necessities. We went on, with a change of clothing, a few francs, bread and cheese for food. Along the way, we gathered what we could; cherries and plums from the orchards, and milk and eggs purchased in villages through which we passed. Ellie and I rode on the big farmcart, drawn by our companions' two grey plough horses. Sometimes we got down to lighten the load, and as we walked I was thankful for all those summers climbing in the Pyrenees, and winters on the high snowfields. Jack and the old man walked side by side. They looked like a pair of brigands, armed and ready, talking together in easy French. Near Montauban, the old man had a cousin with whom he sought shelter. With peasant charity he offered us a refuge there too, but we thanked him and refused, and when we parted, he wept, kissing us all.

From Montauban we went on, on foot. I cannot remember how many days it took; days of endless walking, of occasional fortunate rides in lorries, or horse-wagons, of yearning for as simple a thing as a bicycle. But bicycles were worth their weight in gold, and even had we the money to purchase them, there were none for sale. The whole of the countryside was filled with people moving from one place to another, in search of food, of shelter, of security, which ironically might more likely have been found in the very homes they had left. But a terrible fear was on everyone, and it knew no logic.

Outside Carcassonne an imperious French lady, beautifully dressed, signalled her chauffeur to draw her silver Rolls-Royce abreast of us, as we trudged along the road. They stopped, and she beckoned with one curled finger. Gratefully, we climbed aboard, Jack in the front seat beside the driver and Ellie and I, in our dusty and sweat-stained corduroy trousers, on either side of her immaculate self.

'Carcassonne?' she asked, pointing. We nodded eagerly. Her English was not good, but out of politeness she spoke in our language. All the way into the town, she laid curses on the heads of Daladier and Chamberlain, and every politician and holder of high office who had led to this betrayal of France. She devoted her days to driving back and forth along the roads, aiding refugees, and informed us that if she saw a single Boche she would run him down, and laugh as she did so.

From Carcassonne we could see, at last, the Pyrenees, dressed yet in winter snow, hanging a pale veil across the southern sky. They brought to my mind the white curtain of the Elburz, forever unreachable above Teheran, and amidst the orchards and vineyards and hot sun of the Aude, I longed for their cool refuge.

A vineyard lorry took us out of the city, through Limoux and into a village in the Roussillon, and from there, walking once more, we turned mountainwards, and as we climbed higher, summer rolled back into spring. Cherries gave way to cherry blossoms, and vineyards to high pastures, yet yellowed where the winter drifts had lain. Mist came down, reminding me of Scotland, as we climbed towards winter and the snows. We walked most of the way to Mont Louis.

It was hours after dark when we arrived there. For the last few miles, Jack had carried my pack as well as his own, and walked with an arm about Ellie, supporting her as well. The final few steps, up the cobbled streets within the walls of the town, seemed unsurpassable, like the last few metres of a long, long mountain climb. I have never before, or again, been so tired.

At the mountain inn where we had, in happier times, so often stayed, we were greeted with warmth and affection. All the innkeeper's family, his wife and his two grown sons, and his shy unmarried daughter, got up from their beds to welcome us. They seemed excited, but not terribly surprised to see us, as if our arrival was a logical outcome of events in the wider world. They offered the solemn news that Paris had been surrendered without a shot fired as if they in their far mountain fastness were personally responsible. They were angry, and filled with self-disgust, but I, thinking of May and our friends there, was glad there had been no fighting in the city.

They brought us food that we were too tired to eat, and brandy that we unwisely drank. Perhaps regarding himself likely to become an unfit custodian, Jack unstrapped the holstered military pistol and laid it on the table. Lucien and Raymond, our host's two sons, moved closer, looking upon it with light in their eyes, like children craving a sweet.

'A useful thing,' said their father. Jack slid it across the table and smiled tiredly.

'Have it. It's yours.' The boys pounced upon it at once, taking the pistol from the holster and stroking its smooth metal. 'Don't shoot yourselves,' Jack said, as we rose to retire. They laughed together, black Spanish eyes full of merriment.

'We will shoot nothing but crows,' said Lucien. 'These black crows that come in flocks upon our fields.'

Oh, the relief that night to be in that familiar room, in the old feather bed beneath the time-darkened timbers of the steep slate roof; to be safe, and to fall asleep in the comfort of Jack's arms. We slept much of the following day. When we rose, we each had the luxury of a bath, and dressed in fresh clothes, provided by our generous hosts. I had been offered one of Madame's good dresses, but aware of our current needs, persuaded her to allow me, instead, a pair of Lucien's old trousers, and Ellie the same. She was a little scandalized but bowed to the pressures of wartime. Ellie and I emerged, voluminous, but warm, in corduroy breeches, and thick cotton shirts, wrapped around nearly twice and belted about our waists.

After his bath, Jack sent for fresh water, and soap, and stood in front of the worn grey mirror in the inn's bathroom, and watched his distorted reflection as he carefully shaved off the full beard he had worn for twenty years. I said, 'Why?' and he answered with a smile, 'Changing times.'

I had not seen him thus since we parted in Etaples at the end of the Great War, and I found the result quite disconcerting. He looked remarkably different; surprisingly younger and somehow harder. The change was such that Henri, our host, was quite taken aback, failing to recognize him at all when he came downstairs for dinner that night.

Afterwards, Jack sat with Lucien and Henri, with two

old maps spread out on the table before them, while in a corner of the kitchen, Raymond, the quiet one, worked silently, carefully waxing four pairs of skis. In the high passes into Spain, the snow yet lay too deep to walk.

We left at dawn the next day, Lucien, Jack, Ellie and I. It was not early enough, even then, to avoid the curious gaze of the women out to draw water for the morning's work. But we had little concern. They knew us, and our eccentricities, and we were not the only foreigners to climb to the highest places, with skis on their backs, for the last snow before summer. Our predilection for such nonsense amused them equally in winter; it was not a native sport, and Lucien and Raymond, mountaineers and skiers both, were exceptions.

We laughed and talked freely as we went, as befitted holiday-makers, and although Lucien brought with him the army pistol, he wore it carefully hidden under his coat. Ellie was in high spirits, away from the terrors of the journey from Paris, and teased Jack playfully about his new, strange appearance. I walked behind them, happy and elated; we were together and we were safe. It was all I could ask.

The climb was very beautiful. Lucien took us by a route where no road lay, only a zig-zag path mounting higher and higher, first among dark forests, then into clearings scattered with bright birches and scented boxbrush, and at last to the barren uplands, where no trees grew. We followed the course of a mountain stream that tumbled and fell in foaming waterfalls and silken slides over aeons-worn rock, its waters a luminous glacial grey. A footpath ran beside the stream and we climbed from one delight to another for hundreds of feet until the ground grew arctic, clad only in low alpine mosses and lichens and our stream vanished under a thick bank of winter snow. Yet even there, there were flowers, tiny perfect blossoms of white and pink and blue tucked among the windswept rocks. Ellie stopped to exclaim over them, and gather them to carry with her. She was like a child, lost in an oblivious happy world. Jack climbed beside her, sometimes holding her hand to pull her giggling up the steeper bits, and the sight of them filled me with memories of all our days of play there, with Ellie and with Eithne before her. As he walked, Jack sang to her, the café song, 'Bye, Bye, Blackbird'. It was a joke between them, with which he teased her. He sang prettily in a sweet tenor voice. Lucien walked a little behind us all, with a sure, solemn step, like Hassan Abbas on the hills of my youth.

For a while we climbed beside the tongues of snow extending down the stream beds, but they grew broader and broader until they eventually joined and the ground above us was white wherever it was not black rock. The snow was old and soft, and rotten above the running water; dangerous to walk upon. We stopped and unfastened the skis from our packs, and Lucien and Jack unrolled long strips of silvery seal-skin, and buckled them, with the stiff hairs downward, on to the soles of the skis, and on them we started the climb to the heights of the snowy col.

It was steep and difficult. At first we could hear the stream rushing beneath us in its snow tunnel, but later it grew still, silent in its winter grave. Jack no longer sang, but followed a ski-length behind Ellie, encouraging her, and ready, should she slip, to stop her slide. Lucien and I ski'd upwards side by side, breathing hard and stopping to rest on our poles, and it pleased me that I could match stride for stride with that hardy mountain boy. Once Jack looked over his shoulder to me and he smiled as our eyes met, proud that we had achieved our respective years without yet growing old.

Soon the snow filled all the floor of the high pass, and swept up in drifts against its rocky walls. For a while cliffs bounded us, grey and black, their tops lost in mist and cloud. It was bitterly cold, and the north wind channelled through the gap in the mountains, battering at our backs. It was hard to imagine that we had left Mont Louis amidst spring flowers and that hot summer reigned in the valleys and vineyards far below. When we turned over our shoulders and faced into the wind, we could see far, far down into the blues and greens of the low-lying lands. It was like a vision into Elysium.

Far above, we were in a world without colour, of white and grey and black, before which Ellie's red jacket and hat shone brightly beautiful. Over us, the clouds, so near our heads, swirled and streamed at tremendous speed, just once breaking to reveal the extraordinary blue of a June sky. The walls of rock lowered as we reached the summit of the pass, and at last we were exposed and open, with only distant rises to the great peaks, through which we were passing, to shelter us. The wind was fierce, and when we turned to face into it, light fresh flakes of snow stung against our skin. I looked down the way we had come. The hill fell away, a steep apron of white. Before us, a short stretch of level ground ran out to meet white sky, where the southern slopes of the pass began. We stood silent, joined in a perfect aloneness, remote from all the strife-filled world.

We took off our packs to rest and stripped the seal-skins from the skis for the downhill run. But we kept the skis on our feet, in the deep snow within the pass. Jack ski'd across to the other side and looked down for a long while at our route ahead. When he came back, he talked quietly with Lucien while Ellie and I opened the packs and got out cheese and bread and wine and fresh cherries from the distant summer below.

We ate hungrily, in silence, passing the wine, in a goatskin, from one to the other. Jack and Lucien drank it flamboyantly, with the skin held high, splashing the backs of their throats. But Ellie and I giggled and fumbled and spilled drops in the snow, pink, like drops of blood. While we ate, the cloud lifted, and for a while we could see miles and miles in each direction, to France on one side, and Spain on the other. We finished our meal, and began to refasten the packs.

'Time to go,' Jack said suddenly, nodding to Lucien. I looked up to him. He did not meet my eyes, but seemed suddenly in a restless hurry, checking his bindings, adjusting Lucien's pack for him. I saw him hand his own to Lucien as well. Ellie was fussing with a bootlace, her hands red and cold. Jack bent down, gave her her knitted mittens, and did the lace for her. Then, as she straightened up, he turned his skis opposing hers, so he could put his hands on her shoulders. Solemnly, he tucked two stray black curls within her woollen bonnet. Then he kissed her forehead gently. 'Bye, bye, blackbird,' he said.

'Jack?' I said carefully. Then he came to me, gliding easily across the new soft snow. He stood beside me, facing me, but with his head turned away, bent down over his hands, resting on his poles.

He said, without looking at me, 'Do you know, I *still* wish we'd been seventeen.'

'Jack, why are you saying goodbye to us?' I heard the rise of my voice make the words angry and sharp.

'All those goddam years.'

'You're coming with me.' He raised his head and met

my eyes, and then straightened slowly, so he looked down at me.

'No. Not yet.' His voice was very calm and responsible. When I looked up at him, I saw the lean, hard stranger's face I had seen first at Dernancourt, the fine, blue-green eyes controlled and serene. There was no softening in them any longer, and no compromise.

I shouted suddenly, 'Why? Why?' I waved a hand towards the French valley below. 'Why fight for people who wouldn't fight for themselves?' It was cruel and unfair of me to say it, and in front of Lucien, but Jack deflected my anger gently.

'They'll fight,' he said. 'When they realize what's happened, they'll fight.' He slipped his wrists through the leather loops of the poles and raised his hands to my face. 'Will you be all right?'

'Of course,' I snapped, turning my face. He closed his hands tighter, and did not let me turn. I looked back, and said, more quietly, 'I was all right before I ever met you. I'll be all right now.'

'I remember,' he said with a smile. 'The Rose of No Man's Land.'

'Oh, Jack.' He clutched me suddenly and we leaned awkwardly against each other, arms wrapping each other tight.

'Jesus, don't cry. I've hardly the strength as it is.' I drew back, clumsily, and caught my balance as the skis slipped on the snow.

'Oh, when have I ever cried over you?' I shoved him away. 'Go on. Go. Go on.'

And so he turned, and took two long strides, and was at the edge of the descent. He saluted Lucien, and Ellie, and then rested his poles in the snow. He looked down the long run before him, and looked back at me and we stared at each other in silence. Then he thrust the poles down, and swung his skis into the fall line and ran straight, as fast as he could flee from us, until the steepening hill forced him down into a wide sweeping telemark turn. I watched his descent, graceful and beautiful, turning and turning, like a mountain bird arcing to the valley below. When I could see him no longer, I turned to Lucien and to Ellie who watched unbelieving, her pink-cheeked face streaked with two rivulets of tears. It was only then that I realized I had not kissed him goodbye.

I ski'd across to Ellie and held her while she cried, until Lucien, shouldering the extra pack, said with delicate care, 'Madame Redpath, it is late, and the way is long.'

I nodded and smiled and I dried Ellie's tears with my sleeve. Then I took up my poles, and my pack, and followed him to the southern descent of the col.

'Lucien will lead, and I'll follow you,' I said to Ellie, the way Jack would. 'Use your edges.' She kept staring at me, unable to believe my calm, her mouth trembling. I smiled encouragingly and sent her off behind the Pyrenean boy. I looked back, only once, to the col where we had parted. Then we, too, descended, down and down, in wide smooth curves, until the high col lay between us and the north wind, and the snow grew wet and we could feel the heat rising from the valley below. The sun came out, and our snowfield narrowed into a single long gully and we still ran down, turning and turning, until we could hear the water of the stream rushing beneath us and then the snow ended abruptly in grass. Then we loosened our bindings, and took off our skis, and we were in summer, and in Spain.

29

I heard nothing more of Jack Redpath until the winter of 1943, three and a half years after our flight from France. In those years, I endured London under bombs and blackout, began a new and different career, and watched my daughter Ellie mature into difficult womanhood. They were the years of rations and queueing, of shelters and salvage, firewatch, victory gardens, mending and making do. They were the years of living for the moment and not thinking of tomorrow, or yesterday. And in all those years not one day passed that I did not think of him, or wonder where he was.

I think I always believed he would come back to me, as he had done before, magically, in New York, and in Istanbul. I had enormous faith in him. He was not, like my poor brothers and son, an innocent pawn of politicians or parties. Jack was a very capable man; intelligent, and wily as a cat. He was a survivor. I was certain I would see him again.

That fey certainty no doubt imbued me with the peculiar confident calm in which I arrived in England after the fall of France. It was a calm in which I was quite alone. There was considerable fuss within the family, at the time, and a general outrage directed at Jack, for having, as they saw it, abandoned us to our fate. It seemed beyond my powers to convince them otherwise. I suppose our situation did little to help, and I can envision the sorry sight we made when Clare and Wilhemina collected us from the boat-train, still dressed in the grossly clumsy flowered dresses found for us by a consular official in Portugal as replacement for Lucien's corduroys. Wilhemina, I know, *never* forgave us for returning from Lisbon in 1940, courtesy of the consulate, as 'distressed British subjects', which (stretching a point slightly in Ellie's case), was precisely what we were. She saw the Melrose name demeaned. (Front page of the *Daily Express*!) I thought she was lucky to have us back at all.

Still, she provided us readily with quite sumptuous accommodation, in the Bryanston Square house where, much to my surprise, she chose to ride out the war, leaving Arradale to the staff and a cluster of evacuees. And it was there, the morning after our arrival, that the family gathered to welcome us back into the fold. It was early July when we returned, in that brief lull after Dunkirk. All around, England was bracing herself for invasion. As we sat amidst the blue chintzes of Wilhemina's drawing room, workmen were sawing off the black iron railings outside the windows, and stacking them for scrap. The usual flood of strangers whom Wilhemina entertained came and went, now brusquely official in WVS tunics, carrying gasmasks and tin hats. Wilhemina was the local ARP warden, a post that finally satisfied her lifelong lust for power.

The household was much diminished, only her cook and butler remained, and he was in the Auxiliary Fire Service with other duties of his own. It was Khadija Abbas who served us tea. She had remained with Wilhemina since 1938, forsaking family, homeland, and her promising education, all at the request of my nephew Hugo, who found such sacrifice perfectly natural. They had an understanding that in any house but Wilhemina's would have been an engagement. My sister-in-law, accepting the wonderful convenience of Khadija's dutiful daughterly presence, was not quite ready to accept her as daughter-in-law. If the young couple minded, they did not say. They had larger worries. Hugo, having abandoned the family regimental tradition, was now Pilot Officer Melrose of the RAF, stationed at Uxbridge, and facing an uncertain future. Domestic squabbles would be reserved for a quieter time.

It was Hugo, rakishly handsome in airforce blue, who was my most indignant champion against the perfidy of Jack.

'He just *left* you there?' he declared, his brisk little moustache quivering with outrage. I smiled.

'Why not? We had Lucien. And I was quite capable.'

'But surely, if he *loved* you . . .' Hugo burst out. As if dignity and respect were not part of love. He mumbled an apology for his indiscretion, but shook his head at the same time, dismissing any defence I might make, 'No, no, Aunt Justina, I do say, it's quite unacceptable. I'm sorry. I really am. But the man's an out-and-out cad. If I could get my hands on him . . .'

'Oh, really, Hugo,' Wilhemina said, pained. 'That's hardly practical.' She was no more pleased with Jack than he, but she managed to shift the blame a little, 'The trouble is, and I'm sure Justina *must* agree, these artistic types are just unreliable. What *I* don't understand, my dear, is why you *let* him go off like that. Why didn't you simply *demand* he come with you?' She blinked her eyes, 'I mean he could hardly *refuse*. Of course,' she added, 'I suppose it *is* different when you're not exactly married.'

'Mother,' Hugo said, 'please.' He was still fuming chivalric rage.

I said gently, 'It doesn't matter. He wouldn't have come, anyway.'

'Of *course* he would,' Wilhemina declared. 'The man's

besotted with you.' She looked regretful. 'If only you'd married him. Then he couldn't have refused.'

Clare, who had watched silently, sipping tea, suddenly clunked cup and saucer down together and said sharply, 'Good Christ, Wilhemina, if she'd wanted *that* sort of man she could have married that twit from the Art School.'

But then Ellie spoke, her first words of protest since we left the Pyrenees. 'He *didn't* refuse,' she said. She threw me a quick, bitter glance, amazing me. 'He never refused, because *she* never asked. She never asked him to come.'

'I say, whyever not?' Wilhemina asked baldly.

I shook my head, still watching Ellie glaring at me in anger. 'Jack did what he wanted to do,' I said.

'Jack would do anything for you,' Ellie cried. Her face was fierce. 'Anything. You could have stopped him with a word. One word. If you *loved* him you would have . . .' She wanted to cry, and when I reached to comfort her, she thrust my hand away. 'You didn't even kiss him goodbye.'

'Oh, be quiet, girl,' Clare said. 'They're not *children*, you know.' Then she turned to me and her voice gentled, 'I'm sorry, pet,' she said. She gave me a little hug, the first in uncounted years. I remembered how I used to crave those affections, and silently I hugged her back. Clare proved a good friend in the months that followed.

Clare was the only one of us who had, through her academic achievements and through her quick-witted company, maintained the contacts that our father's position had once ensured. Clare knew people; not the frivolous people that Wilhemina fussed over, but people of influence, and now, as we all aged, people of power. If Clare wanted something done, she knew how to arrange it. Like all who enjoy privilege, she husbanded it carefully, and used it only on rare, necessary occasions. She used it for me now.

Within a month of our arrival, I was offered an appointment under the War Artists' Scheme. Painting, rarely the beloved of officialdom, had found a new champion. The sights and scenes of wartime Britain were to be recorded for a posterity which, from the look of things that lovely and dangerous summer, might quite likely not be British at all. It was a brave and generous act. It provided me, and many others, with work 'throughout the duration' and a new perspective and experience as well. It was a very exciting time that I would not have chosen to miss, and I owed it, most certainly, to Clare. Not that I was unworthy of such an opportunity; I had a certain reputation, and I had the ability. But I had been long out of the country, more a French artist than a British one, and I had not exhibited in Britain since the winter that James Howie died. Clare must have pulled strings, if only to bring me to someone's notice, and I was not the least bit guilty, but quite thoroughly glad.

The work took me everywhere, from the gentle farmland of Kent, with its blue skies criss-crossed with vapour trails, to the factory cities of the North, where women in head-scarves and overalls built the machinery of war. I painted in shelters, in British Restaurants, in bunting-draped village squares.

I painted dogfights in the skies (how deceptively beautiful they were!) and our ack-ack gunners at their posts. I painted ARP wardens, and Home Guard battalions drilling beside the cricket pavilion on village greens, and WVS ladies making jam. It was a peculiar, homey war, with images of almost comical incongruity, this sudden mustering to battle among the familiar cosiness of English towns. Its images suited me perfectly; women's images of the home turned gallantly into war; saucepans for Spitfires. Most of all, those women's faces; in shelters, in food queues, at railway stations; the work-worn gallant faces of the old and unbeautiful; as an artist, I could have been created for this task alone.

I took Ellie with me everywhere; a finer apprenticeship she could not have desired. She worked at my side, often on the same canvas. In the early days of the Blitz, we did crazy, wild things, running about the streets while the sirens blared, dodging the wardens, and finding some useless bits of shelter from which we could watch the bombs fall. There were spectacular sights, quite beautiful, if you divorced them from their destructive reality, the sky dancing with searchlights, and arced with tracer-fire, the blacked-out buildings gracefully delicate against a back-drop of flames. We huddled together under our tin hats, listening to the shrapnel tinkling on the street, glimpsing the alien bombers droning relentlessly through the search beams and cheering shamelessly as our anti-aircraft batteries fired thunderously back. When the dangers overcame our recklessness we waited for a lull and dived for the nearest public shelter, and sat amidst the housewives and children, holding the images of the dark night in our minds. We did a lot of dangerous things in those weeks, things that should have got us both killed; and looking back I see some reaction to what had gone before, some late grasped solidarity with Jack. Though why chancing obliteration in a London street seemed to draw me closer to him, I cannot say.

Later, we were more circumspect. It was looking to be a long war, after all. Some of the early excitement faded as summer retreated into autumn and the raids and the fires grew worse. At home, we had an Anderson shelter sunk into the small and once elegant rear garden, but we were rarely there to use it. Wilhemina spent the nights shepherding neighbours into shelters, enforcing the infuriating blackout, and dousing incendiaries. Khadija drove an ambulance through the dangerous streets. We weren't the only ones taking risks. Nor were all the dangers as simply physical as death.

War is no friend of the honourable mind. I had experienced war before, and seen it turn good people into ogres of prejudice and vengefulness. I had fought hard that it did not do that to me. But that war was very different from this. These were no cannon-fodder soldiers, these determined young knights in the air. Nor below was there the duped civilian hysteria of the past. There was strength and courage and awareness of a truth that was acknowledged only in mockery. There was wit and humour and spirit. This was war on my own land, against my own people, before my own eyes, and I fell hopelessly into its thrall. Our enemy was obvious, his evil undisputed. There was no time for thought and no room for questioning, and I was swept up in pride and in patriotism like everyone else. One day in Kent I saw a Messerschmitt fighter come spiralling down in beautiful flames and smoke and I stood with my daughter and cheered as a young man burned to death. There is in the centre of us all a violent innocence as pure and heartless as that of a child, and when we release it to play in the sun, civilization dies.

Those are the moral dangers of wartime, but they are not the ones that, in wartime, one hears anything about. It was not that loss of integrity that mothers worried over, when their daughters went out with the boys in khaki and airforce blue. But I was more sorry for that spiritual loss than for the more ordinary loss that followed.

Ellie Pyke was nineteen years old when we came to London at the beginning of the war. She was hardly a child, at least not in the terms of the sophisticated thirties and forties. And yet in many ways she was no more aware than I was myself at that age, before that other war. Artistic talent and intelligence advance the spirit, but often retard the physical body. It is the dullards, both male and female, who ripen to ready awareness and find their physical satisfactions early, perhaps because life has little more to offer them. Sometimes I have envied the very simplicity with which they approach such things, remembering the hotly embarrassing nights in East End shelters when youngsters disported themselves in full view of the public eye. I was never like that; nor was Ellie. She was shy and flighty as a pretty young animal with any male creature other than Jack. And having lost Jack, she had no concourse with any man at all. And yet, they sought her avidly.

It is hard to say why. She was certainly no beauty, any more than I ever was; indeed she looked a good deal like me. But she had my mother's wonderful colouring; the glossy black hair and those chador eyes, deep as velvet, and the look in them of something about to take flight. I think it was that very skittishness that excited the men, that look of perpetual wild surprise. Perhaps they thought her capacity for excitement, beginning there, would have no end. Whatever the reason, they courted her. Usually they were airmen; friends Hugo brought home from his daytime war, on quick stand-down leaves to London. They were all lovely, all impossibly handsome it seemed in those days, with their pilots' wings and the shadow of death on their shoulders. What girl could fail to fall for them?

She lost her virginity to a Lancashire lad, a miner's son who talked like Meggie Whyte. I think it was his utter innocence, quite equivalent to her own, that slipped past the barrier of her fear. He was awkward and clumsy in all things but flight, and had downed eleven enemy planes before he died in the wreckage of his own, in September of 1940. It sounds a great lovers' tragedy, as in its way it was. But that was so common then, and they were little more than strangers from beginning to end. And there were others, at once, to take his place.

Then Ellie began a lonely voyage. I do not blame the lads; there are few things sadder than the need of a man to cast his seed before he dies. More so when the man is a boy and the death is so frighteningly near. If they were greedy it was the just greed of all created things, hungry for a snatch of immortality. They asked, and she said yes. They were no more seducers than she.

Of course I worried. I had no Margaret Sanger tracts, no wise sophisticated advice. But I took her aside and taught her what Jack had taught me and hoped she would listen and not fall pregnant. But her eyes roved, resentfully embarrassed, as I spoke, and her whole young form quivered with the need to get away. There was nothing more I could do. Released, she fled from me, as she fled more and more, every day.

It was strange, because in our work we were often inseparable. Sometimes she had projects of her own. She did posters for government ministries, bright idyllic scenes proclaiming the glory of potatoes, the wonder of salvage, the joys of digging for victory. She had a real flair for propaganda, and one of her efforts for the Land Army could have had even me trundling manure for the Greater Good. She did many of those and, for a while, painted sets for ENSA. But mostly, she worked at my side. I could turn a painting over to her, and she would complete it without straying a brush stroke from the lines I would have chosen, nor a shade from the colour. We had fun creating faces, half hers, half mine, quite perfectly balanced. She was to me as the studio apprentice to the Renaissance master, a shadow so perfect that no one today could distinguish her work from mine. How could our minds, our hands, our souls be bound so tight, and our hearts stray so far apart?

I thought for a while it was deliberate. She flaunted her affairs before me, like a naughty child, dressing herself up vampishly, drawing seam-lines down her stockingless legs like a shopgirl, making up too heavily, with clever concoctions from her chalk box, driven by wartime scarcity to the same ruses as my sister Clare a sterner generation ago. Once, as I made some small protest, she laughed richly, dropping her precious hoarded lipstick into her bag. 'Oh Justina, you're so old-fashioned. Imagine, even you.' Which may or may not have been true, but was not relevant at all. After she left, I turned wearily to face Khadija Abbas.

'Why does she hate me so?' I said. The words just came out.

'She doesn't hate,' Khadija said. 'She is angry.'

'But what have I *done*?' I cried desperately.

'Not you,' Khadija said softly. 'She's not angry with you.' I shook my head, bewildered. She said, 'Who does she look for in all those beds? Who will she never find?' I looked up sharply. Her eyes were her father's, wiser than time. *How do you know these things, little girl?* I thought. After that, I let Ellie go her own way.

As such things usually go, the flame of her anger burnt lower, her flightiness eased, and in a few months she settled with one steady lover, her choice over all the rest. He was an odd favourite, a young American adventurer called Ralph Cooper. He had trained with the RAF in Canada, and come on his own to fight a war his country yet resisted. I admired the spirit, and I admired the man, but I did not like him. He was a big West Virginian, with little of culture or grace about him. He adapted well to any company, and fitted easily with Hugo's often elevated friends, but only because their youthful snobberies had no more effect upon him than they would upon a stone. He was that rare thing, a truly confident American. He liked us, but cared not the slightest if we liked him back. He treated Ellie with southern grace, but I sensed beneath it a backwoodsman's unbudging misogyny. He looked upon her painting as a girlish plaything, as the Pykes had looked upon mine.

But he took her out, and kept her happy, and stayed alive and did not desert her, which was more than many men in her life had done. I could not argue, though I watched in prickly resentful fear. I tried to like him. I tried to remember he was some woman's son, as dear to her as Wendell had been to me. But it did not help. He was not worthy of my strange, wonderful daughter; a mother's boast, no doubt, but I was certain it was true.

Still, by the winter of 1943, they were together yet. She seemed happy, and if she had sorrows about the past, she seemed to have forgotten them. I had not heard her speak of Jack for months. He, and May, and our life in France were as far from her as childhood. Which was why it was so strange that she awoke one night in November, in the cramped confines of the Morrison shelter in which we slept, crying his name. Her eyes for several seconds did not focus on my face. When they did, she sobbed and turned away, curling up like a little girl, her face hidden in the dark. She had had a dream. As much as it terrified her, she would not tell me what it was.

In the morning she was quiet and calm, but she would not speak. The whole experience shook me; dark shadows arose, shadows of swan wings I thought forever gone. *I'm too old for this*, I told myself all day, as if the dream had come not to Ellie, but to me. Strange though, as wary and superstitious as I was, I was not convinced. And on that day that Clare came, it had all passed innocently from my mind.

There was a great deal else, most of it quite ridiculous, to take its place. Dissension gripped Bryanston Square. Wilhemina, mine hostess, never the easiest of women, had grown positively truculent with the passage of time, and the corresponding continuance of the war. I think she had made some private contract, that she would allow the Chancellor a year, or possibly two, to indulge his histrionics, and then the whole thing must come to an immediate end. (Quite a few people felt much the same.) Now, however, it had all been going on for four. We were all fed up; things were not looking particularly good; and Wilhemina was more fed up than most. She wanted the lights on, the sirens off, decent food in the shops, decent clothes on her back, and a London rid of all the clamour, indecency and bomb craters. Most of all she wanted an instantaneous return to a social order that any one of us could have told her was dead.

'It's all so *rowdy*,' she proclaimed petulantly that morning at breakfast. '*London's* so rowdy. Not to be a snob but one gets fed up with all those odd faces, and odd uniforms and odd names, and everyone's terrible accents. I want one decent evening with people who know how to behave.' As usual in such outbursts, I said nothing. I did not agree, but beggars cannot be choosy. I had lived as Wilhemina's guest a little too long. Small frictions, symbolic of large spiritual divides, had begun to irritate us both beyond reason.

The previous night, I had returned very late from a

munitions factory in the Midlands. It was a long, tedious rail journey on a packed train. I stood up the entire way, with my easel and paintbox jammed between kitbags and sleeping soldiers, and it was all made worse by the claustrophobia of blacked-out windows and a crawling pace through an air raid, under a bomber's moon. I arrived home exhausted and found the house in civil war.

Ellie and her friends stood accused of misappropriation of an ounce of Wilhemina's cheese ration. Ellie was furiously indignant; Wilhemina was unforgiving, and Khadija was negotiating a truce. I had to pacify each in turn without arousing the wrath of the other. To such nonsense were we driven by the petty deprivation of our lives.

I went to bed with the vague determination that I must find somewhere else to stay; though where in the dwindling housing stock of London, I couldn't imagine. After breakfast, my determination was strengthened: I found Wilhemina preparing a bundle of scrap paper for the WVS salvage; in the midst of it my lifelong collection of personal letters, a treasure so precious that I had carried it with me even in our flight over the Pyrenees.

'For heaven's sake, woman,' I shouted, 'that's *history*.'

'Small use that will be if the Germans get here. They write their *own* history.'

'Not on my bloody letters,' I cried.

'One envelope makes fifty cartridge shells,' Wilhemina said primly, as I snatched them back. I ran with them upstairs and burrowed deep in a drawer and hid them among my knickers. I found a black lacy pair that Jack had bought for me in a lascivious moment and spread them over the top. Wilhemina was just prissy enough not to look beneath.

I calmed down then, and decided to forgive her. It was

all symptoms, anyhow. Hugo had had a scrape the week before. His Spitfire had been shot up and he had to jump, burning his hands and face as he did. They picked him up in a field near Dover, quite cheery, if a bit scorched, disentangling his parachute from a hedgerow. He was fine. But when he got back to base he had a sort of breakdown, and now he was in hospital under observation. I think he was simply exhausted. It was neither unusual, nor likely very serious, and perhaps a lucky thing in that it might relieve him of combat for a while. But it brought the shadow of death too close for Wilhemina's comfort and she was taking it out on us.

I followed her out into the garden, and took up a hoe and began working silently beside her. We had four rows of Brussels sprouts, two of winter cabbage, one each of kale, turnips and leeks, all growing where once had been a terrace with clematis and laburnum and ivy, and a white wrought iron table and chairs. Those, rusted and weary, were stacked in a corner, and each spare hour we hacked away at the indignant city ground, petulantly demanding fertility. Wilhemina smiled once, sheepishly, and I smiled back. She straightened up, and thrust her hands into the pockets of her jacket. It was a good tweed jacket, worn now to threadbare cuffs. Under the jacket she wore a lambswool jumper and pearls.

'I have a question,' she said suddenly. She looked uncomfortable. 'Jolly awkward actually.' I waited, and she worked her mouth in hesitation and then burst out, 'You do know Hugo and Khadija are considering marriage.'

'I *had* rather imagined . . .' I said vaguely.

'Yes. Quite.' She paused again, and tucked a loose hair under her headscarf. 'Well, it's all very well and good,' she stopped again and then faced me with candid eyes, 'I say, Justina, these Persians, what are they exactly?'

'What do you mean?' I asked.

'I mean, are they Arabs or what? Look, old girl, not wanting to put too fine a point on it . . .'

'Don't you like her?' I asked carefully.

'Oh, my word. I like her immensely. She's an absolute gem. But that's not the issue. I mean, there's the family to remember. I've always felt rather responsible . . . the Melrose name, Arradale. I mean we *are* the heirs.'

'I remember,' I said. 'Wilhemina, what's this about?' She looked exasperated.

'You know. Are they *black*, for heaven's sake.'

I was silent for a few moments. Then I said, 'Does she *look* black?'

'Oh, of course she doesn't *look* black. I mean, that would be simple. But what's back in the old pedigree . . . Justina, is Arradale going to fill chock up with piccaninnies?'

'Wilhemina.'

'Yes?'

'Aryan.'

'What?' she bridled.

'They're Aryan. That's where the word comes from. Persia, Iran. They're as snowy white as you, me and Adolf.'

'Justina, don't be miffy. I'm doing my duty, nothing else.' She thrust her fork into the ground and stalked off inside, slamming the garden door behind her. I worked on, laughing to myself, and was still giggling when I heard a voice call my name. It sounded so low and gentle that I did not recognize it as Clare's.

She came slowly into the garden, a tall stern woman in grey, carrying a thin envelope clutched in both hands across her chest. My mind leapt to Wilhemina and her salvage.

'Hello, darling,' I said, amazed. 'Whatever brings you here?'

'A few matters,' she said carefully. 'Can we talk? I should like it to be private.' Her voice was smooth and even.

'I should think so,' I said lightly. 'Wilhemina's off in a huff. I don't expect she'll come back soon.'

'No,' Clare said. 'I spoke to Wilhemina, actually. She's going out. Where's Ellie?'

I looked at Clare thoughtfully, wondering what this was about. I was not even nervous yet. I did not connect her strangeness with myself. 'Ellie's upstairs,' I said, nodding vaguely to the third floor window. 'Painting.'

'I wouldn't want her to come down.'

'I don't think she will; she never leaves work for anything. Clare, what is this? Is Kate in trouble again?' Kate had only just been released, a few weeks before.

'No, dear. Nothing in Ireland this time.' I think then I realized. My body realized. My hands felt cold and my legs began to tremble. 'Shall we sit here?' said Clare. She had moved to the small stone bench at the edge of our Victory Garden, all that remained of its elegant past. I nodded numbly, and sat down. She sat beside me, holding the envelope. We both leaned against the brick garden wall. It was cold and damp, like the wall of the sea-garden at Arradale, and I imagined I could close my eyes and hear the sea, with Clare beside me.

'Tell me,' I said.

'I have to explain something, Justina. What I am going to tell you, I am not meant to know. So I can't be telling you, do you understand? My information is illicitly held. It is also absolutely accurate. So do not hope otherwise.'

Her words were utterly final. I nodded. The far wall of the garden blurred.

'Tell me,' I said again.

'May Howie and Jack Redpath and Jean-Michel Bujold were arrested by the Gestapo three weeks ago in Paris. They were printing an underground newspaper at The Fishing Cat. Among other things. It doesn't matter. That was enough.'

'Oh God,' I said.

'May has been sent somewhere. We don't yet know where. We are trying to find out.'

I said quietly, 'Jack?'

She took my hand, looking straight ahead. 'Jack and Jean-Michel were both shot.'

I sat rigid, my eyes dry. 'No,' I said. 'No.' I gripped her hand. She was ominously quiet.

Then she said carefully, 'Justina, be glad he's dead.'

'What?' I said. '*What?*'

'Just be glad. Don't ask me any more.'

So. Murder had not been enough for them. It never was for those people. I thought of that body I had loved so intimately, how frail and vulnerable before such violence. I wept quietly into my hands. She sat beside me, her awkward bony arms around my shoulders.

'He told them nothing,' she said.

I looked up angrily. 'Oh, what do I care about that?'

'You should,' she said. 'He did.'

I studied her carefully. I felt very calm. 'How do you know all this.'

Clare looked away. 'I told you, I'm not meant to know.'

'Yes. But how do you?' I guess she realized I was no threat to anyone.

'There's a group,' she said. 'Chaps I've met, and some girls. They work in this sort of thing. I've helped out once or twice; a bit of background; history. Translations. They need boffins from time to time. I'm sorry, I can't say much.' She shrugged awkwardly. She had hardly said anything. She was talking about SOE. I only realized after the war, when we learned about such things. Of course, we never heard about them then.

I said carefully, 'How did they know Jack?'

'Through me.' My eyes met hers. I felt growing in me a great hatred.

'You led him into this,' I said.

'No.' She was calm and unrelenting. 'He had his own organization, a year before we made contact, quite independent. I thought he would be useful, and I was right.' She looked down on me sadly. 'He was in London last summer, dear. He would have given the world to see you, but we thought it unwise.' I stared, disbelieving. She held out the envelope she had brought with her. 'He gave me this to keep for you before we dropped him back into France. I think he thought I was reliable.' She handed me the envelope.

'What is it?' I said numbly.

'I don't know, dear. Open it.' When I didn't move, she said, 'Look, darling. It's his will.' I thrust it away.

'I don't want to see this now,' I said. She forced it back into my hands.

'Running from things is not going to help.'

'Oh, you,' I cried, 'you and your damned nanny's tongue.'

She sat back, waiting, and I slowly loosed the seal on the envelope, and drew out two sheets of paper; little enough to sum up a man's life. The first was a simple document, plain-spoken and quite thoroughly legal. It listed all his published works; the poems, the novels, the short stories, the essays, everything, a surprisingly long and respectable sequence. It was properly witnessed, sealed and signed in his familiar disorderly scrawl. He had willed me the copyright to every word he wrote.

The second sheet was a personal letter to me.

My beloved Justina,

God knows if any of this will ever be worth anything, but just in case, I don't want it all going to some goddam turkey farmer in Ohio who happens to carry my name . . .

Do not mourn my love, my life,
Companion of my faithless heart.
No widow now, since never then my wife;
What God has never joined, God cannot part.
Death sunders others; you and I
In spirit wed, cannot in spirit die.
So live for me my forfeit years,
Your love my warmth, your eyes my light,
Your voice my song; That voice endears
The very dust, and ransoms sight,
And soul in silence hears.
Endure this brief deception in the clay,
As you endured each frailty once above,
Who turned with laughter Heaven's wrath away,
And honoured my dishonourable love.

yours for eternity,
Jack

Just before Christmas, I returned to Arradale. I came alone. Ellie did not wish to join me. She said she would come later for her cousin Hugo's wedding to Khadija Abbas. I hoped she meant it. Hugo was stationed now at Wick, in what, in the old war, we would have called 'a quiet sector'. The happy concurrence of his new posting and the fruition of his marriage plans brought Justin Quigley's ungainly mansion its first wedding. Of all Arradale's children, only Douglas and myself had married, and both in London. It was a celebration long overdue.

I had come to assess the state of our neglected home for Wilhemina, and lay groundwork for the wedding. It was all pretence. Wilhemina's capacity for organization was matched only by that of the Yanks. She could orchestrate a wedding with one hand, and run the Italian campaign with the other. But I needed to get away.

So did Ellie, but she would not acknowledge it. She would not acknowledge anything; my grief, nor hers, nor the loss that caused both. When she spoke of Jack's death, which she did rarely, it was as of a death she had read in the newspapers, of a stranger known only by the abstraction of fame. It did not help that, outside of family, because of the nature of our information, we could not share our knowledge at all.

On the day that I learned in that bleak city garden, I waited until Clare had left me, before I told Ellie. I went upstairs to the third floor maids' room we used for a studio, and found her, as I knew I would, enraptured as a child in her work. She looked so young, paint-smudged, chewing on one black wisp of curl, rubbing her nose as she concentrated, smearing paint there. No wonder that brave, shallow man who courted her regarded her a little girl. He had not the eyes to see the woman within.

I did not speak until she had revealed her awareness of me in that sudden start she always gave, as she came out of the reverie of work. 'Oh, it's you,' she said. 'Don't *lurk* like that. You scare me.' She was smiling, though; pleased with the painting before her. I remember it still; a country scene of a railway station, its signposts painted out, made eerie by a row of pale wary faces, London evacuees, awaiting selection. The title was 'Last Chosen'.

'I have something to tell you,' I said. 'Something very sad.' She was hardly listening, her eyes straying to her canvas, and her fingers tapping lightly upon her brush.

And so I told her what Clare had told me. Her face made no change, all the time I was speaking. When I was done, though I was crying, her eyes were calm and dry.

She laid down her brush on her paint table, beside her easel, and said, 'I knew we'd never see him again. I knew it that day in the mountains. That's why I cried then.' There was nothing in the words, or in the tone, that evoked the accusation I knew was there.

'Ellie,' I said, holding my arms out to her.

'I have to go out.'

She turned to me, untied her smock and slipped it off, hanging it casually over a chair, as if she would return at any moment. From numbed, ancient habit I said, 'Clean your brushes.'

'It doesn't matter.' She looked quietly at the canvas, and then turned and went out of the room. I wanted to follow her, but I did not. After a few minutes, I picked up her brushes and began to clean them myself, soothed as always by that patient work. I put them carefully in a glass jar on her table, and tidied the tubes of pigment, the bottle of linseed oil, her charcoals, and her rags. Then I folded her smock and put it away.

A fortnight later, when I left for Scotland, it lay atop the dresser still, precisely where I had placed it. The brushes and paints, the unfinished canvas, remained the same. She had touched none of them since that day she so lightly laid them aside.

As I journeyed northward on that crowded, unheated, shabby train, I comforted myself with the memory of my own defection, after Michael Howie's death, and how time and circumstance had changed all that, and would do the same for her. There was for me no equivalent abandonment; I worked at my easel that same day, and nothing in the finished work would tell that half of it was painted when my love was alive, and half when he was dead. I was far too wise now to relinquish to the enemy my greatest comforter.

I had not been to Arradale for twenty-five years; not since my honeymoon. It is hard to justify that lapse; distance was scarcely sufficient explanation. But I had been rarely in Britain, and then, on fleeting occasions. And Arradale had never been my home since Father died. It was not just the changes wrought by Wilhemina's taste, but the conscious awareness of its passage into other hands and hearts than mine. It was for me nothing but a repository of memories, and as such, was not enhanced by return visits. The longer I stayed away, the further back its image crept, into its earliest days, the Arradale I remembered from the nursery, perfect in every colour and line. Furnishings that had long vanished by my adult years reappeared in those memories; the garden took on the shape it held as the century turned, the rooms took back their old occupants. Jeremy carried me upon his shoulders. Douglas and Geoffrey and Alexander tore about the place like half-grown pups, and Clare stormed and bossed, incongruously pretty in pink ruffles and frills, and followed by the baby feet of William. And I padded about in my silent way, watching, with the wide, startled eyes bequeathed to my daughter, the affairs of my mysterious elders; Father seeking my beautiful reluctant mother, and she rushing for secret comfort to the arms of Persephone.

That was hardly the place I found that Christmas of 1943. Sheep grazed in wire-fenced enclosures right up to the door, and kale and old potato stalks filled the flowerbeds. The family cars slept like princesses in the silence of the garages. I was transported from Achnasheen by an ageing taxi. Behind the house washing lines flapped in a wet sea wind with the ill-assorted garments of the dozen evacuees. Two strange boys on bicycles shouted as I arrived in the incomprehensible accents of Glasgow.

The staff greeted me with silent recrimination. I was the first member of the family to show up for months; Wilhemina's visits home were restricted, as all travel was, by the stringencies of war. Gardeners, housekeeper, cook and remaining maids descended upon me with tales of the horrors of our Glasgow refugees, and the heartless unconcern of their two professional keepers. The news that a family wedding was about to be added to their burdens was not greeted with delight.

I was sympathetic, but not deeply moved by their plight. Arradale, with its green winter fields and bare silent hills seemed a fine and restful place after London. I didn't imagine they were having too terrible a war. Besides, I liked the evacuees. They were bold and friendly and their youth and carelessness was a joy. I wanted to see someone laugh, and play, and ruthlessly forget their elders' grim world. I wanted to do the same myself.

I wandered about the house all the first day, looking into rooms, exploring hallways, rediscovering books in the library, paintings on the walls. I found my old tower studio, later Hugo's nursery, now an empty storeroom. In one corner of a deep highland chest, in which once I kept canvases, there remained, unbelievably, a single black feather of my lost hoody crow. I went up into the loft, and poked among boxes there. I found the wooden tea-chest that held the Christmas treasures, the green and blue and violet hand-painted glass spheres and the star for the top of the tree. I remembered telling Jack about it, that Christmas in Gay Street. I sat for a while on the edge of a kist, lifting them out into the dusty air, seeing them glisten in the bar of sunlight that shot through a chink in the Ballachulish slate, high above my head. *Oh darling*, I thought. *What would you think of this!*

When I came down, I found Donald Angus, Wilhemina's handyman, and asked him to bring the chest down to the shrouded drawing room. Then I went out to persuade the sour old gardener to go up to the hill for a tree. By evening, our dozen evacuees were dashing about the newly opened room, shouting with glee and fumbling those precious Victorian baubles in their rough Gorbals hands. One small, pinched lad who almost never spoke stood all the while by the chest, watching and never touching. When I lifted one ornament and offered it to him he shook his head fiercely. I tried to place it in his hands. But he crumbled them into fists, and muttered, 'Get away. I'll no' do it,' as he began to cry. The tree was very beautiful when it was done.

I was fifty years old on Christmas Day. Someone had found it was my birthday, and the children presented me with a gift at breakfast. It was a wonderful gift, a box in which each had placed some personal treasure, the small wealths of wartime; a single boiled sweet, a pair of woollen socks, a piece of jagged metal from a downed aircraft, a scrap of murky cloth, 'from a dead German pilot; there's *real blood* on it, Miss.' Wealth beyond the dreams . . . I said thank you very much. In the afternoon, the staff and the children's keepers, two stern ladies from Perth, had a Christmas party around the tree. It was a still, grey winter afternoon, turning already to early highland night. I left early, content I would not be missed.

The sea garden had been abandoned for the duration. It was too long and narrow, its beds too intricate, too hemmed in by hedges and trees to serve the roughcast purposes of wartime. Rather than struggle in its elegant confines, the gardeners had let it go to ruin, coming in only to prune the fruit trees and harvest their bounty of apples, plums and pears. Grass filled the borders, and the dried lacy stems of cow parsley clustered about the trees, collapsing in delicate cascades. Along the landward wall, banks of dried willowherb blew gently in the sea wind, trailing soft wisps of seedpods among the dry thistleheads. Nettles, some blackened with frost, others yet greenly growing, swayed in every corner, and thrust up amidst the uncut Elizabethan box. I stood for a long while looking through the rusted wrought iron of the gate, and then I pulled it open on its dragging hinges and went within.

It was so still within the garden, sheltered from the winds off Loch Ewe, warmed by every touch of captured sun. I thought what it would be like to live there, and walked up and down a while, thinking about it, and promising myself that I would look at the sea-cottages where Clare had hoped to retire. There were three. I could come there too. It was all dreaming. There was nowhere I wanted to live, nowhere in this world. All that I loved was free of the earth forever, and I wanted no other home.

When I came to the sea gate, I stood up against it, surprised to find that instead of stretching, I must bend down to look through the tear-shaped slit in the wood. The paint had peeled from the door, and there were two larger splits between rotting planks, but I chose my own. I peered through at the grey sea, and reached to turn the heavy knob and let myself out to the strand. But the door was locked, and the lock rusted shut. I gave up, and sat down on the moss-grown bricks by the foot of the door. I leaned my head against it and drew up my knees, and when I put my hand out to steady myself, it came away stung with the nettles that overgrew the path. I rubbed it, and found a dock leaf growing beside the nettle as it should, and rubbed its cold juices against the sting. I looked up then, to the nettles swaying over me. They were very beautiful, with their soft grey seed heads. They are good to eat, and they say if you take a firm hold they will not sting. But they always, always do. I reached with my two hands and took a great cluster of the soft, webby leaves between my palms. I held them there, my head resting against the sea-gate. Beyond, the hidden sea that ran all the way to Ireland sang in perfect aloneness its utterly innocent song.

Epilogue

Isfahan
17 March 1983

Ezra,

Well, my dear, there you are, and there's certainly enough of it. I trust you received the pages I left with your mother at Arradale in February. Add these, and you have it all. I chose to end that week before your parents' wedding because the rest, all family history, must surely be common knowledge to us both. Anyhow, that was the end of my life with Jack. We had twenty-five years that were never our own, a sleight of hand in the face of God. If we were found out in the end, we could hardly complain . . . He was fifty-three when he died. With him died all the potential of that pure, vivid voice. A terrible waste. The genius of creation is too fine a thing to entrust to frail humanity . . .

I'm sorry about all that rubbish in the beginning about my childhood, but I seemed unable to tell Jack's story without telling my own. (*He* could have done it, no doubt.) Still, it was worth writing down, if only for the sake of our family. It *is* our history, and apart from me, there's no one left who knows half of it any more. As you get older, history, and family, both matter more and more. (Here am I, lecturing you, an historian!) But you'll find out . . . you can't imagine how much I regret *not* learning, as a young person, from those around me who were old . . . whyever did I not ask Mother or even Eugenia something of their life in New York with Justin Quigley? But I didn't . . . lest you suffer the same regrets, here is the collected wisdom of my ninety years in all its verbose majesty. (Jack would have been *scathing*. He *hated* verbosity.)

You do know I have often been asked to write about Jack before, over the years, and I always resisted. I knew I'd feel him looking over my shoulder, thoroughly critical. And he didn't mince words when he criticized. Dear Jack. He's never precisely left me, you know. After all these years, I still dream about him, just as he was, but not in the past at all, but in my present world. He never seems surprised to find me an old lady. And after *all* these years, I must confess I still expect him to walk back into my life . . . I always have . . . you know, some error, a confusion, amnesia or some other cheap novelist's trick . . . I don't fully understand this delusion. There were certainly no doubts. Clare's information, like everything Clare ever said and did, was accurate and to the point. After the war, when that very nice pin-striped gentleman from SOE came and gave me what details they had, it was all substantially the same. And if that wasn't enough, this business in February with Klaus Barbie has come along, and the very real possibility of learning *all* the truth. People have asked me how I feel about it, I mean, do I feel satisfaction or vengeance, or whatever, and the truth is I feel only a desire not to know – I have lived for so many years with his imagined deaths, his imagined murderers. I have come to terms with them all. What I cannot bear to know is the one actual death he died. Perhaps I fear that, knowing that, I would cease to feel, as I have felt for forty years, his continued life. Am I talking rubbish, dear? My friends tell me I have begun to go *on*, when I get on to spiritual matters and I suspect I'm becoming a frightful old bore.

The trouble is I *repeat* myself so. At least on paper I can scratch it out, but that hardly does for when one's speaking. In New York, in January Ellie took me aside very firmly and said I was not to tell stories at all, because I either ruin the endings by giving them away early, or forget them entirely and leave a whole roomful of people hanging in embarrassment. And they won't just tell me to shut up, because they're all in a sort of ridiculous awe, partly of my 'achievements' – that 'Dame' in front of my name works wonders over there – partly of my sheer wondrous decrepitude. Ninety is old enough in the Old World over there amidst the seekers of the Fountain, I'm practically Methuselah. Still Ellie does *fuss* a bit. Details, details. People who've abandoned dreams are great custodians of mundanity. The perfect flowers, the perfect wallpaper. Two days scouring Fifth Avenue for just the right tablecloth. Oh Ellie, my lost lamb.

Which reminds me, dear. I saw your cousin Hannah briefly –

she's in a nice little off-Broadway production of Synge's 'Playboy' that we all enjoyed immensely – and she asked most kindly after you. So she *does* care for you. You must believe me. Even if she never says as much to you. You must understand Hannah. It is not *you* she dislikes, nor is it men. She has lovers, if not a husband, and her lovers are entirely male. It is her situation. *Our* situation. Women do have a frightfully rocky road, everywhere, but particularly in the arts. It makes some of us a little testy. Still, at least she's *using* her abilities, unlike Ellie. Though I can't entirely blame Ellie, or even that fool Cooper, Hannah's father. Things were hard for Ellie at that time, and it was largely my fault. You see, I did not think of her. I knew *I* would be all right without Jack. But I did not think of Ellie. For her sake, I should have spoken, though to be honest, I doubt that would have changed much. Still, it had a powerful effect on Ellie. When death threatens, art is a too rarefied companion. We seek the earth. She never would have married then, were it not for losing Jack. Many marriages are made in wartime for such reasons. Of course, she doesn't trace it to that – she just blames Cooper, and I'm sure he was as stultifying as my own husband, who would likely have smothered all the creativity in me, were it not for Millie Dobbs. But still, she was only married to him for two years, and was *many* years more on her own, before she married Sam Howard, and he's an absolute poppet. And willingly Ellie's champion . . . but now she has endless excuses – it's too late to go back, she's too busy (well *of course* if one spends two days matching a tablecloth to one's curtains), her eyes are not good (as if *mine* were), she has *forgotten* how – well, that may be true; so many, many years; but does one ever forget how to paint? It's like forgetting to breathe. No. The truth is she had no Captain Hartingdon to shame her into life. Hardly a fault of her own, any more than he was a virtue of mine.

Hannah asked if you were married yet, and was quite surprised when I said no. She says she thought you the handsomest thing at Clare's funeral. Leave it to Hannah to say something like that. *I* told her the woman worthy of you has not yet been born, but then, I'm prejudiced. Oh, but I *knew* the woman for you, and how you would have loved her, my sweet cousin May who died in Buchenwald. My pretty blonde angel with the mind of a Jesuit . . . how unkind of Time to abandon you to different generations. How you would have loved each other!

That does bring up another point . . . There is one question everyone wants to ask, but no one dares. So I will ask it for you. Jack and May worked together in France for three years after I left. Were they lovers before they died? The answer is, I hope so. I hope they had that comfort. If you doubt me, you know nothing about love.

I had a letter from your mother the other day, full of concern, and although I have answered it, I am doubtful of my ability to ease her mind. Perhaps, when you are back at Arradale, you will be able to help. I assure you, as I assured her, that I am in excellent health, under the irrefutable circumstance of being my exalted age. The tremor is a nuisance when I paint – I have taken to a wider brush stroke, and a generally more hasty style – if I work quickly I outwit the thing. Like the surgeon Jack and I knew in France who shook like a leaf until he actually had the scalpel in his hand. He was excellent, I understand, though not precisely reassuring! A doctor in New York insisted it was a remnant of the Spanish flu – that it was terribly common amongst my generation – he would not accept that I never *had* Spanish flu. Perhaps it was just being *alive* at that time. There was surely enough in that to make anyone tremble in old age. Aside from that, I am perfectly splendid.

The situation here, upon my return, though certainly not good, is not actually worse than when I left. The border war drags on, sapping the entire nation. But I had little difficulty at the airport – of course, I have lived here for a very long time and am something of an institution. It is unnerving now, leaving each time, and not being sure I will be allowed to return. Still, I go on, as we all do. There has been some unpleasantness – a very nasty incident involving some Europeans; a missionary and his wife, and a young student arrested and then paraded through the streets as arch-criminals. Much shouting and hysteria, and yet my friends here, Muslim as well as Baha'i, came to me to express their deep regrets, as if I myself had been the victim, or of their family. (I did not even know them; they were strangers to me.) Fortunately, no one was hurt and they were actually released after a few days. They have now, not surprisingly, left the country.

Worse, though, has occurred among the population itself. Friends in Isfahan, with whom indeed I had planned to keep the New Year feast, have suddenly been imprisoned. No word of a charge, or of their eventual fate. They have been taken to Teheran, I understand. This sort of thing is very grim, and is making the Baha'i community very edgy. They had associations with the Shah (but then, so did many), which does not help. The truth remains, however, that this is an old argument, come alive under a new guise. We saw this in Europe before the last war. Incidentally, I have no idea if the post is interfered with, or not; if so I daresay I am offending someone, but that will just have to be. Please don't convey the details to Khadija; she is a great worrier. She instructed me solemnly that I must give up the fast, that I am entirely *too* old, and thoroughly exempt. This I knew actually; Abdu'l Baha warns of severity in fasting undermining our mental powers, and mine being frayed at the edges at best, I *am* circumspect. But a *little* fast is good both for the stomach and the soul. I suppose, in theory, I am too old not only for the fast, but for the need to restrain bodily lusts, but actually, the first becomes easier, and as to the last . . . there are yet temptations in old age; anger, impatience, despair . . . more serious perhaps than the playfulness of youth. I'm a little sorry, dear, that you have no religion, neither your father's nor your mother's. It has great value, if only for the discipline, and can be a great comfort.

So do please assure your mother that I am not starving myself to death. I am not, yet, falling to rack and ruin, and as of the present writing am living more or less undisturbed by the tides of revolution sweeping by my door. Poor Khadija, the little mother of all the world.

Perhaps I should mention that I have had an emissary from the Authority. A rather charming man, quite young, American-educated. He took a degree in law at Columbia and was doing further study when the Shah fled. He returned at once. He is also an Islamic scholar of some note. We argued about the Sharia. He was engagingly open at times, faintly ominous at others. He left me with the impression that I must be careful, but I fear I am ignorant of precisely how. He bears the title, 'Proof of Islam', by virtue of his scholarship. I believe he is very young for this honour. It seemed equally appropriate somehow as a *nom de guerre*.

I hope now, with this final segment in hand, you will be able to go forward with your work. Of course I am always ready to answer any question you may raise, and I do urge you to follow the avenues of inquiry I have suggested. I am glad you will attempt to see Sister Jude, when you are in Ireland. Her reminiscences will undoubtedly have a different flavour from mine. I am still attempting to find those photographs. Everything is a ghastly mess, as always. As to your reluctance to query my private feelings over Jack, I do so appreciate your kindness, but please have no fear: I shall be neither upset, nor offended. You must understand that a good many years have passed. Jack Redpath died in France forty years ago. He is as far in my past as Michael Howie. Life is not tidy, like fiction. Our years do not round off together in a neat circle. I was left once more to live on, alone, and I have done so. I have done all my best work since Jack died. Everything I am really known for. It is interesting to remember that. Our lives do not end when love ends, unless we are very foolish souls.

Yours with much love,
Aunt Justina

Isfahan
28 June 1983

Dearest Ezra,

How lovely to hear from you again. I'm so pleased you've been able to make sense of my great scrawl – and you are too kind, and a terrible flatterer. I just see those Persian brigand eyes whenever I read your too-charming prose. Oh, *do* keep it up; such thrills are rare at my age. Still, I should think if you cut it by about half, you'll have the bones of a manuscript.

What good news that Rebecca is to be engaged. I still think of her as your baby sister; it quite amazes me to imagine her married. It amazed me even more when I came to figuring ages and realized she must be thirty. Oh dear, time does get on for us all. Well, with Matthew and Mark both parents twice over, and Rebecca in nuptial mood, my dear, it leaves none but you. Do an old woman a favour, and wait until I've departed. I shall be abominably jealous otherwise. Please give your good parents all the appropriate congratulations, re Rebecca. I am meaning to write, always, but my eyes are so bad, and I like to 'save' them for my work. (This is an exception; writing to you is therapy.)

I have still not quite absorbed your description of Sister Jude. (So glad you were able to see her after all.) 'Bony and spare as a tinker woman, with a laugh that lit up the room.' Yes, well. She would not have gone to fat, and I suppose even nuns grow old. Eithne at sixty-five . . . this one, once the image of Maud Gonne . . . you cannot imagine how *difficult* for me to comprehend. I have not seen her since 1938. I'm not actually sorry, you know. There are some things I have quite given up trying to forgive.

Her memories of Jack were intriguing. I would not have described him as 'rakish'. He wasn't rakish. He was a *little* flamboyant, when he was pleased with himself. But no more. And for heaven's sake, he wasn't tall! Where does she get this from? He was hardly taller than she was – do you know, I think her memory is going back to when she was a child. I think she's just forgotten those years in between. 'The dearest person in my life.' Well, perhaps. But she made his life a misery for a time. Is this what it's always like, Ezra, do you suppose? We become in someone's memory what they would like for us to have been? Is this our immortality? Still, I am so glad she was able to show you that photograph . . . imagine; four decades in holy vows and she keeps it yet! But then, he might have been her father. It was taken, if *my* memory doesn't fail me now, at Mont Louis, on our first visit, by an English visitor on his way to Font-Romeu; Jack and Eithne in a little orchard by the roadside. I do remember.

On the subject of photographs, I have looked out a few. They are surprisingly hard to find, I mean, those of any quality. We just didn't have many, only those like that Eithne showed you, taken by friends or even strangers. There are *some* about. I've seen photographs of Jack in other people's work about Paris – some I didn't know existed. There's one of a great group of people outside the Deux-Magots; McAlmon's in it, I believe, and I think Hemingway. And Jack's there, too, rather by accident. It doesn't really look like him. None of the photographs do. I suppose the best is that one on the jacket of *American Dreamers*, which you have. To tell the truth, and if you'll forgive my immodesty, I much prefer my sketch of him for *A Persian Garden*, you know, the frontispiece. Jack said I flattered him, but it's quite accurate. He was really very handsome, something the photographs never quite show. I have the original here, but I'm afraid I won't let it out of my hands. Still, I'll send this little collection and see if you can find what you need among them. Obviously you have my permission to reproduce the sketch if you'd like; I'm sure the publisher would happily comply.

I'm sorry you were unable to trace Ellen Merryweather's family; though I wonder, dear, if they really could have helped. They knew Jack as a seventeen-year-old farm boy who got Ellen into trouble . . . I doubt they remembered him kindly, if at all. It's a pity now that Millie Dobbs is no longer there, *she* might really have been able to help. She knew them as *children* that first year in New York. But of course she's years dead, now. Most of them are, you know, dear. And Heaven knows what my excuse is! I do understand your difficulties, though. I knew Jack for half of his life, but of the rest I can really tell you very little. He talked so little about it. There are enormous gaps in the story. It's in his books, of course, if you can unravel the truths in the fiction; not easy, I warn you.

It's funny, I'm always sending people back to his books when they want to know about Jack, but so few are willing to look there. He has a reputation quite *apart* from his work, and it is that they seem most drawn to. I must keep reminding them that if he hadn't *written* what he did, no one would care who he was, or how he died.

There is a received wisdom that holds Jack to be a sort of national hero of the Revolution (anybody's). He was a man for sufficient seasons to please all sides; a pacifist who took arms when the cause was right. Even the Left loves a repentant sinner. Then there's the corollary that demands that I take pride in his loss, that I dress in black and bear witness, a sort of Pasionaria of the literary set: I'm sorry, whatever the fashion, I would rather have had the company of that warm, lovely man than forty years' memory of a martyr.

Martyrdom is death turned to victory; but that was not Jack's victory. Jack was victorious those years in Paris, standing against the tide, a solitary man proclaiming the right to live a solitary life. That was the true anti-Fascist. When he gave in to the irresistible violence of our day, he was defeated. So were we all. Every peace we won was lost, every goal we sought cast over, all we believed in laid in the dust. But no one seems to notice. He is proclaimed a hero, anyhow.

Of course, all of it has had a most salutary effect upon his posthumous career. His own story has cast enough reflected light upon his works to give them more fame than they'd ever enjoyed before. I am pleased for that, but I've always resented the reason. I would like him to be read because he wrote well, not because he died heroically. Mind, Jack wouldn't have cared. I can just hear *his* assessment: 'Take the money, sweetheart, and run.' You see, it is very hard for me to see him in an heroic mould – I knew him far too well, and loved him too much. He was far more complex than that; a man of ordinary human courage, and like any imaginative person, with a great capacity for fear. He would not have overcome that easily. If Jack were to become a saint, it would be in the manner of Thomas More; fending off martyrdom to the last possible moment he could.

Still, in the end, he could not. Oh, Ezra, there are times it can all still reduce me to tears. You mustn't pay any attention; I'm finding things rather a trial at the moment. It's Ramadan, of course, and everyone one meets is tense and jumpy. *They* really fast, and all my Muslim friends are exhausted and drained, working all day with neither food nor drink. I don't know how they endure it. The atmosphere in the city is electric. There are fights, demonstrations, all a little unnerving. I suppose it gets to me too; I've been feeling quite depressed and that's not me at all. The truth is, I'm rather fed up with being old. I didn't used to mind so very much; it has all *sorts* of rewards and virtues; but just of late it's become a bore. A *physical* bore. I don't much see the use of occupying a body if it's going to downright refuse to do practically anything you ask of it.

Ah, but I must tell you about the Proof of Islam. He has taken to calling upon me quite regularly, in the course of his duty, as he sees it, or otherwise. I am not certain. Nor do I care. I find him most enchanting. He is such a delectable combination of East and West, this partisan of Ali who can name every rock group prominent in New York. And such charm. We take tea together (he compliments me highly on my tea, a great honour from a Persian) and talk, and I listen dutifully to the dangerous errors of my ways, and try fruitlessly to persuade him of Allah's delight in tolerance, and then, when he feels his duty done, he plies me with questions about London and New York, his face alight with nostalgia. At the end he chides me gently for my immodest dress (and you can imagine just what that might be, at *my age*) and I remind him that Allah being my Creator cannot be shocked at the time-worn reality of his creation. And as for lustful man (for whom such rules were surely devised) I am wrapped sufficiently in the chador of antiquity to suffice. He smiles and nods, and then shakes his head and takes his leave. I am bewitched by the dreamy eyes of revolution.

Do give my best love to all and sundry,
your devoted and decrepit,
Aunt Justina

PS. The portrait of Jack Redpath that I did in 1926 for Millie Dobbs has *probably* gone to her niece, Mrs Winifred MacLeod of Great Barrington, Massachusetts. I'm sorry but that's all the address I have.

Isfahan
17 October 1983

Ezra Darling

I simply must tell you the most extraordinary thing that happened yesterday, and then I'll answer your questions. It was late in the afternoon; I had spent a charming hour with the Proof of Islam discussing the role of martyrdom in Islam and Christianity, interspersed with some lesser ruminations on American television. He had only just left (and it is as well he *had* left), and I had gone back into the courtyard where I was working, when I heard a strange voice calling my name, in what sounded to be English, if only just. I turned and there, standing in the doorway, was a quite ludicrous pair; a tall blond young man, sun-browned as dark as an Iranian, and a short, dumpy young woman with cropped black hair and an enormous smile. 'Mrs Redpath?' he said, all apology and awkwardness. I said, as I usually do, 'Yes, more or less.' I've given up explaining; if the world wants me to have been married to the man, so be it. Apparently they had been knocking at the street door for a full ten minutes, but I never *hear* it any more, so they came right in.

'Terribly sorry, but we've come all the way from Brisbane . . .' Aussies, would you believe.

And they had, too, all the way from Brisbane, via India and Pakistan, and God knows where . . . the very last flowers of the hippy trail . . . can you imagine, in these times, in this place? I rather admired their spunk, or idiocy, if that's more the word . . . Aussies are rather like that, the ferocities of the world just bumble by and they go their happy way. I honestly doubt they were quite *aware* of what was going on in the country. I leave it to more knowledgeable minds than mine to fathom how they even got in. But in they got, and here they were, on a pilgrimage to a Persian garden . . . Do you know, back in the sixties I used to see one or two a week? All with a rucksack full of guidebooks and maps . . . 'Outer Mongolia on Three Roubles a Day' . . . and a wellworn copy of Jack Redpath's verse. They all wanted to see the place where he wrote the poems (I hadn't the heart to tell them it was Paris). The garden is gone, of course, under blocks of housing; the city has grown immensely since those days. I lied a little. I'd send them to the suburbs where similar places remain. Or I'd send them up on to the hills, if they looked fit enough, and *those* are certainly still there.

So we talked a little about Jack, my Aussies and I. They asked me about the meaning of some of the poems; I had to tell them I hadn't any better idea than they; Jack gave me no more clues than he gave anyone else . . . that would be cheating, after all, wouldn't it? They were thrilled to see my 'first edition', signed and all, and would have paid their worldly wealth (not likely very much) for it, had I wanted to sell it, which of course I did not. I couldn't help but laugh. Jack and I used to give them away to anyone; we had a few dozen once. It *was* remaindered after all.

They asked me to autograph their copy. They had the familiar Penguin edition the kids all buy. I had to persuade them not only to forgo my autograph, but to rid themselves of it at once. They could not believe it was a dangerous thing to be carrying, but these days, in this country, it is. Who would imagine anything so innocent would arouse such passions? But the oneness of all faiths is a blasphemy even in the eyes of my genial Proof of Islam . . . and blasphemy is no light charge. Finally, they agreed to leave it with me. (I'm thoroughly compromised already.) For the price of a Penguin paperback one doesn't risk one's life.

They asked me why I stay here, hoping no doubt for some mystic revelation . . . I told them what I've told you; an unholy alliance between my natural stubbornness and my appalling lazy inertia. The very *thought* of going elsewhere quite exhausts me. Besides, I like the climate, the light is excellent at times, and the people, well, the people are like people everywhere, generally charming and occasionally monstrous. Show me the country that is otherwise, and I will show you Paradise.

You are only partially right, you know, that I stay here because of Jack. It is not *just* a matter of living his 'forfeit years' where he might have chosen to live them. I understood what he meant and it was not quite so literal as that. Poets aren't. But I do like to remember him here, sunburnt and happy and intellectually questing – opium dreams and all. *There's* something I would never have told my Australians. But, oh, my dear, at worst a kinder death than that he died. I cannot forget that he left here against his will, and went back to all that was to come, for me.

Anyhow, I gave them tea, and sent them off, back to Australia, presumably, quite happy. They seemed almost an anachronism, like the book itself, as far out of fashion as peace . . . and yet it sells and sells . . . I was just notified of yet another imprint and the royalties still roll in. It has far outsold everything else he wrote. Not that the rest have done badly. You asked me if I have any idea what Jack's work has earned, and quite frankly, I haven't. (Check with my accountants. I'll write them first, if you'd like.) Let us just say (and with no slight intended to your good father's admirable efforts), that the house Justin Quigley built, Jack Redpath has kept in fine repair. Somewhere in Ohio, a turkey farmer curses me yet.

You see, that was Jack, too. He was not all impulse and romanticism as some people portray him. He was a good business man, and he had a finely developed sense of responsibility – he did not *mollycoddle* me, and the family have rather foolishly blamed him accordingly, particularly over that incident in the Pyrenees – but with that one, simple gesture of love and generosity he freed my career forever from the bonds of Mammon. And quite frankly, I was just about old enough to respond to that freedom without self-indulgence. Or at least, so I would like to think. Regardless, it was a supremely thoughtful act, and it took imagination. You must remember his career was virtually over when he died; he was back where he started, with precious little to show for it. That will was an act of faith.

You asked me if the changes in my work since Jack's death are a direct result of it; well, yes, they are, but only in that strictly practical sense. You see I have been *able* to change, to evolve naturally. This is very difficult for artists of any sort. If we are successful commercially we are often driven to continue along the lines of our success. (If we are *un*successful we have no chance to continue at all.) And that implies repetition, not growth. Jack foundered on that bar, along with others. And were it not for his *liberation* of my work, I would undoubtedly have continued on the tried, and not precisely true lines I was following. (Particularly regarding the portraits, which are the most *consumer-oriented* work an artist can do; after all, you don't have to please a flower or a tree, when you paint it.) People are terribly cautious in art because they don't really understand it, and they require the reassurance of the proven. This is stultifying to innovation, naturally enough. Still and all, I dispute that I have changed *that* much. Nor would I at all accept that I have moved into abstraction . . . these are not abstracts, they are just pared down a little. Look at Mr Yeats' quick sketches; look at the clothing in his paintings . . . is this abstraction? Of course not. It's just a dismissal of frippery. In my case, half the reason is this damnable tremor. I get *impatient*. As we get older impatience just overcomes us; abstraction is an expression of our restlessness. It's not at all an attempt to misrepresent the physical. It is an impatience with the physical, an impatience to get closer to the soul. One is searching for a single pure idea. Jack said the same of poetry; that was why he preferred it to any other form . . .

I am glad that you had a chance to see *Seabathers at Sandycove* at the National, when you were in Dublin. It is, frankly, a little gem. I look at it myself with some wonder. It is quite strangely mature; I hardly understand how I did that at such a young age. After, it seems to have taken me years to climb back up to the same height . . . strange. Now, if you get back there soon, I want you to go and look at Jack Yeats' *My Beautiful, My*

Beautiful. (It *is* there, isn't it, not in Sligo?) Then you will see something of what I mean about abstraction and the pure idea. A wonderful thing. Funny, how I remember him, that strange lovely man with his sailing boats on a garden pond in Howth . . .

I'm afraid I can't help much over your desire to see more of my early work for comparison. (There's nothing at all in that league.) I haven't a clue where much of it is. That's Kate's doing, of course. May had husbanded everything so carefully (ridiculously carefully; speaking of acts of faith!) for so many years, but Kate was the ultimate prodigal. Of course it was all hers, in the end, to do what she liked with. There was no one else left. She dismantled Merrion Square with almost as much thoroughness as she managed with Temple House, and there she had the help of the Republicans and a good deal of dynamite. I really think it was deliberate; getting back at her father, or all of us. She was quite twisted in the end. And every penny of profit turned right over to Sinn Fein. How strange for James Howie, the last of his fortune feeding the coffers of the IRA. Remarkably generous, our Kate; she ended up living on charity for her later years. (They *did* look after her well.) So my paintings too have contributed to the Cause, and they would have fetched good prices. Though not half as much as the Pursers and Orpens! Anyhow, there was no changing her. And whatever anyone tells you, have no doubts about that business in Belfast in '74; a carbon copy of Coventry, by the way. She was as guilty as Judas. The only reason there was no sentence was her *epic* age . . . she was eighty-eight! They didn't want to make themselves look like asses so they let her go. To die in her bed at eighty-nine, sustained by the rites of Holy Church, her repentance, if any, known only to God. *Requiescat In Pace*.

Forgive my sarcastic tongue, darling, it's a privilege of age.

On the subject of lost work (and causes), no, dear, I don't believe that there is the slightest chance that a copy of *That Sweet Homeland* might possibly yet exist. I know this is every literary scholar's favourite fantasy, to find a 'lost masterpiece' but I wouldn't waste your time searching. You could *try* to contact someone who might have known Marie Bujold. (I can't imagine she's yet alive herself; she'd actually be older than me. Is *anybody*?) But really, it would lead nowhere. She saved what things she could from May's flat; the paintings, some few papers, books; but everything in the printing house was either taken or destroyed. Just sheer wanton destruction. There were only a couple of copies of the manuscript in existence. May had them both. Jack had quite lost interest in it. He would do that, you see. He just went on to the next thing. *Writing* was his pleasure (if you can call it that). Afterwards, he never seemed to care. It's gone, dear. I have some notebooks that refer to it, but they are quite illegible and incomprehensible. He used a kind of personal shorthand; his notes don't make any sense. I do know you regard this loss a real tragedy and in a way I agree, but not entirely. It was such a *bitter* book, Ezra. I don't mean personally bitter. Jack wasn't bitter about what happened to his career; he just laughed about that. He was bitter about what was happening to the world. It was painful; it hurt me to read his disillusionment. I think it would hurt other readers, too. Let them remember him otherwise. I think fate was kind over this one. Fate is often kinder than we think.

Darling, I do want you to know that I have given careful thought to your very kind advice. Of course I do *know* it would be wise to leave. But we can't always do the wise thing; sometimes we must simply trust and do what appears the right thing, at least, as we see it. I have many friends here, you know, friends of many, many years. I am not alone, and by the same token, I am not without loyalties. We are all very careful, cautious even; the times demand it. I had hoped to keep the October feast with Ja'far Ibrahim and his family, but we have decided such a gathering would be unwise. If I had any doubts, the Proof of Islam personally advised me against it. I am bound to point out that he, too, has suggested that I go. I do not know if this advice was part of his 'brief' or a matter of more personal motivation. He has grown quite protective over me which is pleasurably sweet of him, but he is, like you, a young man, with a young man's easy solutions.

I told him I would give it thought. It is a useful tactic of age, this stalling. The young think time is on their side. They are wrong. It is thoroughly on the side of the old. Only a little longer and no explanations will be required.

Yours quite shamelessly smug,
Justina

Isfahan
11 November 1983

Dearest Ezra,

Thank you so very much for taking the time to write amidst all your concerns. I was deeply sorry to hear of your grandmother's death. She was *such* a character. Memories kept flooding back all day, right back to the earliest days at Arradale, when she had just taken the reins in her iron hands, and I could have throttled her. Oh, dear Wilhemina, what a trial and what a delight. She was an institution. Every family should have one at least. I still cherish your picture of her in the home in Strathpeffer, directing the entire establishment from her Bath-chair, witlessly and unrelentingly, supremely confident even in senility. When Wilhemina decided to go gaga, the world would have been well advised to follow! Oh well, I suppose it's a blessing. Or so they always say. But how do they *know*? So, I imagine she is preparing me a welcome in the next world. In which case, I think I shall go out and do something inspiringly sinful and get sent to the Other Place.

Dearest, I would absolutely *love* to see your first draft of the book, when it is prepared. (How quickly you work!) You are such a poppet to even suggest going to such trouble. But could you? How it would delight me.

I had two very long sessions with the Proof of Islam. On the first, I almost (but not quite) threw him out. I am so *frustrated* by his blindness. It is indisputable that we are all speaking of the same God. (Can there *seriously* be others?) So why this babel in which we all hear his message, that same singular God alone knows. I am quite fed up with it.

Anyhow, he came back the next day, as full of repentance as a Persian male can be. And full of charm. But we are getting into quite serious ground, and we both know it. Instinctively, we both draw back into our No Man's Land of Yankee nostalgia. We had a wonderful discussion about 'fast food' restaurants, a serious philosophical comparison of Wendy's and McDonald's and Taco Bell and Burger King. He adores them. He misses them terribly. They were some happy haven of his student years; bright and friendly, like the nursery. Mind, though, a long way from *his* childhood.

Then we got on to television, of which he is much more

knowledgeable than I. I can never watch it; it disturbs my eyes, that funny flat picture. I think you have to grow up with it for it to work. He gave me a mournful dissertation on the Scheherazade world of *Dallas*, that sad tale ever unwinding . . . he laments the unfortunate Sue Ellen as seriously as if she were his sister; he would reform her, and wrap her in chador if he could. Still he prefers Pam, 'Oh Pom,' he cries in that rich buttery voice and rolls his eyes heavenward as if he spoke of the Prophet's daughter . . .

Quite suddenly he ended the discussion. He grew serious, and placed before me a series of demands; questions, to which I must reply with suitable answers. He is asking me to recant. I told him I could not do it, and he became quite emotional. He laughed a little, and teased, and tried to convince me it was of no import, but he and I both know better. In the end he embraced me, and cried on my shoulder. After he left, I felt, for a while, quite unnerved.

He returned early yesterday in the company of several solemn young men, all handsome as the day is long, all rather devoid of humour. They are his students, I believe. Before them, he carried out an immense diatribe against my beliefs. I think it was not, as would appear, for their benefit, but for mine. When he sent them away, he said to me that I would have a day to change my mind. He was tender and persuasive, coming alarmingly close to a blasphemy himself, in an attempt to show me that embracing *his* version of God's wishes would not compromise my own. I almost agreed, but not quite.

He came back today and he has just left me. We parted amiably, with a display of devotion on his part that was quite genuine and quite touching. I have to inform you that I am going with him, tomorrow, to Teheran. This is not precisely an imprisonment. On the other hand, it is not precisely anything else. Please do not be concerned. I have been in prison before.

Your extremely pigheaded aunt,
Justina

Teheran
The Islamic Republic of Iran
28 November 1983

My dear Ezra,

I want to assure you that the situation is not at all as bad as you might expect. It is not, for a start, as bad as Holloway in

1914. I have no information on Holloway today. It is not, on the other hand, too terribly wonderful. I am comfortable enough, though obviously I would prefer to be elsewhere, but the presence in this place of young innocent women and little children is immensely disturbing. I said as much to the Proof of Islam when he called to see me and, to his credit, he did not argue. He is not in such a position of power as to be able to protest. At times I feel his position is worse than mine.

We are fed reasonably. (At my age one requires so little food, anyhow.) It is warm enough. The security is there, but if not lax, faintly casual. We are allowed out of doors into a courtyard, and over the walls, through a gap in the buildings, I can see the white tops of the Elburz. How they draw me; those mountains beyond my reach. I am allowed to read, and to write, and to sketch. The Proof of Islam brought me charcoals. He bought them himself; very good ones, too. He is also scrupulous about permitting me contact with my family, hence your letter reaching me, and mine presumably to reach you. I think this is an Islamic imperative. Family has high importance, and the care of widows, and orphans . . . I suppose I fit in there somewhere.

Ezra, love, I do immensely appreciate both your concern and that of your parents, but I must be very firm about this: I absolutely forbid you to come here. Your situation would likely prove far worse than mine, and there is absolutely nothing you can do. If the British government cannot achieve anything, it is thoroughly unlikely that you can. Have faith, darling, the whole thing is not settled yet, and the experience is fascinating. 'Once in a lifetime' if you'll forgive the dubious taste. As to your other question, *of course* I'm frightened, darling. Who in their right head wouldn't be?

My companions are immensely brave. It is one thing for me; I have had a good many years to come to terms with what I would have to face quite soon anyhow. But they are young, and the young feel immortal, and quite cheated, accordingly, by an untimely death. Today, as you know, is a solemn feast, and I was thrilled and shaken by their courage in chanting the prayers here . . . it could have led to anything, I suppose . . . but that did not deter them. God, or the compassion of their guards (some are indeed very compassionate, others not) protected them.

The Proof of Islam visits me every day. We have run out of words. We sit across a table and look into each other's eyes. His are as beautiful and passionate as those of my dear Michael. There are tears in them. He pleads with me to recant. I seek desperately to yield but I can find no way.

After he left, I wondered why I characterize him only by his title, and not his name (Hussein Ali). It is because it speaks so clearly of his conscious soul – the direction of his life, the path chosen. The American Indians, I am told, name children only casually until they achieve sufficient distinction to win a name of significance. I think this is what is lacking in our Western World, this linking of word directly to act, of belief to ordinary life. And yet, when you think of it, our names, but words made common by familiarity, have meanings of great import as well. But by choosing them at birth, we lay our paths before we can even walk . . . I had a dictionary, once, that gave the meanings of names, and I followed my curiosity and found much of interest. Your name means *Help*. Did you know? And how appropriate. All your life, since babyhood, you were running to guide, to protect, to teach – to help others through the world. Mine, of course, means *Just*. Well, I hope I have been that; I have honestly tried. But there are surprises. Both Ellie and Clare had names that meant *Bright*. That was an accident. And some are quite obscure. I could not find Eithne anywhere, until I presented it at last to an old minister at Arradale who was a Gaelic-speaking man. He puzzled over dictionaries for quite some while, and found the roots of it in the words for the ashes, the coals of a fire. Quite literally, 'firebrand'. And O'Mordha was from the word for haughtiness. She was in name as well as fact The Haughty Firebrand. And all fortuitous, because neither Kate nor Padraic, for all they'd like to think, had any Irish at all, but chose the name by pretentious accident. So, perhaps our destinies are laid for us, after all.

Mine is here, my dear. I don't think I'm going to elude it. In case I find myself further restricted, I want to tell you something now. You are not to be bitter about this, nor harbour hatreds. For all you may be thinking, these people are not barbarians, not any *more* barbarians than the rest of us. If you had seen our century the way I saw it, you would feel no Western remoteness from savagery. Nothing they can do can match what I saw done in the name of God at Passchendaele and the Somme. It is their turn, now, that is all. There is nothing new under the sun, darling. The very word assassin was born in the mountains of Iran, and the kind of warfare these people often favour was indulged by well-bred lady friends of mine, on the London streets. And what, after all, was Jack Redpath but a terrorist fighting for a holy cause?

Oh Jack, yes. I found his name easily enough, as old as the Bible. Jack, or John, a name by which I never heard him called, means *God is Gracious*. I'll accept that. For twenty-five years, God was gracious to me.

Justina

Christmas Day 1983

. . . I am standing at an arched doorway in a stone wall. There is a plank door, green-painted, and locked, and beyond is a courtyard I do not wish to see. Behind me, the Proof of Islam, in his sweet, passionate voice, begs me to recant. But I will not, for in the name of God, the merciful, the compassionate, I am innocent . . .

Arradale Castle
Wester Ross
Scotland
4 January 1984

Ms Patricia Parkin
Grafton Books
8 Grafton Street
London W1

Dear Ms Parkin,

As I am sadly certain you are quite aware, my great-aunt, Dame Justina Bride Melrose, was executed in the Iranian capital of Teheran on Christmas Day, in the company of four other women and two young girls, all of the Baha'i faith. As you know, the government and all of us did everything in our power to prevent this, and previously everything in our power to convince her to leave, all to no avail. She must in part be held responsible for her own fate; she had been warned repeatedly

of the dangers of her situation, but she was, as you are probably quite aware, extremely stubborn. The charge, if one can call it that, was of 'Crimes against God', a charge which, incidentally, she did not deny.

Yours regretfully
Ezra Melrose